# READER'S DIGEST CONDENSED BOOKS

READER'S DIGEST ASSOCIATION (CANADA) LTD.
CONDENSED BOOKS DIVISION

215 Redfern Ave., Montreal, Que. H3Z 2V9
*Editor:* Deirdre Gilbert
*Assistant Editor:* Anita Winterberg
*Design:* Andrée Payette
*Production Manager:* Holger Lorenzen

FIRST EDITION
PRINTED IN THE U.S.A.

# READER'S DIGEST CONDENSED BOOKS

## 7
### THE PELICAN BRIEF
**John Grisham**
PUBLISHED BY DOUBLEDAY

## 167
### TREASURES
**Belva Plain**
PUBLISHED BY DELACORTE; DISTRIBUTED BY BANTAM

## 325
### EYE OF THE STORM
**Jack Higgins**
PUBLISHED BY PUTNAM; DISTRIBUTED BY BEJO

## 457
### THE ISLAND HARP
**Jeanne Williams**
PUBLISHED BY ST. MARTIN'S; DISTRIBUTED BY MCCLELLAND & STEWART

# In this volume

## THE PELICAN BRIEF
*by John Grisham*

The eagerly awaited new legal
thriller by the author of *The Firm*.
With the murder of two Supreme
Court Justices the White House is
in an uproar. The FBI is searching
its files, scrambling for culprits.
But a brainy and beautiful law
student, Darby Shaw, discovers her
own clues to the killer—clues that
could topple the government. And
take her with it. From the cool
corridors of the White House to
the zesty French Quarter in New
Orleans, a novel that races to a
stunning conclusion. / Page 7

## TREASURES
*by Belva Plain*

The future looks full of promise
for Eddy, Connie and Lara
Osborne—a brother and two sisters
from Ohio. It's the high-flying
1980s, and Eddy is headed for
stunning success on Wall Street.
Connie relishes well-born suitors
and fine homes in big cities. Only
Lara, it seems, will settle for the
treasures close to home. But
as all three discover, life is never
predictable—and its richest
rewards are sometimes found
where we least expect them. A
stirring new novel from a best-
selling author. / Page 167

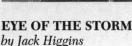

## EYE OF THE STORM
*by Jack Higgins*

Sean Dillon is a master assassin with cold eyes and nerves of steel. His client list reads like a who's who of international menace: the KGB, the PLO, the IRA. So in 1991, with the Gulf war in full fury, he is the top choice as hit man when Saddam Hussein decides to show the world he can strike anywhere. But Dillon runs head-on into his old nemesis, a Special Forces hero, and a fierce clash begins. Outstanding suspense from the author of *The Eagle Has Flown*. / Page 325

## THE ISLAND HARP
*by Jeanne Williams*

It's 1844, on the isle of Lewis in the Scottish Hebrides. Mairi MacLeod's family has lived there for generations, coaxing a living from the windblown moors and rocky coastlines. Then the unthinkable happens: a brutal eviction by a greedy landlord. Many of the islanders flee. But seventeen-year-old Mairi stays, determined to make a new life for her family, determined to overcome all obstacles—including her love for a man who can never be hers. / Page 457

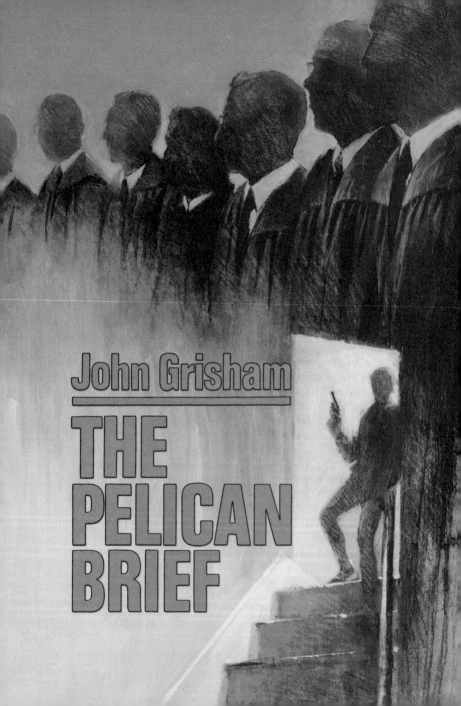

John Grisham

# THE
# PELICAN
# BRIEF

Late one October night two Justices of the Supreme Court are murdered in cold blood. Lone assassin? Conspiracy?

Darby Shaw, a brilliant law student, thinks she has the answer. She calls her theory the pelican brief, and it's so frightening she almost dismisses it. But not before it reaches the ears of very powerful people—people who would kill to silence her.

Alone and terrified, Darby goes underground, melting into the shadows of New Orleans' French Quarter. But she hasn't left her theory behind—or her determination to expose a stunning cover-up.

"[The] Firm fans will find *The Pelican Brief* even more compelling and suspenseful."
—*USA Weekend*

# ONE

H<small>E SEEMED</small> incapable of creating such chaos, but much of what he saw below could be blamed on him. And that was fine. He was ninety-one, paralyzed, strapped in a wheelchair, and hooked to oxygen. His second stroke, seven years ago, had almost finished him off, but Abraham Rosenberg was still alive, and even with tubes in his nose his legal stick was bigger than the other eight's. He was the only legend remaining on the Court, and the fact that he was still breathing irritated most of the mob below.

He sat in a small wheelchair in an office on the main floor of the United States Supreme Court Building. His feet touched the edge of the window, and he strained forward as the noise increased. He hated cops, but the sight of them standing in thick, neat lines was somewhat comforting. They stood straight and held ground as the mob of at least fifty thousand screamed for blood.

"Biggest crowd ever!" Rosenberg yelled at the window. He was almost deaf. Jason Kline, his senior law clerk, stood behind him. It was the first Monday in October, the opening day of the new term, and this had become a traditional celebration of the First Amendment. A glorious celebration. Rosenberg was thrilled. To him, freedom of speech meant freedom to riot.

"Are the Indians out there?" he asked.

Kline leaned closer to him. "Yes! In full battle dress."

"Are they dancing?"

"Yes!"

9

The Indians, the blacks, whites, browns, women, gays, tree lovers, Christians, abortion activists, Aryans, Nazis, atheists, hunters, animal lovers, white supremacists, black supremacists, loggers, farmers— It was a massive sea of protest. And the riot police gripped their sticks.

"The Indians should love me!"

"I'm sure they do." Kline smiled at the frail man with clenched fists. Rosenberg's ideology was simple: Government over business, the individual over government, the environment over everything. And the Indians— Give them whatever they want.

The heckling, singing, chanting, and screaming grew louder, and the riot police inched closer together. The crowd was larger and rowdier than in recent years. Things were more tense. Violence had become common. Churches and priests had been abused by militant gays. White supremacists operating from a dozen paramilitary organizations had become bolder in their attacks on blacks, Hispanics, and Asians. Hatred was now America's favorite pastime.

And the Court, of course, was an easy target. Threats—serious ones—against the Justices had increased tenfold since 1990. The Supreme Court police had tripled in size. At least two FBI agents were assigned to guard each Justice, and another fifty were kept busy investigating threats.

"They hate me, don't they?" Rosenberg said loudly.

"Yes, some of them do," Kline answered with amusement.

Rosenberg liked to hear that. He smiled, and inhaled deeply. Eighty percent of the death threats were aimed at him.

"See any of those signs?" he asked. He was nearly blind. "What do they say?"

"The usual. 'Death to Rosenberg.' 'Retire Rosenberg.' 'Cut Off the Oxygen.' "

"They've been waving those same damned signs for years. Why don't they get some new ones?"

The clerk did not answer. Abe should have retired years ago, but he still insisted on writing his own opinions. He did so with a heavy felt-tip marker, and his words were scrawled across a white legal pad, much like a first grader learning to write. Slow work, but with a lifetime appointment, who cared about time? His three clerks proofed his opinions and rarely found mistakes.

Rosenberg chuckled. "We oughta feed Runyan to the Indians."

John Runyan was the Chief Justice—a tough conservative appointed by a Republican and hated by most minorities. Seven of the nine Justices had been appointed by Republican Presidents. For fifteen years Rosenberg had been waiting for a Democrat in the White House. He wanted to quit, needed to quit, but he could not stomach the idea of a right-wing type taking his beloved seat.

He could wait. He could sit here in his wheelchair and breathe oxygen and protect the Indians, the blacks, the women, the poor, the handicapped, and the environment until he was a hundred and five. And not a single person in the world could do a thing about it, unless they killed him.

The great man's head nodded, then wobbled and rested on his shoulder. He was asleep again. Kline quietly stepped away.

THE door to the office of the Chief Justice was closed. The room was filled with Chief Runyan, three law clerks, the captain of the Supreme Court police, three FBI agents, and K. O. Lewis, deputy director, FBI. The mood was serious, and a serious effort was under way to ignore the noise from the streets below. The chief and Lewis were discussing the latest series of death threats.

In the past sixty days the Bureau had logged more than two hundred—a record. Runyan didn't try to hide his anxiety. From a confidential FBI summary he read the names of individuals and groups suspected of threats—the Klan, the Aryans, the Nazis, the Palestinians, the pro-lifers, the black separatists. Even the IRA.

"What about these Puerto Rican terrorists?" Runyan asked.

"Lightweights. We're not worried," K. O. Lewis answered casually. "Forget them, Chief." Runyan liked to be called Chief. Just Chief. "They're just threatening because everyone else is."

Runyan threw the summary on his desk and rubbed his temples. "Let's talk about security. What about around here?"

Lewis almost smiled. "We're not worried about this building, Chief. It's easy to secure. We don't expect trouble here."

"Then where?"

Lewis nodded at a window. The noise was louder. "Out there somewhere. The streets are full of idiots and maniacs and zealots."

"And they all hate us."

"Evidently. Listen, Chief, we're very concerned about Justice

11

Rosenberg. The director thinks we should place four agents with each Justice, at least for the next ninety days. But Rosenberg refuses to allow our men inside his home; makes them sit in a car in the street all night. He will allow his favorite Supreme Court officer, Ferguson, to sit by the back door, outside, but only from ten p.m. to six a.m. No one gets in the house but Rosenberg and his male nurse. The place is not secure."

Runyan smiled slightly to himself. Rosenberg's death, by any means, would be a relief. "What do you suggest?" he asked.

"Can you talk to him?"

"I've tried. He told me to get lost, then fell asleep."

"So what do we do?" asked Lewis.

"You protect him as best you can, and don't worry about it. If he's not sweating it, why should you?"

"The director is sweating, so I'm sweating, Chief. It's very simple. If one of you guys gets hurt, the Bureau looks bad."

The chief rocked quickly in his chair. The racket from outside was unnerving. "Forget Rosenberg. Maybe he'll die in his sleep. I'm more concerned over Glenn Jensen."

"Jensen's a problem," Lewis said, flipping through his copy of the summary.

"I know he's a problem," Runyan said. "He's an embarrassment. Now he thinks he's a liberal. Votes like Rosenberg half the time. Next month he'll be a white supremacist and support segregated schools. Then he'll fall in love with the Indians and want to give them Montana. It's like having a retarded child. Is he cooperating?"

"Of course not, Chief. He's worse than Rosenberg. He allows us to escort him to his apartment building, then makes us sit in the parking lot all night. He's seven floors up, remember. There are ten ways in and out of the building, and it's impossible to protect him. He likes to play hide-and-seek with us. He sneaks around all the time, so we never know if he's in the building or not. At least with Rosenberg we know where he is all night. Jensen's impossible."

"Where do you suppose Jensen sneaks off to?" Runyan asked.

Lewis glanced at one of his agents. "We have no idea."

The mob on the streets suddenly seemed to come together in one unrestrained chorus. The chief could not ignore it. The windows vibrated. He stood and called an end to the meeting.

THOMAS CALLAHAN WAS ONE OF Tulane's more popular professors, primarily because he refused to schedule classes before eleven a.m. He drank a lot, and the first few hours of each morning were needed for sleep, then resuscitation. Nine- and ten-o'clock classes were abominations. He was also popular because he was cool—faded jeans, tweed jackets with well-worn elbow patches, no socks, no ties. The liberal, chic, academic look. He was forty-five, but with his dark hair and horn-rimmed glasses he could pass for thirty-five.

He was also popular because he taught constitutional law—a required course. Due to his sheer brilliance and coolness, he actually made it interesting. The students fought to sit in on con law under Callahan at eleven, three mornings a week.

Eighty of them now sat in six elevated rows and whispered as Callahan stood in front of his desk and cleaned his glasses. It was exactly five after eleven—still too early, he thought.

"Who understands Rosenberg's dissent in *Nash* versus *New Jersey*?" All heads lowered, and the room was silent. When he started with Rosenberg, it usually meant a rough lecture. "*Nash?*" Callahan looked slowly around the room and waited. Dead silence.

The doorknob clicked loudly and broke the tension. The door opened quickly, and an attractive young female in tight washed jeans and a cotton sweater slid elegantly through it and sort of glided along the wall to the third row, where she deftly maneuvered between the crowded seats until she came to hers and sat down. The guys watched in admiration. For two brutal years now, one of the few pleasures of law school had been to watch Darby Shaw as she graced the halls and rooms with her long legs and baggy sweaters. Her dark red hair fell just to the shoulders. She was that perfect little cheerleader that every boy fell in love with at least twice in high school. And maybe at least once in law school.

"Has anyone read Rosenberg's dissent in *Nash* versus *New Jersey?*" Suddenly Callahan had the spotlight again. Dead silence once more. No volunteers. All heads were bowed. Any movement might attract attention. Someone was about to be nailed.

Callahan revered Rosenberg. Worshipped him. Read books about his opinions. Studied him. Even dined with him once.

Callahan looked around the room. "Can anyone explain the majority opinion in *Nash* versus *New Jersey?*"

13

Silence. Callahan was pacing now, slowly, in front of his desk. He glared at the students. "Did anyone bother to read the case?"

Finally, slowly, Darby Shaw lifted her hand slightly, and the class breathed a collective sigh of relief. She had saved them again. It was sort of expected of her. Number two in their class, she could recite the facts and holdings and concurrences and dissents and majority opinions to virtually every case Callahan could spit at them. She missed nothing. The perfect little cheerleader had graduated magna cum laude with a degree in biology, and she planned to graduate magna cum laude with a degree in law and then make a nice living suing chemical companies for trashing the environment.

Callahan stared at her in mock frustration. She had left his apartment three hours earlier after a long night of wine and law. But he hadn't mentioned *Nash* to her. He wondered if anyone knew he was sleeping with her. Probably not. She'd insisted on absolute secrecy.

"Well, well, Ms. Shaw. Why is Rosenberg upset?"

"He thinks the New Jersey statute violates the Second Amendment." She did not look at the professor.

"That's good. And for the benefit of the rest of the class, what does the statute do?"

"Outlaws semiautomatic machine guns, among other things."

"Wonderful. And just for fun, what did Mr. Nash possess at the time of his arrest?"

"An AK-47 assault rifle."

"And what happened to him?"

"He was convicted, sentenced to three years; then he appealed."

"What was Mr. Nash's occupation?"

"The opinion wasn't specific, but there was mention of an additional charge of drug trafficking."

"So he was a dope pusher with an AK-47. But he has a friend in Rosenberg, doesn't he?"

"Of course."

She was watching him now. The tension had eased. Most eyes followed Callahan as he paced slowly, looking around the room for another victim. More often than not, Darby dominated these lectures, and Callahan wanted a broader participation.

"How about it, Mr. Sallinger? Why do you suppose Rosenberg is sympathetic?"

From the fourth row Sallinger said, "He loves dope pushers."

Callahan smiled at his prey. "You think so, Mr. Sallinger?"

"Sure. Dope pushers, child fondlers, gunrunners, terrorists. Rosenberg greatly admires these people. They are his weak and abused children, so he must protect them."

"And in your learned opinion, Mr. Sallinger, what should be done with these people?"

"Simple. They should have a fair trial with a good lawyer, then a fair, speedy appeal, then punished if they are guilty." Sallinger was perilously close to sounding like a law-and-order right-winger—a cardinal sin among Tulane law students.

Callahan folded his arms. "Please continue."

Sallinger smelled a trap but plowed ahead. "I mean, we've read case after case where Rosenberg has tried to rewrite the Constitution to free an obviously guilty defendant. It's sickening. He thinks all prisons are cruel places, so under the Eighth Amendment all prisoners should go free. Thankfully, he's in the minority now."

"You like the Court's direction, don't you, Mr. Sallinger." Callahan both smiled and frowned. "Are you one of those red-blooded patriotic Americans who wish the old fool would die in his sleep?"

Sallinger knew better than to answer truthfully. "I wouldn't wish that on anyone," he said, almost embarrassed.

Callahan was pacing again. "Well, thank you, Mr. Sallinger. You have, as usual, provided us with the layman's view of the law. I would like now to raise the intellectual level of this discussion. Now, Ms. Shaw, why is Rosenberg sympathetic to Nash?"

"The Second Amendment grants the people the right to keep and bear arms. To Justice Rosenberg it is literal and absolute. Nothing should be banned. If Nash wants to possess an AK-47, the state of New Jersey cannot pass a law prohibiting it."

"Do you agree with him?"

"No. And I'm not alone," said Darby. "It's an eight-to-one decision. No one followed him."

"What's the rationale of the other eight?"

"It's obvious, really. The states have compelling reasons to prohibit the sale and possession of certain types of arms. The interests of the state of New Jersey outweigh the Second Amendment. Society cannot allow individuals to own sophisticated weaponry."

Callahan watched her carefully. Attractive female law students were rare at Tulane, but when he found one, he moved in quickly. Easy work, for the most part. But Darby had been different. He had first spotted her in the library during the second semester of her first year, and it took a month to get her to dinner.

"Who wrote the majority opinion?" he asked her.

"Runyan."

"And you agree with him?"

"Yes. It's an easy case, really."

"Then what happened to Justice Rosenberg?"

"I think he hates the rest of the Court, so he dissents just for the heck of it. His opinions are becoming more indefensible. Take *Nash*. For a liberal like Rosenberg, the issue of gun control is easy. He should have written the majority opinion, and ten years ago he would have. His inconsistencies are almost embarrassing."

"Are you suggesting Rosenberg is senile?" Callahan asked.

Sallinger waded in for the final round. "He's crazy as hell, and you know it. You can't defend his opinions."

"Not always, Mr. Sallinger, but at least he's still there."

"His body's there, but he's brain dead."

"He's breathing, Mr. Sallinger."

"Yeah, with a machine pumping oxygen up his nose."

"But it counts, Mr. Sallinger. He's the last of the great judicial activists, and he's still breathing."

"You'd better call and check." Sallinger lowered his head.

Callahan stared him down, then began pacing again.

# TWO

AT LEAST he looked like an old farmer, with straw hat, bib overalls, neatly pressed khaki work shirt, boots. He chewed tobacco and spit into the black water beneath the pier. He chewed like a farmer. His pickup, parked in the sand at the other end of the pier, had a dusty-road look about it. North Carolina plates. It was midnight, the first Monday in October, and for the next thirty minutes he was to wait in the dark coolness of the deserted pier.

The pickup was not from North Carolina, and neither was the farmer. The license plates and the pickup had been stolen from a scrapyard. The farmer performed none of the thievery. He was a pro, and so someone else did the dirty little deeds.

Twenty minutes into the wait a dark object floated in the direction of the pier. A quiet, muffled engine hummed and grew louder. The object became a small craft with a camouflaged silhouette crouching low and working the motor. The humming stopped, and the black rubber raft stalled thirty feet from the pier.

The farmer carefully placed a cigarette between his lips, lit it, puffed twice, then tossed it down, halfway to the raft.

"What kind of cigarette?" the man on the water asked. He could see the outline of the farmer on the railing, but not the face.

"Lucky Strike," the farmer answered. These passwords made for such a silly game. Silly, but oh, so important.

"Luke?" came the voice from the boat.

"Sam?" replied the farmer.

The name was Khamel, but Sam would do for five minutes until he parked his raft. Khamel started the engine and guided the raft along the pier to the beach. Luke followed from above. They met at the pickup. Khamel placed his black Adidas gym bag between them on the seat, and the truck started along the shoreline.

Luke drove and Khamel smoked, but their eyes did not meet. With Khamel's heavy beard and dark glasses his face was ominous, but impossible to identify. Luke did not want to see it. Part of his assignment, in addition to receiving this stranger from the sea, was to refrain from looking at this face that was wanted in nine countries. In the guarded whispers of his invisible brotherhood, he had often heard of Khamel—an assassin who struck quickly and left no trail, a fastidious killer who roamed the world, but could never be found.

AT DAWN the farm truck stopped at the corner of Thirty-first and M streets in Georgetown. Khamel grabbed his gym bag and hit the sidewalk. He walked east a few blocks to The Four Seasons Hotel, bought a *Post* in the lobby, and casually rode the elevator to the seventh floor. At precisely seven fifteen he knocked on a door at the end of the hall. "Yes?" a nervous voice asked from inside.

"Mr. Sneller?" Khamel said slowly in perfect generic American.

A few seconds passed, and a white envelope eased from under the door. Khamel picked it up.

"It's next door," Sneller said. "I'll await your call." Unlike Luke, he'd never seen Khamel, and had no desire to, really. Luke had seen him twice now and was indeed lucky to be alive.

Khamel's room had two beds. He placed his gym bag on one bed, next to two thick briefcases. He walked to the phone.

"It's me," he said to Sneller. "Tell me about the car."

"It's parked on the street. Plain white Ford with Connecticut plates. Stolen, but clean. The keys are on the table."

"I'll leave it at Dulles shortly after midnight. I intend to leave the gun in the car. Guns leave bullets, and people see cars, so completely destroy the car and everything in it. Understand?"

"Those are my instructions. Yes." Sneller did not appreciate this lecture. He was no novice at the killing game.

Khamel sat on the edge of the bed. "The four million was received a week ago. Now I want the next three."

"It will be wired before noon to the account in Zurich."

"Okay. I'll be in Paris in twenty-four hours, and from there I'll go straight to Zurich. I want all the money waiting for me."

"It will be there if the job is finished."

Khamel smiled to himself. "The job will be finished, Mr. Sneller. By midnight. That is, if your information is correct."

"Our people are in the streets. Everything is in the briefcases—maps, diagrams, schedules, the articles you requested."

Khamel glanced at the briefcases behind him. "Okay." He placed the receiver on the phone.

THE streets were clear and quiet for day two of the fall term. The Justices spent their day on the bench listening to lawyer after lawyer argue complex, dull cases. Rosenberg slept through most of it. In years past he was a tiger, a ruthless intimidator who tied even the slickest lawyers in knots. But no more. It was almost four p.m. when he informed his clerks he wanted to go home. Jason Kline, his senior clerk, notified the FBI, and moments later Rosenberg was wheeled into his van. Two FBI agents watched. A male nurse, Frederic, strapped the wheelchair in place, and Sergeant Ferguson of the Supreme Court police slid behind the wheel of the van.

On Volta Street in Georgetown, the van slowed, and backed into the driveway of Rosenberg's town house. Frederic, the nurse, and

Ferguson, the cop, gently rolled him inside. The agents watched from the street in their black government-issue Dodge Aries.

After a few minutes Ferguson made his mandatory exit and spoke to the FBI agents. A week earlier Rosenberg had finally acquiesced and allowed Ferguson to quietly inspect each room upstairs and down upon his arrival home in the afternoons.

"Everything's fine," Ferguson said. "I'll be back at ten p.m."

By ten Rosenberg was fast asleep. The bed was a narrow reclining army-hospital job with push-button controls and collapsible rails. It was in a room behind the kitchen that Rosenberg had used as a small study for thirty years, before the first stroke. It smelled of antiseptic and looming death. Next to the bed was a large table with a hospital lamp and at least twenty bottles of pills. Thick, heavy law books were stacked in piles around the room. Frederic sat close by in a worn recliner. He was tired, and as soon as the Justice was snoring, he lowered the lights. The room was almost dark. Frederic jerked backward, and the recliner unfolded. He closed his eyes.

SHORTLY after ten, with the house dark and quiet, the door to a bedroom closet upstairs opened slightly, and Khamel eased out. His wristbands, nylon cap, and running shorts were royal blue. His long-sleeved shirt, socks, and Reeboks were white with royal trim. Perfect color coordination. Khamel the Jogger. He was clean-shaven, and under the cap his very short hair was now blond, almost white.

The stairs creaked slightly under the Reeboks. He was five ten and weighed less than a hundred and fifty pounds, so the movements were quick and soundless. The stairs landed in a foyer not far from the front door. He knew there were two agents in a car by the curb. He knew Ferguson had arrived seven minutes before.

He slid through the foyer into the kitchen, dipping under a window, and looked into the backyard. He could not see Ferguson, though he knew he was seventy-four inches tall, sixty-one years old, had cataracts, and couldn't hit a barn with his .357 Magnum.

Rosenberg and his nurse were snoring. Khamel smiled to himself as he crouched in the doorway and quickly pulled the .22 automatic and silencer from the Ace bandage wrapped around his waist. He screwed the four-inch tube onto the barrel and ducked into the room. The nurse was sprawled deep in the recliner, mouth open.

19

Khamel placed the tip of the silencer an inch from his right temple and fired three times. The hands flinched and the feet jerked, but the eyes remained closed. Khamel quickly reached across to the wrinkled and pale head of Justice Abraham Rosenberg and pumped three bullets into it.

He watched the bodies and listened for a full minute. The nurse's heels twitched a few times; then the bodies were still.

He wanted to kill Ferguson inside the house. It was eleven minutes after ten—a good time for a neighbor to be out with the dog for one last time before bed. Khamel crept through the darkness to the rear door and spotted the cop strolling benignly along the fence, twenty feet away. Instinctively Khamel opened the back door, turned on the patio light, and said, "Ferguson," loudly.

He left the door open and hid in a dark corner next to the refrigerator. Ferguson obediently lumbered across the patio and into the kitchen. Khamel fired three bullets into the back of his head, and he fell loudly onto the kitchen table.

Khamel turned out the patio light, unscrewed the silencer, and stuffed it and the pistol into the Ace bandage. He peeked out the front window. The dome light was on, and the agents were reading. He stepped over Ferguson, locked the back door, and disappeared into the darkness of the small lawn. He jumped two fences without a sound and found the street. He began trotting. Khamel the Jogger.

IN THE balcony of the Montrose Theatre, Supreme Court Justice Glenn Jensen sat by himself eating popcorn from a large box and watching the naked men on the screen below. He was dressed conservatively—navy cardigan, chinos, Loafers. Wide sunglasses to hide his eyes, and a suede fedora to cover his head. He was blessed with a face that was easily forgotten, and once camouflaged, it could never be recognized—especially in a deserted balcony of a near-empty gay movie house at midnight.

It had become a challenge, really—this cat-and-mouse game with the FBI and the rest of the world. On this night they had dutifully stationed themselves in the parking lot outside his building, with another pair parked by the rear exit. He'd allowed them to sit for four and a half hours, before he disguised himself, walked nonchalantly to the garage in the basement, and drove away in a friend's car. The building had too many points of egress for the poor Fibbies to monitor him. He was sympathetic to a point, but he had his life to live. If the Fibbies couldn't find him, how could a killer?

The balcony was divided into three sections with six rows each. It was very dark, the only light being the blue stream from the projector behind. It was a marvelous place to hide.

Jensen was forty-eight, the youngest of the nine Justices. When he was first appointed, six years before, he used to worry about getting caught. But he told himself that if he was recognized, or in some awful way exposed, he would simply claim he was doing research for an obscenity case. There was always one on the docket.

Two old men in the center section whispered and giggled. Jensen glanced at them occasionally but concentrated on the movie.

A fourth person soon walked quietly, with his draft beer and popcorn, to the top row of the center section. He sat by the aisle, dressed appropriately—tight jeans, black silk shirt, earring, horn-rimmed shades, neatly trimmed mustache. Khamel the Homosexual.

At twelve twenty the two old men stood arm in arm and tiptoed away. Jensen did not look at them. Khamel moved like a cat to a seat three rows behind the Justice; then he quickly moved down a row.

Khamel set the beer and popcorn on the floor and pulled a three-foot strand of nylon ski rope from his waist. Wrapping the ends around both hands, he stepped over the row of chairs in front of him. The attack was quick and brutal. Khamel looped the rope just under the larynx and wrenched it violently, snapping the head over the back of the seat. The neck broke cleanly. He tied the rope behind the neck, slid a six-inch steel rod through a loop in the knot, and wound the tourniquet. It was over in ten seconds.

Jensen slumped in his seat. Khamel was not one to admire his handiwork. He left the balcony, walked casually through the lobby, then disappeared onto the sidewalk.

THE President was a heavy sleeper. The phone rang twelve times before he heard it. He grabbed it and stared at the clock. Four thirty a.m. He listened to the voice, jumped to his feet, and eight minutes later was in the Oval Office. No shower, no tie. He stared at Fletcher Coal, his chief of staff, and sat properly behind his desk.

Coal was smiling. His perfect teeth and bald head were shining.

21

Only thirty-seven, he was the boy wonder who four years earlier had rescued a failing campaign and placed his boss in the White House. He was a guileful manipulator and nasty henchman who had cut and clawed his way through the inner circle until he was now second-in-command. Many viewed him as the real boss.

"What happened?" the President asked slowly.

Coal paced in front of the President's desk. "Two FBI agents found Rosenberg around one a.m. Dead in bed. His nurse and a Supreme Court policeman were also murdered. All three shot in the head. A very clean job. While the FBI and D.C. police were investigating, they got a call that Jensen had been found dead in some queer club. Voyles called me at four, and I called you. He and Gminski should be here in a minute."

"Gminski?"

"The CIA should be included, at least for now."

The President folded his hands behind his head and stretched. "Rosenberg is dead."

"Yes, quite. I suggest you address the nation in a couple of hours."

"The press—"

"Yes. It's out. They filmed the ambulance crew rolling Jensen into the morgue."

"I didn't know he was gay."

"Not much doubt about it now. This is the perfect crisis, Mr. President. Think of it. We didn't create it. No one can blame us. And the nation will be shocked into some degree of solidarity. It's rally-around-the-leader time. It's just great. No downside."

The President sipped a cup of coffee and stared at the papers on his desk. "And I'll get to restructure the Court."

"That's the best part. It'll be your legacy. I've already instructed Attorney General Horton to begin a preliminary list of nominees."

The President nodded his approval. "Any suspects?"

"Not yet. I told Voyles that you would expect a briefing."

"I thought the FBI was protecting the Supreme Court."

Coal smiled wide. "Exactly. The egg is on Voyles' face."

A security guard knocked on the door, then opened it. Directors Voyles and Gminski entered together. The mood was suddenly somber as all four shook hands. The two sat before the President's desk as Coal took his customary position standing near a window to the side of the President. He hated Voyles and Gminski, and they hated him. Coal thrived on hatred. He had the President's ear, and that was all that mattered.

"I'm very sorry you're here, but thanks for coming," the President said. They nodded grimly. "What happened?"

Voyles described the scene at Rosenberg's home when the bodies were found. The killings were clean and professional. Jensen had been found by another character in the balcony. No one saw anything. Voyles was not as gruff and blunt as usual. It was a dark day for the Bureau, and he could feel the heat coming. But he'd survived five Presidents, and he could certainly outmaneuver this one.

"The two are obviously related," the President said, staring at Voyles.

"Maybe. Certainly looks that way, but—"

"Come on, Director. Within two hours two Supreme Court Justices are assassinated. And you're not convinced they're related?"

"I didn't say that. There must be a link somewhere. It's just that the methods were so different. And so professional. You must remember, we've had thousands of threats against the Court."

"Fine. Then who are your suspects?"

No one cross-examined F. Denton Voyles. He glared at the President. "It's too early for suspects. We're still gathering evidence. We'll have ballistics and autopsies by late this afternoon."

"I want to see them here as soon as you have them. I also want a shortlist of suspects by five p.m. today."

"Certainly, Mr. President."

"And I would like a report on where your security broke down."

"You're assuming it broke down."

"We have two dead judges, both of whom were being protected by the FBI. The American people deserve to know what went wrong, Director. Yes, it broke down." The President then turned to Robert Gminski, director of the CIA. "Bob, I want a straight answer."

Gminski tightened and frowned. "Yes, sir. What is it?"

"I want to know if these killings are in any way linked to any agency, operation, group—whatever—of the U.S. government."

"Come on! Are you serious, Mr. President? That's absurd." Gminski appeared to be shocked, but the President, Coal, even Voyles, knew anything was possible these days at the CIA.

"Dead serious, Bob. Check it out. I want to be damned certain. Rosenberg did not believe in national security. He made thousands of enemies in intelligence. I want a report by five today."

"Sure. Okay. But it's a waste of time."

Fletcher Coal moved to the desk, next to the President. "I suggest we meet here at five, gentlemen. Is that agreeable?"

They both nodded, and stood. Coal escorted them to the door without a word. He closed it.

"You handled it real well," he said to the President. "Voyles knows he's vulnerable. I smell blood."

"Rosenberg is dead," the President repeated to himself. "I just can't believe it."

"I've got an idea for television." Coal was pacing again now, very much in charge. "We need to cash in on the shock of it all. You need to appear tired, as if you were up all night handling the crisis. Right? The entire nation will be watching. I think you should wear something warm and comforting. Let's relax a little. How about a cardigan and slacks? No tie. Sort of the grandfather image."

The President was listening intently. "You want me to address the nation in this hour of crisis in a sweater?"

"Yes. A brown cardigan with a white shirt. The image is good. Look, Chief, the election is a year from next month. This is our first crisis in ninety days, and you need to look casual but in control. It'll be worth five, maybe ten points in the ratings. Trust me, Chief."

"I don't like sweaters."

"Just trust me."

# THREE

DARBY Shaw awoke in the early darkness. After fifteen months of law school her mind refused to rest for more than six hours, and she was often up before daybreak. She watched the ceiling and listened to Callahan snore.

October in New Orleans is still muggy and warm. The heavy air rose from Dauphine Street, below, across the small balcony outside the bedroom, and through the open French doors. It brought with it the first stream of morning light. Darby stood in the doors and covered herself with Callahan's terry-cloth robe.

Downstairs in the kitchen, she brewed a pot of thick French Market chicory, poured a tall mugful, then climbed the stairs and eased back into the bed. It was ten minutes before six. She flicked the remote controls to an NBC News special report, and suddenly there was the President sitting behind his desk, looking somehow rather odd in a brown cardigan with no tie.

"Thomas! Wake up!" She pressed a button, and the volume roared. The President said good morning.

"Thomas!" She leaned toward the television. Callahan sat up, rubbing his eyes and trying to focus. She handed him the coffee.

The President had tragic news. He looked deep into the camera and explained to the American people the tragic events of the night before. After announcing the deaths, he launched into a flowery obituary for Abraham Rosenberg. A towering legend, he called him. It was a strain, but the President kept a straight face while lauding the career of one of the most hated men in America.

Callahan gaped at the television. "Rosenberg? Murdered?"

"Check out the sweater," Darby said, staring at the face with heavy orange makeup, and the brilliant silver hair plastered carefully in place. The President was a wonderfully handsome man with a soothing baritone voice; thus he had succeeded greatly in politics. He was even sadder now as he talked of Justice Glenn Jensen.

"The Montrose Theatre at midnight," Callahan repeated.

"Where is it?" she asked. Callahan had finished law school at Georgetown.

"Not sure. But I think it's in the gay section."

"Was he gay?"

"I've heard rumors. Evidently."

The President rambled for a few more minutes, still deeply saddened, even shocked, and very human, but nonetheless the President and clearly in charge. He signed off with his patented grandfather smile of complete trust, wisdom, and reassurance.

Callahan turned off the set and sat in a wicker chair by the French doors. "No suspects," he mumbled.

"I can think of at least twenty," Darby said.

"Yeah, but why the combination? Rosenberg is easy, but why Jensen?" Callahan fluffed his hair. "I think I'll cancel class. I'm not in the mood. Damn, I can't believe this. That fool has two nominations. That means eight of the nine will be Republican choices."

"They have to be confirmed first," Darby said.

"We won't recognize the Constitution in ten years' time."

"That's why they were killed, Thomas. Someone or some group wants a different Court—one with an absolute conservative majority. The election is next year. A Democrat may be elected President. Why take a chance? Kill them now, before the election. Makes perfect sense if one was so inclined."

"But why Jensen?"

"He was an embarrassment. And obviously an easier target."

"Yes," said Thomas, "but he was basically a moderate with an occasional leftward impulse, and he was nominated by a Republican."

Darby reclined on the bed, watching the sunlight filter across the balcony. "Think of it. The timing is beautiful. Think of the radicals, the zealots, the pro-lifers, and gay haters. Think of all the groups capable of killing, and all the threats against the Court, and the timing is perfect for an unknown, inconspicuous group to knock them off."

"And who is such a group? The Underground Army?"

"They're not exactly inconspicuous. They killed Judge Fernandez, in Texas. They use bombs, plastic explosives."

"Scratch them."

"I'm not scratching anybody right now." Darby stood and retied the robe. "Come on. I'll fix you a Bloody Mary."

"Only if you drink with me. I've got a book of Rosenberg opinions. Let's read them, sip Bloody Marys, then wine, then whatever. I miss him already."

"Thomas, I have federal procedure at nine, and I can't miss it."

"I intend to call the dean and have all my classes canceled. Then will you drink with me?"

"No. You're a professor. You can cancel your classes if you want to. I am a student." He followed her down to the kitchen.

WITHOUT removing the receiver from his shoulder, Fletcher Coal punched another button on the phone on the desk in the Oval Office. Three lines were blinking, holding. He paced slowly in front of the desk and listened while scanning a two-page report from Attorney General Richard Horton. Then he growled something into the receiver and slammed it down.

"That was Nellson. He ran two polls, beginning at noon. The computer is digesting it now, but he thinks the approval rating will be somewhere around fifty-two or fifty-three."

The President smiled. "What was it last week?"

"Forty-four. It was the cardigan. Just like I said. This is a wonderful crisis, Chief." Coal punched a blinking button and picked up the receiver. He slammed it down without a word. "It's five thirty, Chief. Voyles and Gminski are waiting."

"Show them in."

As usual, the President had changed clothes six times since breakfast, and now wore a glen plaid double-breasted suit with a red-and-navy-polka-dot tie. Office attire. He nodded at Voyles and Gminski, but neither stood nor offered to shake hands. They sat across the desk, and Coal took his usual sentrylike position.

"It's been a long day, Mr. President," Bob Gminski said to break the ice. Voyles looked at the windows.

Coal nodded, and the President said, "Yes, a very long day, so let's be brief. Let's start with you, Bob. Who killed them?"

"I do not know, Mr. President. But I assure you we had nothing to do with it."

The President glared at Voyles, whose stocky figure was still draped with a bulky trench coat. "Ballistics? Autopsies?"

"Got 'em," the director said as he opened his briefcase.

"Just tell me. I'll read it later."

"The gun was small caliber, probably a twenty-two. Point-blank range for Rosenberg and his nurse; no farther than twelve inches away for Ferguson. Three bullets into each head. They picked two out of Rosenberg; found another in his pillow. Same type slugs, same gun—same gunman, evidently. Complete autopsy summaries are being prepared, but there were no surprises."

"How'd he get into the house?"

"No apparent signs of entry. No fingerprints. I suspect the killer was hiding when the Justice returned and Ferguson walked through. I think he entered sometime in the afternoon and simply waited, perhaps in a closet, or in the attic, upstairs."

"What about Jensen?" the President asked.

"Strangled with a piece of nylon rope. No fingerprints. No witnesses. Time of death was around twelve thirty this morning. We

27

don't know when he left his apartment. We're relegated to the parking lot, remember. We followed him home around six p.m., then watched the building for seven hours, until we found out he'd been murdered. He sneaked out of the building in a friend's car."

Coal took two steps forward with his hands clasped rigidly behind him. "Director, do you think one assassin did both jobs?"

"Who knows? Give us a break. There's little evidence. It'll take time to piece this thing together." Voyles paused. "Could be the same guy, but he must be superman. Probably two or three, but regardless, they had to have a lot of help. Someone fed them a lot of information, such as how often Jensen goes to the movies, where does he sit, what time does he get there, does he go by himself."

"You're suggesting a conspiracy," Coal said intelligently.

"I'm not suggesting a damned thing."

"Then who are your suspects?" the President asked.

Voyles breathed deeply. "We don't have a prime suspect at the moment—just a few good possibilities. This must be kept quiet."

"Of course it's confidential," Coal snapped. "You're in the Oval Office."

"And I've been here many times before. In fact, I was here when you were running around in dirty diapers, Mr. Coal. Things have a way of leaking out."

The President raised his hand. "You have my word, Denton."

Voyles watched the President. "Court opened Monday, as you know. For the past two weeks we've been monitoring various movements. We know of at least eleven members of the Underground Army in the D.C. area. The group has the capability and the desire. It's our strongest possibility for now. They're just the people who would hate Rosenberg and Jensen."

Coal was not impressed. The Underground Army was on everyone's list. "Other suspects?" he asked.

"There's an Aryan group called White Resistance that we've been watching for two years. It operates out of Idaho and Oregon. The leader was spotted Monday in the demonstration outside the Supreme Court. We'll try to talk to him tomorrow."

"But are these people professional assassins?" Coal asked.

"I doubt if any group performed the actual killings. They just hired the assassins and provided the legwork."

"So who're the assassins?" the President asked.

"We may never know, frankly."

The President stood, and smiled at Voyles across the desk. "You have a difficult task." It was the grandfather voice, filled with understanding. "I don't envy you. If possible, I would like a two-page typewritten report by five p.m. each day on the progress of the investigation. If something breaks, call me immediately."

Voyles nodded and stood, tying the strap around his trench coat. He handed the ballistics and autopsy reports to Coal.

"Thanks for coming, gentlemen," the President said warmly. Coal closed the door behind them.

The President stared at the carpet. After a moment he said, "I want to talk to Horton. These nominations must be perfect."

"He's sent a shortlist of ten. Looks pretty good."

"I want young conservative white men opposed to abortion, pornography, queers, gun control, racial quotas, and all that. I want judges who hate dope and criminals and are enthusiastic about the death penalty. Understand?"

Coal was on the phone, punching numbers and nodding.

K. O. LEWIS sat with the director of the FBI in the back of the quiet limousine as it left the White House and crawled through rush-hour traffic. So far, in the early hours of the tragedy, the press had been brutal. The buzzards were circling. No less than three congressional subcommittees had already announced hearings and investigations into the deaths of the Justices. And the bodies were still warm.

They rode in silence in the direction of the Hoover building. It would be a long night.

"Are you sure you want three hundred agents on this case?" Lewis finally asked his boss.

Voyles lit a cigar and opened his window. "Yeah—maybe four hundred. We need to crack this baby before the press eats us alive."

"It won't be easy. These guys left almost nothing."

Voyles blew smoke. "I know. It's almost too clean."

IN A cluttered study carrel on the fifth level of the Tulane law library, Darby Shaw scanned a printout of the Supreme Court's docket. It was loaded with controversy, but none that interested her.

There was a child pornography case from New Jersey, a dozen death penalty appeals, and the usual array of civil rights, tax, zoning, Indian, and antitrust cases. From the computer she had pulled summaries of each, then reviewed them. But the suspects she compiled would be obvious to everyone. The list was now in the garbage.

Callahan was certain it was the Aryans or the Nazis or the Klan; some easily identifiable collection of right-wing domestic terrorists, he felt. Darby was not so sure. The hate groups were too obvious. They needed Rosenberg alive because he kept them in business. She thought it was somebody much more sinister.

Callahan was sitting in a bar on Canal Street waiting for her, though she had not promised to join him. She had checked on him at lunch and found him on the balcony upstairs, drunk and reading his book of Rosenberg opinions. He had decided to cancel con law for a week; said he might not be able to teach it anymore now that his hero was dead. She told him to sober up, and left.

Now, at a few minutes after ten, she walked to the computer room, on the fourth level of the library, and sat before a monitor. The room was empty. She pecked away at the keyboard, found what she wanted, and soon the printer was spewing forth page after page of appeals pending in the eleven federal appellate courts around the country. An hour later she possessed a six-inch-thick summary of the eleven dockets. She hauled it back to her cluttered study carrel. It was after eleven, and the fifth level was deserted.

She sipped a warm Fresca and stared blankly at the printout before her. The first assumption was easy: the killings were done by the same group for the same reasons. If not, then the search was hopeless. The second assumption was difficult: the motive was not hatred or revenge, but rather manipulation. There was a case or an issue out there on its way to the Supreme Court, and someone wanted different Justices. The third assumption was a bit easier: the case or issue involved a great deal of money.

The answer would not be found in the printout. She flipped through it until midnight, and left when the library closed.

IN THIRTY-FOUR years Abraham Rosenberg wrote no fewer than twelve hundred opinions. He wrote majority opinions, concurrences to majorities, concurrences to dissents, and many, many dissents. Often he dissented alone. Every hot issue had received an opinion of some sort from Rosenberg, and the scholars and critics loved him. On Thursday, Darby found five hardback compilations of his opinions. One book contained nothing but his great dissents.

Darby skipped class Thursday and secluded herself again in the study carrel at the library. The computer printouts were scattered neatly on the floor. The Rosenberg books were open, marked, and stacked on top of each other. She found no books on the writings of Justice Glenn Jensen. In six years he had authored only twenty-eight majority opinions—the lowest production on the Court.

Darby studied Jensen's opinions. His ideology swung radically from year to year. He was generally consistent in protecting the rights of criminal defendants, but there were enough exceptions to astound any scholar. In seven attempts he had voted with the Indians five times. He had written three majority opinions strongly protective of the environment. He was near perfect in support of tax protesters. But there were no clues. Jensen was too erratic to take seriously. Compared to the other eight Justices, he was harmless.

## FOUR

THOMAS Callahan slept late. He had gone to bed early, sober, and alone. For the third day in a row he had canceled classes. It was Friday, and Rosenberg's service was tomorrow, and out of respect, he would not teach con law until his idol was properly put to rest.

He fixed coffee and sat on the balcony. On these late mornings—and there were many—he cherished his freedom. He was twenty years out of law school, and most of his contemporaries were strapped into seventy-hour weeks in pressurized law factories.

He had lasted two years in private practice. A behemoth in D.C. with two hundred lawyers had hired him fresh out of Georgetown. But Callahan wanted to live past fifty, so he retired from private practice, earned a master's in law, and became a professor. He slept late, worked five hours a day, wrote an occasional article, and for the most part enjoyed himself immensely. With no family to support, his salary of seventy thousand a year was more than sufficient to pay for his two-story bungalow and his Porsche.

One of his best friends from law school was Gavin Verheek,

another dropout from private practice, who had gone to work for the FBI. He was now special counsel to the director. Callahan was due in Washington on Monday for a conference of con law professors. He and Verheek planned to get together Monday night.

Callahan needed to call and confirm this, and to pick Verheek's brain. He dialed the number from memory. The call was routed, then rerouted; then the man was on the phone.

"How are you, Thomas?" Gavin asked.

"It's ten thirty, I'm not dressed, and I'm sitting here in the French Quarter sipping coffee and watching pedestrians on Dauphine."

"What a life. Here it's eleven thirty, and I haven't left the office since they found the bodies Wednesday morning."

"I'm just sick, Gavin. He'll nominate two Nazis."

"Well, of course, in my position I cannot comment on such matters. But I suspect you're correct."

"You've already seen his shortlist of nominees, haven't you, Gavin? Come on, you can tell me. Who's on the list? I'll never tell."

"Neither will I, Thomas."

"So who killed them? I'm a taxpayer. I have a right to know."

"Don't you read the papers? We have no suspects. *Nada.*"

"Surely you have a motive."

"*Mucho* motives. Lots of hatred out there, Thomas."

"Are we on for Monday?"

"Maybe. Voyles wants us to work around the clock until the computers tell us who did it. I plan to work you in, though."

"Thanks. I'll expect a full report, Gavin. Not just the gossip."

"Thomas, Thomas. Always fishing for information. And I, as usual, have none to give you. Gotta run, pal. The tension is so thick around here you can smell it."

Callahan punched the number for the law school library and asked if Darby had been seen. She had not.

DARBY parked in the near-empty lot of the federal building in Lafayette and entered the clerk's office, on the first floor. It was noon Friday, court was not in session, and the hallways were deserted. She stopped at the counter and waited. A deputy clerk walked to the window. "Can I help you?" she asked in the tone of a lowly civil servant who wanted to do anything but help.

Darby slid a strip of paper through the window. "I would like to see this file."

The clerk glanced at the name of the case. "Why?" she asked.

"I don't have to explain. It's public record, isn't it?"

"Semipublic."

Darby took the strip of paper and folded it. "Are you familiar with the Freedom of Information Act?"

"Are you a lawyer?"

"I don't have to be a lawyer to look at this file."

The clerk opened a drawer in the counter and took out a key ring. She nodded, pointing with her forehead. "Follow me."

The sign on the door said JURY ROOM, but inside, there were no tables or chairs, only file cabinets and boxes lining the walls.

The clerk pointed to a wall. "That's it. This file cabinet has the pleadings and correspondence. The rest is discovery, exhibits, and the trial."

"Where's the appeal?"

"Not perfected yet. I think the deadline is November first. Are you a reporter or something?"

"No."

"Good. As you obviously know, these are public records. But the trial judge has placed certain restrictions. First, I must have your name and the precise hours you visited this room. Second, nothing can be taken from this room. Third, nothing in this file can be copied until the appeal is perfected. Fourth, anything you touch must be put back where you found it. Now, what's your name?"

"Darby Shaw."

The clerk scribbled it on a clipboard hanging near the door. "We close at five. Find me at the office when you leave."

Darby opened a drawer full of pleadings and began flipping through files and taking notes. The lawsuit was seven years old, with one plaintiff and thirty-eight corporate defendants who had collectively hired and fired no less than fifteen law firms from all over the country. Big firms, many with hundreds of lawyers.

Seven years of expensive legal warfare, and the outcome was far from certain. Bitter litigation. The trial verdict last summer was only a temporary victory for the defendants. It had been purchased or in some other way been illegally obtained, claimed the plaintiff

33

in its motions for a new trial. Boxes of motions. Accusations and counteraccusations. Pages and pages of affidavits detailing lies and abuses by the lawyers and their clients. One lawyer was dead.

Another had tried suicide, according to a classmate of Darby's who had worked on the fringes of the case when she was employed in a summer clerkship with a big firm in Houston.

Darby stared at the file cabinets. It would take her five hours just to find everything.

CALLAHAN was irritated on Saturday night when he knocked on the door to Darby's apartment. She had avoided him for four days now while she played detective and barricaded herself in the law library. She had skipped classes and failed to return his calls and in general neglected him during his hour of crisis. But he knew that when she opened the door, he would forget about being neglected.

He knocked again. The chain rattled from inside, and he instantly smiled. The feeling of neglect vanished.

"Who is it?" she asked through the chain.

"Thomas Callahan, remember? Begging you to let me in."

The door opened, and Callahan stepped in. He held a liter of wine, and a pizza from Mama Rosa's. Darby took the wine and pecked him on the cheek. "Are we still buddies?" he asked.

"Yes, Thomas. I've been busy." He followed her through the cluttered den to the kitchen. A computer and an assortment of thick books covered the table.

"I called. Why didn't you call me back?"

"I've been out." She opened a drawer and removed a corkscrew.

He looked at her. "It's been three nights, Darby."

"What kind of pizza?" She removed the cork and poured two glasses. Callahan watched every move.

"Oh, it's one of those Saturday-night specials where they throw on everything headed for the garbage. Shrimp tails, eggs, crawfish heads. Cheap wine too. I'm a little low on cash, and I'm leaving town tomorrow, so I have to watch what I spend."

Darby was opening the box. "Looks like sausage and peppers."

He took his wineglass and the bottle and followed her to the den, where she turned on the stereo. They relaxed on the sofa.

"Let's get drunk," he said.

"You're so romantic. You've been drunk for a week."

"Eighty percent of a week. It's your fault, for avoiding me."

"What's wrong with you, Thomas?"

"I'm all keyed up, and I need companionship."

"Let's get half drunk." She sipped her wine and draped her legs across his lap. "What time is your flight?"

"One thirty. Nonstop to National. I'm supposed to register at five, and there's a dinner at eight."

"What's up for Monday?"

"The usual eight hours of airhead debate on the future of the Fifth Amendment. Then a committee will draft a proposed conference report. More debate Tuesday, another report; then we go home. I'd like a late date at a very nice restaurant."

"Why do you go to these conferences?"

"I'm a professor, and I'm expected to. If I didn't go, the dean would think I was not contributing to the academic environment." She refilled the wineglasses. "You're uptight, Thomas."

"I know. It's been a rough week. I hate the thought of a bunch of Neanderthals rewriting the Constitution. We'll live in a police state in ten years, and I can't do anything about it."

The music was soft and the lights low. Callahan had more wine and sank deeper into the sofa. "So, Ms. Shaw, who done it?"

"Professionals. Haven't you read the papers?"

"Of course. But who's behind the professionals?"

"I don't know. The unanimous choice seems to be the Underground Army. But there have been no arrests. I'm not convinced."

"And you've got some obscure suspect unknown to the rest of us."

"I had one, but now I'm not so sure. I spent three days tracking it down, even summarized it in my computer and printed out a thin rough draft of a brief, which I have now discarded."

Callahan stared at her. "You're telling me you skipped classes for three days, ignored me, worked around the clock playing Sherlock Holmes, and now you're throwing it away."

"It's over there, on the table."

"I can't believe this. While I sulked around in loneliness all week, I knew it was for a worthy cause. I knew my suffering was for the good of the country, because you would peel away the onion and tell me tonight or perhaps tomorrow who done it."

"It can't be done—at least not with legal research. There's no pattern, no common thread in the murders. I almost burned up the computers at the law school."

"Ha! I told you so. You forget, dear, that I am a genius at constitutional law, and I knew immediately that Rosenberg and Jensen had nothing in common but black robes and death threats. The Nazis or Aryans or Kluxers or Mafia killed them because Rosenberg was Rosenberg and because Jensen was the easiest target."

"Well, why don't you call the FBI and share your insights with them? I'm sure they're waiting by the phone."

"Don't be angry." Callahan placed his glass on the table and stroked her. "Look, baby, I'll read your brief. And then we'll talk about it, okay? But I'm not thinking clearly right now. . . ."

"Forget my little brief." She grabbed his neck and pulled him to her, and they kissed long and hard.

THE cop stuck his thumb on the button next to the name of Gray Grantham and held it down for twenty seconds. Then a brief pause. Then another twenty seconds. Pause. Twenty seconds. Pause. It was almost dawn, Sunday. The cop pushed again and looked at his patrol car, parked on the curb under the streetlight.

The mike crackled. "Who is it!"

"Police!" answered the cop, who was black and emphasized the *po* in police just for the fun of it.

"What do you want?" Grantham demanded.

"Maybe I got a warrant." The cop was near laughter.

Grantham's voice softened. "What time is it, Cleve?"

"Almost five thirty."

"It must be good."

"Don't know. Sarge didn't say, you know. He just said to wake you up 'cause he wanted to talk. He said be there at six."

"Where?"

"There's a little coffee shop on Fourteenth near the Trinidad Playground. It's dark and safe, and Sarge likes it."

"Where does he find these places?"

"You know, Grantham, for a reporter, you can ask the dumbest questions. The name of the place is Glenda's. Can you find it?"

"Yeah. I'll be there as soon as I can."

SARGE WAS OLD AND VERY BLACK, with a head full of brilliant white hair. He wore thick sunglasses, and most of his co-workers in the White House thought he was half blind. He held his head sideways and smiled like Ray Charles. He sometimes bumped into door facings and desks as he unloaded trash cans and dusted furniture. He walked gingerly, as if counting his steps. He worked patiently, always with a smile, and for the most part he was ignored as just another friendly, old, partially disabled black janitor.

Sarge's territory was the West Wing, where he had been cleaning for thirty years now. Cleaning and listening. Cleaning and seeing. He picked up after some terribly important people who were often too busy to watch their words, especially in the presence of poor old Sarge. He knew which walls were thin, which air vents carried sound. He could disappear in an instant, then reappear in a shadow where the important people could not see him.

No one ever suspected Sarge of leaking stories to the press. There were enough bigmouths within any White House to lay blame on one another. It was hilarious, really. Sarge would talk to Grantham, at the Washington *Post,* then wait excitedly for the story, then listen to the wailing in the basement when the heads rolled. He was an impeccable source, and he talked only to Grantham. His son, Cleve, the cop, arranged the meetings.

Grantham arrived at Glenda's a few minutes after six and walked to a booth in the rear. There were three other customers.

"Good to see you, my friend." Sarge had a raspy voice that was difficult to suppress with a whisper. No one was listening.

Grantham gulped coffee. "Busy week at the White House."

"You could say that. Lot of excitement. Lot of happiness."

"You don't say."

"Yes. The President and his boys are quite happy Rosenberg was murdered. There was almost a festive mood around the place Wednesday. Fate has dealt the President a wonderful hand. He now gets to restructure the Court, and he's very excited about that."

Grantham listened hard as Sarge continued.

"There's a shortlist of nominees. The original had twenty or so names; then it was cut to eight."

"Who did the cutting?"

"Who do you think? The President and Fletcher Coal. They're

terrified of leaks at this point. Evidently the list is nothing but young, staunchly conservative judges, most of whom are obscure."

"Any names?"

"Just two. A man named Pryce, from Idaho, and one named MacLawrence, from Vermont. I think they are both federal judges."

"Anything else?"

"No. But I'll keep my ears open. When will you run it?"

"In the morning. Thanks." Grantham headed for the door.

VERHEEK was late as usual. In the twenty-three-year history of their friendship, he had never been on time. He had no concept of time. Late for Verheek meant at least an hour.

So Callahan sat for an hour in the bar, which suited him just fine. After eight hours of scholarly debate he needed Chivas Regal in his veins, and after two doubles on the rocks he felt better.

When the third double was served, an hour and eleven minutes after seven p.m., Gavin Verheek strolled to the bar.

"Sorry I'm late," he said, and ordered a Moosehead.

"You look tired," Callahan said as he inspected his friend. Old and tired. Verheek was aging badly and gaining weight. There were heavy circles under his eyes. "Did you come from work?"

"I live at work now. The director wants a hundred hours a week until something breaks. I told my wife I'd be home for Christmas."

"How is she?"

"Fine. A very patient lady."

Gavin gulped the beer, and they followed the maître d' to a small table in the corner. Callahan ordered another round.

"Did you see that thing in the *Post*?" Verheek asked.

"I saw it. Who leaked it?"

"Who knows. Voyles got the shortlist Saturday morning, hand-delivered by the President himself, with rather explicit demands about secrecy. He showed the list to no one over the weekend; then this morning the story hit with the names of Pryce and MacLawrence. Voyles went berserk when he saw it, and a few minutes later the President called. Voyles rushed to the White House and had a huge fight with Fletcher Coal. Very nasty."

Callahan hung on every word. "This is pretty good. Keep going."

"Anyway, there's no way the leak came from us. Impossible. It

39

had to come from the White House. It's leaking like rusty pipes."

"Coal probably leaked it."

"Maybe so. He's a sleazy one."

"I've never heard of Pryce and MacLawrence."

"Join the club. They're both young, radically conservative, with precious little experience on the bench."

"And the rest of the list?"

"Don't ask, Thomas. I'll never tell. Let's say that Pryce and MacLawrence seem to be reflective of the entire list."

The drinks arrived. "I want some of those stuffed mushrooms," Verheek told the waiter. "Just to munch on."

"Bring me an order too," said Callahan, slowly sipping his Scotch.

Verheek removed his jacket and loosened his tie. "Let's talk about women. How's the girl?"

"Which one?"

"Come on, Thomas. The girl . . ."

"She's beautiful and brilliant and soft and gentle—"

"What's her name again?"

"Darby. She's from Denver."

"I love western girls. They're so independent, and they tend to wear Levi's and have long legs. Do you have a photo?"

"No. She's not a grandchild or a poodle."

"It must be nine, ten months now. The great Thomas Callahan, he of the disposable women, has fallen hard."

"I have not."

Verheek was leaning halfway across the table, grinning stupidly. "Don't lie to me, Thomas. I think you're in love with this gal but too cowardly to admit it. I think she's got your number, pal."

"Okay, she does. Do you feel better?"

"Yeah, much better."

The mushrooms were served in simmering skillets. Verheek stuffed two in his mouth and chewed furiously.

Four Arabs noisily filled a table next to them, yakking and jabbering in their own language. All four ordered Jack Daniel's.

"Who killed them, Gavin?"

Verheek chewed for a minute, then swallowed hard. "If I knew, I wouldn't tell. But I swear I do not know. It's baffling. Not a clue."

"Why the combination?"

"Simple. It's so simple, it's easy to overlook. Rosenberg had no security system in his town house. Any decent cat burglar could come and go. And poor Jensen was hanging around those places at midnight. They were exposed. That's why they were selected."

"Then who selected them?"

"Someone with a lot of money. The killers were professionals, and they were probably out of the country within hours."

"How much would these killers charge?"

"Millions. And it took a bunch of money to plan it all."

Callahan reached into his coat pocket and removed a thick envelope. He laid it down. "Take a look at this when you get a chance. It's sort of a brief. Darby wrote it."

"I'll read it tonight. What's it about?"

"She took off four days last week, totally ignored the rest of the world, and came up with her own theory, which she has now discarded. But read it anyway. It's fascinating. She is very intelligent. Her passion, other than me of course, is constitutional law."

"Poor thing."

The Arabs erupted in screaming laughter, slapping each other and spilling whiskey. Callahan and Verheek watched them for a minute until they died down.

Verheek stuffed the envelope into his coat, on the back of his chair. "What's her theory?"

"It's a bit unusual. But read it. I mean, it can't hurt, can it? You guys need the help."

"I'll read it only because she wrote it. I'd love to meet her."

## FIVE

THE phone rang four times, and Gray Grantham grabbed it from bed. He sat on a pillow trying to focus.

"Who is it?" he asked.

The voice on the other end was low and timid. "Is this Gray Grantham with the Washington *Post?*"

"It is. Who's calling?"

Slowly, "I can't give you my name."

The fog lifted, and Grantham focused on the clock. It was five forty. "Okay, forget the name. Why are you calling?"

"I saw your story yesterday about the nominees."

"That's good. Why are you calling me at this obscene hour?"

"I'm sorry. I'm on my way to work and stopped at a pay phone. I can't call from home or the office."

The voice was clear and articulate. "What kind of office?"

"I'm an attorney."

"Private or government?"

A slight hesitation. "Uh . . . I'd rather not say."

"Okay. Look, I'd rather be sleeping. Why exactly did you call?"

"I may know something about Rosenberg and Jensen."

Grantham sat on the edge of the bed. "Such as . . ."

A much longer pause. "Are you recording this? I'm really very scared and confused, Mr. Grantham. I prefer not to record this."

"Whatever you want. I'm listening."

"Can this call be traced?"

"Possibly. But you're at a pay phone. What difference does it make?"

"I don't know. I'm just scared."

"It's okay. I swear I'm not recording, and I swear I won't trace it. Now, what's on your mind?"

"Well, I think I may know who killed them."

Grantham was standing. "That's pretty valuable knowledge."

"It could get me killed. . . ." The voice trailed off, as if he were looking over his shoulder.

"Relax," Grantham said, pacing now. "Why don't you tell me your name, okay? I swear it's confidential."

"Garcia. That's not a real name, but it's the best I can do."

"Okay, Garcia. Talk to me."

"I'm not certain, okay? But I think I stumbled across something at the office that I was not supposed to see."

"Do you have a copy of it?"

"Maybe."

"Look, Garcia, you called me. Do you want to talk or not?"

"I'm not sure. What will you do if I tell you something?"

"Check it out thoroughly. If we're gonna accuse someone of the assassinations of two Supreme Court Justices, believe me, the story will be handled delicately." There was a very long silence. Grantham froze and waited. "Garcia, are you there?"

"Yeah. I need to think about this. I haven't slept in a week, and I'm not thinking rationally. I might call later." He hung up.

Grantham looked at the row of numbers on his phone and punched seven digits, waited, then six more, then four more. He scribbled a number on a pad by the phone and hung up. The pay phone was on Fifteenth Street in Pentagon City.

GAVIN Verheek slept four hours and woke up drunk. When he arrived at the Hoover building an hour later, the alcohol was fading and the pain was settling in. He cursed himself, and he cursed Callahan, who no doubt would sleep until noon. They had left the restaurant at midnight, when it closed, then hit a few bars.

He had a meeting with Director Voyles at eleven, and it was imperative to appear sober and alert. He told his secretary that he had caught a nasty virus—maybe the flu—and that he was to be left alone at his desk unless it was awfully important. She closed the door behind her. He opened his briefcase and found the envelope.

The brief was thirteen pages of computer paper, all double-spaced with wide margins. Her name, address, and phone number were typed on the cover sheet. She wrote well, in the scholarly legal fashion of long sentences with large words. But she was clear.

Gavin had never heard of her suspect and was certain it was not on anyone's list. Technically it was not a brief, but more of a story about a lawsuit in Louisiana. She told the facts succinctly and made them interesting—fascinating, really.

The facts took four pages; then she filled the next three with brief histories of the parties. He was hooked. On page 8 the brief summarized the trial. On 9 it mentioned the appeal, and the final three pages laid an implausible trail to the removal of Rosenberg and Jensen from the Court. Callahan said she had already discarded this theory, and she seemed to lose steam at the end. But it was readable.

There was a soft knock at the door. It was Verheek's secretary. "I hate to bother, but the director wants you in his office."

He rubbed his eyes. "Do you have any aspirin?"

"Well, yes, I believe so."

He sat holding his head in his hands. He heard her banging drawers, and then she was before him with the goods.

"Thanks." He pointed at the brief. "Send this to Special Agent

43

Eric East. He's in charge of the murder investigation. Write a note from me. Tell him to look it over when he has a minute."

She left with the brief.


FLETCHER Coal opened the door to the Oval Office and spoke gravely to K. O. Lewis and Eric East. The President was in Puerto Rico viewing hurricane damage, and Director Voyles now refused to meet with Coal alone. He sent his underlings.

Coal waved them to a sofa, and he sat across the coffee table. For a week now they had brought daily reports of their investigation to this office and handed them to Coal, who devoured the material and memorized it for the next meeting. He had perfect recall. If they misstated something, he would terrorize them.

Lewis placed a four-inch stack of the latest reports on the table. "Anything new?" Coal asked.

"Maybe. The French authorities were routinely reviewing footage taken by the security cameras at a Paris airport, and they thought they recognized a face. They reported to Interpol. The face is disguised, but Interpol believes it is Khamel, the terrorist. I'm sure you've heard of—"

"I have."

"They've studied the footage at length and are almost certain he exited a United plane that arrived nonstop from Dulles last Wednesday, about ten hours after Jensen was found."

"And Interpol contacted the CIA?"

"Yes. They talked to Gminski around one this afternoon."

Coal's face registered nothing. "How certain are they?"

"Eighty percent. Khamel's a master of disguise, and it would be a bit unusual for him to travel in such a manner. So there's room for doubt. We've got photos and a summary. Frankly, I've studied the pictures, and I can't tell anything. But Interpol knows him."

"He hasn't been photographed in years, has he?"

"Not that we know of. And rumor has it he goes under the knife and gets a new face every two or three years."

Coal pondered this for a second. "Okay. What if it's Khamel, and what if he was involved in the killings? What does it mean?"

"It means we'll never find him. There are at least nine countries, including Israel, actively stalking him right now."

"What else do you have?"

Lewis glanced at Eric East. "Well, maybe a small new wrinkle."

"What is it?" Coal asked.

East shifted uncomfortably. The brief had been passed upward all day, until Voyles read it and liked it. He viewed it as a long shot, but the brief mentioned the President, and Voyles loved the idea of making Coal and his boss sweat. He had instructed Lewis and East to deliver the brief to Coal and to treat it as a theory the Bureau was taking seriously. For the first time in a week Voyles had smiled. "Play it up," he had said. "Tell them we intend to pursue it."

"It's a theory that has surfaced in the last twenty-four hours, and Director Voyles is quite intrigued by it," East said. "He's afraid it could be damaging to the President."

Coal was stone-faced, never flinching. "How's that?"

East placed the brief on the table. "It's all here in this report."

WHEN Air Force One landed at Andrews a few minutes after ten p.m., the President bounced off the plane and darted into his limousine. Coal was waiting. The President sank low in the seat. "I didn't expect you," he said.

"We need to talk." The limo sped away toward the White House.

"It's late and I'm tired. What's so important?"

Coal handed over a copy of what was now known as the pelican brief.

"I don't want to read," said the President. "Tell me about it."

"Voyles and his motley crew have stumbled across a suspect that no one has mentioned until now. An eager-beaver law student at Tulane wrote this thing, and it somehow made its way to Voyles, who decided it had merit. The theory is so farfetched, it's incredible, and on its face it doesn't worry me. But Voyles worries me. He's decided he must pursue with enthusiasm, and the press is watching every move he makes. There could be leaks."

"We can't control his investigation."

"We can manipulate it. Gminski is waiting at the White House."

"Gminski!"

"Relax, Chief. I personally handed him a copy of this three hours ago and swore him to secrecy. He may be incompetent, but he can keep a secret. I trust him much more than Voyles."

"I don't trust either one of them."

Coal liked to hear this. He wanted the President to trust no one but him. "I think you should ask the CIA to immediately investigate this. I would like to know everything before Voyles starts digging. Neither will find anything, but if we know more than Voyles, you can convince him to back off. It makes sense, Chief."

The President was frustrated. "It's domestic. The CIA has no business snooping around. It's probably illegal."

"It is illegal, technically. But Gminski will do it for you, and he can do it quickly, secretly, and more thoroughly than the FBI."

The President took the brief and tossed it onto the empty seat next to him. "Is it someone we know?"

"Yes."

BECAUSE it is a city of the night, New Orleans wakes slowly. It's quiet until well after dawn, then eases into the morning. There's no early rush except on the corridors to and from the suburbs, and the busy streets downtown. But in the French Quarter—the soul of New Orleans—the smell of last night's whiskey, jambalaya, and blackened redfish lingers not far above the empty streets, until the sun can be seen. An hour or two later it is replaced with the aroma of coffee and beignets, and the sidewalks reluctantly show signs of life.

Darby curled herself in a chair on the small balcony, sipping coffee and waiting on the sun. Callahan was a few feet away through the open French doors, still wrapped in sheets and dead to the world. She pulled his robe closer around her and inhaled the richness of his cologne. She thought of her father and his baggy cotton button-downs, which he let her wear when she was a teenager.

Her father was her friend. By the time she finished high school, she had the run of his closet. If he were living now, he would be four years older than Thomas Callahan. Her mother had remarried and moved to Boise. Darby had a brother, in Germany. The three seldom talked. Her father had been the glue in a fractious family, and his death had scattered them.

Twenty other people had died in the plane crash, and before the funeral arrangements were complete, the lawyers were calling. It was her first real exposure to the legal world, and it was not pleasant. A slick ambulance chaser got next to her brother, and he persuaded the family to sue quickly. His name was Herschel, and for two years the family suffered as he stalled and lied, and bungled the case. They settled a week before trial for half a million—after Herschel's cut—and Darby got a hundred thousand.

She had decided to be a lawyer. If a clown like Herschel could do it and make big bucks while wreaking havoc on society, then she could do it for a nobler purpose. She wanted to work for an environmental firm. Finding a job, she knew, would not be a problem.

Darby's hundred thousand had doubled. She had placed most of it in mutual funds, but only those without holdings in chemical and petroleum companies. She lived modestly. Callahan cared little for money and never pressed her for information.

She laid the ground rules for the relationship, and he agreed to them. There would be no other women. They would be very discreet. And he had to stop drinking so much.

He stuck to the first two, but the drinking continued. There were heavy drinkers in his family, and it was sort of expected of him. Still, for the first time in his life, Thomas Callahan was madly in love, so he was careful about the drinking. With the exception of last week and the trauma of losing Rosenberg, he never drank before five p.m.

When she was dressed, Darby kissed him on the cheek and covered him with a quilt. She locked the front door quietly behind her. The sun was up now, peeking through the buildings across Dauphine. The sidewalk was empty.

She had class in three hours, then con law at eleven. It was time to be a student again. She had wasted four days playing detective.

THEY watched her, and it was enjoyable. Tight jeans, baggy sweater, long legs, sunglasses. They watched her close the door and walk quickly along Royal, then disappear around the corner. The hair was shoulder length and appeared to be dark red.

It was she.

THE monitor was on a cluttered table in the center of the newsroom, and Gray Grantham glared at it amid the hum and roar of the gathering and reporting. The words were not coming. The phone rang, and he grabbed the receiver. "Grantham."

"It's Garcia."

47

He forgot the monitor. "Yeah, so what's up?"

"I have two questions. First, do you record these calls, and second, can you trace them?"

"No and yes. We don't record until we ask permission, and we can trace, but we don't."

"Okay. I'm just scared, that's all. I'll talk to you as long as I can trust you, but if you ever lie to me, Mr. Grantham, I'll quit talking."

"It's a deal. When do you start talking?"

"I can't talk now. I'm in a hurry. I'll call during lunch tomorrow."

"I'll be waiting right here."

Garcia was gone. Grantham punched seven digits, then six, then four. He wrote the number, then flipped through the yellow pages to Pay Phones Inc. The Vendor Location listed the number as being on Pennsylvania Avenue near the Justice Department.

THE argument started with dessert. She clicked off the drinks Callahan had already consumed with dinner: two double Scotches while they waited for a table, one more before they ordered, and, with the fish, two bottles of wine, of which she'd had two glasses. He was drinking too fast, and by the time she finished rattling off this accounting, he was angry. He ordered Drambuie for dessert because it was suddenly a matter of principle. She was furious.

Darby spooned her coffee and ignored him. Mouton's was packed, and she just wanted to leave without a scene and go home.

The argument turned nasty on the sidewalk. He pulled the keys to the Porsche from his pocket, and she said he was too drunk to drive. Give her the keys. He staggered on in the direction of the parking lot, three blocks away. She said she would walk, and followed a few steps behind, embarrassed at the stumbling figure in front of her. She pleaded with him. He would kill someone. He yelled something about driving better drunk than she could sober. She'd never seen him this drunk.

She yelled at him as he approached the Porsche. "Thomas! Please! Let me drive!" She was on the sidewalk across the street and would go no farther. He stumbled on, waving her off. He unlocked the door, squeezed downward, and disappeared between the other cars. The engine started and roared as he gunned it.

Next to the parking lot was a greasy little dive with neon beer signs covering the windows. Darby leaned on the side of the building, looked at the street, and almost hoped for a cop.

The explosion knocked her to the sidewalk. She landed on all fours, face down, stunned for a second, then immediately aware of the heat and the tiny pieces of fiery debris falling in the street. She gaped in horror at the parking lot. The Porsche had flipped in a perfect violent somersault and landed upside down. The car was a brilliant fireball, roaring away with flames instantly devouring it.

Darby started toward it, screaming for him. Debris fell around her, and the heat slowed her. She stopped thirty feet away, screaming with hands over her mouth.

Then a second explosion flipped it again and drove her away. She tripped, and her head fell hard on the bumper of another car. The pavement was hot to her face. That was the last she remembered.

The dive emptied, and the drunks were everywhere. They stood along the sidewalk and stared. Thick, heavy smoke billowed from the fireball, and within seconds two other cars were on fire. There were shouts and voices in panic.

"Whose car is it?"

"Is anybody in it?"

"Call 911!"

They dragged her by the elbows back to the sidewalk, to the center of the crowd. She was repeating the name Thomas. A cold cloth was placed on her forehead. Sirens. She heard sirens as she came around. "Thomas," she repeated, her mouth dry. "Thomas."

"It's okay. It's okay," said a black face just above her. He was carefully holding her head and patting her arm. Other faces stared.

The sirens were screaming now. She gently removed the cloth, and her eyes focused. There were red and blue lights flashing from the street. She sat up. They leaned her against the building, beneath the neon beer signs. They eased away, watching her carefully.

"You all right, miss?" asked the black man.

She couldn't answer. Didn't try to. "Where is Thomas?" she asked.

The first fire truck screamed to a halt twenty feet away, and the crowd parted. Firemen scrambled in all directions.

"Miss, who is Thomas?" asked the black man.

"Thomas Callahan," she said softly, as if everyone knew him.

"Was he in that car?"

She nodded, then closed her eyes. The sirens wailed and died, and in between she heard the shouts of anxious men and the popping of the fire. She could smell the burning.

A cop shoved his way through the crowd. "Police. Outta the way. Police." He pushed and shoved until he found her. He waved a badge under her nose. "Ma'am, Sergeant Rupert, NOPD."

He was in her face, this Rupert with bushy hair, a baseball cap, black-and-gold Saints jacket. She stared blankly at him.

"Is that your car, ma'am? Someone said it was your car."

She shook her head. No.

Rupert was asking if she was all right, and at the same time pulling her up. It hurt like mad. Her head was busted, and she was in shock, but what did this moron care. She was on her feet. Her knees wouldn't lock, and he kept asking if she was all right. The black man looked at Rupert as if he were crazy.

There, the legs worked now, and she and Rupert were walking through the crowd to an unmarked cop car. She lowered her head and refused to look at the parking lot. Rupert opened the front door and gingerly placed her in the passenger's seat.

Another cop squatted in the door and started asking questions. He wore jeans, and cowboy boots with pointed toes. Darby placed her head in her hands. "I think I need help," she said.

"Sure, lady. Just a coupla questions. What's your name?"

"Darby Shaw. I'm very dizzy, and I think I'm in shock."

"The ambulance is on the way."

Another cop car, one with decals and lights, squealed to a stop in front of Rupert's. Rupert disappeared for a moment. The cowboy cop suddenly closed her door, and she was all alone in the car. She started crying. She was cold. She slowly laid her head on the driver's seat and curled into a knot. Silence. Then darkness.

SOMEONE was knocking on the window above her. She opened her eyes. The man wore a uniform, and a hat with a badge on it.

"Open the door, lady!" he yelled.

She sat up and unlocked the door.

"Is this your car, lady?"

"No!" She glared at him. "No, it's Rupert's."

"Okay. Who the hell is Rupert?"

There was one fire truck left, and most of the crowd was gone. This man in the door was obviously a cop. "Sergeant Rupert. One of you guys," she said.

"Get outta the car, lady."

Darby crawled out and stood on the sidewalk. In the distance a solitary fireman hosed down the burned frame of the Porsche.

Another cop joined them on the sidewalk.

The first cop asked, "What's your name?"

"Darby Shaw."

"Why were you passed out in the car?"

She looked at the car. "I don't know. I got hurt, and Rupert put me in the car. Where's Rupert?"

"Who's Rupert?" the first cop asked.

This made her mad, and the anger cleared away the cobwebs. "Rupert said he was a cop."

The second cop asked, "How'd you get hurt?"

Darby glared at him. She pointed to the parking lot across the street. "I was supposed to be in that car over there. But I wasn't, so I'm here listening to your stupid questions. Where's Rupert?"

They looked blankly at each other. The first cop said, "Stay here," and he walked across the street to another cop car, where a man in a suit was talking to a small group. They whispered; then the first cop and the man in the suit walked back to Darby.

The man in the suit said, "I'm Lieutenant Olson, New Orleans PD. Did you know the man in the car?" He pointed to the parking lot.

The knees went weak, and she bit her lip. She nodded.

"What's his name?"

"Thomas Callahan."

"That's what the computer said. Now, who's this Rupert?"

Darby screamed, "He said he was a cop!"

Olson looked sympathetic. "I'm sorry. There's no cop named Rupert."

She was sobbing loudly. Olson helped her to the hood of Rupert's car and gently held both her shoulders with his hands while the crying subsided and she fought to regain control.

"Check the plates," Olson told the second cop, who quickly scribbled down the tag number and went to call it in.

Olson looked at her eyes. "Were you with Callahan?"

51

She nodded, still crying but much quieter.

"How did you get in this car?" Olson asked slowly and softly.

She wiped her eyes and stared at Olson. "This guy, Rupert, came and got me. He put me in the car, and this other cop, with cowboy boots, started asking questions. Another cop car pulled up, and they left. Then I guess I passed out. I would like to see a doctor."

The second cop was back with a puzzled look. "The computer has no record of this tag number. Must be fake tags."

Olson took her arm and led her to his car. He spoke quickly to the two cops. "I'm taking her to Charity. Wrap this up and meet me there. Impound the car. We'll check it later."

She sat in Olson's car, staring at the parking lot. Four cars had burned. The Porsche was upside down in the center; nothing but a crumpled frame. A cop was stringing yellow crime-scene tape around the lot. Tears dripped off her chin.

Olson slammed his door, and they eased through the parked cars and headed for St. Charles, with the blue lights on, but no sirens.

"He's dead, isn't he?" she said.

"Yes, Darby. I'm sorry. I take it he was the only one in the car."

"Yes." He gave her a handkerchief, and she wiped her eyes. "Please, tell me who Rupert is," she said.

"I have no idea. I don't know a cop named Rupert, and there was no cop here with cowboy boots."

She thought about this for a block and a half.

"What did Callahan do for a living?"

"A law professor at Tulane. I'm a student there."

"Who would want to kill him?"

She shook her head. "You're certain it was intentional?"

"No doubt about it. It was a very powerful explosive."

She tried to speak, but could not hold the tears. She buried her head in the handkerchief.

Olson parked near the emergency entrance at Charity and helped her quickly inside. Darby found a seat, and Olson talked to the lady behind the window, then crouched in front of Darby. "It'll be a few minutes. Sit tight. I'm gonna move the car."

He was gone. Darby waited, then walked through a pair of double doors and down a hall. The hall was a zoo, with nurses and orderlies and the wounded yelling and moving about. She turned a corner and saw an EXIT sign. Through the door, and she was in an alley. Don't run. Be strong. It's okay. No one's watching. She was on the street, walking briskly. She refused to cry.

When Olson returned, he would figure they had called her and she was back there getting worked on. He would wait. And wait.

She turned corners. The French Quarter was just ahead. She could get lost there. She felt safer. She entered the Holiday Inn on Royal, paid with plastic, and got a room. After the door was bolted and chained, she curled up on the bed with all the lights on.

# SIX

VERHEEK emerged from the bathroom with shaving cream on half his face and grabbed the phone. "Hello," he snapped.

It was a female voice he'd never heard before. "This is Darby Shaw. Do you know who I am?"

He smiled. "Well, yes. I believe we have a mutual friend."

"Did you read the little theory I wrote?"

"Ah, yes. The pelican brief, as we refer to it."

"And who is we?"

Verheek sat in a chair by the bed. This was no social call. "Why are you calling, Darby?"

"I need some answers, Mr. Verheek. I'm scared to death."

"It's Gavin, okay?"

"Gavin. What did you do with the brief?"

"Well, I read it, then sent it to another division within the Bureau; then it was shown to Director Voyles."

"Has it been seen outside the FBI?"

"I can't answer that, Darby."

"Then I won't tell you what's happened to Thomas."

Verheek pondered this for a long minute. "Yes, it's been seen outside the FBI. By whom and by how many, I don't know."

"Thomas is dead, Gavin. He was murdered around ten last night. Someone planted a car bomb for both of us. I got lucky, but now they're after me."

"Darby, are you certain? I mean, who would want to kill him?"

"I met a couple of them."

"Are you hurt?"

"Physically I'm okay."

"Where are you, Darby?"

"New Orleans."

"How'd you—"

"It's a long story. Who saw the brief, Gavin? Thomas gave it to you Monday night. Forty-eight hours later he's dead. And I'm supposed to be. It fell into the wrong hands, wouldn't you say?"

"Are you safe? Where are you staying?"

"Not so fast, Gavin. I'm moving real slow right now. I'm at a pay phone, so no cute stuff."

"Come on, Darby! Thomas Callahan was my best friend. We'll have a dozen agents pick you up. You can't stay on the streets."

"Why, Gavin? Who's after me? Talk to me, Gavin."

"I'll talk to you when I get there."

"I don't know. Thomas is dead because he talked to you. I'm not that anxious to meet you right now."

"Darby, look, I don't know who or why, but I assure you you're in a very dangerous situation. We can protect you."

She hesitated. "Maybe later." The voice was cracking.

He breathed deeply. "You can trust me, Darby."

"Okay, I trust you. But my brief has someone awfully upset."

"Will you call me at the office? I'll give you an inside number."

"Give me the number, and I'll think about it."

"Please, Darby. I'll go straight to the director when I get there. Call me at eight, your time."

Darby hung up. The shock of it all—the fatigue, the fear, the pain. Darby buried her head in the pillow. She hated crying, and this would be the last of it for a while. Mourning would only get her killed.

EVEN though it was a wonderful crisis, with the ratings up and Rosenberg dead, with the Democrats running for cover, and reelection next year in the bag, the President was sick of this crisis and its relentless predawn meetings. He was sick of F. Denton Voyles and his smugness, his squatty little figure in a wrinkled trench coat sitting on the other side of his desk. He would be here in a minute for another tense encounter before breakfast, in which Voyles would tell only a portion of what he knew.

He was sick of Coal too. Sick of his brilliance. Coal was happiest on mornings when the tension was thick and a nasty meeting was planned. He was standing beside the desk now, going through the mail, while the President scanned the *Post*. The President glanced at him. Perfect black suit, white shirt, red silk tie, a bit too much grease on the hair.

"Voyles said he wouldn't come if I was here. That's hilarious," Coal said. He was clearly amused.

"I don't think he likes you," the President said.

"He loves people he can run over."

"I guess I need to be sweet to him."

"Lay it on thick, Chief. He has to back off. This theory is so weak it's comical, but in his hands it could be dangerous."

"What about the law student?"

"We're checking. She appears harmless."

A secretary on the intercom announced the arrival of Voyles.

"I'll be going," Coal said. He would listen and watch from around the corner. At his insistence three closed-circuit cameras had been installed in the Oval Office. The monitors were in a small locked room in the West Wing. He had the only key. The cameras were invisible and supposedly a big secret.

The President met Voyles at the door with a warm handshake and guided him to the sofa for a warm, friendly little chat. Voyles was not impressed. He knew Coal would be listening. And watching.

Voyles removed his trench coat and laid it properly on a chair.

The President crossed his legs. He was wearing the brown cardigan. The grandfather. "Denton," he said gravely, "I need a favor."

Voyles stared with rigid and unblinking eyes. "Yes, sir."

"I need the scoop on this pelican thing. It's a wild idea, but it mentions me, sort of. How serious are you taking it?"

Oh, this was funny. Voyles fought off a smile. It was working. Mr. President and Mr. Coal were sweating the pelican brief. They had received it late Tuesday, worried all day Wednesday, and now, in the waking hours of Thursday, were on their knees begging about something one notch above a practical joke.

"We're investigating, Mr. President." It was a lie, but how could he know? "We are pursuing all leads, all suspects."

"What have you learned?"

"Not much, but we just started," Voyles said. "I assigned fourteen

55

agents in New Orleans to start digging." The lies sounded so good.

Fourteen! The President sat up straight. Fourteen Fibbies out there flashing badges, asking questions, and it was just a matter of time before this thing got out. "Sounds like it's pretty serious."

Voyles was unyielding. "We're very serious, Mr. President. They've been dead a week, and we're tracking leads as fast as we can. My men are working around the clock."

"I understand all that, but how serious is this pelican theory?"

This was fun. "I doubt if there's anything to it, Mr. President. But we've got to check it out."

There was a touch of a smile. "I don't have to tell you, Denton, how much this nonsense could hurt if the press found out. I just wish you would back off this thing. I mean, it's absurd, and I could really get burned. Know what I'm saying?"

"Mr. President, are you asking me to ignore a suspect?"

The President shifted and recrossed his legs. "Come on, Denton, you know what I'm saying. There are bigger fish in the pond. The press is watching this investigation, just dying to find out who's a suspect. You know how they are. Forget about it for a while. This little brief is a joke, but it could embarrass the heck out of me."

Denton Voyles looked hard at him. Relentless.

The President shifted again. "What about this Khamel thing? Since we're talking numbers, how many men are assigned to him?"

Voyles said, "Fifteen," and almost laughed.

The President's mouth fell open. The hottest suspect in the game gets fifteen, and this damned pelican thing gets fourteen.

Coal smiled, and shook his head. Voyles had been caught in his own lies. On the bottom of page 4 of the Wednesday report Eric East and K. O. Lewis gave the number at thirty, not fifteen. "Relax, Chief," Coal whispered to the screen. "He's playing with you."

The President was anything but relaxed. "Good Lord, Denton. Why only fifteen? I thought this was a significant break."

"I'm running this investigation, Mr. President."

"I know. And you're doing a fine job. I'm not meddling. I just wish you'd consider spending your time elsewhere, that's all."

"So you're asking me to back off?"

The President stared fiercely at Voyles. "Ignore it for a couple of weeks, Denton. If it flares up again, take another look."

Voyles relented and managed a tiny smile. "I'll make you a deal. Your hatchet man Coal has done a number on me with the press over the security we provided to Rosenberg and Jensen. You keep that pit bull away from me, and I'll forget the pelican theory."

"I don't make deals."

Voyles kept his cool. "Good. I'll send fifty agents to New Orleans tomorrow. And fifty the next day. We'll be flashing badges all over town and doing our damnedest to attract attention."

The President jumped to his feet. "All right, all right. It's a deal."

Voyles stood. "I don't trust Coal, and if I smell him one more time during this investigation, the deal's off and we investigate the pelican brief with all the weight I can muster."

The President held up his hands and smiled. "It's a deal."

Voyles was smiling, and the President was smiling, and in the closet near the Cabinet Room, Fletcher Coal was smiling at a screen. Hatchet man. Pit bull. He loved it. Those were the words that created legends. He turned off the screens and locked the door behind him. He had some typing to do.

Occasionally Coal found it necessary to resort to the phantom memo. These were always widely circulated in the West Wing and usually dripped to the press. They could be found lying on almost every desk. Coal would scream and accuse. He had fired people for phantom memos, all of which came from his typewriter.

It was four paragraphs, and it summarized what he knew about Khamel and his recent flight out of Washington. And there were vague links to the Libyans and Palestinians. Coal admired it. How long before it would be in the *Post* or the *Times?*


From the White House the director would fly to New York and return tomorrow. Gavin camped outside K. O. Lewis' office until there was an opening in his schedule. He was in.

"You look scared," Lewis said.

"I've just lost my best friend, Thomas Callahan—the guy from Tulane who brought me the pelican brief. It got passed around, then sent to the White House and who knows where else, and now he's dead. Blown to bits by a car bomb last night in New Orleans."

"I'm sorry."

"It's not a matter of being sorry. Evidently the bomb was intended for Callahan and the student who wrote it—a girl by the name of Darby Shaw. They've been dating and were supposed to be in the car together when it exploded. But she survived, and I get this call this morning at five, and it's her. Scared to death."

Lewis listened. "And you think there's a connection between Callahan's death and the brief?"

"Yes, I think so. Don't you?"

"Doesn't matter, Gavin. I just got off the phone with the director. Pelican's off our list. I'm not sure it was ever on it."

"But my friend's been killed with a car bomb."

"I'm sorry. I'm sure the authorities there are investigating."

"Listen to me, K.O. I'm asking for a favor."

"Listen to me, Gavin." Lewis was walking around the desk. "I don't have any favors. We're chasing enough rabbits right now, and if Director Voyles says stop, we stop. Voyles was explicit."

"So was the girl, K.O. He was murdered, and now she's hiding somewhere in New Orleans, calling for help, and we're too busy."

"I'm sorry, Gavin." Lewis placed his hand on Verheek's shoulder, as if his time were up. Gavin jerked away and headed for the door.

"I'm not giving up, K.O." He slammed the door behind him.

SHE entered Rubinstein Brothers from Canal Street and got lost between the racks of men's shirts. No one followed her in. She quickly picked out a navy parka—men's small—a genderless pair of aviator sunglasses, and a British driving cap. She paid with plastic. As the clerk ran the card through she put the parka on and stuffed her hair under the hooded collar. The clerk watched discreetly.

She exited. Back on Canal. A busload of tourists swarmed into the Sheraton, and she joined them. She went to the wall of phones and called Mrs. Chen, her neighbor. Had she seen or heard anyone? Very early there had been a knock on the door. Mrs. Chen hadn't seen anyone, just heard the knock. Darby's car was still on the street. Everything okay? Yes, all's fine. Thanks.

She watched the tourists and punched the inside number for Gavin Verheek. After three minutes of refusing to give her name, and repeating his, she had him.

"Where are you?" he asked.

"Let me explain something. For the moment I will not tell you or anyone else where I am. So don't ask. What did Mr. Voyles say?"

"Mr. Voyles was at the White House and unavailable. I'll try to talk to him later today."

"That's pretty weak, Gavin. You have nothing. I expected more."

"Be patient, Darby."

"Patience will get me killed. What would you do if you knew you were supposed to be dead, and the people trying to kill you had assassinated two Justices, knocked off a law professor, and have billions of dollars they obviously don't mind using to kill with?"

"Go to the FBI."

"Thomas went to the FBI, and he's dead."

"Thanks, Darby. That's not fair."

"I'm not worried about fairness or feelings. I'm more concerned with staying alive until noon."

She saw a face. He walked among the tourists at the registration desk. He held a folded newspaper and tried to appear at home, just another guest, but his walk was a bit hesitant and his eyes were searching. The face was long and thin with round glasses.

"Gavin, listen to me. Write this down. I see a man I've seen before—maybe an hour ago. Six feet two or three, thin, thirty years old, glasses, receding hair, dark in color. He's gone. He's gone."

"Did he see you? Where are you?"

"In a hotel lobby. I don't know if he saw me. I'm gone."

"Darby, listen to me! Whatever you do, keep in touch, okay?"

"I'll try."

THE photographer's name was Croft, and he did a little of this free-lance work—this slithering around, shooting people who did not know they were targets of a private investigator. Many of his clients were divorce lawyers who needed dirt for trial.

Another client was Gray Grantham. Grantham was a serious, ethical reporter with just a touch of sleaze, and when he needed a dirty trick, he called. Croft liked Grantham because he was honest about his sleaziness. The rest were so pious.

It was noon, and Croft was in Grantham's Volvo because it had a phone. He was on Pennsylvania, parked illegally. The booth was a block and a half ahead, and with his telephoto lens he could almost read the phone book hanging from the rack.

At twenty after twelve a young man with a nice suit appeared from nowhere and closed the door. Croft got his Nikon and rested the lens on the steering wheel. The sidewalk bustled with lunch traffic. The shoulders and heads moved quickly by. A gap. Click. A gap. Click. The subject was punching numbers and glancing around.

The car phone rang three times and stopped. It was the signal from Grantham, at the *Post*. This was their man, and he was talking. Croft fired away. Click. Click. Full face, full figure. Beautiful.

GARCIA was shadowboxing. He had a wife and child, he said, and he was scared. There was a career ahead with plenty of money, and if he kept his mouth shut, he would be a wealthy man. But he wanted to talk. He rambled on about how he had something to say, but just couldn't make the decision. He didn't trust anyone.

Grantham let him ramble long enough for Croft to do his number. Garcia would eventually spill his guts. He had called three times now and was growing comfortable with his new friend, Grantham, who'd played this game many times and knew how it worked.

The pictures were outstanding. Croft had blown them to five by seven. Garcia was under thirty, a very nice looking, clean-cut lawyer. Dark, short hair. Dark eyes. Maybe Hispanic, but the skin was not dark. Navy suit—expensive. White collar, silk tie.

Grantham studied the pictures and kept an eye on the door. Sarge was never late. It was dark, and the club was filling up. Grantham's was the only white face within three blocks.

Garcia, he could see, was too well dressed to be a government lawyer. So he was a private one in a firm for about three or four years now and hitting somewhere around eighty grand. Great. That narrowed it down to fifty thousand lawyers.

The door opened, and Cleve, Sarge's son, walked in through the smoke and haze. He sat in the booth across from Grantham.

"Where's Sarge?" Grantham asked.

"Sarge didn't want to talk tonight. He gave me an urgent message for you. I've got an envelope in my car, sealed real tight."

"Let's go."

They made their way through the crowd to the door. The patrol car was parked at the curb. Cleve opened the door and pulled the envelope from the glove box. "He got this in the West Wing."

Grantham stuffed it into his pocket. "Thanks, Cleve. Tell Sarge I love him."

"I'm sure that'll give him a thrill."

The patrol car drove away, and Grantham hurried to his Volvo. He locked the door, turned on the dome light, and ripped open the envelope. It was clearly an internal White House memo, and it was about an assassin named Khamel.

Grantham flew across town toward central Washington. It was almost seven thirty, and if he could put it together in an hour, it would make the late city edition, which began rolling off the presses at ten thirty. Thank goodness for the car phone. He called a friend at the foreign desk and asked him to pull everything on Khamel.

He was suspicious of the memo. The words were too sensitive to sling around the office like the latest policy on coffee or vacations. Someone, probably Fletcher Coal, wanted the world to know that Khamel had emerged as a suspect in the killings of Justices Rosenberg and Jensen, and that he was an Arab of all things and had close ties to Libya and Iran and Iraq—countries led by fiery idiots who hated America. Someone in the White House of Fools wanted the story on the front page.

It was a helluva story. He and Smith Keen, the assistant managing editor of investigations, had it finished by nine.

TWENTY-FOUR hours after hitting the street Darby was still alive. If she could make it to morning, she could start another day with new ideas about what to do and where to go. For now, she was tired. She was in a fifteenth-floor room of the Marriott, with the door bolted. Her thick, dark red hair was now in a paper sack.

It had taken two painful hours with dull scissors to cut it off, yet leave some semblance of style. It took another two hours to color it black. She could've bleached it and gone blond, but that would be obvious. She assumed she was dealing with professionals, and for some unfathomable reason, she determined at the drugstore that they might expect her to do this and become a blonde.

She was dead tired, but afraid of sleep. She had not seen her friend from the Sheraton during the day, but he was out there, she knew. And he had friends. If they could assassinate Rosenberg and Jensen and Thomas Callahan, she would be easy.

She couldn't go near her car, and she didn't want to rent one. Rentals leave records. She could fly, but they were stalking the airports. After they realized she had disappeared, they would expect her to run. She was just an amateur, a little college girl brokenhearted after watching her man blown to bits. If she tried to make a mad dash somewhere, get out of the city, they would pick her off.

She rather liked the city at this moment. It had a million hotel rooms; almost as many alleys and dives and bars. She knew it well—especially the Quarter. She would stay off the streets in the mornings and try to sleep then. She would change clothes and hats and sunglasses. She would move until she got tired of moving; then she might leave. She had to keep thinking. She would survive.

She wanted to talk to Alice Stark, her best friend. Alice would be worried she was missing and would go to the cops. She would call Alice tomorrow.

She dialed room service and ordered a Mexican salad and a bottle of red wine. She would drink all of it, then sit in a chair and watch the door until she fell asleep.

# SEVEN

GMINSKI'S limo made a wild U-turn on Canal as if it owned the street, and came to a sudden stop in front of the Sheraton. Both rear doors flew open. Gminski was out first, followed quickly by three aides, who scurried after him with bags and briefcases.

It was almost two a.m., and the CIA director did not stop at the front desk, but went straight for the elevators. The aides ran behind him. No one spoke as they rode up six floors.

Three of his agents were waiting in a corner room. One of them opened the door, and Gminski barged through it.

"Where is she?" he snapped at an agent by the name of Hooten. The one named Swank opened the curtains and pointed to the Marriott, across the street and down a block.

"She's on the fifteenth floor, third room from the street. Lights are still on. We saw her go in. She paid with a credit card."

"Poor kid," Gminski said. "Has anyone followed her?"

"No."

Gminski sat on the edge of the bed, laced his fingers together, and cracked every conceivable knuckle. "What do you think?" he asked Hooten, the oldest of the three agents.

"They're chasing her. They're looking under rocks. She's using credit cards. She'll be dead in forty-eight hours."

"She's not completely stupid," Swank inserted. "She cut her hair and colored it. She's moving around. I'll give her seventy-two."

"This means her little brief is directly on point," Gminski said. "And it means our friend is a very desperate man. Where is he?"

Hooten answered quickly. "We have no idea."

"We have to find him."

"He hasn't been seen in three weeks."

Gminski picked up a room key. "So what do you think?"

"Do we bring her in?" Hooten asked.

"It won't be easy," Swank said. "She may have a gun."

"She's a scared kid," Gminski said. "She's also a civilian. We can't go snatching civilians off the sidewalk. How do we take her?"

"There are ways," Hooten answered. "Catch her on the street. Go to her room. It's not that difficult. She's not a pro."

Gminski paced slowly around the room, and everyone watched him. "I'm not inclined to take her. Let's sleep four hours and meet here at six thirty. If you can convince me, I'll say do it. Okay?"

They nodded obediently.

THE wine had worked. She had dozed in the chair, then made it to the bed and slept hard. Now the phone was ringing. Five times, ten, fifteen, twenty. It would not stop. The eyes opened but saw little. The sun was up, and the lights were on. She stared at the phone. Could be a wrong number. With the exception of the registration clerk and maybe his boss and perhaps room service, not a single living soul knew she was in this room.

It stopped ringing. Good. Wrong number. She walked to the bathroom, and it began ringing again. She counted. After the fourteenth ring she lifted the receiver. "Hello."

"Darby, it's Gavin Verheek. Are you okay?"

She sat on the bed. "How'd you get the number?"

"The credit card. The paper trail. It's the FBI, Darby. We have ways. It's not that difficult."

"Then they could do it too."

"I suppose. Stay in the small joints and pay with cash."

There was a thick knot in her stomach. Just like that. The paper trail. She could be dead. Killed along the paper trail.

"Listen, Darby. We've got some information. There will be a memorial service tomorrow at three on campus, with burial afterward in the city. Callahan's family wants me to serve as a pallbearer. I'll be there tonight. I think we should meet. Your life is in danger right now, and you need to listen to me."

"What did Director Voyles say?"

"I haven't talked to him." There was a pause. "We're taking no action at this time."

"And what might that mean, Gavin? Talk to me."

"That's why we need to meet. I don't want to do this over the phone. We're on your side, Darby. I swear."

She thought about this. It made sense, but they had found her so easily. "I'm listening. You haven't talked to the director, but the FBI's taking no action. Why not?"

"I'm not sure. He made the decision yesterday to back off the pelican brief and gave instructions to leave it alone."

"That's not very much. Does he know about Thomas? Does he know that I'm supposed to be dead because I wrote it, and forty-eight hours after Thomas gave it to you, they—whoever they are—tried to kill both of us? Does Voyles know all this, Gavin?"

"No, Darby."

"Okay, listen. Do you think he was killed because of the brief?"

"Probably."

"Thanks. If Thomas was murdered because of the brief, then we know who killed him. And if we know who killed Thomas, then we know who killed Rosenberg and Jensen. Right?"

Verheek hesitated. "I'll say probably."

"Fine. *Probably* means yes for a lawyer. It's a very strong *probably*, yet you're telling me the FBI is backing off my suspect."

"Settle down, Darby. Let's meet tonight and talk about it. I could save your life."

She carefully laid the receiver under a pillow and walked to the bathroom. She brushed what was left of her hair, then threw a change of clothes into a new canvas bag. She put on the parka, cap, and sunglasses, and quietly closed the door behind her.

FRIDAY MORNING IN THE QUARTER. The air was cool and clean. Eight a.m.—too early for people. She walked a few blocks, and on Dumaine near Jackson Square she found a coffee shop. It was nearly empty and had a pay phone in the back. She poured her own thick coffee and set it on a table near the phone. She could talk here.

Verheek was on the phone in less than a minute.

"Where will you stay tonight?" she asked, watching the door.

"Hilton, by the river."

"I know where it is. I'll call late tonight or early in the morning. Don't track me again. I'm into cash now. No plastic."

"That's smart. Can you find this morning's Washington *Post?* Nice story about Rosenberg and Jensen and perhaps who done it."

"I can't wait. I'll call later."

She zigzagged toward Canal, covering her tracks, along the antiques shops on Royal, and finally to the French Market. She was quick but nonchalant. She bought a *Post* and a *Times-Picayune* from a vendor and found a table in a deserted corner of Café du Monde.

Front page. Citing a confidential source, the story dwelt on the legend of Khamel and his sudden involvement in the killings. Many thought he was dead. But Interpol believed he had killed as recently as six months ago. He had not been photographed in over a decade, said an expert. The FBI had him at the top of their list.

She opened the New Orleans paper slowly. Thomas' picture was on page 2, with a long story. The cops were treating it as a homicide, but there wasn't much to go on. The law school was in shock, according to the dean. Services were tomorrow on campus. A horrible mistake had been made, the dean said. If it was murder, then someone had obviously killed the wrong person.

Her eyes were wet, and suddenly she was afraid again. Maybe it was simply a mistake. It was a violent city with crazy people, and maybe someone got their wires crossed and the wrong car was chosen. Maybe there was no one out there stalking her. She put the sunglasses on and looked at Thomas' photo. He was so handsome.

GRANTHAM'S Khamel story electrified Washington that morning, and the hottest game in town was speculating about the source.

The game was especially hot in the Hoover building. In the office of the director, Eric East and K. O. Lewis paced nervously about while Voyles talked to the President for the third time in two hours. Voyles was cussing—not directly at the President, but all around him. He cussed Coal, and when the President cussed back, Voyles suggested they set up the polygraph, strap in everyone on the President's staff, beginning with Coal, and just see where the damned leaks were coming from. And they cussed back and forth.

Voyles hung up, and spoke with his eyes closed. "He wants us to place that *Post* reporter under surveillance. We've done it before."

"What type of surveillance?" asked K.O.

"Let's just follow him. Around the clock, with two men. See where he goes, who he sleeps with. He's single, isn't he?"

"Divorced seven years ago," Lewis answered.

"Make sure we don't get caught. Do it with plainclothes."

"Does he really believe the leaks are coming from us?"

"No. I don't think so. If we were leaking, why would he want us to trail the reporter? I think the President knows it's his own people. And he wants to catch them."

"It's a small favor," Lewis added helpfully.

THE office of Matthew Barr was tucked away on the third floor of a tacky and decaying office building on M Street in Georgetown. There were no signs on the doors. An armed guard in a coat and tie turned people away at the elevator. The carpet was worn.

Fletcher Coal nodded at the security guard and made his way through the small maze of dingy offices in the direction of Barr's. Coal did not fear any man in Washington, with the exception of this one. Matthew Barr was an ex-marine, ex-CIA, ex-spy, with two felony convictions for security scams from which he had earned millions. Coal had personally recruited him to head the Unit—an unofficial, hidden little division of the Committee to Reelect the President, which officially did not exist. It had an annual budget of four million—all cash from various slush funds—and Barr supervised a small band of highly trained thugs who quietly did the work.

Barr's door was always locked. He opened it, and Coal entered.

"Let me guess," Barr started. "You want to find the leak."

"In a way, yes. I want you to follow this reporter, Grantham, around the clock and see who he's talking to. He's getting some awfully good stuff, and I'm afraid it's coming from us."

"You're leaking like cardboard."

"We've got some problems, but the Khamel story was a plant. Did it myself."

Barr smiled at this. "I thought so. It seemed too clean and pat."

"Did you ever run across Khamel?"

"No. Ten years ago we were sure he was dead. He likes it that way. He has no ego, so he'll never get caught. He can live in a paper shack in São Paulo for six months, eating roots and rats, then fly off to Rome to murder a diplomat. Why are you interested?"

"I think I know who hired him to kill Rosenberg and Jensen."

"Oh, really. Can you share this bit of gossip?"

"No. Not yet," Coal replied.

"Okay. This is all legend, you understand. He can kill with either hand, either foot, a car key, a pencil, whatever. He's an expert marksman with all weapons. Speaks twelve languages. He's believed to be the most proficient and expensive assassin in the world. Let me guess. You want me to bring Khamel back alive."

"You leave Khamel alone. I sort of like the work he did here. I want you to follow Gray Grantham, find out who he's talking to."

"Any ideas?"

"A couple. There's a man by the name of Milton Hardy, a janitor in the West Wing. He appears to be half blind, but I think he sees and hears a lot. Follow him for a week or two. Everyone calls him Sarge." Coal threw an envelope on the desk. "Make it three weeks."

"So you know who hired the killer?" Barr said.

"We're getting close."

"The Unit is more than anxious to help."

"I'm sure."

MRS. Chen owned the duplex and had been renting the other half to female law students for fifteen years. She was picky but private, and lived and let live as long as all was quiet.

It was dark when she answered the door. The person on the porch was an attractive young lady with a nervous smile.

"I'm Alice Stark, a friend of Darby's," the young woman said. "May I come in?" Mrs. Chen lived alone, with the doors and windows locked tightly. But if Alice was Darby's friend, she could be trusted. Mrs. Chen opened the door, and Alice was inside.

"Something's wrong," Mrs. Chen said.

"Yes. Darby is in a bit of trouble, but I can't talk about it. Did she call this afternoon?"

"Yes. She said you would look through her apartment."

Alice breathed deeply and tried to appear calm. "It'll just take a minute. She said there was a door through a wall somewhere. I prefer not to use the front or rear doors."

Mrs. Chen frowned, and her eyes asked, Why not?

"Has anyone been in the apartment in the last two days?" Alice asked. She followed Mrs. Chen down a narrow hallway.

"I've seen no one. There was a knock early yesterday before the sun, but I didn't look." She moved a table away from a door, pushed a key around, and opened it.

Alice stepped in front of her. "She wanted me to go in alone. Okay?" Mrs. Chen nodded, and closed the door behind Alice.

It opened into a tiny hallway that was suddenly dark. Alice fumbled through a purse and found a pencil-thin flashlight. Darby had been specific. No lights could be seen through the windows. They could be watching. Darby said she would explain later.

Alice tiptoed around a corner in the direction of the den. Darby said there was a small lamp next to the television that was always on. She used it as a night-light. Either the bulb was gone, or someone had unscrewed it. The den was pitch-black.

The flashlight glowed with all the energy of a fading match. Alice inched toward the kitchen. The computer was on the table. With her little light, she examined it, pushed the power switch, and the screen slowly warmed up, emitting a greenish light.

Alice sat down in front of the keyboard and studied the directory closely. There were supposed to be around forty entries, but she saw no more than ten. Most of the hard-drive memory was gone. She turned on the laser printer, and within seconds the directory was on paper. She tore it off and stuffed it into her purse.

She stood and inspected the clutter around the computer. Darby had estimated the number of floppy disks at twenty, but they were all gone. The red expandable files were stacked neatly, but empty. It was a clean, patient job. He or they had spent hours erasing and gathering, then left with no more than one bag of goods. Alice turned the computer off and eased through the den to the hall.

Mrs. Chen was waiting for her. "Okay?" she asked.

"Everything's fine," Alice said. "Just watch it real close. I'll call you in a day or two to see if anyone has been by. And please, don't tell anyone I was here."

Mrs. Chen listened intently as she moved the table in front of the door. "Is she all right?"

They were almost to the front door. "She's gonna be fine. She'll be back in a few days. Thank you, Mrs. Chen."

Mrs. Chen closed the door, bolted it, and watched from the small window. The lady was on the sidewalk, then gone in the darkness.

FRIDAY night in the Quarter! Tulane played in the Dome tomorrow, then the Saints on Sunday, and the rowdies were out by the thousands roaming in noisy mobs, crowding bars, and raising hell.

Alice was an hour late when she arrived at the oyster bar on St. Peter. It was packed. She retreated to a corner and surveyed the people. Darby was in a tiny booth, crouched over a beer bottle, with sunglasses and a hat.

Alice went over and squeezed her hand. "It's good to see you." She studied the hairdo and was amused by it. Darby removed the sunglasses. The eyes were red and tired.

"Someone tried to kill me, Alice. My name's on a list that some very nasty people are holding. I think they're following me."

"Kill? Did you say kill? Who would want to kill you, Darby?"

"I'm not sure. What about my apartment?"

Alice handed her the printout of the directory. Darby studied it. This was not a dream or a mistake. The bomb had found the right car. Rupert and the cowboy had had their hands on her. The face she had seen was looking for her. They had gone to her apartment and erased what they wanted to erase. They were out there.

"What about floppies?"

"None. Not a single one. The expandable files, on the kitchen table, were empty. Everything else appears to be in order."

Darby stuffed the printout into a pocket. "Look, Alice, you don't need to be seen with me. Maybe this wasn't a good idea."

"Who are these people?"

"I don't know. They killed Thomas, and they tried to kill me."

"But why, Darby?"

"You don't want to know. The more you know, the more danger you're in. Trust me, Alice. I can't tell you what I know."

Alice stared at her friend. They had studied hours together, shared notes, sweated exams, teamed up for mock trials, gossiped about men. Alice was hopefully the only student who knew about Darby and Callahan. "I want to help, Darby. I'm not afraid."

Darby had not touched the beer. "Well, I'm terrified. I was there when he died, Alice. The ground shook. He was blown to pieces."

"Then go to the cops."

"Not yet. Maybe later. I'm afraid to." She stared at the table. "Alice, if you want to help, go to the memorial service tomorrow. Spread the word that I called you from Denver, where I'm staying with an aunt whose name you don't know, and that I've dropped out but will be back in the spring. Make sure that rumor gets started."

"Okay, Darby. You're smarter than I am. Then what?"

"Start the rumor, and I'll call you within two days."

"Where are you staying?"

"Here and there. I move around a lot."

Alice stood and pecked her on the cheek. Then she was gone.

VERHEEK sat on the bed sipping a beer and staring at the phone. She said she would call. He could save her life if she would

At midnight he left the hotel room. An agent in the New Orleans office had given him a couple of law school hangouts close to campus. He would go there, mix and mingle, and listen. Maybe he would hear something—make a friend who knew her or maybe knew someone who knew her. A long shot, but a lot more productive than staring at the phone.

He found a seat at the bar in a joint called Barrister's, three blocks from campus. The crowd was rowdy and under thirty.

The bartender looked like a student. At half past one, after two beers, Verheek asked him, "Are you a law student?"

"Afraid so."

"I'm a lawyer," Verheek said. "Special counsel, FBI."

"So you're from Washington?"

"Yeah. In town for the game Sunday. Where do you go to school?"

"Here. Tulane. I'll finish in May. You need a beer?"

"No. Did you have Thomas Callahan?"

"Sure. You knew him?"

"I was in law school with him at Georgetown." Verheek pulled a card from his pocket and handed it to the kid. "I'm Gavin Verheek." The kid looked at it, then politely laid it next to the ice.

"Do you know a student by the name of Darby Shaw?"

"I haven't met her, but I know who she is. I've seen her a few times. She's hard to miss." A long, rather suspicious pause. "Why?"

"We need to talk to her." Gavin pulled a dozen cards from his pocket and laid them on the bar. "I'll be at the Hilton for a few days. If you see her or hear anything, drop one of these."

"Sure. There was a cop in last night asking questions. You don't think she was involved in Callahan's death?"

"No, not at all. We just need to talk to her."

Verheek paid for the beer, thanked the kid again, and was on the sidewalk. It was almost two, and he was dead tired.

# EIGHT

Garcia called for the last time. Grantham took the call before dawn Saturday, less than two hours before they were to meet. He was backing out, Garcia said. The time was not right. If the story broke, then some very powerful lawyers and their very rich clients would fall hard. These people were not accustomed to falling, and they would take people with them. And Garcia might get hurt. He had a wife and little daughter. Why take chances?

"Then why do you keep calling me?" Grantham asked.

"I think I know why they were killed. I saw something, okay?"

"We've had this conversation for a week now, Garcia. It's all useless unless you show it to me."

"Yeah. But there's a chance they know that I know."

"These are the guys in your firm?"

"Yeah. No— Wait— How'd you know I was in a firm?"

"It's easy. You go to work too early to be a government lawyer. You're in one of those two-hundred-lawyer firms where they expect the associates and junior partners to work a hundred hours a week. The first time you called me, you said you were on the way to the office, and it was something like five a.m."

"Well, well. What else do you know?"

"Not much. We're playing games, Garcia. If you're not willing to talk, then hang up and leave me alone. I'm losing sleep."

"Sweet dreams." Garcia hung up.

Grantham stared at the receiver. He fumed for thirty minutes before he fell asleep. He was dead to the world when the phone rang again.

It was a female. "Is this Gray Grantham with the Washington Post?"

"It is. And who are you?"

"Are you still on the story about Rosenberg and Jensen?"

He sat in the darkness and stared at the clock. Five thirty. "We've got a lot of people on it, but yes, I'm investigating."

"Have you heard of the pelican brief?"

He tried to think. "The pelican brief. No. What is it?"

"It's a harmless little theory about who killed them. It was taken to Washington last Sunday by a man named Thomas Callahan, a professor of law at Tulane. He gave it to a friend with the FBI, and it was passed around. Things snowballed, and Callahan was killed in a car bombing Wednesday night in New Orleans."

The lamp was on, and Grantham was scribbling. "Where are you calling from?"

"New Orleans. But I'm at a pay phone, so don't bother."

"How do you know all this?"

"I wrote the brief."

He was wide awake now. "If you wrote it, tell me about it."

"I don't want to do that, because even if you had a copy, you couldn't run the story. It'll take some thorough verification."

"Okay. We've got the Klan, the terrorist Khamel, the Aryans—"

"Nope. A bit obvious. The brief is about an obscure suspect."

"Why can't you tell me who it is?"

"You seem to have magical sources. Let's see what you find."

"Give me twenty-four hours."

"I'll try to call Monday. If we're gonna do business, Mr. Grantham, the next time I call, tell me something I don't know."

"Are you in danger?"

"I think so. But I'm okay for now."

She sounded young—mid-twenties, maybe. She wrote a brief. She knew the law professor. "Are you a lawyer?" he asked.

73

"No. And don't spend your time digging after me. You've got work to do, Mr. Grantham, or I'll go elsewhere."

"Fine. You need a name."

"Just call me Pelican."

FOR half an hour students and faculty had streamed into Rogers Chapel for Thomas Callahan's memorial service. In a dark room on the third floor of Newcomb Hall, the Pelican sat with her face to the window and watched. She'd been there for two hours. She was certain the bad guys were lurking in the bushes around the chapel. If they found her, maybe they would do it quick and it would be over. She gripped a wadded paper towel and dried her eyes.

She had selected this moment to run. She would get out of the country, hide for a year, and hope the crime would be solved and the bad guys would be put away. But it was a dream. The quickest route to justice ran smack through her. She knew more than anyone. The Fibbies had circled close, then backed off. Verheek had gotten nowhere. Her little brief had killed Thomas, and now they were after her. She knew the identity of the man behind the murders of Rosenberg, Jensen, and Callahan. This made her rather unique.

Suddenly she leaned forward. There he was! The thin man with the narrow face. He was wearing a coat and tie and looked properly mournful as he walked to the chapel. It was him! The man she'd last seen in the lobby of the Sheraton when she was talking to Verheek.

He stopped at the door and jerked his head nervously around. He was a klutz, a giveaway. He stared at three cars parked innocently on the street, less than fifty yards away. He opened the door and was in the chapel. Beautiful. The fools killed Thomas, and now they join his friends for last respects.

Ten minutes later the thin man came out by himself, lit a cigarette, and strolled toward the three cars, his hands stuck deep in his pockets. He was sad. What a guy. When he was out of sight, a man in a green Tulane sweatshirt emerged from the middle car. He walked down the street after the thin one. He was short, thick, and powerful. A regular stump.

He disappeared down the sidewalk, behind the thin man, behind the chapel. Within a minute they emerged from behind the building. They were together now, whispering, but for only a moment, because the thin man peeled off down the street. Stump walked quickly to his car and got in. He just sat there waiting for the service to break up and to get one last look at the crowd on the off-chance that she was stupid enough to show up.

THIS little victim would go unnoticed. No one would suspect him. It was such a small job, but his client was adamant. Khamel happened to be in the neighborhood, having just arrived from Havana by boat and car, and the money was right.

Edwin Sneller did not open the door, but slid the key under it. Khamel picked it up and opened the door to the next room. He walked in and moved quickly to the bed, where he placed his bag, then to the window, where he studied the lights of the French Quarter, below.

He walked to the phone and punched Sneller's number. "Tell me about her," Khamel said softly to the floor.

"There are two photos in the briefcase."

Khamel opened it and removed the photos. "I've got them."

"They're numbered one and two. One we got from the law school yearbook. It's about a year old and the most current we have. The other is two years old, from a yearbook at Arizona State."

Khamel held both pictures. "A beautiful woman."

"Yes. Quite beautiful. All that lovely hair is gone, though. Thursday night she paid for a hotel room with a credit card. We barely missed her Friday morning. We found long strands of hair on the floor and a small sample of black hair color. Very black."

"What a shame."

"We haven't seen her since Wednesday night. She's proven elusive. Credit card for a room Wednesday, credit card at another hotel Thursday. Nothing last night. She withdrew five thousand in cash from her checking account Friday, so the trail is cold."

"Maybe she's gone."

"I don't think so. Someone was in her apartment last night. We've got the place wired, and we were late by two minutes."

"Moving sort of slow, aren't you?"

"It's a big town. We've camped out at the airport and train station. We're watching her mother's house, in Idaho. No sign. I think she's still here. The police talked to her after the bomb Wednesday, then lost her. We're looking; they're looking. She'll turn up."

"What happened with the bomb?"

"Very simple. She didn't get in the car."

Khamel smiled slightly and picked up the most recent photo. He liked this face. Even with short dark hair it would be an intriguing face. He could kill it, but it would not be pleasant.

AFTER two nights of barhopping, Gavin Verheek was drained and weakened. Saturday night he prowled five or six bars. Tulane lost again, and after the game the bars filled with rowdies. Things got hopeless, and he quit at midnight.

He was sleeping hard when the phone rang. He lunged for it.

"Gavin?" she asked.

"Darby! Is this you? Why haven't you called before now?"

"Please, don't start asking a bunch of stupid questions. I'm at a pay phone, so no funny stuff."

"Come on, Darby. I swear you can trust me."

"Okay, I trust you. Now what? Who's after me, Gavin?"

"Could be a number of people. I don't know who they are."

"You're playing games, Gavin. How can I trust you if you won't talk to me?"

"Okay. I think it's safe to say your little brief hit someone in the gut. You guessed right— The wrong people learned of the brief, and now Thomas is dead. And they'll kill you the instant they find you."

"We know who killed Rosenberg and Jensen, don't we?"

"I think we do."

"Then why doesn't the FBI do something, Gavin?"

"We may be in the midst of a cover-up."

"Bless you for saying that. Bless you," Darby said.

"I could lose my job."

"Who would I tell, Gavin? Who's covering up what?"

"I'm not sure. We were very interested in the brief until the White House pressed hard. Now we've dismissed it."

"I can understand that. Why do they think they can kill me and it will be kept quiet?"

"I can't answer that. Maybe they think you know more."

"Can I tell you something? Moments after the bomb, while Thomas was in the car burning and I was semiconscious, a cop named Rupert took me to his car and put me inside. Another cop, with cowboy boots and jeans, started asking me questions. I was in shock. They disappeared, Rupert and his cowboy, and they never returned. They were not cops, Gavin. They watched the bomb and went to plan B when I wasn't in the car. I didn't know it, but I was probably a minute or two away from a bullet in the head."

Verheek listened, his eyes closed. "What happened to them?"

"I think they got scared when the real cops swarmed on the scene. They vanished. I was in their car, Gavin. They had me."

"You have to come in, Darby. Listen to me."

"Do you remember our phone chat Thursday morning when I suddenly saw a face that looked familiar and I described it to you? Well, that face was at the memorial service yesterday."

"Where were you?"

"Watching. He walked in a few minutes late, stayed ten minutes, then sneaked out and met with Stump."

"Stump?"

"Yes. He's one of the gang. Stump, Rupert, Cowboy, and the Thin Man. Great characters. I'm sure there are others, but I haven't met them yet."

"The next meeting will be the last, Darby. You have about forty-eight hours to live."

"We'll see. How long will you be in town?"

"A few days. I'd planned to stay until I found you."

"Here I am. I may call you tomorrow."

Verheek breathed deeply. "Okay, Darby. Whatever you say."

She hung up. Verheek threw the phone across the room and cursed it.

Two blocks away and fifteen floors up, Khamel stared at a television movie about people in a big city. They spoke English, his third language, and he repeated every word out loud. He did this for hours. He had watched thousands of American movies. He had been told his English could pass for that of an American's. But one slip—one tiny mistake—and she would be gone.

THE VOLVO WAS PARKED IN A LOT a block and a half from its owner, who paid one hundred dollars a month for what he thought was security. They eased through the gate, which was supposed to be locked. It was a 1986 GL without a security system, and within seconds the driver's door was open. One sat on the trunk and lit a cigarette. It was almost four a.m. Sunday.

The other one opened a small tool case and went to work on Grantham's car phone. He installed a tiny transmitter and glued it in place. A minute later he eased out of the car. The one with the cigarette handed him a small black cube, which he stuck under the car and behind the gas tank. It was a magnetized transmitter, and it would send signals for six days before it needed replacing.

They were gone in less than seven minutes. Monday, as soon as Grantham was spotted entering the *Post* building, on Fifteenth, they would enter his apartment and fix his phones.

HER second night in the bed-and-breakfast was better than the first. She slept until midmorning. Maybe she was used to it now.

She tried to be disciplined about her thinking. This was her fourth day as the Pelican, and to see number five she would have to think like a fastidious killer. But after her eyes opened and she realized there was no gunman lurking in the closet and she was safe, her first thought was always of Thomas.

He had loved her madly, had fallen hard. She loved him too. And it hurt so much. She wanted to stay in bed and cry for a week. The day after her father's funeral a psychiatrist had explained that the soul needs a brief, very intense period of grieving; then it moves to the next phase. But it must have the pain. It must suffer without restraint before it can properly move on.

It wasn't working with Thomas. She couldn't scream and throw things the way she wanted. Rupert and Thin Man and the rest of the boys were denying her a healthy mourning.

Where would they be today? Did they know where she was? No. She would be dead. Did they know she was now a blonde?

The hair got her out of bed. She walked to the mirror over the desk and looked at herself. It was even shorter now—and very white. Not a bad job. She had worked on it last night. If she lived for another two days, she would cut some more and go back to black.

A hunger pain hit, and for a second she thought about food. It was almost ten. Oddly, this bed-and-breakfast didn't cook on Sunday mornings. She would venture out to find food and a Sunday *Post* and to see if they could catch her now that she was a butch blonde.

She put on new army fatigues and a new flight jacket, and she was ready for battle. The eyes were covered with aviator shades. She crept through the dark kitchen, unlocked the rear door, and stepped into the alley behind the little inn. It was cool enough to wear the flight jacket without being suspicious. Silly, she thought. In the French Quarter she could wear the hide and head of a polar bear and not appear suspicious.

He saw her when she stepped onto the sidewalk next to Burgundy Street. The hair under the cap was different, but the legs were still long. She walked a certain way, and after four days he could pick her out of a crowd regardless of the hair. The cowboy boots—snakeskin with pointed toes—hit the sidewalk and started following. She was a smart girl, turning every corner, changing streets every block. She walked quickly, but not too fast, with her hands deep in the fatigues and her eyes darting behind the shades. He figured she was headed for Jackson Square, where there was a crowd on Sundays and she thought she could disappear.

He was sitting at a table in a crowded sidewalk café at the corner of St. Peter and Chartres, and he was less than ten feet away when she saw him. A split second later he saw her, and she probably would have made it if she hadn't hesitated for a step. But the slight hesitation gave her away. She kept walking, faster now.

It was Stump. He was on his feet and weaving through the tables when she lost sight of him. At ground level he was anything but chubby. He seemed quick and muscular. She lost him for a second on Chartres. She kept moving, hung a left on St. Ann, and was almost to Royal when she took a quick glance behind her. He was on the other side of the street, but very much in pursuit.

Get to Bourbon Street, she decided. Kickoff was four hours away, and the Saints fans were out in force celebrating before the game. She turned on Royal and ran hard. He turned on Royal, trotting now. She turned left on Dumaine. Bourbon was ahead, and there were people everywhere.

She could hear him now. No sense looking anymore. He was back there running—and gaining. When she turned onto Bourbon, Mr. Stump was fifty feet behind her, and the race was over.

She saw her angels as they made a noisy exit from a bar. Three large, overweight young men dressed in a wild assortment of black-and-gold Saints garb stepped into the street as Darby ran to them.

"Help!" she screamed wildly, and pointed at Stump. "Help me! That man is after me! He's trying to rape me! Help!"

Suddenly the street was silent. Everyone froze, including Stump, who stopped, then rushed forward. The three Saints stepped in front of him with folded arms and glowing eyes. It was over in seconds. Stump used both hands at once—a right to the throat of the first one, and a vicious blow to the mouth of the second. They squealed, and fell hard. Number three was not about to run. His two buddies were hurt, and this upset him. Number three, Mr. Benjamin Chop of Thibodaux, Louisiana, kicked Stump squarely in the crotch, and Stump was history. As Darby eased back into the crowd, she heard him cry in pain.

While he was falling, Mr. Chop kicked him in the ribs. Number two, with blood all over his face, charged wild-eyed into Stump, and the massacre was on. They kicked him without mercy until someone yelled, "Cops!" and this saved his life. Mr. Chop and number two helped number one to his feet, and the Saints were last seen darting into a bar. Stump crawled away like a dog hit by a Mack truck but still alive and determined to die at home.

Darby hid in a dark corner of a pub on Decatur, drinking coffee. Her hands shook and her stomach flipped. The po'boys smelled delicious, but she could not eat. After three hours, she ordered a plate of boiled shrimp, and it settled her. She was safe in here, she thought, so why not watch the game. The pub was packed at kick-off. She was a Saints fan now, and she hoped her three buddies were okay and enjoying the game.

AT SOME point in the fourth quarter, with the Saints down by four field goals, Edwin Sneller called Khamel, next door.

"She's here," Sneller said. "One of our men saw her this morning at Jackson Square. He followed her, then lost her. But she's here. Her hair is very short and almost white. She was wearing green

81

army pants and a brown bomber jacket. Somehow she recognized him, and took off."

"How would she recognize him? Has she seen him before?"

"I can't answer that. There's a small card under your door you need to see."

Khamel laid the phone on a pillow and walked to the door. In a second he was back on the phone. "Who is this?"

"The name is Verheek. Works for the FBI in Washington. Evidently, he and Callahan were friends, and Verheek was a pallbearer at the memorial service yesterday. Last night he was hanging out in a bar not far from the campus, asking questions about the girl. Two hours ago one of our men was in the same bar posing as an FBI agent. The bartender produced the card. Look on the back. He's in room nineteen oh nine at the Hilton."

"A five-minute walk." The street maps were scattered on the bed.

"Yes. We've made a few phone calls to Washington. He's just a lawyer. He knew Callahan, and he's trying to find the girl."

"She would talk to him, wouldn't she?"

"Probably."

"How's my English?"

"Perfect."

KHAMEL waited an hour and left the hotel. With the coat and tie, he was just an average Joe strolling along Canal at dusk. He carried a large gym bag and smoked a cigarette, and five minutes later entered the lobby of the Hilton. He worked his way to the elevator through the crowd of fans returning from the Dome.

There was no answer at 1909. His new pal, Verheek, was probably hanging around a bar, passing out cards, talking about Darby Shaw. What a nut.

He knocked again, and while he waited he slid a plastic ruler between the door and the facing and worked it gently until the bolt clicked. Locks were minor nuisances for Khamel.

Inside, he locked the door behind him and placed his bag on the bed. Like a surgeon, he picked the gloves from a pocket and pulled them over his fingers. He laid a .22 and silencer on the table. He plugged the recorder into the phone jack under the bed, then called the weather station twice to test it. Perfect.

Khamel covered his tracks and settled low in the closet. He held the .22 just in case Verheek happened to barge into the closet and he had to kill him with bullets. If not, he would just listen.

GAVIN quit the bars Sunday. He was getting nowhere. He couldn't find her in this city, and it wasn't his fault. If she didn't call again, he was finished playing detective. He had done his best.

He was stretched on the bed in nothing but boxer shorts, flipping through a magazine and ignoring the television. It was almost eleven. He would wait on her until twelve, then try to sleep.

It rang at exactly eleven. He killed the television. "Hello."

It was her. "It's me, Gavin."

"So you're alive."

"Barely. They saw me today, and one of their goons—my friend Stump—chased me through the Quarter."

"But you got away."

"A small miracle. Stump was just a few steps from me when he picked a fight with the wrong guys. I'm scared, Gavin."

Verheek paused a second. Her voice was shaking. She was losing her cool. "Look, Darby, I can't hang around New Orleans for the next month hoping you'll trust me. I've got a flight out of here tomorrow, and I think you need to go with me to Washington."

"What happens then?"

"Well, you get to live, for one thing. I'll plead with the director, and I promise you'll be safe. We'll do something, dammit."

"What makes you think we can just fly out of here?"

"Because we'll have three FBI agents surrounding you. Look, Darby, tell me where you want to meet right now, and within fifteen minutes I'll come get you with the agents. These guys have guns, and they're not afraid of Stump and his pals. We'll get you out of the city tonight and to Washington tomorrow."

She thought for a moment. "Behind your hotel is a place called Riverwalk. It's a shopping area. On the second level is a clothing store called Frenchmen's Bend. At noon tomorrow I want you to stand by the entrance and wait for five minutes."

"Come on, Darby. You won't be alive at noon tomorrow. Enough of this cat-and-mouse."

"Just do as I say, Gavin, or we call it off. I have no idea what you

83

look like, so wear a black shirt and a red baseball cap. Stand by the door and hold a folded newspaper. I'll be watching. After five minutes, walk inside to the right rear corner, where there's a rack of safari jackets. Browse around a bit, and I'll find you."

"Okay, okay. Then what do we do?"

"You and I—and only you and I—will leave the city. I don't want anyone else to know of this. Do you understand, Gavin? No one else. Agreed?"

He closed his eyes. "This is not what I wanted. But I'll be there at noon. I just hope you make it."

"How tall are you, Gavin? How much do you weigh?"

"Five ten. And two hundred, but I plan to lose it."

"I'll see you tomorrow."

"I hope I see you, dear."

She was gone. He hung up, walked to the bathroom, closed the door, and turned on the shower. For ten minutes he cussed her in the shower, then stepped out and dried himself.

He opened the door. The room was dark. Dark? What? He had left the lights on. He headed for the switch next to the dresser.

The first blow crushed his larynx. It was a perfect blow. He grunted painfully and fell to one knee, which made the second blow so easy. It hit like a rock at the base of the skull, and Gavin was dead.

Khamel flipped on a light and looked at the pitiful nude figure on the floor. He lifted the corpse onto his shoulders and laid it across the bed. Working quickly, he turned the television to full volume, unzipped his bag, removed a cheap .25-caliber automatic, and placed it on the right temple of the late Gavin Verheek. He covered the gun and the head with two pillows and pulled the trigger. Now the critical part: he placed one pillow under the head, threw the other on the floor, and carefully curled the fingers of the right hand around the pistol, leaving it twelve inches from the head.

He took the recorder from under the bed, punched a button, listened, and there she was. He turned off the television.

With a little luck the cops would look around the room and declare it to be another suicide. Because this guy was an important FBI lawyer, an autopsy would be done in a day or so, and probably by Tuesday an examiner would discover it was not a suicide.

By Tuesday the girl would be dead; he would be in Managua.

# NINE

GRANTHAM's official sources at the White House denied any knowledge of the pelican brief. Sarge had never heard of it. A friend at Justice denied ever hearing about it. Grantham dug all weekend with nothing to show for it. The Callahan story was verified when he found a copy of the New Orleans paper. When her call came in at the newsroom Monday, he had nothing fresh to tell her.

"I'm still digging," he said. "If there's such a brief in town, it's being closely protected."

"I assure you it's there, and I understand why it's being protected," the Pelican said.

"I'm sure you can tell me more."

"Lots more. The brief almost got me killed yesterday, so I may be ready to spill my guts sooner than I thought."

"Who's trying to kill you?"

"Same people who killed Rosenberg, Jensen, and Thomas Callahan. I've seen at least four of them since Wednesday. They're here in New Orleans hoping I'll do something stupid."

"How many people know about the pelican brief?"

"Good question. Callahan took it to the FBI, and I think from there it went to the White House, where it evidently caused quite a fuss, and from there, who knows. Two days after he handed it to the FBI, Callahan was dead. I, of course, was supposed to have been killed with him."

"Do the police have your name?"

"My name is Darby Shaw. I'm a law student at Tulane. Thomas Callahan was my professor and lover. I wrote the brief, gave it to him, and you know the rest. Are you getting all this?"

Grantham scribbled furiously. "Yes, I'm listening."

"I'm rather tired of the French Quarter, and I plan to leave today. I'll call you from somewhere tomorrow. Can you get a list of all major contributors to the President's last election?"

"It's public record. Not difficult. I can have it by this afternoon. Do you have a copy of the brief?"

She hesitated. "No, but it's memorized."

"And you know who's doing the killing?"

"Let's take it slow. I'll call you tomorrow."

THIS WAS NOT FORTY-BUCKS-AN-HOUR work. Not even thirty. Croft knew he'd be lucky to squeeze fifteen out of Grantham for this needle-in-the-haystack Mickey Mouse rubbish.

The photographer stuck his sunglasses over his ears and entered the hallway that led to the atrium, where four escalators carried a thousand lawyers up to their little rooms. He had Garcia's face memorized. He was even dreaming of this kid with the bright face and good looks, the slim physique. He would know him if he saw him.

He stood by a pillar, holding a newspaper. Lawyers everywhere, scurrying upward with their smug little faces and carrying their smug little attaché cases. Why did they all dress alike? Dark suits. Dark shoes. An occasional nonconformist with a daring little bow tie. Two hours at lunch, and then Grantham would have another building for him to patrol. He told Grantham this was hopeless, just shooting in the dark. Grantham said it's all they could do. He said Garcia was scared and wouldn't call anymore. They had to find him.

FOUR blocks away, Fletcher Coal paced back and forth in front of the President's desk. He frowned. "Bad news, Chief. Really bad news. Gray Grantham called thirty minutes ago and asked if we had any knowledge of the pelican brief."

"Wonderful. Fabulous. How'd he get a copy of it?"

Coal sat in a chair across the desk and thought for a moment.

"Voyles leaked it?" the President finally asked.

"Maybe, if it was leaked. Grantham is known for bluffing. We can't be certain he's seen the brief. Maybe he's fishing."

"Maybe, my eye. What if they run some crazy story about it? What then?" The President slapped his desk and bolted to his feet. "What then, Fletcher? That paper hates me!"

"They can't run it unless they can confirm it with another source, and there can't be another source, because there's no truth to it. It's a wild idea that's gone much further than it deserves."

The President sulked. "How did Grantham find out about it?"

"Who knows. No one here knows about it but you and I. They brought one copy, and it's locked away in my office. I personally Xeroxed it once and gave it to Gminski. I swore him to secrecy."

The President sneered.

"Okay, you're right. There could be a thousand copies out there by now. But it's harmless, unless of course our friend actually did these dirty deeds. Then—"

"Then I'm finished. How much money did we take?"

"Millions—directly and indirectly." And legally and illegally. But the President knew little of these transactions, and Coal chose to stay quiet.

The President walked slowly to the sofa. "Why don't you call Grantham? Pick his brain. See what he knows. If he's bluffing, it'll be obvious. What do you think?"

"I don't know. If I call out of nowhere, he'll be suspicious."

"Yeah, I guess you're right." The President thought for a second. "What's the downside?" he finally asked.

"Our friend could be exposed by the press. Voyles covers his tail and says you told him to back off. The *Post* goes berserk with another cover-up smear. And we can forget reelection."

"Anything else?"

"Yeah. The brief is fantasy. Grantham will find nothing, and I'm late for a meeting." Coal walked to the door. "I'll be back at one."

The President watched the door close and breathed easier. He had eighteen holes of golf planned for the afternoon, so forget the pelican thing. If Coal wasn't worried, neither was he.

He punched numbers on his phone and finally had Bob Gminski on the line. The director of the CIA was a terrible golfer, but the President invited him to play. Certainly, said Gminski.

"By the way, Bob, what about this pelican thing?"

Gminski cleared his throat. "Well, Chief, I told Fletcher Coal that it was a fine work of fiction. I think its author should forget about law school and pursue a career as a novelist. Ha, ha, ha."

"Great, Bob. Nothing to it, then."

"We're digging."

"See you at three." The President hung up.


RIVERWALK runs for a quarter of a mile along the water and is always crowded. It is packed with two hundred shops, cafés, and restaurants, on several levels, with doors leading onto a boardwalk. It's a stone's throw from the Quarter.

Darby arrived at eleven and sipped espresso in a tiny bistro. Frenchmen's Bend was one level down. She was nervous, and the espresso didn't help. She could not trust Gavin Verheek. He was employed by a law-enforcement agency that at times operated by its own rules. But at this moment there was no one else to trust. After five days and two near misses, she was throwing in the towel.

Eleven forty-five. She paid for the espresso and fell in behind a crowd of shoppers. A dozen people were browsing in Frenchmen's Bend as she eased into a bookstore two doors down. First she looked at magazines; then with three minutes to go she stepped between two rows of cookbooks and watched for Gavin.

She expected him at precisely noon, and there he was—black sweatshirt, red baseball cap, folded newspaper, a bit thinner than she expected, but he could lose a few pounds. Her heart pounded away. Be cool, she said. Just be cool.

She held a cookbook to her eyes and peered over it. He had gray hair and dark skin. The eyes were hidden behind sunglasses. He fidgeted and looked irritated, the way he sounded on the phone.

He was okay. She liked the way he looked. He had a vulnerable, nonprofessional manner about him that said he was scared too.

After five minutes, he walked through the door as he'd been told and went to the right rear of the store.

KHAMEL had been trained to welcome death. And after thirty years of expecting it, nothing—absolutely nothing—made him afraid. He picked through the safari jackets and tried to appear nervous.

She was behind him, but very close when she said, "Gavin."

He jerked quickly around. She was holding a white Panama hat and speaking to it. Her hair was a gold color, and shorter than his.

"Darby," he said. "Let's get out of here." He had listened to the recording a hundred times, and he was confident he had Verheek's inflection and slight upper-midwest accent.

"Follow me," she said. They left the store. She took his hand, and they walked quickly down a flight of stairs to the boardwalk.

"Have you seen them?" he asked.

"No. Not yet. But I'm sure they're around."

"Where are we going?"

They were on the boardwalk, almost jogging, talking without looking at each other. "Just come with me," she said.

"You're going too fast, Darby. We look suspicious. Slow down.

Look, this is crazy. Let me make a phone call, and we'll be safe. I can have three agents here in ten minutes." This was working. They were holding hands, running for their lives.

"Nope." She slowed. The boardwalk was crowded, and a line had formed beside the *Bayou Queen,* a paddle wheeler. They stopped at the end of the line.

"What is this?" he asked. "Are we getting on this boat?"

"Yes."

"This is stupid." He could take her out now with one hand, but there were people everywhere. People in front, people behind.

"I've got a car a mile upriver at a park. We'll stop in thirty minutes," she explained in a low voice.

The line was moving now. "I don't like boats. They make me seasick. This is dangerous, Darby." He looked around, like a man pursued, and tugged at his pants. They were thirty-six inches in the waist, and covered eight layers of briefs and gym shorts. Instead of weighing one fifty, he could pass for one ninety.

"Relax, Gavin. It's gonna work."

They were almost to the steps of the *Bayou Queen.*

The man with the gun ran to the end of the line and elbowed his way through the tourists. He had killed before, but never in such a public place as this. The back of her head was visible through the crowd. He shoved his way desperately through the line. A few cursed him, but he couldn't care less. The girl was almost on the boat when he knocked the last person out of the way and stuck the gun into the base of the skull just below the red baseball cap. He fired once, and people screamed and fell to the ground.

Gavin fell hard into the steps. Darby screamed and backed away in horror. Voices were yelling and people were pointing. The man with the gun was running toward a row of shops.

"He's got a gun!" a woman near the boat yelled, and the crowd backed away from Gavin, who was on all fours with a small pistol in his right hand. He rocked pitifully back and forth like an infant, blood streaming from his nose and chin. He started yelling in a language Darby did not recognize.

Two crew members from the boat hovered on the steps, afraid to move. A woman was crying, then another. Darby inched farther back. "He's Egyptian," a small dark woman said.

89

He lunged forward to the edge of the boardwalk. The gun dropped into the water, and he collapsed with his head hanging over the river. Shouts came from the rear, and two policemen rushed to him. A hundred people now inched forward to see the dead man. Darby shuffled backward, then left the scene.

SHORTLY after dark she left Riverwalk and flagged a cab at Poydras. Her clothes were different, and hidden under a new black trench coat. The sunglasses and hat were also new. It was time to run, but she couldn't get careless.

An elderly black man sat low behind the wheel.

"I need to go to Baton Rouge," she said. "How much?"

"Lord, honey, that's a heckuva ride. A hundred and fifty."

She crawled into the back seat and threw two bills over. "There's two hundred. Get there as fast as you can."

He turned off the meter and stuffed the money into his pocket. Darby lay down in the back seat and closed her eyes. The old man was a fast driver, and within minutes they were on the expressway.

She still heard the gunshot and saw him on all fours rocking back and forth, trying to live just a moment longer. Thomas had once referred to him as Dutch Verheek, but said the nickname was dropped after law school. Dutch Verheek was not an Egyptian.

She had caught just a glimpse of his killer as he was running away. There was something familiar about him. He had glanced to his right just once as he was running, and something clicked. But she had been screaming and hysterical, and it was a blur. Everything blurred. Halfway to Baton Rouge she fell into a deep sleep.

DIRECTOR Voyles listened to the receiver, mumbled a few instructions, and hung it up. It was nine p.m., and judging from the wrinkled shirt, he had been at the office at least fifteen hours.

"That was Eric East," Voyles said to K. O. Lewis, who sat across the desk in Voyles' office. "He's been there about two hours, and they just finished the autopsy. Single bullet to the right temple, but death came sooner, from a single blow at C-two and C-three. The vertebrae were shattered. No powder burns on his hand. Another blow severely bruised his larynx. He was nude. Estimate of between ten and eleven last night." Voyles rubbed his red eyes.

"How could he go down for a simple funeral and end up dead?"

"He was snooping around on this pelican thing. One of our agents—guy named Carlton—told East that Gavin was trying to find the girl, that the girl had called him, and that he might need some help bringing her in. Carlton talked to him a few times."

"Has anyone seen the girl?" Lewis asked.

"She's probably dead. I've instructed New Orleans to find her."

"Her little brief is getting folks killed right and left. When do we take it seriously?"

The director was standing now, cracking his knuckles and thinking aloud. "We have to cover ourselves. I think we should assign at least two hundred agents to pelican, but try like hell to keep it quiet. There's something really nasty there, K.O., but the President asked me to back off, remember. I said we would, in part because we thought the brief was a joke." Voyles managed a smile. "Well, I taped our little conversation. I figure he and Coal tape everything, so why can't I? I had my best body mike, and the tape's clear as a bell."

"I'm not following," Lewis said.

"Simple. We go in and investigate like mad. If the press gets wind of the investigation, and if the pelican brief is on target, then I'll make sure the country knows the President asked us to back off because it's one of his pals."

Lewis was smiling. "It'll kill him. The election is next year."

Denton Voyles walked slowly behind his chair. "We'll look under every stone, K.O., but it won't be easy to solve this thing. We've got a very wealthy man in a very elaborate plot to use very talented killers to take out two Justices. These people don't talk, and they don't leave trails. Look at our friend Gavin. We'll spend two thousand hours digging around that hotel, and I'll bet you there won't be a shred of useful evidence."

"I'm somewhat responsible, Denton. Gavin came to me Thursday morning after he learned of Callahan, and I didn't listen. I knew he was going down there, but I just didn't listen."

"Look, I'm sorry he's dead. Gavin was a fine lawyer, and I trusted him. But he got himself killed because he stepped out of bounds."

Lewis stood. "How much do I tell Mrs. Verheek?"

"Let's say it looks like a burglary . . . cops ain't sure down there . . . still investigating. Tell her I'm devastated."

COAL'S LIMO WAS WANDERING aimlessly through the city—a ritual not unusual when he and Barr met to talk about dirty business.

"I must know what Grantham knows," Coal was saying. "He's hot on this pelican brief."

"You think he's seen it?"

"No, not at all. If he knew what was in it, he wouldn't be fishing for it. But dammit, he knows about it. That's what worries me. He's good, he's tenacious, and he smells blood with this story."

"Of course, it would be asking too much if I wanted to know what was in the brief."

"Don't ask. It's so confidential it's frightening."

"Then how does Grantham know about it?"

"That's what I want to know. Where are his sources?"

"We got his car phone, but we haven't been inside the apartment yet. Almost got caught this morning by his cleaning lady. We'll try again tomorrow."

"Don't get caught, Barr. Remember Watergate."

"They were morons, Fletcher. We are quite talented."

"That's right. So tell me, can you and your quite talented associates bug Grantham's phone at the *Post*?"

Barr frowned at Coal. "Have you lost your mind? That place is busy at all hours. They have security guards. Impossible."

"Then tap his apartment," Coal instructed. "I want a report twice a day on all his calls."


BREAKFAST at Dupont Circle. It was quite chilly. A few winos lay about like driftwood. But the sun was up, and he felt safe, and, anyway, he was still an FBI agent, with a shoulder harness and a piece under his arm. His name was Trope, a very special assistant to Mr. Voyles. He was so special that no one except he and Mr. Voyles knew about these secret little chats with Booker from Langley. He sat on a bench and unpacked a breakfast of banana and muffin.

Booker strolled near the fountain with a cup of coffee. He glanced around, then sat down next to his friend. They were both office boys now, far into their twilights but close to their bosses, who from time to time grew weary of trying to figure out what the other was doing, or just needed to know something quickly.

"We lost a man in New Orleans," Trope said.

Booker sipped the hot coffee. "He got himself killed."

"Were you there?"

"Yes. We were close but watching others. What was he doing?"

Trope unwrapped the cold muffin. "We don't know. Went down for the funeral, tried to find the girl, found someone else, and here we are. It was a clean job, wasn't it?"

Booker shrugged. What did the FBI know about killing? "It was okay. Pretty weak effort at suicide, from what we hear."

"Where's the girl?" Trope asked.

"We lost her at O'Hare. Maybe she's in Manhattan, but we're not certain. We're looking."

"And they're looking." Trope took a bite of the banana.

"I'm sure they are." Booker checked his watch. These meetings were extremely brief. "What are Mr. Voyles' plans?"

"He's going in. He sent fifty troops last night, with more today."

"What about the White House?"

"Maybe they won't find out. What do they know?"

"They know Mattiece."

Trope managed a tight smile. "Where is Mr. Mattiece?"

"Who knows. He's been seen little the past three years. He owns at least a half-dozen homes in as many countries, so who knows."

"The brief nailed him, didn't it?"

"It's beautiful. And if he'd played it cool, the brief would have been ignored. But he goes berserk, starts killing people, and the more he kills, the more credibility the brief has."

This was good stuff. "Voyles says we may need your help."

Booker nodded. "Done. But this will be a very difficult matter. First, the probable gunman is dead. Second, the probable bagman is very elusive. There was an elaborate conspiracy, but the conspirators are gone. We'll try to find Mattiece."

Trope ate the muffin. "Can't you bring the girl in?"

"No. We don't know where she is, and we can't just snatch innocent civilians off the street. She doesn't trust anyone right now."

Trope stood. "I can't blame her." He was gone.

GRANTHAM held a cloudy fax photo sent from Phoenix. It was of Darby as a junior at Arizona State, a very attractive twenty-year-old coed. A second fax, sent by an Associated Press stringer in New

Orleans, was a copy of her freshman photo at Tulane, and somewhere in the yearbook the stringer had found a photo of Darby drinking a Diet Coke at a law school picnic. She wore a baggy sweater with jeans that fit just right. The photo looked like something out of *Vogue*. She was laughing, and the face was warm. Grantham had tacked this one onto the small corkboard beside his newsdesk. There was a fourth photo, of Thomas Callahan.

Grantham placed his feet on the desk. It was almost nine thirty, Tuesday morning. The newsroom hummed. He had made eighty calls in twenty-four hours and had nothing to show but four photos and a stack of campaign finance forms. He was getting nowhere.

He skimmed the *Post* and saw the strange story about one Gavin Verheek and his demise. The phone rang. It was Darby.

"Seen the *Post*?" she asked.

"I write the *Post*, remember."

She was not in the mood for small talk. "The story about the FBI lawyer murdered in New Orleans— Have you seen it?"

"I'm just reading it. Does it mean something to you?"

"You could say that. Listen carefully, Grantham. Callahan gave the brief to Verheek, who was his best friend. Friday, Verheek came to New Orleans for the funeral. I talked to him by phone. He wanted to help me, but I was scared. We agreed to meet yesterday at noon. Verheek was murdered Sunday night. Got all that?"

"Yeah, I got it."

"Verheek didn't show for our meeting. He was, of course, dead by then. I got scared and left the city. I'm in New York."

"Okay." Grantham wrote furiously. "Who killed Verheek?"

"I do not know. There's a lot more to the story. I've read the *Post* and *The New York Times,* and I've seen nothing about another killing in New Orleans. It happened to a man I was talking to who I thought was Verheek. It's a long story."

"Sounds like it. When do I get this long story?"

"When can you come to New York?"

"I can be there by noon."

"That's a little quick. Let's plan on tomorrow. I'll call you at this time tomorrow with instructions. Be careful, Grantham."

He admired the jeans and the smile on the corkboard. "It's Gray, okay? Not Grantham."

"Whatever. There are some powerful people afraid of what I know. I saw a man die yesterday, and I have no idea who he was or why he was killed, except that he knew about the pelican brief. When you get here, I'll tell you everything I know, but you can never use my name. I don't want to ask for more trouble, okay, Gray? If I ever doubt you, I'll disappear."

"You have my word, Darby. I swear."

"I think you're making a mistake. This is not your average investigative job. This one could get you killed."

"By the same people who killed Rosenberg and Jensen?"

"Yes."

"Do you know who killed Rosenberg and Jensen?"

"I know who paid for the killings. I know his name, his business, his politics. I'll tell you tomorrow, if I'm still alive."

There was a pause. "Perhaps we should talk now," he said.

"Perhaps. But I'll call you in the morning."

Grantham hung up, and admired the slightly blurred photo of this beautiful law student who was convinced she was about to die. For a second he succumbed to thoughts of chivalry and gallantry and rescue. She suddenly trusted him to the exclusion of all others. He would make it work. And he would protect her.

THE taxi stopped at the corner of Fifth and Fifty-second, and Gray paid quickly and jumped out with his bag. The car behind was honking, and he thought how nice it was to be back in New York.

It was almost five p.m. Wednesday, the pedestrians were thick on Fifth, and he figured that was precisely what she wanted. Move quickly, she had told him. Wear sunglasses and watch for everything, because if he was being followed, he could get them killed.

He fought the crowd and walked as fast as possible to The Plaza Hotel, up the steps and through its lobby, then out onto Central Park South. As he neared Sixth Avenue he walked even faster. He was keyed up, and regardless of how restrained he tried to be, he was terribly excited about meeting her.

On the phone she had said to duck into the St. Moritz, at the corner of Sixth, and he did. She had reserved a room for him under the name of Warren Clark. He paid cash for the room and rode the elevator to the ninth floor. He was to just sit and wait, she'd said.

95

He stood in the window for an hour and watched Central Park grow dark. The phone rang. "Mr. Clark?" a female asked.

"Uh, yes."

"It's me. Take the elevator to the eighteenth, then walk down to the fifteenth. Room fifteen twenty."

Ten minutes later he was standing before room 1520. He felt like a sophomore on his first date. He knocked and waited.

"Who is it?"

"Grantham," he said to the door.

She opened the door. The hair was gone, but she smiled, and there was the cover girl. She shook his hand firmly. "Come in."

She bolted the door behind him. "Would you care for a drink?"

"Sure. What do you have?"

"Water, with ice."

"Sounds great."

She walked into a small sitting room, where the television was on with no sound. "In here," she said. He set his bag on the table and took a seat on the sofa. She was standing at the bar, and for a quick second he admired the jeans. No shoes.

She handed him the water and sat in a chair by the door.

"Thanks," he said.

"Have you eaten?" she asked.

"You didn't tell me to."

She chuckled. "Forgive me. I've been through a lot. Let's order room service. I'd love a cheeseburger with fries, and a cold beer."

He nodded, and smiled at her. "Perfect."

She picked up the phone and ordered. Grantham walked to the window and watched the lights crawling along Fifth Avenue.

She looked at him carefully, then said, "I'm twenty-four. How old are you?" She was on the sofa now, sipping ice water.

He took the chair nearest to her. "Thirty-eight. Married once. Divorced seven years and three months ago. No children. Live alone with a cat. When did you leave New Orleans?"

"Monday night. I took a cab to Baton Rouge, and flew to Chicago, where I bought four tickets to four cities, including Boise, where my mother lives. I jumped on the plane to La Guardia at the last moment. I don't think anyone followed."

"You're safe."

"Maybe for the moment. We'll both be hunted when this story is published. Assuming it's published."

Gray rattled his ice and studied her. "Depends on what you tell me. And how much can be verified from other sources."

"I'll tell you what I know, and the verification is up to you."

"Okay. When do we start talking?"

"After dinner, on a full stomach. You're in no hurry, are you?"

"Of course not. I've got all night, all day tomorrow, and the next day. I mean, you're talking about the biggest story in twenty years, so I'll hang around as long as you'll talk to me."

Darby smiled and looked away. Exactly a week ago she and Thomas were waiting for dinner in the bar at Mouton's. She had lived a year in the past seven days, and she was having a real conversation with a live person who did not wish her dead. She crossed her feet on the coffee table. It was not uncomfortable having him here in her room. She relaxed. His face said, "Trust me." And why not? Whom else could she trust?

"What are you thinking about?" he asked.

"It's been a long week. Seven days ago I was just another law student busting my tail to get to the top. Now look at me."

He was looking at her. The hair was dark and very short, and quite stylish, but he liked the long version in yesterday's fax.

"Tell me about Thomas Callahan. Isn't he part of the story?"

"Yeah. I'll get to it later."

Suddenly Grantham realized she was not just a hot little coed, but a widow in mourning. "I'm very sorry about Thomas," he said.

She smiled, but said nothing.

There was a loud knock. Darby jerked her feet off the table and glared at the door; then she breathed deeply. It was the food.

"I'll get it," Gray said. "Just relax."

# TEN

For centuries a mammoth battle of nature raged without interference along the coastline of what would become Louisiana. From the south the ocean pushed inland. From the north the Mississippi River hauled down an inexhaustible supply of fresh water and sediment and fed the marshes with the soil they needed to vegetate and thrive. The salt water from the Gulf eroded the coastline and burned the freshwater marshes by killing the grasses that held them together. The river responded by draining half the continent and depositing its soil in lower Louisiana. It slowly built a long succession of sedimentary deltas, each of which, in turn, eventually blocked the river's path and forced it to change course yet again. The lush wetlands were built by the deltas.

The marshlands were a marvel of natural evolution. Using the rich sediment as food, they grew into a green paradise of cypresses and oaks, of pickerelweeds, bulrushes, and cattails. The water was filled with crawfish, shrimps, oysters, red snappers, flounder, pompano, bream, and crabs. The coastal plain was a sanctuary for wildlife. Hundreds of species of migratory birds came to roost.

The wetlands were vast and limitless, rich and abundant.

Then oil was discovered there in 1930, and the rape was on. The oil companies sliced the marshes to ribbons to get to the riches. They drilled, found oil, then dredged like maniacs to get to it. Their canals were perfect conduits for the Gulf and its salt water, which ate away at the marshes.

Since oil was found, tens of thousands of acres of wetlands have been devoured by the ocean. Sixty square miles of Louisiana vanishes every year. Every fourteen minutes another acre disappears.

In 1979 an oil company punched a hole deep in Terrebonne Parish and hit oil. A lot of oil. They backed off a mile, drilled, and hit another big one. Three miles away they struck gold again. The oil company capped the wells and pondered the situation, which had all the markings of a major new field.

The oil company was owned by Victor Mattiece, a Cajun from Lafayette who'd made and lost several fortunes drilling for oil in south Louisiana. In 1979 he happened to be wealthy, and more important, he had access to other people's money. He began buying land around the capped wells.

A man of infinite patience and planning, Mattiece huddled with his lawyers and other advisers and devised a plan to methodically form new companies and buy the surrounding land under a myriad of corporate names. The plan was to consolidate territory, then dredge yet another channel through the beleaguered marshlands so that the oil could be brought out with haste. The canal would be thirty-five miles long and twice as wide as the others.

Because Victor Mattiece had money, he was a popular man with the politicians and bureaucrats. He played their game skillfully. He sprinkled money around where needed. He loved politics but hated publicity. He was paranoid and reclusive.

The land acquisition sailed smoothly along. Mattiece did the sprinkling act, and obtained official permission to gouge his way through the delicate marshes and cypress swamps. The pieces were falling majestically into place, and Mattiece could smell a billion dollars. Maybe two or three.

Then an odd thing happened. A lawsuit was filed to stop the dredging and drilling. The plaintiff was an obscure environmental outfit known simply as Green Fund.

The lawsuit was unexpected, because for fifty years Louisiana had allowed itself to be devoured and polluted by oil companies, and people like Victor Mattiece. It had been a trade-off. The oil business employed many and paid well. Oil and gas taxes paid the salaries of state employees. The small bayou villages had turned into boomtowns. The politicians took the oil money and played along. All was well, and so what if the marshlands suffered.

Green Fund filed the lawsuit in the U.S. District Court in Lafayette. A federal judge halted the oil project, pending a trial.

Mattiece spent weeks with his lawyers, plotting and scheming. Break any rule, cut any throat, spend any amount of money, he instructed them. Just win the damned lawsuit. Never one to be seen, he assumed an even lower profile. He moved to the Bahamas and operated from an armed fortress at Lyford Cay.

Though invisible now, he made certain his political contributions increased. His jackpot was still safe beneath Terrebonne Parish, and he would one day extract it.

By the time the two Green Fund lawyers waded in, they had identified over thirty separate defendants. Some owned land. Some did exploring. Others laid pipe. Others drilled. The joint ventures, limited partnerships, and corporate associations were an impenetrable maze. The defendants and their legions of high-priced lawyers answered with a vengeance. They filed motions by the truckload, and when they were all denied and it was evident there would one day be a trial by jury, the oil lawyers dug in and played dirty.

Luckily for Green Fund's lawsuit, the heart of the new oil reserve was near a ring of marshes that had been for years a natural refuge for waterfowl. Ospreys, egrets, pelicans, ducks, cranes, geese, and many others migrated to it. Though Louisiana has not always been kind to its land, it has shown a bit more sympathy for its animals. So the Green Fund lawyers played heavy on the birds.

The pelican became the hero. After thirty years of insidious contamination by DDT and other pesticides, the Louisiana brown pelican perched on the brink of extinction. Almost too late, it was classified as an endangered species, and afforded a higher class of protection. Green Fund enlisted experts from around the country to testify on behalf of the majestic bird.

Seven years after Mattiece first buzzed over Terrebonne Bay in his jet helicopter, the pelican suit went to trial. It was a bitter trial that lasted ten weeks. Green Fund sought damages for havoc already inflicted and a permanent injunction against further drilling.

They lost the trial, and it was not altogether unexpected. The oil companies spent millions. Their fancy litigator from Houston wore elephantskin boots and a Stetson, and could talk like a Cajun when necessary. The jurors were not impressed with the dire warnings about pollution and the frailness of wetland ecology. Oil meant money, and folks needed jobs.

But the judge kept the injunction in place for two reasons. First, he thought Green Fund had proved its point about the pelican, a federally protected species. And it was apparent to all that Green Fund would appeal, so the matter was far from over.

The dust settled for a while, and Mattiece had a small victory. But he knew there would be other days in other courtrooms.

THE tape recorder was in the center of the small table, with four empty beer bottles around. Grantham made notes as he talked.

"Who told you about the lawsuit?"

"A guy named John Del Greco. He's a law student at Tulane who clerked last summer for a big firm in Houston that was on the periphery of the hostilities."

"What's the status of the lawsuit?"

"From the trial level it will be appealed to the fifth circuit court of appeals. That appeal should be perfected in a month or so."

"Where's the fifth circuit?"

"New Orleans. About twenty-four months after it arrives there a three-judge panel will hear and decide. The losing party will undoubtedly request a rehearing by the full panel, and this will take another three or four months. There are enough defects in the verdict to ensure a reversal or a remand."

"What's a remand?"

"The appellate court can affirm the verdict, reverse the verdict, or find enough error to send the whole thing back for a new trial. If it goes back, it's been remanded. They can also affirm part, reverse part, remand part—sort of scramble things up."

Gray shook his head in frustration as he scribbled away. "Any idea what the fifth circuit might do?"

"None. The plaintiffs are alleging a multitude of procedural sins by the defendants, and given the nature of the conspiracy, a lot of it's probably true. It could be reversed."

"Then what happens?"

"The fun starts. If either side is unhappy with the fifth circuit, they can appeal to the Supreme Court."

"Surprise, surprise."

"Each year the Supreme Court receives thousands of appeals but is very selective about what it takes. Because of the money and issues involved, this one has a decent chance of being heard."

"From today, how long would it take for the case to be decided?"

"Anywhere from three to five years."

"Rosenberg would have died from natural causes."

"Yes, but there could be a Democrat in the White House," Darby said. "So take him out now, when you can predict his replacement. It's beautiful. If you're Victor Mattiece, and you've only got fifty million or so, and you want to be a billionaire, and you don't mind killing a couple of Supremes, then now is the time."

"But what if the Supreme Court refused to hear the case?"

"He's in good shape if the fifth circuit affirms the trial verdict. But if it reverses and the Supreme Court denies certiorari, he's got problems. My guess is that he would go back to square one, stir up some new litigation, and try it all again. There's too much money involved to just go home. When he took care of Rosenberg and Jensen, one has to assume he committed himself."

101

"Where was he during the trial?"

"Invisible. Keep in mind it is not public knowledge that he's the ringleader of the litigation. By the time the trial started, there were thirty-eight corporate defendants. Of the thirty-eight, seven are traded publicly, and he owns no more than twenty percent of any one. The other thirty-one are privately held, and I couldn't get much information. But I did learn that many of these private companies are owned by each other. It's almost impenetrable. I suspect Mattiece owns or controls eighty percent of the project. Del Greco heard he operates from behind offshore banks and companies."

"Do you remember the seven public companies?" Gray asked.

"Most of them. They were footnoted in the brief, a copy of which I do not have. But I've rewritten most of it in longhand."

"Can I see it?"

"You can have it. But it's lethal."

"I'll read it later. Tell me more about the brief."

"Mattiece is from a small town near Lafayette, and in his younger years was a big money man for politicians in south Louisiana. He spent big bucks on Democrats locally and Republicans nationally, and over the years he was wined and dined by big shots from Washington. Seven years ago, when the President was the Vice President, he was in New Orleans for a Republican fund-raiser. A photographer snapped a picture of Mattiece shaking hands with the V.P., and the New Orleans paper ran it. It's wonderful. They're grinning at each other like best friends. I stuck it on the last page of the brief, just for the fun of it. This is fun, isn't it?"

"I'm having a ball."

"Mattiece dropped out of sight a few years ago and is now believed to live in several places. He's very eccentric."

The recorder beeped, and Gray changed tapes. Darby stood and stretched her long legs.

"Are you tired?" he asked her.

"I haven't been sleeping well. How many more questions?"

"How much more do you know?"

"We've covered the basics. We can fill in the gaps tomorrow."

Gray turned off the recorder and relaxed on the sofa. "So who selected Rosenberg and Jensen? Mattiece is not a lawyer."

Darby sat in a chair and pulled her feet under her. "Rosenberg is easy. Jensen wrote little on environmental issues, but he was consistent in voting against all types of development. If they shared common ground, it was protecting the environment."

"And you think Mattiece figured this out by himself?"

"Of course not. A pretty wicked legal mind presented him with the two names. He has a thousand lawyers."

"Any in D.C.?"

Darby shrugged. "I can think of at least two D.C. firms that I ran across as I went through the file. One is White and Blazevich, a very old, powerful, rich Republican firm with four hundred lawyers."

Gray was suddenly wired. He was on his feet. "This may fit. This may be it, Darby. Last week I got three phone calls from a lawyer in D.C. named Garcia. But that's not his name. He said he knew something about Rosenberg and Jensen, and he wanted to tell me what he knew. Then he got scared and disappeared."

"There are a million lawyers in D.C."

"Two million. But I know he works in a private firm. We had a meeting planned for last Saturday, and he called and said forget it. I think he has something that he was about to show me."

"He could be your verification."

"What if he works for White and Blazevich? We've suddenly narrowed it to four hundred lawyers. Garcia could be our link to Mattiece."

"Our link?"

"Yes, our link. I thought you wanted to nail Mattiece."

"I want him to pay, but I'd rather leave him alone. I've seen enough blood to last me a long time, Gray. You take this ball and run with it. You're the investigative reporter."

He didn't hear this. He walked over to the window. "You mentioned two firms. What's the other?"

"Brim, Stearns, and somebody."

"Are they as big as White and Blazevich?"

"I doubt it. I'd guess two hundred lawyers."

"Okay. Now we're up to six hundred lawyers in two firms. You're the lawyer, Darby. How can we find Garcia?"

She was yawning. They had been talking for almost three hours, and she was exhausted. "I really haven't given it much thought. I'll sleep on it and explain it to you in the morning."

"I'll get my things," Grantham said, picking up the tapes.

"Would you do me a favor?" she asked. She paused, and looked at the sofa. "Would you mind sleeping on the sofa tonight? I haven't slept well in a long time, and I need the rest. I'm spooked, and it would . . . well, be nice if I knew you were in here."

He swallowed hard and looked at the sofa—a five-footer at most. "Sure," he said. "I don't mind. No problem."

"Thanks." She smiled demurely, and Gray melted. She smiled again, then closed the door to her bedroom. She didn't lock it.

He sat on the sofa in the darkness. Sometime after midnight he dozed and slept with his knees not far from his chin.

JACKSON Feldman was the executive editor at the *Post,* and at five thirty on Thursday afternoon Gray Grantham was standing in his office. Smith Keen, the assistant managing editor, was also standing, and holding the four-page outline of a story, along with a copy of Darby's handwritten reproduction of the pelican brief. Feldman's copy was lying on the desk. They appeared dazed.

Gray sat on the edge of a table. No one spoke.

Feldman rubbed his eyes roughly, then looked at Keen. "Wow," he finally said.

Gray smiled. "You mean, that's it? I hand you the biggest story in twenty years, and you are so moved you say, 'Wow.' "

"Where's Darby Shaw?" Keen asked.

"I can't tell you. It's part of the deal."

"When did you talk to her?"

"Last night, and again this morning. She talked. I listened. I flew home. I wrote the outline. So what do you think?"

Feldman slowly folded his thin frame into his chair. "How much does the White House know?"

"The brief was delivered to the White House last week, and at the time, the FBI thought it should be pursued. After the White House had it, the FBI backed off. That's all I know."

"How much did Mattiece give the President three years ago?"

"Millions, through a myriad of political action committees. This guy is very smart. He's got all kinds of lawyers. It's probably legal."

The editors were thinking slowly. They were stunned, as if they'd just survived a bomb blast. Grantham was quite proud. Feldman flipped through the papers until he found the photograph of Mattiece and the President. He shook his head.

"It's dynamite, Gray," Keen said. "We just can't run without a bunch of corroboration. Hell, you're talking about the world's greatest job of verifying. How can you do it?"

"I've got some ideas. First we'll try to find Garcia."

"We? Who's we?" Keen asked.

"Me, okay? Me. I'll try to find Garcia."

"Is the girl in on this?"

"I can't answer that. It's part of the deal."

"Answer the question," Feldman said. "Look at where we are if she gets killed helping you with the story. It's much too risky."

"She's a source, and I always protect my sources. No, she's not helping with the investigation. She's just a source, okay?"

They stared at him in disbelief.

"Do you want some help?" Feldman finally asked.

"No. She insists on me doing it alone. She's very scared."

"I got scared just reading the thing," Keen said. "I see every word you write, okay?"

"And I want a daily report, okay?" Feldman said.

"No problem." Gray opened the door.

Feldman glared at him. "Don't get hurt, and don't allow her to get hurt. Understand, Grantham?"

Gray smiled and left the office.

HE WAS almost to Thomas Circle when he saw the blue lights behind him. The cop did not pass, but stayed on his bumper.

He parked in a small lot next to an apartment house. It was dark, and the blue lights flashed in his mirrors. He rubbed his temples.

"Step out," the cop demanded from the bumper.

Gray opened the door of his Volvo and did what he was told. The cop was black and was suddenly smiling. It was Cleve. He pointed to the patrol car. "Get in."

They sat in the patrol car, under the blue lights.

"Sarge can't talk anymore, Grantham," Cleve said. "He smells something around the place. He's caught a few strange looks, and he's heard a thing or two."

"Such as?"

"Such as they're talking about you and how much they need to know what you know. He thinks they might be listening."

"Come on, Cleve. Is he serious?"

"He's heard them talk about how you're asking questions about the pelican something or other. You've got 'em shook up."

"What has he heard about this pelican thing?"

"Just that you're hot on it and they're serious about it. These are mean and paranoid people, Gray. Sarge says to be careful."

"I need his help, but tell him this is very touchy."

"What is this pelican business?"

"I can't say. But tell Sarge it could get him killed."

RUPERT paid for his cinnamon roll and sat on a barstool overlooking the sidewalk. It was midnight, and Georgetown was winding down. The coffee shop was busy, but not crowded. He sipped black coffee.

He recognized the face on the sidewalk, and moments later the man was sitting on the next barstool. He was a flunkie of some sort. They had met a few days before, in New Orleans.

"So what's the score?" Rupert asked.

"We can't find her. And that worries us because we got some bad news today, unconfirmed, that the bad guys have freaked out and that the number one bad guy wants to start killing everybody who happens to know about that little paper. He's sending in big boys with big guns. Money can kill a lot of people."

This killing talk did not faze Rupert. "So what's my plan?"

"Hang around. We'll meet here tomorrow night, same time. If we find the girl, it'll be your show."

"How do you plan to find her?" Rupert asked.

"We think she's in New York. You can live there for years and never be seen. It's the perfect hiding place." The messenger was on his feet. "We have ways to find her."

## ELEVEN

BRIM, Stearns, and Kidlow had a hundred and ninety lawyers, according to the latest edition of the *Martindale-Hubbell Law Directory*. And White and Blazevich had four hundred and twelve, so hopefully Garcia was only one of a possible six hundred and two.

But if Mattiece used other D.C. firms, they didn't have a chance.

As expected, White and Blazevich had no one named Garcia. It was filled with Ivy Leaguers with long names that ended in numerals. There were no Hispanics in the firm. Brim, Stearns, and Kidlow was a smaller version of White and Blazevich, but four Hispanic names were listed. Darby wrote them down. Two men and two women.

She sat in a corner of the Fordham University law library for an hour. It was Friday morning, ten in New York and nine in New Orleans. She missed the quiet mornings sipping coffee on Thomas' balcony. She missed the smell of cologne on his bathrobe.

She left the building, and on Sixty-second headed east toward Central Park. It was a brilliant October morning, with a perfect sky and cool wind. She wore new Ray Ban sunglasses, and a muffler up to her chin. She was determined to walk without looking over her shoulder. They probably weren't back there, but she knew that it would be years before she could stroll along a street without a doubt. She would leave tomorrow and spend a few days in Washington. If she survived, she would then leave the country; go maybe to the Caribbean.

She found a phone in the rear of a bagel shop on Sixth Avenue and punched Gray's number at the *Post*. "It's me," she said.

"Well, well. I was afraid you had skipped the country."

"Thinking about it. I'll be there tomorrow. What do you know?"

"I'm just gathering junk. I've got copies of the annual statements for the seven public corporations involved in the suit."

"It's lawsuit, not suit. A suit is something you wear."

"How can you ever forgive me? Mattiece is neither an officer nor director of any. Otherwise, I'm just sitting here waiting on you."

"I've got a better idea. I'll call you when I get there."

"Don't call me at home."

She paused for a second. "May I ask why not?"

"One of my best sources thinks I've ruffled enough feathers to get myself placed under surveillance."

"Fabulous. And you want me to team up with you?"

"We'll be safe, Darby. We just have to be careful."

She gripped the phone and clenched her teeth. "How dare you talk to me about being careful! I've been dodging bombs and bullets for ten days now. Maybe I should stay away from you, Grantham!"

There was a pause as she looked around the tiny café. Two men at the nearest table looked at her. She was much too loud.

Grantham spoke slowly. "I'm sorry. I—"

"Forget it. Just forget it."

He waited a moment. "Are you okay?"

"I'm terrific. Never felt better."

"Are you coming to D.C.?"

"I don't know. I'm safe here, and I'll be much safer when I get on a plane and leave the country. I have this burning desire to see my twenty-fifth birthday. My thirtieth too. That would be nice."

"I understand."

"I'm not sure you understand. I think you're more concerned with Pulitzers and glory than my pretty little neck."

"I assure you that's not true. Trust me, Darby. You'll be safe. You've told me the story of your life. You must trust me."

"I'll think about it. Give me some time."

She hung up, and ordered a bagel. The café was suddenly packed. Run, baby, run, her good sense told her. Take a cab to the airport. Let Grantham dig. He was very good, and he'd find a way to break the story.

Stump limped by on the sidewalk. She caught a glimpse of him through the crowd and through the window. Her mouth was suddenly dry, and she was dizzy. He didn't look inside. He just ambled by with a slight limp, looking rather lost.

FELDMAN was looking for him, another reporter said, and Gray walked quickly to the office. Smith Keen and Howard Krauthammer, the managing editor, were waiting with Feldman. Keen closed the door and handed Gray a newspaper. "Have you seen this?"

It was the New Orleans paper—the *Times-Picayune*—and the front-page story was about the strange deaths of Verheek and Callahan, just days apart. It mentioned Darby Shaw, who had disappeared. But no link to the brief.

"I guess the cat's out of the bag," Feldman said.

"It's nothing but the basics," Gray said. "We could've run this three days ago."

"Why didn't we?" asked Krauthammer.

"There's nothing here. It's two dead bodies, the name of the girl, and a thousand unanswered questions. They've found a cop who'll talk, but he knows nothing beyond the blood and gore."

"But they're digging, Gray," Keen said.

"*The New York Times* has picked it up," Feldman said. "They'll run something tomorrow or Sunday. How much can they know?"

"Why ask me? Look, it's possible they have a copy of the brief. But they haven't talked to the girl. We've got her, okay? She's ours."

"We hope," said Krauthammer.

Feldman rubbed his eyes. "Let's say they have a copy of the brief and they know she wrote it. They can't verify it right now, but they're not afraid to mention it without naming Mattiece. Let's say they know Callahan was her professor and that he brought the brief here and gave it to his friend Verheek. And now they're dead and she's on the run. That's a pretty good story, wouldn't you say, Gray?"

"It's peanuts compared to what's coming," Gray said. "I don't want to run it, because it's the tip of the iceberg and it'll attract every paper in the country. We don't need a thousand reporters bumping into each other."

"I say we run it," Krauthammer said. "If not, the *Times* will."

"We can't run the story," Gray said.

"Why not?" asked Krauthammer.

"Because I'm not going to write it, and if it's written by someone else here, then we lose the girl. She's debating right now about whether to leave the country. One mistake by us and she's gone."

"But she's already spilled her guts," Keen said.

"I gave her my word, okay? It's very simple. I will not write the story until it's pieced together and Mattiece can be named."

"And how long might that take?" Feldman asked.

"A week, maybe."

"They're running something tomorrow or Sunday," Feldman said again.

"Let 'em run it. I'll bet money it'll be the same story. You guys are assuming they've got a copy of the brief, but its author doesn't have a copy of it. We don't have a copy of it. Let's wait and read their little story, then go from there."

The editors studied each other. Krauthammer was frustrated. Keen was anxious. But the boss was Feldman, and he said, "Okay.

If they run something in the morning, we'll meet and look at it."

"Fine," Gray said quickly, and reached for the door.

"You'd better move fast, Grantham," Feldman said.

THE limousine moved patiently in the beltway rush hour. It was dark, and Matthew Barr read the brief with the aid of a reading light in the ceiling. Coal watched the traffic.

"Very nasty," Barr said. "How true is it?"

"I'd love to know."

"When did you first see it?"

"Tuesday of last week. It came over from the FBI. The President was not happy with it, but there was no cause for alarm. Just a wild shot in the dark, we thought. He talked to Voyles, and Voyles agreed to leave it alone for a while. Now I'm not so sure."

"That's awfully close to obstruction of justice. If the brief turns out to be true, the President has problems."

They rode in silence. Coal wasn't worried about criminal charges. The President had had one little chat with Voyles, asked him to look elsewhere for the time being, and that was it. Hardly the work of felons. But Coal was terribly concerned with reelection, and a scandal involving a major contributor like Mattiece would be devastating. The thought was sickening: a man the President took millions from had paid money to have two Supreme Court Justices knocked off. His pal the President could then appoint more reasonable men to the bench so that oil could be harvested. The Democrats would be howling with glee. Every newspaper would run it every day for a year. The Justice Department would be forced to investigate. Coal would be forced to take the blame and resign. Hell, everyone in the White House except the President would have to go. It was a nightmare.

"We've got to find out how much of the brief is true," Coal said. "I want you to talk to Mattiece."

"And you think he will tell me his secrets."

"Yes, eventually. He's desperate, and he's killing people. What if you told him the press had the story and the end was near, and if he is inclined to disappear, now's the time. You're coming to him from Washington—from the inside. Or so he thinks. He'll listen to you."

"Okay. What if he tells me it's true? What's in it for us?"

"Damage control. The first thing we'll do is immediately appoint two nature lovers to the Court. I mean, wild-eyed radical bird watchers. It would show that down deep we're good little environmentalists. Almost simultaneously the President will call in Voyles and the Attorney General and Justice and demand an immediate investigation into Mattiece. We'll leak copies of the brief to every reporter in town, then hunker down and ride out the storm."

Barr was smiling with admiration. "So how do I find Mattiece?"

"I've got a man working on that. Be ready to go on Sunday."

Barr smiled to the window. He would like to meet Mattiece.

IT WAS Saturday morning, and the President wanted to sleep late. But he was sitting at his desk wearing a tie, listening to Richard Horton, the Attorney General. Fletcher Coal stood nearby.

"We are seriously considering a formal grand jury investigation into the deaths of Rosenberg and Jensen," Horton announced gravely. "In light of what's happened in New Orleans, we think this should be pursued immediately."

"The FBI is investigating the case," the President said. "Why should we get involved?"

"Are they investigating the pelican brief?" Horton asked. He knew the answer. He knew Voyles was in New Orleans at this moment with hundreds of agents, collecting a pile of useless evidence. He knew the President had asked Voyles to back off, and he knew Voyles was not telling the President everything.

"They are pursuing all leads," Coal said. "They gave us a copy of the brief almost two weeks ago, so we assume they're pursuing it."

Exactly what Horton had expected out of Coal. "I feel strongly that the administration should investigate this matter at once. What if the brief is on target? If we do nothing and the truth eventually surfaces, the damage will be irreparable."

"Do you honestly believe there's any truth to it?" asked the President.

"It's awfully suspicious. The first two men who saw it are dead, and the person who wrote it has disappeared."

Horton's investigations leaked worse than the White House basement, and Coal was terrified of this clown impaneling a grand jury. "Don't you think it's a bit premature?" he asked.

"I don't think so."

"I've looked at the morning papers," Coal said. "There's not a word anywhere about those two dead lawyers or the girl or Mattiece or anything related to the brief."

"We don't normally sit back and wait for the press to do our investigating, Mr. Coal."

"What's wrong with waiting a week?" asked the President.

"Nothing," shot Coal.

"Wait a week," the President ordered. "We'll meet here next Friday. I'm not saying no, Richard. Just wait seven days."

Just that quick the decision was made. Horton shrugged. He'd covered his rear. He would go straight to his office and dictate a lengthy memo detailing everything he could remember about this meeting, and his neck would be protected.

Coal handed him a sheet of paper. It was the bird-watcher list: four judges who were much too liberal for comfort. But plan B called for radical environmentalists on the Court.

Horton blinked several times. "You must be kidding."

"Check 'em out," said the President.

"These guys are off-the-wall liberals," Horton mumbled.

"Yes, but they worship the sun and moon, and trees and birds," Coal explained helpfully.

Horton caught on and suddenly smiled. "I see. Pelican lovers."

GRAY arrived at his desk in the newsroom at nine, and Darby called within minutes. "I'm here," she said. "I don't know how many I've brought with me, but I'm here and alive."

"Where are you?"

"Tabard Inn, on N Street. I saw an old friend yesterday. Remember Stump, who was grievously wounded on Bourbon Street? Well, he's walking again. A slight limp, but he was wandering around Manhattan yesterday. I don't think he saw me."

"Are you serious? That's scary, Darby."

"It's worse than scary. I left six false trails when I left New York last night, and if I see him in this city somewhere, I intend to surrender. I'll walk up to him and turn myself in."

"I don't know what to say."

"Say as little as possible, because these people have radar. I'll play private eye for three days, and I'm out of here. If I live to see Wednesday morning, I'm on a plane to some beach."

"When do we meet?"

"I'm thinking about that. Where do you park your car?"

"Close to my apartment."

"Leave it there and go rent another one—a generic Ford or something. Go to the Marbury Hotel, in Georgetown, and get a room under another name. They take cash. I've checked."

Grantham took notes and shook his head.

"Sneak out of your apartment after dark. Take a cab to the Marbury. Have them deliver the rental car there. Take two cabs to the Tabard Inn, and walk into the restaurant at nine tonight."

"Okay. Anything else?"

"Bring clothes. Plan to be away from your apartment for at least three days. And plan to stay away from the office."

"Yes, ma'am. I assume there's a master plan rattling around somewhere in your brain."

"Maybe. We'll talk about it over dinner."

"Is this sort of like a date?"

"Let's eat a bite and call it business."

"Yes, ma'am."

"I'm hanging up now. Be cautious, Gray. They're watching."


SHE was sitting at a table in a dark corner of the tiny restaurant when he found her at exactly nine. The first thing he noticed was the dress, and as he walked to the table he knew the legs were under it, but he couldn't see them. Maybe later, when she stood. He wore a coat and tie, and they were an attractive couple.

He sat close to her in the darkness so they could both watch the small crowd. "Where'd you get the dress?" he asked.

"I shopped a little this afternoon. You like it?"

"It's very nice."

The waiter was before them with menus. They ordered drinks. The restaurant was quiet and harmless.

"How'd you get here?" he asked.

"Around the world. I took a train to Newark, a plane to Boston, a plane to Detroit, and a plane to Dulles. I was up all night."

"How could they follow that?"

113

"They couldn't. I paid with cash—something I'm running out of. I'd like to wire some from my bank, in New Orleans."

"We'll do it Monday. I think you're safe, Darby."

"I've thought that before."

She looked at her menu, and he looked at his.

"You changed your hair again." It was light brown, and she wore a trace of mascara and blush. And lipstick.

"It's going to fall out if I keep seeing these people."

The drinks arrived, and they ordered. As Gray squeezed the lime in his gin and tonic a party of six entered from the bar, and Darby watched them carefully. When she talked, her eyes darted quickly around the room.

"I think you need a couple of drinks to relax," Gray said.

She took a long drink of white wine and inched closer to him.

THE lobby of the Marbury Hotel was empty at six a.m. Sunday, when Gray found a copy of *The New York Times*. He raced back to his room, on the eighth floor, spread the paper on the bed, and skimmed it intensely. The front page was empty, and this was crucial. If they had the big story, it would of course be there.

But there was nothing. And the less he found, the faster he skimmed, until he was down to sports and classifieds, and he stopped and sort of danced to the phone. He called Smith Keen, who was awake. "Have you seen it?" he asked.

"Ain't it beautiful," Keen said. "I wonder what happened."

"They don't have it, Smith. They're digging like crazy, but they don't have it yet. Who did Feldman talk to?"

"He never says. But it was supposed to be reliable."

"Are you busy?" Gray asked.

"Well, not exactly. It's almost six thirty on Sunday morning."

"We need to talk. Pick me up outside the Marbury Hotel."

"The Marbury Hotel?"

"Yes. In fifteen minutes. I'll explain."

"I'll be there."

Gray nervously sipped coffee from a paper cup and waited in the lobby. He half expected thugs to be hiding on the sidewalk. When he saw Keen's Toyota ease by on M Street, he walked quickly to it.

"What would you like to see?" Keen said as he drove away.

"Oh, I don't know. It's a beautiful day. How about Virginia?"

"As you wish. Did you get kicked out of your apartment?"

"Not exactly. I'm following orders from the girl. She thinks like a field marshal. I'm in room eight thirty-three until Tuesday, if you need me, but don't tell anyone."

Keen smiled. "I assume you want the *Post* to pay for this."

"I'm not thinking about money right now. The same people who tried to kill her in New Orleans turned up in New York on Friday. They have amazing talent in pursuit, and she's being painfully cautious. She's leaving here Wednesday morning for good. So we've got two days to find Garcia."

"What if you find Garcia and he won't talk, or knows nothing?"

"I've had nightmares about that. But I think he knows something big. I'm convinced there's a document or something tangible."

They crossed the Potomac and cruised by Arlington National Cemetery. Keen lit his pipe and cracked a window. "What if you can't find Garcia?"

"Plan B."

"So what's plan B?"

"I don't know yet. Darby hasn't gotten that far."

SHE had instructed him to stay off the streets and to eat in his room. He had a sandwich and fries in a bag and was obediently walking to his room, on the eighth floor of the Marbury. An Asian maid was pushing her cart near his room. He stopped at his door and pulled the key from his pocket.

"You forget something, sir?" the maid asked.

Gray looked at her. "Well, no. Why?"

"You just left, sir, and now you are back."

"I left four hours ago."

The maid shook her head and took a step closer to him. "No, sir. A man left your room ten minutes ago." She studied his face intently. "But sir, now I think it was another man."

Gray glanced at the number on the door: 833. He stared at the woman. "Are you certain another man was in this room?"

"Yes, sir. Just minutes ago."

He panicked. He walked quickly to the stairs and ran down eight flights. What was in the room? Nothing but clothes. Nothing about

Darby. He stopped and reached into a pocket. The note with the Tabard Inn address and her phone number was there. He caught his breath and eased into the lobby. He had to find her.

THE Edward Bennett Williams Law Library, at Georgetown, was quickly filling with Sunday students now thinking of final exams.

Darby found an empty table, opened volume five of *Martindale-Hubbell*, and found the section for D.C. firms. White and Blazevich ran for twenty-eight pages. Of four hundred and twelve lawyers, eighty-one were partners and the rest were associates. She grouped them all by alphabet and wrote every name on a legal pad.

The work was boring, but she memorized names until she knew more about White and Blazevich than anyone outside the firm.

MATTHEW Barr went to New Orleans, where he met with a lawyer who instructed him only to fly to a certain hotel in Fort Lauderdale. Barr checked in Sunday night and found a room waiting for him. A note at the desk said he would receive a call in the early a.m.

He called Fletcher Coal at home and briefed him on the journey so far.

Coal had other things on his mind. "Grantham's gone crazy. He and a guy named Rifkin, with the *Times*, are making calls everywhere. They could be deadly."

"Have they seen the brief?"

"I don't know if they've seen it, but they've heard of it. Rifkin called one of my aides yesterday and asked about the brief. The aide knew nothing, and got the impression Rifkin knew even less. But we can't be certain."

"Damn, Fletcher. We can't keep up with a bunch of reporters. Those guys make a hundred phone calls a minute."

"Just two guys—Grantham and Rifkin. You've already got Grantham wired. Do the same for Rifkin."

"Grantham's wired, but he's using neither the phone in his apartment nor the one in his car," Barr said. "He hasn't been home in twenty-four hours, but his car's still there. We were following, and so were the Fibbies. I think he got wind of it."

"You must find him."

"He'll turn up. He can't get too far away from the newsroom."

"Do you think you'll see Mattiece tomorrow?"

"I don't know. These guys are very secretive. I just don't know."

"Call me in the morning."

SHE stepped on the note when she opened her door. It said, "Darby, I'm on the patio. It's urgent. Gray." She took a deep breath, crammed it into her pocket, and locked the door. She followed the narrow hallways to the lobby, then through the dark sitting room, by the bar, through the restaurant, and onto the patio. He was at a small table partially hidden by a brick wall.

"Why are you here?" she whispered as she sat close to him. "You're not supposed to come here unless I say so."

He looked tired and worried as he gave her a quick summary of his morning, from the phone call to Smith Keen to the maid in the hotel. He'd spent the rest of the day darting all over the city in various cabs—almost eighty bucks' worth of cabs—and he'd waited until dark to sneak into the Tabard Inn.

"I have no idea how anyone could find my room," he said.

"Did you tell anyone your room number?"

"Only Smith Keen. But he'd never repeat it."

"Where were you when you told him?"

"In his car."

She shook her head slowly. "I distinctly told you not to tell anyone. Didn't I?"

He would not answer.

"It's all fun and games, isn't it, Gray? Just another day at the beach. I've tried to impress upon you how dangerous these people are. But hey, you're Gray Grantham, of the Washington *Post*. You're fearless, and the bullets will just bounce off, won't they?"

"Come on, Darby. I'm convinced, okay?"

"Listen, hotshot, you'd better be convinced. One more screwup and we're dead. I'm out of lucky breaks. Get a room here. Tomorrow night, if we're alive, I'll find you another small hotel."

He felt like a first grader who'd just received his first spanking. "So how'd they find me?" he asked.

"I would assume the phones in your apartment are tapped and your car is bugged. And I would assume Smith Keen's car is also wired. These people are not amateurs."

# TWELVE

HE SPENT the night in room 14, but slept little. The restaurant opened at six, and he sneaked down for coffee, then sneaked back to his room.

It would be a long and tiresome day, but it would all be spent with her, and he looked forward to it. He'd made a mistake—a bad one—but she'd forgiven him. At precisely eight thirty he knocked on the door to room 1. She quickly opened it, then closed it behind him.

She was a law student again, with jeans and a flannel shirt. She poured him coffee and sat at the small table where the phone was surrounded by notes from a legal pad.

"Did you sleep well?" she asked, but only out of courtesy.

"No." He threw a copy of the *Times* onto the bed. He'd already scanned it, and it was empty again.

Darby took the phone and punched the number of the Georgetown law school. She looked at him, listened, then said, "Placement office, please." There was a long pause. "Yes. This is Sandra Jernigan. I'm a partner with White and Blazevich, here in town, and we're having a problem with our computers. We're trying to reconstruct some payroll records, and the accountants have asked me to ask you for the names of your students who clerked here last summer." She listened for a second. "I see. How long will it take?" A pause. "And your name is . . . Joan. Thank you, Joan."

Gray watched intently, but with an admiring grin.

"Yes, Joan. Six of them. Our records are a mess. Do you have their addresses and Social Security numbers? We need it for tax purposes." . . . "Sure. How long will it take?" . . . "Fine. We have an office boy in the area. His name is Snowden. He'll be there in thirty minutes. Thank you, Joan." Darby hung up, and breathed deeply.

"You're wonderful," he said. "I guess I'm the office boy."

"You could pass for one. You have an aging law school dropout look about you." And you're sort of cute, she thought to herself. She took a drink of cold coffee. "This could be a long day."

"So far, so good. I get the list and meet you afterwards, right?"

"Yes. The placement office is on the fifth floor of the law school.

I'll be in room three thirty-six, a small conference room on the third floor. You take a cab first. I'll meet you there in fifteen minutes."

"Yes, ma'am." Grantham was out the door. Darby waited five minutes, then left with her canvas bag.

They would start with the law school at Georgetown. If it was a dead end, they would try the one at George Washington. If there was time, they would try American University. Three strikes, and she was gone. By late Wednesday she would be on a beach.

The cab stopped at the law school, at the grungy base of Capitol Hill. She took the stairs to the conference room and closed the door behind her. She spread her notes on the table and was just another law student preparing for class.

Within minutes Gray eased through the door. "Joan's a sweet lady," he said as he placed the list on the table. "Names, addresses, and Social Security numbers. Ain't that nice."

Darby looked at the list and pulled a phone book from her bag. They found four of the names in the book. She looked at her watch. "It's five after nine. I'll bet no more than half of these are in class at this moment. I'll call these four and see who's at home. You take the two with no phone number and get their class schedules from the registrar."

Gray looked at his watch. "Let's meet back here in fifteen minutes." He left. Then Darby went to the pay phones on the first level and dialed the number of James Maylor.

A male voice answered, "Hello."

"Is this Dennis Maylor?" she asked.

"No. I'm James Maylor."

"Sorry." She hung up. Maylor's address was ten minutes away. He didn't have a nine-o'clock class, and if he had one at ten, he would be home for another forty minutes. Maybe.

She called the other three. One answered, and she confirmed. There was no answer at the other two.

Gray waited impatiently in the registrar's office. A part-time student clerk informed him that she wasn't sure if they could give out class schedules. Gray said he was certain they could if they wanted to.

The registrar walked around a corner. "May I help you?"

"Yes. I'm Gray Grantham, with the Washington *Post*, and I'm

119

trying to find two of your students—Laura Kaas and Michael Akers. Are they in class this morning?"

"Is there a problem?" she asked nervously.

"No. Just a few questions." He was smiling. It was a warm, trusting smile that he usually flashed at older women. It seldom failed him.

"Well, I really should talk to the dean, but he's out of town."

"I just need their class schedules so I can find them. I'm not asking for grades or transcripts. Nothing confidential."

"Just a minute," she said, and disappeared around the corner.

Darby was waiting in the small room when Gray laid the computer printouts on the table. "According to these, Akers and Kaas should be in class right now," he said.

Darby looked at the schedules. "Akers has criminal procedure. Kaas has administrative law; both from nine to ten. I'll try to find them." She showed Gray her notes. "Maylor and Reinhart were at home. I couldn't get Ratliff and Linney."

"Maylor's the closest. I can be there in a few minutes."

"What about a car?" Darby asked.

"I called Hertz. It should be delivered in fifteen minutes."

MAYLOR answered the door shortly after the first knock. He was intrigued when Gray Grantham, of the Washington *Post,* pulled a photograph from his coat pocket. It was of Garcia on the sidewalk. But White and Blazevich covered twelve floors, most of which Maylor had never been on, and he did not recognize Garcia.

Darby found Laura Kaas as the admin-law classroom emptied. She said she was Sara Jacobs, from the Washington *Post,* asked a few questions, and handed Laura the photo. Laura spoke slowly, suspiciously. She said she'd never left the tax section on the fifth floor at White and Blazevich. She did not know Garcia.

At exactly ten thirty Darby and Gray met again in room 336. Gray had caught Ellen Reinhart in the driveway as she was leaving for class. She had worked in the litigation section of White and Blazevich, but Garcia's face did not register, and she said she was in a hurry. They scratched off Maylor, Kaas, and Reinhart, whispered their plans, and split again.

Gray left to find Edward Linney, whose address was north of

Georgetown's main campus. Darby, the investigative reporter, located JoAnne Ratliff in the offices of the *Georgetown Law Journal*, but Ratliff did not recognize Garcia. When the ten-o'clock classes were over, Darby spoke with Michael Akers. It was an awfully big firm, he said. The partners wore name badges to their meetings. It was a rotten place to work too, and they were all a bunch of thugs, really. Everything was political. He had never seen Garcia.

DARBY jumped into the new Hertz Pontiac as it stopped at the corner, and they were off in traffic.

"I struck out," Gray said. "Linney wasn't home."

"I talked to Akers and Ratliff, and both said no. That's five of six who don't recognize Garcia."

"I'm hungry. You want some lunch?"

"That's fine."

"Is it possible to have five clerks work three months in a law firm and not one of them recognize a young associate?" Gray asked.

"Not only possible, very probable. This is a long shot, remember."

"Could we have the wrong firm?"

"Maybe the wrong firm, maybe the wrong law school."

Gray parked illegally behind a row of small buildings off Mount Vernon Square, and they walked to a deli. She waited at a table by the window as he stood in line and ordered club sandwiches. Half the day had flown by, and though she didn't enjoy this kind of work, it was nice to stay busy and forget about the shadows.

Gray brought a tray of food and iced tea, and they ate.

"What if you can't link Mattiece? What'll you write about the story?" she asked.

"Depends on how far I get. We could've run that story about Verheek and Callahan, but it only scratched the surface."

"And you're going for the big bang."

"Hopefully. If we can verify your little brief, this will be the biggest story since—"

"Watergate?"

"No. Watergate was a series of stories that started small and kept getting bigger. This, my dear, is very different. Watergate was a stupid burglary and a bungled cover-up. These are masterfully planned crimes by very rich and smart people."

"And the cover-up?"

"That comes next. After we link Mattiece to the killings and run the big story, half a dozen investigators will crank up overnight. This place will be shell-shocked—especially at the news that the President and Mattiece are old friends. As the dust settles we go after the administration and try to determine who knew what and when."

"But first Garcia."

"Ah, yes." Gray looked at his watch. "It's twelve fifteen. Do you want to wire the money before we call Edward Linney? We can start the wire now and pick the money up later."

"Let's go," Darby said. "I'm finished."

THEY found a pay phone at a convenience store three blocks from the bank, and Gray called Linney's number. No answer. He slammed the phone down and got in the car. "He wasn't at home this morning, and he's not at home now."

"Could be in class," Darby said. "We need his schedule. You should've picked it up with the others. So back to the law school. I'll wait in the car while you march in there and get it."

"Yes, ma'am. Whatever."

A DIFFERENT student was behind the desk in the registrar's office. Gray asked for Linney's class schedule, and the student went to look for the registrar. Five minutes later the registrar walked around the corner and glared at him.

He flashed the smile. "Hi. Remember me? Gray Grantham, with the *Post*. I need another class schedule."

"The dean says no."

"I thought the dean was out of town."

"He is. The assistant dean says no. No more class schedules."

"Where is the assistant dean's office?"

The registrar dug in and folded her arms. "He will not allow you to have any more class schedules. Our students are entitled to privacy. You've already gotten me in a lot of trouble. One of the students you talked to this morning called White and Blazevich, and they called the assistant dean, and the assistant dean called me and said no more schedules will be given to reporters."

"Why should they care?"

"They care, okay? We've had a long relationship with White and Blazevich. They hire a lot of our students."

Gray tried to look pitiful and helpless. "Edward Linney's not in trouble. I just need to ask him a few questions."

She smelled victory. She had backed down a reporter from the *Post*, and she was quite proud. So offer him a crumb. "Mr. Linney is no longer enrolled here. That's all I can say."

Gray backed toward the door and mumbled, "Thanks."

He was almost to the car when someone called his name. It was the student from the registrar's office.

"Mr. Grantham," he said as he ran toward Gray, "I know Edward. He's sort of dropped out of school for a while. Personal problems."

"Where is he?"

"His parents put him in Parklane Hospital, in Silver Spring. He's being detoxified."

Grantham shook his hand. "Thanks."

They stopped at the bank, and Darby left with fifteen thousand in cash. Carrying the money scared her. Linney scared her. White and Blazevich suddenly scared her.

PARKLANE was a detox center for the rich, a small building surrounded by trees and sitting alone a half mile off the highway. This might be difficult, they decided.

Gray entered the lobby first. Then Darby entered, and strolled to the water fountain for a very long drink. Gray asked the receptionist for Edward Linney's room number.

"He's in room twenty-two, but you can't see him."

"They told me at the law school I could see him."

"And who might you be?"

He was so friendly. "Gray Grantham, with the Washington *Post*. They told me I could ask him a couple of questions."

"I'm sorry they told you that, Mr. Grantham."

"This is a very important matter, and I must see Mr. Linney this afternoon," Gray said, still courteous. "If you won't allow it, then I have to talk to your boss."

She gave him her best get-lost look and backed away from the counter. "Just a moment. You may have a seat."

123

She left, and Gray turned to Darby. He pointed to a set of double doors that appeared to lead to the only hallway. She took a deep breath and walked quickly through them. They opened into a large junction from which three dark carpeted corridors branched out. A brass plate pointed to rooms 18 through 30.

This would get her arrested. Her name would be in the paper, and Stump, if he was literate, would see it, and they'd get her.

The door to number 22 was closed and had the name Edward L. Linney tacked on it. She knocked.

A voice answered softly, and she stepped into the room. The carpet was thicker, and the furniture was made of wood. He sat on the bed in a pair of jeans, no shirt, reading a thick novel.

"Excuse me," she said as she closed the door behind her.

"Come in," he said with a soft smile. It was the first nonmedical face he'd seen in two days. What a beautiful face. He closed the book.

She walked to the end of the bed. "I'm Sara Jacobs, and I'm working on a story for the Washington *Post*."

"How'd you get in?" he asked, obviously glad she was in.

"Just walked. Did you clerk last summer for White and Blazevich?"

"Yes, and the summer before."

She handed him the photo. "Do you recognize this man?"

He took it and smiled. "Yeah. He works in the oil-and-gas section on the ninth floor. His name is, uh, wait a minute."

Darby held her breath.

Linney tried to think, and said, "Morgan. Yep. It's Morgan."

"His last name is Morgan?"

"That's him. I can't remember his first name. It's something like Charles, but that's not it. I think it starts with a C."

"And you're certain he's in oil and gas?"

"Yeah. I worked in the bankruptcy section, on the eighth floor, and oil and gas covers half of eight and all of nine." He handed the photo back. "What's this guy done?"

"Nothing. We just need to talk to him." She was backing away from the bed. "I have to run. Thanks. And good luck."

"Yeah. No problem."

Darby quietly closed the door and scooted toward the lobby.

Grantham was preaching to the administrator about the cost of health care when she walked quickly through the double doors. She was through the lobby and almost to the front door when the administrator said, "Miss! Oh, miss! Can I have your name?"

Darby was out the front door, headed for the car. Grantham shrugged at the administrator and casually left the building. They jumped in and sped away.

"Garcia's last name is Morgan. Linney recognized him immediately, but he had trouble with the first name. Starts with a C." She was digging through her notes from *Martindale-Hubbell*. "He works in oil and gas on the ninth floor."

Grantham was speeding away from Parklane. "Oil and gas!"

"That's what he said." She found it. "Curtis D. Morgan, oil-and-gas section, age twenty-nine."

"Garcia is Curtis Morgan," Gray said with relief. He looked at his watch. "It's a quarter till four. We'll have to hurry."

RUPERT picked them up as they turned out of Parklane's driveway. The rented Pontiac was flying all over the street. He drove like an idiot just to keep up, then radioed ahead.

MATTHEW Barr had to be cool. They wouldn't dare hurt him. He had been escorted to a black Lear by a man named Larry, who was at least six six, with a neck as thick as a utility pole. Barr sat by himself in the cabin. The windows were covered, and this annoyed him. But he understood. Mr. Mattiece treasured his privacy. Larry and another heavyweight were at the front of the cabin flipping through magazines and completely ignoring him.

After the Lear began its descent, Larry lumbered toward Barr. "Put this on," he demanded as he handed over a thick cloth blindfold.

At this point a rookie would panic. An amateur would start asking questions. But Barr had been blindfolded before. While he had doubts about this mission, he calmly covered his eyes.

THE man who removed the blindfold introduced himself as Emil, an assistant to Mr. Mattiece. He was a small wiry type with dark hair and a thin mustache. He sat in a chair and lit a cigarette.

"Our people tell us you are legitimate, sort of," he said with a friendly smile. Barr looked around the room. There were no walls, only windows in small panes, and the sun was bright. A plush garden surrounded a series of fountains and pools outside the room. They were in the rear of a very large house.

"I'm here on behalf of the President," Barr said. "I have orders to speak directly to Mr. Mattiece."

"I see. Mr. Mattiece is not well. He prefers not to meet you." Emil never stopped smiling. "He wants you to talk to me."

Barr shook his head. He would hold firm. "I am not authorized to talk to anyone but Mr. Mattiece," he said properly.

The smile almost disappeared. Emil pointed beyond the pools and fountains to a large gazebo-shaped building with tall windows. "Mr. Mattiece is in his gazebo. Follow me."

They left the sun room and walked along a narrow boardwalk to the gazebo. Rows of perfectly manicured shrubs surrounded it.

"I'm afraid you must remove your shoes," Emil said. He was barefoot. Barr untied his shoes and placed them next to the door.

"Do not step on the towels," Emil said gravely.

The towels?

Emil opened the door for Barr, who stepped in alone. The room was perfectly round, about fifty feet in diameter. There were three chairs and a sofa, all covered with white sheets. Thick cotton towels were on the floor in perfect little trails. A door opened, and Victor Mattiece emerged from a small room.

Barr froze, and gawked at the man. He was thin and gaunt, with long gray hair and a dirty beard. He wore only a pair of white gym shorts, and walked carefully on the towels without looking at Barr.

"Sit over there," he said, pointing at a chair. "Don't step on the towels."

Barr avoided the towels and took his seat. Mattiece turned his back and faced the windows. His skin was leathery and dark bronze. His toenails were long and yellow.

"What do you want?" he asked quietly to the windows.

"The President sent me."

"He did not. Fletcher Coal sent you. I doubt if the President knows you're here. I know about Coal. And I know about you and your little unit. Now, what do you want?"

"Have you read the pelican brief?" Barr asked.

The frail body did not flinch. "Why is Mr. Coal so concerned about the pelican brief?"

"Because a couple of reporters have wind of it. And if it's true, then we need to know immediately."

"What if it is true?" Mattiece said to the windows.

"Then we have problems."

Mattiece had not moved an inch. "Do you know what I think?" he said. "I think Coal is the problem. He gave the brief to too many people. He handed it to the CIA. He allowed you to see it. This really disturbs me."

Barr could think of no response. It was ludicrous to imply that Coal wanted to distribute the brief. The problem is you, Mattiece. You killed the Justices. You panicked and killed Callahan. You're the greedy fool who was not content with a mere fifty million.

Mattiece turned slowly and looked at Barr. The eyes were dark and red. He looked nothing like the photo taken with the Vice President at the Republican fund-raiser in New Orleans, but that was seven years ago. He'd aged twenty years in the last seven, and perhaps gone off the deep end along the way.

Barr could not look at him. "Is it true, Mr. Mattiece? That's all I want to know."

Behind Barr a door opened without a sound. Larry, in his socks and avoiding the towels, eased forward two steps and stopped.

Mattiece walked on the towels to a glass door and opened it. He looked outside and spoke softly. "Of course it's true." He walked through the door and closed it slowly behind him.

Barr watched the idiot shuffle along a sidewalk. What now? he thought. Perhaps Emil would come get him. Perhaps.

Larry inched forward with a rope, and Barr did not hear or feel anything until it was too late. Mattiece did not want blood in his gazebo, so Larry simply broke the neck and choked him.

THEY had engaged in a healthy debate over this elevator ride, and here she was. Gray was right; this was the quickest route to Curtis Morgan. And she was right; it was a dangerous route to Curtis Morgan. But the other routes could be just as dangerous. The entire game plan was deadly.

She wore her only dress and her only pair of heels. Gray said she looked really nice. The elevator stopped on the ninth floor, and she walked across a plush lobby. The name WHITE AND BLAZEVICH covered the wall in thick brass lettering. Her knees were weak, but she made it to the receptionist. It was ten minutes before five.

"I have an appointment with Curtis Morgan," Darby managed. "My name is Dorothy Blythe."

The receptionist was stunned. She couldn't speak.

Darby's heart stopped. "Is something the matter?"

"Well, no. I'm sorry. Just a moment." The receptionist stood quickly, and disappeared in a rush.

Darby's legs were rubbery. She looked around trying to be nonchalant, as if she were just another client waiting on her lawyer.

He came first, followed by the receptionist. He was about fifty, with bushy gray hair and a terrible scowl. "Hi," he said, but only because he had to. "I'm Jarreld Schwabe, a partner here. You say you have an appointment with Curtis Morgan."

Keep it up. "Yes. At five. Is there a problem?"

"When did you make the appointment?"

"I don't know. About two weeks ago."

The elevator opened, and a man in a cheap suit approached quickly to join the conversation. Darby scowled at him.

"You can't see Curtis Morgan," Schwabe said.

"And why not?" she demanded, sounding genuinely irritated.

Schwabe was inching closer. "He's dead."

Her knees were jelly and about to go. But, she thought quickly, it was okay to looked shocked. "Why didn't anyone call me?"

"We don't have any record of such an appointment."

"What happened to him?" she asked, stunned.

"He was mugged a week ago. Shot by street punks."

The guy in the cheap suit took a step closer. "Do you have any identification?"

"Who are you?" she snapped loudly.

"He's security," said Schwabe.

"Security for what? Is this a law firm or a prison?"

"Why don't you leave, Ms. Blythe?" Schwabe said.

"I can't wait!"

"I'll see you down," the security man said, reaching to assist her.

"Touch me and I'll sue you! Get away from me. I know how to

129

leave. I'm amazed you clowns have any clients." The closer she got
to the elevator, the louder she yelled. She was a crazy woman. They
watched her until the elevator door opened and she was gone.

GRAY paced along the end of the bed, holding the phone and
waiting for Smith Keen. Darby was stretched out on the bed with
her eyes closed.

Gray stopped. "Hello, Smith. I need you to check something."

"Where are you?" the editor asked.

"A hotel. Look back six or seven days. I need the obituary for
Curtis D. Morgan."

"Who's he?"

"Garcia."

"Garcia! What happened to Garcia?"

"He died, obviously. Shot by muggers. Can you check it quick?
I need his wife's name and address if we have it. We'll try to talk to
his widow tonight."

"Garcia's dead. This is weird, baby. Do you think you're safe?
What if they're watching his house?"

"We'll have to take that chance," Gray said. "I'll call you back."

He placed the phone on the floor and sat in an antique rocker.
He watched her. A forearm covered both eyes. She was in jeans and
a sweatshirt. The dress was thrown into a corner.

"You okay?" he asked softly.

"I've got a headache. A real genuine pounding headache."

"You've worked for it. Can I get you something?"

"Yes. A one-way ticket to Jamaica."

"You can leave tonight. I'll take you to the airport right now."

She removed the forearm from her eyes and gently massaged
both temples. "I'm sorry I cried."

"You earned the right." She had been in tears when she stepped
off the elevator. He was waiting like an expectant father, except he
had a .38 in his coat pocket—a .38 she knew nothing about.

"So what do you think of investigative reporting?" he asked.

"I'd rather butcher hogs."

He kicked his shoes off and placed his feet on the bed. She
breathed deeply. Minutes passed without a word. "Do you know
that Louisiana is known as the Pelican State?" she asked finally.

"No, I didn't know that."

"It's a shame, really, because the brown pelicans were virtually wiped out in the early 1960s from pesticides in the fish they ate. Then Louisiana began transplanting brown pelicans from southern Florida, and the population has slowly increased. But the birds are still very much in danger. The cypress swamp that Mattiece wants to destroy is home to only a few dozen pelicans."

Gray pondered these things.

"What day is it?" she asked after a while.

"Monday."

"I left New Orleans a week ago today. Thomas and Verheek had dinner two weeks ago today. That, of course, was the fateful moment when the pelican brief changed hands. Three weeks ago I was an innocent little law student minding my own business. I guess those days are gone."

"What're your plans?" he asked.

"I'll hide somewhere for a few months, maybe a few years. I've got enough money to live for a long time. If and when I reach the point when I'm not looking over my shoulder, I might come back."

"To law school?"

"I don't think so. The law has lost its allure."

"Why'd you want to be a lawyer?"

"I thought I could change the world and get paid for it."

"Most lawyers I know would rather be doing something else."

"But they can't leave, because of the money," Darby said.

"I detest lawyers."

"And I guess you think reporters are adored."

Good point. Gray looked at his watch, then dialed Smith Keen's number. Keen read him the obit, and Gray took notes.

"A couple of other things," Keen said. "Feldman is very concerned about your safety. Report to him before noon tomorrow."

"It's the *Times*, isn't it?"

"I'm not worried about the *Times*. I'm much more concerned about you and the girl. We're very nervous over here."

"We're fine. Everything's lovely. What else have you got?"

"Three messages from a man named Cleve. Says it's urgent."

"I'll call him later."

"Okay. You guys be careful. We'll be here late, so check in."

Gray hung up and looked at his notes. It was almost seven. "I'm going to see Mrs. Morgan. I want you to stay here."

She sat up and crossed her arms on her knees. "I'd rather go."

"It's too risky, Darby. What if they're watching the house?"

She thought about this for a minute. "No. I'm going. I've survived in the minefields for twelve days. This is easy."

THE private jet with Edwin Sneller aboard landed at National in Washington a few minutes after seven. He was delighted to leave New York. For almost a week his men had checked hotels and watched airports and walked streets. They knew they were wasting their time trying to find the girl in Manhattan, but orders were orders. They had to stay close in case she made a mistake, like a phone call or a transaction that could be traced.

She had made no mistakes until two thirty this afternoon, when she needed money. They knew that at some point she would have to wire cash, since the bank was in New Orleans and she wasn't. Sneller's client owned eight percent of the bank, a nice little twelve-million-dollar holding that could make things happen. A few minutes after three Sneller had received a call from the Bahamas.

They did not suspect her to be in Washington. And they certainly didn't expect her to link up with the reporter. Fifteen thousand went from her account to his, and suddenly Sneller was back in business. He had two men with him, a dozen en route from Miami. He was not hopeful. With Khamel on the team, everything had seemed possible. He had killed Rosenberg and Jensen so cleanly, then disappeared without a trace. Now he was dead—shot in the head because of one little innocent female law student.

THE Morgan house was in a neat suburb in Alexandria. The neighborhood was young and affluent, with bikes and tricycles in every yard.

Three cars were parked in the drive. Gray rang the doorbell and watched the street. Nothing suspicious.

An older man opened the door slightly. "Yes," he said softly.

"I'm Gray Grantham, with the Washington *Post,* and this is my assistant, Sara Jacobs." Darby forced a smile. "We would like to speak with Mrs. Morgan. It's very important."

"Wait a minute." He closed the door and disappeared.

The narrow wooden porch had a small veranda over it. They were in darkness and could not be seen from the street. A car passed slowly.

He opened the door again. "I'm Tom Kupcheck, her father, and she doesn't want to talk."

Gray nodded as if this were understandable. "I know what she's been through, but we won't be five minutes. I promise."

"I guess you're hard of hearing. I said she doesn't want to talk."

Gray kept calm. "Her husband called me three times before he died. I talked to him on the phone, and I don't believe his death was a random killing by street punks."

"He's dead. My daughter's had a bad day. Now get out of here."

"Mr. Kupcheck," Darby said warmly, "we believe your son-in-law was a witness to some highly organized criminal activity."

Gray handed him a business card. "If your daughter wants to talk, use the number on the back. I'll call around noon tomorrow."

"You do that. For now, just leave. You've already upset her."

"We're sorry," Gray said as they walked off the porch. Mr. Kupcheck watched them as they left.

They hurried to the parked car. There was no traffic on the street. Gray zigzagged his way out of the neighborhood, through the short suburban streets, watching the mirror until he was convinced they were not being followed.

"End of Garcia," Darby said as they headed for the city.

"Not yet. Maybe she'll talk to us tomorrow."

"If she knew something, her father would know. And if he knew, wouldn't he cooperate? There's nothing there, Gray."

This made sense. They rode in silence for a few minutes.

"We can be at the airport in fifteen minutes," he said. "I'll drop you off, and you can take a plane anywhere. Just vanish."

"I'll leave tomorrow. I need some rest, and I want to think about where to go. Thanks."

"Do you feel safe?"

"At this moment, yes. But it's subject to change in seconds."

"I'll be glad to sleep in your room tonight. Like in New York."

"You didn't sleep in my room in New York. You slept in the sitting room." She was smiling, and this was a good sign. Slowly she

133

lay down on the seat and placed her head in his lap. He gently rubbed her shoulder, and she clutched his hand. "I'm scared to death," she said quietly.

HE HAD left her room around ten, after egg rolls and a bottle of wine. He was tired and discouraged. And he was unhappy, because she would leave tomorrow. The *Post* owed him six weeks of vacation, and he was tempted to go with her. Mattiece could have his oil. But she hadn't invited him to join her getaway. She was grieving.

He was now at the Jefferson Hotel, on Sixteenth, pursuant, of course, to her instructions. He called Cleve at home.

"They put Sarge on medical leave," Cleve said, irritated.

"What's wrong with him?"

"Nothing. He says they want him out of the place for a while. They're scared to death. No one except the President can talk to the press without Coal's approval. He's obsessed with you and how much you know. Sarge thinks you could be in serious danger."

"Tell Sarge I'm fine. I'm hiding."

"I wish you'd tell me when you disappear. Call me tomorrow."

"Okay. I'll check in. And thanks, Cleve."

# THIRTEEN

H E SLEPT four hours and was awake when the phone rang. It was dark outside. He stared at the phone and picked it up on the fifth ring. "Hello," he said suspiciously.

"Is this Gray Grantham?" It was a very timid female.

"Yes. Who is this?"

"Beverly Morgan. You stopped by last night."

Gray was on his feet. "Yes. I'm sorry if we upset you."

"No. My father is very protective. I hope he didn't offend you." The voice was hollow and detached, yet trying to be strong.

"Not at all."

"He's asleep now, so we can talk. He told me Curtis called you, and I've thought about it all night. What did Curtis say?"

"He never identified himself. He used the code name of Garcia. Don't ask how I learned his identity—it'll take hours. He said he possibly knew something about the assassinations of Justices

Rosenberg and Jensen, and he wanted to tell me what he knew."

"Randy Garcia was his best friend in elementary school."

"I got the impression he had seen something at the office. He was very nervous, and he thought he was being followed. We had planned to meet, but he called and said no, he was scared. He had to protect his family. Did you know any of this?"

"No. I knew he was under a great deal of stress. He hated the office, really. He worked for a bunch of cutthroats. They spend tons of money on this marvelous façade of respectability, but they are scum—complete monsters to work with. Very unethical."

"Why did he stay with the firm?"

"The money kept getting better. He was very unhappy, but he tried to keep it to himself."

"How much life insurance did he have?" Grantham asked.

She paused for a second. "You're a smart man. Two weeks ago he bought a million-dollar term policy with double indemnity for accidental death. I guess you're right. I guess he was suspicious."

"I don't think he was killed by muggers, Mrs. Morgan."

"I can't believe this." She choked a little, but fought it off. "If he had something to show you, what would it be?"

He was the reporter. He was supposed to ask the questions. "I have no idea. He never hinted."

"Where would he hide such a thing?" The question was sincere, but irritating. Then it hit him. She was going somewhere with this.

"I don't know. Where did he keep his valuable papers?"

"We have a lockbox at the bank for deeds and wills and stuff. I looked at the lockbox last Thursday with my father, and there was nothing unusual in it. Then Saturday morning I was going through his desk in the bedroom, and I found something a bit unusual."

Gray was staring wildly at the floor, a lump in his throat. "What is it?" he asked as coolly as possible.

"It's a key to another lockbox. First Columbia. We've never banked there. I was puzzled by it, but I found all of our legal papers in the old lockbox, so I had no reason to check this one. I figured I'd run by when I felt like it."

"Would you like me to check it for you?"

"What if you find what you're looking for?"

"I don't know what I'm looking for. But what if I find something

135

Curtis left behind that proves to be very, let's say, newsworthy?"
"Use it. When do you want the key?"
"Stand on the front porch. I'll be there in about three seconds."


THE private jet from Miami had brought only five men, so Edwin
Sneller had only seven to plan with. Seven men, and no time. His
hotel suite was a mini–command center as they tried to plan the
next twenty-four hours. A few things were certain: Grantham had
an apartment, but he was not there. He had a car he was not using.
He worked at the *Post,* and it was on Fifteenth Street. White and
Blazevich was in a building on Tenth near New York, but the girl
would not return there. Morgan's widow lived in Alexandria. Beyond that, they were searching for two people out of three million.
They would concentrate on the Post building. It was the one spot
Grantham had to come back to.


THE downtown traffic was bumper to bumper, and that suited
Darby just fine. She was in no hurry. The bank opened at nine
thirty, and sometime around seven, over coffee in her room, he had
convinced her that she should be the one to visit the vault. Beverly
Morgan had told Gray that her bank, First Hamilton, froze their
box as soon as they learned of Curtis' death, and that she was
allowed only to view the contents and make an inventory. So the
question was whether or not First Columbia knew Curtis was dead.
It was a huge bank, with a million customers, and they decided that
the odds were against it.
Darby was tired of playing the odds. And now here she was about
to be Beverly Morgan matching wits with First Columbia.
"I don't know if I can do this, Gray. What if they call security on
me? I have this sudden phobia of security guards."
"You can do it, okay? Play it cool. Be assertive. It should come
natural. I'll come blaring through the lobby like a SWAT team."
"We'll all be killed."
"Relax, Darby. It'll work."
"Why are you so chipper?"
"I smell it. Something's in that lockbox, Darby. And you have to
bring it out, kid. It's all riding on you."
Gray slowed the car, then parked illegally in a loading zone forty

feet from the front entrance of First Columbia. Together they walked quickly to the door. It was almost ten. "I'll wait here," he said, pointing to a marble column. "Go do it."

She disappeared inside the revolving door. The lobby was as big as a football field, with columns and chandeliers and fake Persian rugs. It was the largest bank in the city, and no one noticed her.

The vault was behind a set of massive polished bronze doors that were slightly open to allow a select few in and out. To the left an important-looking lady of sixty sat at a desk with the words SAFE-DEPOSIT BOXES across its front. Her name was Virginia Baskin.

"I need access to a box," Darby said without breathing.

"The number, please," Ms. Baskin said. There was no smile as she hit the keyboard and turned to the monitor.

"F five six six."

She punched the number and frowned. "That was rented just two weeks ago."

Run! Darby thought. She frowned. Run before she calls the guards. Run before the alarms go off.

"I assume you're Mrs. Morgan," Ms. Baskin said, pecking on the keyboard.

Keep assuming, baby. "Yes. Beverly Anne Morgan."

She pecked again. "Who rented this box?"

"My husband, Curtis D. Morgan."

"And his Social Security number?"

Darby casually opened her new leather shoulder bag and pulled out her wallet. How many wives memorized their husband's Social Security number? She opened the wallet. "It's five one oh, nine six, eight six eight six."

Ms. Baskin liked this. She placed a wide card on a clipboard on the desk and pointed at it. "Sign here, Mrs. Morgan."

Darby nervously signed.

Ms. Baskin glanced at the signature. "Do you have your key?"

"Of course," Darby said with a warm smile.

Ms. Baskin took a key from the drawer and walked around the desk. "Follow me." They went through the bronze doors. Designed along the lines of a mausoleum, the vault was a maze of hallways and chambers. Two men in uniform walked by. The women passed four identical rooms with walls lined with lockboxes. Ms. Baskin stepped into the fifth room, and Darby looked nervously behind her.

Virginia was all business. She walked to F566, which was shoulder high, and stuck in the key. Darby inserted her key next to the other one. Virginia then turned both keys, slid the box two inches from its slot, and removed the bank's key. She pointed to a small booth. "Take it in there. When you finish, lock it back in place and come to my desk."

"Thanks," Darby said. She waited until Virginia was out of sight, then slid the box from the wall. Inside were two items: a thin brown legal-sized envelope and an unmarked videotape. She stuffed them into her bag, slid the box back, and left.

Virginia had rounded the corner of her desk when Darby walked behind her. "My, that was quick."

"I'm finished," Darby said. "I found what I needed. Thanks."

Her step was a bit quicker the second time through the lobby. Gray was guarding the marble column. The revolving door spun her onto the sidewalk, and she was almost to the car before he caught her. "Get in the car!" she demanded.

"What'd you find?"

"Just get outta here." She yanked the door open and jumped in. He started the car and sped away.

"I cleaned out the box," she said. "Is anyone behind us?"

He glanced in the mirror. "How do I know? What is it?"

She opened her purse, pulled out the envelope, and opened it.

"What's in the envelope?" Gray asked.

"I don't know! I haven't read it yet."

She pulled out a document and started reading it aloud. It was a four-page affidavit, typed, and sworn to under oath before a notary public. It was dated Friday—the day before the last phone call to Grantham. Under oath Curtis Morgan said he worked in the oil-and-gas section of White and Blazevich. Since he joined the firm, five years earlier, he had worked for a client named Victor Mattiece, who was engaged in a huge lawsuit in south Louisiana. Mr. Mattiece, whom he'd never met, but who was well known to the senior partners of White and Blazevich, wanted desperately to win the lawsuit and eventually harvest millions of barrels of oil from the swamplands of Terrebonne Parish, Louisiana. The partner supervising the case for White and Blazevich, F. Sims Wakefield, was very close to Victor Mattiece and often visited him in the Bahamas.

The lawsuit was very important to White and Blazevich. The firm was not directly involved in the trial and appeal, but everything crossed Wakefield's desk. He worked on nothing but the pelican case, as it was known, spending most of his time on the phone with either Mattiece or one of a hundred lawyers working on the case. Morgan averaged ten hours a week on the case, but always on the periphery.

On or about September 28 Morgan was in Wakefield's office. He walked in with two files and a stack of documents unrelated to the pelican case. Wakefield was on the phone. Morgan stood around waiting for a few minutes, but the conversation dragged on. Finally Morgan picked up his files and documents from Wakefield's cluttered desk and left. He went to his office at the other end of the building and started working. As he reached for a file, he found a handwritten memo, inadvertently taken from Wakefield's desk, on the bottom of the stack of documents he had just brought to his office. He read it. Then he read it again. He was stunned by the memo, and immediately terrified of it. He walked down the hall to the nearest Xerox and copied it. He returned to his office and placed the original in the same position, under the files. He would swear he'd never seen it.

A copy was attached to the affidavit. It was handwritten on White and Blazevich internal stationery, and it was directed to Wakefield from Marty Velmano, a senior partner. It was dated September 28.

> Sims:
>
> Advise client, research is complete—and the bench will sit much softer if Rosenberg is retired. The second retirement is a bit unusual. Einstein found a link to Jensen, of all people. The boy, of course, has those other problems.
>
> Advise further that the pelican should arrive here in four years, assuming other factors.

There was no signature.

Gray was chuckling and frowning at the same time. His mouth was open. Darby was reading faster now.

Marty Velmano, according to Morgan, was a ruthless shark who worked eighteen hours a day and felt useless unless someone near him was bleeding. He was the heart and soul of White and Blazevich. A tough operator with plenty of money, he lunched with Congressmen and played golf with Cabinet members. He did his throat cutting behind his office door.

Einstein was the nickname for Nathaniel Jones, a demented legal genius the firm kept locked away in his own little library, on the sixth floor. He read every case decided by the Supreme Court, the eleven federal appellate courts, and the fifty state supreme courts.

Morgan folded his copy of the memo and placed it in a desk drawer. Ten minutes later Wakefield stormed into Morgan's office, very disturbed and pale. They scratched around Morgan's desk and found the memo. Wakefield was angry, and asked if Morgan had read this. No, he insisted. Evidently, he'd mistakenly picked it up when he left his office, he explained. Wakefield was furious. He lectured Morgan about the sanctity of one's desk, but finally realized he was overreacting. He left with the memo.

Morgan hid the copy in a lawbook in the library on the ninth floor. He was shocked at Wakefield's paranoia. Before he left that afternoon, he precisely arranged the articles and papers in his desk and on his shelves. The next morning he checked them. Someone had gone through his desk during the night.

Morgan became very careful. He assumed his office was wired and his phones were bugged. He caught suspicious looks from Wakefield. Then Justices Rosenberg and Jensen were killed. There was no doubt in his mind it was the work of Mattiece and his associates. The memo did not mention Mattiece, but it referred to a client. Wakefield had no other clients. And no one client had as much to gain from a new Court as Mattiece.

On two occasions after the assassinations, Morgan was followed. He was taken off the pelican case. He was afraid of being killed. If they would kill two Justices, they would kill a lowly associate.

He had signed the affidavit under oath before Emily Stanford, a notary public. Her address was typed under her name.

"Sit tight. I'll be right back," Gray said as he pulled into a tow-away zone. He opened his door, jumped out, and dashed across E Street. There was a pay phone outside a bakery. He punched Smith Keen's number.

"Smith, it's Gray. Listen carefully and do as I say. I've got another source on the pelican brief. It's big, Smith, and I need you and Krauthammer in Feldman's office in fifteen minutes. Get a TV with a VCR. I think Garcia wants to talk to us."

"He left a tape?"

"Yes. Fifteen minutes."

"Are you safe?"

"I think so. I'm just nervous as hell, Smith." Gray hung up and ran back to the car.

THE Thin Man hid under a ragged fedora. His pants were rags, his shoes were torn, and he sat in his wheelchair in front of the Post and held a sign proclaiming him to be hungry and homeless. There was a bowl with a few coins in it in his lap, but it was his money. He looked pitiful sitting there like a vegetable, wearing green Kermit the Frog sunglasses. He watched every move on the street.

He saw the car fly around the corner and park. The man and the woman jumped out. He had a gun under the ragged quilt, but they were moving too fast. And there were too many people on the sidewalk. They entered the Post building.

He waited a minute, then rolled himself away.

SMITH Keen was pacing and fidgeting in front of Feldman's office. He saw them weaving hurriedly down the aisle, between the rows of desks. Gray was leading and holding her hand.

"Smith Keen, this is Darby Shaw," Gray said between breaths.

They shook hands. "Hello," she said, looking around at the sprawling, cluttered newsroom.

"My pleasure, Darby. From what I hear, you are a remarkable woman."

"Right," Grantham said. "We can chitchat later."

"Follow me," Keen said. "Feldman wants to use the conference room." They cut across the cluttered newsroom and walked into a plush room full of men, with a long table in the center.

Feldman closed the door and reached for her hand. "I'm Jackson Feldman, executive editor. You must be Darby." He pointed around the table. "This is Howard Krauthammer, managing editor; Elliot Cohen, assistant managing editor; and Vince Litsky, our attorney."

She nodded, forgetting each name. They were all at least fifty, all

141

in shirtsleeves, all deeply concerned. She could feel the tension.

The television and VCR were on a portable stand. Gray pushed the tape in. "We just got this, so we haven't seen it."

Darby sat in a chair against the wall. The men inched toward the TV and waited. On a black screen was the date—October 12. Then Curtis Morgan was sitting at a table in a kitchen. He held a switch that evidently worked the camera.

"My name is Curtis Morgan, and since you're watching this, I'm probably dead." The men grimaced, and inched closer. "Today is October twelfth, and I'm alone. My wife knows nothing about any of this. I've told no one. I've signed an affidavit, and I plan to leave it with this video in a safe-deposit box in a bank downtown."

"We've got the affidavit," Gray said. He was standing next to Darby. No one looked at him. They were glued to the screen.

Morgan slowly read the affidavit. It took him ten minutes. When he had finished, he laid it on the table and looked at some notes on a legal pad. He was a handsome kid who looked younger than twenty-nine. He was at home, so there was no tie. Just a starched white button-down. White and Blazevich was not an ideal place to work, he said, but most of the lawyers were honest and probably knew nothing about Mattiece. In fact, he doubted if many besides Wakefield, Velmano, and Einstein were involved in the conspiracy. There was a partner named Jarreld Schwabe who was sinister enough to be involved, but Morgan had no proof. (Darby remembered him well.) There was an ex-secretary who'd quit abruptly a few days after the assassinations. Her name was Miriam LaRue, and she lived in Falls Church. She might know something.

Morgan finished with a chilling farewell: "I don't know who will see this tape. I'll be dead, so it won't really matter. I just hope you use this to nail Mattiece and his sleazy lawyers."

Gray ejected the tape. He smiled at the group. "Well, gentlemen, did we bring you enough verification, or do you want more?"

Feldman was walking. "How'd you find Morgan?"

"We found a law student who clerked for White and Blazevich last summer. He identified a photograph of Morgan."

"How'd you get the photograph?" Litsky, the attorney, asked.

"Don't ask. It doesn't go with the story."

"I say run the story," Krauthammer said loudly.

"Run it," said Elliot Cohen. "Run it with the biggest headline since Nixon Resigns."

Feldman stopped near Smith Keen. The two friends eyed each other carefully. "Run it," said Keen.

He turned to the lawyer. "Vince?"

"There's no question, legally. But I'd like to see the story after it's written."

"How long will it take to write it?" the editor asked Gray.

"The pelican brief portion is already outlined. I can finish it up in an hour or so. Give me two hours on Morgan—three at the most."

Feldman paced to the other side of the room and stood in Gray's face. "What if this tape's a hoax?"

"Hoax? We're talking dead bodies, Jackson. I've seen Morgan's widow. He's dead. Even his law firm says he's dead. And that's him on the tape, talking about dying. I know that's him. Everything he said verifies the pelican brief. Everything. Mattiece, the lawsuit, the assassinations. Then we've got Darby, the author of the brief. And more dead bodies. And they've chased her all over the country. There are no holes, Jackson. It's a story."

Feldman finally smiled. "It's more than a story. Have it written by two. It's eleven now. Use this room and close the door. We'll meet here at exactly two and read the draft. Not a word."

The men stood and filed from the room, but not before each shook hands with Darby Shaw. She kept her seat. When they were alone, Gray sat beside her and they held hands.

"How do you feel?" he asked.

"I don't know. I've had better months. I'm happy for you."

He looked at her. "Why are you happy for me?"

"You put the pieces together, and it hits tomorrow. It's got Pulitzer written all over it."

"I hadn't thought about that."

"Liar."

"Okay, maybe once. But yesterday, when you told me Garcia was dead, I quit thinking about Pulitzers."

"It's not fair. I do all the work. We used my brains and looks and legs, and you get all the glory."

"I'll be glad to use your name. I'll credit you as the author of the

143

brief. We'll put your picture on the front page, along with Rosenberg, Jensen, Mattiece, the President, Verheek, and—"

"Thomas? Will his picture run with the story?"

"It's up to Feldman. He'll edit this one."

She thought about this, and said nothing.

"Well, Ms. Shaw, I've got three hours to write the biggest story of my career. A story that will shock the world. A story that could bring down a presidency. A story that will solve the assassinations. A story that will make me rich and famous."

"You'd better let me write it."

"Would you? I'm tired."

"Go get your notes. And some coffee."

THEY closed the door. A news aide rolled in a personal computer with a printer. They sent him after a pot of coffee, then some fruit. They outlined the story in sections, beginning with the assassinations. Darby preferred to write in longhand. She scaled down the litigation and the brief and what was known of Mattiece. Gray took the rest and typed out rough notes on the machine.

At twelve thirty Smith Keen sent in food. Darby ate a cold sandwich and watched the traffic below.

She saw him. He was leaning on the side of a building across Fifteenth Street, and he would not have been suspicious, except he had been leaning on the side of the Madison Hotel an hour earlier. He was sipping something from a Styrofoam cup and watching the front entrance to the Post. He wore a black cap, denim jacket, and jeans. He was under thirty. She nibbled on her sandwich and watched him for ten minutes. He never moved.

"Gray, come here, please."

He walked over. She pointed to the man with the black cap.

"Watch him carefully," she said. "Tell me what he's doing."

"He's drinking something, and he's watching this building."

"What's he wearing?"

"Denim from head to toe. A black cap. Boots. What about it?"

"I saw him an hour ago standing over there by the hotel. He was sort of hidden, but I know it was him. Now he's over there."

"So?"

"So for the past hour he's been watching this building."

Gray nodded. This was no time for a smart comment. She was concerned. She'd been tracked for two weeks now, and she knew more about being followed than he did.

The man looked at his watch and walked slowly along the sidewalk. Then he was gone. Darby looked at her watch. "It's exactly one. Let's check every fifteen minutes, okay?"

"Okay. I doubt it's anything," he said, trying to be comforting.

Gray returned to the computer, typed furiously for fifteen minutes, then walked back to the window. "I don't see him," he said.

But he did see him at one thirty. "Darby." He pointed to the spot where she'd first seen him. She looked out the window and focused on the man with the black cap. Now he had on a dark green Windbreaker, and he was not facing the Post. He watched his boots, and every ten seconds or so glanced at the front entrance.

"Why do I have this knot in my stomach?" Darby said.

"How could they follow you? It's impossible."

"They knew I was in New York. That seemed impossible."

"Maybe the guy's following me. Have you seen him before?"

"They don't introduce themselves."

"Look, we've got thirty minutes and they're back in here with knives to carve up our story. Let's finish it, then we can watch the dude out there."

They returned to their work. At one forty-five she stood in the window again, and the man was gone. The printer was rattling the first draft, and she began proofing.

THE editors read with their pencils. It was a long story, and Feldman was busy cutting like a surgeon. Smith Keen scribbled in the margins. Krauthammer liked what he saw.

Darby was at the window. Dude was back again, now wearing a navy blazer with the jeans. He looked at the Post, then back at the street. He was in front of a different building, and at exactly two fifteen he began looking north along Fifteenth.

A car stopped on his side of the street. The rear door opened, and there he was. The car sped away, and limping ever so slightly, Stump walked casually to the man with the black cap. They spoke for seconds; then Stump walked south. Dude stayed in place.

She glanced around the room. They were immersed in the story.

Stump was out of sight, so she couldn't show him to Gray. No, they were not watching the reporter. They were waiting on her.

And they had to be desperate. They were standing on the street hoping somehow a miracle would happen: that she would emerge from the building and they could take her out. They had to be scared. She was inside spilling her guts and waving copies of that damned brief. Tomorrow the game would be over. Somehow they had to stop her. They had their orders.

She was in a room full of men, and suddenly she was not safe.

Feldman finished last. He slid his copy of the story to Gray. "Minor stuff. Should take about an hour. Let's talk phone calls."

"Just three, I think," Gray said. "The White House, FBI, and White and Blazevich."

"Wait until four thirty or five before you call the White House and White and Blazevich," Feldman said. "If you do it sooner, they may go nuts and run to court."

"Okay. I'll rework it by three thirty, then call the FBI for their comment. Then the White House, then White and Blazevich."

Feldman was almost out the door. "We'll meet again here at three thirty. Stay close to your phones."

When the room was empty again, Darby locked the door and pointed to the window. "You've heard me mention Stump?"

"Don't tell me."

"Afraid so. He met with our little friend, then disappeared. I know it was him. I really want to get out of here."

"We'll think of something. I know some cops."

"Great. And they can just walk over and beat him up. They can't bother these people. What are they doing wrong?"

"Just planning murder."

"How safe are we in this building?"

Gray thought a moment. "Let me tell Feldman. We'll get two security guards posted by this door."

FELDMAN approved the second draft, at three thirty, and Gray was given the green light to call the FBI. Four phones were brought in, and the recorder was plugged in. Feldman, Smith Keen, and Krauthammer listened on extensions. Gray spoke with Phil Norvell, a sometime source within the Bureau.

"Phil, Gray Grantham, with the *Post*. I've got the recorder on. We're running a story in the morning detailing a conspiracy in the assassinations of Rosenberg and Jensen. We're naming Victor Mattiece—an oil speculator—and two of his lawyers here in town. We also mention Verheek—not in the conspiracy, of course. We believe the FBI knew about Mattiece early on but refused to investigate at the urging of the White House. We wanted to give you guys a chance to comment."

There was no response on the other end.

"Phil, are you there?"

"Yes. I think so. I'm sure we will have a comment. Let me see Mr. Voyles, and I'll call you back."

They waited eight minutes, and Voyles himself was on the line. He insisted on speaking to Jackson Feldman.

"Look, Jackson, this is crazy. You guys are jumping off a cliff. We've investigated Mattiece—still investigating him—and it's too early to move on him. Now, what's your boy got?"

"My boy has the pelican brief, Denton, and I'm sitting here looking at Darby Shaw."

"I was afraid she was dead," Voyles said simply.

"No. She's very much alive. She and Gray Grantham have confirmed the brief from another source. It's a large story, Denton."

Voyles sighed deeply and threw in the towel. "We are pursuing Mattiece as a suspect," he said. "We need to talk. I mean, man to man. I may have some deep background for you. I'll be there in twenty minutes."

The editors were terribly amused at the idea of the great F. Denton Voyles hopping into his limo and rushing to the *Post*. He hated the press, and this willingness to talk on their turf and under their gun meant only one thing: he would point the finger at someone else. And the likely target was the White House.

Gray punched the number for the White House, and they picked up the extensions. Keen turned on the recorder.

"Fletcher Coal, please. This is Gray Grantham, with the Washington *Post*, and it's very urgent."

He waited. The secretary returned with the message that Mr. Coal was on his way. Please hold.

Finally, "Fletcher Coal."

"Yes, Mr. Coal. Gray Grantham, at the *Post*. I am recording the conversation. Do you understand that?"

"Yes."

"Mr. Coal, we're running a story in the morning, which in summary verifies the facts set forth in the pelican brief. Are you familiar with the pelican brief?"

Slowly, "I am."

"We have confirmed that Mr. Mattiece contributed in excess of four million dollars to the President's campaign, three years ago."

"Four million, two hundred thousand—all legal."

"We also believe the White House intervened and attempted to obstruct the FBI investigation into Mr. Mattiece."

"Is this something you believe, or is it something you intend to print?"

"We are trying to confirm it now."

"And who do you think will confirm it for you?"

"We have sources, Mr. Coal."

"Indeed you do. The White House emphatically denies any involvement with this investigation. The President asked to be apprised as to its status after the tragic deaths of Justices Rosenberg and Jensen, but there has been no direct or indirect involvement from the White House. You have received some bad information."

"Does the President consider Victor Mattiece a friend?"

"No. They met on one occasion. Mr. Mattiece was a significant contributor, but he is not a friend of the President."

"Any other comment?"

"No. The press secretary will address this in the morning."

They hung up. Feldman rubbed his hands together. "I'd give a year's pay to be in the White House right now," he said.

# FOURTEEN

F. DENTON Voyles wore his customary wrinkled trench coat, with the belt tied tightly around the center of his short and dumpy physique. He swaggered as humbly as he could through the newsroom, with K. O. Lewis and two agents in tow. All dressed in dark coats, they resembled a Mafia don with bodyguards. The busy newsroom grew silent as they walked quickly through it.

A small, tense group of editors huddled in the hallway outside Feldman's office. Howard Krauthammer knew Voyles and met him as he approached. They shook hands and whispered. Smith Keen joined the conversation and shook hands with Voyles and Lewis. The two agents kept to themselves, a few feet away.

Feldman opened his door, saw Denton, and motioned for him to come in. K. O. Lewis followed. They exchanged routine pleasantries until Smith Keen closed the door, and they took a seat.

"I take it you have confirmation of the pelican brief," Voyles said.

"We do," Feldman answered. "Why don't you and Mr. Lewis read a draft of the story? It will explain things. The reporter, Mr. Grantham, wants you to have the opportunity to comment."

"I appreciate that."

Feldman handed a copy of the draft to Voyles. K. O. Lewis leaned over, and they immediately started reading. "We'll step outside," Feldman said. "Take your time."

He and Keen walked across the newsroom to the conference-room door. Two large security guards stood in the hall. Gray and Darby were alone inside when they entered.

"You need to call White and Blazevich," Feldman said.

They picked up the extensions, and Keen handed a phone to Darby. Gray punched the numbers.

"This is Gray Grantham, with the Washington *Post*, and I need to speak to Mr. Velmano, please. It's very urgent."

"He's in a meeting," the secretary said.

"So am I," Gray said. "Go to the meeting and tell him his picture will be on the front page of the *Post* at midnight tonight."

"Well, yes, sir."

Within seconds Marty Velmano said, "Yes, what's going on?"

Gray identified himself and explained about the recorder.

"I understand," Velmano snapped.

"We're running a story in the morning about your client, Victor Mattiece, and his involvement in the assassinations of Justices Rosenberg and Jensen."

"Great! We'll sue you for the next twenty years. You're out in left field, buddy. We'll own the *Post*."

"Yes, sir. Remember, I'm recording this."

"Record all you want! You'll be named as a defendant. This will

149

be great. Mattiece will own the Washington *Post!* This is fabulous!"

Gray shook his head in disbelief. "Have you heard of the pelican brief? We have a copy." The editors smiled at the floor.

Dead silence.

"Mr. Velmano, we also have a copy of a memo you sent to Sims Wakefield, dated September twenty-eighth, in which you suggest your client's position will be greatly improved if Rosenberg and Jensen are removed from the Court. We have a source that tells us this idea was researched by someone called Einstein."

More silence.

Gray continued. "We have the story ready to run. Would you care to comment, Mr. Velmano? Are you there?"

"Will you run the memo word for word?"

"Yes."

"You idiot. You've waited until five o'clock. An hour earlier, and we could've run to court and stopped this damned thing."

"Yes, sir. It was planned that way."

"You don't mind ruining people, do you?"

"No, sir. Anything else?"

"Tell Jackson Feldman the lawsuit will be filed at nine in the morning, just as soon as the courthouse opens."

"I'll do that. There's no lawsuit, Mr. Velmano, and I think you know it."

The phones clicked, and they were listening to the dial tone. They smiled at one another in disbelief.

Feldman stood. "I wouldn't use any of that."

"But I sort of liked the part about ruining lives. And what about the lawsuit threats?" Gray asked.

"You don't need it, Gray. The story takes up the entire front page now. Maybe later."

There was a knock at the door. It was Krauthammer. "Voyles wants to see you," he said to Feldman.

"Bring him in here."

Gray stood quickly, and Darby walked to the window. The sun was fading, and the shadows were falling. There was no sign of Stump and his band of confederates, but they were there, no doubt plotting one last effort to kill her, either for prevention or revenge.

Voyles entered with K. O. Lewis. Feldman introduced them to

Gray Grantham and Darby Shaw. Voyles walked to her, smiling and looking up. "So you're the one who started all this."

"I think it was Mattiece," she said coolly.

He turned away and took off the trench coat. "Can we sit?" he asked in general.

They sat around the table—Voyles, Lewis, Feldman, Keen, Grantham, and Krauthammer. Darby stood by the window.

"I have some comments for the record," Voyles announced. "First, we received a copy of the pelican brief two weeks ago today and submitted it to the White House on the same day. It was delivered by the deputy director—K. O. Lewis—to Mr. Fletcher Coal. Special Agent Eric East was present during the meeting. We thought it raised enough questions to be pursued, but it was not pursued for six days, until Mr. Gavin Verheek, special counsel to the director, was found murdered in New Orleans. At that time the FBI immediately began a full-scale investigation of Victor Mattiece. The investigation is continuing in full force. We believe Mattiece to be the prime suspect in the assassinations of Justices Rosenberg and Jensen, and we are attempting to locate him."

"What will you do if you find Mattiece?" Grantham asked.

"Arrest him."

"Did the White House interfere with your investigation?"

"I'll discuss it off the record. Agreed?"

Gray looked at the executive editor. "Agreed," Feldman said.

Voyles stared at Feldman, then Keen, then Krauthammer, then Grantham. "You cannot use this under any circumstances."

They nodded, and watched him carefully.

"Twelve days ago, in the Oval Office, the President asked me to ignore Mattiece as a suspect. In his words, he asked me to back off. He said it would be very embarrassing and would seriously damage his reelection efforts. He felt there was little merit to the pelican brief, and if it was investigated, then the press would learn of it and he would suffer politically."

"Are you certain?" Gray asked.

"I recorded the conversation. I have a tape, which I will not allow anyone to hear unless the President first denies this."

A tape! Feldman cleared his throat. "You just saw the story. There was a delay by the FBI from the time it had the brief until

151

it began its investigation. This must be explained in the story."

"You have my statement. Nothing more."

"Who killed Gavin Verheek?" Gray asked.

"I will not talk about the specifics of the investigation."

"But do you know?"

"We have an idea. That's all I'll say."

Gray glanced around the table. It was obvious Voyles had nothing else to say now, and everyone relaxed at the same time.

"What do you do now?" Krauthammer asked.

Voyles loosened his tie and almost smiled. "There'll be a grand jury tomorrow. Quick indictments. We'll try to find Mattiece, but it'll be difficult. He's spent most of the past five years in the Bahamas, but owns homes in Mexico, Panama, and Paraguay." Voyles glanced at Darby. She was leaning against the wall by the window, hearing it all.

"Which edition will this story run in?" Voyles asked.

"Late city—a few minutes before midnight," said Keen.

"Will it have Coal's picture on the front?"

Keen looked at Krauthammer, who looked at Feldman. "I guess it should. We'll quote you as saying the brief was personally delivered to Fletcher Coal, who we'll also quote as saying Mattiece gave the President four point two million. Yes, I think Mr. Coal should have his face on the front, along with everyone else."

"I think so too," Voyles said. "If I have a man here at midnight, can I pick up a few copies of it?"

"Certainly," Feldman said. "Why?"

"Because I want to personally deliver it to Coal. I want to knock on his door at midnight, see him in his pajamas, and flash the paper in his face. Then I want to tell him I'll be back with a grand jury subpoena and, after that, an indictment. And shortly after that, I'll be back with the handcuffs."

He said this with such pleasure it was frightening.

"You think he'll be indicted?" Krauthammer asked innocently.

"He'll take the fall for the President. He'd volunteer for a firing squad, to save his boss."

Feldman checked his watch and pushed away from the table.

"Could I ask a favor?" Voyles asked.

"Certainly. What?"

"I'd like to spend a few minutes alone with Ms. Shaw."

Everyone looked at Darby, who shrugged her approval. The editors and K. O. Lewis filed out of the room. Darby took Gray's hand and asked him to stay. They sat opposite Voyles at the table.

"I wanted to talk in private," Voyles said, looking at Gray.

"He stays," she said. "It's off the record. If you plan to interrogate me, I won't talk without an attorney present."

He was shaking his head. "Nothing like that. I was just wondering what's next for you."

"Why should I tell you?"

"Because we can help."

"Who killed Gavin?"

Voyles hesitated. "Off the record I'll tell you who we think killed him, but first tell me how much you talked to him before he died."

"We talked several times over the weekend. We were supposed to meet last Monday and leave New Orleans."

"When did you last talk to him?"

"Sunday night. He was in his room at the Hilton."

"And you discussed the meeting on Monday?" Voyles asked.

"Yes."

"Had you met him before?"

"No."

"The man who killed him was the same man you were holding hands with when he lost his brains. The Great Khamel."

She choked, and covered her eyes and tried to say something. But it wouldn't work.

"This is rather confusing," Gray said, straining to be rational.

"Rather, yes. The man who killed Khamel is a contract operative hired independently by the CIA. He was on the scene when Callahan was killed, and he made contact with Darby."

"Rupert," she said quietly. "Do you have any idea how confusing this is?"

"I can imagine. Rupert's not his real name, of course, but that'll do. He's probably got twenty names. If it's who I think it is, he's a British chap who's very reliable."

"Why was Rupert in New Orleans? Why was he following her?" Gray asked.

"It's a very long story, and I don't know all of it. I try to keep my

153

distance from the CIA, believe me. I have enough to worry about. It goes back to Mattiece. A few years ago he needed some money to move along his grand scheme. So he sold a piece of it to the Libyan government. I'm not sure if it was legal, but enter the CIA. Evidently, they watched Mattiece and the Libyans with a great deal of interest, and when the litigation sprang up, the CIA monitored it. I don't think they suspected Mattiece in the Supreme Court killings, but Bob Gminski was handed a copy of your little brief just a few hours after we delivered a copy to the White House. Fletcher Coal gave it to him. I have no idea who Gminski told of the brief, but the wrong words hit the wrong ears, and twenty-four hours later Mr. Callahan is dead. And you, my dear, were very lucky."

"Then why don't I feel lucky?" she said.

"And that doesn't explain Rupert," Gray said.

"I suspect Gminski immediately sent Rupert to follow Darby. I think the brief initially scared Gminski more than the rest of us. He probably sent Rupert to trail her—in part to watch, and in part to protect. Then the car exploded, and suddenly Mr. Mattiece just confirmed the brief. I have reason to believe there were dozens of CIA people in New Orleans hours after the car exploded."

"If the CIA moved so fast, why didn't you?" Darby asked.

"Fair question. We didn't think that much of the brief, and we didn't know half as much as the CIA. I swear, it seemed like such a long shot, and we had a dozen other suspects. We underestimated it. Plain and simple. Plus, the President asked us to back off, and it was easy to do because I'd never heard of Mattiece. Then my friend Gavin got himself killed, and I sent in the troops."

"Why would Coal give the brief to Gminski?" Gray asked.

"It scared him. And, truthfully, Gminski is . . . well, he's Gminski, and he sometimes does things his way without regard for little obstacles like laws and such. Coal wanted the brief checked out, and he figured Gminski would do it quickly and quietly."

"So Gminski didn't level with Coal."

"He hates Coal," Voyles said, "which is perfectly understandable. Gminski dealt with the President, and no, he didn't level with him. It all happened so fast. Remember, Gminski, Coal, the President, and I first saw the brief just two weeks ago today."

Darby pushed her chair away and walked back to the window. It was nice to have these mysteries revealed to her, but they created more mysteries. She just wanted to leave. She was tired of running and being chased, tired of the guilt for writing the thing. She longed for a small house on a deserted stretch of beach, with no phones and no hiding. She wanted to sleep for three days without nightmares and without seeing shadows. It was time to go.

Gray watched her carefully. "She was followed to New York, then here," he said to Voyles. "Who is it?"

"They were on the street all day watching the building," Darby said, nodding to the window.

Voyles seemed skeptical. "Have you seen them before?"

"One of them. He watched Thomas' memorial service, in New Orleans. He chased me through the French Quarter. He almost found me in Manhattan, and I saw him chatting with another fella about five hours ago. I know it's him. Who is he?"

"I don't think CIA would chase you. Do you see them now?"

"They disappeared two hours ago. But they're out there."

Voyles stood and stretched his thick arms. He walked slowly around the table. "We can help," he said.

"I don't want your help," she said to the window.

"What do you want?"

"I want to leave the country, but I want to make sure no one follows. Not you, not them, not Rupert nor any of his pals."

"You'll have to come back and testify before the grand jury."

"Only if they can find me. I'm going to a place where subpoenas are frowned upon."

"What about the trial? You'll be needed at trial."

"That's at least a year from now. I'll think about it then."

Voyles paced. "I'll make you a deal. I've got a plane and plenty of men who carry guns and are not the least bit afraid of those boys playing hide-and-seek. First, we'll get you out of the building, and no one will know it. Second, we'll fly you anywhere you want. Third, you can disappear from there. You have my word we won't follow. But, and fourth, you allow me to contact you through Mr. Grantham here if, and only if, it becomes urgently necessary."

She was looking at Gray as the offer was made, and it was obvious he liked the deal. She kept a poker face, but it actually sounded good. If she had trusted Gavin after the first phone call, if she'd left

155

New Orleans with him when he suggested, he would not have been murdered. And she would never have held hands with Khamel.

There comes a time when you give up and trust people. She didn't like this man, but he was being remarkably honest with her.

"Let's do it like this. I get on your plane, headed for Denver. No one is on it but me, Gray, and the pilots. After we take off I instruct the pilot to go to, let's say, Chicago. Can he do that?"

"Okay. What happens when you get to Chicago?"

"I get off the plane alone, and it returns with Gray. I get lost in a busy airport and catch the first flight out."

"It's a deal. We won't follow. When do you wish to leave?"

She looked at Gray. "When?"

"It'll take me an hour to revise the story again and add Mr. Voyles' comments."

"An hour," she said to Voyles.

"I'll wait."

"Could we talk in private?" she said, nodding at Gray.

"Certainly." Voyles grabbed his trench coat and stopped at the door. He smiled a chubby smile at her. "You're a helluva lady, Ms. Shaw. Your brains and guts are bringing down one of the sickest men in this country. I admire you. And I promise I'll always level with you." He left the room.

The door closed. "Do you think I'll be safe?" she asked.

"Yes. I think he's sincere. It's okay, Darby."

"You can leave with me, can't you?"

"Sure."

She walked to him and put her arms around his waist. He held her tightly and closed his eyes.

AT SEVEN the editors gathered around the table for the last time. They quickly read the section Gray had added to include Voyles' comments. Feldman walked in late, with an enormous smile.

"You will not believe this," he said. "I've just had a call from Judge Roland, an old friend of mine. Seems as though the boys at White and Blazevich called him away from the dinner table and requested permission to file an injunction tonight with an immediate hearing. Judge Roland quite impolitely declined."

"Let's run this baby!" Krauthammer yelled.

# FIFTEEN

THE takeoff was smooth, and the jet was headed due west, supposedly for Denver. Gray found two Sprites in the refrigerator and handed one to Darby. She popped the top of the can.

The jet appeared to be level. The copilot appeared in the door of their cabin. He was polite, and introduced himself.

"We were told we'd have a new destination after takeoff. We'll need to know something in about ten minutes."

"Okay," Darby said.

The copilot smiled and returned to the cockpit.

Darby and her long legs consumed most of the small sofa, but Gray was determined to join her. He lifted her feet and sat at the end of it. They were in his lap. Red toenails. He rubbed her ankles and thought only of this first major event—the holding of the feet. It was terribly intimate for him, but didn't seem to faze her. She was smiling a little now, unwinding. It was over.

"Were you scared?" he asked.

"Yes. And you?"

"Yes, but I felt safe. I mean, it's hard to feel vulnerable with six armed buddies using their bodies as shields."

"Voyles loved it, didn't he?"

"He was like Napoleon, making plans and directing troops. It's a big moment for him. He'll take a shot in the morning, but it'll bounce off. The only person who can fire him is the President, and I'd say Voyles has control of him at the moment. I think we've added ten years to his career. What have we done!"

"I think he's cute," Darby said. "I didn't like him at first, but he sort of grows on you. And he's human. When he mentioned Verheek, I saw a trace of water in his eyes."

"A real sweetheart."

Her feet were long and thin. Perfect, really. They were pale and needed sun, and he knew that in a few short days they would be brown, with sand permanently stuck between the toes. He had not been invited to visit later, and this was disturbing. He had no idea where she was going, and this was intentional.

The jet hummed, and shook softly. Grantham rubbed along the tops of Darby's feet. He'd been cocky and abrasive at first, she thought—a typical reporter. But he was thawing rapidly, and she was finding a warm man who obviously liked her very much.

"Tomorrow's a big day for you," she said. "What'll happen?"

"A lot of people will be in early. We'll gather in the conference room, and they'll bring more televisions. We'll spend the morning watching the story break. It'll be great fun listening to the official White House response. White and Blazevich will say something. Voyles will be very visible. The lawyers will assemble grand juries, and the politicians will hold press conferences. It will be a rather significant news day. I hate that you'll miss it."

She gave a little sarcastic snort. "What's your next story?"

"Probably Voyles and his tape. You have to anticipate a White House denial of any interference, and if the ink gets too hot for Voyles, he'll attack with a vengeance. I'd like to have the tape."

"And after that?"

"Depends on a lot of unknowns. After six o'clock in the morning the competition gets much stiffer. There'll be a million rumors. Every paper in the country will be wedging in."

"But you'll be the star," she said with admiration.

"Yeah, I'll get my fifteen minutes."

The copilot knocked on the door and opened it.

"Atlanta," Darby said, and he closed the door.

"Why Atlanta?" Gray asked.

"Ever changed planes at Atlanta? Ever gotten lost changing planes at Atlanta? It's huge and wonderfully busy. I rest my case."

He emptied the can and set it on the floor. "Where to from there?" He knew he shouldn't ask, but he wanted to know.

"I'll do my four-airports-in-one-night routine. I'll feel safer. Eventually I'll land somewhere in the Caribbean."

Somewhere in the Caribbean. That narrowed it to a thousand islands. Why was she so vague? Didn't she trust him?

"I'll call you when I get there. Or I might drop you a line."

Great! They could be pen pals. He could send her his stories, and she could send postcards from the beach.

"Will you hide from me?" he asked, looking at her.

"I don't know where I'm going, Gray."

"But you'll call?"

"Eventually, yes. I promise."

BY ELEVEN P.M. ONLY FIVE lawyers remained in the offices of White and Blazevich, and they were in Marty Velmano's room, on the tenth floor. Velmano, Sims Wakefield, Jarreld Schwabe, Nathaniel "Einstein" Jones, and a retired partner named Frank Cortz. Two bottles of Scotch sat on the edge of Velmano's desk. One was empty, the other almost there. Einstein sat alone in one corner, mumbling to himself. He had wild curly gray hair, and indeed looked crazy.

Cortz finished a phone chat with an aide to Victor Mattiece. He handed the phone to Velmano, who placed it on the desk.

"They're in Cairo, in the penthouse suite of some hotel," Cortz reported. "Mattiece will not talk. He's locked himself in a room, and needless to say, he ain't coming to this side of the ocean. They've told the boys with the guns to get out of town. The chase is off."

"So what're we supposed to do?" asked Wakefield.

"We're on our own," said Cortz. "Mattiece has washed his hands of us."

They spoke quietly and deliberately. The screaming had ended hours before. Wakefield blamed Velmano for the memo. Velmano blamed Cortz for bringing in a sleazy client like Mattiece in the first place. That was twelve years ago, Cortz screamed back, and we've enjoyed his fees ever since. Schwabe blamed Velmano and Wakefield for being so careless with the memo. They dragged Morgan through the mud again and again. It had to be him. Einstein sat in the corner and watched them. But that was all behind them now.

"I'll be in New York at six a.m.," Velmano said. "Then to Europe for a month on the trains. It was time to retire anyway."

"I can't run," Wakefield said. "I've got a wife and six kids. I don't know what I'll do. I just don't know." He stood weakly and started for the door. He was unbalanced at the moment. He didn't have a lot of money, and his wife was a spendthrift with a penchant for babies.

"Where are you going, Sims?" asked Schwabe.

"To my office. I need to lie down."

Wakefield walked deliberately to the stairway and down one flight to his office, on the ninth floor. He was crying when he locked the door behind him. Forget the note. If you write it, you'll talk yourself out of it. There's a million in life insurance. He opened a desk drawer and pulled the .38 from under a file. Do it quick!

He stuck it in his mouth and pulled the trigger.

THE limo stopped abruptly in front of the two-story home in Dumbarton Oaks, in upper Georgetown. Voyles and two agents jumped from the rear of the car and walked quickly to the front door. Voyles held a newspaper. He banged the door with his fist.

It was twenty minutes after midnight. Coal was not asleep. He was sitting in the darkened den in his pajamas and bathrobe, so Voyles was quite pleased when he opened his door.

"Nice pajamas," Voyles said, admiring his pants.

Coal stepped onto the tiny concrete porch. "What do you want?"

"Just brought you this." Voyles stuck the paper in his face. "Nice picture of you, right next to the President hugging Mattiece."

"Your face'll be in it tomorrow," Coal said.

Voyles threw the paper at his feet and walked off. "I got tapes, Coal. You start lying, and I'll jerk your pants off in public."

Coal stared at him, but said nothing.

Voyles was at the car. "I'll be back in two days with a grand jury subpoena," he yelled. "Next I'll bring an indictment. Of course, by then you'll be history and the President'll have a new bunch of idiots telling him what to do." The limo sped away.

GRAY and Smith Keen sat alone in the conference room, reading the words in print. Gray was many years beyond the excitement of seeing his stories on the front page, but this one brought a rush with it. The faces were lined neatly across the top: Mattiece hugging the President, Coal talking importantly on the phone in an official White House photo, Velmano sitting before a Senate subcommittee, Verheek smiling at the camera in an FBI release, Callahan from the yearbook, and Morgan in a photo taken from the video.

Around three a.m. Krauthammer brought a dozen doughnuts and promptly ate four of them while he admired the front page. Feldman arrived fresh and hyper. By four thirty the room was full and four televisions were going. CNN got it first, and within minutes the networks were live from the White House.

They bounced back and forth between the White House, the

Supreme Court, and the newsdesks. And though she wasn't quoted in the story, there was no secret about the identity of the author of the brief. There was much speculation about Darby Shaw.

At seven the room was packed and silent. The four screens were identical as the President's press secretary walked nervously to the podium in the White House pressroom. He was tired and haggard. He read a short statement in which the White House admitted receiving over fifty million in campaign money from Victor Mattiece, but he emphatically denied any of the money was dirty. The President had met Mr. Mattiece only once, and that was when he was the Vice President. He had not spoken to the man since being elected President, and had handled none of the money. He had a committee for that. No one in the White House had attempted to interfere with the investigation of Victor Mattiece as a suspect, and the President welcomed a full investigation into the allegations contained in the *Post* story. If Mr. Mattiece was the perpetrator of these heinous crimes, then he must be brought to justice.

It was a weak performance by a troubled press secretary, and Gray was relieved. He suddenly found himself crowded, and needed fresh air. He found Smith Keen outside the door.

"Let's go eat breakfast," he whispered.

They flagged a cab on Fifteenth and enjoyed the crisp autumn air rushing in through the open windows.

"Where's the girl?" Keen asked.

"I have no idea. I last saw her in Atlanta, about nine hours ago. She said she was headed for the Caribbean."

Keen grinned. "I assume you'll want a long vacation soon."

"How'd you guess?"

"Right now we're in the middle of the explosion, Gray. The pieces start falling to earth very soon. You're the man of the hour, but you must keep pushing. You must pick up the pieces."

"I know my job, Smith."

"You've got this faraway look in your eyes. It worries me."

"You're an editor. You get paid for worrying."

They stopped at the intersection at Pennsylvania Avenue. The White House sat majestically before them. It was almost November, and the wind blew leaves across the lawn.

AFTER EIGHT DAYS IN THE SUN, the skin was brown enough and the hair was returning to its natural color. Maybe she hadn't ruined it. She walked miles up and down the beaches and ate broiled fish and island fruit. She slept a lot the first few days, then got tired of it.

A travel agent in San Juan, who claimed to be an expert on the Virgin Islands, had found her a room in a guesthouse in downtown Charlotte Amalie, on the island of St. Thomas. Darby wanted crowds, at least for a couple of days, and Charlotte Amalie was perfect. The guesthouse was on a hillside four blocks away from the harbor, and her room was small but clean.

She'd seen the paper in Miami, and she'd watched the frenzy on a television in the airport, and she knew Mattiece had disappeared. If they were stalking her now, it was simply revenge. And if they found her after the crisscrossing journey she had taken, then they were not human, and she would never lose them. She vowed to stop looking over her shoulder.

The small room served its purpose, and for two days she never ventured far. She cried over Thomas, and was determined to do it for the last time. She wanted to leave the guilt and pain in this tiny corner of Charlotte Amalie and exit with the good memories and a clean conscience. It was not as difficult as she tried to make it, and by the third day there were no more tears.

On the fourth morning she packed her bags and took a ferry to the island of St. John. She took a taxi along the North Shore Road. The windows were down, and the wind blew across the back seat. The music was a rhythmic mixture of blues and reggae. She tapped her foot and closed her eyes to the breeze. It was intoxicating.

They left the road at Maho Bay and drove slowly toward the water. She'd picked this spot from a hundred islands because only a handful of beach houses were permitted in this bay. The driver stopped on a narrow treelined road, and she paid him.

The house was almost at the point where the mountain met the sea. The architecture was pure Caribbean—white wood frame under a red tile roof—and built barely on the incline, to provide for the view. She walked down a short trail from the road, and up the steps. It was a single-story with a porch facing the water. She had it for a month.

She placed her bags on the floor of the den and walked to her porch. The waves rolled silently to the shore, thirty feet below her. Two sailboats sat motionless in the bay, which was secluded by mountains on three sides. A rubber raft full of kids splashing moved aimlessly between the boats.

The nearest dwelling was down the beach. She could barely see its roof above the trees. A few bodies relaxed in the sand. She quickly changed into a tiny bikini and walked to the water.

IT WAS almost dark when the taxi finally stopped at the trail. He got out, paid the driver, and the cab disappeared. He had one bag, and he eased along the trail to the house. The lights were on. He found her on the porch sipping a frozen drink and looking like a native with bronze skin.

She was waiting for him, and this was so important. He didn't want to be treated like a houseguest. Her face smiled instantly, and she set her drink on the table.

They kissed on the porch for a long minute.

"You're late," she said as they held each other.

"This was not the easiest place to find," Gray said. He was rubbing her back, bare down to the waist, where a long skirt began and covered most of the legs.

"Isn't it beautiful?" she said, looking at the bay.

"It's magnificent," he said. He stood behind her as they watched a sailboat drifting. He held her shoulders. "You're gorgeous."

"Let's go for a walk."

He changed quickly into a pair of shorts and found her waiting by the water. They held hands and walked slowly.

"Those legs need work," she said.

"Rather pale, aren't they?" he said.

Yes, she thought, they were pale, but they weren't bad. Not bad at all. The stomach was flat. A week on the beach with her, and he'd look like a lifeguard. They splashed water with their feet.

"You left early," she said.

"I got tired of it. I've written a story a day since the big one, yet they want more. Keen wanted this, and Feldman wanted that, and I was working eighteen hours a day. Yesterday I said good-bye."

"I haven't seen a paper in a week," she said.

"Coal quit. They've set him up to take the fall, but indictments look doubtful. I don't think the President did much, really. He's just dumb and can't help it. You read about Wakefield?"

"Yes."

"Velmano, Schwabe, and Einstein have been indicted. Mattiece, too, of course, along with four of his people. There'll be more indictments later. It dawned on me a few days ago that there was no big cover-up at the White House, so I lost steam. I think it killed his reelection, but he's not a felon. The city's a circus."

They walked in silence as it grew darker. She'd heard enough of this, and he was sick of it too. There was half a moon, and it reflected on the still water. She put her arm around his waist, and he pulled her closer. They were in the sand, away from the water. The house was half a mile behind them.

"I've missed you," she said softly.

He breathed deeply, but said nothing.

"How long will you stay?" she asked.

"I don't know. A couple of weeks. Maybe a year. It's up to you."

"How about a month?"

"I can do a month."

She smiled at him, and his knees were weak. She looked at the bay, at the moon's reflection in the center of it as the sailboat crawled by. "Let's take it a month at a time, okay, Gray?"

"Perfect."

"Like a ride on a magic carpet." That's what the past two years have been for John Grisham. In December 1990, in the wake of the phenomenal success of his novel *The Firm* (a popular Condensed Books selection), Grisham closed his law practice in Southaven, Mississippi, to devote himself full time to writing. He and his wife, Renée, moved south, to the city of Oxford, where they bought a seventy-acre former horse farm. Here, on a hilly section of the property, they built their dream house— a butter-yellow Victorian.

*John Grisham*

Grisham's office is above the garage. He works at an oak desk, often with his Labrador, Bo, standing guard at the door. Each of his novels is meticulously outlined before he actually starts to write. "You should see the walls of my office," he says. "They are covered with flowcharts, notes, street maps, diagrams." When he wants inspiration, he goes out and rides his tractor until the muse strikes.

*The Pelican Brief* was not based on any single event, says Grisham. The idea came to him when he started thinking about how many 5–4 Supreme Court decisions there have been. One vote in either direction could mean a major shift in American law. That in turn set him thinking about the power of the individual Justices. But when asked if he thinks their terms should be limited, Grisham comes out with an emphatic no. "There can be a brilliant decision by an eighty-five-year-old Justice," he says, "and a bad one by a forty-year-old."

And what is the best thing about the fame and fortune that has come his way? "It frees me from financial worries, so that I can just enjoy my family—Renée and our two children, Ty and Shea. Family is the number one priority in my life."

The ties that bind
can also fashion life's truest

# TREASURES

## Belva Plain

*One* of Peg Osborne's children was happy with small-town life and love. Two wanted more: wealth, status, expensive artwork. But everything has its price. And how does one find life's greatest treasures?

From a well-loved author, the unforgettable story of a family whose ambition brought them to the heights, only to threaten them with the deepest despair.

THE two United States marshals, who had come to make an arrest, parked their inconspicuous black car, got out, and looked up at the ornamental neomodern roof of the sixty-five-storied tower. Somber rain clouds drooped over the city, releasing their first drops just as the pair in their plain dark suits reached the bronze doors that fronted the avenue. The younger man, who seemed almost imperceptibly to hesitate, followed the other across the marble floor to the long rank of elevators. This was no ordinary assignment today, nor was this a part of New York into which he usually was sent, and he was feeling a certain tension. It bothered him that he did. It was unprofessional.

"It seems funny, in a way, to handcuff the guy," he said. "Guy'll be wearing a Brooks Brothers suit probably. You know what I mean? He's not an armed thug."

"But you can't ever tell what a person will do. He could go off his nut and start punching. Or he could even head for the window. Press the forty-first floor, will you?"

The elevator slid upward silently, as if on silken cords, while a red light efficiently marked each number as it passed.

"Smells of money, doesn't it, Jim?" remarked the younger.

"Sure does. And lots of it."

"Wonder what the guy really did. Really, I mean."

"Lord knows. Got to be a high-priced lawyer to figure it out."

"Seems kind of sad, being hauled off from a place like this."

169

"It's always sad, no matter where it is. You never feel good about it," Jim said seriously. "But it's a job, Harry."

The door opened, and they stepped out in front of a long glass wall with many glass doors.

"Which way, Jim? Which is his?"

"He owns the whole floor. I'll get you there. Don't worry."

Receptionists are always pretty, reflected Harry, allowing his senior to do the talking to her while he himself examined the surroundings. He didn't know anything about rich living, and yet, when the brief opening and shutting of a door gave him a view of quiet gray carpeting and a corridor lined with paintings, he knew that he was seeing the real thing. Gold was gaudy, and quietness was expensive. Maybe he had read that somewhere.

He thought, In one of these rooms, perhaps a room at the end of that very corridor, a man is going to have a terrible shock.

The receptionist must have telephoned, because now a woman came rushing in. A fussy-looking matron with fuzzy gray hair.

"What? United States marshals?" she cried, confronting Jim.

He showed his badge, and Harry did the same.

The woman's eyes, enlarged by her glasses, sprang tears. "It's got to be a mistake. This isn't right! You're not going in."

"Ma'am," said Jim, "here's the warrant. Read it. We can force our way in. You don't want us to do that, do you?"

They were moving through the door toward the gray carpet, following the frantic woman. They entered a room, spacious, with many windows, more paintings, and a great desk at which a man was seated. Upon seeing them, he stood.

The woman was almost babbling. "I couldn't stop them. I—"

The man was young. He's about my age, thought Harry, and all this place is his. And somehow the pity he had been feeling for this stranger now turned to anger. To be my age and own all this!

The man was standing on dignity, but he was scared to death, his face had gone blue white. He stammered.

"There's— There's a mistake here. A terrible mistake. My lawyer's working on the matter right now."

"You'll be able to call your lawyer," Jim said. "But you'll have to come along now." He took out the cuffs. "I'm sorry, but you'll need to wear these."

"You don't understand," the man said. "I'm not the sort—"

"Please. Make it easy for yourself," Jim told him patiently.

The woman was openly weeping. "He's a good man. Be gentle with him."

In five minutes they were out of the building with their prisoner, whose handcuffs were hidden by the raincoat the woman had dropped over them. Silently, stunned and proud, the prisoner climbed into the car and was driven away through the dreary rain.

The event made the front pages of all the papers, as well as the television news. Telephones rang in the offices of the city's prestigious corporations. At dinner parties all up and down Fifth Avenue, Park Avenue, out on the North Shore of Long Island, and in Connecticut it was the topic of the moment.

"Everybody loved him," people said, commiserating. "So bright, so charming, so kind. I can't believe it! How can you explain it?"

## PART ONE
### 1973–1981
### Chapter One

THE downstairs neighbors had provided hot soup, cold meats, salad, and a home-baked pie—food enough for a dozen hungry eaters, Eddy Osborne remarked to himself. But there were only his sisters Connie and Lara and Lara's husband Davey at the kitchen table, none of them able to swallow more than a few mouthfuls. If anyone had told me I'd swallow even that much on the day of my mother's funeral, I wouldn't have believed it, he thought.

He stood up, poured a cup of coffee from the pot on the stove, and went to stare out the rain-beaded window at the bleak March afternoon. A shudder chilled his shoulders. Here was the ultimate desolation—the gray gloom and the grief.

Poor Peg, poor Mom! Sometimes the wig had tilted to the side, mocking her gaunt face with a rakish, jaunty look. She had been so vain, too, about the thick, tawny hair all three of her children had inherited. . . . And Eddy's heart broke. Making a little sound like a sob, he covered it with a cough and turned his face.

Lara said softly, "One thing, anyway, should be a comfort. She was never alone. One of us was always with her. And she did appreciate that private room, Eddy. Remember how she kept asking whether you really could afford it?"

"She'd have had that if it had taken my last penny, so help me!"

"Oh," Lara cried. "She must have known there was no hope for her, yet she never said a word. How brave she was!"

"No," Connie said. "The real reason is that she was afraid to admit how lousy life can be."

The grim, harsh comment shocked. But there was no sense in challenging it. Connie would say that she was merely looking truth in the face. She had few illusions, young Connie. The elder sister felt that was a pity, but answered only, "Let's go inside. No, leave the dishes, Connie. I'll clear them later."

The living room was dominated by the television, whose great blank eye was staring as they all sat down. Connie pulled down the shades, complaining, "Rotten weather!" as if, on this day at least, the rain need not have been so furious.

"Your mother would say," Davey responded in his mild way, "that rain like this nourishes the earth."

No one answered. Yes, Eddy knew, that would be typical of her. But I'm not like her, he thought, nor is Connie.

Too restless to be still, he went back to a window again and raised the shade that Connie had lowered. The houses across the street were mirror images of this one where Lara lived—a tall, shingled Victorian with a second door cut into its front to accommodate an upstairs flat. Before each house lay a woebegone yard with neglected, weedy shrubs and piles of soiled, melting snow.

What a miserable way to live, he thought. So many years gone by already in this confining town!

He turned around. Davey was reading the newspapers. The two women had laid their heads back and closed their eyes. They were exhausted. And Eddy felt compassion for them, for their tenderness in a tough, hard world. He knew how desperately Lara longed for a child and would probably never have one; he knew how Connie, like himself, longed for betterment, for color, for life. He knew that her feet, like his, wanted to run.

Now as they rested, unaware of his scrutiny, he observed his sisters. Connie had a 1920s look—her lips a bold Cupid's bow, her nose short and straight, her eyebrows two narrow graceful curves above alert gray eyes. She was unusually vivacious and knew how to make the best of herself. People looked at her. Yet it was always said that Lara was the beauty, having what were called good bones. Her face was a pure oval, and she had contemplative sea-blue eyes, the same color as Eddy's own.

His, however, were not contemplative, any more than Connie's were. Their eyes were quick. Everything about us two, for better or for worse, is quick, he thought suddenly. And it seemed to him that now was as good a time as any to say what had to be said.

"I've something to tell you. I hope you won't be too shocked, but I'm going to be leaving town, leaving Ohio."

"You're what?" cried Connie, sitting up straight.

"There's a guy I've known since college who's in New York now. He's an accountant, like me, only he happens to have an uncle who's lent him enough to start in brokerage. He wants a partner, and he's willing to take me in with him."

A gleam of interest shot through Connie's eyes. "Wall Street?"

"Yes, ma'am. You bet. Wall Street."

"Leaving us!" Lara cried. "Oh, Eddy."

"Minutes away by plane, honey. I'm not leaving you. Not ever." And he repeated, "A matter of minutes. All right, a couple of hours. Not the end of the world." His smile coaxed.

Lara was dismayed. "But you've been building up so nicely! I can't understand why you'd want to leave it all behind like that."

"Building? Yes. But it's too gradual, too slow, compared with this opportunity. It's small potatoes."

She thought, We're splitting apart already. Peg's six hours in her grave. Then it's true what they say: When the mother dies, the family breaks up. Couldn't he think of that—Eddy, Peg's golden boy, with the bright hair, the sea-blue eyes, and the nonchalant stance? She felt suddenly hopeless.

Davey asked quietly, "How long have you known this?"

"About three months. I probably should have told you sooner, but I thought . . . well, we were all going through enough."

Davey had another question. "Don't you have to put up any money at all, Eddy?"

"Sure, but not much. I've saved twelve thousand dollars out of my earnings, and I was incredibly lucky at cards one night a while back. Made another fifteen, believe it or not. So I've got enough to put down for my share of the partnership, and I'll pay off the balance out of what I make in the market."

"*If* you make it in the market, you mean," Davey said.

"I'll make it. I have a feel for the market. It's on the rise, a long rise. Anybody can see that. Besides, you don't get anyplace in life without taking a few chances. You have to be willing to risk. All the great inventors, all the industrialists took risks."

Davey glanced at Lara, and she saw that he was reading her mind, feeling her sadness, as he always could and did.

Then he said quietly, "To each his own. I guess New York will agree with you, Eddy. It's no place for us. Lara and I have our places here. The shop's doing a whole lot better than it did when my dad had it, and I've got some inventions, some ideas I'm working on—" He stopped, took Lara's hand, and pressed it.

Lara could read her brother's mind. How good is "a lot better"? Eddy must be thinking as he glanced around. It was a pretty room, furnished with secondhand pieces that she had slipcovered herself in pink, red, and cream. But the carpet was threadbare. . . .

Eddy used to come home starry-eyed over some house he had seen or a car he had ridden in. Like Pop before him, he *aspired;* like Pop, too, he'd been quick to imitate the upper class—its dress, its speech. But unlike Pop, he was smart. He might do very well. Yes, it was possible. Oh, this was a blow all the same! To lose Eddy, to lose his invaluable good humor, the sparkle he brought into the room.

Connie, in her practical way, asked how soon he planned to go.

"I thought in about two weeks. First I want to help you get out of that apartment, find something nicer. It's too large for you alone, without Mom, and too glum besides. Do you feel up to going out with me tomorrow to look?"

"Well," she answered. "Well." Her eyes moved about the room, as if searching, then to Davey and Lara. Finally, looking down at a tear in the carpet, she said, "It looks as if we've both picked the same time to surprise each other."

Alarmed again, Lara cried, "What are you talking about?"

"Well, you see—you see— Oh, Lara, how I've been wanting to just . . . just *go* somewhere! I've never really *been* anywhere."

"Will you get to the point, Connie, please?"

"Texas. I've been hearing so much about it. It's booming. You can always get a job. There's something exciting just in the sound of it. Texas. Houston. I want to see it."

Lara's mouth went dry. "You don't know a soul there, Connie. To go alone, leaving the only family you've got—it doesn't make any sense. And you're only twenty! What kind of a job do you think you'll get without a single contact? Where will you live?"

"Darling, don't be a mother hen. I'll buy a newspaper and read the ads—what do you think?"

Lara's thoughts were sad and bitter. Yes, I was a mother hen. I had to be, hadn't I? All the years Mom was too sick from chemotherapy to take charge, and I with a teenage sister eight years younger than I and a lively brother five years younger than I.

"It's not so easy to find a job, Connie. You have no training. At least you do have a job here that you can depend on."

"What—selling slacks and skirts in a tenth-rate department store, when there's so much in the world to do and see?"

"You might take some courses and learn something better."

"I haven't the will just now, or the patience." Connie stood up and laid her hand on Lara's shoulder. "Don't look so hurt," she said. "I'm not staying away forever. Can't you make believe we're very rich and I'm taking a year off to travel around the world?"

"She's right," Eddy said. "A young woman wants a change, a touch of adventure in her life. It's natural, Lara. If you hadn't fallen in love with Davey, probably you would have felt the same way."

Lara, knowing she was expected to smile, did so, faintly. "We'll talk some more," she replied.

Davey agreed. "Good idea. Tomorrow's another day, so let's try to lighten up a little. As Eddy says, it's not the end of the world."

Lara got the message. "Stay here for the night, Connie. Don't go back to the apartment. I'll get some blankets for the spare room."

THE spare room, Lara thought as she straightened the bed, was meant to be the nursery. It was to have had lemon-yellow walls, a frieze of Mother Goose figures going all around, and white furniture. The crib would have had a canopy of dotted organdy.

She hated the room. Seven years married, and nothing. Doctors, thermometers, hormones, sperm analyses—and nothing.

"Why don't you fix this room? You could have a nice little den," Connie remarked as she came in.

She doesn't know how that hurts, Lara thought.

On the dresser stood the room's sole ornament, a photograph of their parents taken on their wedding day. The two sisters stood looking at it now. Their parents had been handsome people— Vernon dark, with a sporty boutonniere and flashing teeth; Peg's sweet face tiny in its frame of lavish hair.

Connie sighed. "How happy they were!"

"Mom loved Pop no matter what. Remember how he used to call her Peg o' My Heart?"

"I don't see how she could have kept on loving him. I guess it was noble of her, but I'm not made that way. Life's too short."

"He was a good man, except for the booze," Lara said, "and that ran in his family. Thank God none of us has inherited it."

Pop had been a salesman, traveling back and forth through the Midwest, selling anything from shoes to used tires. As often as he lost his jobs, the family moved from one flat to another, always in the oldest part of a town, above a hardware store or a Laundromat. The longest period they ever stayed in one place was when his liver and then his heart finally failed; then Peg opened her little beauty parlor and eked out a living for her children.

And yet . . . "He was a good man," she repeated.

Connie's look was a mingling of pity and disbelief. "I guess you've forgotten the nights when he came staggering home."

"No, but I remember the nights he read poetry aloud to us."

Then Peg, who knew nothing about books, had nevertheless smiled in pleasure because her children were being taught to love them. Lara sighed. The ache lay heavy within her. Through all this dreadful day the memories had been aching.

Connie had begun to strip off her clothes. In bra and panty hose she stood and stretched.

"I'm so tired, I hardly have enough strength to take a shower."

"Wait till the morning, then. You need your rest."

Connie smiled. "You always used to say that. Oh, Lara darling, don't look so miserable! Don't worry about me. I'll do fine."

"I can't help worrying, can I? Besides, I'll miss you. I've never been without you."

176

"Don't you think I'll miss you, too?"

"Are you really sure you're doing the right thing?"

"Lara, I need a chance to meet people. In this town—you know what's here. I don't want a life like . . ."

Like mine, Lara said to herself. I know that. Walking home beneath the trees on a summer night, Davey asked me, "Are you willing to share almost nothing with me? I'll do my best for you, Lara. Only, my best isn't all that good." Was I willing? To go to the ends of the earth with you, Davey, to live in a tent or under the open sky. It was true then, and it is true still.

"I love you, Lara," Connie said.

"Of course you do. We all love each other. Go to sleep, dear. I'll go out and say good night to Eddy."

He was already in his overcoat. "I waited to see whether you were feeling any better. Davey's gone out to his workbench."

"I feel all right. I guess I have to. But why did you encourage her?"

"Lara, you're a rock. Do you think Connie and I don't remember how you watched over us? But honey, a time comes when one can't cling to the rock anymore, and Connie's time has come."

"Whom have we got?" Lara blurted. "Two second cousins too old and poor even to make the trip for the funeral. We have no roots, and I'm trying to establish some, that's all."

"Money will help," Eddy said. "And I'm trying to make some."

"We're not speaking the same language tonight, Eddy."

"Maybe not. We're both too tired to think." He kissed her. "I'll be going. Get some rest."

Through the window that overlooked the yard she saw a light burning in Davey's shed behind the garage. The rain had slackened to a drizzle, and throwing an old coat on, she ran out back.

Davey's workroom was a cramped jumble of shelves before which stood a battered table covered with tubes, filaments, calipers, chisels, fuses, rolled copper wire. Bent over these now was Davey's dark head; he was apparently intent on writing in a notebook.

Even if nothing was ever to come of any of his inventions, she would always be proud of him. He was the first friend she had made on her first day in a strange high school in a new town. The tall boy with the odd name, Davey Davis, the basketball star of the school.

She went in and put her arms around him. He stroked her hair.

177

"I know. It's been a cruel day. Cruel months," he murmured.

"I've been thinking over and over how Connie and Eddy will never come back again."

"Lara! This isn't like you. You're always the family optimist."

"I know. But sometimes I get to thinking that one can be a fool of an optimist, too." She sighed. "You know what I mean, Davey."

"The baby," he said gently.

"The baby we wait for every month and who never comes."

He put his cheek on hers, holding her close. After a moment he said, "We could adopt."

"But that's not easy either. One doesn't just walk in and select a baby. One waits for years, and even then—"

"Perhaps not a baby, Lara, but an older child who needs a home? Sad to say, there are plenty of those."

"I want a baby! I want to be the mother from the very start."

"Darling," Davey said, holding her tighter. "Then we should wait a little more. Won't you try some of your optimism again?"

She felt that she was weighing him down with her obsession, while he was striving to lift her up. It wasn't fair of her.

"Okay, okay, no more. Let's go upstairs," she said.

Later, in the familiar bed, under the quilts, they lay quietly and warmly.

"You're still the most beautiful woman I've ever seen," Davey murmured. "In a gingham apron or, better, in nothing at all."

And so, after a little time, desire moved them. It fled across Lara's mind as they turned into each other's arms that this was the deepest joy and comfort of all, this total, trustful merging. This was the reality of life. All else faded away.

In the aftermath she curved herself into Davey's back, feeling unity, feeling the safety of his presence in the silent room.

## Chapter Two

HOUSTON was *hot*. Like a metal dome, the bronze sky burned above the city. Dusty leaves hung through the long afternoon. Coming into the hotel from the street was like walking into a freezer room; the sweating body received a shuddering shock.

Connie's hotel was a huge commercial establishment in the

downtown business district. Neither expensive nor cheap, it suited the funds Eddy had advanced.

She had moved the chair in her room over to the window. The outlook here, some fifty feet to a bank of similar windows on the opposite side of the meager courtyard, was depressing, but even such dim daylight was less depressing than the sullen yellow lamplight next to the dingy brown bed.

At her feet lay a pile of newspapers. Column after column of help wanted ads confirmed her judgment: Texas was truly booming. With a feeling of challenge and elation she ran her eyes to the top of a page and down. Suddenly she read:

> Young vendeuse for exclusive shop, experienced European fashions for demanding clientele, well spoken, attractive appearance. Salary and commissions.

"Vendeuse." From her slight experience with high-school French, Connie summoned up a verb: *vendre,* to sell. So what this verbiage boiled down to was being a saleswoman in a fancy dress shop. "Experienced." Three years' worth, although not doing exactly what they were looking for. "Young . . . well spoken, attractive." She stood up and went to the full-length mirror on the bathroom door.

The sight was reassuring. Her heavy hair hung at a becoming length almost to her shoulders. The beige linen suit with coral shirt, Lara's going-away gift, was smartly slender; the gold earrings, Eddy's extravagant birthday present, were eighteen karat. Connie examined her face, no match for Lara's classic near perfection. She knew that well and was not at all bothered, for she had the greater power to attract.

The important thing was to know how to use this power to a practical end. So before going to be interviewed, Miss Osborne, go buy a stack of magazines and make yourself familiar with European fashion. Then tomorrow morning do your hair, hail an air-conditioned taxi, and arrive coolly unruffled and speak up.

THE shop, situated in a grand mall, was spacious and serene, carpeted in silver gray and ornamented with sprays of gladioli. Here and there a circular rack held a dozen garments on display.

Slowly and keenly, for half an hour, Connie was examined.

179

"You say you've had experience with merchandise like this?"

"Yes. In Cleveland."

"Have you a recommendation from them?"

"Unfortunately, no. The owner died of a heart attack, and everything fell apart the next day." Connie touched a lavender suit that hung where she was standing. "What they've been doing with Chanel is delightful, isn't it? Adding new touches without changing the traditional charm one bit."

"Ah, yes, of course." And finally, "Well, if you're available to start soon, we can go over the formalities in the office."

"That would be wonderful."

So it was settled, an auspicious start on the third day in this vast, energetic city. It would be pleasant to work surrounded by beautiful, rich things. Granted, it would be still more pleasant to have the beautiful, rich things for oneself, Connie reflected. But one day at a time. Next she must find herself a car and a place to live.

LATE in the afternoon she stopped her little red car in front of a neat brick house shaded by oaks. Before climbing the steps to the front door, she looked back at the car. A good buy, only two years old. Davey always tried to get a demonstration car, and today she had found one. This further success now gave her confidence.

A heavy woman with short blue-gray curls answered her ring.

"Mrs. Raymond?" asked Connie. "I'm Consuelo Osborne. I'd like to see the room."

"You sounded older on the telephone this morning."

"Did I?" Connie replied, smiling.

"Well, come in."

At the rear of the house, looking out on the garden, was a bedroom furnished with a Grand Rapids bed and dresser, a comfortable chair, and maroon cretonne curtains. It was unmistakably clean. Connie's fastidious nose detected the very freshness of the air.

"It's lovely," she said.

"You're not a Texan."

"I'm from Ohio."

"What made you leave?"

"I can't stand the cold winters."

"Not sick, are you?"

"No, no," Connie said. You had to think fast in this world, or you'd be tripped up. "I'm perfectly healthy."

"To tell you the truth, we're retired and were looking for a more settled woman, someone older. But I can see you're a lady, and we do have to give youth a chance, don't we?"

Connie smiled.

"Osborne? English stock."

"With a touch of Dutch on my mother's side."

Mrs. Raymond seemed satisfied. "Would you like a cold drink? I keep iced tea ready all the time in this weather."

The two sat down at the table in the immaculate kitchen. And Connie saw that the woman, now that her suspicions had been dispelled, was lonesome.

"So you said there was Dutch on your mother's side?"

"Yes. Mom always said we were cousins"—Connie laughed—"very distant cousins, of the Vanderbilts. That's how I got the name Consuelo." The story unfolded, rolling easily from her lips. Who knew? There might even be something to it. "Dad was in the furniture business. He died just when I was about to leave for the University of Michigan, so I couldn't leave my mother alone. Not that there wasn't plenty of money. It was a question of caring for her."

"Poor dear, losing your mother so young."

The afternoon wore on. At the end of it Consuelo got up, drove back to the hotel for her luggage, and by nightfall was comfortably established in the room with the garden view.

HOUSTON was *rich*. In spite of all she had ever read, Connie had not been able to imagine how so much money could be so lavishly, so gorgeously spent. Women bought without even asking the price: ski clothes for Vail or Gstaad, beach garb for the Caribbean, British tweeds, Italian suits, French silks and ball gowns. The very feel of the fabrics was a pleasure to Connie and was communicated to her customers, bringing more sales and commissions.

The owner was delighted with her. "You deserve a little something for your good work," she said one day. "Look in the back and pick out a couple of dresses for yourself. I'll let you have them at cost. Just be sure to mention us when you're out on the town."

Connie, however, wasn't going out on the town at all. After four months in the city she still knew almost no one. How did you get to know people? Especially the kind of people who came into the shop and talked about the Hermitage in Leningrad and about hearing Placido Domingo at the Metropolitan in New York. Those were the people she wanted to know. The truth was, Connie was feeling more deprived here in Houston than she had felt back home.

Pride wouldn't let her admit it, however. Whenever she called Eddy, he was so full of enthusiasm that she was forced to respond in kind. With Lara she dared not even hint at anything less than perfect satisfaction, for Lara would only urge her to come home.

One Sunday she got into the car and drove. Idling along through the bleak downtown, she emerged upon a wide avenue on which stood great hotels among brilliant flowers blazing in the sunlight. She swung the car into a hotel driveway and got out.

As people came and went in the lofty lobby, she felt a touch of amusement at herself for acting as if she had walked into a palace. It was only a hotel, and she was a hick, a rube, a bumpkin, staring at the chandeliers, the silk tapestries, the diamond-studded watches in the jeweler's display window—staring at everything.

She went farther in, sat down, ordered tea, and watched the parade. She had been sitting long enough to have a second cup when a young woman on the banquette beside her spoke up.

"I hope you won't think me awfully rude, but I've been admiring your dress. I've been looking all over without finding a thing."

Obviously, she was hoping that Connie would say where she had bought the dress, and so Connie did.

"I might have guessed. That place is too rich for my blood."

The honest admission brought forth an honest response. "For mine, too. I work there, and sometimes I get something at cost."

"Lucky you! I've just given notice on my job. I'm getting married and moving to Dallas."

"And lucky you! Getting married, I mean."

"He's wonderful. By the way, my name's Margaret Ames."

"Connie Osborne."

Connie was starved for talk, and soon intimate opinions, about clothes and hair and life in general, were being exchanged.

"I hope I can find a job in Dallas as good as the one I've had," said Margaret Ames. "I work at a country club, where I'm in charge of parties, lunches, weddings, dinners, stuff like that. I go over menus with people. I do it all. It's really great."

"Well, my job's pretty good, but I wouldn't call it great," Connie confided. "If I could make a change, I wouldn't mind." And she struck out boldly. "I suppose your work must be very complicated. Don't you have to know a lot about food and serving and—"

"Not really. You pick it up from the cooks and waitresses as you go along. Actually, all you need is to be friendly, have a good memory, and be good-looking. You do meet a top class of people. The best. As a matter of fact, I met my fiancé there when his company sent him to do an estimate for a new roof."

"It sounds wonderful."

"Hey! Would you be interested? I'd be glad to recommend you."

"Really? You're an angel!"

"No trouble at all. You know, I have a feeling you'd just fit."


EVERY day, in the beginning, was magical. To look out every morning on acres and acres of green, over the golf course and the low hills beyond, then down where the pool and the tennis courts lay in a grove of cool trees! All was peace and ease; everything was beautiful. The airy rooms were shaded restfully against the glare of the afternoons. At dinnertime the blue-and-white dining room sparkled. At night, on the terrace, candles flickered in hurricane globes and lanterns hung among the trees.

Connie's heart expanded. Her normally high spirits soared higher. People liked her. She had a dependable memory for names and faces, and the guests were pleased when she remembered where they liked to be seated and what they liked to drink. The staff, many of them older women who had been there for years, were almost motherly toward her.

"Don't put the Darnley table near to the Exeters'. Mrs. Exeter was Darnley's first wife, and the two women hate each other."

"If Mr. Tory says seven thirty, he means seven twenty-eight. That man's so prompt, he'll be early to his own funeral."

The headwaitress, Celia Mapes, who was handy with such advice, was kindly but could be meddlesome, too.

"I've got a daughter about your age, living with some guy she says she'll probably marry. I suppose you are, too, aren't you?"

"Living with some guy? No, I live by myself."

"What happened? Did you break up?"

"I've never had anybody to break up with."

"Never had a boyfriend? Nothing wrong with you, is there?"

"Not that I know of." Connie laughed. "I've just never met anybody. There was an awfully nice guy once, but he had acne, and it turned me off." And there had been others, like the floor manager in the store back home. That one had been good to look at. But he was flat, without ambition. And all he could talk about was sports.

"Well, my dear, it's no good being so fussy or you'll find yourself behind, one of these days." Celia Mapes looked at Connie with quizzical eyes. "You're pretty as a picture, but if you're thinking of teaming up with any of the members here, forget it. Money sticks to money, you know."

There were a good many young men among the club's membership, and Connie's glance often met frank male compliment in mischievous eyes. But nothing ever came of it. As the months passed, the job's first glamour inevitably began to dwindle. And Connie seemed to be looking down a long, long road with a dead end.

At the same time, in New York, Eddy had been climbing, with no shortness of breath, a long, easy hill. He and his partner, Pete Brock, bolstered by Pete's uncle, had been advancing steadily, amassing both brokerage accounts and social contacts.

"It's a case," Pete said in the office one afternoon, "of which comes first, the chicken or the egg. The guy you meet on the tennis court becomes your customer, or your satisfied customer invites you to play at his club. Not bad for a pair from Ohio, is it?"

"Not bad at all," Eddy replied.

But not remarkably good either. Leaning back in the swivel chair, he surveyed the office, which consisted of four decently furnished rooms in a mediocre 1920s building, on a dingy street halfway between the garment district and the theater district. There was nothing wrong at all with the setup if one was content with security and a modest living. Obviously, Pete Brock was.

"I have to tell you something," Eddy said. "It's something I've been putting off. Pete, I want to strike out on my own."

The other sat up straight. "Hey! I thought we were going along like a house afire! What is it? Give me the truth, Eddy. On the level."

"On the level. You're my friend, Pete, and I don't want you to think that I don't appreciate a thousand times over that you chose me for your partner. But you and I go at different speeds, and—"

"Oh, because I don't want to take money out of the firm and invest, because I don't want a fancier office, because I'm satisfied with—"

"You're satisfied with less than I want out of life, Pete."

"You've got a regular income, an apartment, friends, this whole fantastic city to play in. What's the more that you want out of life?"

The "more." It was almost impossible to explain. What good was it to walk on Fifth Avenue or Madison gazing at the galleries filled with paintings of such beauty that you could hardly tear yourself away; what good to look at the airlines' posters of Paris, Hawaii, and Morocco, stare at splendid women as they stared into the windows of splendid jewelers' shops, when every one of these was beyond one's reach? There was no use in trying to explain.

So he simplified his thoughts. "I'd like to expand, that's all. Remember how I talked about tax shelters? You said positively no."

"And I still do. We're stockbrokers, Eddy."

"We're not limited to that, though. That's the way I see it. And you don't. But that's okay. Friends don't always have to see things the same way."

"Eddy, you're a gambler at heart." The tone was mildly reproachful. "You've got a gambling streak, and it's dangerous."

"Who, me? A gambler? You're all wrong, Pete. I've saved a nice fat nest egg. That's why I'm in a position to go out on my own. Osborne and Company. Brokerage and tax shelters. There's a tremendous call for them. Perfectly legal. You have to know just how to structure them for big write-offs."

Pete shook his head. "Big. It looks like big trouble to me."

Eddy laughed. "No, no, no. But you know what's wonderful? That we can part with no hard feelings. Not on my part, at least."

Pete stood up and put out his hand. "Nor on mine, Eddy."


You had to spend money to make money. To Eddy that was axiomatic. The decoration of the new office, in a well-kept building on Madison Avenue, had cost somewhat more than he had intended, but the result was totally pleasing.

185

"It's foolish to skimp on quality," the decorator had told him. "You can actually feel the richness of good carpet underfoot." And it was true, Eddy thought as he glanced about the new domain, from the dark green carpet to the elegantly framed etchings of classical Rome. What a relief after that dump of Pete's!

It was also true that a man's suit conveyed an unmistakable impression. He stroked his arm, now encased in the best British worsted. What a difference a custom-made suit could make!

At three Eddy had an appointment with a builder. Hastening up Madison Avenue, he reflected upon the nice way things could mesh. This builder, Mr. Hartman, was planning a shopping center on Long Island and needed investors. At the same time some of the brokerage accounts who had left Pete to follow Eddy were looking for investments, shelters by which to cut their income taxes. It was encouraging to note how many customers had chosen him over Pete. But Pete had never been especially sociable. You had to be upbeat, you had to smile, if you wanted to attract people.

He was smiling when he entered Mr. Hartman's office.

"Let's get down to business, Eddy. I'm swamped today, so let's waste no time. I hope you haven't come empty-handed."

"No, sir. I've got five names, and I'll have more by Wednesday."

The two men sat down, with papers spread out between them.

"These are all responsible people, Mr. Hartman. I'm about through checking their references, and they're all top drawer."

"I see they are. Always stick with the top drawer, young man." The older man placed Eddy's papers in a tidy pile. "And speaking of that, how would you like me to put you up for membership in my tennis club on the Island?"

"That sounds great, Mr. Hartman!"

"They've got nice accommodations. You can spend weekends there next summer. Get out of the city, play tennis, have a swim. The fee's pretty steep, but it'll be worth it to you."

"I know it will, Mr. Hartman. I'm honored you'll endorse me."

"No problem, Eddy. My pleasure."

They shook hands, and Eddy went down onto the street. It was all he could do not to whistle. He saw a long vista ahead, a bright corridor lined with opening doors.

In such a mood he walked uptown and stopped before the window of an art gallery. There, all by itself, hung a small watercolor of a pond, with catkins along the shore. Neo-Impressionist, he decided. He had been buying art books, teaching himself against the day when he would be a buyer of art. And he went inside to inquire of a rather distinguished gentleman the price of the painting.

"Twelve thousand dollars. The artist has been doing very well."

Eddy's attention was suddenly attracted by another watercolor, on the wall. He moved closer to it. Here, too, was water—a cove or inlet where sailboats were at anchor in the evening. So deft, so real was it that one could almost hear the soft lapping of the water and feel the cool air. Yet for all its realness there was something else the artist had put there. A marvelous excitement rose in him.

"This one is much the better of the two," he said.

"You're right, of course. He's a finer artist than the other."

"Naturally, it must be more expensive?"

"Actually, two thousand less. The other man has a bigger name."

"I see." He knew he had spent a lot on the office, and he was due to move out of his walk-up flat next month. He would need to furnish the new place, but he wanted this picture.

"I'm going to buy it," he said. "I really want it."

"I congratulate you on your taste. You have a fine eye. And you won't be sorry. In a few years you could get twice the price back, should you ever decide to sell it."

Eddy carried his happy purchase home, where he hung it on the wall opposite his bed. He smiled. This beautiful thing was his. I'm really moving up, he thought. I'm moving up.

## Chapter Three

ONE morning a young man knocked at the open door of Connie's little office and introduced himself. "I'm Richard Tory, and I understand you're the person to see about a surprise luncheon for my mother. You are Miss Osborne, aren't you?"

"I am, but I'm always called Connie here."

"I didn't know. I hardly ever come to the club."

His was, indeed, an unfamiliar face. If she had seen him before, she would have remembered him, for he had a distinctive crown of light, very curly hair, fair skin, and aquiline features.

He gave her a smile that was almost shy. "I've never done anything like this before. I hope you'll help me."

"No problem at all. You want to give a luncheon?"

"Yes. It's my mother's fiftieth birthday, and I thought of assembling her best friends, about fifty in all. Do you know my folks?"

"Yes. They've been here quite often."

"Well, my mother likes things simple. What I mean is, no favors or balloons, nothing like that. It wouldn't be her style. I'll leave it to you. Plenty of flowers on the tables—she loves flowers."

"Any special color?" Connie said.

He considered. "She likes blue. Cornflowers, maybe? And daisies?"

"You have good taste. I can get blue-and-white-checked tablecloths, a country-garden-party effect. How does that sound?"

"Good, good! And you'll know what the ladies like to eat?"

"Oh, most of them are dieting. Why don't you let me talk to the chef and make up a menu? Then I can phone you."

"Of course. Here's my office number. And thanks a lot."

What a nice person, Connie thought when he left. *Nice.* She looked at his business card: MCQUEEN-BARTLETT ADVERTISING. The telephone directory listed it at a prestigious address downtown. Then, turning pages to the residential listings, she found Roger Tory at a River Oaks address and Richard Tory with a separate number at the same address.

River Oaks. Grand stone houses under grand old trees. Jaguars and Mercedes before impressive entrances. Lawns green as a billiard table. Sighing, she put the directory back on the shelf.

THE party went well. Fifty middle-aged ladies in silks and linens came bearing gifts, drank champagne, sang "Happy Birthday," and went home satisfied. At the end Mrs. Tory summoned Connie to compliment her cordially on the arrangements.

"Your son had as much to do with it as I did," Connie told her.

It had occurred to her that he might drop in to see how the party was going. But since he had not done so, it was hardly likely that she would see him again. It was absurd to think it would make any difference in her life even if she were to. So it was with surprise that she looked up from her desk one morning the following week to find him at the door. He was wearing tennis whites and carrying a racket.

"I hear the party was a great success. Thank you."

"It was a pleasure to do it," she replied.

He stood in the doorway as if uncertain whether to say more, to come farther, or to retreat.

"I haven't played tennis here in a couple of years," he said then. "It's handier to play at home. But I thought I'd give this a try for a change to see whether I could beat the pro."

"And did you?"

"No, but I gave him a run for his money."

"You must be pretty good."

"Well, I'm not bad."

His face was open, with a wide forehead and a friendly mouth. He had a vital look. Wholesome, she thought.

"I'm not bad either," she said immodestly. "My brother taught me, and he's marvelous."

"Then would you like to have a game sometime?"

"I'd love to, but don't forget I'm a working girl."

"And I'm a working man. This is my three-week vacation. Otherwise I'd be in the office."

How could this be happening? It seemed as if she were delicately balancing, teetering on a narrow plank. The wrong word, either too eager or too indifferent, could bring about the fall.

She said carefully, "I have Sundays and usually Mondays, unless there's a wedding or something, and—well, it's flexible time, depending on the schedule. They're very considerate here."

"They should be. So, when are you free? Anytime this week?"

"It happens that I've got this afternoon off. But you won't want any more tennis today, will you?"

"No. It's gotten beastly hot. I will want lunch, though, won't you? There's a great place down the road. I'll go change, and then how about meeting in the parking lot at half past twelve?"

I CAN'T believe this, Connie kept thinking. He's so easy to talk to. He reminds me of Davey. Lara would like him. He's not at all what I'd expect from anyone who lives in River Oaks. He doesn't seem like the men I've been watching at the club, with their skeptical, suave faces. The restaurant was emptying out, and she and Richard were still settled in a booth, with iced coffee before them.

189

"I usually like to travel someplace for my vacation," Richard was saying, "even if it's only up to New York. The company has me spending so much time there that I've got myself a small apartment near the U.N. building. My parents like to fly up for theater weekends, so they can use it, too. Do you like New York?"

"I've never been there. I've never been anywhere, actually." Then, because that sounded pathetic, Connie fell back upon the explanation she had devised. "First my father always said he couldn't leave his business. A large furniture business. Then when he got sick, naturally . . ." She made a pretty gesture with her hands. "After that Mom got sick, too, and we couldn't leave her."

"It must have been awful for you," he said kindly. "Well, I'm sure you'll get to see the world. If you want to, you will."

"I'd especially love to see England. My family was always so aware of roots, and they were all in England except for a bit of Dutch, way back—distant relatives of the Vanderbilts."

"Gosh, I'm a plebeian compared with you. Most of my folks were Irish who came over during the potato famine. And I've got a Polish great-grandfather who worked in the coal mines."

Connie spoke lightly. "What difference does it all make? People are people."

"Right you are. When shall I see you again? Sunday?"

"Sunday would be lovely."

"Okay. Write down your address, and I'll pick you up. And bring your swimsuit. You'll want a swim in our pool before lunch."

He had asked her to his house. She was scared to death.


IN BACK of a long white brick house with symmetrical wings and a classical façade lay the perfect lawn, the tennis court, and the pool that one would expect to find there.

"We have the place to ourselves today," Richard said.

He led her to the tennis court. She had bought something new, a short Wimbledon skirt. It looked traditional, as shorts did not, and this tiny flounce was becoming, too, as it whipped above long, tanned legs.

"Hey, you're a great player. You didn't tell me how good you were," Richard called over the net.

He won the set, although not easily. Next came the pool, where she dove and raced with ease. Connie was thankful again for Eddy's tough, insistent training. "The more skills you have, the farther they'll take you." That had been his constant admonition, and she saw now that it had been worth heeding, for Richard was a graceful athlete, and he was plainly admiring her.

"You're terrific," he kept saying. "Terrific!"

He had an enthusiastic way of speaking, with superlatives and exclamations, so that she had to wonder how old he might be; his manner seemed extraordinarily young.

So she asked him, and he told her. "Twenty-four. Why? Were you wondering why I'm still living here at home?"

Before she could reply, he said, "Actually, I'm planning to leave. I've applied for transfer to the New York office." He smiled. "Not that it's been a hardship for me to live here."

"I wouldn't think so," Connie said, looking at the terrace with its white wrought-iron furniture, its cobalt-blue awnings, and its petunias trailing out of stone urns. One would want to think it over before departing from such a pleasure island as this.

"Come on, I'll show you the house," Richard offered.

One large cool room, dimmed by blinds drawn against the noon heat, opened onto another. They had walked into the eighteenth century. She might have foreseen that chairs would be Sheraton, sofas Chippendale, and that the dining room would be papered with Chinese peonies. On the table stood a crystal Lalique swan.

"It's lovely," Connie said. "A lovely house."

In the hall Richard said, "The cook's left lunch for us in the refrigerator. I thought we might take it outside."

She helped him carry the lunch: a seafood salad, strawberry tarts, and a bottle of white wine, properly chilled. The umbrella and the shrubbery gave shade. If a pair of mourning doves had not been cooing at the feeder, the garden would have been completely still. Connie sighed with pleasure.

"I think I know what you're feeling," Richard said. "Sometimes I think I'm crazy to give this up for a couple of rooms thirty floors above the New York sidewalks. And yet I want to. New York's the fount of good things. Not that we haven't got them here, too—music, art. But then I guess you've found them for yourself."

"I'm ashamed to say I haven't."

191

"Really? Well then, we'll have to do something about it."

So today was to be only a beginning! Connie's heart acknowledged this with a small eager leap. "I'd like that very much."

"There's an exhibit of western art on right now. I went last week, but I wouldn't mind going again. Southwestern things are especially good—red rocks and canyons and Indian faces."

"Do you collect art?"

He shook his head. "I'm not a collector of anything except books. I feel that great art belongs in museums, where thousands of people can see it. Besides, I couldn't afford great art."

"I agree with you—about art belonging in museums, I mean."

"Do you? I'm glad. People around here use paintings for status. And some of what they buy is nothing but fad stuff. Why, I was at a house last week when the funniest thing— Oh, I shouldn't bore you."

"Please. I want to hear it."

"But you don't know the people I'm talking about. You don't know the way they think, and so my story loses its point."

"No names, but just tell me. Do they belong to the club?"

"Yes. Most of the people I know belong to it."

"Then I have a pretty good idea how they think."

She met his glance, and in the same instant they both laughed. Oh, I like him, she thought. He's smart and funny and honest.

The afternoon went fast. "I've had a great day," he said when they arrived at her door. "I hope you did, too."

"It was wonderful," she answered.

His good-bye kiss was gentle, a chaste kiss.

They saw each other every day of his vacation. When she had to go to work early, he called for her and returned to bring her home. On late nights he waited for her. It was remarkable how easily one could fall into dependence on such attentions.

He took her to the exhibit of southwestern art, to some concerts and a ballet. All of these were enchantments for Connie. She had known they existed, yet was astonished when they materialized before her eyes and ears, as if they were a kind of lovely magic.

She thought about Richard almost all the time. Who could tell whether anything more was to follow these few bright days? Nothing was sure, she told herself. Was she falling in love with him? There flashed before her a picture of Lara at her wedding, of her face turned toward Davey, of the trust, the joy, the adoration. And Davey had had nothing to give Lara except himself.

But I am not like Lara, she thought.

For a moment she felt guilty.

DAYS passed. They went on picnics. They spent a day in San Antonio. They danced at country barbecues and dined at sumptuous French restaurants. By the third week they were still what they had been in the first week, a congenial couple having a wonderful time, who ended their pleasant hours with a tender kiss.

One night, however, there came a difference. Suddenly, over the coquilles St. Jacques and the wine, Richard fell into silence. His eyes, empty of their customary humor, fixed themselves on Connie.

"You're the most beautiful woman I've ever seen," he said.

She responded lightly, "Beauty is in the eyes of the beholder."

"Ah, don't be flippant, Connie. Let's get out of here. Can't talk in this place."

When they were in the car, he commanded, "Now listen to me." He grasped her two hands. "They're finally transferring me to New York, and I can leave next week. But I can't go without you, Connie. I'm in love with you. I never thought—I mean, that a person could feel this way, be so sure of wanting to spend the rest of his life with someone. And yet I'm more sure about this than about anything. What about you, Connie? Can you love me? Can you marry me?"

How could she not love a man who looked at her, who touched her as if she were the most precious object ever made? The moment was brilliant, exquisite. Her heartbeat thundered in her ears.

"Oh, yes," she said. "Oh, yes."

After a few minutes he released her, turned on the motor, and drove her home. In front of her house they kissed again. The night was calm and bright. When, still held against his warm chest and shoulder, she opened her eyes, she saw the sky was filled with stars. It seemed she had never seen so many before.

After Richard left, she was too overwhelmed to sleep. Consuelo Tory, she thought. She sat down at the dressing table and stared into the mirror. Astonished eyes stared back at her. Why me? they asked. How can it be possible to get what one wants so easily, so soon? People always tell me life isn't like that.

Disconnected fragments floated through her head. The wedding ring: Dare she ask for a diamond band? No. Just be delighted with anything you get. Eddy will be happy for me. And we'll be seeing each other in New York. . . .

She prepared for bed, and the air conditioner's sleep-inducing hum took hold. Still, in dreams the fragments floated, dreams such as children have on the long, impatient night before Christmas.

By eight o'clock the next morning she had already been on the telephone with Lara for half an hour.

"You can't do this," Lara kept crying. "You hardly know him."

"Peg knew Pop six weeks before she married him, and they'd still be together if they'd lived. You know that."

After a moment Lara asked what Richard did for a living.

"He's in the advertising business, and we're moving to New York." Hastily Connie added, "But he's not at all what you think of when you hear 'Madison Avenue'—sharp and competitive, you know? Richard's got a kind of innocence that's very appealing. Lara, he's wonderful, he's everything you'd want for me, and I love him."

"Well, if you're sure . . . When shall I meet him?"

"He wants to be married next week. Can you get down here?"

"Honey, I can't do it on such short notice. Davey's having trouble with his father, another stroke, and— Can't you wait?"

"Richard doesn't want to. But it's okay. Obviously, we're not having a big wedding. We'll come visit you afterward. Will you tell Eddy? I tried to phone him just now, but there was no answer."

"He's probably at his club for the weekend. Our Eddy seems to have made contact in high places."

Not as high as mine, I'll bet, Connie thought, but did not say.

THE minister performed the marriage at the Torys' house, with Mr. and Mrs. Tory, in brass-buttoned blazer and printed silk, as the witnesses. The five participants stood before a small table within the semicircle of a bow window.

This is the high peak of my life, and it will be over in ten minutes, Connie was thinking. I have to remember everything: The sonorous words. Richard's parents. Richard. The light streaming through the curtains, turning his face pink. Now he's smiling at me. I don't know him at all, and it scares me. Yes, of course I know him. He's everything that's good. And here's the ring, a diamond band after all. Is this happening to me? To me? I love him. I'm not scared at all. I love him. . . .

"Richard, I love you," she said the moment it was over.

THIRTY-THREE floors beneath the windows of the New York apartment, lights moved along the East River Drive. In every direction the lights of the city glimmered and gleamed, dazzling Connie's astounded eyes. Tomorrow Richard was going to start her education: the museums, Broadway, Lincoln Center, Fifth Avenue. . . . No words, no pictures, had ever begun to realize the marvel of it all!

It was still some time before midnight, and Richard had gone to sleep, but she, wakeful, sat down at the dinette table and drank a cup of hot milk. Her mind spun back over the hours since yesterday, living and reliving this beginning of her new life.

It had seemed fitting, like closing a circle, to spend their first night at the Houston hotel where she had learned of the position at the country club. Events had made an orderly pattern: the farewell to the parents, the entrance into the hotel wearing the unmistakable bride's going-away suit. The new luggage. The deluxe suite with the champagne in the bucket and the roses on the table. The white lace nightgown. The groom's removal of the nightgown. The bodies intertwined on the wide, soft bed.

She had thought that the night would be long and slow, a dream of repeated delight. It had been neither long nor slow. To be sure, Richard had been eager enough, but it was all over in minutes, after which he immediately fell asleep.

Still, that was the first night, she told herself. As she had read in books and magazines, sex is not always an automatic triumph. And Richard was really a darling. They had had breakfast in their room before taking the plane to New York, and in a tiny box between the folds of her napkin she found diamond studs for her ears.

"I saw you once admiring them on someone," he told her.

On the plane her conscience had done a queer thing: it rose up and hit her. There were things she had to say to this good man, and she fumbled for a way to begin.

"Richard, I lied. I lied to you about myself," she said.

"I know that. I was only sorry you felt it necessary."

"Let me tell you the truth. My father was an alcoholic. We grew up dirt poor and miserable all the time—"

"I don't need to hear that," Richard interrupted gently. "You are you, and I don't care about another soul."

So that ended the subject, and she had felt a certain relief.

She stretched out her hand now to observe the sparkle on her finger. Then she got up and went into the living room. Furnished in modern chrome, steel, and glass, it had a sparkle of its own, and she was satisfied with what she saw. The future had arrived, and it was good.

## *Chapter Four*

THE round little table in the dining ell had been pushed toward the window so that Davey and Lara might have a view of Manhattan at night. Connie, who had found to her surprise that she liked to cook, had made a fine, festive dinner—crown roast of lamb, vegetables cut like flowers, and a French dessert.

Richard raised his wineglass and touched the others' glasses.

"To celebrate our first dinner all together," he said.

Even Eddy became serious, and Connie's mouth trembled. It was such a beautiful moment! These dear people gathered here in this gleaming apartment.

"Such a pretty table," observed Lara. "You're going to be a good housewife," she said almost tenderly.

"She is already," Richard said. "Connie's a perfectionist."

"She always was. She was the neatest little girl in school."

"And now you're a positively shining bride," said Eddy.

"Am I? Well, I'm happy. And who wouldn't be in this wonderful brand-new city?"

"With your wonderful brand-new husband," Lara said.

Richard laughed. "I get a kick out of her enthusiasm. She's walked my feet off every weekend and gone everywhere from the Bronx Zoo to the botanical gardens to the Statue of Liberty."

"I've been here over a year now," Eddy said, "and I haven't seen any of those except the statue."

"But you've been working," Connie said.

Eddy's sigh was satisfied. "Damn hard. It's been well worth it, though. I've got more business than I can handle by myself. I've hired a bright young M.B.A., and I'm thinking of taking on a second. When I redouble the business, in another couple of years, I'll have to move again, to a real spread."

Richard leaned an elbow on the table, a look of genuine interest on his face, as Eddy gave an exuberant description of Wall Street. Eddy raised his hand, revealing fine gold cuff links, and gave his familiar grin.

"I've always loved numbers. I can feel them—I can feel the market." He paused a moment. "We're family, so I can tell you. I'm worth almost nine hundred thousand dollars." He turned to Davey and the two sisters. "And you all know what I started with."

"You're way out of my league, Eddy," said Richard. "Oh, I make a good salary in advertising, but I'm conservative. I put everything into treasuries and tax exempts and watch it slowly grow."

"That's fine enough if you feel comfortable that way."

"I do now. I'm still paying off the mortgage on this co-op."

"You've made a good investment. It's a great location down here near the U.N. I'm thinking of a co-op myself, but I can wait."

"The way you're going, you won't have to wait long." Richard stood up. "Will you excuse me? I'm watching out for Texas time. I have to make a call to a Houston client."

"Very very likable," Eddy said when Richard had closed the bedroom door. "He's very modest, isn't he?"

"Richard's a gentleman," Connie said.

"He must make a fortune. McQueen is an international firm."

"I guess so. I never thought about it."

"A love match, then! Just like Lara and Davey here. But it's nice to have a few luxuries thrown in, too, like your watch."

"You see everything, Eddy."

He laughed. "Hold out your arm."

Connie pulled her sleeve back to reveal a wide glitter of gold and diamonds on her wrist.

"Beautiful," Eddy said. "You know what? I think you're going to lead a charmed life from now on."

"Speaking of love matches," Lara asked, "what about girls, Eddy? Anything serious?"

Eddy laughed. "Don't rush me. It's too soon for a love match."

"It's never too soon when it's real," Lara said.

Eddy shrugged. "Time will tell. Meanwhile, I've no problem meeting girls, especially at my club on Long Island." He turned to Davey. "So what have you two been doing since I saw you?"

"Just more of the same," Davey replied quietly.

Lara corrected him as Richard came back into the room. "Not so. Davey's working on something new that looks very important. He showed it to a doctor in town who thought—"

"No, no," Davey interrupted. "Don't make a big deal out of it."

"You never talk about yourself," his wife countered. "Dr. Lewis was impressed. If you don't tell them, I will."

Davey gave in. "Oh, all right. It's a funny thing how ideas come. I'd been working half a year on something to do with credit cards and wasn't getting anywhere. Then one day I saw a kid pumping up his bike tires, and this thing popped into my head."

"The moment he explained it, I knew, I just knew, that Davey had something important." Lara's face was vivid with excitement.

"My wife," Davey said, looking not unpleased, "thinks I'm a genius. All it is, is a kind of improvement, a little gimmick, for a heart pump. The balloons that push blood through the arteries, you know? Here, I'll show you."

The five heads leaning across the table almost touched each other as Davey drew a rough sketch on a scrap of paper.

"What I've done is figure out a timing device. It's like a computer really, you set it and"—he crumpled the paper—"I can't make it clear this way, but it's really a fairly simple concept. I've been thinking I ought to take my working model to one of the big university research centers and let them see what they can do with it."

"Now, wait a minute! Hold it," Eddy cried. "You don't mean you'd just hand it over and let somebody else get all the benefit?"

"Benefit?" Davey's tone was puzzled. "If the idea's really any good, heart patients will be the ones to get the benefit, I hope."

"Of course," Eddy agreed impatiently. "But don't you understand that other people might take your idea and make a fortune out of it? Money. Everything comes down to money. Why, you have no patent. I can't make head or tail out of that sketch, Davey, but if there's any chance it's worth something, you have to protect yourself."

"I'm not thinking of it that way." Davey's voice, always low, was

198

even lower than usual. "I'm not looking to make money. I only want to do something worthwhile if I can."

"I admire your ideals," Richard put in gently. "But you can do something good for the world and for yourself, too."

"Listen to me. I'm taking charge of this," Eddy said. "You keep this idea under your hat, hear me? No talking about it to anyone. I'm going to find the best patent lawyer in Ohio."

Connie had to smile. Here was the familiar brother again, taking control as he used to do when Pop had drunk too much or when Peg was sick, breezing into the house, organizing everybody.

"After you get the patent," Eddy went on, "you'll need financing to set up a small plant and start producing. You'll need plenty of cash. You'll need bank credit. You'll need collateral." He jumped up and began to pace the room. "I can lend you whatever you need. A pure loan, mind you. I only want to see you two get ahead, that's all." He stopped in front of Lara. "And if this thing is really good, you ought to quit teaching and help Davey. You've got the head for figures. Now's your chance to help Davey's brainchild get born."

"I feel sort of as if I'd been gone over with a steamroller," Davey said. "I don't know why I don't just say no to the whole business."

"Because this steamroller is painless," Connie replied. "Go sit down," she commanded Lara, who had begun to clear the table. "You're company."

"No. I haven't had a chance to be alone with you."

There was barely room for two in the kitchen. Lara perched on a stool while Connie stacked the dishwasher. It crossed Connie's mind that most of their conversations since they had grown up had been held in kitchens after an evening meal.

"Oh, I do like Richard," Lara exclaimed. "He's delightful."

"You see? You didn't trust me, did you?"

Lara laughed. "Oh, you're as smart as they come, Connie, but even smart people can make mistakes." Lara glanced around the kitchen. "Tell me what you do all day," she said.

"Well, Richard has married friends, and I've been going around with some of the wives to the art galleries and places, and oh, frankly, spending money for the first time in my life. Not on junk either; I've bought clothes and a few antiques and loads of books. I can afford them, and it's a good feeling, let me tell you."

"Guess it must be."

"Lara, I hope you'll keep after Davey and make him listen to Eddy. This may be your chance to get up in the world."

"We're all right. We have enough. But for Davey's sake I hope something does come of his idea. He's worked so hard on things that came to nothing, and I don't want him to get discouraged."

"You're an angel, Lara."

"Of course I'm not. People aren't meant to be angels."

"Well, whatever you are, you're not like me."

Lara gave her sister a tender look. "I'm so glad you have someone to love you. Nothing else really matters very much in the end."

"I suppose not," Connie said, irritated somehow by the cliché.

An odd silence came momentarily between the sisters, so that Connie was relieved when the men appeared to remind them that it was time to go home.

"Next time at our house," Davey said. "And make it soon. You should show Richard where your roots are, Connie."

"Not for a couple of months," replied Richard. "Connie and I are going to Europe for six weeks."

"We are?" cried Connie. "We are?"

"Yes. I was going to keep the surprise a little longer, but it just won't keep. We haven't had a honeymoon, and this will be it."

Connie's astonishment, Richard's satisfaction, and the others' generous pleasure on their behalf warmed the space in which they stood together. And this warmth seemed to linger in the rooms even after all the guests had gone home.

"But can you afford to take six weeks off?" asked Connie, while they were undressing. "It'll be frightfully expensive, won't it?"

"I get the money from my grandmother's trust next month, when I turn twenty-five. And we're going to do this in grand style. See a bit of Italy and France, maybe Belgium, finish in England, and come back on the *Queen Elizabeth*. How does that sound?"

"Like heaven," she said dreamily.

Richard was stretched out on the bed, while she still had to remove makeup and brush her hair. This routine had already formed itself: he watched her prepare for bed while they talked over the day. There was something very comfortable about it.

"Nice people tonight," he said. "I like your family."

"I'm glad."

It was good to have some cause for pride before him, and she had been very proud of her family this evening. Eddy's bravado was a little overdone, to be sure, but nobody was perfect, and one could only respect Davey's and Lara's quiet dignity.

She thought aloud. "Lara's a sweet, simple soul."

"Not that simple. She's smart and strong. Her manner fools you."

And Connie became aware of how perceptive Richard was; it was only *his* own manner that fooled you. People were made in layers, she reflected, and as you peeled them away one by one, you could be astonished by what you found each time. She wondered whether he could be peeling her away, layer by layer. It might be that he would learn more about her than she knew herself.

She began vigorously to brush her hair.

## Chapter Five

THEY stayed on the forward deck all afternoon as the *Queen* slid from The Solent into the English Channel and out to sea. Richard had gotten a deck chair, a blanket against the raw wind, and a book; but Connie stood at the railing until the coast receded.

Behind her lay all the quaint and ancient places, the castles, lakes, and gardens, the cobblestoned alleys and the marbled palace-hotels of Europe, all of them as far removed from her Manhattan apartment as was that apartment from Peg's flat. No, farther, farther. Willingly she would turn the ship around and go back. She was already feeling the ache of nostalgia, an urgent restlessness. It was the same feeling that had swept over her when, in Houston, she had seen her first ballet and felt the world so filled with wonders.

Travel with Richard was rewarding but also frustrating. After a morning at the Jeu de Paume and the Rodin Museum she was envious. I must learn about art, she told herself, and I know almost nothing of European history. I know almost nothing at all.

Richard had bought Connie dresses in Paris, assuring her that the dark red velvet and the emerald satin would be right for dinner on the ship. In England she had fallen in love with country antiques and old landscapes. After seeing flowery Cotswold inns and burnished London shops, she began to envision old mahogany and old

201

paintings, a library with leather chairs. She had a new awareness that the rooms near the U.N. were not so grand after all—that as a matter of fact they were ordinary.

So on the homeward voyage that compelling sense of restlessness came sweeping back.

In the dining salon Richard and Connie found themselves seated next to Mrs. Dennison Maxwell, a lady well into her sixties. By the final night she was on intimate terms with the young Torys.

"It's a pleasure to see a pretty young woman with a good-looking young man for a change. In New York these days the prettiest young women all seem to be married to dreadful old men. You haven't said, but this is your honeymoon, isn't it?" And when informed that it was, she continued, "I had mine on the *Queen Mary*. There's no comparison. Your parents must have told you about the old *Queens,* I'm sure. Now, *they* had elegance."

"Oh, yes," Connie answered. "So wonderfully Old World."

"I do love your Texas accent," Mrs. Maxwell told her.

"But Connie doesn't—" began Richard, and stopped when Connie's foot brushed his.

"You must meet my granddaughter-in-law," the woman went on. "She's practically a bride, like you—only married a year. You'd like each other."

Connie smiled. "That's so kind of you, Mrs. Maxwell."

"She's terribly busy, Bitsy is. She raises more money for her charities than any three women. I don't know where she gets the energy or time." Mrs. Maxwell took a small silver pen from her bag. "Do write your phone number, dear. I'll tell Bitsy to be sure to call and introduce you around town. People adore Texans."

"Why on earth did you want her to think you came from Texas?" Richard asked Connie when they were alone.

"Because. You heard what she said. People adore Texans."

He laughed. "Maxwell. I wonder whether that can be Maxwell Knox International. We do their advertising. She might be. She has that *air.* Couldn't you smell it?"

"I smelled the very good perfume. That's all."

"Not the disgusting smell of snobbery?"

"Not at all. She was interesting. And meeting her granddaughter might be a look into another world. What's there to lose?"

IT WAS INDEED ANOTHER WORLD. And to Connie's surprise it accepted her at once. But then, people had always taken a liking to Connie. She was bright and quick, friendly and obliging.

Sondra Maxwell—called Bitsy—was known for her independence. She wore a mink coat over a woolen skirt and sweater, sneakers, and on her wrist a gold bracelet whose value Connie, having seen enough by now to know, estimated at ten thousand dollars. Her hair hung long enough to be tossed as she walked. She owned a small poodle of a rare red color and persuaded Connie to buy its sister, named Delphine. The two young women with the two small dogs soon made a striking pair as they moved along the opulent streets of the Upper East Side.

Now, with Bitsy's group, Connie went to exercise classes, played tennis, went shopping, took art appreciation classes, had lunch at Le Cirque, and eventually came to see her picture on the society page of a popular magazine. Toward the end of the winter the Torys were even invited to the Maxwell house—five spacious rooms in a solid old building on Park Avenue.

"Don't blame me for the furnishings," said Bitsy. "They're all my grandmother's, foisted on us by the family when she died. But we've outgrown this place, and as soon as we move, we'll refurnish."

This apology astonished Connie, who had been about to remark, and now did not, how handsome the apartment was.

The evening ended early, for all the young men had to get up early to appear in court, at the bank, the investment office, or wherever else it was that they had to appear in Manhattan.

Connie and Richard were reading in bed later when presently Connie laid down her book.

"I've been thinking," she said. "We need to do some serious entertaining. It's part of getting ahead, as you saw tonight."

"Those people didn't need to get ahead by entertaining, Connie. They were born ahead."

"I know, but we really should be able to have a dinner party, or at the very least give a big brunch, and we can't do it here. Don't you think we need a larger apartment, Richard?"

"Hey, I'm not the president of my firm, you know."

"Of course I know. I don't mean anything outrageous." And very carefully, very delicately, she proceeded. "But this place doesn't do

justice to your taste. And it's complicated, having always to say no
to friends and make excuses. For instance, Bitsy's asked me to be
on the committee for the hospital ball. It's really a prestigious thing,
but one has to make a sizable donation or, better still, take a whole
table. And I really don't know how to keep on refusing when we've
become such good friends."

"Those people go to three or four affairs like that every month
during the season, Connie. We don't belong with them. It makes no
sense for us to try keeping up."

There was a long pause, during which Richard appeared to be
waiting for some acknowledgment while she was inwardly coming
to terms with her expanding knowledge of the world. Richard's
parents were not rich, not really. They were very prosperous, but
not rich. The house in River Oaks had good furniture, but no rare
antiques; the paintings were not of museum quality.

Taking her hand, Richard said softly, "What's the least you'd
need to give?"

"Well, fifteen hundred would do. I think maybe it would."

"Okay. I'll write a check in the morning."

"Oh, you're sweet! Thanks so much. You're so sweet."

He reached across to turn off the lamp and then, reaching back,
put his arm around her. His lips brushed her neck.

"Feel happier now, do you?"

"Oh, yes, oh, yes."

Richard was tightening his hold. He wanted sex. She wanted to
go to sleep. And it crossed her mind that her original desire for him,
which had been disappointed often and which had slowly been
cooling toward indifference, might possibly be turning into active
rejection. His three minutes, or maybe it was a minute and a half,
of pleasure were worse than nothing for her, far worse. . . .

We have to have a new apartment, she was thinking as he sighed,
brushed her ear with his lips, and rolled over to sleep.

WITH the package tucked under his arm, Eddy headed into the
bright afternoon feeling a marvelous sense of well-being. Business
was big now, really big; it swelled like a balloon. One satisfied client
recommended another. From real estate czars came theater people, a big-time boxer, a rock-and-roll singer, rich Park Avenue

widows—anybody and everybody. He kept their money growing and his own with it.

Strolling along in the late spring sunshine and filled with such thoughts, he almost bumped into Connie on Fifty-seventh Street.

"Whatever are you doing here in the middle of the afternoon?" she demanded. "And with that twinkle on your face."

"Shopping. You don't think women are the only ones who can take an hour off to go shopping, do you?"

"What are you buying?"

"Silver. I'm collecting. It's an investment, but I'm doing it for pleasure, too. I'm also collecting ivory carvings."

"And where do you plan to put all this stuff?"

"Come on with me, and I'll tell you. I'll take you to tea at The Plaza. I worked right through lunch, and I'm starved."

Having settled himself into the restful shelter of the Palm Court, from which the hectic streets seemed to be miles removed, he explained, "I'm still waiting for the right co-op to come along, but in the meantime my new place isn't all bad."

"I should think not." Connie sounded almost indignant, he thought.

"I'll need more money than I want to spend now if I want the perfect place on Fifth, with a view of Central Park."

"Very wise of you, as always."

Eddy squeezed lemon into his cup, raised it, and studied his sister over the rim. Then, aware that for some inexplicable reason she was angry, he gave her his most appealing smile.

"There's something wrong with you. You're either mad or sad."

"Nothing's wrong."

"Yes. I've sensed something different these last few weeks. You've lost your glow. I'm used to seeing you glow."

"Glow!" she mocked, and fell into a glum silence. Eddy could not know that she was ashamed to be envious of her beloved brother. He had succeeded at everything he had ever tried. If there were pleasures to be had anywhere, Eddy would have them. If there were things to be known, he would know them. Yet nothing could have induced her to reveal herself to him.

Gently he asked, "Anything wrong between Richard and you?"

"No, no. What makes you think that?"

"I only asked. I like Richard. He's interesting and kind."

"He is kind." And then she blurted her complaint. "It's so expensive living here! I didn't expect it to be like this."

"It surely is. But it also depends on the way you want to live."

"Well, I want a decent apartment, that's all. I hate being cooped up in that cramped little box. You should understand."

"Don't forget I'm making money, not living on a fixed salary. Even a good one like Richard's doesn't go far after taxes. The thing is, you have to know how to make your money grow."

"And just how am I to do anything about that?" she asked.

"You know," he said, "I've been doing great things for strangers. Tax shelters, arbitrage, futures, whatever. So why shouldn't I be doing something for Richard too?"

"He's keeping his grandmother's trust with the same bank that the family's been with for three generations, that's why."

"One can be too conservative, letting the money lie there doing next to nothing. I never can get over how you have to prod people to do things for their own good. Take Davey. Now, thanks to me, he's got his patent approved, and I've made him a loan so he can establish credit for a mortgage. He tells me he's found a neat little building and he's begun to hire help. If I hadn't pushed, he'd be just where he's always been, and Lara would be wasting a very good business head. The two of them always think they have enough. And somehow they do! You know," he mused, "when I think back to the way we lived at home, the way Peg managed, I don't understand how she did it. It's funny how fast you get used to having more."

"Yes," Connie said soberly. "Funny."

"Listen," Eddy said. "I'm going to call Richard. There's no sense in his creeping along when it's possible to fly."

"You're a good soul, Eddy. With all your faults." Connie patted his hand, and he knew that her anger had vented itself.

"Well, I try. I'll have my little talk with Richard tonight."

Two weeks later Eddy was off to Long Island for a vacation at the club. It had quickly assumed the feel of home. When a young man has a sense of humor, plays excellent tennis, is friendly, and has money, he can be at home anywhere, Eddy reflected as he lay alongside the pool surrounded by pleasant chatter. On his left the golf course, a glaze of green, undulated toward distant hills.

"Gosh, it's beautiful!" he exclaimed.

Terry, his friend and tennis partner, answered with a deprecation. "This place? I can show you a club that makes this look like a dump. This place is vulgar. Nouveau riche."

Eddy set his cold beer aside. "If it's that bad, how come you're a member?"

"Frankly, because they wouldn't take me into Buttonwood. I'm nouveau riche." Terry laughed. "And not all that 'riche' either."

Eddy wanted to know more. "What's the difference?"

"Oh, it's the people, I guess—the way they look, who they are."

"How do you know all this?"

"My sister married a member of Buttonwood." Terry laughed again. "She married up. I'll tell you what. I'll ask her to get two girls for us and invite us to their Saturday dinner dance. It'll be fun, and you'll see for yourself what I mean."

BUTTONWOOD really was different. Age and sober elegance registered their immediate impression upon Eddy's sharp eyes. The house had very likely been the summer mansion of some railroad, oil, or banking tycoon back in the 1890s. No contemporary decorator had had anything to do with this dark carved paneling or these gently faded English chintzes. No contemporary fashion dictator had had contact with the women either. They looked . . . well, underdressed. At Eddy's club the women glittered in jewels and dresses fit for an opera ball.

Terry, having found his sister's party, was making introductions. "And this is my good friend Eddy Osborne."

The sister was a cordial feminine copy of Terry. Her husband, whose name Eddy had not quite caught—it sounded like Truscott—was thin and bald; he had a lordly manner and cold eyes. The two young ladies, Marjorie Somebody and Pamela Somebody, were both tall; they had attractive faces and straight hair fastened with barrettes. Preppy types. One wore white linen, the other yellow.

"I'm Pamela," the one in white said, giving Eddy a quick smile, "in case you've gotten the names mixed, for which I wouldn't blame you. Pamela Granger. You have no drink," she added.

Truscott—or was Truscott the last name?—overheard. "There's not much time for drinks. You're late as usual, Terry."

"I'm sorry, but I come here so seldom that I forget the way."

Touché! There's no love lost between those two, Eddy thought. Unexpectedly he met Pamela's eyes. They were laughing. Her lips formed words silently: Old prude. Icicle. He winked, she winked back, and he went in to dinner feeling rather happy.

An older couple, almost certainly the Truscotts' original guests before Terry had invited himself, sat at the table. The gentleman was apparently a stockbroker, because Truscott and he launched at once into an informed discussion of the market. Eddy was torn between the attractions of Pamela and the attractions of that discussion. "Federal Reserve," "gross national product," and "earnings ratio" kept meeting his ears.

Finally he had to express an opinion.

"I couldn't help but hear," he said to the two men. "You're right—there's no doubt about hotel stocks or limited partnerships in hotels. This is the new age of travel."

Truscott's cold eyes stared at Eddy's striped tie. "It's good to know you agree with us," he said.

"Are you in the market these days?" asked the other man.

Terry gave a boom of a laugh. "Oh, slightly, just slightly." Shaking with delight, he turned to his brother-in-law. "Osborne and Company? You've never heard of Osborne and Company?"

"Certainly I have," Truscott answered stiffly. "Is—"

"He is. Vernon Edward Osborne himself."

Truscott flushed. "You didn't say—"

"I know. I introduced him as Eddy, which is what he's called."

"Well," said Truscott, recovering. "I had no idea."

No, Eddy said to himself. If you hadn't assumed I was just one of Terry's insignificant friends, you'd have looked at me very differently. But aloud, in his most gracious manner, he replied that he was happy to be here and to meet Terry's family and friends.

Money, money, he thought as he turned back to Pamela. Eddy Osborne without it is nothing. But I knew that, didn't I? And that's why I left Ohio.

"What's Osborne and Company? Is it stupid of me not to know?" Pamela asked now.

"Finance. Investments. And it's not stupid of you. Why should you know? You probably know a hundred things that that old fossil doesn't know."

"Well . . . horses, dogs, animals, the environment. All that stuff. That's what I'm involved with."

He looked into the clear gaze of long, almond-shaped gray eyes under a rosy-tanned forehead. "Dogs and horses, you said?"

"I love horses. I teach at a riding school—"

"How old are you? Where do you live? Do you mind my questions?"

"I'm twenty-two, and I live with my mother, not far from here. And no, I don't mind your questions."

"I'm twenty-seven, and I live and work in New York. I live alone. I'd like to get out of here so we can talk, Pamela. If you'd like to."

"I would, but obviously, we can't. And I'm called Pam."

"How about tomorrow? May I take you to dinner?"

She nodded. "Fine. And now we'd better join the conversation."

He understood the propriety. She had breeding and manners. The eastern Establishment, that was the expression. She had that air. And heart, too. The way she'd seen through the old snob.

She's something new, he thought when he left that night.


THE back road was not far from the Sound. He had driven through here before and knew his way. The houses were far apart, most of them the bulky brown-shingled summer "cottages" built by New York families in the early years of the century. Turning into a secluded lane, he passed through a tunnel of overgrown dark shrubbery and stopped in front of a wraparound porch from which the paint was peeling. The place had seen better days.

Pam, with a shining smile, came down the steps.

"I hope you're hungry," he said. "I've made a reservation at what I'm told is the best French restaurant within fifty miles."

"I'm always hungry."

"It certainly doesn't show," he answered, with a quick appraisal of her body, which was lean, well curved, and taut.

"Exercise. I'm a sports freak, but mostly I ride. Do you?"

"Ride?" Eddy, having never been on a horse, hesitated. "I haven't ridden in years, but I'd like to start doing it again."

"Oh, do! It's marvelous. There's nothing like getting up early,

209

while the world's still asleep except for yourself, the horse, and the birds. What I like best is riding along the beach."

She had a pleasing, animated way of speaking, so he encouraged her with comments and questions. He had insisted on having a very private table at a corner window overlooking the twilight garden, and there they sat undisturbed until long after darkness fell. By that time he had learned many things, among them that she had been a debutante, that her father had died, and that her mother had given up their New York apartment to economize.

"Our family had money a couple of generations ago, but somehow it just ebbed away. I never understand how that can happen."

"Oh, it happens easily," Eddy said. "Takes no effort at all."

They both laughed.

"I really don't mind," Pam said. "I like my life here. The riding lessons pay well enough, and what can be better than getting paid for doing what you love to do?"

"And what do you do when you're not busy around horses?"

"Oh, I'm a volunteer. I work at the animal shelter, and I'm on a committee to save the wetlands. I get really enraged when I see developers tearing into this earth. There'll be nothing green left. We people who live here all year round love this place."

In his daily travels between the office tower and the apartment tower, Eddy had to confess, he had been giving very little thought of late to whether the earth was green or not. He tried to think of another woman or man he had ever met who was worried about wetlands or stray animals, and could not. Interesting. And he wondered what she might be thinking about him.

Driving back to his club, he reviewed the evening. Should he try to see her again? It was a long way out there from his club, and he certainly had no dearth of women who were more conveniently situated. She wasn't a tremendous beauty. In spite of the fact that she obviously had a splendid body, he had a feeling that she would be rather cool. And yet there was something about her . . .

He was still in this state of mild concern when he walked into the club and up to his room. Then all of a sudden he made a connection. He could almost hear it click in his head. The reason for his hesitation was a very simple one: he was afraid of rejection. He was afraid that she was, after all, too different, too far out of his reach.

A strange insecurity for Eddy Osborne, who would have said that insecurity was one feeling from which he rarely suffered!

He reached for the telephone.

"Pam? I hope I didn't wake you."

"No. I'm reading in bed."

In bed. Long hair loose on the pillow. White nightgown sheer enough to see through it to the rosy flesh.

"I don't know about you, Pam, but I had a great time tonight. Would you care to repeat it tomorrow?"

"Why, I'd love to, Eddy."

"Fine. Shall I pick you up at six?"

"I have a thought," she said. "How would you like to meet me at the stables and go riding? I'm free all afternoon."

Whatever had he told her? He seemed to remember having given the impression that he knew all about horsemanship but had simply been away from it for a time. What a fix!

"Eddy? Are you there?"

"Yes. I was only thinking, my riding clothes are at home." He thought quickly: Buy an outfit, then wing it. It can't be that hard. "I'll buy some stuff in the morning. My old stuff's probably moth eaten anyway. And be prepared. I'll be stiff as a board."

"It'll all come back to you. Besides, I'm an instructor."

So began a memorable week. Because he had assured himself that his first attempt to ride a horse would be successful, so it was. Armed beforehand with an hour's worth of study from a paperback book of instructions, Eddy managed to give a fair performance.

"For somebody who hasn't ridden in years, you're doing well," Pam said as they walked their horses. "All you need is practice."

The city, in the days that followed, might as well have been on another planet for all the differences between its noisy, melting streets and the bliss of fresh winds and airy lawns. Pam and Eddy went exploring. They sailed, swam, played tennis, and laughed a good deal. To Pam's surprise Eddy wanted to take a tour of historic houses; she was even more surprised at how much he knew about furniture periods and architectural styles.

"I like to have beautiful things around me," he said simply, "so I need to learn about them."

She took him to an antiques shop, where they both browsed, and

211

he bought a pair of charming Staffordshire figures. One evening they went to an Italian movie, on another to an outdoor concert, and on one had a backyard supper at Pam's house, then sat on the porch with her mother, who went upstairs after a proper interval.

On the sixth night, under a bright moon, they came back to the porch. The house was already dark, and there was no sound as they came up the steps but for the thumping of an old dog's tail.

"I haven't seen him before," said Eddy.

"This is Buster. I rescued him from the pound. His owners left him there after twelve years. Can you believe it? It could have broken your heart to see the look in his eyes."

I really like her. I really do, he said to himself. And curiously, he asked, "Tell me. Do you ever look far ahead? Plan what you want to do with your life, I mean?"

"Oh, I'd like to live pretty much as I'm living now. And someday have a husband and children, but not for a long time."

He pressed her. "You don't feel that you're missing anything?"

"No. I like being independent. What should I miss?"

He hesitated and then took a chance. "Well, sex, for instance."

She laughed. "I don't deprive myself. Not when I meet the right person."

He pressed again. "How do you recognize him?"

And she, laughing again, replied, "Now, you know better than to ask a silly question like that!"

Their chairs were so close that their knees almost touched. The sweetest, most alluring fragrance lay on the air—her perfume or that flowering vine climbing the railing? He stood up and took both her hands. Her body, yielding easily, rose up to meet his.

"Where shall we go?" he whispered.

"Here, in the swing. Don't worry. It doesn't creak."

His head swam with an explosion of fire that came from the very depth of him, from the racing of his blood. Clothes dropped in an instant to the floor; an instant later he lay with her. And then there was only that fire exploding, and afterward the sweetness. The sweetness.

"And I thought— I just didn't think you would be like this."

She was lying with her head on his shoulder and now sat up.

"Like what? What am I like?"

He sat up, too, shaking himself. "You won't believe me. You'll think it's just a line, but the truth is that I've never felt anything quite like this. I don't know what you did, but . . ."

"And if I tell you that I don't make a habit of sex with someone who's practically a stranger, will you believe me? It happens to be the truth. I need to have real feeling, real and quick and deep. And that happens very very rarely." Pam took his hand.

He looked into her eyes, which shone.

"I believe you," he said.

After that, he knew he could not forget her. All the way back to New York, when the vacation week was over, he thought about her. He wanted to give her a present and decided on flowers, the most lavish roses that could be ordered.

She had said quite plainly that she was not ready for marriage, which was perfect because he was not either. Not yet. But when I am ready, he thought, it will be Pam.

ABOUT six months later Richard Tory was able to say, "He's a financial whiz, your brother is. Do you know, with those futures he bought for me I added ten percent to my capital? It's incredible. I think," he proposed cautiously, "I think we're in a position now to look for that apartment you've been wanting."

Warmth like a glow from liquor surged through Connie's chest. "How large can we go?"

"Well, four rooms, perhaps?"

She thought of Bitsy's ten new rooms. "How about five, so we can spread out? You wanted to bring your books from Houston."

"Well, all right. It'll come high, especially where Eddy's looking, and I guess that's where you want to be, too." Richard got out a pad and pencil, and she waited, looking over his shoulder, with an anxious tilt to her head. "Let's see. With my salary I can pay as high as five or six hundred. I can handle the mortgage. And I'll pay it off as fast as Eddy can make my money grow."

"What about furniture? The only things we own are the antique screen and the Venetian mirror I bought on Third Avenue."

"We'll shop there again. We'll go slowly, take our time."

Not too much time, Connie thought. Richard was so slow and deliberate. Not like Eddy, who went right after what he wanted.

## *Chapter Six*

EDDY and Connie had flown out to see Davey's brand-new plant. It was a day for celebration.

"I've got a turkey in the oven," Lara said. "Before we go, we'll have a big lunch. Then we can see the plant later."

"But not too late. Eddy and I are taking a six-o'clock plane."

"I thought you were staying over Sunday. Such a flying visit—"

"I know. But Eddy changed his mind. You know he's a workaholic, and as for me, I do have a husband. By the way, Richard said to tell you he's terribly sorry he couldn't make it. He's bogged down with evening meetings."

Connie looks extraordinarily pretty today, Lara thought. Her hair was lighter, almost ash blond, and she was wearing a mink jacket. One didn't have to be experienced in the wearing of mink to know that this was no ordinary department store bargain, nor were the claret-colored shoes and the matching woolen dress.

"You look lovely," she said. "And happy, too."

Connie replied lightly. "It's probably the new apartment."

"Tell me about it."

"Well, it's between Madison and Park, a prime neighborhood. Two of the rooms at the rear are rather dark, but it's a dream compared with the old dump. All we have to do now is furnish it." Connie sighed. "We've got the bedroom finished and a lot of other stuff on order. English country things, mostly—mahogany and oak, lots of chintz and linen."

There was a casual air of authority in her tone, a subtle change from the last time Lara had seen her. It always seemed strange to Lara that money changed people so abruptly. Although, she reflected, if Davey's new enterprise works out, it won't change him.

Then she said shyly, "I'm rather happy today. Happy and hopeful. I missed this month. I might be pregnant, I think."

Connie got up and hugged her. "Oh, darling, I hope so! A person really ought to get something she wants so much!"

"And you? Or shouldn't I ask?"

"All in good time. I'm in no rush."

"It looks as if Eddy's in no rush either. I wish he'd get married."

"Why? He couldn't be happier than he is now, although I do think he has a girl he sees a lot. Pam." Connie laughed. "She likes horses, so he's taken up riding in a big way. I think she's in the Social Register or something."

After lunch they all got into Davey's new Jeep and drove across town to the plant. It was a neat, low building that had been a small warehouse, behind a wire fence. Above the white-painted entrance was a dignified sign saying only THE DAVIS COMPANY. The open space had been divided into various work areas, where sundry pieces of machinery, some still disconnected, had been placed.

Lara made a proud comment. "A little different from the workbench in the shed out back."

Offices had been partitioned off at the far end of the building. Davey pointed them out. "This one's mine, and that's Lara's. She takes a load of paperwork off my shoulders, let me tell you."

"You've got a first-class accountant, I hope," Eddy said. "You've got to watch those taxes, watch those dollars."

Davey nodded. "I watch them," he said.

"You've got to make them grow faster and bigger."

"What do you mean?"

"Listen to me, Davey. You can't afford to lag behind. It's time to go public, to issue stock. You need capital so you can expand."

"I'm comfortable with the size we are. Lara and I—well, she manages the office, wages, and orders, while I'm out in the shop. And three salesmen are out traveling."

"If you got as few as twelve stockholders, each with fifty thousand dollars, you'd have over half a million for improvements."

"I don't want to get involved with strangers and give them a vote in the running of my affairs. I'm a small-town guy, Eddy."

"Listen. You wouldn't have to sell stock to strangers. There must be a dozen well-heeled people in this town, maybe even friends of yours, who would jump at a chance to invest in a growing company." Eddy looked around. "This place is nice, yes, but it can use a lot of fixing up. And you'd have cash to buy the equipment you'll need."

"Well, yes," Davey acknowledged. "I was hoping to get a loan."

"Then you'd be saddled with interest payments. Will you please do it my way, Davey? I can set up the whole thing for you. Finance

215

is my business, isn't it? Go home and start thinking about whom you can approach to buy shares."

Davey and Lara looked hesitantly at one another. After a moment Lara spoke. "Dr. Donnelly? He's been Davey's family doctor since Davey was a baby," she explained. "And your friend Tony? What do you think, Davey? His aunt Alma left a pile of money."

"That's great!" Eddy said. "Those are the kinds of contacts you need. I'll talk to my lawyers and get back to you by the end of the week. I see a big future here, Davey. Bigger than you probably realize. But you've got to put it on the road. You understand?"

"I guess I do," Davey said. "You are convincing, I must say."

Their route to the airport passed the new housing development on the south end of town. When they came to it—a scattering of unoriginal yet pleasing shingled colonials on a huge sloping field— Eddy insisted on seeing the model house. So they all trooped through empty rooms that had the fresh smell of new wood, through picture-book bathrooms and a magnificent kitchen with a barbecue.

"This," Eddy declared, "is what you two should buy."

"This isn't the time," Davey said.

"This is exactly the time, Davey. I always tell you, people should enjoy life as they go along. Today won't come again. It's now that you're young." Eddy pointed toward the window. "Look at the space out there. Fence it in, make a hedge of evergreens. You'd have room for a pool eventually. What have you got now? A dingy yard and a shabby screened-in porch."

"He's right," asserted Connie. "After all, he's not talking about a mansion, just a pretty simple house."

Lara considered the lemon-yellow appliances, the European cabinets, the butcher-block island, and the brass chandelier. In her estimation these were hardly simple, and she said so.

With slight impatience in her voice Connie rebuked her. "You never want anything!"

Just so had Connie used to speak, with that frown, when she was in grade school. And Lara, countering that impatience with the patience she had used back then, replied, "It's no use wanting what you can't afford."

Eddy clapped Davey on the back. "Go for it! You can afford it. I'll be your mortgagor. I'm flooded with cash right now."

"Thanks, Eddy, but the answer is no," Davey said.

"Okay, brother-in-law. You're a stubborn customer and always were. But I don't have to tell you that I never give up either." He looked at his watch. "We don't have a lot of time. Let's go, folks."

At the local airport the Davises watched Eddy and Connie climb the steps to board the plane. At the top they both turned and waved, Connie's newly bright hair streaming out in the wind. And Lara, along with a sense of loss at this departure, had a curious sense of relaxation. They were both so—so energetic. The two of them were alike, bright and lovable and quick to fill every hour, with no rest. It made you tired just to think of living like that.


THE taxi turned into Connie's street. It felt good to be home, even after such a short time. Tomorrow there was the art class at the museum, and after that an appointment with the rug people about the dining room. Richard wanted to make do with carpeting, but Bitsy Maxwell's Oriental had the muted shimmer of stained glass. Richard would just have to be convinced.

The taxi stopped at the door, and the old doorman saluted her.

"Good evening, Higgins," Connie said. "Mr. Tory home?"

"Yes, ma'am. He came in a couple of hours ago."

It was only ten thirty. The big meeting must have broken up very early, then. There was no light in the foyer when she opened the apartment door; no light anywhere. He must be already asleep.

The poodle whimpered in its basket. She turned on a lamp and picked up the dog and kissed it. Then, removing her shoes so as not to disturb Richard, she crossed the bare floor to the bedroom. The door was open. A weak shaft of light from the lamp fell directly on the bed, where Richard lay naked and face down.

She felt a shock, as though her hand had touched a spark. The thought struck: He's *dead,* and her hand went to her heart.

She must have made a sound. Afterward she remembered only that she turned on the switch at the door, illuminating the room with rosy lamplight, that he started up, that she saw his horrified face, all eyes, and that there was not one but two men on the bed.

She stood there absorbing the total truth of what was before her. Richard was cowering behind the blanket, absurdly covering his nakedness. The other man slid beneath its far side, absurdly hiding. Connie's laugh was a shrill falsetto shriek that ended in a gasp.

She fled. She sat at the kitchen table, the kitchen being the only other room that was complete, and put her head down on it.

"Oh, my God," she wailed. "Oh, my God!"

After a long while she sat up and rocked her body back and forth, bent over, with her hands on her elbows, rubbing and rubbing her arms. Her head was empty, numb.

Finally she heard whispers at the outer door and the soft thud of its closing. Without turning, she knew when Richard came to the kitchen door. He would be wondering, in his desperation, what to say to her. Although, after her first shock, she was beginning to feel the rise of fury—she, desirable and young, to be so cheated, so tricked—she could not help but feel pity for him.

As he approached, she had to look at him. He had put on pajamas. His voice was barely audible.

"Listen. Please listen to me. This was my first time, I swear it. And I can't explain it—except that we had a business meeting, then it was a nice night, so we walked uptown together, and I asked him in for a drink. A perfectly natural thing to do."

She could not answer. Her tears welled. This is unreal, she was thinking. This isn't happening to me. To me, Connie Osborne.

"The thing is, I guess— I knew we had too much to drink." He had an imploring look upon his face. "Connie, I don't make a practice of this. I'm sorry. I'll spend the rest of my life being sorry."

"Your being sorry doesn't help very much. Oh!" she cried. "I should have had some inkling, I should have been smarter!" And she bent over again in pain, rubbing her arms.

"We've been so happy together," she heard him say. "Traveling, listening to music, making a home. We've been so happy." He moved closer, looming tall above where she still huddled, so close that she smelled the fresh scent of his cologne. "Connie . . . you're not going to leave me, are you?"

She looked up then, straight into his eyes, which were pleading.

"Is it true? Will you swear that you never did this before?"

"Connie, I swear it. And I never will again. Never."

She sighed. It was as if her heart were crying, heavy with its confusion of anger, shame, and pity for him.

He went to a chair, and for a long time they sat not speaking. The silence, like a heavy sea, swelled over them both. Finally Richard opened his mouth and made a slight sound, then closed it again.

"Is there something else you want to tell me?" she asked.

He looked past her, out toward the nighttime sky stained rusty pink by the city's million lights. Sweat dampened his forehead, and tears stood in his eyes.

"Will you give me another chance? Will you? Will you?"

How could she just throw him away? "Yes, I will."

"Oh, bless you, Connie. Bless us both." He got up then, saying gently, "You're worn out." Realizing she wouldn't sleep in the bed, he pulled out the folding cot and set it up for her there.

When she lay down on it, she could see, high at the top of the window, an oblong of sky. Pink, obscuring what should have been deep, soothing black, looked dirty now, like a silky blot on the enormous world and on her own small life.

## Chapter Seven

THE little old white inn on a dirt road just beyond the little old white village was framed with autumn reds and yellows. In a warm New England wind leaves sank slowly onto the still green grass. A sweet, fruity fragrance tinged the air. There were tennis courts at the inn, there were canoes, and there was a section of the Appalachian Trail to hike on.

It was a few weeks later, and the two had agreed to put the sorry episode away forever, so nothing was said to impede a return to normal living. On their third night at the inn Connie was even able to shut out that appalling scene in their beautiful bed at home and to respond to Richard's wish for sex. In the morning at breakfast he reached suddenly across the table and clasped her hand. She was sure she read gratitude in the clasp.

They drove back to the city feeling reconciled and renewed. Their pleasant routines were waiting for them: Richard's at the office and Connie's, for the next few months at any rate, at the shops, acquiring possessions for the new apartment.

They had begun afresh.

And then on a fair Saturday afternoon in the following month, Connie entered Central Park to enjoy the walk home, away from the traffic on the streets. The day was closing; perambulators, bicycles, and dog-walkers were all heading for home, but here and there a few people still sat on benches in the warm sun. Connie was smiling. What a wonderful city in all its variety! How wonderful to be young here, to have some money in one's pocket, and to be able to buy such heavenly Chinese blue lamps as she had just found today!

This was the moment she saw two men on a bench, only partly hidden in a cluster of long-needled pines—two men in an embrace, arms encircling and lips joined. . . . How disgusting.

One of the men was Richard. She froze. Her heart made such a frantic leap that for an instant she thought it would stop. But her legs kept moving. It was as if her legs knew enough to carry her away from there as fast as they could go. As if they understood she must get home to shelter and safety. Get home. Get home.

Shut the door and sit down, still with coat on, sit gasping, numb. You tried, you did what you should. How could he have lied to you? Rotten. Rotten.

After a while she got up and made a cup of coffee. She was drinking it, warming her cold shaking hands around the cup, when Richard came in, looking as cheerful as always.

"How was your day? I had more to do at my desk than I'd thought, or I'd have been home by noon."

"At your desk?" she said. "Try Central Park."

He stared. "What do you mean?"

"Richard, I saw you, so don't lie. You've lied enough already."

He looked away from her. A flush like a disease swept over him.

"It wasn't your first time, that night." She waited and, as anger mounted, cried out fiercely, "Answer me! It wasn't, was it?"

"Well, not quite. But there haven't been a lot of times. I mean . . ."

He floundered. The strength drained from him. It was visible in the sag of his shoulders. And within Connie's chest hung the heavy weight of disillusionment.

Her voice was thick in her throat. "I believed you. How could you have done this to me? To a person who trusted you?"

He sighed. "I guess I couldn't help it."

"Then you should never have married me. Why did you?"

"I loved you, Connie," he answered simply. "I still do. Your beauty, your intelligence and curiosity, your drive."

Connie shook her head. Tears stung, but she did not want to let them fall. In crises one must keep one's control. And this was crisis. This was the end of the road that had begun that morning when he had walked in, sun bronzed and tall, in his tennis whites.

Then a tear fell. And Richard cried out, "Oh, Connie, I'm so sorry! What can I do? Can I ask you again for another chance?"

She wiped the tear with the back of her hand. "It wouldn't do any good. It wouldn't work, and you know that."

"What then? Divorce?"

"I have no choice, the way things are."

"Whatever you do, just please . . . If there's some way . . ."

"I won't say anything to anyone, Richard, except my brother. You can depend on my word."

"I know I can. And you can keep this apartment. It's paid for, free and clear. The rest of my cash is invested with Eddy."

"I don't want blood money," Connie said stiffly.

"You won't have to fight me for anything."

"I don't want to fight you at all, Richard. I just want to talk to Eddy. He'll know what to do. Now I can't talk anymore. I'm exhausted. Wrung out."

"I'M IN no mood for explanations or commiserations from friends like Bitsy Maxwell," Connie said. "They'll just have to wait. I'll tell Lara myself, so don't tell her, Eddy. She'll be heartbroken for me, but other people will ask only out of curiosity."

They were in Eddy's office, waiting for Richard to arrive. Laid in readiness on the desk was a tidy stack of papers, a white island on a mahogany sea—Richard's portfolio of securities.

Now Richard entered. He had been sleeping for the last week at a hotel, or very likely had been lying awake there. Gray pouches made semicircles beneath his eyes.

Eddy rose, offered his hand, and smiled. "Come in, Richard. I'm glad to see you but awfully sorry about the reason."

Connie twirled a ring around her little finger and did not look up.

Richard, stifling a quiver in his throat, rushed to begin. "I suppose Connie's told you everything. I don't know how you will regard me now, Eddy. This is hardly what you expected—"

"She's told me. As to how I regard you—well, I'm not here to judge anybody. All I can say is, people make mistakes. What can you do? You're both decent and honorable, so there's no reason why this business shouldn't be agreeably settled."

Eddy was in a hurry to finish "this business" as fast as possible. The thing now was to look ahead. That this marrying business could end in such a mess was appalling. Connie, poor girl, had been in such a rush to get married, too. Pam, now, was just the opposite, he reflected thankfully. A modern woman, she was happy enough to be on her own, earning her own few dollars, taking each day as she found it. She was a perfect complement to himself. Freedom. Freedom was the ticket, and no binding ties, only loose ones that can be dropped when the time for dropping comes. One had only to look at this poor pair of mismatched—

"As to alimony," Richard was saying to Eddy, "well, just give me the figures. And remember, Connie's got expensive tastes."

"You make me feel disgusting when you talk like that!" Connie gasped. "We have no children, and I don't need alimony. Just make some sort of fair settlement."

Eddy put up a hand before Richard could answer. "Enough. Enough. Let me just say there's plenty for you both. Richard, your shelters got you a four-to-one write-off this year, remember? Connie, why don't you read a magazine in the waiting room while we run over some figures? It won't take all that long."

Connie sat and tried to read. But unable to concentrate, she laid the magazine aside and allowed her mind to wander. The conclusion of the wandering was that you can depend on nothing. Why should Peg, still in her forties, have died of cancer? Why should Richard have turned out like this? The only thing you can depend on is money. That's tangible. It doesn't die young or disillusion you. Take care of it and it lasts. It's there to keep you warm and safe and give you honor, besides. That receptionist thinks I don't know that she's looking me over, envying my mink and my alligator shoes. I used to do that, too, when I worked at Richard's club; I used to see the rings on their hands when I gave out menus. I know—

The receptionist was speaking to her. "Mr. Osborne just buzzed. You can go back in."

As she opened the door Eddy's cheerful voice rang out, too loud. "I give her two years before she'll be married again."

SOME SIX WEEKS LATER CONNIE stood on the sidewalk in the cold white winter sunshine with a slip of paper in her hand. It's not possible, she thought. Given the way I lived with Richard and careful as I always was, especially after that awful night, how can this be? It must have been that weekend in the country.

"You're not happy about it," the doctor had said, observing Connie's face.

"My marriage just broke up. This is absurd. I can't have a baby."

The doctor, a quiet, elderly woman, kept a neutral manner, saying calmly, "You mean you don't want to."

Although her mind was quite made up, Connie's heart had begun to flutter in a small panic of its own.

"It's nothing to look forward to, is it? An abortion, I mean."

"True enough," the other woman said. "That's why you need to go home and think it over for a couple of days."

"I don't have to think it over. I'm not in a position to have a child. I don't want it!" she cried, twisting her damp hands in the strap of her pocketbook. "I particularly don't want this child. I wouldn't welcome it, and would that be fair to it? I don't even know where my own life is going, let alone somebody else's. No, I can't."

The doctor stood up. "Well, then, you can make your appointment at the desk. They'll give you your instructions."

So Connie folded the instruction sheet and started home. Her heart was still fluttering when she opened her apartment door. For a minute or two she stood still in the foyer and just looked around, as if to orient herself. Then, still wearing her coat, she picked up her patient little dog and walked through the rooms.

It was almost impossible to believe that a life was growing in her body. She did not feel any different, but the life was there, a minute heart already throbbing. And she was about to let them rip it out! A violent shaking overcame her. And as she clasped Delphine she felt the little dog's heart beating, beating. . . . She sat down and cried. The dog in her lap looked up at her face and licked her hand.

Presently, cried out, she got up and looked around. The living room was almost complete, an English oak stretcher table stood in the dining room, and the cabinets that were to have held Richard's books in the den were finished. She would simply have to fill them one by one with books of her own. A new bed stood in the bedroom now, covered in yellow quilted chintz. The sight of these accumulating possessions began to soothe her. They were curiously comforting, enfolding her and reassuring her that she was, after all, safe.

There was no reason for panic. If you just kept your head, you could get through almost anything. By tomorrow the simple operation would be over. After that, go forward, she told herself.

Thus Connie passed the evening, and in the morning was calm.

ON THAT same afternoon, Lara, too, had been seeing a doctor. She said wanly, "I felt so sure this time. I can't explain, but I was so sure, when I missed, that this was it. I just don't know."

"I know only that we've tried everything possible, Mrs. Davis." The doctor had a kindly manner. He was genuinely sorry. "Adoption? It can work out beautifully, you know."

Lara wiped her eyes. "It takes years to get a baby, Doctor. There aren't nearly enough for all the people who want them."

"That's true of infants. But if you would take an older child who needs parents—and there are many such, shunted from one foster home to another—you might be very happy, I think. You and your husband would make wonderful parents."

I wanted Davey's baby, our baby, Lara told herself. Not a child who remembers her own mother. But she said nothing.

"Think about it," the doctor added. "Go home and talk it over."

So all that evening she and Davey talked it over, sitting together on the sofa. He had his arm around her when finally he said, "There comes a time, no matter what the problem, when one has to face the hard truth. And I think we've come to it. As a matter of fact, at the last stockholders' meeting, Don Schultz happened to mention that a cousin of his adopted a boy from a home somewhere in Minnesota. It's a church-run place, and they give you the child's background. We should try it, Lara. It's time we made a decision."

Of course, he was right. She knew that. And she said, "I'm ready. Yes. Will you get the name of the place tomorrow?"

"I will. And Lara darling, listen. Things aren't all bad. We'll find a child in need of love, and we have a lot of love to give. Think of poor Connie, married three years and finished."

"I know. She's pretty shaken by it, too."

"Why don't you go to her? You haven't seen her since it happened, so why not get on a plane tomorrow and surprise her? Stay for a couple of days and cheer her up. See a few shows, have fun together. Meanwhile, I'll talk to the people in Minnesota."

IN THE white room, with its rows of flashing instruments, the doctor and nurse in white, and its cold white light, Connie thought, Lie back. Be confident. Clench your fists and hold on. The room whirled. You're not here. You're far away on a beach, under a tree. You're sweating, but you haven't made a sound. Almost finished, someone says. Now vast relief. . . . It's over.

They told her to rest, gave her a long, cool drink, and she fell asleep. When she awoke, the short winter day was ending, and they told her she might go home. There really was nothing to it.

The first person she saw in the lobby at home was Lara, sitting on a bench near the elevator.

"Oh," Lara said, rushing to Connie. "I've been here for hours! They wouldn't let me into your apartment."

"Why didn't you say you were coming? Is anything wrong?"

"No, not with us. But you— Oh, Connie, I just couldn't stay away. I've been thinking and thinking about you and Richard."

Of all times for her to come here! Connie said to herself. Any other day I would have been overjoyed to see her.

"Come up," she said almost peremptorily.

She switched on the lights, bringing to life the living room and the den beyond, all thickly carpeted, the furniture gleaming.

"Oh, how beautiful!" Lara cried, clasping her hands like a child.

The gesture irritated Connie, whose legs were suddenly going weak. She wanted only to lie down again. But then Lara put her arms around her.

"Darling, I would have come to you if I had known you and Richard were having problems. I might even have helped straighten things out between you. Who knows."

Connie gave a brittle laugh. "You don't know what you're talking about. It was not preventable. I never told you the whole story. I planned to do it soon, but I just haven't felt like talking."

Lara looked stricken. "I'm so sorry. I can't tell you how sorry. We were shocked, Davey and I. We really liked Richard." She gave Connie a quick look. "You don't look well, darling."

"As a matter of fact, I'm not feeling well." Her legs were shaking now. "Maybe I'm coming down with something."

"No," Lara said decisively. "It's your nerves, and no wonder. I'll make you some tea. You must be starved, too. Sit down and stay right there. I can find my way around your kitchen."

Connie soon heard the slam of the refrigerator door and the clink of a pot—cheerful domestic sounds reminding her of Peg. And she was ashamed of having been so unwelcoming to Lara. I really am wrung out, she thought, and closed her eyes.

When she opened them, Lara was standing in front of her holding a tray with a lamb chop, a salad, and a cup of tea.

"It's lovely. You're too nice to me," Connie said. The kindness made her eyes tear. "You always were."

"Come on, come on. Now I'll sit here with you, and if you feel like talking, do. And if you don't, don't." Seating herself with a tray of her own on her lap, Lara began to eat, while at the same time anxiously observing Connie. "Do you want me to talk? I don't mean about your troubles, either. If you want quiet, just say so."

"Talk, of course. But as to my divorce, I'll tell you tomorrow. It's a long story."

"All right, then, I'll tell you something about myself. First, we've decided to buy that house. Eddy convinced us we can afford it."

"Really? Oh, I'm glad! It's a lovely house."

"Wait. There's bigger news. I almost don't want to talk about it until it comes true. We think— We expect to have a child."

"You do? Oh, how wonderful! You've wanted one so. But you don't look it, you don't show. When will it be?"

Lara shook her head. "No, darling. I'm not pregnant. We've finally made up our minds to adopt, that's all."

"Oh. Well. That's wonderful, too, isn't it? Tell me about it. I've heard one has to be on a waiting list for years, though."

"Well, I hope not. It's much easier if one agrees to take an older child. So it won't be a baby. But we don't mind. In the meantime we're getting the spare bedroom ready until we can move."

Connie had a swift double vision: the sterile glare of that room this morning, when something had been taken away, and the bright clutter of another room, which Lara would be filling now with toys and noise and . . .

"I hope it won't take too long to leave that dreadful flat behind," she said.

Lara smiled. "I've never found it so dreadful," and Connie smiled back and said, "You wouldn't. You never complain."

It was pleasant to be there in the quiet with her sister, and she was glad, after all, that Lara had come. The food and the hot tea began to revive her. An odd thought, possibly induced by Lara's concern, crossed Connie's mind: I have always been cared for. First there was my mother, then Lara, and then Richard. From this thought came a sudden desire to tell everything to Lara now. And starting at the end of her tale, she said bluntly, "The reason I'm weak is that I've just come back from having an abortion."

Lara's fork clattered onto the plate. "You what?"

"I didn't know I was pregnant when I left Richard, not that it would have made any difference," Connie explained. Her heart began that panicked fluttering again. "You don't know about him. He wasn't a bad person, but I couldn't stay because he was—"

Lara flung up her hand. "What does Richard matter? I don't care what he was or what he did, but you—you killed your baby!"

Of course. This was how Lara would see it! And Connie reproached herself: I should have kept my mouth shut.

"I didn't exactly love doing it," she said quietly. "But it was necessary, Lara. And anyway, it wasn't even a baby yet. It was the size of my little finger." Seeing Lara's eyes gone dark with horror, she stammered, "Or something like that."

"You're lying to yourself. The size! It was alive and growing, and you murdered it. I— Damn you, Connie! I'd have given years of my life to have a child of my own."

"Can't you understand?" Connie cried. "I'm not psychologically prepared to have a child right now! I'm in the middle of a divorce. What kind of a home could I offer it?"

"*I* would have given it a home. That baby—that baby was a part of Peg, a part of her that would have gone on, and you destroyed it. I'll never get over this. Never."

"That's your problem! I'm going to *make* myself get over it."

Lara's flushed face was mottled. She fumbled for a handkerchief. And Connie pleaded, "Why are we quarreling over this, Lara? If you think I was wrong, well, it's your privilege to think so. Let's

227

understand each other. But I can't undo what's done, can I? And anyway," she finished gently, "it really was my business, my decision, my sorrow. I'm not the little sister now, taking advice at your knee. You mustn't try to run my life anymore."

Lara shook her head. "I never tried to run your life, Connie."

"You're trying now."

"That's what you think of me? Well, I've heard everything." Lara sobbed. "I came here to help you, Connie, came out of love, and this is what I get for it. This."

Suddenly the sight of Lara's futile tears infuriated Connie. She lashed out. "If there's anything I despise, it's people feeling sorry for themselves."

"I'm not sorry for myself. I'm sorry for you, Connie."

"Well, don't be! I'll get along fine," she said, not meaning it.

"This is what you call fine? You're a terrible disappointment, Connie. I can only hope you'll straighten out your life."

"Will you just please let me alone? Let me alone!"

"Oh, I'll let you alone. Indeed I will. I'll bother you no more." Lara ran to the closet. "Where's my coat? I'm leaving, Connie. You just go run your life your own way. And good luck to you."

"Wait, Lara!" Connie gasped. "What are you doing?"

"Taking the first plane home," said Lara, fastening her coat.

"You won't get one at this hour. Wait."

"Then I'll sleep at the airport." The door clicked shut.

For a while Connie sat staring at the door's blank face, the pain within her a knot in her chest. The room was absolutely still, the charming room that she had planned. The curtains were drawn for the night, accentuating the stillness. She sprang up and pulled them open onto the city, onto the street below.

Tomorrow she would tell Eddy what had happened. Or maybe she'd just ask him for some advice. It would be a long time before her art courses materialized into a really important job. So in the meantime should she think of going back to work in a boutique? There had to be something to fill the days. She needed advice.

The little dog crept around her feet, and she bent to stroke it. Its love was pure and simple. It neither judged nor disappointed.

"Without you, Delphine," she whispered aloud, "I don't know how I'd get through this night."

# Chapter Eight

LARA looked across the parlor to where Davey was sitting, as if for affirmation. This was the final moment, the climax, after some months' journey through time and some miles' journey through a fading autumn countryside to this Minnesota town. Now here they were. And she was suddenly conscious of her thundering heart.

Mrs. Elmer was an unpretentious gray-haired woman, who for the last half hour had been relating a sad, simple story.

"Susanna is an intelligent little six-year-old girl, but she's lived through what I call a war. Her father died in a factory accident while her mother was pregnant. The mother, an immigrant from Eastern Europe without family, was so devastated that she was not able to provide the happiest environment. Then when she herself fell ill with leukemia— Well, you can imagine."

Lara's eyes never left Mrs. Elmer's face. "Who took care of Susanna then?" she asked.

"Neighbors. First one family, then another. But after the mother died, the state took charge and she went to a foster home. Now I've had her here for the last two weeks, after the path was cleared for a possible adoption. I'm sort of a way station. What she needs now is permanence and a lot of patient love."

"There are no relatives on the father's side?" Davey asked.

Mrs. Elmer understood. "No, not a soul. If you adopt Sue—she likes to be called that—she'll be your child without question."

Davey smiled. "I think we're ready to see her, Mrs. Elmer."

"I'll go get her. They're all playing in the yard."

He came and laid his hand on Lara's shoulder. Feeling it tremble, she thought, This is how he would be if I were giving birth, only he would be walking the length of the corridor, getting in people's way.

At that moment the door opened and the woman returned, urging a small girl ahead of her—a thin child with extraordinary blue-black eyes in a delicate face, and a long brown ponytail.

"Sue," said Mrs. Elmer, "these are Mr. and Mrs. Davis. Will you shake hands with them?"

Fearfully the child raised her gaze from her own scuffed shoes and looked down at Lara's shoes. A small, cold hand was held out, and an almost indistinguishable word was murmured.

Softly Lara said, "Sue . . . We've heard so much about you, about what a lovely girl you are. So we wanted to bring a present for you. It's in this box. Do you want to open it, or shall I?"

As if unsure what answer would be the right one, Sue waited, and Lara said quickly, "Here, we'll do it together. You hold one end of the bow, and I'll pull it open."

Under layers of tissue paper lay the most extravagant, the most beautiful doll, a perfect little girl with real blond hair, an expressive face, and a party dress of ribbons and white lace.

The child stared, not touching it.

"Take it, pick her up," urged Lara.

Still the child just stared. Lara and Davey glanced at one another with a common thought between them: She's terrified. And lifting the doll out of the box, Lara placed it in Sue's arms.

"She's yours, dear. She wants you to love her. What would you like to name her?"

This time a reply came promptly and clearly. "Lily."

"Oh, I like that name," Lara said, while above Sue's head Mrs. Elmer's lips moved silently to say, That was her mother's name.

Suddenly, passionately, Sue clutched the doll to her chest and ran with it to the armchair at the other end of the room.

Davey's raised eyebrows, furrowing his forehead, asked a question of his wife: Should we? Will this child's problems be more than we want to undertake?

Mrs. Elmer drew her chair close to Davey's and Lara's.

"Well, what do you think?" she whispered. "Do you think you want her? She's really a sweet child."

Davey was paying no attention to Mrs. Elmer. And Lara, following his look, saw that Sue was rocking the doll in her arms and smiling. The smile, most feminine and most endearing, went, Lara saw, straight to Davey's heart.

That unselfconscious smile went straight to Lara's heart, too. She had a sudden revelation: I can make happiness bloom again in this child. Almost gaily she thought, I will braid her hair when it grows longer. I'll make a thick braid with a ribbon bow at the tip. I will—

"Of course," Mrs. Elmer was saying very low, "your taking her depends on whether she wants to go. I will not send an unwilling child away from here." She raised her voice. "Sue, will you come

over? We want to ask you something. Would you like to go home with Mr. and Mrs. Davis?"

Lara made a correction. "Aunt Lara and Uncle Davey. That's what we'd be if you would come to live with us."

Those eyes, so black and lustrous! The piteous plea as they were raised to Lara, studying Lara's face. Were they saying, Take me! Take me! Or were they saying, I don't want you. Let me alone.

"We've been wanting a little girl like you," Lara said, trying not to coax too blatantly, wanting just to seem friendly. "We have no children in our house. You'd have your own room. The shelves have wonderful toys, a carriage for Lily, a little kitchen."

Solemn, the child said, "I'd like that."

"You'll go to school," said Lara, "and have lots of friends. I know some nice girls for you to play with. We shall love you very much, Sue. Will you come with us? It will be a nice long ride home, and we'll stop for ice-cream cones on the way. Will you come?"

Sue paused. The pause seemed very very long. Oh, I want this child! Lara cried to herself. There's something about her. . . .

"All right," said Sue.

Davey spoke with a catch in his throat. "How fast can we get the basic legal preliminaries over with so we can get back to Ohio?"

"It won't take long," said Mrs. Elmer.

And so it was that Susanna Davis went to her new home.

THE first hours went well enough. The drive home was enlivened by many stops for food, a sailboat ride on Lake Michigan, and shopping in Chicago, which was most necessary since Sue's entire shabby wardrobe fitted into one suitcase.

Trying on a winter jacket, she pranced in front of the mirror. Pleasure in the totally new experience of receiving things lessened her shyness, and like any normally secure young girl, Sue actually rejected one of Lara's suggestions. This touch of spirit encouraged Lara.

"But I like the red one. I want the red one."

"The red one it shall be then, Miss Sue."

Saying so, Lara heard an echo in her head, an echo of her own voice years before saying something like that to a little girl who always had decided ideas: "Whatever you say, Miss Connie."

It was a year since that tragic night in New York. After it, weeks had passed during which the hurt and smart of Connie's words had increased. She should have called me, Lara thought. All these months . . . I know Eddy told her we were going to fetch this child. She could have called us to wish us luck. For an instant her throat was choked; then the lump receded, leaving an ache of grieving resignation. And she turned back to her new little girl.

They arrived home, and Sue was shown to her room. The new clothes were put away, and Lily went to sit on the doll's chair by the bed. Lara made a quick dinner for them all, which Sue ate hungrily.

Afterward, Lara gave her a bath, observing that she was none too clean and that her ribs stuck out. She had had minimal care, poor little girl. When Lara had brushed Sue's hair and teeth and put on a new white nightgown, she put her into bed.

"Would you like me to read a story, Sue? This is a lovely book. *Winnie-the-Pooh*, it's called. Let's begin," said Lara confidently.

"I don't want a story, Mrs. . . . I forgot your name."

"Mrs. Davis. But to you I'm Aunt. Aunt Lara. Will you say that?"

"Aunt Lara." The girl yawned.

"You're sleepy." The delicate face was so white, so wan. "It's been a long day," Lara said softly, "and we've lots to do tomorrow. We have to get you registered at school. Let me hug you good night."

When she had left the room, Davey asked, "How is she doing?"

"Very well, I think. So far, so good."

But in the middle of the night, loud crying awakened them in their room across the hall. Lara ran. Sitting up in the little bed, Susanna was shaking with deep sobs. Lara took her into her arms.

"There, there," was all she could say. Banal words, yet they had the utmost meaning when warm arms and a warm voice went with them.

Anxious, Davey asked from the doorway, "Does anything hurt her, do you think?"

"Everything does," Lara answered, and he nodded.

For long minutes she sat with the child's tears wetting her shoulders, her own tears brimming. And they stayed holding each other until the sobbing ceased and Sue was laid back under the quilt to fall asleep. But Lara, not leaving her, sat dozing, crumpled and cold, in the rocking chair until the morning.

Patience, patience was all. And little by little, day after day, small changes, almost imperceptible, began to occur.

Lara's friends brought their children to play. At first when Sue was invited back, she refused to go. *She's afraid that I'll leave her there, and she'll be given away again,* Lara knew. *It's not that she loves us. Of course not. It's that she's afraid of another change.*

Lara spoke openly. "Tell me, Sue, is that why you won't go to Jennifer's house? That you're afraid you'll be kept there?"

Sue's silence was the answer.

"Will you go if I stay there with you?"

A nod of the head was the answer.

After half a dozen trials of this sort, one day Lara left her to go down to her office, which Davey and she had agreed must be turned over temporarily to someone else while Sue got adjusted and while they made the move into the new home. When she returned to the friend's house, Sue was playing in the yard. She hadn't missed Lara at all.

"Now," Lara said, hugging her tightly, "you see that I always come back to you. Uncle Davey and I will never let you go."

Fortunately, the first-grade teacher was especially understanding. "In the beginning, Mrs. Davis, I did see tears starting but always held back. She's a proud little girl. But the improvement in attitude is really wonderful. She's going to be fine. You people are obviously doing something right."

Lara felt a flood of beaming warmth. As the months passed and Sue grew closer she often had to remind herself not to sing out, for fear of boring people with the repetition of her hope and joy.

Mrs. Evans appeared in Eddy's office with a silver tray upon which stood a plate of thin-sliced whole wheat sandwiches and a little silver pot of coffee.

"Do you realize, Mr. Osborne, that you had no lunch and it's after four o'clock?"

Eddy smiled sheepishly, as if he were a boy being reprimanded by a loving mother. He enjoyed having a dignified gray-haired widow with an upper-class British accent in his service. Most men looked for a secretary on the right side of thirty who was curved in the right places. But Eddy had a different sense of the suitable.

"You take too good care of me, Mrs. Evans."

"Well, if I didn't keep after you the little bit that I do, you'd work yourself to death. Now, I'll put this down. Relax and unwind."

"I'm starting to do it right now. As soon as I eat, I'm heading out to the country. It's worth the Friday traffic to have two grand summer days when you get there. And you go home, too, Mrs. Evans. You could do with some unwinding yourself."

"Thank you, Mr. Osborne. I believe I will. And I'm leaving orders that you're not to be disturbed."

Eddy stretched. It had been a wearying day, and yet he felt exhilarated. For here he was, established at last in the perfect office he had dreamed about, filling a floor and a half of the building. He had an able staff of forty, and the business hummed like a dynamo, making money. Every minute, every second counted. Phones rang, the ticker rolled, computers wrote. These were the exciting '80s, and Eddy Osborne was at the very center of the excitement!

When he looked out the window, westward to the Trump Tower, southward to Rockefeller Center and the Empire State Building, eastward to Sutton Place, northward to Central Park, it resembled a diorama of miniature gray-white towers. Leaving this private oasis to plunge down in the elevator and emerge onto the pavement, into enormity and a cacophony of horns and fire sirens, was total shock. Yet he loved that shock.

This room is marvelous, he thought. The decorator had read Eddy's mind. The burnished mahogany paneling was such as one would find in a London club. The enormous Oriental rug was richly dark, too, faded in areas that daylight had touched for half a century or more. The tall clock in the corner was an authentic piece out of the 1700s. It had cost him almost two hundred thousand dollars.

His affairs were going well enough, he reflected, to warrant his buying almost anything he might want. Anything at all. He was worth, he calculated, not quite nineteen million dollars, after just seven years. His income had reached eleven million a year. The firm's securities portfolio now topped six billion. And he mused over the old cliché: Nothing succeeds like success. How true it was!

His feel for the market had not failed him yet. Even in a rising market there were plenty of investors who, snaillike, got almost nowhere; even in such a market you had to know when and where to move. But the firm's chief business was still tax shelters—in real estate, oil, cattle, anything to produce losses that would reduce one's taxable income. That was where the real money lay. And that was why people were flocking to Osborne and Company.

It still surprised him to be so easily accepted. The social Establishment invited him into its homes and clubs. He was also on the boards of half a dozen important philanthropies, all entailing lavish donations. Far from begrudging these, Eddy actually welcomed making grand gestures. Even making loans to friends made him content with himself. It made him feel in charge.

The tall clock chimed. Calculating swiftly, he allotted his time: an hour to go home, shower, and throw some clothes into a bag, then two hours, if he was lucky, to head out to Pam's place, in the country. But first came the Friday call to Lara that he never missed. And he reached for the telephone.

When Sue's voice answered, he played the expected game.

"Hi. This is Uncle Eddy. Let me guess. Is this you, Davey?"

A giggle and a protest. "Uncle Eddy! You know who it is!"

"Oh, of course. You're Sue. I should have recognized you by your pink shirt, anyway."

"Not today! I'm wearing my Snoopy shirt. Can't you see?"

"I can't see so well. I left my glasses somewhere."

Lara's voice cut in. "My turn, Susie. Uncle Eddy's probably in a hurry. Hang up, dear."

"I can't get over the way that child can kid me right back. She's got real wit," Eddy said.

"I know it. And to think that in the beginning we were worried that she'd never be happy again!"

"Where are you this minute? What room?"

"In the kitchen, getting dinner. Why?"

"Because. I just like to imagine you cooking up a storm in that picture-book kitchen." He had an instant picture of her standing at the island, where the copper pots hung. The last time he had been there, she had a row of African violets up on the windowsill.

"I'm using the barbecue right now. It's marvelous."

"Aren't you glad I made you buy that house?" he demanded. "Don't you love it?"

"Of course I do. Who wouldn't?"

And again he felt that glow of pure pleasure, a glow that spread, tingling as it rose up into his throat, to end with a chuckle of laughter. Because of him, Lara and her little family were in the home they deserved, modest as it was. He had lent Davey enough for the down payment, a sum that Davey, in the healthy growth of his new prosperity, had already repaid.

"Is Davey home yet?" he asked now.

"He just came in. Here he is. Davey, it's Eddy."

"Hi, Davey! A new gadget in the works?"

"Well, I hope so. An instrument for bone surgery. It looks promising, but I can't tell yet." That was Davey, prudent and cautious.

"I looked over that copy of your accountant's report yesterday, and it looks mighty good."

"Yes, things are going well. Orders keep coming in, and I took on five new men last week. Even at that, we can barely keep up."

"Do you still not want to talk about investments with me? I can make you rich, Davey, if you let me."

"Eddy, again I tell you, we're not interested in being rich."

"Okay, okay. Some other time. I'm in the usual rush. Kiss Lara for me, and give Sue an extra hug from Uncle Eddy."

When he hung up, he felt good. He always felt good after his call to Ohio, knowing that Lara was solidly placed for the first time in her life, with a tidy interest in a steady, flourishing business. If Davey would only let me invest for him, Eddy reflected. He's the finest guy in the world. But to actually not want to have money, real money, with all the liberty and power and delight it gave!

A short time later he was in his car, heading toward the Queens Midtown Tunnel. It was a fair, cool evening, and the air rushed softly through the open windows of the new gray Mercedes two-seater. The car was superb. It responded like a living thing, like a fine horse. As he drove, maneuvering fleetly through the traffic, his mind kept clicking, his mental processes as finely tuned as the piece of machinery beneath him.

If only his sisters would get together again! He was stumped by each of them. It wasn't in his nature to comprehend how pain could be nurtured for so long. They were both anguished and angry, he knew. The words they had spoken to each other had apparently cut as harshly as knives. It was a pity, a sad, sad pity.

At least, though, he had seen Connie out of a profound slump. At least now she had her boutique on Madison Avenue to keep her busy. It puzzled him that she wasn't married yet. She was highly selective, of course, but she had a right to be; she was stunning and she had a brain, a pair of qualities that didn't always go together.

Now Eddy's thoughts slid naturally to his own most private affair, the Pamela affair. Recently he had sensed a growing impatience within himself, a feeling that things had been drifting for too long. Undoubtedly there was substance in what Pam always said, that she wanted independence before making a commitment. But there were too many attractive men hanging around her. He both knew it and didn't want to know it. Too often he saw men's glances at her, glances quickly turned away when Eddy intercepted them.

Ah, but I am probably making a mountain out of a molehill, he began to assure himself. I'm imagining. I'm exaggerating. Pam cares about me. There can't be any mistake about that, about the way we are together, and not only in bed. . . .

He drove down Pam's long gravel drive, parked the car, and got out, reaching for a magazine on the seat, a popular business weekly. This issue, which had come out only yesterday, contained the long-anticipated article about himself, the "Young Prince of Wall Street." A few years ago he would have bounded into this house waving it in his hand, but now he thought carefully before acting. Yes, he decided, there would be far greater impact if people were to discover the article for themselves, as they were sure to do. He walked up the porch steps without it and knocked on the screen door.

When Pam's mother's cool voice called, "Come in," he followed it to the dining room, where he found her on a step stool changing bulbs in the chandelier.

"Oh, Eddy! It's good to see you. Pam's upstairs showering, and I'm struggling here. If only I were three inches taller . . ."

"Here, let me." He took off his jacket, revealing smartly striped braces and a shirt pocket with a small, tasteful monogram.

"What three extra inches can do!" he said gaily as Mrs. Granger handed up the bulbs.

"More than three. Oh, I don't care what women's lib people say, a woman needs a man around. A husband." The tone was wistful.

He kept the talk light. "What for? To change light bulbs?"

She was shrewd. At once her retort became equally light. "Oh, to mix drinks and cope with the plumber. All that sort of thing."

They were on to each other. Yet he liked the woman. Her prattle was both amusing and interesting.

"It must seem foolish to you that two women live alone sur-rounded by so much empty space. But my great-grandfather built this house, and the best parts of my life were lived here. Besides, Pam loves it as much as I do. She's got her horses just down the road and . . . well, you know."

He knew. The place had its charm and dignity. He looked over to the sideboard—original Sheraton, he was sure. On it stood a George II tea service. Old silver acquired a special soft gleam, and it felt like silk in the hands. These pieces must have been in the family for five generations. It would feel nice to be part of such a family, he thought. It would make you feel solid, rooted.

As he screwed in the last of the bulbs Pam came clattering down the stairs and into the dining room, waving a magazine. "Hey, you, with your secrets. Mom, look what they've written about Eddy!"

The two women leaned over the magazine, reading the double-page spread. Evening light sifted through the screen and passed through Pam's pink silk housecoat, outlining her long legs and giving rise in Eddy to certain very warm recollections. He stood waiting until they finished, and listened modestly to their praise.

"Eddy!" Pam cried. "I never dreamed what really big things you were doing. You never talk about yourself."

"All these articles exaggerate," he said. "Writers have to make them sensational. It's their living, after all. Anyway, everybody has a talent for something and should try to live up to it. And that's all I do, the whole story," he concluded with an easy smile.

Mrs. Granger complained, "If I'd only known, I'd have had a celebration for you. We're just having hamburgers and salad."

"Sounds great enough to me, Mrs. Granger."

"I think you two had better eat without me. I'm invited to my cousin Mona's, and I'm not dressed yet. I'm running late." At the foot of the stairs she turned around. "As a matter of fact, I'm going to spend the night there. It's too far to be driving home by myself."

So he had just been handed a nice little present, a welcome comfort for the night.

"I'll be staying at the club," Eddy said, "but I'll make sure to see that Pam turns on the burglar alarm before I leave her."

239

Pam's eyes beamed straight toward his. "Let's eat and then go riding. We'll ride western, in jeans. Somebody's boarding a pair of pintos, and I thought it would be fun to ride along the beach tonight. There's a moon, and it'll be gorgeous. Are you game?"

"Sure am."

THE stable was fragrant with hay and the natural smell of clean, well-tended animals. In two stalls, facing each other, stood a pair of brown-and-white mares. Pam stroked their long cheeks.

"Aren't they lovely? The owner's starting a ranch upstate."

They put the western bridles and saddles on, then led the mares outside and mounted.

Night riding was one of the exhilarating pleasures she had taught him. The beach was deserted, and the quiet, except for the sound of waves and horses' hoofs slapping the sand, was an amazement to a New Yorker's ears. They rode without talking, in single file, with Pam at the head. When she put the mare into a gallop, her hair flew out behind her. The total effect of girl and animal, both so lean and agile, was as graceful as any ballet. Pam's strength and beauty fired Eddy. He had never before been so bothered, so possessed.

Once they were back in the house and having coffee in the kitchen, Eddy asked abruptly, "Have you ever slept—steadily, I mean—with anybody but me?" What he wanted to ask and could not bring himself to ask was, Do you ever sleep with anybody now when I'm not here?

"What makes you ask such a question, for goodness' sake?"

"You're a very very sexy lady," he said. There was a pause before he brought forth another bold question. "How many men have you had besides me? If you don't want to tell me, I'll understand that I don't matter to you, and that will be that."

Pam stood up and laid her face against his. "You matter very much to me, and I'll tell you whatever you want to know. I've had two men before I met you. But why bring all this up now, Eddy?"

He felt that she was being truthful and, moved, took her hand.

"We've never talked seriously about things, have we? I just felt that the time had come for us to do so."

She smiled. "I'll talk about anything you want."

He smiled back. "Later. I'd rather go upstairs. Shall we?"

"Just let me get ready. I'll call you."

He had never seen her room or even been upstairs. When he heard her call, he entered a blue-and-white bedchamber, all summer sky and silk clouds. On a little couch at the foot of the canopy bed, Pam sat naked among white lace pillows. Her expression as she looked at him was absolutely serious, different from anything he had ever seen upon her face before. Startling impressions and sensations raced across his mind. Even this room of hers was something he would not have imagined, it was so soft and womanly. It might well be the place where Lara slept with Davey. It was matrimonial. "Our bedroom is the most important room in the house," Lara had said of her new home. And a queer yearning ran now through Eddy's very bones at the recollection. He had never felt such a yearning. To come home every night to a lovely woman, to share this bed with her, to belong to each other in total trust!

He felt a little catch in his throat, and he held out his arms.

"Would you— Could you make this permanent, do you think? What I mean is . . . marry me?"

"Oh," she said. "Oh, oh, yes, I could. Yes, yes, I will. I want to."

She was laughing, she was crying. She was live and perfect. Almost as tall as he, she fitted into his arms. She was right for him.

LAUGHTER, their familiar mood, took over in the morning.

"Do you suppose you'd better clear out before my mother comes home?" asked Pam.

"Lord no. She knew I was going to stay here. She practically invited me. She's probably figuring out the wedding date."

Pam looked out over the lawn, where sprinklers were showering drops as bright as sparks.

"Whenever I thought about it," she said slowly, "and not being in a hurry, I never thought about it often, I pictured a huge reception on that lawn. A dance floor under a marquee. A marvelous dress, six bridesmaids, the works. You know."

"Fine with me."

"Darling, my mother couldn't possibly afford it."

"I'll pay! What's the difference?"

"A lot of difference. She wouldn't hear of it. A matter of pride, much, much pride, darling. Maybe we could elope."

Disappointed, Eddy replied, "That's not very festive."

"I know. Well, let me think a little."

"Okay, think. But I want you to meet me in the city this week. Somebody was telling me about a grand apartment for sale—twelve rooms, prewar, with high ceilings. A beauty. Let's take a look."

"You talk as if money didn't matter! Are you that rich, Eddy?"

He grinned. "I do all right. Enough for you not to worry about money. Enough for you to have anything you want."

Wonderingly she said, "I don't want a lot, Eddy. I never have. This seems so strange. I can't get used to it."

The grin turned into a laugh. "You will. You'll love it, too."

Eddy's plans developed as rapidly as a roll of film unwinds. The apartment was magnificent: paneled walls, marble fireplaces that worked, a far view of the East River, a near view of private gardens. Pam, looking down at this green enclave, found it hard to understand how anyone could part with a place like this one.

"They want to sell the furniture," Eddy told her, "but we surely don't want it." He surveyed the long drawing room. "Now, I'd have a cabinet on either side of the fireplace, to house my silver. The collection's grown, so that I've even got boxes under my bed."

"That's a handsome piano, though. I think it's rosewood."

"Hey, you're right! You want to buy it?"

"I don't play."

"That doesn't matter. It looks wonderful where it is. Enormous rooms need a piano. It'll be a showpiece. Next to you."

Sometime later he said thoughtfully, "You know, maybe it's not such a bad idea after all for us to get married by ourselves. I've been thinking that a big wedding would be a problem for me, too. I've told you about my sisters' feud—it would be awkward, painful, to have them together. The whole thing hurts my heart, Pam. They're both such good people." Eddy sighed. "What about an elopement to Paris? Your mother's pride is intact, my family problem is solved, and we have a great vacation. What do you say?"

"Why, I say yes," Pam answered promptly. "Double yes."

THEY were married at the American Church in Paris. Afterward they had dinner at the Grand Véfour, then returned to their suite at the Hotel Ritz. In the morning they walked out onto the Place

Vendôme and in wonderful slow leisure, at Van Cleef and Arpels, bought a diamond ring.

Pam knew Paris rather well, having been there frequently with her parents during the good times before her father's death, and she led Eddy easily to all the sights, from the Eiffel Tower to the Louvre. The fall season had begun, restoring the beautiful city, after the summer lull, to a thrilling life of concerts, theater, gallery openings, and discotheques.

In total companionship the two of them rollicked through three splendid weeks. They walked, danced, shopped, laughed, and thought in identical rhythms. And he was proud, swelling within, when men turned to glance at the healthy young woman, so unmistakably American even in her new French clothes, with her long hair, her confident long stride, and her white, perfect teeth.

## Chapter Nine

IT HAD been Eddy's idea to have a housewarming, a real smash. On the day of the party it was sleeting outdoors, and the cold was intense, so that in contrast Eddy and Pam's apartment was a southern garden, fragrant and warm. Connie arrived early, just as preparations were being completed.

The foyer walls were lined with flowering trees in marble tubs; the staircase leading to the second floor was decked with ropes and garlands of smilax. Casual overflowing bouquets of roses and freesia stood on tables and mantels in the library and the dining room, in Pamela's sitting room and Eddy's den. Back in the immense and still unfurnished drawing room, caterers had arranged gilt chairs and tables in a circle, leaving space for those who wanted to dance.

Connie felt awestruck. You could fit her apartment five times over into this one and still have space left. She walked back into the library. Its walls of French boiserie and the needlepoint rug were precious. Above the fireplace a new painting had been hung: a Sargent? The pearllike flesh, the dusky velvet, the woman's very pose were unmistakable. This was what you could do when you had *real* money. How ever had Eddy managed to achieve it all?

"Admiring the lady?" Eddy inquired from the doorway.

"Of course. When did she arrive?"

"Just in time for tonight. Isn't she a beauty? And the art nouveau lamp cost two hundred thousand. Don't worry, I know it's vulgar to talk prices. But come look—" he began, then Pam interrupted him.

"Darling, do leave your sister alone. When Eddy gets enthusiasms, I don't have to tell you how he throws himself into them with all his strength. Connie, you look beautiful as always."

Connie's sheer apricot silk dress was a column of Fortuny pleats in the style of ancient Greece.

"And how smart of you to wear no jewelry except earrings!"

"Thank you." I've learned, Connie thought. The sumptuous diamond tassels, an extravagance she had not resisted, were made to dazzle by themselves, without competition. "You look lovely, too."

"Well, white satin is the nearest I could get to wedding regalia," said Pam, who looked aristocratic and elegant. "I suppose I'll always be a trifle sorry that we didn't have a big wedding."

The doorbell rang, and Eddy said quickly, "We're having a varied crowd, Connie. There should be some interesting people for you."

It was difficult to tell who was "interesting" and who was not while drifting from room to room with the buzz of chatter in one's ears, a drink in one hand and a canapé in the other. There were the usual elderly married men wanting to strike up a conversation apart from their wives, and the usual hunters, some of them very attractive, jostling each other for a chance to take a young woman home and spend the night. Mostly Connie found herself standing on the fringe of some group gathered around Eddy. He was to be marveled at, she thought, as men, some of them twice his age, showed their regard for him. Her heart swelled with joy for her brother.

When dinner was announced, she located her place card on one of the tables in the library. The unaccompanied man seated next to her stood up and pulled out her chair. His dark, wavy hair was flecked with gray; he had remarkably fine brown eyes—watchful eyes—and a strong frame marred by a slight paunch.

"Martin Berg," he said, introducing himself.

"Connie Osborne. I'm Eddy's sister."

"Ah! Somebody said he had a beautiful sister. I had no idea I'd be lucky enough to have you as my dinner partner."

Beyond that, the man had little to say. When the first course came, a lobster bisque, he announced that he was hungry and began to eat. The others at the table, chiefly middle-aged married couples, apparently all knew one another. Several voluble conversations sprang up.

"Oh, were you at their Southampton affair? I hear they had flowers flown in from Europe. . . ."

". . . speaks French like a native, after school in Switzerland."

"Of course, it's all the thing to have a *mas* on some isolated hillside in Provence. She had a decorator from Paris do it."

Beneath this trivial, loud prattle came a soft voice, a whisper.

"You look far away," said Martin Berg.

"Do I? I didn't mean to."

"I think you're bored. I think it's your nature to be friendly."

"How can you tell?"

"I saw you before dinner, in the other room. Am I right?"

"Well, I usually do more talking than I've done here, but—"

"But these people are boring, and you wouldn't have had a chance to break in if you'd wanted to. So talk to me."

The mellow bass of the voice was, curiously, both appealing and demanding. She answered, "I'd like to. What shall I talk about?"

"About yourself. Are you married?"

"Divorced. And you?"

"Soon to be. We've been a long time separated, but there've been complications. Two children. Have you got babies?"

"Fortunately, no."

"You notice I said babies, not children. You can't be long out of school yourself."

"Thank you, but I'm not all that young. I'm twenty-seven."

"I'm forty-seven. My son's in college at the Sorbonne. And I have a little girl, a dear little girl, whom I miss most terribly."

Such a candid, pained admission from a stranger was unusual. He seemed a person so sure of himself that he could afford to say whatever he pleased, whenever and wherever his mood moved him. She glanced again from his face with its firm, narrow lips, to his fine, tasteful tie, to the equally tasteful watch.

"Where does your girl live?" she asked.

"In Paris, with her mother." Berg's manner turned brisk. "Let's talk about something cheerful. About your brother," he said deliberately. "Of course, you know they're all calling him the young

245

prince. And he really is a wonder. It took me years to get a footing on Wall Street, and look where he's gotten almost overnight."

"Oh, you're in finance, too?"

"Yes. Stocks and bonds." And for a moment he toyed with his dessert, a baked Alaska with a mound of meringue and a thick chocolate sauce. "I shouldn't eat this stuff, although sweets are my weakness. How do you manage to keep so thin?" he asked, for Connie had not left a particle on her plate.

"Exercise, daily workout."

"I should do it, too, but I hate exercise. The only kind I like is dancing. Would you like to dance now?"

They excused themselves and went to the drawing room. A little alcove in the semicircle of palms near the piano had been prepared for the musicians. Their pulsing music had brought almost everybody to the dance floor, gyrating to the tom-tom rhythm.

Berg danced well, and Connie saw by his smile that he was enjoying himself. Then the music changed from rock and roll to show tunes from *My Fair Lady,* and she had to move into his arms. She was almost as tall as he, so that their cheeks met. And when she turned her head, their eyes met. They were friendly eyes, like Richard's, except that there was no humor in them, or shyness either. Nor was there shyness in his firm hold around her waist.

When the music switched back to the tom-tom rhythm, Martin paused. "I've had enough of that for tonight, haven't you? How about going somewhere else for some real old-fashioned dancing? Or would you rather just go someplace for a quiet drink?"

He was obviously very very interested. And with a difference. What it was that made his interest different from the usual none-too-subtle bid for a night in bed she could not have said. She told him that a quiet drink would be very nice.

"Where shall it be, Connie?"

"My place," she told him.

"This is a pleasing room," he said, looking around the library.

"No Sargent over the fireplace. No fireplace, for that matter."

He shrugged. "What's the difference? Your brother's a rich man. He can afford a Sargent. And this is very nice. In good taste."

They were on their second glass of champagne. She was beginning to feel the wine's potency; her blood ran hot, and her words were coming too slowly. It became absolutely necessary to keep from falling asleep.

"We could put some music on and roll up the rug in the hall," she suggested.

"A great idea. Let's."

Firmly held again, she followed in perfect rhythm. Coming face to face, they regarded each other solemnly; then he placed a light kiss on her lips. His mouth was pleasing, with its fragrance of fruity wine. He kissed her again. Her head spun; they pressed more closely to each other. Presently the tape stopped. And still they stood together in a quiet so thick and deep that she could hear the throbbing of his heart. There was no question about what must follow.

In the bedroom, they undressed slowly, not taking their eyes away from each other. At last she stood naked of everything except the long diamond earrings.

Expertly he unscrewed the earrings and drew her onto the bed.

He knew how to please, how to prolong pleasure. Indeed, Connie had never had as much pleasure with anyone before. Quickly she grasped the fact that Berg was passionate and would want a passionate response from her. Not getting it, he might never come back. She hoped he would, for he was unmistakably a man, and she had had her fill of boys.

Sex was an art. Very well, then, she would practice it.


"You are," Martin said in the morning, "the best I've ever known." His eyes were bright with happiness and admiration.

It was late on a dark gray Sunday. But the kitchen, where they were having breakfast, was cheerful, the feeling companionable.

"So you're from Ohio?"

"A small-town girl."

"You surely don't look it. You look like Fifth Avenue. As for me, I'm from Flatbush—Brooklyn, that is. My parents were Polish immigrants. My father drove a taxi. . . . But that's of no interest to you."

"Oh, but it is." And it was, for in a startling instant she became aware that this man was the first person she had met since leaving Texas who had made his own way—that he had come, as she had, from the class that is called working. "Go on," she said.

"My parents are dead now. I'm the youngest of seven, one of only two born here. There's nothing unusual to tell, all considered. I worked hard. I've been a waiter, and I've pushed a handcart in the garment district. But I was also lucky, I know that. I got a scholarship to Yale and after that to the Wharton School."

"That's hardly the result of luck, Martin."

He shrugged. "My brother Ben is the remarkable one. He teaches economics in a community college. You'd expect him to be a freethinker, he's so antibourgeoisie and all, and yet he's religious, practically Orthodox. We're Jews, of course."

He wasn't concealing his origins; he was, in fact, being prideful about them, while hers were so repugnant to her that she must hide them not only from others but from herself as well. This became clear to her for the first time, and she heard herself saying to this stranger, "I always lie about myself. I let people think I'm from a Texas oil family. If I told you what my life was really like—"

Martin put up his hand. "You don't need to tell me anything. I'm only curious about why you're not lying to *me*."

"I don't really know." She played with the bacon and egg on her plate. Why? Perhaps because he created confidence, because he was so calm and composed and confident himself.

She said, "I suppose I feel that you won't care about backgrounds and families, the way other people do. And I trust you."

"I hope you don't trust everybody as quickly. It's dangerous."

There was a silence so prolonged that Connie, feeling uneasy, broke it by suggesting that they move out of the kitchen, onto more comfortable chairs in the library.

A small stack of books lay on a table next to a bowl of early tulips. Martin examined them. "You're reading *history*?" he asked. "Napoleon? The French Revolution?"

"I'm trying, a little at a time. I'm curious about history, art, music—everything."

He nodded. "My wife is crazy about France. She's gone off to live permanently in Paris. In the winter she takes an apartment in Cannes, though I don't know why. It can be freezing in the winter, and the beach is awful anyway."

Connie was curious. "Did she come from Brooklyn, too?"

"No. Doris' people were a couple of steps higher on the ladder.

They lived on the Upper West Side. She was a social worker when I met her. She's a fine person, very sensible. So why, then, the divorce?" Two dark furrows cut Martin's forehead, and his eyes looked suddenly weary. "It's insidious, this process of growing apart. Hard to analyze. Anyway, I've moved out of the apartment, though I still own it, and taken two rooms in a hotel, a far more cheerful place. But I miss my little girl. Let me show you a picture."

He got up and returned with his wallet. "Here she is. Melissa."

A plain child, a homely child, with Martin's dark eyes, looked up at Connie while he waited for a comment.

"She's sweet. She doesn't look like you, though, does she?"

"She looks like Doris. But she's *like* me. Her mind, her ways . . . she's like me. She was here for Christmas, and we had a great time. It broke my heart when I had to put her on the plane."

Connie felt the man's pain. "I'm sorry, Martin," she said gently. "I wish I could say something to make you feel better."

He caught her hand and held it between both of his. "You've done other things to make me feel better, Connie. I never expected— Honestly, I swear I never expected what happened last night. But you're a beautiful, vibrant, and passionate woman."

"I don't make a habit of things like this, I assure you."

"Nor do I. I was never a man for one-night stands. I want a relationship, a feeling for each other, with no holding back. I suppose you might as well hear this now, because we're going to be seeing a whole lot of each other, I think."

When Eddy telephoned that evening, Connie said, "I was just going to call and tell you both what a marvelous party that was."

"You left early."

"I didn't really want to, but Martin Berg—"

"I saw. You must have made a hit with him."

"He's very nice. He reminded me of you, in a way. Started out poor like you. Finance, securities— Isn't that what he does?"

"Oh, my Lord. You don't know who he is? He's Frazier, DeWitt, Berg! They've got five thousand employees and branch offices all over the world. It's one of the oldest white-shoe firms on the Street."

"And just what, pray tell, is a 'white-shoe firm'?"

"Old-line aristocrats. Firms that go back a couple of generations.

In this case Frazier's dead, but they keep the name. DeWitt took Berg in twenty years ago, in spite of his Brooklyn background, because he happens to be absolutely brilliant. They deal in billions. Hostile takeovers. Big, big fees, whichever side of the deal they happen to take. Where did you two go?"

"To my house. He's nice to talk to, very modest. You'd never think he was what you've told me."

"You think you'll see him again?"

"Maybe. You never can tell about men, can you?" Connie said cautiously. "But he's a sweet man. Really sweet."

THE months unfolded. Martin was extraordinary. He had prodigious energy, at work eighteen hours out of twenty-four. Every morning at half past six his chauffeur drove him from his rooms to a breakfast meeting at his office, at some other office, or at a hotel.

"I don't know where you get your energy," she would whisper when, half asleep, she heard him move through the room on tiptoe.

"As long as I have enough left for you," he would answer.

He had that, too. She would have been satisfied had he been much less ardent, but he would never know that, for her purpose was to please. His kindness, intelligence, and immaculate appearance made it easy to do the pleasing.

Joyously Martin bought and bought for Connie: a sable coat, a Burmese ruby from Harry Winston, a pair of diamond-studded bracelets from David Webb. She understood how much it meant to this man to make an entrance with a splendidly dressed young woman on his arm. What she did not understand were his ultimate intentions. Was she to be a cherished mistress or, finally, a wife?

He was unmistakably a powerful, attractive man. It would hurt to lose him. . . . A little shiver of fear would run down Connie's back while the essential question trembled, waiting to be asked. But she dared not ask it.

THE seasons flowed. In early spring they went to Vail in Martin's firm's private jet, and Connie learned to ski. In the summer there were open-air concerts in the city, and delightful sidewalk cafés. Sometimes on weekends they met Eddy and Pam on Long Island. The fall brought parties again—charity benefits and balls. Martin bought tickets and took tables for everything.

When Christmas approached, Martin announced that his daughter would spend the week with them in Palm Beach.

"I haven't used the house in two years, but I've been letting friends use it. I've invited Ben this time, too." Martin chuckled. "My brother doesn't approve of the house, you know. Says he doesn't approve of me either. But we get along fine, anyway."

These last words held a sting for Connie. Although she mentioned Eddy quite freely and happily, she had never told Martin anything about Lara except to say that she had a sister in Ohio, for she could not have mentioned the separation without tears. There was too much pain for her to enter into explanations.

In Palm Beach, at the end of the vast lawn stretching up from the ocean, immured by gates and shrubbery from public view, lay a long pink stucco house with a red tile Spanish roof. Striped awnings shaded the tall windows. Hibiscus and oleander blazed in the sunshine. Enormous rooms led to loggias, terraces, and a Mediterranean courtyard, where a fountain splashed.

Connie was looking over Martin's shoulder toward the pool and the guest wing. "How many rooms are there?" she inquired.

"Sixty-four. Not counting the separate quarters for gardeners."

Ben Berg and Melissa arrived within an hour of each other, and shortly afterward were seated at a little table in the courtyard having dinner. Three pairs of identical dark, heavy eyes surrounded Connie. All three Bergs had the same thick hair; the girl's was just a tangle of coarse black silk. The two brothers had the same alert and vigilant face, but Melissa's expression seemed either worried or perhaps just absentminded. At any rate, she was badly dressed, in sallow green with a loose wide collar. Her mother ought to know better or to care more, Connie thought pityingly.

The fountain trickled. No leaf stirred.

"A perfect night," Martin murmured. He reached across the table for his daughter's hand and held it. Melissa did not let go.

Long after the dessert was cleared away, the men were still talking about industry, arguing mildly now. Melissa did not speak, but Connie felt her furtive glances. She was wondering, probably, what Connie's position here might be, and could not know that Connie was wondering the same about herself.

251

The melancholy began to weigh heavily, and Connie stood. "We're forgetting about jet lag. For Melissa it's already past midnight."

"Of course," Martin said at once. "Go to bed. You, too, Connie. Maybe you ladies might want to do some shopping tomorrow."

With Melissa in the house Martin would of course stay in his own bed. So Connie lay awake in a room that was too large for one person to occupy alone. Her memory spun.

"How are things between Martin and you?" Eddy had recently inquired, meaning, You're starting the second year. When is he going to marry you? She had answered only, "Things are fine."

The divorce proceedings were taking their time, it was true. Still, there was no guarantee that Martin had anything else in mind but to continue as they were, even after the divorce became final. There were no guarantees of anything in this world, and nothing lasted forever. She should not be taking for granted this protected life, this gold-lined cocoon. Indeed, she should not have let herself grow fond of the man. And as she lay looking up at the dim ceiling a tightness came to her throat, as though she were about to cry.

THE day's purchases were spread on Melissa's bed, clothes for every possible occasion in the life of an eleven-year-old girl. Regarding herself in the mirror, Melissa allowed a timid smile to brighten her sober eyes. Peach-colored linen brought color to her pale cheeks. Her thick hair was smoothed back with a bandeau.

Connie, from her seat on the chaise longue, observed the change and remarked, "You like yourself. That's good."

"I'm going to wear this tonight. Daddy will like it."

"I'm sure he will."

The girl sat down on the edge of the bed and began to fold sweaters. Connie looked at her, round-shouldered and ungainly despite the improvements. It was absurd that this child should make her feel awkward. Yet as she was thinking of a way to make a smooth exit, Melissa spoke.

"Are you a special friend of Daddy's?"

"I'm a friend. I don't know what you mean by 'special.' "

"Oh, special. A lady who lives here."

Connie flushed; nevertheless, she pursued the subject. "Why? Do special friends usually live here?"

"Not always. But Daisy did. She was very pretty. When we left and went to live in Paris, I guess Daddy was lonesome, so Daisy moved in. But then I think he stopped liking her after a while."

"What makes you think that?" Connie kept her voice careless.

"She didn't want to go away, but Daddy told her to. I was here, and I heard them."

"I see. He told her to."

"Yes. I think I'll go swimming. Want to come?"

"Not just now. Maybe later I will."

For long minutes Connie stood in the bathroom staring at herself in the mirror. The flush had receded, leaving her face pale and shocked. He told her to go! Had that other woman—Daisy—also stood here before the mirror contemplating herself and her future? Had she, too, been "fond" of Martin Berg before she was cast out?

For a long time she stood absorbed by her own deliberations. Finally she fetched her cosmetic case from the bedroom, took out her birth control pills, and poured them down the toilet.

## Chapter Ten

MIDWAY through the spring Connie's guess was confirmed.

"You'll have a December baby," the doctor said.

She thought how ironic it was that, pregnant for the second time in uncertain circumstances, she should now find herself reassured. But it still remained for her to inform Martin, who might not be pleased at having fatherhood thrust upon him by his lover.

As it turned out, he was more astonished than anything else.

"But you were using the pill!" he exclaimed.

"I'm afraid it's not infallible."

"When will it be?"

"December."

After an ominous silence Martin looked thoughtful. "At least the timing is convenient. My divorce is final in thirty days. I found out this morning. I picked this place for dinner to celebrate."

They were at La Grenouille, one of their favorite choices for dining out. She looked past him at a mass of yellow hyacinths.

"We can be married over the Memorial Day weekend. We'll have a seventh- or eighth-month baby."

253

She understood. He had his position to maintain. Modern times or no, the world of finance was not the world of theater or the arts.

He smiled. "Now that I've absorbed the shock, it's really rather nice, you know. Let's order champagne."

They toasted each other. Martin became talkative; once he had accepted a reality, he always began to organize projects around it.

"We'll have to move into my apartment. Wait till you see it. It's spectacular, a whole floor overlooking Fifth Avenue. Of course, it needs to be completely done over. Melissa needs a proper room, no matter how seldom she uses it. And bear in mind a room for my son. He may never sleep in it, but do it anyway. And guest rooms. I suppose your sister will want to bring her family sometimes."

"Perhaps not. They're so busy building up the business. . . ."

Pictures flashed: Lara as she must look standing in the doorway of the new house; standing with Davey in front of the proud façade of the Davis Company; Lara bringing her supper tray on the last night; Lara . . . The trouble was that the longer one waited to make a healing move, to write a letter or to pick up the telephone, the more difficult it became, until finally it was impossible.

"Well, I'll be having people fly in now and then. Still, we'll have the wedding—a garden wedding—at my place in Westchester. It will need a little freshening up, that's all. It's in good shape."

"I wondered why you've never shown it to me, or the apartment either," Connie said.

"Because I didn't remember much joy in either one of those places. But now you'll bring joy. And beauty. And life."

There were twenty-seven rooms in the apartment. Passing piles of furniture draped in sheets, Connie followed Martin into a gymnasium, a poolroom, a music room, a restaurant-size kitchen, and more. The dining-room floor was marble, but the Victorian chairs were ugly, as was a gigantic painting of men and horses whirling in battle among half-naked women. Connie wrinkled her nose.

Martin laughed. "Yes, it's awful. Get rid of it. I want you to hire the best decorator in town, give him carte blanche. It's our home. His home." He poked her gently in the stomach. "Or hers."

Connie felt the excitement as she looked about the grand rooms. The new life she was nurturing within her would enter the world in possession of all this, the safety and the grandeur.

Now began a friendly rivalry between Connie and Eddy, who had long since discovered the lure of the auction galleries. "Although," Martin grumbled good-naturedly, "I don't understand how your brother finds time for such stuff." And then he added, "I hope he's on firm ground, Connie. He's soared like a Roman candle."

"Don't worry about Eddy. He's always known what he's doing."

Often the brother and sister went together, seeking treasures. Connie bought a pair of Tang horses, eighth century. Eddy bought a Tiffany desk. She bought a Chinese vase for twelve thousand dollars and two jewel-studded Fabergé eggs.

"You're spending a fortune," he said. "Berg doesn't mind?"

"He told me to."

The brother and sister stared at each other. "Can you believe what we're doing? That it's really us?"

"And that you're going to be Mrs. Martin Berg!" cried Eddy.

Things changed. From having lived, albeit luxuriously, in the background of Martin's life as an almost anonymous feminine companion, now Connie was made visible. Early one morning she accompanied him to his office on Wall Street.

A private elevator took them to the trading floor. Row upon row of desks faced a large electronic board where numbers flickered in a continuous march. More lights blinked from telephones on the desks, at each of which sat a man with piles of papers in front of him.

"Block trading." Martin spoke just above a whisper. "Huge blocks for institutions and pension funds. They can move millions of dollars in minutes. Fascinating, don't you think?"

She thought it more static than fascinating to watch a man sit like a zombie, a telephone stuck in his ear. But she agreed.

"Trading is the core of the business, Connie. Mergers and acquisitions are the big thing these days, of course, and I'm in the midst of them, from Zurich to Tokyo, but I never forget that right here is where I began. Okay, let's go on to mergers and acquisitions."

As they walked through the floor above, Martin continued. "Behind every one of these doors sits some bright young M.B.A. working on a deal that can either earn millions for the firm or go bust. If too many of his deals go bust, he goes, too. He's got to produce to earn his six hundred thousand a year, let me tell you. These fellows

255

*work*. Twenty-four hours at a stretch sometimes when they're near to a closing. Well, here's my lair."

The room was modern, neat, and spare. It was utilitarian, with its own electric quote board at one end. The only decoration was a ficus tree. Connie walked to the bank of windows and saw the narrow stretch of Manhattan from river to river, saw the harbor, the twin towers of the World Trade Center, the Statue of Liberty.

Martin smiled at her. "Come meet my partner, across the hall."

Preston DeWitt stood up at his desk when they came in. He was very tall and thin; his close-shaven narrow cheeks were pink, and his lavish white hair sprang crisply on either side of the part.

Martin made the introduction. "I'm playing hooky, Preston. Taking Connie to lunch at '21' in honor of our engagement."

"Splendid." The accent was crisp, too, verging on the British, Connie thought. "And when's the wedding?"

"Memorial Day weekend, in the country," Martin said.

"You can bet I'll be there. It's all just splendid."

In these few moments Connie appraised Preston DeWitt. The keen black eyes, so odd in contrast to the fair skin, were calculating. The suit looked absolutely starched, as if he never sat down. He's handsome, really startling, Connie thought.

"Do you see each other socially?" she asked Martin when they were in the elevator.

"Rarely. But don't get me wrong. We like each other. I have a lot of respect for Preston. He works hard, and he doesn't even have to. He inherited this firm, but he's also got independent wealth from his mother's family. Mines and lumber for three generations."

"It's remarkable you fit so well together, being so different."

"Hey, I've quadrupled the assets since I came in! This was purely and simply a brokerage firm, and I'm the one who's turned it into a powerful investment bank. Preston knows that."

Once in the car, they rolled along Wall Street. A cold April rainstorm had arisen, a brief return of winter. People were hurrying along the windy streets, crowding the subway entrances, pushing through the crowds. But inside the car as it rolled uptown to "21," it was warm and dry. Connie sighed and stretched her legs in comfort. To be so safe, and so removed from the poor souls in the streets and in the subways, was bliss.

Forty-three acres surrounded Cresthill, Martin's residence among the low hills of northern Westchester County. From the window of the room where Connie stood, she could see the tennis courts, the heated pool, the stables, and the woods beyond. When the door opened, she turned toward Martin.

"Are you sure you feel all right?" he asked.

"I feel absolutely wonderful. I don't look pregnant?"

"No one could possibly guess."

"I've gained eight pounds. It would show if this skirt weren't so full." She smoothed the diaphanous pink silk.

Martin put his arm around her waist. In the mirror that faced them she could see the white carnation in his buttonhole; she could see his happiness.

"The judge is already here, but we've got half an hour. People are still arriving. And Eddy just came. Shall I send him up?"

"Do. I'm getting nervous up here all by myself."

One could hear Eddy's approach even on carpeted stairs and floors. His running steps thudded; he rattled keys, cleared his throat, made *noises.* Now he almost leaped into the room.

"Wonder why you haven't gotten my wedding present yet?" he shouted. "Go to the front window. Look down on your right."

Cars were lined up in the big graveled circle and all down the driveway as far as she could see.

"Where am I supposed to look?"

"Behind where the Rolls' chauffeur stands. What do you see?"

"What a question! I see a station wagon."

He corrected her. "A Mercedes station wagon. Like it?"

"Of course. It's stunning."

"Well, it's yours. From Pam and me."

"Eddy! You're a darling! I love it. You're both darlings," Connie said. "Why doesn't Pam come up so I can thank her?"

"You can thank her later." Eddy hesitated, grew grave, and exclaimed softly, "What a pity that you never invited Lara!"

Connie drew a sharp breath and sat down. "Oh, Eddy! How can you do this to me today? I did invite her. I sent a letter last week, with such fears, I can't tell you! I didn't know how she would take it. And I haven't heard a word. I knew she wouldn't come."

Eddy threw his head back in delighted laughter. "Oh, but you're wrong! She's here waiting, Connie. She wanted to surprise you."

"Oh, Eddy. Where is she? Bring her in!"

Connie's eyes, brimming with tears all mingled with mascara, stung so sharply that Lara seemed to be wavering in the doorway. She's grown older, Connie thought. And she held out her arms.

Lara cried. Then, murmuring, "I mustn't crush your dress," she let go of Connie, saying over and over, "But I am so glad, so glad."

"You didn't answer me, so I thought you weren't coming."

"Oh, I was hoping you would invite us. Davey said, and Eddy said so many times, long before this, that I should call you." Lara's eyebrows drew together. "I wanted to, but I dreaded a rejection."

Eddy, who was watching them like a proud, tender parent, said quickly, "I'm going to leave you two now, but I'll be back."

The sisters were left with years' worth of living to disclose.

"Eddy tells me your little girl is darling," Connie began.

"Oh, she is. I am so grateful for the way my Sue's growing."

"And he tells me Davey and you have a fabulous business."

"Well, he ought to know. He's had enough to do with it. But *fabulous* is a big word."

"Doesn't Eddy always use big words? Big—that's Eddy. But I'm impressed, anyway. When I think of that shed in your backyard, when I think of so many things we lived through together . . ."

"Sometimes it doesn't do to remember too much. I wish I could forget the things I said to you. I was too harsh, Connie. I guess it was just that after all those years of wanting a baby, I went crazy because you could have one and didn't want it."

"Don't," Connie said gently. "It's past, it's over."

"You're right." Lara glanced around the room. "This house! I've never seen anything like it. You're living like a princess, Connie."

"Did you meet Martin when you came in?"

"Briefly. Eddy introduced us."

"He's very sweet. You'll see. You'll really like him."

"If you love him, of course I will."

The conversation came to a stop. They were examining each other. She is sturdy and comforting, Connie said to herself. She copes.

"What are you seeing when you look at me so gravely?" asked Lara.

Connie shook her head. "No, no, I was only seeing your dress. I like the color, the blue. But you have put on some weight."

"Fifteen pounds."

"As much as that! How did you let it happen?"

"Guess." Lara's eyes were very bright. "I'm pregnant. I'm in my sixth month. So you see, I'm really not all that fat."

Connie got up and put her arms around Lara. Moved to the heart, she could find nothing to say.

"Connie, no tears," Lara protested gently. "Your makeup."

"Did Eddy tell you I was pregnant, too?"

Eddy, appearing just then at the door, denied that. "Definitely not. I considered that your secret if you wanted to keep it. Now, take a look at who's here."

"Davey!" There he stood, almost shyly, with a twinkling smile. "Come in and let me hug you. You look surprised. . . . You heard what I said."

"It seems as if an awful lot's happening at once. That's why."

"When is it to be?" asked Lara.

"Not till December."

And Davey said, "We're happy for you."

"Yes, both of them are making an uncle out of me," Eddy said. "Or I should say 'again,' because I am one already. Where is she? Where are you, Sue?"

"Here." And from behind Davey stepped a dark-haired little girl in a party dress.

"This is Aunt Connie," Lara announced. "Isn't she pretty in her bride dress?"

Great solemn eyes stared at Connie. "She's not as big as you are, Aunt Lara."

"Her baby's not as near to being born as ours is. That's why."

"The baby's room is pink," Sue interposed, "and I'm giving her a pink cat when she comes. I bought it with my allowance."

They've worked some sort of miracle here, Connie thought, recollecting Eddy's first accounts of a frightened orphaned waif and Lara's patient struggles. Bending to kiss Sue on either cheek, she said, "I think your baby will be the luckiest baby in the world to have a sister like you."

Connie's eyes met Lara's over Sue's head. The emotion inside the room was tangible, almost too much to be borne.

Eddy must have sensed the need to lighten the moment, for with mock brusqueness he gave orders: "Come on, everybody, hurry down. I'm giving the bride away, and I'll be ready and waiting to make our grand entrance."

Connie floated. In her long pink dress, the color of evening clouds, she floated down the spiral stairs to Eddy, then into the drawing room and down the aisle between the guests, on their little gilt chairs, to where Martin stood waiting. Beside her hovered a singular creature, her own spirit, cannily observing the event and everyone in it, including herself.

The judge is wizened; his voice is as dry as his words. In a few minutes the ring is given, and it is all over. Martin bends down and kisses Connie; it is a long kiss on the mouth, and she is embarrassed before all these people. She catches Bitsy Maxwell's eye. Now she is infinitely richer than Bitsy, which is what counts.

They are walking back down the aisle between two rows of smiles. Eddy winks, and Pam blows a kiss. There's Preston's white patrician head. Martin's son is sullen; he came unwillingly. There's Melissa in a beautiful French dress with real lace, but green again. Her mother must not like her. Connie will help her. Connie will be good to Martin's children, will do everything right.

Now they stand in the receiving line to be kissed and congratulated. The guests disperse among the airy rooms and out into the gardens. Music strikes up, music for happiness.

How Connie loves all this! She is glowing.

TABLES were set up under flowered umbrellas on the terraces and lawns. Waiters bearing silver trays offered hors d'oeuvres so lavish as to make superfluous the dinner that followed inside.

So large and so diverse was the crowd that friends had a hard time finding each other. Meanwhile Pam, in a black-and-white print dress, was saying to Eddy, "This must be wonderful country for horses. We ought to buy a place like this, Eddy. I'm getting tired of Long Island. It's gotten too crowded, even in the best parts of it. I visited Kentucky once, and I loved it, loved all that space—"

"Kentucky? I can't live there, honey. It's too far."

"It could be an investment. Horses can make a lot of money."

"You'd really like it?"

"I'd adore it."

"All right, then. When I retire. I promise I'll keep it in mind."

And why not? Make her happy. That's what life is all about, what money is for, he thought. And he imagined himself saying someday, "Our place in Kentucky"; he imagined himself riding over hundreds of acres, all his own; he imagined, too, the people who would be their friends and neighbors, the southern gentry.

"Your sister's done well for herself," Pam remarked now, "taking a big step farther up with each marriage." She mused, "It's remarkable how different your two sisters are. I mean temperamentally. Lara's so strong, much more so than Connie."

"I wouldn't say that."

"I would." She nodded. "Sometime you'll see that I'm right."

At that moment Lara was not feeling especially strong. Her feet, in the new shoes bought for this occasion, had begun to hurt. And the baby under her skirt's flounce had been doing some vigorous exercise. So Davey and she had scurried for two vacant seats in the shade of the laurel hedge, while Sue, who had found a boy about her own age, went wandering off with him.

Before long, however, they joined the movement up the rise toward the house for dinner. By the time they found Pam and Eddy, the bride and groom were already alone on the dance floor. Connie's pale dress floated, and her pale hair tumbled as they whirled. Frankly exuberant and frankly triumphant, she sang, *"I could have danced all night,"* into the faces of the smiling crowd.

To Lara, as she watched, there came memories—first of the small, demanding sister, then of the young woman leaving home because "there had to be more to life" and "I'm not like you, Lara."

She took her husband's hand. "Isn't she beautiful? I hope she'll be happy this time, Davey!"

"Oh, Connie gets what Connie wants. But happy? That's something else," he replied.

## Chapter Eleven

THE week-old baby lay sleeping in a bassinet beside the bed on which Lara rested. Afternoon sunlight touched her little round head and glinted on a soft red-gold fuzz.

Eddy observed, "She's going to have Peg's hair."

Pam asked, "Are you going to call her Peggy, or will you be formal and stay with Margaret?"

Lara laughed. "Whatever comes naturally, I guess, though we seem to have begun with Peggy."

Eddy focused his Polaroid camera on the baby. "Connie said to take some pictures. She was so angry that her doctor doesn't want her to fly. . . . What time is that stockholders' meeting?"

"Half past three. Davey's picking Sue up at school, and then you and he can go on to the plant. We're all off our schedules this week on account of Miss Peggy." And Lara felt a smiling warmth from head to toe. "Oh, there they are. I hear the car."

A moment later came a clattering on the stairs. Sue and another little girl, followed more quietly by Davey, tore into the bedroom.

"Mom! Mom! I've brought my friend to see our baby. She didn't believe we have one, so I brought her."

The two children glanced briefly into the white bassinet.

"Can we touch her hand?" asked Sue.

"If you're very gentle. Babies are very soft. You haven't told me your friend's name, Sue."

"Oh, yes. This is Marcy. And this is my mom. And my sister's name is Peggy. Are there any ice-cream sticks in the freezer?"

"Yes, darling. Daddy will get them for you."

When the little group had clattered back downstairs, Lara reached for a handkerchief. "Excuse me. I feel a bit teary."

"Why, what's the matter?" asked Pam.

"You didn't notice, of course. But this was the first time she called me Mom." Lara looked toward the bassinet. "I'm so happy that I'm in a daze. Nothing seems quite real. How can happiness like this last?"

"It's real, and it will last," Eddy declared heartily.

With that he went downstairs to join Davey.


"So you've got friendly stockholders," Eddy said on the way into town. "That's one of the nice things about a small community. Sometimes I miss it."

"Sure you do!" Davey laughed. "You couldn't wait to get away from here, you know that. I happen to be comfortable with small-ness. I've known every one of my stockholders practically from the

cradle up: Doc Donnelly and Henry Baker—he's the superinten-
dent of schools, and he was a friend of my father's—and my best
friend, Tony. They have total confidence in me. It's a good feeling,
Eddy. Sometimes I think I'm the luckiest man in the world."

"I wonder," Eddy said, "whether after your meeting—incidentally,
it's very nice of you to let me listen in—if you would have any
objection to my presenting a few of my ideas about personal fi-
nances? Some of your people might be interested. Of course, this
is totally apart from your company."

"Sure. Go ahead. It's fine with me if anybody wants to stay."

This, Eddy reflected as he watched the proceedings, is unlike any
stockholders' meeting I've ever attended. There were no challenges, no arguments, no hostile questions from the handful of men
and one decorous middle-aged lady. He saw distinctly what Davey
had described. He recognized the honest, forthright personalities.

Davey in his plain, frank way introduced Eddy.

"This is the man who is really responsible for the birth of the
company. He made me put my ideas to work. And now Mr. Vernon
Osborne, whom we all call Eddy, would like to say a few words."

After a few enthusiastic remarks about Davey and the Davis
Company, Eddy came quickly to the point.

"I can't tell you how happy I was just now to learn of your fine big
dividend. However"—and here Eddy made a significant pause—
"let's just take a second look at your personal income tax returns.
Oh, my! How many of those beautiful dollars will be yours to keep
and how many belong to Uncle Sam? Now, I would like to explain
to you a way in which, by buying a limited partnership, you can
keep a larger part of that income—or even the whole of it—legally.
Yes, no tax at all! Possibly you're not familiar with ten-to-one write-
offs and tax deferrals. The write-offs in some investments can be
tremendous. Cattle, movies, lithographs. . . ."

He was in his usual top form. His presentation extended an hour,
and by the end of it he had convinced all twelve of his listeners, who
agreed to invest sums ranging from fifteen thousand to seventy-
five. A very satisfactory meeting came to a close.

On the way home Eddy asked, "What about you, Davey?"

"I don't think so. I'd rather pay my taxes and sleep nights."

Eddy did not reply. Best to drop the subject instead of using one's valuable energy trying to move this—this *mule*. Sometimes Davey could be infuriating.

When Pam and Eddy had gone home that night, Davey sat on the edge of the bed and talked.

"I wouldn't touch that stuff with a ten-foot pole. Ten-to-one write-offs! Why, it's not even moral. The losses are fabricated, they're artificial. It's just a gimmick—the whole thing!"

Lara spoke mildly. "It's apparently a legal gimmick, Davey."

"I don't care whether it's legal or not. It's indecent. I'm going to advise everybody who was there today not to send his check in."

"You're not!" Lara stood beside the bassinet, hands on her hips. "You can't be going to tell them you don't trust Eddy!"

"Of course I wouldn't say that. I'll say I don't believe in the deal. Lithographs—good Lord! These are my friends, Lara. My friends."

"But Eddy's my brother! How can you go behind his back? How can you? It's all right if you personally don't want to invest, but to tell other people not to is unconscionable."

The argument went on a long time. In the end Davey agreed.

"Maybe I'm making a mountain out of a molehill," he said.

## PART TWO
### 1981–1990
### Chapter Twelve

GOLDEN times these were, spent in health and comfort. The sisters, in spite of living so far apart, were closer than ever. Connie, too, had had a daughter, named Thérèse, who had come into the world with little fuss on a blustering December afternoon. If Peg could know, Connie thought, she would be so thankful to see us and to see another generation growing up. Even the two husbands got along well. Their backgrounds and experiences were surely different enough; yet because both were busy men with many interests, they were compatible. Martin's charities were on a colossal scale that frequently were front-page news. But Davey, too, could take pride, and did, in his contributions to his town: a day-care plan for his workers, a library fund drive, and more.

Sometimes, on a weekend when Davey was free, Martin would send the company plane to pick up the Davises and bring them to

Westchester for sports or to New York for the theater, for which he was always able to procure the best seats. He loved putting his ample houses to use, and they were rarely empty.

One fall afternoon the little girls, now three, were playing in Connie's Fifth Avenue drawing room while their mothers, along with Thérèse's Scottish nurse, watched over them. Thérèse was like Melissa—pale, small-sized, and serious. The child looked up at Connie now out of Martin's brown eyes; but unlike his, hers were wistful. And within Connie two feelings struggled with each other: resentment and a fierce, determined love. She must protect Thérèse, teach her how to take care of herself.

Lara's child was chuckling over a ball that kept rolling out of reach. Two large dimples appeared in her cheeks; her red-gold hair curved loosely about her charming face. And Connie wondered what Lara would be feeling if Thérèse were hers. . . .

EDDY strode rapidly across Madison Avenue to his office. Bad luck, that's all it was. It had always worked before. But dealing with the IRS was like sticking your hand into a grab bag. And it would have to be those folks out in Ohio who got caught.

Well, Abner Saville would know. He was one of the smartest accountants in the city. Eddy hastened his steps. Abner, in his calm, rational way, would surely quiet his jangling nerves.

"You sounded awfully upset when you asked me to come over," Abner began as soon as Eddy entered the room.

"Did I? Well, I guess I was a little upset. It's not like me, is it? But I've had a couple of nasty telephone calls these last few days."

Abner's black eyebrows rose in surprise. "Nasty? What about?"

"I sold a bunch of tax shelters a few years back in Ohio. My sister's husband has a business with twelve stockholders, all his friends. They bought limited partnerships from me. Now it seems the IRS will disallow the deductions. These people are in a frenzy." Eddy sighed. "The deal was so beautiful, too. Ten to one."

The black eyebrows rose higher into a troubled forehead.

"Ten to one! They can't have been real estate partnerships."

"No. Lithographs."

"I could have told you that would never wash, Eddy."

"It has washed."

"Yes? How many times."

"Well, once. It's been several years now, and not a word."

"So it slipped by once. A fluke. You should have known that deductions like those make no financial sense and that the government was bound to catch up with them. Eddy, the IRS is starting to go after fake losses in a big, big way."

"They're not 'fake' losses!"

"Eddy, you know better. You've been my client for a long time, a very important one, and a very good friend besides. It's no pleasure for me, I assure you, to disagree with you."

"All I want to know is, can these people sue me for anything?"

Abner grimaced. "No. It wasn't fraud on your part. You just gave them terrible advice. But it surely doesn't do much for your reputation, and it will be bad for them. Back taxes, penalties, and interest besides. No fun." Abner stood up. "Before I leave, Eddy, I'd like to give you some advice."

Eddy managed a smile. "What? Again?"

"Yes, again. I'm not happy about your tax deferrals. Some of your figures puzzle me. I need to go over your books very very carefully, but I advise you to stop playing at brinkmanship, Eddy."

Saville gave with one hand and took away with the other. It was a vast relief to know that he wasn't going to be sued. But the talk of "brinkmanship" left Eddy feeling insecure, and resentful at being challenged. Arriving in the outer hall at home, he did not announce himself with his customary signal whistle.

Pam greeted him with a kiss. "Smell the paella? We've got a marvelous cook at last. Why, what's the matter? You look bushed."

He answered merely, "I'm fine, but it was a long day."

They were having their after-dinner coffee when the phone rang. Pam answered, then said, "It's Davey. He wants to talk to you."

Anticipating another long, defensive explanation, Eddy settled into an armchair in the den and, cheerfully covering his dread, began, "Hello, Davey. How's everything?"

Davey was glum. "Bad. Very bad, Eddy. Every person who bought a partnership has been called for an audit. And every one has been told by his accountant that he doesn't stand a chance."

"Wait, hold on! I think you're jumping at conclusions. The principals here in New York, the guys who produce the litho-

267

graphs, I know they'll put up a fight. They've got more to lose—"

"That's bunk, Eddy." The accusing voice grew louder. "My friend Tony will lose the whole inheritance from his aunt, and more besides because he borrowed from his cousin. Look, the details don't matter. But Tony's not speaking to me."

"That's ridiculous. Why should he be sore at you?"

"I'm the one who recommended your judgment, remember?"

"Davey, I'm very sorry," Eddy said softly. "Lord knows my intentions were of the best. But you have to admit there are risks in any investment, whether it's a horse, a house, or—anything."

"It seems that this was less an investment than a gamble. I am resentful, Eddy. Every one of my stockholders, my trusting friends, is my enemy now because of this. Lara can't walk into Ben Levy's store to buy the kids socks, she's so ashamed to face him."

Never in all their years had Eddy known Davey to be so agitated. Davey, gone over to the attack! This thing was escalating.

"I'm sorry. I've said I am. But those people made an investment, it went sour, and that's too bad. I have no legal obligation to them."

"So you don't intend to do anything. That's it, is it?"

What a day! Eddy's nerves—those steady, healthy nerves that so seldom even made their presence known—were quivering.

"Look, Davey, I've never known you to be so unreasonable. Frankly, you're driving me to my wits' end over this sorry business, which I deeply regret. How many times do I have to tell you? So will you kindly let me alone, will you—"

"Oh, I'll let you alone, all right. You can bet I'll do that."

Who first hung up the telephone it was impossible to say. For a long minute Eddy sat still. He was angry; he was humiliated and sad. How could this have happened to Eddy Osborne, the conciliator, who avoided argument, above all in his family?

THESE were dark wintry days in Ohio, miserable days.

"Is this to be another wasteful feud like the one between Connie and me?" demanded Lara. "Every time I talk to Pam, it looks more hopeless, and we feel terrible about it. She can't get anywhere with Eddy, and I can't get anywhere with you."

"I'm tired of talking about it," Davey answered wearily. "And I have to think you don't really understand my position."

"Well, I'm not the only one. Connie says that Martin's position is Let the buyer beware.'"

"Oh, beautiful! I wonder how Martin would like to confront our stockholders and feel their outrage directed straight at him!"

It was after supper, and the late February evening was still fairly light. Peggy asked to go outside, and Lara fastened her snowsuit and showed her to the door while talking furiously over the child's head.

"All right, the IRS disallowed the deductions, and they have to pay up. Oh, it's not fun, but it's not the worst thing in the world either. They have no right to be blaming you or Eddy."

Davey had no more heart for analyzing; this night was a repetition of a dozen other nights. And yet he had to add something new.

"If I had invested with them, it would be different. This way it looks suspicious, as if I should have advised them not to believe in the project. As if I didn't believe in it! Only *you* wouldn't let me, Lara, remember? You said it would be awful to undermine him—"

"Yes. And he's done a lot for us, hasn't he?"

"Anybody in your family you'll defend. Especially Eddy."

"He's the salt of the earth. He's entitled to a mistake."

"Some mistake!"

"I never thought you'd be an ingrate, Davey Davis. Oh, for heaven's sake, who's at the back door?"

Someone was pounding, rattling the knob. Lara ran.

"Whatever do you want?" she began. And then at the sight of Sue's face at the door she cried, "What? What happened?"

The child was terrified. "Peggy! She fell down the Burkes' stairs." She began to cry. "Oh, Mom, she won't move!"

They flew. In the neighbor's floodlit front yard a little group had already gathered at the bottom of the long flight of stone steps. Lara thrust through the barricade of legs and stooped backs to reach her baby—her baby, whose cap had fallen off, whose hair lay spread upon the snow, whose eyes were closed. Lara fell on her knees.

A voice said, "Don't move her. You're not supposed to."

More voices babbled. "The ambulance ought to be here in a minute." "They take so long." "Don't touch her. . . ."

Sue wept on Lara's shoulder. "Mom, Mom, I was in Amy's house next door, and Peggy must have been looking for me at the Burkes' and slipped on the ice— Oh, Mom!"

269

But Lara said nothing as she knelt there staring at her child.

Davey put his head against Peggy's chest. As if one could hear a heartbeat through that thick snowsuit! He looked up at Lara.

"She's just fainted. That's all it is." Then with a queer, awkward gesture he put his hands over his face, and someone led him away.

People helped Lara climb into the ambulance, where she and Davey sat beside the stretcher. Endlessly they rode through the darkening empty streets. Lara had never been so cold. Davey put his hand over hers, and they sat, still without speaking, never taking their eyes away from Peggy, who had not yet moved.

Lights from the emergency wing glared into the courtyard. Once they got inside there, it would somehow be all right. People there would know at once what to do. Yes, yes, Peggy would be fine again. Lara's thoughts spun.

Such a tiny body in her overalls and T-shirt, such a small body next to such big ones all in white! Doctors, nurses, interns; who was who? Low, hurried voices spoke and came back again to look, to touch and listen. Peggy's labored breathing was like a snore—a dreadful sound, but at least it proved that she was alive.

They were taking her blood pressure, listening to her heart.

"No blood in the lungs," announced a young man with a stethoscope around his neck.

But surely that was blood seeping out of her ears? Still almost speechless, Lara pointed.

"That's from the skull fracture," the young man said, adding kindly, "It need not be as dreadful as it sounds."

Now Peggy's little face began to swell. One could almost see it happening as the flesh rose, black and blue. A crust of blood had hardened on one cheek. Lara bent to wipe it away.

"Will she wake up soon?" It was her first question—a foolish one, she knew as she was asking it.

Davey shook his head and said, "Darling, it takes time."

Suddenly the little body stiffened. It rose into an arc, straightened, then arched again with head thrown back and arms and legs frantically flailing from side to side.

"My God!" cried Lara, grasping Davey's arm.

They were putting a tongue depressor into Peggy's mouth and holding her firmly.

"A seizure," a nurse told Lara. "Look away. It will be over in a minute or two."

"But why?" Lara wailed. "Why?"

The seizure ended as abruptly as it had begun, and the child lay back, inert. The slow, noisy breathing resumed. Davey was motioned aside. After swift talk at the far end of the room, he came back to Lara.

"They'll be taking her for X rays of the chest and skull. And after that, an electroencephalogram."

So she knew. She knew enough about brain damage to understand. If she had had any thoughts—and she had had them—about swift repairs in this emergency room, after which they would take Peggy home as good as new, she now knew better.

HOURS in the intensive care unit were to follow. Now came the specialists—the otolaryngologists, the ophthalmologists, and the neurologists—to observe, to test, to prescribe, and in the end to speak less frequently of hope. The child was still unconscious. Every third hour the parents were allowed to see her.

They had almost forgotten Sue. That night each had asked the other whether they had told Sue to watch Peggy in the yard, and each answered, "No. I thought you had."

"So that's why she was at Amy's. Peggy left a bit later, I remember now. We were arguing," Lara said, weeping. "Arguing like fools."

On the second day Connie flew in to stay a few days. And the next day Eddy arrived with Pam. Pam took Lara into her arms, but Eddy went first to embrace Davey.

"Davey, Davey, there are no words for this. I take back every mean word I said to you that night. God help us all."

Davey's eyes were wet. "It's all unimportant, not worth a breath. Only our baby matters. . . . Thank you for being here, Eddy."

From everywhere came an outpouring of concern and help. Neighbors took Sue to school and watched the house. The telephone rang, the mail flowed; there were fifty names on a huge card from Peggy's nursery school. Even those who had felt so bitterly unforgiving toward Davey came through. As Henry Baker, meeting Davey at the gas station, said as he took his hand, "One thing has nothing to do with the other. I pray for the child."

271

At the end of the third week Peggy was moved to the subacute floor. The threat of infection was past, the swelling was down, and her face looked normal. It was the face of a child asleep.

"In a way it's worse," Lara said to Davey. "When she looked so awful, we could blame everything on that and look forward—as if as soon as she looked like herself, she would really be herself. And now there's nothing . . ." The words trailed off.

"I know," Davey said. And then, perhaps to give his wife some encouragement that he himself did not feel, he reminded her that "all the doctors say it will take time, darling. Patience."

Connie flew in once or twice every week, making, without intending to, a small stir in the hospital every time.

A nurse said to Lara, "Your sister's beautiful," and then almost apologetically added, "Well, you do look alike. Her clothes are what I meant. They're so—well, you know—so New York. Is it true she comes in a private plane?"

Yes, it was true.

"Such a good sister! So devoted."

That was true, too.

"Martin says you should get another opinion," Connie reported one day.

"We've had a half dozen, and they all say the same thing. Wait."

But nothing was happening. The weeks went by, the snow melted, spring came, with lilac and forsythia, and still Peggy lay asleep, the sweet head quiet on the pillow.

In the beginning of the third month they were summoned to the hospital. The doctor, obviously troubled, spoke somberly.

"We'll have to face it. There's nothing more we can do for Peggy here. I think you should look at a chronic-care facility."

Davey let that sink in for a second or two. Then he whispered, "Chronic? You mean she could spend the rest of her life there?"

"She could."

No longer did Lara or Davey spend the whole day at the hospital. An anxious young girl at home still had to be cared for and cooked for. The Davis Company had to be looked after, too. They were both as keenly aware of these realities as of the dreadful reality that waited on the fourth floor of the hospital. And so, like walking ghosts, they did what was necessary, day after day, and waited.

From her office window one afternoon Lara looked out onto the parking lot, where a long bank of weeping willows that had been little more than sprouts a few years ago stood like green fountains. Idly, because it was so hard for her tortured mind to concentrate, she wondered about the young man in the impeccable suit who had jumped so briskly from his car and gone into Davey's office. The door opened, and Davey brought him into the room.

"This is Mr. Harrison. He represents the P.T.C. Longwood Company," he told her. "And since you're an officer of the Davis Company, I think you should hear what he has to say."

"Happy to meet you," Mr. Harrison said to Lara.

"Mr. Harrison has a proposal. I'm not at all interested, but—"

"If you're not," said Lara, "then I won't be either."

"It won't take long," the man said. "I'd just like you to listen for five minutes, no more. My company—I'm sure you know it's one of the top hundred corporations in the country—is interested in patents that you hold for several surgical items. Cardiac, orthopedic and— You're familiar with them, I'm sure, Mrs. Davis?"

"Very familiar. My husband invented them all."

Harrison smiled. "Of course. Here are some of our products. We are a conglomerate, as you must know. We make rubber footwear, hospital supplies, electronic parts, and, of course, our soft drinks. Well, that's enough to give you an idea of our spread. Our hospital supply division is connected, quite naturally, with our electronic parts division. And that's where your patents come in. Not just the patents, but your whole operation. I'm talking, of course, about a merger. Two fine firms tying up together."

Davey smiled. "It would hardly be a tying, Mr. Harrison. It would be more like a swallowing. Ours is a small operation."

"We have a niche for you, Mr. Davis, just the right niche. And once you are a part of P.T.C. Longwood, you wouldn't be small anymore, would you?"

"Perhaps we like being small," Lara said.

Mr. Harrison agreed at once. "Oh, I can understand that it has its advantages. But it has disadvantages, too. Bigness can afford to take risks, the risks that have made this country move ahead."

"I know about risk," Davey said. "This whole business was a risk. It started in my backyard."

"I'm sure it was a struggle, too. And nobody knows more about struggle than we do. Our president, Franklin Bennett, pulled himself up all the way to where he is today. So we do understand. But think how much more you could be doing even now if you had almost unlimited funds and efficient management behind you. I'd like you to fly out and see our main plant, in Michigan, where we would move you. Then you'd know what I'm talking about."

Davey said, "Even if I were interested, which I'm not, Mr. Harrison, I have an obligation to my employees and to this community. They—we—don't want to move. We have roots here."

"You're saying we can't do business?"

"I'm afraid so." And Davey walked toward the door.

Harrison followed. "This has been sudden, I realize, but it's not fair to yourself to dismiss the whole thing without some more thought. I'd like very much to go back and tell Mr. Bennett that you're going to give it some."

When Harrison had gone, Davey commented, "Smooth talker."

"I didn't know we were so famous. Did you?"

"I could do with less fame of that sort," Davey remarked somewhat darkly.

At home that evening, he told Eddy and Pam, who had come to visit Peggy, of the day's event.

"Why do you dismiss it like that?" asked Eddy. "Leveraged buyouts are the thing now. You'd come away with a fortune."

"I don't want a fortune," Davey grumbled. "Bankers! Brokers! They trade businesses as if they were baseball cards. They only understand numbers, not people. Not the hopes and the sweat that go into a place like mine. Talks of moving to . . . Where was it, Lara?"

"Michigan."

"Close this down and walk away from it, just like that! And who knows, after they'd bought us, what they'd do? Who's to say they can't sell you again and send you somewhere else? Vagabonding all around the country," Davey finished indignantly.

Eddy resumed his cautions. "I still don't think you people understand who Bennett is. He's a legend, one of the most powerful corporate executives in America."

"I've read enough about him," Lara said, "to make out he's a heartless, greedy tough guy, who doesn't care who he steps on."

"What do you care, if he can improve the quality of your family's life? Money's the ticket and always will be."

"Yes and then again, no," Lara said. "But mostly no."

ONE Saturday Martin Berg arrived. Davey was at work, and Lara had just lain down for a few minutes on the sofa in the den when the doorbell rang.

"Oh, I've startled you." Martin's eyes examined her acutely. "You look beat. And why not? Let me make you a cup of tea."

She smiled. There was always something commanding about Martin; one didn't disagree with him. So she went back to the sofa. When he returned with two cups of tea, he got right to the point.

"These doctors, they've done their best, but Connie's told me their verdict, and we just can't accept it, Lara. Now, there's a place not far from us in Westchester, a famous place where they specialize in head injuries. I made some contacts this morning, and we can get the baby in. I think we should give it a try."

She stirred her tea, watching the milk swirl in the cup as her thoughts swirled in her head. Without being willing to confess it even to Davey, she had almost no hope left. Ever since they had spoken of chronic care, she had known this was the end of the road. It was as if her child had died. No, it was worse.

She looked up at Martin. His eyes were filled with sadness. And he had said "we" when, after all, the child was not his.

"I suppose there isn't anything to lose, is there?" she replied.

He paused, waiting. "Shall I talk to Davey, then?"

"You needn't. If I want to try it, he'll want it, too. That other place would be . . . would be like a warehouse, he said."

Berg nodded. "I'll call him tonight anyway, when I'm home." He rose. "I'll be going now, flying back. I guess I could have done this on the phone, but I didn't expect you'd accept so promptly."

She smiled. "You're a good man, Martin."

A good man, and so competent. It was a relief, in a way, to let him take over, to make this decision for them.

"By the way," Martin said as she accompanied him to the door, "have you thought about that offer of Bennett's? I know this is a terrible time to talk about business, but I just wondered."

"Not really," she replied. "So Eddy told you about it?"

"No, not Eddy. I get around. I hear things. And rumors float fast in my business."

"Then you must have heard that we're not interested."

"Not even enough to think it over?"

"We just dismissed the whole idea."

"They won't dismiss it, you may be sure. As soon as all their financing is arranged, they'll be back. I know how it works."

## Chapter Thirteen

THEY took Peggy, then, to the new place, a smaller one surrounded by pleasant, expensive trees; otherwise, nothing was different, for when at the end of the day they walked away from her, she was still lying in a bed connected to monitors and tubes. Lara asked no questions anymore, and Davey, too, was silent. It was as if they both had learned that there were no answers.

"Lara, you'll stay with us here, of course," said Connie. "Davey can fly in weekends. We'll keep the plane available."

"Oh, but I can't. There's Sue at home. School isn't out yet, and besides, she's been through enough as it is. I will accept the offer of the plane rides, though. Martin and you are godsends, Connie."

So a routine began. As the plane descended toward the Westchester Airport, Lara, looking down, would see her sister waiting and waving. Then there would be an embrace, an anxious question, and an answer: "I went yesterday. The same."

The hospital visit would follow, and that, too, would be the same. Lunch would be brief so that Lara could fly home early.

One day, while at the lunch table at Cresthill, it occurred to Lara that she had not seen Thérèse for weeks. She asked why.

Connie hesitated. "I thought— To tell the truth, I thought it might be too hard for you to see her."

Lara's eyes filled. "Oh!" she cried. "Oh, the world mustn't stop because of Peggy. Do call her. I want to see her."

When Thérèse came, Lara took her on her lap. The child, wriggling, turned to look up at her.

"Where's Peggy?" she demanded.

"Peggy's sick, darling."

"When is she going to get better?"

"We're not sure yet."

"Oh. Can I have that cake?"

Connie was feeling a particular shame. How often on behalf of her own little girl had she not envied the beauty of her sister's child! And here sat her Thérèse, healthy and bright, on Lara's lap. What must be Lara's pain as she made the comparison?

They were to drive to the city that day, and Lara was to fly home from La Guardia Airport instead of Westchester.

"I ordered some summer things on Madison Avenue," Connie said. "And anyway, a little window-shopping will do you good."

The shopping accomplished, they stopped to give Thérèse an ice-cream treat, then walked slowly back up Fifth Avenue to the apartment. The car was already waiting at the curb for Lara. When the driver opened the door, Connie laid a hand on her arm.

"Lara . . . try to take care of yourself. Did you ever think living could be so damned hard?"

"It's just as well we didn't think."

Connie sighed. She kissed her sister, saying, "Get home safely," then stood watching while the car merged with traffic on Fifth Avenue.


"IF BY some miracle Peggy should be well again . . ." Too often Lara had caught herself saying the words and had reprimanded herself because sensible people didn't count on miracles.

And yet it happened.

It was Connie who witnessed it. One afternoon when she was making her regular stop at the hospital, she saw Peggy open her eyes. Then they closed again.

Still in a state of shock, she described the happening. "I don't know how I even had enough strength to run down the hall. I just screamed at the first nurse I met. And the doctors came running, and more nurses. Then I telephoned you, Lara."

Within the hour Martin's plane flew to Ohio. Davey left the plant in the middle of discussing an order, Sue left school, and Lara, trembling and laughing, joined them at the airport.

Before they arrived at the hospital, in the early evening, Peggy had awakened for a second time.

"Mommy," she had whispered. Her frightened gaze had swept

the room, and finding the faces all strange except for Aunt Connie's and Uncle Martin's, she had begun to cry.

Connie stroked her hair. "Mommy's coming soon. She's on the way," she whispered over and over.

And Mommy came. By now they had Peggy propped against pillows. Lara came rushing. She saw no one, spoke to no one; the little crowd parted to let her through, and she fell on her knees beside the bed. Davey, behind her, reached down and curved Peggy's arms around the mother's neck.

"How do you explain this?" Martin asked Peggy's doctor. "It's incredible, a miracle."

"Well, it's so rare a happening," Dr. Jonathan Bayer said, "that you might as well call it one. The swellings that come with head injuries seldom take this long to subside. This coma has lasted an extraordinarily long time."

"When may we take her home?" asked Davey.

The doctor shook his head. "Not for a long time yet. We can't be sure how much of her mental function has been restored. She'll need extensive therapy." As the parents' faces fell, he added kindly, "What's very much in her favor is her age."

And so the families entered the next phase.

Peggy was to spend another three to eight weeks in intensive care; then if all went well, she might be taken home and brought back every day for two to three months for rehabilitation therapy.

"But we live in Ohio," Lara cried out in dismay.

Martin said at once, "She'll stay with us, and Connie will drive her over here every day for her treatment."

Lara looked at Davey, reading his mind. "I know you think it's too much to accept," she told him in front of everyone, "but you would do it for them, Davey."

"Of course," Davey said.

The routine was established. It seemed to Lara as if the little person who was Peggy Davis was being reinjected with life through the sheer loving will of the many who were concentrating all their strength upon her. Now hope at last came pouring through Lara's veins, to surge out in sudden bursts of happy tears or reckless laughter. Peggy began to walk, tottering a little between the nurses' hands, then taking her first steps unaided down the hall. Memory came back and she began to ask about Sue and her friends in school. As the days passed, she demanded attention, and even lost her temper when Connie refused to give her a candy bar before dinner.

Dr. Bayer, who happened to walk in on the tantrum, was amused and pleased. "An excellent sign. A return to normalcy."

He swooped down on Peggy and lifted her above his head. "My friend! Aren't you my best friend? Come on, I'll show you something. You, too," he told Connie. "There's something to see."

In the glass-walled sun-room at the end of the hall, he pointed outdoors. Blurred by the soft rain, a magnificent rainbow arched across the sky and disappeared behind a tree.

"Oh, beautiful. Beautiful," Connie whispered.

"The pot of gold must be right in back of those trees," he said.

"I won't even bother to look for it. We've already found its pot of gold." And Connie stroked Peggy's arm.

"You're right, of course," the doctor said seriously.

Something in his voice, a richness or a compassion, made her look into his face. For all these weeks she had seen him in Peggy's room and had noted only that he was authoritative in a kindly way and that the child had begun to adore him. Now suddenly she saw him as if for the first time: a man about her own age, with a long, narrow face, narrow eyes, and a markedly cleft chin that softened the angularity of his bones.

Spontaneously she said, "I hope you know how grateful we all are. And not only for your skill. You are so tender with Peggy!"

"You're very tender with her yourself."

"She's my niece. We're a close family."

"You're fortunate."

"You have no children?"

"I'm not married. I have no parents, brothers or sisters. No ties." He smiled. "Still, there are always compensations. At the drop of a hat I can pick up and go wherever I want to go in the world."

"I hope you aren't planning to leave us before Peggy's all well again."

"No. I've no plans now. I've been everywhere from Vietnam to Egypt studying head wounds and injuries, so it's time to stay put for a while. Come, Peggy, we're going back to your room. You'll have dinner, and then your candy."

279

Connie, as she followed them, had a fleeting thought: He's someone I'd like to know. But their paths, their ways, were far apart, and the thought vanished.

THE day came when Peggy was discharged from the hospital. A room had been prepared for her at Cresthill, a rosy shelter filled with welcoming toys: a dollhouse like a Swiss chalet, a stuffed polar bear, a real fishtank, and a panda taller than Peggy herself. It was a mirror image of Thérèse's room across the hall.

Lara gasped. "What have you done here? I can't believe it."

Connie was pleased. "Do you like the goody packages?"

In shining white boxes were a powder-blue velvet dress, a monogrammed snowsuit, and embroidered pajamas for Peggy, two Norwegian ski sweaters and a British camel-hair coat for Sue.

"I had such fun shopping. You know how I love to shop."

"You're a dear, and they're all wonderful," Lara said, wondering where and when Peggy would get to wear a powder-blue velvet dress back home. "But what can I say to all this?"

"Say nothing," Martin answered as he came into the room. He smiled with satisfaction. "She ought to feel at home here."

From the window they could see the two little girls bobbing on the seesaw while the nanny carefully watched.

Connie read Lara's mind. "Nanny's been told to be careful of Peggy, not to let her get too tired or to fall. Although really, Lara, that child has to be made of iron. She's almost back to herself."

And indeed, compared with Thérèse, Peggy was far the sturdier and the tougher of the two. Peggy had Connie's drive and energy and sparkle; maybe that was why Connie, without realizing it, had become so attached to the child. So Lara mused as she watched them playing on the stately lawns of Martin Berg's great house.

SUMMER was fading when they finally brought Peggy home.

Connie was very emotional about the parting. "We'll miss her so," she kept saying. "Thérèse will be an only child again."

They had all grown very close these last hard months, and the separation hurt. Loaded down with parting gifts, the Davises climbed aboard Martin's plane. As they rose into the air, Martin, Connie, and Thérèse were still visible—tiny figures waving.

"Dear, wonderful people," Lara said.

At home, in Ohio, more dear, wonderful people waited for them. Neighbors had prepared a feast. Men from the plant had brought their marching band to parade around the yard, to Peggy's huge delight. The weekly newspaper was out with an item on the editorial page about the marvelous recovery of Peggy Davis.

And on this night the Davis parents made real love for the first time since that terrible hurt so many months before. Once Lara turned out the light, Davey raised the blankets, making a warm little cave, just tight enough for the two of them. Enormous gratitude, incredible joy enveloped her as she slid into the cave.

## Chapter Fourteen

As EDDY hastened toward his office he felt a chill. It would be one of those interminably uncomfortable meetings like the last few, with reams of paper spread out before his splitting head. He felt like telephoning with an excuse.

"Mr. Hendricks has been here almost half an hour," Mrs. Evans told him, somewhat reproachfully, when he arrived. So Abner Saville had sent someone in his place. What could that mean? Perhaps he was out of town or not feeling well.

Eddy entered his office. Mr. Hendricks was already at the conference table, with papers spread out. The two men shook hands.

"Sorry I'm late, Hendricks. The cab got caught in traffic on the way back from Wall Street. What happened to Abner?" he inquired pleasantly as he went to his desk. "Not that I mind seeing you. I meant, I'm used to your partner. We've been friends for years."

"I know that. Abner thought it advisable to get another opinion. Sometimes friendship can confuse things." Ominous words, Eddy thought. "Would you mind coming to the table," Hendricks added, "so we can look over these papers together?"

"Of course. No problem."

"I have here," Hendricks began in a flat tone, "our work sheets for the firm and also your personal tax returns." His black-rimmed glasses with their thick lenses were bent on Eddy. "I don't like to say it, but frankly, Mr. Osborne, some of this material is very distressing. You know, of course, that we've had a suspicious feeling the last few months that things are not altogether in balance."

Eddy raised his chin and met the man's somber gaze. "Suspicious? I don't like the word, Mr. Hendricks. Give me the bottom line." His head had begun to throb. Quick darts of pain, needle pricks, ran down his arm.

"The bottom line is this: Osborne and Company is too highly leveraged. Your liabilities exceed your assets."

"All right, all right, I know that!" Eddy exclaimed. "A couple of big investors happened to take their money out, and that played a little havoc with the cash flow, that's all. Nothing to worry about."

"I wouldn't say that. If any more of your clients decide to pull out, you'll be facing disaster."

"But why should they want their money?" Eddy retorted. "There's no reason in the world why they should."

Hendricks sighed. "I don't like being the bearer of bad news, Mr. Osborne. There's been a commingling of funds—"

Eddy's pains grew sharper. "What are you talking about?"

"Your personal checkbook." Hendricks looked away. "There are entries that don't match, or rather they do match up to withdrawals from general funds. For example, on June seventeenth you made out a check to the Winterheim Galleries for six hundred eleven thousand dollars that you didn't have in the account. But on the eighteenth you deposited an exact amount to cover the check and withdrew it from the account of Mr. Sidney—"

Eddy's heart pounded. "All right! I did a damn fool thing, I'll admit it. I go a little crazy sometimes, mostly buying art. But everything I buy—securities, real estate, whatever—is prime stuff, investment quality. That's how I've achieved what I have. Look, I know it wasn't right, but it's just cash flow. I need a couple of months to straighten things out, that's all. And I won't let it happen again."

"It's more than a question of time, I'm afraid." Hendricks' monotone was mournful. "There are questions that have to be answered. How to explain, for instance, why you opened a separate personal account with another stockbroker, in which you deposit money that you've taken—borrowed—from your own customers? This is the way the IRS or the SEC will talk when the time comes. You see, we really wanted you to look over these records so you'd understand why we can't file this income tax return."

Eddy grasped the arms of his chair. "Can't file? Why can't you?"

"Please. You can't expect us to put our name to these declarations when they are not true, can you? I think you should get a lawyer. And a very good one. I'm truly sorry, Mr. Osborne."

As Hendricks put his papers away and went to the door, Eddy called to his back, "Why didn't Abner come and tell me himself?"

And from the doorway the mournful voice replied, "He's been trying to tell you all along, but you haven't been hearing him."


IN THEIR bedroom that night, Pam undressed very slowly, taking time to walk around in her white chiffon chemise. Then she went to a drawer and drew out a black lace nightgown. She stepped out of the chemise, stretched languidly and then, with a pretty gesture, picked up the slithering black gown and slid it over her head. Eddy understood that it was a well-meant effort to cajole him out of his cross mood, more than just a signal of her usual desire. But sex was the last thing he wanted.

He dropped onto the bed and groaned. "I'm awfully tired!"

She got in beside him and touched his arm. "You're sure you're not sick? It's so unlike you."

"I'm not sick," he said.

"The truth, Eddy?"

"The truth. Now will you let me sleep?" he asked.

But he was sick, truly, with a rising fear that ran like ice water through his blood and bones. Cash flow, that's all it was. Sometimes the flow dried up a little, but only temporarily. His mind strove, but when you were handling so many accounts, investments, and clients, it was hard to recall each separate transaction. He could recall, to be sure, the Fragonard, the excitement of the frenetic bidding at the auction gallery, and then taking it home, the treasure, fine as any Fragonard in any museum anywhere. Yes, and Fifth Avenue in Christmas week, when the rubies, glistening like dew on roses, had beckoned from their black velvet bed in the window. So the millions flew, millions upon millions, before you knew it.

He could hear his heart pound. That small, pathetic thudding was the only sound in the room. And he was conscious, as he had never been before, of the immensity of the world—or rather of his own smallness within its enormous, threatening expanse.

The first thing he'd have to do was to find a new lawyer.

Somewhere in the apartment a clock struck. The place was full of clocks Eddy had collected: old English tall clocks, a rare eighteenth-century skeleton clock whose marvelous mechanism was fascinating to observe. Ten strokes. Morning was only hours away. If he could only stay here in this dark room. If he could only tell Pam! Yet he didn't want to pour his fears out before her. A man had pride, after all. A man wanted to be a hero in his wife's eyes.

On sudden impulse he reached for her hand, whispering, "Are you asleep?" although he knew well that she was not.

"Of course I'm not. What's the trouble, Eddy? Tell me."

He sighed. "I'm tired of the rat race. It's been getting to me."

She waited.

"I've been thinking." Thoughts were forming as he spoke. "You've always had that idea of buying a place in Kentucky, and I've always said, 'Someday.' You know, it's come to me that maybe 'someday' should be now. I wouldn't mind living there for good."

She was astonished. "Leave everything here? The office? The business? Whatever put it into your head right now?"

"Oh, I don't know. I guess there's a time for everything. Time to begin and time to end. So how about our going down to look? If we find a wonderful place, we'll buy it. Or rather, you will."

Put everything into her name. All the treasures in this apartment and the apartment itself. Sell it to her for a few dollars, five or ten thousand, make it a bona fide sale. Just in case . . .

There was sudden alarm in Pam's voice. "But why, Eddy? This is too sudden. Something has to be wrong. You look so worried."

No, he thought again, I will not tell her. I'm not going to frighten the life out of her. A good lawyer will iron the whole problem out.

"Honey, there's not all that much to explain, nothing to worry over. It'll be a great thing for us. We can go down and raise horses. We'll live longer, be healthier. It makes a lot of sense. Believe me."

And with that Pam had to be satisfied.

IT TOOK almost no time at all to buy a fine old house enriched by six hundred acres of woods and fields, because they fell in love with it on sight. It stood at the end of a long drive lined with dogwoods and redbuds, a perfect picture-book house, with columns, a veranda, and a fanlight over the door. Eddy's pulses beat; he was captivated. For one marvelous minute, as he rested his eyes upon that house, he forgot that this was to be a hideout, an escape.

"Well," he said. "Well, what do you think?"

"I'll bet there's a fireplace in every room," Pam said.

In a happy kind of daze they followed the caretaker through the rooms, Pam murmuring, "Oh, it's too good to be true! I'd love to hang your Rowlandson prints in the little upstairs hall. This corner bedroom should be ours. I'd do it in pale blue, very cool."

She's thrilled, he thought. This is her rightful setting; she'll have a dozen dogs running all over the place.

The caretaker had some comments as they went outside again.

"Back there's a pond, and behind it the woods. The orchard, the cornfield, and vegetables are on that side. Some folks might think the stables are too close to the main house, but," he added regretfully, "I sure would hate to see them torn down."

"Torn down!" Pam exclaimed. "Absolutely never!"

Two long, handsome buildings faced each other across a courtyard. On one a clock, and on the other a gilded weather vane twinkled in the sunlight.

"There's room for thirty horses," the man said.

The expression on Pam's face was rapturous.

"So you love it, darling?" Eddy said. "Let's waste no time, then, closing the deal and getting workmen in here to fix it up."

For time was pressing. Time was of the essence.

CONNIE's silver heels clicked over the stone floors through the long, dim sculpture galleries of the Metropolitan Museum as she hurried back toward the Temple of Dendur from the ladies' room. Round tables covered with lace cloths over turquoise petticoats surrounded the temple, which still, some thousands of years after its conception on the Nile, held a powerful dark mystery. The shrubbery and the flowers, the gilded candelabra, the poached lobster, and the Haut-Brion all were magnificent, as befitted both the setting and the marriage of one of the most important financiers in America. Oh, it was wonderful to be among grand events in the heart of the city! These were the people who kept the city moving, and she was part of them. Often when she gave her name,

Mrs. Martin Berg, in a shop, she would hear awed whispers among the salesgirls. And then, remembering her days in the Houston dress shop, she would jubilate, as now at this moment.

Bitsy Maxwell was at the Bergs' table. "I hear," she said, "that you've just bought a marvelous house in London."

"Yes. It's in Belgravia. It's one of those early-nineteenth-century terrace houses and needs a lot of work. I wanted the house for Martin. He goes back and forth from London so much that I really thought he should have a place of his own. The Savoy is a perfect hotel, but still, a hotel isn't a home, is it?"

Connie caught Martin's eye just as he was rising from the table.

"I see Simmonds over there," he whispered. "He's supposed to get some more publicity on the neurology wing I'm donating."

"Darling, sit down and relax. You work too hard."

"I have to if I want to keep up with your expenditures." Martin smiled. "But I don't mind. Do you know you're the most beautiful woman in this whole room, including the bride?"

She watched him walk away. He really looked well, thanks to her unrelenting supervision of his exercise and diet. She had been good for him; even his sisters had told her so. Ben, the disapproving brother, they fortunately saw quite seldom. As to Martin's children, she was careful to be as loving to Melissa as to her own Thérèse.

Now and again she still wondered what it was like to be "in love," to feel the euphoria, the willingness to die for another that one read about and that she saw between Lara and Davey. . . . Well, it was immaterial. She was here tonight in pride and splendor.

Her husband was standing now in the center of a cluster of men. Something had happened, for the group around him was enlarging. Men were putting their napkins aside and rising to join it. Presently Martin came back toward her and beckoned.

She stood up and followed. "What is it? Is something wrong?"

Martin was glum. "I'm afraid there is, and I wanted to tell you before we go back to the table, in case anyone says something. It's about your brother. He's to be indicted by the U.S. attorney. The news is all over Wall Street."

A wave of shock swept over her. "Indicted? For what?"

"I don't know all the details. Insider trading, defrauding Internal Revenue. I'm not sure."

Eddy! But he was so clever and so good. Surely this had to be a mistake, some sort of unjust accusation. Oh, poor Eddy!

"Honey, don't cry here. Don't let it show."

She took a long, deep breath. Then very softly she asked, "Martin, if it's true, what's going to happen to him?"

"If it's true," Martin said grimly, "he'll go to prison."

## Chapter Fifteen

HENRY Rathbone was one of the most celebrated and expensive lawyers in the city, and he had counseled Eddy to keep calm and go to work as usual. Naturally, Rathbone had made no promises, but his general demeanor had suggested a modified optimism. And so Eddy dressed himself that morning to his usual perfection, ate his usual breakfast, and was now seated at his desk with the usual pile of papers before him.

Abruptly the door opened, revealing Mrs. Evans in dismay.

"Mr. Osborne! Two men are here. They say they're United States marshals. They showed me their badges. I couldn't stop them. I—"

Eddy stood up. "Let them in," he said, with immediate awareness that his heart had begun to pound.

Two men entered, men so ordinary as to be indescribable.

"Mr. Osborne," one said, "we have a warrant for your arrest."

Arrest. But Rathbone said— These were paper proceedings, weren't they? Things settled by words between lawyers, settled in offices, at desks and on telephones, not physically! Arrest was *seizing*. Seizing your body.

Eddy stammered. "What for? I mean I don't understand. There's a mistake. My lawyer's working on it right now."

"You can call your lawyer. But you'll have to come along first."

"You'll have to put these on," the second man said.

Mrs. Evans was staring at the handcuffs. Her lips hung open, and her faded, neatly waved hair was rumpled.

"I'll go with you," Eddy said. "You don't have to put those on me. I'm not the sort of person who'll make trouble."

"Make it easy for yourself," the man told him. "Put out your hands."

Good Lord, Eddy thought, not through the main door. Not to be marched past all those desks and all those eyes!

"Can we go out the back door?" His voice faltered badly.

"There's a private entrance," Mrs. Evans said, weeping now. "It's not the way you came in. Please," she pleaded, "it's quicker."

Eddy's hands just hung at the ends of his too stiff arms. There was no place to put them. Mrs. Evans leaped for the Burberry raincoat in the closet and draped it over them, then kissed him.

"God bless you, Mr. Osborne. He's a good man," she warned the intruders. "Be gentle with him," she said fiercely.

So Eddy departed from the offices of Osborne and Company with one man ahead of him and one behind him. A plain black sedan was parked below, and no one in the hurrying crowd on the sidewalk saw the three men get into the back seat and drive away.

When they had traveled a few blocks, Eddy brought himself to ask where they were going.

"The United States Courthouse at Foley Square," he was told.

THEY had held his splayed fingers to an inked pad. They had taken his picture with a number placard, as if he were a rapist or a murderer. But when Rathbone came in, Eddy put on the face that the world knew best and was jocular Eddy Osborne again.

"Well, Henry, here I am. What happens next—the guillotine?"

"No, no, Eddy. We'll have you out on bail in no time. Come—we have to appear before a United States magistrate. He sets the bail. The U.S. prosecutor will be there, too."

Rathbone had authority in this place, and his walk showed it. That's the way I used to walk through the bull pen at Osborne and Company, Eddy said to himself, and then realized that he had already said "used to."

The magistrate sat high in a small courtroom wearing his black robes. Even in that dingy, unimpressive room he looked—well, magisterial. Perhaps it was the robe that did it. The United States attorney was a handsome man, whose vote-getting face was perfect for television. Eddy stood waiting while the three men talked.

"The charges," said the handsome prosecutor, "warrant high bail, Your Honor. This man is charged on five separate counts involving more than three hundred million dollars. So far."

"Your Honor," responded Rathbone, "my client is not a hardened criminal. This is a first offense. If it is an offense at all."

"Your Honor," said the prosecutor, "I would like to ask that bail be set at five million dollars."

The magistrate's black eyebrows went up.

"That is most excessive, Your Honor," Rathbone argued. "Mr. Osborne has a home and a wife. He has relatives. His sister is married to one of the most prominent men in the city. He has roots. He's not going to run away. I would ask that reasonable bail be set. One hundred thousand dollars would be reasonable."

"Your Honor, in light of the charges, that makes no sense. It is out of proportion, entirely out of proportion."

Rathbone persisted. "He is not going to flee, Your Honor."

There was a long silence while the magistrate pondered. At last he made his decision. "Bail will be two million dollars."

"May I consult with my client?" asked Rathbone. They went to the back of the room. "Can you get it?" he whispered to Eddy.

"No. You know I'm strapped. All the accounts were in Pam's name." Thank heaven he'd been smart enough to do that.

"Your relatives? Berg? A bail bondsman would take time."

Eddy was silent. He looked off into the thick, smoky air beyond the window, then back at Rathbone. "I dread asking Berg."

"I understand. Would it be easier if I were to ask instead?"

"It would help. Thank you, Henry. Thank you very much."

Rathbone left, and Eddy remained gazing out the window at nothing. It seemed hours, but actually it was only twenty minutes before Rathbone returned and at once addressed the court. Bail had been arranged and would be delivered within the hour.

IN THE library, Eddy sat in a vague sort of daze. Pam had gone to her mother's and wouldn't be home before dinnertime.

Then, as if obeying some peremptory command, he sprang up. In a pantry closet he found cardboard cartons, rolls of tissue paper, brown wrapping paper, and balls of heavy twine. The house was well stocked with such practical items, for Pam was a good housekeeper, an efficient keeper of the home that was now being destroyed. For no matter what Rathbone had said—something like "I'll do my best"—Eddy felt disaster in his bones.

Back in the library, he set to work taking pictures down from the walls. There went the Sargent lady in her velvet dress; Winslow Homer's palm trees bending in a southern wind; Pissarro's crowded, rainy street in Paris. These were his treasures, and he was ripping them off his walls. For three hours he worked, going from room to room, lifting, padding, cutting his fingers on twine. He wrapped small objects, porcelains and ivories; he began to take down his first editions, the leather-bound Dickens, the Walt Whitman, the—

"Have you gone crazy? Crazy?" Pam screamed.

He pulled himself erect and, ankle-deep in paper, regarded his wife, his cherished wife, in her camel-hair coat.

Stupidly he said, "We're moving to Kentucky, you remember. I had some time, so I thought I'd get a few things ready."

She grabbed his shirtfront. "Eddy, do you think I'm an idiot? Sit down here and tell me what's wrong. I want to know. Now!"

His Adam's apple seemed to swell until it hurt. Nevertheless, he had to begin. "I'm in trouble with the government, Pam. Some tax trouble. I was arrested this morning."

"Arrested?"

"Yes. It was quite an experience." He managed a weak smile.

"But what have you done?" she cried.

"A few foolish things, I have to admit. But nothing criminal. I haven't hurt anybody. It's a tax mess, that's all. Very complicated."

"But if you were arrested, you must be out on bail."

"Yes. Martin put it up."

She was standing above him, waiting. And he looked up at her.

"I got in too deep," he said. "I don't know how it happened. I thought I had a magic touch. I always did have." He put his head in his hands. "Maybe I lost my touch. Things started to drain away. Pam, I think it's possible that I might go to prison."

The doorbell rang, making Eddy start. He supposed, after the morning's experience, that he would never again feel secure about who might be on the other side of a door. But Pam had gone to answer it, and he heard the voices of Martin and Connie.

"Lord, look at this ruin!" Connie stared about her.

Martin waved her to silence. "How're you doing, Eddy?"

"I want to thank you, Martin. If I can thank you, that is."

"Just see how you can work your way out of your troubles. That'll

291

be thanks enough. Your sisters are beside themselves with worry. Lara phoned just now." Martin shoved aside a pile of tissue paper and sat down on the sofa. "I only spoke ten minutes with Rathbone, so tell me, how deep in the hole are you?"

"I don't know exactly. A lot. I'd have to figure. It's complicated."

Martin frowned slightly. "But you must have some idea. Rathbone says one of the counts against you is that you played the stock market with your clients' funds. Haven't you any conception of your personal stock holdings?"

"I don't know. Maybe thirteen million. It varies. Good Lord," he blurted, "I saved fortunes for my clients, all the same! And now they remember only my mistakes and won't give me the time to correct them. All I need is some time! I haven't committed murder, have I?"

"Well, if you've ruined people, that's almost the same thing, isn't it?" Connie said, sounding bitter. "Some of my good friends that I sent to you, too."

Martin stopped her. "There's no point in that sort of talk."

Pam sat rigidly looking toward the window, where lights twinkled across the street. Holding tears back, she blinked, and Eddy knew that the truth had finally just reached her.

"I don't understand," he said, "what started this government crackdown in the first place. What happened all of a sudden?"

"Somebody wrote an anonymous letter," Martin replied. "It was mailed from Vancouver to the SEC. Somebody who'd apparently lost money because of insider trading. I heard it from a man who has a brother with the SEC. Oh, it wasn't about you at all, but it started the ball rolling."

"Do you think I really have cause to be terribly worried?"

Martin stood up. "I think I'm glad you have a top-notch attorney. Meanwhile, use your head. Head over heart, you know."

Eddy nodded ruefully. "My mother used to say that."

"Well, you do it. Take a stiff Scotch and go to sleep." When Martin gave Eddy his hand, the grip was comforting. "Call me if you need me. Come on, Connie."

When they had left, Pam let a few tears fall, whispering into Eddy's shoulder, "Life was a ball, wasn't it? Such fun, being young and healthy and with no worries. Now I feel a hundred years old."

"Life will be a ball again," he said.

Smile, Peg always told her children. Smile even when you don't want to, and it'll actually make you feel like smiling.


"HE SWINDLED people, didn't he? Tell the truth," Connie said on the way home. "How could he have been so stupid?"

"One word," Martin said. "Greed. He got too greedy."

"How will it end?"

Martin shrugged. "My guess is that it'll end badly. From what I can see, he's committed four or five felonies."

"I'm angry at him, but I'm heartbroken, too. Poor Eddy! He's got to be terrified. And I'm awfully sorry for Pam."

"He told me once that everything belongs to her. Six paintings alone will give her twenty million. So I wouldn't worry."

"All the same, they'll be ruined socially. Utterly ruined."


THE federal court judge had the stern expression of a cancer surgeon about to operate. The jury's twelve chairs looked solemn even when they were vacant. Eddy wondered whether his heart, which had now subsided into an irregular beat—after all, how could it possibly have kept hammering this long?—would ever beat normally again.

All the chairs behind him, in row after row, were filled. Directly behind him, in the second row, sat his wife and his sisters. Lara, every week that his trial lasted, kept going back and forth from Ohio. Connie came in a sable coat, at least fifty thousand dollars' worth of coat, he knew; Pam, most sensibly, had worn her camel-hair coat. She was a princess, no doubt of it, in her dignity and reassuring calm. Pam was royalty.

Once he saw the puzzled, mournful face of Mrs. Evans, and from her brief words during recess he gathered that Osborne and Company had been taken over by the government's examiners, who occupied almost every desk. And he hoped, although he did not say so, that no one would put his feet on his private desk, which was a treasure brought from an ancient house in Yorkshire.

As he sat beside Rathbone the hours dragged and the voices droned. The judge made a lengthy explanation to the jury about the securities business. The prosecutor pointed at Eddy and spoke of "the life-style, ladies and gentlemen, which this man maintains—palatial suites in the finest hotels, in Florida and in Cannes and Gstaad. One of the finest art collections in this city. An East Side apartment you could probably fit all twelve of your homes into. And whose money bought all these marvels? Not his! No, it was money he received from investors who trusted him, whom he strung along using fake accounts. And I'll tell you who else's money." Here, the long finger swiveled back toward the jurors. "Your money!"

When it was Rathbone's turn, he told the jury, "These financial transactions are very complicated, but you are all intelligent people. Do not be misled by name calling. The practice of deferring taxes is quite legal; neither my client nor his firm are the only ones who do this. It is by no means an evasion of taxes." He directed them to a large chart. "Let me show you. . . ."

And so it went on and on, day after day. Eddy, well primed and well rehearsed, went on the stand and was carefully led by Rathbone. He performed well. Then on cross-examination he still kept his calm demeanor, but he knew that he was floundering, and he was forced to answer some questions that condemned him. These hours were an interminable torture, and when the end came, the verdict was guilty.

Some weeks later, in the same courtroom, Eddy stood with Rathbone to hear the sentence. His Honor meted out the words with no inflection and no emotion.

"You have been found guilty on eight separate counts of conspiracy to defraud the Internal Revenue Service. . . . Your greed has been inordinate and without conscience. . . . However, I do take into some account the letters I have received from character witnesses who testify to your charitable acts, your personal generosity. Therefore, I sentence you to four years' imprisonment on each of the eight charges, the sentences to run concurrently. Furthermore, you will pay a fine of one million dollars in addition to back taxes. And you are forbidden ever to engage in the securities business as long as you live. Court is dismissed."

There was a scrape and shuffle of chairs and feet. Pam kissed him. Lara and Connie were stricken.

Rathbone asked softly, "Are you okay?"

Eddy nodded. "Okay."

"We'll appeal, of course."

"And if we lose?"

"I don't believe in thinking in those terms, you know that."

"But if we do," persisted Eddy.

"You're out in two years. You could have gotten a lot worse."

"You're saying I got off easy?"

Rathbone shrugged. "I didn't say that, Eddy. I only meant that it could be worse."

The two men, followed by the three women, moved downstairs and out onto the sidewalk.

"If I do get sent up," Eddy questioned in a low voice, "where will I go?"

"Minimum security. I'll ask for Allenwood—it's in Pennsylvania. It's the least harsh. Not harsh at all."

VERNON Edward Osborne lost his case on appeal and was given three days to report to Allenwood Federal Penitentiary. Rathbone had obtained permission to take his client there himself, but Eddy didn't want Pam to come with them.

"I don't want you to see me in that place," he told her.

"Not me?" she cried.

"No, Pam. I don't want you to remember me all our lives like that. I'm going to tell my sisters too. Just write to me."

"Eddy, I don't care what you say. I'm going to visit you."

They spent the last night in a suite at the Hotel Pierre in New York, for their apartment had been emptied out and its contents trundled away to Kentucky. Pam ordered flowers, as if this were a bridal night, and a feast of a dinner with champagne. Afterward they sat together in front of the television set, watching a comedian who wasn't funny. Eddy lay with his head on her lap while she stroked his hair.

After a while she said, "It's going to be terrible without you."

"The time will pass." He wanted to comfort her and himself, too. "It will go by faster than we think, and we'll have the rest of our lives after that."

"We need something to remember," she murmured in his ear. "Something to last us."

"Darling, I don't think I—"

"Yes, yes. You will."

So he followed her to the bed, and her hands, soft and burning, moved upon him. Slowly, slowly he let everything go.

Afterward, once Pam had fallen asleep, he got up and went to the window. The city lay sparkling, wide awake below, and limousines were moving down Fifth Avenue, transporting people to late gala functions. On Madison they would be transporting people uptown to their silken homes. Suddenly the city with all its glamour seemed to Eddy like a place he had never known and would never know again. He shook himself. The feeling was too strange, too eerie. He said aloud, "Hey, Eddy Osborne, get hold of yourself! You're down, but you're not out yet."

## Chapter Sixteen

ON A dark Sunday after Thanksgiving, men had started to arrive at Cresthill. So far Connie had counted fifteen of them in the red leather library. Obviously, some tremendous deal must be approaching its climactic hour to have brought all these bankers, lawyers, accountants, and principals together. From past experiences she knew that they might well be here all day.

Cigar smoke was seeping out of the library now, past closed doors and into the adjoining sitting room, where Connie was. Yes, this deal had to be something extraordinary, she reflected, for Martin had been unusually tense during the last few weeks.

Restless now, she got up and went to the window. Far down the slope a bright orange spot slid across the snow where Nanny was pulling Thérèse on her sled. And Connie had a curious recollection of being pushed down a little hill in a cardboard carton. It might have been Lara who had pushed her, or perhaps her mother. How Peg would marvel today at the grandchild to whom all this splendor belonged, these wide, quiet fields and this great house!

Then she thought of Eddy. Poor Eddy, in that awful place. She had gone once with Lara to see him, and their presence had upset him terribly; it had crushed his pride. But over the telephone he still talked with his old bravado, as if he really hadn't done anything. Two years ago he had been here with them, happy and boisterous, loaded as usual with gifts. Just there near the front door he had parked and called the butler to help him carry Thérèse's dollhouse.

Poor Eddy. She remembered him presenting her with the Mercedes on her wedding day, bidding for a Matisse at a spectacular auction, answering respectful questions at a fashionable dinner party. What had it all meant in the end? A strange, sick feeling of loss swept through her, as if there were no purpose in anything. And Connie shook herself, as if to rid herself of a dismal foreboding.

HOURS later the meeting broke up, and Martin, with his partner, Preston DeWitt, brought a man to meet Connie—a broad, bulky man in an ankle-length mink coat. Martin made the introductions.

"Pleased to meet you," said Franklin Bennett. The famous Franklin Bennett. His eyes touched her from head to foot. "Berg, you sure know how to pick them. Nothing like a young woman to make you feel like a rooster again. How old are you, Connie?"

Appalled, she answered, "I'm in my mid-thirties."

"My wife— My new wife's younger. Twenty-seven. You remind me of her. Say, Berg, you've got a beautiful spread here."

"Well, it's home," Martin said modestly. "We like it."

"Why on earth wouldn't you? So I'll be going." Bennett turned toward the door. "Can't keep the young missus waiting too long."

When the door had closed, Preston sighed in disgust. "What a horror that man is! He started in a cereal factory, but within eleven years he was P.T.C. Longwood's president," he told Connie. "He's climbed, he's clawed. He's got eyes in the back of his head."

Preston, too, was soon out the door, and when Connie brought coffee into the library and set it on the table, which was still littered with papers, Martin said, "By the way, Bennett wants to include your brother-in-law's plant in the deal we've been discussing."

"What? Davey's place? Whyever would he?"

"It seems that they've some patents that fit into Bennett's medical-supply division. He wants them badly."

"It's funny you never told me about it before. Davey will hate it if anyone tries to interfere with his plant."

Martin laughed. "That's irrelevant when there's a conglomerate to be assembled. Bennett intends to make them a fantastic offer. He may even fly out there himself to see the plant."

"He must want it awfully, then. Funny. A little place like that."

297

"Now, who can that be?" Lara wondered, looking up from her desk, at which she was going over the monthly bank statement. It was not often that a stretch limousine drew up to the factory door.

A bulky man wearing, of all things, a long mink coat got out and picked his way up the walk through puddled, melted snow. A minute later she was summoned to Davey's office, across the hall.

"Franklin Bennett," said the newcomer, "but call me Frank. I'm informal." He sat down, stretching his legs. "I never thought I'd find myself in the wilds of Ohio. Haven't been in a small burg like this since I grew up in one. The weather's nice today, at least."

Neither Davey nor Lara had any comments to make to that.

Bennett lit a cigar. "I don't usually visit every small operation," he began, leaning back so far that the chair creaked. "But I hear you gave my man a hard time a while back."

"I wouldn't say that," said Davey very calmly. "I've never been known to give people a hard time."

"Well, you turned him down flat, didn't you?"

"That's my privilege, Mr. Bennett. This is our place, and we want to keep it that way."

Now Bennett switched to a smile. "I guess I can understand that. Your brother-in-law, Martin," he said, indicating Lara, "has told me how you people worked to get this operation under way."

Martin! Lara's eyes met Davey's. Martin, the benefactor, the rock of strength. She felt as if she had been struck in the chest.

"You've done a nice job, too. Very nice. But you don't want to stop here, do you? You want to grow, don't you? To expand?"

"It wouldn't be expanding," Davey said. "It would be breaking up, Mr. Bennett, and I don't want to do that."

"You could find yourself worth millions in a couple of years."

"Mr. Bennett, you probably won't understand this, but neither my wife nor I have the least desire to be worth millions."

Bennett leaned forward, so that cigar smoke rose into Lara's face. "You may not care about money, but your stockholders will care, and you can bet on that. All I need is to present my offer at a stockholders' meeting, and they'll vote to sell out."

Davey was silent. His eyes met Lara's, speaking to her. Don't be afraid, they said. I've met bullies before.

"I'll give you time to think it over, Davis. I'd like to avoid a fight, on account of Berg." Bennett rose. "He's financed some sweet deals for me, and I appreciate it when people cooperate." A smile flashed across the florid face. "Well, my plane is waiting. Be seeing you."

"Not if I can help it," Davey declared as the door closed. He stood still a moment. "It's a raid, that's what it is, Lara."

"And Martin's part of it! I'm numb. Can you believe this?"

"Calm down. We have to take our time and think."

"But I'm just awfully awfully scared. That man Bennett—he's brutal, Davey. What are we going to do?" she asked.

"Right now? Go home and eat."

Dropping the subject, she made the dinner hour as normal as ever. At the table Sue discussed a problem in math with Davey. Now at the head of her junior high school class, Sue wanted to be a scientist. Lara watched her draw a diagram on a paper napkin. Such a serious girl she was. And yet she had a delightful giggle, too.

Sue was cutting Peggy's chicken. The care she took of Peggy was beautiful to see. Sue sometimes has more patience with her than I have, reflected Lara.

After dinner Lara and Davey took their coffee to the den. Lara looked around the comfortable room. Home. The curtains, warm rose-flowered linen, were drawn against the evening; the children's photographs were ranked on the bookshelves. Home. They'd planned it so well, made it so snug. And now total strangers had come, daring to invade this chosen life. The outrage!

The telephone rang, and Davey picked it up.

"Hello, Martin. . . . Yes, he was here. . . . What?" He nodded to Lara. "Take the phone in the kitchen. Martin wants you to listen."

Martin's voice had a powerful ring. "So what happened?"

"The first thought that came to me, Martin, was amazement that you're a part of this. You never told us."

Davey's voice trembled so faintly only Lara would be aware of it. Only she could know the sense of outrage he was suppressing.

"It's a very recent involvement, that's why. We weren't in it at the start. Bennett switched from some other people and then came to us to do a leveraged buyout."

"Well, either way," Davey said, "it's come as a shock."

"I'm sorry to hear that. It's a coincidence, that's all. And yet, not such a strange one. We are, after all, well-known investment bankers, and P.T.C. Longwood is naturally looking for the best help it can get." Martin spoke lightly, easily.

If only, Lara was thinking, we could speak our minds. But there are all the ties, the ramifications, the favors we accepted. And Connie. How to endure another breach with Connie?

"So tell me, what did you think?"

"I thought he was an awful man," Davey said.

Martin laughed. "I can't disagree with that. But if you had to love everyone you met in the business world, you'd do mighty little business."

"True. Only I don't want to do business of this kind with anyone."

"If you don't like the deal, I can get him to sweeten it. You know that. Leave it to me. What part of it didn't you like?"

"We didn't get to any of the parts. I didn't want to hear them. I'm not interested."

There was a pause until Martin said, sounding incredulous, "That's impossible."

"It's true, Martin."

"Listen, Davey. I realize that he must have turned you off. Nobody likes the man, but everyone admits he's a phenomenon. In the entire corporate world there's nobody who can even come close to what Bennett's accomplished so fast." Martin sighed. "You can't win, Davey. Take my word for it."

TALK of a leveraged buyout spread through the town. Someone from P.T.C. Longwood had planted an item in the local paper, which was repeated and expanded. Davey was interviewed, but carefully avoided any definite conclusions. Stockholders and employees wrote letters to the editor, nine out of ten of which were against any change in the Davis Company.

Rumors were picked up by the statewide press in a series of articles about the takeover mania. From these it was deduced that the Davis Company's plant was to be shut down and five hundred people put out of work. The news resulted in a great protest rally in the high school stadium, attracting a crowd as large as the one for the Thanksgiving Day football game.

At an emotional meeting of his employees and their families, Davey promised to fight Bennett and whip him. But driving home with Lara afterward, he said to her, "I've had the stockholders canvassed. The stock's already risen on rumors alone, so what do you think will happen when the offer's on the table? They'll take the lollipop instead of the good bread, I'm certain of it. The damage has been done; they don't trust me."

"Davey, I don't believe it for one minute. The business with Eddy is past and over. Everybody understands what really happened. People don't hold anger forever." She waited for comment, but since none came she asked thoughtfully, "Don't you think it's mighty strange that we've heard nothing from Martin?"

"Not at all. Undoubtedly he's angry. They're going full steam ahead, and he doesn't want another useless discussion with us." Davey put a hand on hers. "Everything all right between Connie and you? You haven't said, and I've been afraid to ask."

"We spoke three times last week, but not about this. Anyway, I have the definite impression that she has no idea what's going on." Lara hesitated. "Do you think we'll know anything by Christmas?"

"I imagine so. I imagine we'll receive the final offer at the stock-holders' meeting next week."


THE principals sent their representatives to the meeting. A fleet of rented cars came from the airport and disgorged a dozen or more prosperous young men with bulging burnished-leather briefcases. No Bennett or Berg appeared. These lawyers, bankers, accountants, and corporate executives of the upper-middle echelon did their work well, however, lucidly presenting in essence one simple choice: Do you want to take your golden dollars now, or are you satisfied with modest gains and future hopes?

In vain did Davey, when his turn came, point out that the golden dollars and the whole edifice of P.T.C. Longwood were founded on a gigantic pyramid of debt.

"Whereas here," he said, "you have four tangible, debt-free walls where men work and make things that you can see and touch with your hands. You've been earning a good return on your money. We're growing, providing products for which there is real need. And there are more plans on the drawing board. Why else do you think this monstrous megacorporation is so eager to engulf us?"

But the audience, Lara saw, was unmoved, even though Davey

was speaking more eloquently than he had ever spoken before. She was stricken. These were the people who had been so eager to buy stock, so confident of his talent. Such intelligent people, too, or so one would think—a banker's widow, a doctor, an architect. . . .

"Have you lost all confidence in me?" Davey pleaded. "We're prospering, aren't we, under my direction?"

And he looked from face to face, but the faces were either blank or turned away. They were impatient. The evening was late; they were in a hurry to vote for their quick money and go home.

So, close to midnight, the vote was called. They hardly needed to take the trouble to count it. In the hall afterward Ben Levy and Doc Donnelly were the only ones to even look in Davey's direction.

"I'm sorry I had to do what I did, Davey," the doctor said. "I know I personally feel some guilt about deserting the ship, but frankly, the way most of us see it is that if you could be taken in by that Osborne fellow, why then, it's a question of judgment."

"We all lost a big bundle on him," Ben added. "This is a chance to recoup in a big, big way."

Davey's face, Lara saw, was stone white. And she spoke sharply to the men. "Enough's been said, hasn't it? Good night."

Alone with Davey, she asked, "What happens now?"

"Berg and his people will meet in New York with Bennett and his people to finalize it. It shouldn't take more than a month, if that. And then they'll send me a check for our share of the stock. And then I guess I'll start hunting for a job somewhere."

Yes, she thought bitterly, it's my family that's done this to him. Eddy and Martin—but Eddy first—have brought him down. She could not look at him.

## Chapter Seventeen

"Why don't we change the subject?" Ben Berg suggested to his brother.

The two had been having a wild argument all through dinner. It had been Martin's idea to invite Ben—just arrived for a semester of study at the London School of Economics—to the house in Belgravia. Connie had objected to dining here in this lofty hall, with the stiff new butler in attendance, when Ben would have been far more comfortable in a restaurant. Nevertheless, Ben was here, as earnest as ever.

"Brokerage fell way off after the crash," Martin said. "The only business that's really holding up is the leveraged buyout."

Ben's eyebrows rose. "A poor excuse, especially from a man who already has more than enough of the world's goods."

"What's 'enough'? Does anyone ever have it, even in academia?"

Like a bulldog, Martin hangs on to the final word, Connie thought. Bored, she took another spoonful of raspberry sorbet, sliding the satisfying sweetness over her tongue, and concentrated on her surroundings, which were also satisfying.

The entire house had been restored to its early-nineteenth-century splendor. From the Palladian windows to the classical moldings and the crystal drops that festooned the chandeliers, all was perfection. In the hall, statues stood in marble niches and the floor was laid with enormous marble squares. Between one drawing room and another, interior columns copied the temples of ancient Greece. Nowhere but in Britain would one find a house like this. There was surely nothing like it in the States, she declared silently.

"We get rid of deadwood. We tighten production when we buy out," Martin was saying.

"That's why we're doing so well in world markets," Ben countered. "Why, our whole manufacturing capacity is oozing away across the Pacific." The sweep of his arm upset a water goblet.

"Coffee in the little rose room," Connie directed then.

In the rose room, so named because of the carpet and the still life over the mantel, a genial fire snapped behind the screen, accentuating by its heat and brilliance an awareness of a dingy, wet fog outside, chilling the streets.

Martin shivered and held his hands toward the flame. "I wish I didn't have to go flying back home," he grumbled.

"I wish you didn't either. Why must you?" asked Connie.

"I told you, I've got a deal on. What else? It's finally gotten all its pieces together, and the principals want to close it fast, before Christmas. Anyway, I'll be back in a couple of days."

Connie became suddenly alert. "You're not talking about that man Bennett's deal, are you?"

Martin nodded.

"Are Davey and Lara still one of the pieces?"

"They are, and struggling to the very end."

"I thought the deal was dead."

"What made you think that?"

"You never talked about it."

"Do I usually discuss my deals with you?"

"Do you usually make deals that involve my sister?"

Martin lit a cigar and took a few puffs on it.

"Connie, I kept you out of it on purpose. I foresaw the possibility of trouble, and I wanted to avoid a family squabble."

"So you thought sneaking was the better way," she said sharply.

A picture seemed to rise out of the fire and hover there before her eyes: Bennett in the mink coat; all the clever men in their dark suits in the library of the Westchester house; superimposed somehow upon these were Lara and Davey standing over Peggy's bed.

"How can you do this?" she cried. "Forcing people. . . . You might as well hold a gun to their heads."

"Gun? Gun? You make a fool of yourself, Connie. Davey's stockholders voted in our favor. It's not my fault if he can't see reason."

"Whether it's reasonable or not isn't the point, Martin. Davey's worked years to build that business, and you're taking it away. Can't you get it through your head that Davey and Lara are different from you and me? They don't want the money."

"The more fools they." Martin turned to his brother, who had withdrawn into a copy of *Country Life*. "You should approve of Connie's brother-in-law, Ben. He's got this dinky little company he hates to let go of even though it's to his best advantage."

Ben laid the magazine down. "I may be a professor of economics, but I still can't understand why America's top businessmen want to wreck American business. To say nothing of the human factor, the cruelty."

Connie broke in. "You're on their side? Lara and Davey's?"

"I would have to be," Ben said quietly.

An odd melancholy settled in the room. "We are not in never-never land," Martin said. "This is a practical world, and Davey's been outvoted, that's all."

Bitterness was a taste in Connie's mouth. "You don't care. You take away the thing he built, break his heart, and you don't care."

Martin tossed the cigar into an ashtray. "You know what I think? I think you're crazy. Making much ado about nothing."

Ben got up and began to walk toward the door.

"Oh, good Lord. Ben, where are you going?" Martin said.

"I've got early classes tomorrow, but this is between you and Connie, anyway. Thanks for the good dinner."

When they had seen Ben to the door, they went upstairs.

Irritably Martin began to undress, talking as if to himself, pacing from closet to bathroom and back again. "I wonder how early the airline offices are open. And how am I going to get a seat? There must be a couple of thousand students going home for Christmas. I wish I had our plane here. Just my luck the fool thing has to be in for overhauling. Just when I need it."

"Where's the company plane?"

"Preston has it in Vail. He'll be flying back for the closing tomorrow." Martin stopped in front of the dressing-table mirror, before which Connie was sitting removing her makeup. "Look at me," he said. "I look terrible."

Two deep lines had carved themselves into his cheeks, lines that she had really not been aware of until this minute.

"Well, don't I look terrible?" he demanded.

"You look tired, that's all."

"This business is wearing me down. And this whole evening was a bomb. Ben, with his holy conscience, making me feel like a—like a thief or something. And you—you fall right in with him. Lara and Davey, all evening. Maybe that's the reason I feel so wrung out."

"I doubt it," she said coldly.

"Well, I don't. And now I'm tired. I want some sleep."

In the morning there would be no time to talk. Then the next day, in New York, the deal would be closed. In Ohio, Lara would be waiting with Davey for the telephone to ring with the news.

"Martin, listen to me. Personally, in Davy and Lara's position, I might go along with the offer and be glad about it. But that isn't the point." Floundering, Connie felt herself overcome by a sense of futility. For the first time ever, she was furious with him. She cried out, "I'm not going to let you hurt them, Martin. I'm not! If you make people wretched, if you destroy them in their hearts, it doesn't matter much whether what you did is legal or not."

"Damn you, Connie!" He whirled upon her. "You and your hard-luck family! Nothing but trouble."

"That's not true. And at least we care about one another."

"Leave me alone. I've heard enough," Martin said. "I need some rest. I'm sleeping across the hall."

The door closed sharply behind him.

She wanted—she needed—to fling herself onto the bed and cry out her frustration. And for a moment she stood undecided. But no, Connie, no. Cream your face as you always do. Drink some hot milk, climb into bed, and swallow the tears. Be sensible.

THE plane roared up out of Heathrow and climbed northward toward Scotland and the Atlantic. Every seat in every class on every westbound plane had been filled, and Martin had spent hours waiting for this lucky cancellation.

He laid his head back but was too perturbed to sleep. He hadn't said good-bye to Connie that morning. She had been asleep when he had gone into their room to get his clothes. He felt bad about leaving like that. He'd said some nasty things last night to his good-natured, good-hearted Connie. As to her family, the fact was that he admired their warmth; to their credit they stood fast to each other in a chilly world.

A vague sadness, an unfamiliar pity, filled Martin's chest. Connie, his joyous Connie. He wished now he could turn the plane around, go back to London, and tell her how much he loved her. The moment I land, he said to himself, I'll phone her. Then—

Pan American Flight 103 went down over Scotland in clear weather at three minutes after seven o'clock in the evening.

IN THOSE terrible minutes during which one airplane blew apart in the sky, another one headed toward a smooth landing at the airport outside of Louisville, Kentucky.

Anyone who had not seen Eddy Osborne for the past two years would have noticed at once as he emerged from this plane that he had altered. His vivid eyes were as striking as ever, and his hair was still as thick and fair, but there was a reserve, a quietness, about his expression that one had never associated with Eddy in the past. His posture and his gait were different, too; the jaunty step was no more. He walked through the airport toward the car-rental counter with the deliberate manner of a thoughtful man.

There was no one to meet him. Having been discharged from the prison a few days earlier than he had expected, he had thought he would surprise his wife. As he began to drive under a wide, light winter sky, his heart beat faster at the thought of home and Pam.

He reached the stone pillars, the long graveled drive that led up to his house. A sudden fear struck him that he would show tears and seem foolish. He parked the car and looked up at brilliant green shutters. On the second floor on the far side was the room where he would sleep tonight. He blinked and steadied himself. And another fear almost overwhelmed him—that perhaps he was dreaming all this, that he wasn't really here, but was still in Allenwood. He walked up to the front door and seized the brass knocker.

"Oh, my Lord," said Pam when she opened the door.

He stood for a moment, awkward at the sight of her, then his eyes filled and he took her in his arms.

"Oh, you shocked me," she murmured against his cheek. Kissing, they trembled against each other. "Oh, Eddy. I'm glad," she said.

They held each other apart, examining each other.

"You haven't changed," he told her. "What about me? Have I?"

"I can't tell yet. Come sit down."

He leaned back against the pillows in the corner of the sofa. And he remembered how many hundreds of times he had imagined his homecoming, bounding into the house, carrying her off to bed, there to quench an unbearable desire. And now that the moment had come, he wanted only to sit here and look at her.

"You do look different," she said. "I didn't notice it so much when I visited you—up there."

"A lot happens in two years."

She said softly, "I know." And she gave him the encouraging smile that one gives to an invalid or to a troubled child, and he saw how hard this hour was for her, too. She took his hand and held it between both of hers. "Things are going to come right."

He gave her a small wan smile. "You guarantee it?"

"Absolutely! You and I are going to have fun again. I promise."

Her eyes were anxious; she was appealing to him.

"I believe you. Now tell me things. Tell me about the horses."

307

"Oh, we have some beauties in the stalls! Yesterday we had two foals born, both treasures. And I've finally found a perfect man for the stables after having three absolute disasters in a row, one too lazy to get up in the morning, one more . . ."

He was only half listening. He felt suddenly flattened, and tried to analyze his feelings—some vague trace of fear inside him.

Pam was saying, "I'll come right back and bring a tray of goodies for you. You can't have had a decent meal since—"

"Since I went to prison, you mean. It's all right to say it, Pam."

"We are going to forget it, Eddy Osborne." She kissed him. "Now stay there and rest. I won't be long."

When she had gone, he began to look around the room. It was scented with the pine branches, garlanded for Christmas, that hung from the mantel. It was odd how he had to look twice to recognize some things. For that matter, the house itself was strange to him. He had been in it so briefly, after all, and then it had been in disarray, with painters and plumbers coming and going.

He walked out into the hall, which was airy and light. The staircase curved up to a landing, where stood a tall clock from his collection. The Waterford chandelier that had once hung in Pam's sitting room now descended from a thick silk rope two stories long.

Restless, he went upstairs to explore. It pleased him to see his Rowlandson prints in the hall, his pink jade Chinese horse on Pam's chest of drawers. By the braided trim on all the curtains he recognized the hand of their New York decorator, who had been persuaded—for a handsome fee, no doubt—to come to Kentucky.

Then something caught his attention, a pipe lying in an ashtray on a small lamp table in the bedroom at the end of the hall. For a moment he stood blankly seeing the thing, not comprehending it. Then, despising the immediate unworthy, cheap suspicion, he turned away. But it happened also that the closet door that faced him was ajar, and the unworthy, cheap suspicion drove him to reach out to the knob and seize it.

In a tidy row hung a man's riding clothes, half a dozen suits, a raincoat, an overcoat, tweed jackets, and a silk bathrobe—an entire wardrobe. Pajamas hung on a hook. And then Eddy became frantic; he ran to the chest and opened drawers. There were underclothes; there were socks, sweaters, and shirts with London labels. In the adjoining bathroom were shaving things, a brush and a comb.

He understood. For the first time in his life he thought he would go mad. He ripped the pajamas off the hook and tore the trousers from waist to ankle. Then, shaking with rage, he sank down on the chair and covered his face with his hands.

He was still sitting there when he heard Pam calling from the downstairs hall.

"Where are you? I've got soup and a smoked salmon sandwich. Eddy? Where are you?"

He did not answer. Then he heard her come up the stairs in search of him. And still he did not move.

Her glance—from shocked, wide-open eyes—took in the closet, the bureau drawers, and the clothes on the floor. Then it came to rest on Eddy, who looked back in silence.

"Oh," she said very softly. "Oh. But you've misunderstood! Sometimes I have a guest who stays overnight, that's all. He likes to ride on these trails, so he leaves his riding clothes here."

"And his suits and his underwear and a stack of shirts?"

She said nothing.

"I see that at least you have enough decency to blush."

She began to cry. "You don't believe me. I know how this might look to someone who didn't know me—"

"But that's just it, Pam. I do know you. Be truthful with me now. At least you can do that much for me."

Presently, in a harsh whisper, she spoke. "He's nobody. I mean *nobody* to me. He's nothing. He was nice to me when I came here, not knowing a soul. It was so lonely. It's one thing for a bright young couple to arrive together in a new place and start fresh. But for a woman to come alone, without a husband—"

"Or a husband in jail."

He walked to the window. The grass on this winter afternoon was still bright, but he was only half seeing it, was only barely conscious of this pastoral sweetness. He was numb.

"I didn't plan for it," Pam began again. "It just happened. And not as often as it may seem, either. He never lived here. I don't love him, Eddy. I never did, not for one minute. And I'm so ashamed." Now, with piteous eyes, she looked fully at him. "I've been thinking for weeks how the minute you got here— And now it's all spoiled!"

309

Our twisted lives. How is it possible for everything to go wrong? he asked himself. Everything.

Pam held out her arms. "But I won't let it be spoiled. I won't let it, Eddy! Come. Come here. Please. Can you? Please."

He felt himself flinch. "I can't," he said very low. It was an effort to speak. "I'm so incredibly sorry for us both, that's all."

For a minute or two he stood and looked at her trembling shoulders. Then carefully he closed the door behind him and went downstairs. He had no idea where he was going.

He walked through many rooms, down long passageways. Wall after wall displayed his treasured paintings, and precious sculpture stood in lighted niches. Beautiful they were, each one a marvel; and yet he stared about him feeling empty. The zest of ownership had gone. It would be enough to see these things in a museum.

After a while he went out onto the veranda. The sun had moved far to the west. He sat down—waiting for what, he did not know.

Presently, after an hour or more had passed, he heard the door open. Pam came out and sat down. Her eyes were swollen.

"What now, Eddy?" she asked quietly.

He answered, "I guess you'll want a divorce."

"Why? Do you really think that's what *I* want?"

"I don't know. I know I can't stay here." There was such a heaviness in his chest that he could hardly breathe. "I guess I'll go back to Ohio. There was a fellow in . . . in that place, whose brother-in-law has a large firm of accountants in Columbus. They offered me a job. I turned it down, but now I'll take it. I'll get an apartment and live within the salary. No worries. It'll feel good."

A silence, sorrowful and heavy, fell between them. After a while Pam broke it softly. "You'll be needing things for the apartment. There's plenty of stuff here. The attic's full. Even though I sold five million dollars' worth, there's enough left for another big sale."

"Sell it, then. Get the cash."

"I'm hardly in need of cash."

And now an idea struck Eddy, an illumination, as if a light that had been flickering had flared into a brilliance. "I was thinking, if it were sold, some of the people I took from could be paid back."

"You don't have to do that. You've been discharged in bankruptcy. You're cleared."

"I know that, but I don't feel cleared."

"I don't see why not, Eddy. What about the paintings? You could take some of them to sell. Then *you* sock away the cash."

"I'll have no use or space for treasures in the kind of little place I'll have, and I don't want the cash. I need to be free and clean."

"Isn't there anything I can give you? Anything at all that I can do?" Pam asked in a rising, wavering little voice. And he understood how sorry she was for him, for everything.

"Yes. Yes, there is something. I was thinking about Davey and Lara. You've kept in touch. Would you be willing to lend them enough to buy back the stock? Or you could buy it yourself and then release it to Davey, so he can beat those people who want to take him over. You know Davey. He'll pay you back ahead of time."

"I'll think about it. I've always loved Lara. You know that."

"It would mean so much. They've struggled so."

"I think Martin Berg's too rotten for words."

"I don't know. I don't judge anybody anymore." Eddy could hear the rueful sound of his own voice. "I only know how easy it is to get caught up in the rat race. Business is business, after all."

"Lara held out to the end. Didn't I always say she's the tough one? I told you so long ago. I wish—I wish I had her guts."

The short afternoon was coming to a close. Rusty clouds edged with silver fled toward the horizon. Pam stood up.

"It's getting cold. Come in and get ready for supper."

"I'm not hungry, and I have to see about getting back."

"You have to eat, Eddy."

"Okay. I'll just take a little walk around first."

It felt good to walk, to know he could keep on walking, if he chose, to the end of the earth and meet no barrier, no locked gate. No one was watching him. His feet crunched on gravel, then trod on grass, and following a track, he seemed to recall that it led to a pond. At the edge of the pond all was still; even the wind had died. He stood there hearing the stillness. "I loved her so," he said aloud.

After a while, as thick dusk fell, he walked back toward the barns and the house. A horse at the stable-yard fence whinnied softly, and Eddy went up to lay his hand on the warm head. On some impulse, then he put his own head against the animal's long cheek, and rested there. He had a sense of kinship, of perfect trust.

311

"What are you doing here?" Pam said. "I thought I heard steps on the gravel."

He started. "Nothing much. Just talking to the horse."

"I've come to tell you something. I will pay. Not just Davey and Lara, but the people who lost through you. Just let me know whom you owe, and I will pay. Of course, it will mean selling this place."

He was astonished.

"You're really willing to do that, Pam?"

"Yes, if you're willing to try to forgive what I've done, and begin again with me. No, Eddy, hear me out," she said as he started to reply. "I've been thinking about us. We were never very grown up, were we? Not even grown up enough to start a family, to be responsible for kids. At least I wasn't. I married you because you were handsome and we had great sex. I never really thought about *you*, about what drove *you*. If I had, maybe I could have helped you."

He was infinitely moved. And I, he thought, I married you because you were beautiful and you had a family tree that I didn't have and that I envied. Crazy, wasn't it?

"Eddy?" Her voice trembled. "Can we ever be what we were?"

"I don't know. There's so much I don't know anymore."

"I'm willing to try if you are. If you would just stay for a while. We'll be selling this place, and there'll be the moving and—"

"You'll need help, I know."

She did not answer. She's giving up all this because I asked her to, he was thinking. And it seemed to him that he owed her something in return. Why not stay, then, if that's what she needed?

"I'll stay awhile," he said. "Just fix a room for me."

## Chapter Eighteen

THE first person whom Connie saw among the little crowd that awaited her plane's arrival at Kennedy was Preston, whose silver-white head loomed above all others. He stepped back to let Melissa, just in from Paris, reach her first.

"Oh, Connie! Oh, Daddy!" Melissa said as they embraced.

The girl's homely face was swollen with weeping. It flashed across Connie's mind that here was the one person who had really deeply adored Martin. And this thought, this genuine pity, added to her own shock and grief, brought tears to Connie also.

Preston grasped her hand. "You must be exhausted. I've made special arrangements to get you through customs first. And I thought you'd like to keep together in one car, so I've got a stretch limo waiting. Seats for six." Preston counted: Connie and the two girls, Nanny, Connie's secretary, and himself. "Yes, just right. Come. We'll be out of here in no time."

"So good of you," she murmured, following him.

"We're all just devastated, Connie. There are no words for it."

Outside the car, on the way to the apartment, the bleak December day rolled past: joggers along the waterfront, high-rise apartments, rows of uniform houses with plastic snowmen in their yards and windblown tinsel decorations. Connie was thinking, I was reading to Thérèse at the very instant the plane went hurtling in pieces through the sky, and I was thinking how many hours it would take before I could phone Martin in New York and say how sorry I was.

Oh, Lord! How sorry! Gulping, she closed her eyes. That awful fight! And then the horror. The horror. Such a good man, a kind man! No woman could have wanted a more devoted husband. The terribly sad thing was that she had never returned his love, not in her heart, although, thank goodness, he could have had no way of knowing that. But she had tried to be a good wife; that much at least was undeniable. Impulsively she reached forward for Melissa's hand and squeezed it, vowing, I will take care of Martin's daughter, for she needs me. That much I can do for his memory.

By the beginning of spring Connie's telephone began to bring discreet invitations for small, quiet dinner parties. She was not interested. Still numbed by the unpredictability of death, by the daily immanence of it, which she had quite forgotten since the long-ago death of her mother, she was now feeling a need only for the protective comfort of the familiar. Lara and Eddy had, of course, come at once to New York and thrown their arms around her. It was then that she learned how Pam, through Eddy, had rescued the Davis Company. Her feelings on learning of it were a mixture of tenderness toward her brother—how changed he was, still optimistic, but with the boastful swagger gone!—and a sense of shame that it had been Martin who had driven Davey to the wall.

What a year it had been for Eddy, for Lara—for the three of them, each in his own way! A year of trials and tests. It seemed to Connie now that they were merely pausing, resting as the world rests when a terrible winter seems to have passed, but there is still no certainty that another storm might not be on the way.

Drawn by this need for the familiar, she made a few impulsive trips in Martin's plane to Ohio and Kentucky.

Davey's plant was going full blast, but still Lara worried.

"The debt load is horrendous, Connie. To think that Davey had to borrow such a sum to save his own place! We're making just about enough to meet the payments he promised Pam. And after that, we barely squeeze by. It doesn't seem to make any sense."

"I can't believe Pam would press him, though."

Lara shook her head. "No, no. But I don't understand it. Ninety percent of their splendor's gone. It's very queer. It's almost as if she'd stripped herself when she made the loan to us."

"That's too saintly to be real. Nobody does that."

"Well, wait till you go there and see," said Lara.

What Connie saw that first time was a neat white house of moderate size surrounded by ten level acres of grazing grounds, stables, and riding rings. By the side of the country road, above the mailbox, a sign read OSBORNE HORSE FARM, RIDING, BOARDING, SCHOOLING. Pam, familiar in boots and breeches, came out and led her around, explaining the new order of things.

"We don't raise racers, only a few horses for show. Eddy's turned against racing, and I see his point, because it's just gambling, really. Riding for its own sake is the true sport."

Connie, feeling dainty and citified, hurried to keep up with Pam's long stride. "How's Eddy getting on in the new job?"

"Very well. It's only a three-member firm of accountants."

Pam's tone was flat. Connie thought she sensed a reluctance to touch on Eddy's work. But that was probably understandable.

"Quite a change," she said sympathetically.

"Yes. Come see the house. You'll find that quite a change, too."

Here indeed was no southern mansion, merely the usual basic rooms, with simple though tasteful furniture, along with an office decorated by framed photographs of horses. Still, Connie was gratified to recognize some familiar things that Eddy had cherished.

"Oh, the Winslow Homer!" she cried on entering the living room. "I always loved that so."

"Yes," Pam said. "Would you like the whole tour? Upstairs?"

"Of course. You know how I love to see houses."

On the second floor, off a narrow hall, there opened a sunny master room, three more bedrooms, and a small office.

"Eddy's office," Pam said. "Eddy's bedroom next to it."

The women's eyes met. Connie turned hers away. Was there something Pam wanted her to know? If so, why not tell her?

But no more was said. They went downstairs, had tea with small talk, and waited for Eddy to come home to dinner.

After dinner, when Pam had to talk to a customer in the stables, the brother and sister were, for a while, alone. And presently, after many circumlocutions, Connie came to her point.

"This retrenchment— I don't mean that you aren't living very nicely, but the change is dramatic, isn't it? What's the reason?"

Eddy's faint smile was wry. "Reason? Have you any idea what it cost Pam to outbid P.T.C. Longwood for Davey's company?" Then as Connie's flush rose to her face he said quickly, "It's a painful subject, I know, but you mustn't let it pain. It's past and done with. Business is business. It always was."

"But I don't understand why she made such a sacrifice," Connie said in a low, hurt voice. "It's staggering."

"Because I asked her to." Eddy's mouth closed in a hard line.

"Extraordinary." She looked around the room. "And you are back where you started, living on what you earn from day to day."

"As most people do. Although we have Davey's payments."

All the way home Connie was bothered by what she had seen and heard. It seemed to her that in some way she had inherited a responsibility for making good the damage that Martin's firm had done. And she said as much when she next saw Preston.

"Frankly, I can't see why you should feel responsible," he said. "Your brother-in-law chose to take the hard way. To my mind he was foolish. Now he's struggling."

"I hate to see him struggling. I've been thinking that I want to buy the loan from Pam. I really do."

"Go ahead. You can certainly afford to. Especially if you plan to sell all that property. Do you?"

"Yes. What do I want with a huge house in London? It's just a responsibility. And I'm selling Palm Beach, and the ski house. It's so much easier to take a suite in a hotel when you want to go somewhere. All I want to keep are the apartment and Cresthill."

"You've done well for yourself in this world, Connie. But you deserve it. You've got heart."

"Thank you. I was thinking, Preston, I could take Davey's repayments, after I've assumed the loan, and put part away for Lara's children. It would have to be secret because he and Lara would never accept it otherwise. Can that be done?"

"Easily. We'll set up a trust. Just tell me when."

ONE day in early fall Connie happened to drive past the hospital where Peggy had been cared for. Quite naturally, then, the whole experience raced like a motion picture through her memory.

*He was a nice man, that doctor, Jonathan Bayer. I remember thinking,* she said to herself, *that I'd like to know him. I can't say why exactly, but he just seemed interesting.*

And driving on with the top down and a fresh breeze blowing, she felt a sudden heat rise to her cheeks. *Absurd, Connie. Where do you think you are? In junior high school?*

There was a choice of three routes from Cresthill to the village, the most circuitous of which passed the hospital. Nevertheless, driving one day with Thérèse in the car, she took that route again.

"Look, Mommy. That's where Peggy was when she was sick. We used to bring toys and cookies for the children there."

"You're right, we did. Would you like to buy some toys and bring them there again?"

"Yes, let's."

*The project was a good one, and it ought to be carried out. Besides . . . But how foolish! He probably wasn't even there anymore. And if he was—so what?*

"We'll go tomorrow," Connie said.

They had half a dozen cartons filled with toys when they returned the next day. It took several trips to carry all of these indoors. On the last one Connie, dropping a carton, was rescued as Jonathan Bayer came hurrying through the parking lot.

"What's going on? It's not Christmas yet," he said.

Connie explained. "We have a special feeling for this place, because of Peggy. My sister's child, if you remember."

"Remember? Of course I do!" He looked surprised.

What a stupid remark! Naturally he remembered. And annoyed with herself for being so awkward, she made amends.

"When she came, she might as well have been dead, and when she left, she was whole again. It was a miracle."

"Yes, miracles do happen, but not often." They set the bundles down in the front hall and stood there for a moment, uncertain.

"Shall I have these distributed, or do you want—" began the doctor, when Connie interrupted hastily, "No, no, I don't want to. That's too much like Lady Bountiful. Oh, no."

He laughed. "Good for you. I'll see to it, then. We're always in need of toys, and we surely thank you. Especially you, Thérèse."

He went down the hall fast, almost running, as Connie remembered he used to do.

Outside on the lawn, patients singly and in groups, with nurses or relatives, sat in wheelchairs or made arduous efforts to walk. A little boy about Thérèse's age was sitting on the grass with a woman, fumbling over a game.

Thérèse stopped. "I'll show you how to do it," she told him.

Connie said quickly, "No, no. Don't bother the little boy."

The other woman looked up, smiling. "She just wants to be friendly. We don't mind, if you don't."

So the two mothers sat watching while Thérèse, with astounding patience, demonstrated to the boy how to tilt the box so that the silver ball would run through the maze into the hole.

Presently Dr. Bayer came down the walk and stopped to watch the children. When at last the silver ball fell into the hole, the boy laughed, and Thérèse clapped and stood up.

"Time to go now," said Connie.

Dr. Bayer, also going in the direction of the parking lot, remarked as Thérèse ran ahead, "You have an unusual child."

"Yes. She's always been quick and bright."

"Like you."

"Thank you. But she's like her father."

"I see the kindness, too."

"I'm lucky to have her, I know." And she added, "We live alone now, the two of us. Her father was on Flight 103 that went down over Scotland last winter."

"Oh!" he cried. "Your husband—that vital man!"

There was such genuine pain in his single "Oh!" that she turned to look at him. She saw an expression of extraordinary gentleness.

They reached Connie's car. When he had seen them into it, Dr. Bayer stood at the window. She had not yet started the motor.

She said, "The things you do here . . . When I remember my little niece, I feel so grateful. I wish I could do something to show it. Better than bringing a few toys, I mean."

"You could volunteer," he told her. "You could do pretty much what Thérèse did just now. The nurses don't have enough time for all that should be done, especially on weekends."

"Really? I think I'd like to do that."

"If you're interested, come see me about it. They've made me medical director since you were here. I'm on the ground floor."

"Let's go, Mommy!" Thérèse cried impatiently.

For once, Connie was glad of the child's impatience.

SHE asked to be with children, so on the following Saturday she was given charge of a ten-year-old girl who needed someone to walk with her around the grounds. This was such simple work that it was hardly work at all, and yet how valuable it was. It might, in another sense, be thought odd for Connie to be spending the afternoon with a strange child while her own child was being cared for by a nanny. And she knew, of course, that the only reason she was not at home with Thérèse was Jonathan Bayer.

He came upon her just after she had returned her charge.

"Well, how do you like this work?"

"It's hardly work, but I feel I've done something worthwhile."

"You have." He looked at her quizzically. "I'm off for the rest of the day. Would you like to have a drink with me?"

"That would be nice."

"There's a place down the road. We can sit out under an umbrella, if you'd like."

"That would be nice."

Where was her vaunted personality? She was as tongue-tied as a girl on a first date. They got into his car, drove, and found themselves at an umbrella table on a gilded September afternoon, with nothing but silence swelling between them. Her heart pounded. She did not understand, knew only that something powerful had taken hold of her, that she felt eased while she was drawn to him, and yet that she feared this thing, so fearfully unfamiliar.

After a few awkward attempts at conversation they finished their drinks and drove back to the hospital. He took her hand on parting.

"This is only our first time," he said. "We'll do better next time."

THERE were three more times—a tea, a lunch, and a dinner. And the talk began to flow between them, talk about places Connie had never seen, such as a hospital for Cambodian refugees in Thailand. She learned that he had always wanted to be a doctor. She learned that he had never been married; for some reason that pleased her. But then she had to give him in turn the bare facts of her own life, about her family and her marriages.

After the dinner date, in the dark of the hospital parking lot where she had kept her car, he kissed her. It was a light brush on the lips, and that was all it was. He couldn't know it, but if he had asked her to, if there had been a private place for them to go, she would have lain down there on the grass with him, would have cried out the marvel that it had taken all these years for her to feel, really to *feel*, at last. . . . She scarcely recognized herself. And driving home alone through the quiet night, she wept.

Then for two weeks there was no word from him. I don't understand it, she thought over and over. She felt a cold sense of loss. The man had reached her as no man ever had; yet that was not to say that she had reached *him* in the same way, was it?

One night, not sleeping well, she got up and walked through the house, from room to room. The place was lonely. The place was a museum crammed with brilliant objects collected in superfluity, that all might see how well their owner had "made it." The place was useless. It was dead. How strange it was that living here, she had never before felt its deadness!

"I will telephone him in the morning," she said aloud into the midnight silence. "Pride or not, what more have I got to lose?"

If he agreed, they would have dinner together here tomorrow.

319

IT WAS STILL LIGHT ENOUGH WHEN Jonathan arrived to see the gold leaves tremble slowly onto the leaf-speckled grass. From the window nook in the library, where they dined simply at a small round table, he gazed out at a vast view of lawns emblazoned with ornamental trees, with gazebos, ponds, and statuary. During the last few minutes, after an animated start, he had become quiet.

Connie had told herself she would be very open; for the first time in her life she would bring no wiles, no calculations to bear upon a man. And so she asked bluntly, "What are you thinking?"

He turned to her with equal honesty. "I am thinking that this place reminds me of Versailles."

"I want to sell it," she said abruptly.

"I thought you loved it."

"I did once." She hesitated. "It was a binge. An addiction."

He listened while she let her thoughts speak, thoughts that not long ago she would have said she could never have. All that money, flowing in and spilling over . . .

"In the end," she said softly, "it has no meaning. The treasures, the rich prizes, have no meaning."

Without answering, he gazed at the darkening scene beyond the window. With every one of her senses she was aware of him, aware of the black, curving eyelashes, of the cleft chin that gave a sweetness to the powerful face, of the long hand that rested on the table.

He stood up suddenly. The coffee had grown cold in the cups. "Connie, I need to talk to you."

Fifty people could sit comfortably in the library. At one end a fire was lit against the early autumn chill, and there she led him to sit.

"Connie," he began, "I know you wondered why I didn't call you. You knew, we both knew, that something was happening to us. But I was so afraid." He waved his hand toward the enormous room. "I don't belong here. I knew who Martin Berg was—a decent man, I'm sure, but worlds apart from me—and I thought that a woman who coveted all this couldn't possibly be happy with my ways."

Connie's heart was hammering. "Go on," she said.

"You don't know how I fought with myself. I remember thinking how warm you are, with all your vital joy. And still I asked myself whether I really knew you."

"And do you think you do now?"

"Oh, much better. What you said just then about the treasures, the rich prizes, seemed to open the way for me to see you clearly."

She got up and stood before him, trembling. "What do you see?"

"I see a woman. A real one. Oh," he said, "I kept thinking I mustn't lose you. Then I thought, but what if we start out together and then I lose you? How much worse that would be!"

"You won't lose me, Jonathan."

"Oh," he cried, and rose to meet her.

For minutes then they stood together, clasped while he kissed her eyes, her cheeks, and her mouth, his hands moving gently on her body, and neither of them able to stop or to let go. So this had been here in the world all the time, and she had never known it!

And she said to him, "I wanted it to turn out like this. I wanted it so. With all my heart."

THANKSGIVING, one year later.

With huge pleasure Lara looked down the long table. At the far end sat Davey; ranked on either side were Eddy and Pam, Melissa Berg, Connie and Thérèse and Jonathan, then Lara's own two children. In the center was a splendid mound of chrysanthemums, baby pumpkins, and dried Indian corn.

"I always wanted a really big tableful, really big," Lara said.

"Next year, if you invite us," Eddy said, looking significantly at Pam's visible, enormous pregnancy, "it will be even fuller."

A sliver of pie remained on the plate in front of Lara. "Does anyone want the last piece?" she asked. "If not, I guess we can all get up and stretch."

At the living-room window, Connie stood looking out at the yard. At the far end of the property stood Davey's new workroom, much like the shabby original in size and shape but painted white, with green window boxes that Lara would plant with geraniums again. Connie smiled to herself.

"He gets his best ideas when he can work at home in a quiet place," Lara said, coming up beside her. "The plant's too busy."

Davey overheard. "Thank heaven it's busy. I hired ten new men last week. Have you heard about P.T.C. Longwood, Connie?"

"No, I don't hear about those things anymore."

"Well, it was in the papers. Bennett's selling to the Japanese."

"A few more billions for his coffers," said Connie, scoffing.

"Connie, you've become an idealist," Lara observed tranquilly.

"Well, I have. It's disgusting when people pile up millions."

"It's an easy addiction to get," Eddy said, "and hard to break."

"None of us is exactly impoverished." That was Davey.

"We've finally sold Cresthill," Connie announced abruptly. "The apartment, too. We close on our new house this week."

It pleased her that they all wanted to know about the new one.

Jonathan replied with a smile. "It's a beautiful colonial near the hospital and Thérèse's new school, a little larger than I wanted and a little smaller than Connie wanted, so we compromised, since each of us paid for our half of it."

"There's just enough room for you all, including Melissa when she's home from college, and even a nursery for Pam's baby," Connie said. "Are you positive you haven't twins in there, darling?"

"I'd be delighted if she had," said Eddy, taking his wife's hand.

"What a wonderful day it's been," sighed Lara with that same lovely, tranquil look on her face.

"I've been thinking of Peg," Connie murmured. "If she knows that we're here together like this, she's very very happy."

And Eddy added typically, "Yes, we haven't done too badly. We've had our ups and our downs, and nobody's won a Nobel Prize either, but we haven't done too badly."

Connie caught her husband's eye. So you like us? went her silent question.

Yes. And you, you I love came his silent answer.

The moment caught Connie's heart. She must remember it exactly, its familiar faces, its well-known voices, and even the way the late sun fell, to touch with its blessed light these whom she held most dear—all these, her living treasures.

Belva Plain has been called the "queen of family-saga writers" by *The New York Times*, and her countless fans would undoubtedly agree. Time and again she has taken the strands of one family's tale and deftly woven them across the generations, and time and again those efforts have landed her books squarely on best-seller lists. With the publication of *Treasures,* her ninth novel— and sixth to appear in Condensed Books—there are now sixteen million copies of her books in print worldwide.

*Belva Plain*

The author claims that when she first started writing, the family theme was an "unconscious emphasis," yet it has long been a key ingredient in her life. "One of the reasons family is so important to me is because I was an only child and I never had lots of relatives nearby," she explains. She was delighted when she married and had a family of her own. She and Dr. Irving Plain, an opthalmologist, were married for forty-two years, until his death in 1982, and their marriage produced three children. As her novels demonstrate, families can be a wonderful source of strength and joy. And of course, most families experience enough challenges and struggles to provide fascinating story material.

While several of Mrs. Plain's earlier books, including *Evergreen* and *Crescent City,* had a historical flavor, for *Treasures* the author decided to tackle a contemporary theme: pursuit of material wealth at the expense of personal integrity and family. Herself a hard worker at her craft, the author firmly believes that family should take precedence over work. As she's noted, "I feel very fortunate that my own grandchildren are growing up surrounded by cousins and aunts and uncles." And with the love and attention of their devoted grandmother as well.

Belva Plain, who lives in suburban New Jersey, is already hard at work on her next novel.

# JACK HIGGINS

# EYE OF THE
# STORM

# The mortar attack
## on number Ten
### Downning Street when the

War Cabinet was meeting at

ten a.m. on Thursday, 7 February

1991, is now a matter of history.

It has never been satisfactorily explained.

Perhaps it went something like this. . . .

# One

I T WAS just before dark as Dillon emerged from the alley and
paused on the corner. Rain drifted across the Seine in a flurry of
snow, sleet mixed with it, and it was cold, even for January in Paris.
He wore a reefer coat, a peaked cap, jeans and boots—just another
sailor off one of the barges working the river, which he very definitely was not.

He lit a cigarette in cupped hands and stayed there for a moment
in the shadows, looking across the cobbled square at the lights of
the small café on the other side. After a while he dropped the
cigarette, thrust his hands deep in his pockets and started across.

In the darkness of the entrance two men waited, watching his
progress. One of them whispered, "That must be him."

He made a move. The other held him back. "No. Wait till he's
inside."

Dillon, his senses sharpened by years of entirely the wrong kind
of living, was aware of them but gave no sign. He paused at the
entrance, slipped his left hand under the reefer coat to check that
the Walther PPK was securely tucked into the waistband of his
jeans against the small of his back; then he opened the door and
went in.

It was typical of the sort of place to be found on that part of the
river: half a dozen tables with chairs, a zinc-topped bar, bottles
lined against a cracked mirror behind it. The entrance to the rear
was masked by a bead curtain.

The barman, a very old man with a gray mustache, put down the magazine he was reading and got up from the stool.

"Monsieur?"

Dillon unbuttoned his reefer coat and put his cap on the bar. He was a small man, no more than five feet five inches, with fair hair and eyes of no particular color at all, though they were the coldest the old man had ever looked into. He shivered, unaccountably afraid, and then Dillon smiled. The change was astonishing—suddenly nothing but warmth there and immense charm. His French, when he spoke, was perfect.

"Would you have such a thing as half a bottle of Champagne?"

The old man stared at him in astonishment. "Champagne? You must be joking, monsieur. I have two kinds of wine only. One is red and the other white." He placed a bottle of each on the bar.

"All right," Dillon said. "The white it is. Give me a glass."

He put his cap back on, went and sat at a table against the wall from where he could see both the entrance and the curtained door. He poured some of the wine into the glass and tried it.

He said to the barman, "And what vintage would this be? Last week's?"

"Monsieur?" The old man looked bewildered.

"Never mind." Dillon lit another cigarette, sat back and waited.

THE man who stood peering through the curtain was in his mid-fifties, of medium height, with a slightly decadent look to his face, the fur collar of his dark overcoat turned up against the cold. He looked like a prosperous businessman—right down to the gold Rolex on his left wrist—which in a way he was, as a senior commercial attaché at the Soviet embassy in Paris. He was also a colonel in the KGB—one Josef Makeev.

The younger, dark-haired man in the expensive vicuña overcoat who peered over his shoulder beside him was called Michael Aroun. He whispered in French, "This is ridiculous. He can't be our man. He looks like nothing."

"A serious mistake many people have made, Michael," Makeev said. "Now wait and see."

The outer door swung open, rain blowing in, and two men entered. They had been waiting in the doorway as Dillon crossed the square.

One of them was over six feet tall, bearded, an ugly scar near the right eye. The other was much smaller. They were dressed in reefer coats and denims. They looked exactly what they were—trouble.

They stood at the bar as the old man looked worried. "No trouble, Pierre," the smaller one said. "We only want a drink."

The big man turned, looked at Dillon and crossed to his table. "It seems as if we've got one right here." He picked up Dillon's glass and drank from it. "Our friend doesn't mind, do you?"

Without getting out of his chair, Dillon raised his left foot and stamped downwards against the bearded man's kneecap. The man went down with a choked cry, grabbing at the table, and Dillon stood. The other man took a knife from his pocket, springing the blade, and Dillon's left hand came up holding the Walther PPK.

"On the bar. You never learn, people like you, do you? Now get this piece of dung out of here while I'm still in a good mood."

The small man went to his friend and struggled to get him on his feet. They stood there for a moment, the bearded man's face twisted in agony. Dillon went and opened the door, the rain pouring relentlessly down outside.

As they lurched past him he said, "Have a good night," and then he closed the door.

Still holding the Walther, he called in English, "All right, Makeev. I know you're there, so let's be having you."

The curtain parted, and Makeev and Aroun stepped through. "My dear Sean, it's good to see you again."

"And aren't you the wonder of the world," Dillon said, just the trace of an Ulster accent in his voice. "One minute trying to stitch me up, the next all sweetness and light."

"It was necessary, Sean," Makeev said. "I needed to make a point to my friend here. Let me introduce you."

"No need," Dillon told him. "I've seen his picture often enough. If it's not on the financial pages, it's usually in the society magazine. Michael Aroun, isn't it? The man with all the money in the world."

"Not quite all, Mr. Dillon." Aroun put a hand out.

Dillon ignored it. "We'll skip the courtesies, my old son, while you tell whoever is standing on the other side of that curtain to come out."

"Rashid," Aroun called, then said to Dillon, "It's only my aide."

The young man who stepped through had a dark, watchful face and wore a leather car coat, his hands thrust deep in the pockets.

Dillon knew a professional when he saw one. He motioned with the Walther and said, "Plain view." Rashid actually smiled and took his hands from his pockets. "Good," Dillon said. "I'll be off, then."

He turned and got the door open. Makeev said, "Sean, be reasonable. We only want to talk. A job, Sean."

"Sorry, Makeev, but I don't like the way you do business."

"Not even for a million, Mr. Dillon?" Michael Aroun said.

Dillon paused and turned to look at him calmly. Then he smiled with enormous charm. "Would that be in pounds or dollars, Mr. Aroun?" He walked out into the rain.

As the door banged, Aroun said, "We've lost him."

"Not at all," Makeev said. "A strange one this, believe me." He turned to Rashid. "You have your portable phone?"

"Yes, Colonel."

"Good. Get after him. Stick to him like glue. When he settles, phone me. We'll be at Avenue Victor-Hugo."

Rashid didn't say a word, simply went. Aroun took out his wallet and extracted a thousand-franc note, which he placed on the bar. He said to the barman, who was looking totally bewildered, "We're very grateful." Then he turned and followed Makeev out.

Aroun slid behind the wheel of the black Mercedes. As they drove away Makeev said to him, "A remarkable man, Sean Dillon. He first picked up a gun for the IRA in 1971. Twenty years, Michael, and he hasn't seen the inside of a cell once. Then he became too hot for his own people to handle, so he moved to Europe. He's worked for everyone—the PLO, the Red Brigade in Germany in the old days, the Basque national movement."

"And the KGB?"

"But of course. He's worked for us on many occasions. We always use the best, and Sean Dillon is exactly that. He speaks English and Irish, fluent French and German, reasonable Arabic, Italian and Russian."

"And no one has ever caught him in twenty years. How could anyone be that lucky?"

"Because he has the most extraordinary gift for acting, my friend. A genius, you might say. As a boy, he was awarded a scholarship to the Royal Academy of Dramatic Art, in London. By nineteen he was working for the National Theatre. I have never known anyone who can change personality and appearance so much just by body language. Makeup helps when he wants. He's a legend that the security services of most countries keep quiet about because they can't put a face to him, so they don't know what they're looking for. I doubt if there's a recent photo of him anywhere."

"And you think he might undertake this business if I offer him enough money?"

"No. Money alone has never been enough for this man. It always has to be the job itself where Dillon is concerned. How can I put it? How interesting it is. This is a man to whom acting is everything. What we are offering him is a new part." Makeev smiled as the Mercedes joined the traffic moving around the Arc de Triomphe. "Let's wait and see. Wait until we hear from Rashid."

AT THAT moment Captain Ali Rashid was by the Seine at the end of a small pier jutting out into the river. The floodlights were on at Notre-Dame, and the effect with the rain falling was of something seen through a net curtain. Rashid watched Dillon turn along the narrow pier to the building on stilts at the far end, waited until he went inside, and followed him.

The sign over the door said LE CHAT NOIR—the Black Cat. He peered through the window cautiously. There was a bar and several tables, just like the other place. The only difference was that people were eating, and there was even a man sitting on a stool against the wall, playing an accordion. All very Parisian. Dillon was standing at the bar speaking to a young woman.

Rashid moved back, walked to the end of the pier, paused by the rail in the shelter of a small terrace and dialed the number of Aroun's house in the Avenue Victor-Hugo on his portable phone.

There was a slight click as the Walther was cocked and Dillon rammed the muzzle painfully into Rashid's right ear. "Now then, son, a few answers," Dillon demanded. "Who are you?"

"My name is Rashid," the young man said. "Ali Rashid. I'm a captain in the Iraqi army, assigned to protect Mr. Aroun."

"And Makeev and the KGB?"

"Let's just say he's on our side."

"The way things are going in the Persian Gulf, you need somebody on your side, my old son." There was the faint sound of a voice from the portable phone. "Go on, answer him."

Makeev was saying, "Rashid, where is he?"

"Right here," Rashid told him, "outside a café called the Black Cat. It's on the river, near Notre-Dame."

"Put him on," Makeev ordered. Rashid handed the phone to Dillon, and the Russian said, "A million pounds, Sean."

"And what would I have to be doing for all that money?"

"The job of a lifetime. Let Rashid bring you round here, and we'll discuss it."

"I don't think so," Dillon said. "I think what I'd really like is for you to get yourself into gear and come and pick us up."

"Of course," Makeev said.

Dillon handed the phone to Rashid and smiled. "Now let's you and me go inside and have ourselves a drink in comfort."

IN THE sitting room on the first floor of the house in Avenue Victor-Hugo, overlooking the park—the Bois de Boulogne—Josef Makeev put down the phone and reached for his overcoat.

"Was that Rashid?" Aroun demanded.

"Yes. He's with Dillon now, at a place on the river. I'm going to get them. You hold the fort, Michael. I won't be long."

He went out. Aroun lit a cigarette, then turned on the television. He was halfway into the news. There was direct coverage from Baghdad of Tornado fighter-bombers of the British Royal Air Force attacking at low level. It made him bitterly angry, for, surprising in one so self-centered, he was a patriot. Infinitely more important was the fact that his father, retired as a general from the Iraqi army, had been killed in a bombing raid on the third night of the air war. Aroun switched off the television, poured himself a brandy, and went and sat by the window.

Michael Aroun was forty years of age and a remarkable man by any standards. Born in Baghdad of a French mother, he'd had a maternal grandmother who was American. Through her, his mother had inherited ten million dollars and a number of oil leases in Texas. She had died the year he graduated from Harvard Law School, leaving everything to him because his father, the general, was happy to spend his later years at the old family house in Baghdad with his books.

Like most great businessmen, Aroun had no academic training in the field. He knew nothing of financial planning or business administration. His favorite saying, one much quoted, was: When I need a new accountant, I buy a new accountant.

His friendship with Saddam Hussein had been a natural development. The Iraqi President had been greatly supported in his early days in politics by Aroun's father, who was also an important member of the Baath Party. It had placed Aroun in a privileged position as regards the development of his country's oil fields, brought him riches beyond calculation.

Now he was faced with disaster. He was far from ruined in personal terms—he still had oil interests in the United States. But that portion of his wealth that stemmed from Iraq had dried up, was finished, as a result of the coalition's massive air strikes against his country since the seventeenth of January. There was also a great secret in his life. In August, shortly after Iraq's invasion of Kuwait, Aroun had been sent for by Saddam Hussein himself. Sitting here by the open French window, a glass of brandy in one hand, rain slanting across the terrace, he gazed out across the Bois de Boulogne in the evening light and remembered that meeting.

SADDAM Hussein was in uniform, sitting at a large desk, writing slowly. He looked up and smiled, putting down his pen.

"Michael." He came round the desk and embraced Aroun like a brother. "Your father—he is well?"

"In excellent health, my President."

"Give him my respects. You look well, Michael. Paris suits you."

He sat down behind the desk again, and Aroun sat opposite. Against the wall in the darkness stood the young intelligence captain named Rashid, who had escorted Aroun to the presidential palace. Rashid was one of the new breed, trained by the British at the military academy at Sandhurst.

"Paris was fine," Aroun said, "but my place is here now, in these difficult times."

Saddam Hussein shook his head. "Not true, Michael. I have soldiers in plenty but few men such as you. You are rich, famous, accepted at the highest levels of society and government anywhere in the world. More than that, because of your beloved mother of blessed memory, you are not just an Iraqi but also a French citizen. No, Michael. I want you in Paris."

"But why, my President?" Aroun asked.

"Because one day I may require you to do a service for me and for your country that only you could perform."

Aroun said, "You can rely on me totally, you know that."

Saddam Hussein got up and paced to the nearest window. "I still hope our friends in America and Britain stay in their own backyard, but if not"—he shrugged—"then we may have to fight them in their own backyard. Remember, as the Prophet instructs us in the Koran, there is more truth in one sword than in ten thousand words." He paused. "One sniper in the darkness, Michael. Bush or the Thatcher woman. The proof that my arm reaches everywhere. The ultimate coup. Would you be capable of arranging such a thing if necessary?"

Aroun had never felt so excited in his life. "I think so, my President. All things are possible, especially when sufficient money is involved. It would be my gift to you."

"Good." Saddam nodded. "You will return to Paris immediately. Captain Rashid will accompany you. He will have the codes we will be using on the radio, that sort of thing. The day may never come, Michael, but if it does . . . " He shrugged again, and turned to Rashid. "That KGB colonel at the Soviet embassy in Paris?"

"Colonel Josef Makeev, my President."

"Yes. Like many of his kind, he is not happy with the changes now taking place in Moscow. He will assist in any way he can. He's already expressed his interest." Saddam Hussein embraced Aroun again. "Now go. I have work to do."

SINCE his return to Paris, Aroun had got to know Makeev well, meeting mainly at various embassy functions. Saddam Hussein had been right. The Russian was definitely on their side, willing to do anything to cause problems for the United States or Great Britain.

The news from home, of course, had been bad. The buildup of such a gigantic army—who could have expected it? And then in the early hours of the seventeenth of January the air war had begun. One bad thing after another, and the ground attack still to come.

Aroun poured himself another brandy now, remembering his

despairing rage at the news of his father's death. The feeling of impotence had been like a living thing inside him. And then came the morning when Ali Rashid had rushed into the great ornate sitting room, a notepad in one hand, his face pale and excited.

"It's come, Mr. Aroun. The signal we've been waiting for. I just heard it on the transmitter from Baghdad." He held out the pad.

> The winds of heaven are blowing. Implement all that is on the table. May God be with you.

Aroun had gazed at the words in wonder, and his voice was hoarse when he said, "The President was right. The day has come."

"Exactly," Rashid said. "Implement everything that is on the table. We're in business. I'll get in touch with Makeev and arrange a meeting as soon as possible."

DILLON stood at the French windows and peered out across the Avenue Victor-Hugo to the Bois de Boulogne. He was whistling softly to himself, a strange eerie little tune.

"May I offer you a drink, Mr. Dillon?"

"Champagne wouldn't come amiss. Krug would be fine."

"A man of taste, I see." Aroun nodded to Rashid, who opened a side door and went out.

Dillon unbuttoned his reefer coat. "So you need my services, this old fox tells me." He nodded at Makeev. "A million pounds, he said. Now what would I have to do for all that?"

Rashid entered quickly with the Krug in a bucket, three glasses on a tray. He put them on the table and opened the bottle.

Aroun said, "I'm not sure, but it would have to be something very special. Something to show the world that Saddam Hussein can strike anywhere."

"He needs something, the poor old sod," Dillon said cheerfully. "Things aren't going too well." As Rashid finished filling three glasses the Irishman added, "And what's your trouble, son? Aren't you joining us?"

Rashid smiled, and Aroun said, "In spite of Sandhurst, the captain remains a very Muslim Muslim. He does not touch alcohol."

Dillon raised his glass. "I respect a man with principles."

Makeev said, "This would need to be big, Sean. No point in

anything small. We're not talking blowing up five British army paratroopers in Belfast."

"Oh, it's Bush you want, is it?" Dillon smiled. "The President of the United States flat on his back with a bullet in him?"

"Would that be so crazy?" Aroun demanded.

"It would be this time, son," Dillon told him. "President Bush has the finest security in the world, believe me. A ring of steel, and in present circumstances he's going to stay home while this whole Gulf thing works through, mark my words."

"What about their Secretary of State, James Baker?" Aroun said. "He's been indulging in shuttle diplomacy throughout Europe."

"Yes, but knowing when—that's the problem. You'll know he's been in London or Paris when he's already left and they show him on television. No. You can forget the Americans on this one."

There was silence, and Aroun looked glum. Makeev was the first to speak. "Where does one find the weakest security, Sean, as regards national leaders?"

Dillon laughed out loud. "Oh, I think your Sandhurst man here can answer that."

Rashid smiled, pouring some more Champagne into Dillon's glass. "He's right. The British are the best in the world at covert operations, but in other areas . . . " He shook his head.

"It's not all that many years ago that the Queen woke up in Buckingham Palace and found an intruder sitting on the bed," Dillon told them. "And how long ago—six years—since the IRA almost got Margaret Thatcher and the entire British Cabinet at a Brighton hotel during the Tory Party conference." He put down his glass and lit a cigarette. "The Brits even have to go softly-softly on terrorists, up to a degree anyway, not like French intelligence. Jeez, if the lads in Action Service got their hands on me, they'd have me wired up for electricity before I knew what was happening. Mind you, even they are prone to the occasional error."

"What do you mean?" Makeev demanded.

"Have you got a copy of the evening paper handy?"

"Certainly," Aroun said. "Ali, on my desk."

Rashid returned with a copy of Paris *Soir*. Dillon said, "Page two. Read it. You'll find it interesting."

Rashid read the item aloud.

"Mrs. Margaret Thatcher, until recently Prime Minister of Britain, is staying overnight at Choisy, at the old Royal Hunting Lodge, as a guest of President Mitterrand. They are to have further talks in the morning. She leaves at two o'clock for an air force emergency field at Valenton, where an RAF plane returns her to England."

"Incredible, isn't it, that they could have allowed such a press release. But I guarantee the main London newspapers will carry that story also."

There was a heavy silence, and then Aroun said, "You're not suggesting . . ."

Dillon said to Rashid, "You must have some road maps handy. Get them."

Rashid went out quickly. Before Aroun could reply, Rashid came back with three maps and opened one on the table. They looked at it.

"There we are—Choisy," Rashid said. "Thirty miles from Paris, and here is the air force field at Valenton, only seven miles away."

"Good," Dillon said. "It's perfectly clear that only one country road links Choisy to Valenton, and here, about three miles before the airfield, there's a railway crossing. Perfect."

"For what?" Aroun demanded.

"An ambush. There'll be one car—two at the most—and an escort. Maybe half a dozen CRS security police on motorbikes."

"My God!" Aroun whispered.

He turned in appeal to Makeev, who shrugged. "He means it, Michael. You said this was what you wanted, so make up your mind."

Aroun took a deep breath. "All right."

Dillon calmly reached for a pad and pencil on the table and wrote quickly. "Those are the details of my numbered bank account in Zurich. You'll transfer one million pounds to it first thing in the morning. On successful completion I'll expect a further million."

"Now look here," Rashid started, but Aroun held up a hand.

"Fine, Mr. Dillon. Now what else can we do for you?"

"I need operating money. I presume a man like you keeps large supplies of the filthy stuff around the house."

"Very large," Aroun said, smiling. "How much?"

"Can you manage dollars? Say twenty thousand?"

"Of course." Aroun nodded to Rashid, who went to the far end of the room and swung a large oil painting to one side, disclosing a wall safe, which he started to open.

Makeev said, "And what can I do?"

"The old warehouse in Rue de Helier, the one we've used before. I've got most things I need stored there, but for this job I'd like a light machine gun. A tripod job. A Heckler and Koch or an M60—anything like that will do." He looked at his watch. "Eight o'clock. I'd like it there by ten. You've still got a key?"

"Of course," Makeev said.

Rashid came back with a small briefcase. "Twenty thousand. In hundred-dollar bills."

"Good. And I'll take the maps."

Dillon walked to the door, opened it and started down the curving staircase to the hall. Aroun, Rashid and Makeev followed him.

"But is this all, Mr. Dillon?" Aroun said. "Is there nothing more we can do for you? Won't you need help?"

"When I do, it comes from the criminal classes," Dillon said. "Honest crooks who do things for cash are usually more reliable than politically motivated zealots. Don't worry, you'll hear from me one way or another. I'll be on my way, then."

Rashid got the door open. "One thing, Mr. Dillon," he said. "What happens if things go wrong? I mean, you'll have your million in advance and we'll—"

"Have nothing? Don't give it a thought, my old son. I'll provide an alternative target. There's always the new British Prime Minister, this John Major. I presume his head on a plate would serve your boss back in Baghdad just as well."

Dillon smiled once, then stepped out into the rain.

## Two

DILLON paused outside the Black Cat on the end of the small pier for the second time that night. It was almost deserted. A young man and woman at a corner table were holding hands, a bottle of wine between them. The accordion was playing softly, and the musician talked to the man behind the bar at the same time. They were the Jobert brothers, gangsters of the second rank in the Paris underworld.

As the door opened and Dillon entered, the musician stopped playing. "Ah, Monsieur Rocard," he said. "A long time."

"Gaston." Dillon shook hands and turned to the barman. "Pierre."

"See," Gaston said, "I still remember that little tune of yours, the Irish one." He played a few notes on the accordion.

"Good," Dillon said. "A true artist."

Behind them the young couple got up and left.

"And what may we do for you, my friend?" Pierre inquired.

"Oh, I just want to put a little business your way." Dillon nodded at the door. "It might be an idea if you closed."

Gaston put his accordion down, went and bolted the door, and pulled down the blind. He returned and sat on his stool. "Well?"

"This could be a big payday for you boys." Dillon opened the briefcase, took out the road map and disclosed the stacks of hundred-dollar bills. "Twenty thousand American. Ten now and ten on successful completion."

"My God!" Gaston said in awe, but Pierre looked grim.

"And what would be expected for all this money?"

Dillon spread the road map on the bar. "I've been hired by the Union Corse," he said, naming the most feared criminal organization in France, "to take care of a little problem—a business rivalry."

"Ah, I see," Pierre said. "And you are to eliminate the problem?"

"Exactly. The men concerned will be passing along this road here towards Valenton shortly after two o'clock tomorrow. I intend to take them out at the railway crossing—a simple ambush. You two are still in the transport business, aren't you? Stolen cars, trucks?"

"You should know," Pierre told him.

"A couple of vans—that's not too much to expect, is it?"

"And then what?"

"We'll take a drive down to this place tonight." Dillon glanced at his watch. "Eleven o'clock, from here. It'll only take an hour."

Pierre shook his head. "Look, this could be heavy. I'm getting too old for gunplay."

"No gunplay. You two will be in and out so quickly you won't know what's happening. A piece of cake." He took several stacks of hundred-dollar bills from the briefcase and put them on the bar counter. "Ten thousand. Do we deal?"

And greed, as usual, won the day as Pierre ran his hands over the money. "Yes, my friend, I think we do."

"Good. I'll be back at eleven, then." Dillon closed his briefcase. Gaston went and unlocked the door for him, and the Irishman left.

Gaston closed the door and turned. "What do you think?"

Pierre poured two Cognacs. "I think our friend Rocard is a very big liar."

"But also a very dangerous man. So what do we do?"

"Wait and see." Pierre raised his glass.

DILLON walked all the way to the warehouse in Rue de Helier, twisting from one street to another, melting into the darkness occasionally to check that he wasn't being followed. Honest crooks who did things for cash—that was the phrase he'd used with Aroun. Unfortunately, it didn't always hold true, and there had been something in big Pierre's manner.

There was a small Judas gate set in the larger double gates of the warehouse. He unlocked it and stepped inside. There were two cars—a Renault saloon and a Ford Escort—and a police BMW motorcycle covered with a sheet. He checked it all, then moved up the stairs to the flat in the loft above. It was not his only home—he also had a barge on the river—but it was useful on occasions.

On the table in the small living room was a canvas holdall with a note on top that simply said, "As ordered." Inside was a Kalashnikov PK machine gun, its tripod folded, the barrel off for easy handling. There was a large box of belt cartridges, a similar box beside it. From a drawer in the sideboard he took a folded sheet and put it in the holdall. He checked the Walther in his waistband and, bag in hand, went down the stairs.

He locked the Judas and went along the street, excitement taking control, as it always did. It was the best feeling in the world when the game was in play. He turned into the main street, and a few minutes later he hailed a cab and told the driver to take him to the Black Cat.

THEY drove out of Paris in Renault vans, exactly the same except for the fact that one van was black and the other white. Gaston led the way—Dillon beside him in the passenger seat—and Pierre followed. It was very cold, snow mixed with the rain now. They talked very little, Dillon lying back in the seat, eyes closed so that the Frenchman thought he was asleep.

Not far from Choisy the van skidded, and Gaston cursed and wrestled with the wheel.

Dillon said, "Easy. Wrong time to go in a ditch. Where are we?"

"Just past the turning to Choisy. Not long now."

Dillon sat up. It had stopped snowing. The night sky had cleared, showing a half-moon, and below them, at the bottom of the hill, was the red light of the railway crossing. There was an old boarded-up building at one side, a stretch of cobbles in front of it.

"Pull in there," Dillon said.

Gaston did as he was told and braked to a halt, switching off the motor. Pierre came up in the white Renault, got down from behind the wheel and joined them.

Dillon stood looking at the crossing a few yards away and nodded. "Perfect. Give me the keys."

Gaston did so, and the Irishman unlocked the rear door of the black van, disclosing the holdall. He unzipped it as they watched, took out the Kalashnikov, put the barrel in place expertly, then positioned it so that it pointed to the rear. He filled the ammunition box, threading the cartridge belt in place.

"That looks a real killer," Pierre said.

"Seven-point-two-millimeter cartridges mixed with tracer and armor piercing," Dillon said. "It's a killer all right. Kalashnikov. I've seen one of these take a Land-Rover full of British paratroopers to pieces."

"Really," Pierre said. "And what's in the other box?"

"More ammunition."

Dillon covered the machine gun with the sheet from the holdall, then locked the rear door. He got behind the wheel, started the engine and moved the van a few yards, positioning it so that the tail pointed on an angle towards the crossing. He got out and locked the driver's door.

"So you leave this here?" Pierre asked him. "What if someone checks it?"

"What if they do?" Dillon knelt down at the offside rear tire and poked it with a knife he took from his pocket. There was a hiss of air, and the tire went down rapidly.

Gaston nodded. "Clever. Anyone gets curious, they'll just think a breakdown."

"But what about us?" Pierre demanded. "What do you expect?"

"Simple. Gaston turns up with the white Renault just after two this afternoon. He blocks the road at the crossing, gets out, locks the door and leaves it. You follow in a car, pick him up and go straight back to Paris."

"And what about you?" the big man asked.

"I'll be here, waiting in the van. I'll make my own way. Now, back to Paris. You can drop me at the Black Cat, and that's an end of it. You won't see me again."

"And the rest of the money?" Pierre demanded as he got behind the Renault's wheel, and Gaston and Dillon joined him.

"You'll get it, don't worry," Dillon said. "I always keep my word, just as I expect others to keep theirs. A matter of honor, my friend. Now let's get moving."

Pierre glanced at his brother, started the engine and drove away.

It was just on half past one when they reached the Black Cat. "I'll be off, then," Dillon said.

He got out and walked away, turning into a side street. Pierre said to his brother, "After him, and don't lose him. I want to know where he's staying. This thing stinks, Gaston, like bad fish, so get moving."

DILLON moved rapidly from street to street, following his usual pattern. He had intended returning to the warehouse, but pausing on the corner of an alley to light a cigarette, he glanced back and could have sworn he saw a movement. He was right.

Dillon had had a feeling about Pierre all night, a bad feeling. He turned left, worked his way back to the river and walked along the pavement and past a row of trucks, their windscreens covered with snow. He came to a cheap hotel—the kind used by prostitutes or truckers stopping overnight—and went in.

The desk clerk was very old and wore an overcoat and scarf against the cold. His eyes were wet. "Monsieur?"

"I brought a load in from Dijon a couple of hours ago. Intended to drive back tonight, but the truck's giving trouble. I need a bed."

"All right. Twenty francs, monsieur. Number eighteen, on the second landing."

Dillon took the key, paid the twenty francs and went upstairs.

The room was as disgusting as he expected. He closed the door, moved carefully through the darkness and looked out the window cautiously. There was a movement under a tree across the road. Gaston Jobert stepped out and hurried away along the pavement.

"Oh, dear," Dillon whispered, then lit a cigarette and thought about it.

PIERRE, sitting at the bar of the Black Cat waiting for his brother's return, was leafing through Paris *Soir* when he noticed the item on Margaret Thatcher's meeting with Mitterrand. His stomach churned, and he read the item again with horror. It was at that moment the door opened and Gaston hurried in.

"What a night. I'm frozen to the bone. Give me a Cognac."

"Here." Pierre poured some into a glass. "And you can read this interesting tidbit while you're drinking."

Gaston did as he was told and suddenly choked on the Cognac. "She's staying at Choisy!"

"And leaves from that old airfield at Valenton. Leaves Choisy at two o'clock. How long to that railway crossing? Ten minutes?"

"We're done for," Gaston said. "This is out of our league, Pierre. If this takes place, we'll have every cop in France on the streets."

"But it isn't going to. I knew Dillon was bad news. Always something funny about him. You managed to follow him?"

"Yes. He doubled around the streets for a while, then ended up at that fleapit old François runs just along the river." He shivered. "But what are we going to do?" He was almost sobbing. "This is the end, Pierre. They'll lock us up and throw away the key."

"No, they won't," Pierre told him. "Not if we stop him, they won't. They'll be too grateful. Who knows, there might even be a reward in it. Now, what's Inspector Savary's home number?"

INSPECTOR Jules Savary came awake cursing as the phone rang at his bedside. He'd had a long night and had only just managed to get to sleep. He picked up the phone. "Savary here."

"It's me, Inspector. Pierre Jobert."

Savary glanced at the bedside clock. "For heaven's sake, Jobert, it's two thirty in the morning."

343

"I know, Inspector, but I've got something special for you."

"You always have. Can't it wait till the morning?"

"I don't think so, Inspector. Margaret Thatcher—she's staying at Choisy tonight, leaves for Valenton at two tomorrow afternoon. I can tell you all about the man who's going to see she never gets there."

Jules Savary had never come awake so fast. "Where are you?"

"At the Black Cat," Jobert told him.

"Half an hour." Savary slammed down the phone, leaped out of bed and started to dress.

IT WAS at exactly the same moment that Dillon decided to move on. He left the room, locking the door, found the back stairs and descended cautiously. There was a door at the bottom, which opened easily enough and gave access to a yard at the rear.

An alley brought him to the main road. He crossed, walked along a line of parked trucks, chose one with a good view of the hotel. He got his knife out, worked away at the top of the passenger window until he could get his fingers in and exert pressure. A minute later he was inside. He sat back—collar up, hands in pockets—and waited. It was half past three when the four unmarked cars eased up to the hotel. Eight men got out—none in uniform, which was interesting.

"Action Service, or I miss my guess," Dillon said softly.

Gaston Jobert got out of the rear car and stood talking to them for a moment. Then they all moved into the hotel. Dillon wasn't angry, just pleased that he'd got it right. He left the truck and started to walk to the warehouse in Rue de Helier.

THE French secret service, notorious for years as the SDECE, had its name changed under the Mitterrand government to Direction générale de la sécurité extérieure—DGSE—in an attempt to improve its shady and ruthless image. Measured by results, however, few intelligence organizations in the world are so efficient.

The service, as in the old days, was still divided into five sections, the most famous—or infamous, depending on your point of view—being Section Five, more commonly known as Action Service.

Colonel Max Hernu, as ruthless as anyone, was sixty-one years of age, an elegant white-haired man who now sat at his desk in the first-floor office in DGSE's headquarters, on the Boulevard Mortier. It was just before five a.m., and Hernu, wearing horn-rimmed reading glasses, studied the report in front of him.

Inspector Savary watched respectfully. "What do you think, sir?"

"These Jobert brothers—you believe what they're telling us?"

"Absolutely, sir. I've known them for years. They do well in stolen cars."

"So this would be out of their league?"

"Very definitely. They're second-rate hoods, really. They've admitted to me that they've sold cars to this man Rocard in the past."

"Of course they are telling the truth. The ten thousand dollars speak for them there. But this man Rocard— You're an experienced copper, Inspector. Give me your opinion."

"His physical description is interesting, sir, because according to the Jobert boys, there isn't one. He's small, no more than five feet four or five. No discernible color to the eyes, fair hair."

"Go on," Hernu said.

"Pierre says his French is too perfect."

"What does he mean by that? That he isn't French?"

"Exactly," Savary said. "Two facts of interest there. He's always whistling a funny little tune. Gaston picked it up because he plays accordion. He says Rocard told him once that it was Irish."

"Now, that is interesting."

"A further point. When he was assembling the Kalashnikov in the back of the Renault, he told the boys he'd seen one take out a Land-Rover full of British paratroopers. Pierre didn't ask him where."

"So you smell IRA here? And what have you done about it?"

"Got your people to get the picture books out, Colonel. The Joberts are looking through them right now."

"Excellent." Hernu got up, went to the electric pot on the stand and poured himself some coffee. "What do you make of the hotel business? Do you think he's been alerted?"

"Perhaps, but not necessarily," Savary said. "I mean, what have we got here, sir? A real pro out to make the hit of a lifetime. I think he may have used the hotel because he suspected that Gaston might follow him. But then he'd want to know why. Was it the Joberts just being curious, or was there more to it?"

"So you think he could have been up the street watching our people arrive?"

"Very possibly. I got a bad feeling about this guy."

Hernu nodded. "Right. Let's see if they've finished. Have them in."

Savary went out and returned with the Jobert brothers. They stood there looking worried, and Hernu said, "Well?"

"No luck, Colonel. He wasn't in any of the books."

"All right," Hernu said. "Wait downstairs. You'll be taken home. We'll collect you again later."

"But what for, Colonel?" Pierre asked.

"So that your brother can go to Valenton in the Renault and you can follow in the car, like Rocard told you. Now go." They hurriedly left, and Hernu said to Savary, "We'll see Mrs. Thatcher is spirited to safety by another route, but a pity to disappoint our friend Rocard."

"If he turns up, Colonel."

"You never know—he just might. You've done well, Inspector. Go and get some breakfast." Hernu checked his watch. "I'm going to ring British intelligence and disturb the sleep of a very old friend of mine. If anyone can help us with our mystery man, it should be he."

THE special number that Max Hernu rang was of a section of the British security service known as Group Four, located on the third floor of the Ministry of Defense, in Park Lane. It had been set up in 1972 to handle matters concerning terrorism and subversion in the British Isles. It was responsible only to the Prime Minister. Its chief, Brigadier Charles Ferguson, was asleep in his flat, in Cavendish Square, when the telephone beside his bed woke him.

"Ferguson," he said, immediately wide awake.

"Paris, Brigadier," an anonymous voice said. "Priority one. Colonel Hernu."

"Put him through, and scramble." Ferguson sat up, a large, untidy man of sixty-five, with rumpled gray hair and a double chin.

"Charles?" Hernu said in English.

"My dear Max, what brings you on the line at such an hour?"

"Mrs. Thatcher overnighting at Choisy. We've details of a plot to hit her on the way to Valenton this afternoon."

"Good God!"

"All taken care of. The lady will now take a different route home. We're hoping the man concerned will show up, though I doubt it."

"Who is it? Anyone we know?"

"From what our informants say, we suspect he's Irish, though his French is good enough to pass as a native. The thing is, the people involved have looked through all our IRA pictures with no success."

"Have you a description?"

Hernu gave it to him. "Not much to go on, I'm afraid. This one is special. You're the expert on the IRA, so what do we do?"

"You're wrong there, old chap," Ferguson said. "The greatest expert on the IRA is right there in Paris—Martin Brosnan, our Irish American friend. After all, he carried a gun for them till 1975. Very respectable these days. Writes books and lives rather well. I heard he was a professor of political philosophy at the Sorbonne. If you've a mystery on your hands, he might be the man to solve it."

"Thanks for the suggestion," Hernu said. "I'd forgotten about Brosnan. But first we'll see what happens at Valenton."

Ferguson put down the phone, pressed a button on the wall and got out of bed. A moment later the door opened, and his man-servant, an ex-Gurkha corporal, came in.

"Emergency, Kim. I'll ring Captain Tanner and tell her to get round here; then I'll have a bath. Breakfast when she arrives."

The Gurkha withdrew. Ferguson picked up the phone and dialed a number. "Mary? . . . Ferguson here. Something big. I want you at Cavendish Square within the hour. Oh, better wear your uniform. We've got that thing at the Ministry of Defense at eleven. You always impress them in full war paint."

He put the phone down and went into the bathroom feeling wide awake and extremely cheerful.

IT WAS six thirty when the taxi picked up Mary Tanner on the steps of her Lowndes Square flat. The driver was impressed, but then most people were. She wore the uniform of a captain in the Women's Royal Army Corps, the wings of an army air corps pilot on her left breast. Below them the ribbon of the George Cross—a gallantry award of considerable distinction—and campaign ribbons for Ireland and for service with the United Nations peacekeeping force in Cyprus.

She was a small girl, black hair cropped short, undeniably attractive in a grave, rather quiet way. Twenty-nine years of age and a lot of service under the belt. A doctor's daughter who'd taken an

English degree at London University, tried teaching and hated it. After that came the army. Cyprus for a while, then three tours of duty in Ulster, in Northern Ireland. It had been the affair in Londonderry that had earned her the George Cross and left her with the scar on her left cheek, which had brought her to Ferguson's attention. She'd been his aide for two years now.

She paid off the taxi, hurried up the stairs to the flat on the second floor and let herself in with her own key. Ferguson was sitting on the sofa in the elegant drawing room, a napkin under his chin, while Kim served him poached eggs.

"Just in time," he said. "What would you like?"

"Earl Grey tea, Kim, please. Now, what have we got?"

He told her while he ate and Kim brought her tea and toast. She sat opposite listening. When he finished, she said, "This Brosnan— I've never heard of him."

"Before your time, my love. He must be about forty-five now. He was born in Boston. One of those filthy rich American families. High society. His mother was a Dubliner. He did all the right things—went to Princeton, then volunteered for Vietnam as an enlisted man. Airborne Rangers. Quite something for someone with his social standing. He was discharged a sergeant and was heavily decorated."

"You're just an old snob. What happened to him after that?"

"He went to Trinity College, Dublin, to work on a doctorate. In August '69 he was visiting an uncle on his mother's side, a priest in Belfast. Remember what happened? How it all started?"

"Orange mobs burning Catholics out?" she said.

"And the police not doing too much about it. The mob burned down Brosnan's uncle's church and started on the Falls Road. A handful of old IRA men with a few rifles and handguns held them off, and when one of them was shot, Brosnan picked up his rifle. Instinctive, I suppose, with Vietnam and all that."

"And from then on he was committed?"

"Very much so. He's killed a few in his time but always up front, I'll say that for him. He became quite famous. There was a French war photographer, Anne-Marie Audin, whose life he saved in Vietnam. Quite a romantic story. She turned up in Belfast, and Brosnan took her underground for a week. She got a series out of it for *Life* magazine. The gallant Irish struggle. You know the sort of thing."

"Sorry, sir. I've seen too much blood on the streets of Derry to go for that one."

"Yes, well, I'm not trying to whitewash him. In 1975 he went to France to negotiate an arms deal. As it turned out, it was a setup and the police were waiting. Unfortunately, he shot one of them dead. They gave him life. He escaped from prison in '79—at my instigation, I might add."

"But why?"

"Someone else before your time—a terrorist called Frank Barry, an evil genius if ever there was one. Started off in Ulster, later tried to get Lord Carrington on a trip to France when he was foreign secretary. The French hushed it up, but the Prime Minister was furious. Ordered me to hunt Barry down whatever the cost."

"Oh, I see now. You needed Brosnan to do that?"

"Set a thief to catch a thief and so forth, and he got him for us."

"And this Anne-Marie Audin—did they marry?"

"Not to my knowledge, but she did him a bigger favor than that. Her family is one of the oldest in France, and enormously powerful politically. Thanks to her pressure behind the scenes, President Mitterrand granted him a pardon. Wiped the slate clean."

"Which is how he's at the Sorbonne now," she said. "But does the leopard ever change its spots?"

"Oh, ye of little faith. You'll find his file in the study if you want to know more." He passed her a piece of paper. "That's the description of the mystery man. Not much to go on, but run it through the computer anyway."

She went out as Kim entered with a copy of *The Times*. Ferguson read the headlines immediately, then turned to page two, where his attention was briefly caught by the item concerning Mrs. Thatcher's visit to France.

"Well, Max," he said softly, "I wish you luck."

## Three

IT WAS much warmer in Paris later that morning, most of the snow clearing by lunchtime. It was clear in the countryside, too, as Dillon moved along the back roads towards Valenton. He was riding the BMW motorcycle from the warehouse and was dressed as a CRS policeman—helmet, goggles, a MAT 49 machine gun slung across the front of the dark uniform raincoat.

Madness to have come, of course, but he couldn't resist the free show. He pulled off a narrow lane by a farm gate and, after consulting his map, followed a track through a small wood and came to a low stone wall on a hill. Way below him was the railway crossing, the black Renault van still parked where he had left it.

He checked his watch. Two fifteen. He focused his Zeiss glasses on the scene below, and then the white Renault came down the road, half turning to block the crossing. There was a Peugeot behind it, Pierre at the wheel, and he was already reversing, turning the car as Gaston ran towards him. Gaston climbed in, and the Peugeot disappeared up the road.

"Now for the cavalry," Dillon said softly.

It was perhaps ten minutes later that a large truck came down the road and braked to a halt, unable to progress farther. It had high canvas sides on which was emblazoned STEINER ELECTRONICS.

"Electronics, hell," Dillon said.

A heavy machine gun opened up from inside the truck, firing through the side, raking the Renault. When the firing stopped, a dozen men in black overalls and riot helmets, all clutching machine carbines, jumped out. As they approached the Renault, Dillon pressed the electronic detonator he'd taken from his pocket. The self-destruct charge in the second black box—the one he had told Pierre contained extra ammunition—exploded instantly, the vehicle disintegrating, parts of the paneling lifting into the air in slow motion. There were several men on the ground, others running for cover.

"There you are. Chew on that, gentlemen," Dillon said.

He walked back to the BMW, swung a leg over and drove away.

DILLON opened the door of the warehouse on Rue de Helier, rode the BMW inside and parked it. As he turned to close the door, Makeev called from above, "It went wrong, I presume?"

"I'm afraid so. The Jobert brothers turned me in."

As he went up the stairs Makeev said, "The disguise—I like that. A policeman is just a policeman to people. Nothing to describe."

"Exactly. I worked for a great Irishman called Frank Barry years ago. He used the CRS copper on a motorcycle a lot."

Dillon followed the Russian into the sitting room. "Tell me," Makeev said, "now what?"

"As I said last night, I'll provide an alternative target. I mean, all that lovely money." Dillon lit a cigarette. "And I don't like to be beaten. I'll think of something for you, and I'll pay my debts."

"The Joberts—are they worth it?"

"Oh, yes," Dillon said. "A matter of honor, Josef."

Makeev sighed. "I'll go and see Aroun, give him the bad news. I'll be in touch."

"Here or at the barge." Dillon smiled. "Don't worry, Josef. I've never failed yet—not when I set my mind to a thing."

MARTIN Brosnan's apartment was by the river on the Quai de Montebello, opposite Île de la Cité, and had one of the finest views of Notre-Dame in Paris. It was within decent walking distance of the Sorbonne, which suited him perfectly.

It was just after four as he walked towards it, a tall man with broad shoulders and dark hair that was far too long, giving him the look of some sixteenth-century brave. Martin Aodh Brosnan. The Aodh was Gaelic for Hugh, and his Irishness showed in the high cheekbones and gray eyes.

It was getting colder again, and he shivered inside his trench coat as he hurried along to the apartment block. His was the apartment on the corner of the second floor. Scaffolding ran up the corner to the fifth floor, where some sort of building work was taking place.

As he was about to go up the steps to the ornate entrance a voice called, "Martin?"

He glanced up and saw Anne-Marie Audin leaning over the balcony rail. "Where in the world did you spring from?" he asked in astonishment.

"Cuba. I just got in."

He went up the stairs two at a time, and she had the door open as he got there. He lifted her up in his arms in an enormous hug. "How marvelous to see you. Why Cuba?"

She kissed him and helped him off with the trench coat. "Oh, I had a rather juicy assignment for *Time* magazine. Come in the kitchen. I'll make your tea."

Surprising in an American, but he couldn't stand coffee. He sat at the table and watched her move around the kitchen, her short hair as dark as his own, this supremely elegant woman who was the same age as he was and looked twelve years younger.

"You look marvelous," he told her as she brought the tea. He sampled it and nodded in approval. "That's grand. Just the way you learned to make it back in south Armagh, in 1971, with me and Liam Devlin showing you the hard way how the IRA worked."

"How is the old rogue?"

"Still living in Kilrea, outside Dublin. Gives the odd lecture at Trinity College. Claims to be seventy, but that's a wicked lie."

"He'll never grow old, that one."

"Yes, you really do look marvelous," Brosnan said again. "Why didn't we get married?"

It was a ritual question he had asked for years, a joke now. There was a time when they had been lovers, but for some years now, just friends. Not that it was by any means the usual relationship. He would have died for her, almost had in Vietnam the first time they met.

"Now that we've got that over, let's go into the drawing room," she said.

It was a magnificent room. There was an ornate gold mirror over the marble fireplace, plants everywhere, a grand piano, comfortable sofas and a great many books. She had left the French windows to the balcony standing ajar, and Brosnan went to close them. At that moment the doorbell sounded.

He opened the door and found Max Hernu and Jules Savary standing there, the Jobert brothers behind them.

"Professor Brosnan?" Hernu said. "I am Colonel Max Hernu."

"I know very well who you are," Brosnan said. "Action Service, isn't it? What's all this? My wicked past catching up with me?"

"Not quite, but we do need your assistance. This is Inspector Savary, and these two are Gaston and Pierre Jobert."

"Come in, then," Brosnan said, interested in spite of himself.

On Hernu's orders the Jobert brothers stayed in the hall while he and Savary followed Brosnan into the drawing room. Anne-Marie was frowning slightly as Brosnan made the introductions.

Hernu kissed her hand. "A great pleasure."

She looked worried now. "Martin, you're not getting involved in anything?"

"Of course not," he assured her. "Now, what can I do for you, Colonel?"

"A matter of national security, Professor. I hesitate to mention the fact, but Mademoiselle Audin is a photojournalist of some distinction."

She smiled. "Total discretion—you have my word, Colonel."

"We're here because Brigadier Ferguson, in London, tells us you are an expert in matters relating to the IRA. Let me explain."

Which he did, covering the whole affair as rapidly as possible. "You see, Professor," Hernu concluded, "the Jobert brothers have combed our IRA picture books without finding him. We know nothing more than that we think he's Irish and he speaks fluent French."

"So what do you want me to do?"

"Speak to the Joberts."

Brosnan glanced at Anne-Marie, then shrugged. "All right. Wheel them in."

He sat on the edge of a table while they stood awkwardly before him. "How old is he?"

"Difficult, monsieur," Pierre said. "He changes from one minute to the next, like he's more than one person. I'd say late thirties."

"And description?"

"Small, with fair hair."

"All right. He's small, fair-haired, late thirties. What makes you think he's Irish?"

"He's always whistling a funny sort of tune," Gaston said. "A bit eerie. I managed to follow it on my accordion. He said it was Irish."

Brosnan's face had gone quite still. He stood there, and Anne-Marie put a hand on his arm. "You know him, Martin?"

"Almost certainly. Could you pick that tune out on the piano?" he asked Gaston.

"I'll try, monsieur." He lifted the lid, tried the keyboard gently, then played the beginning of the tune with one finger.

"That's enough," Brosnan said. "An old Irish folk song—'The Lark in the Clear Air'—and you've got trouble, gentlemen."

They sent the Jobert brothers home; then Brosnan turned to Hernu and Savary. "The man you're looking for is Sean Dillon."

"Dillon?" Hernu said. "Of course. The man of a thousand faces, someone once called him."

"A slight exaggeration," Brosnan said, "but it will do. He never looks back. God knows how many he's killed."

"Why does he do it?" Anne-Marie asked. "Not for any political ends."

"Because he likes it," Brosnan said. "Because he's hooked."

"I get the impression that you don't care for him very much," Hernu said. "In personal terms, I mean."

"Well, he once tried to kill me and a good friend of mine," Brosnan told him. "Does that answer your question?"

"It's reason enough, certainly." Hernu got up, and Savary joined him. "We must be going. I want to get this to the brigadier as soon as possible. We may count on your help, I hope, Professor?"

Brosnan glanced at Anne-Marie, whose face was set. "Look," he said, "I don't mind talking to you again if that will help, but I don't want to be personally involved. You know what I was, Colonel. I won't go back. I made someone a promise a long time ago."

"I understand perfectly, Professor." Hernu turned to Anne-Marie. "Mademoiselle, a distinct pleasure."

"I'll see you out," she said, and led the way.

When she returned, Brosnan had the French windows open and was standing looking across the river. He put an arm around her. "All right?"

"Oh, perfect," she said, and laid her head against his chest.

AT THAT precise moment Ferguson was sitting by the fire in the Cavendish Square flat when the phone rang. Captain Mary Tanner answered it in the study. After a while she came out. "That was Downing Street. The Prime Minister wants to see you. Now, sir."

Ferguson got up. "Call the car. You come with me and wait."

She picked up the phone, spoke briefly, then put it down.

"Let's go," he said, and led the way out.

They arrived quickly and were checked through the security gates at the end of Downing Street. Mary Tanner stayed in the car while Ferguson was admitted through the most famous door in the world. An aide led him up the main staircase, and when they reached the corridor, he knocked on the door and opened it.

"Brigadier Ferguson, Prime Minister."

The last time Ferguson had been in that study, it had been Mrs.

Thatcher's, the feminine touches unmistakably there. Things were different now, more austere. John Major put some sort of report aside and sat back. He was a pleasant gray-haired man in horn-rimmed glasses, the youngest Prime Minister of the twentieth century. Yet his handling of the crisis in the Gulf had already marked him out as a leader of genuine stature.

"Please sit down, Brigadier. I'll get right to the point. The business affecting Mrs. Thatcher in France. Obviously, very disturbing."

"Indeed so, Prime Minister. Thank God it all turned out as it did."

"Yes, but that seems to have been a matter of luck more than anything else. I've spoken to President Mitterrand, and he's agreed that in all our interests there will be a total security clampdown."

"What about the press, Prime Minister?"

"Nothing will reach the press, Brigadier," John Major said. "I understand the French failed to catch the individual concerned?"

"I'm afraid that is so, according to my latest information. But Colonel Hernu of Action Service is keeping in close touch."

"Good. Your first task is to run down whoever was behind this affair. If he's IRA, then he's our business, wouldn't you agree?"

"Absolutely."

"I'll let you go and get on with it, then. Keep me informed of every significant development on an eyes-only basis."

"Of course, Prime Minister."

The door behind opened as if by magic, the aide appeared, and Ferguson was ushered out.

THE limousine drove away, taking Mary Tanner and Ferguson back to his office. It was on the third floor of the Ministry of Defense on a corner overlooking Horse Guards Avenue, with a view of the Victoria Embankment and the Thames River at the far end. He had hardly got settled behind his desk when Mary hurried in.

"Coded fax from Hernu. I've put it through the machine. You're not going to like it one little bit."

It contained the gist of Hernu's meeting with Martin Brosnan: the facts on Sean Dillon—everything.

"Couldn't be worse," Ferguson said. "He's like a ghost—this Dillon chap. Does he exist or doesn't he? There's nothing to go on."

"But we have one thing, sir. Brosnan."

"True, but will he help? It's the girlfriend, you see. Anne-Marie Audin. She has a horror of him becoming what he once was."

"Yes, I can understand that."

"But never mind. We'd better get a report on latest developments to the Prime Minister. Let's keep it brief."

Mary produced a pen and took notes as he dictated. "Anything else, sir?" she asked when he had finished.

"I don't think so. Get it typed. One copy for the file, the other for the P.M. Send it round to Number Ten by messenger. Eyes only."

She did a rough type of the report herself, then went along the corridor to the typing-and-copying room. The copier was clattering as she went in. The clerk standing in front of it was in his mid-fifties, white hair, steel-rimmed army glasses.

"Hello, Gordon," she said. "A priority one here. Your very best typing. One copy for the personal file. You'll do it straightaway?"

"Of course, Captain Tanner. Fifteen minutes. I'll bring it along."

She went out, and he sat down at his typewriter, taking a deep breath to steady himself as he read the words FOR THE EYES OF THE PRIME MINISTER ONLY.

Gordon Brown had served in the intelligence corps for twenty-five years, reaching the rank of warrant officer. On his retirement from the army he had been employed by the Ministry of Defense, and everything had been fine until the death of his wife from cancer the previous year. They were childless, which left him alone in a cold world at fifty-five years of age, and then something miraculous happened. At an art display at the German embassy he'd met Tania Novikova, a secretary-typist at the Soviet embassy.

They'd got on so well together. She was thirty and not particularly pretty, but when she took him to bed on their second meeting at his flat, in Camden, it was like a revelation. Brown had never known sex like it, was hooked instantly. And then it started—the questions about his job, about the Ministry of Defense. He knew what was happening, but didn't care. There was a series of reports passing through on British army changes in view of political changes in Russia. It was easy to run off spare copies. When he brought them round to her flat, she took him to heights of pleasure such as he had never known.

From then on he would do anything. FOR THE EYES OF THE PRIME

MINISTER ONLY. How grateful would she be for that? He finished typing and ran off two extra copies, one for himself and one for Tania Novikova, who was, of course, not a secretary-typist at the Soviet embassy as she had informed Brown, but a captain in the KGB.

IT WAS just before eight, the streets deserted because of the cold, as Pierre and Gaston drove off from the Black Cat in the old Peugeot. They planned to have dinner and go to a nightclub. They came to a small square, and as they started to cross it a CRS man on his motorcycle came up behind them, flashing his lights.

"There's a cop on our tail," Gaston said.

Anonymous in helmet and goggles, the cop waved them down. "A message from Savary, I suppose," Pierre said, and pulled over.

"Maybe they've got him," Gaston said excitedly.

The policeman halted behind them, pushed his bike up on its stand and approached. Gaston got the door open and leaned out. "Have they caught the fool?"

Dillon took the Walther with a Carswell silencer from inside his raincoat and shot him twice in the heart. He pushed up his goggles.

Pierre crossed himself. "It's you."

"Yes, Pierre. A matter of honor."

The Walther coughed twice more. Dillon pushed it back inside his raincoat, got on his bike and drove away.

TANIA Novikova's flat was just off the Bayswater Road, not far from the Soviet embassy. She'd had a hard day, had intended an early night. It was just before nine thirty when her doorbell rang. She was toweling herself down after a nice relaxing bath. She pulled on a robe and went downstairs.

Gordon Brown stood at the door ringing the bell impatiently, hugely excited. When she opened the door and saw who it was, she was immediately angry and drew him inside.

"I told you never to come here, Gordon."

"But this is special," he pleaded. "Look what I've brought you."

In the living room she took the large envelope from him, opened it and slipped out the report. Her excitement was intense as she read through it. Incredible that this fool could have delivered her such a coup.

"It's good stuff, isn't it?" he demanded.

"Excellent, Gordon. You *have* been a good boy."

"Really?" His arms were around her waist, pulling her to him. "I can stay over, then?"

"Oh, Gordon, it's such a pity. I'm on the night shift."

"Please, darling. Just a few minutes, then."

She had to keep him happy, she knew that. "Quarter of an hour, Gordon, that's all, and then you'll have to go." She took his hand and led him into the bedroom.

AFTER she'd got rid of him, she dressed hurriedly, debating what to do. Tania Novikova was a hard, committed Communist, and she served the KGB with total loyalty. For a young woman she was surprisingly old-fashioned. Had no time for Gorbachev or the glasnost fools who surrounded him. Unfortunately, many in the KGB did support him, and one of those was her boss at the Soviet embassy, Colonel Yuri Gatov.

What would his attitude be to the failed attempt to assassinate Mrs. Thatcher? she wondered. She left her flat and started to walk to the embassy, in Kensington Palace Gardens. Probably the same outrage the British Prime Minister must feel. So what to do?

It came to her as she arrived at her office that there was someone who might very well be interested, and not only because he thought as she did but because he was in Paris, right in the center of all the action. Her old boss, Colonel Josef Makeev. That was it. Makeev would know how best to use such information.

She called his office. By chance, he was working late. "Tania," he said when he picked up the phone, "what can I do for you?"

"I understand there was an incident affecting Empire over there yesterday," she said.

Empire was an old KGB code phrase referring to assassination attempts at high government level in Britain. Makeev was immediately alert. "That's correct."

"Have you an interest?"

"Very much so."

"There's a coded fax on the way. I'll stand by in my office if you want to talk."

Tania Novikova put down the phone. She had her own fax cod-ing machine at a second desk. She went to it, tapping the required details out quickly, and inserted the report. She stood waiting.

A few minutes later her phone rang.

"You've done well, Tania," Makeev said. "This one was my baby."

"I'm so pleased."

"Does Gatov know about this?"

"No, Colonel."

"Good. Let's keep it that way. Cultivate your contact. Let me have anything else on the instant. There could be more for you. I have a friend coming to London. The particular friend you've been reading about."

"I'll wait to hear." She put down the phone, totally elated.

In Paris, Makeev sat there for a moment frowning, then picked up the phone and rang Dillon. There was a slight delay before the Irishman answered, "Who is it?"

"Josef, Sean. I'm on my way there. Utmost importance."

Makeev put down the phone, got his overcoat and went out.

## Four

BROSNAN had taken Anne-Marie to a small restaurant in Montmartre that evening. They had just finished the main course when Max Hernu appeared, Savary standing behind him.

"Snow in London, snow in Brussels, and snow in Paris," said Hernu, brushing it from his sleeve and opening his coat.

"Do I deduce from your appearance here that you've had me followed?" Brosnan asked.

"Not at all, Professor. We called at your apartment, where the porter was kind enough to mention three or four restaurants he thought you might be at. This is the second."

"Then you'd better sit down and have a Cognac and some coffee," Anne-Marie told Hernu and Savary. "You both look frozen."

They took off their coats, and Brosnan nodded to the headwaiter, who hurried over and took the order.

"I'm sorry, mademoiselle, to spoil your evening, but this is most important," Hernu said. "About two hours ago the bodies of the Jobert brothers were found in their car, not far from the Black Cat."

"Murdered—is that what you are saying?" Anne-Marie put in.

"Oh, yes, mademoiselle," he said. "Shot to death."

"Two each in the heart?" Brosnan asked.

"Why, yes, Professor. How did you know?"

"Dillon, without a doubt. It's a real pro's trick, Colonel. You should know that. Never one shot—always two, in case the other man manages to get one off at you as a reflex."

Hernu stirred his coffee. "Did you expect this, Professor?"

"Oh, yes. He'd have come looking for them sooner or later. A strange man. He never goes back on a contract, and he expects the same from those he deals with. What he calls a matter of honor."

"I've known killers in plenty," Savary said. "And not just the gangsters who see it as part of the job, but the man who's killed his wife because she's been unfaithful. Dillon seems something else. I mean, all those hits and not even in his own country. Why?"

"I'm not a psychiatrist," Brosnan said, "but I knew men like him in the army in Vietnam in Special Forces. Good men, some of them, but once they started the killing, it seemed to take over like a drug. They became driven men. It was as if people had become— how can I put it?—just things."

There was silence. Finally Hernu said, "We must catch him, Professor. Will you join us in hunting him down?"

Anne-Marie put a hand on Brosnan's arm, dismay on her face, and she turned angrily to the two men. "That's your job, not Martin's."

"It's all right," Martin soothed her. "Don't worry." Then he said to Hernu, "Any advice I can give, any information, but no personal involvement. I'm sorry, Colonel. That's the way it has to be."

Savary said, "You told us he tried to kill you once. You and a friend."

"That was in '74. He and I both worked for this friend of mine, Liam Devlin. He was what you might call an old-fashioned revolutionary. Thought you could still fight it out like the old days—an undercover army against the troops. He didn't like bombs, soft target bits, that kind of stuff."

"What happened?" the inspector asked.

"Dillon disobeyed orders, and the bomb that was meant for the police patrol killed half a dozen children. Devlin and I went after him. He tried to take us out." His voice had changed in a subtle way. Harder, more cynical. "Left me with a groove in one shoulder, and I gave him one in the arm. That was when he first dropped out of sight in Europe."

"And you didn't see him again?"

"I was in prison for over four years from 1975, Inspector. You're forgetting your history. He worked with a man called Frank Barry for a while, another refugee from the IRA. Do you remember him?"

"I do indeed, Professor," Hernu said. "As I recall, he tried to assassinate Lord Carrington, the British foreign secretary, in circumstances very similar to this recent affair."

"Dillon was probably doing a copycat of that operation. He worshipped Barry."

"Who you killed on behalf of British intelligence, I understand."

Anne-Marie said, "Excuse me." She got up and walked down to the powder room.

Hernu said, "We've upset her." He got up and buttoned his coat. "We've taken up enough of your time. My apologies to Mademoiselle Audin."

Brosnan watched them go, and Anne-Marie returned. "Sorry about that, my love," he told her.

"Not your fault." She looked tired. "I think I'll go home."

"You're not coming back to my place?"

"Not tonight. Tomorrow perhaps."

The headwaiter brought the bill, then helped them into their coats and ushered them to the door. Outside, snow sprinkled the cobbles. She shivered and turned to him. "You changed, Martin, back there. You started to become the other man again."

"Really?" he said, and knew that it was true.

"I'll get a taxi," she said.

"Let me come with you?"

"No, I'd rather not."

He watched her walk down the street. Then he turned and went the other way, wondering about Dillon, where he was and what he was doing.

DILLON's barge was moored in a small basin on Quai St.-Bernard. The interior was surprisingly luxurious: a stateroom lined with mahogany, sleeping quarters in a cabin beyond, and a small shower room. The kitchen on the other side of the passageway was small but very modern. He was in there now, waiting for the kettle to boil, when he heard footfalls on deck. He opened a drawer, took out a Walther, cocked it and slipped it into the back of his waistband. Then he went out.

Makeev came down the companionway and entered the stateroom. He shook snow from his overcoat and took it off. "What a night. Filthy weather."

"Worse in Moscow," Dillon told him. "Coffee?"

"Why not."

When he came back, a china mug in each hand, Dillon said, "Well, what's happened?"

"My sources tell me the Joberts have turned up very dead indeed. Was that wise?"

"To use an immortal phrase from one of those old James Cagney movies, 'They had it coming.' Now, what else?"

"Oh, an old friend from your dim past has surfaced—Martin Brosnan."

"Brosnan?" Dillon seemed transfixed for a moment. "Where in the hell did he turn up from?"

"He's living right here in Paris, just up the river from you, on Quai de Montebello, the block on the corner opposite Notre-Dame. Very ornate entrance. Within walking distance of here. You can't miss it. Has scaffolding on the front."

"All very detailed." Dillon took a bottle of Bushmills whiskey from the cupboard and poured a drink. "What's it got to do with me?"

Makeev told him about Max Hernu, Savary, Tania Novikova in London—everything. "So," he said as he finished, "at least we know what our friends are up to."

"This Novikova girl could be very useful to me," Dillon said. "Will she play things our way?"

"No question. She worked for me for some years. A very clever young woman. Do I take it this means you want to go to London?"

"When I know, I'll let you know."

"And Brosnan?"

"I could pass him on the street, and he wouldn't recognize me," Dillon said. "Have you come in your car?"

"Of course not. Taxi. I hope I can get one back."

"I'll get my coat and walk some of the way with you."

The snow was only a light powdering on the ground; barges passed on the river; and Notre-Dame, floodlit, floated in the night. They reached Quai de Montebello without seeing a taxi.

Makeev said, "Here we are—Brosnan's place." Dillon looked across at the scaffolding, and Makeev said, "Apartment four, the one on the corner, on the second floor."

"Does he live alone?"

"Not married. Has a woman friend, Anne-Marie Audin." A taxi came out of a side street then, and moved towards them. Makeev raised an arm. "We'll speak tomorrow."

The taxi drove off, and Dillon was about to turn away when Brosnan came round the corner and went up the steps. Dillon recognized him instantly. He turned, smiling, and walked away, whistling to himself softly.

AT HIS flat in Cavendish Square, Brigadier Ferguson was just getting ready to go to bed when the phone rang. It was Hernu. "Bad news, Charles. He's knocked off the Jobert brothers."

"Dear me," Ferguson said. "He doesn't mess about, does he?"

"I've been to see Brosnan, but I'm afraid he's refused to come in with us on this. Offered to give us his advice and so on, but he won't become actively involved."

"Nonsense," Ferguson said. "We can't have that."

"What do you suggest?"

"I think it might be an idea if I came over to see him. Possibly tomorrow afternoon. We'll let you know."

"Excellent. I couldn't be more pleased."

Ferguson sat there thinking about it for a while, and then he phoned Mary Tanner at her flat. He brought her up to date. "I think I'll go over tomorrow, have a chat with Hernu, then speak to Brosnan," he said. "He must be made to realize how serious this is."

"Do you want me to come?"

"Naturally. I can't even read a menu over there, whereas we all know that one of the benefits of your rather expensive education is fluency in the French language. Get in touch with the transport officer at the ministry, and tell him I want the Learjet standing by tomorrow."

"I'll handle it. Anything else?"

"No. I'll see you at the office in the morning." He put down the phone, got into bed and switched off the light.

ONE of the first things Ferguson did on reaching his office was to dictate a further brief report to the Prime Minister, bringing him up to date and informing him of the Paris trip. Mary took the draft to the copy room. The duty clerk, a Mrs. Alice Johnson, typed the report and had just finished putting it through the copier when Gordon Brown came to take over from her. He was on a split shift, from ten a.m. until one and from six p.m. until ten in the evening.

"You go whenever you like, Alice. Anything special?"

"Just this report for Captain Tanner. It's a Number Ten job. I said I'd take it along."

"I'll take it for you," Brown said, and she passed him both copies of the report and started to clear her desk.

No chance to make an extra copy, but at least he could read it as he went along to Mary Tanner's office.

She was sitting at her desk when he went in. "That report you wanted, Captain Tanner. Shall I arrange a messenger?"

"No, thanks, Gordon. I'll see to it."

When he went back to the copy room, Alice Johnson was still there. "I say, Alice," he said, "would you mind hanging on for a little while? Something's come up. I'll make it up to you."

"That's all right," she said. "You get off."

He hurried downstairs to the canteen and went into one of the public telephone booths. Tania Novikova was still at the flat because she had left the embassy late the previous night. "I've told you not to ring me here. I'll ring you," she told him.

"I must see you. I'm free at one."

"Impossible."

"I've seen another report. The same business."

"I see. Have you got a copy?"

"No. That wasn't possible, but I've read it."

"What did it say?"

"I'll tell you at lunchtime."

Her voice was cold and hard when she said, "Don't waste my time, Gordon, or I'll hang up."

He panicked instantly and told her. "Just that the two French criminals involved had been murdered—they presumed by the man Dillon. Oh, and Brigadier Ferguson and Captain Tanner are flying over to Paris in the Learjet at noon. They're hoping to persuade this man Martin Brosnan to help them."

"You've done well, Gordon. I'll see you tonight at your flat. And bring your work schedule for the next couple of weeks."

Brown went upstairs, full of elation.

FERGUSON and Mary Tanner touched down at Charles de Gaulle Airport just after one. By two o'clock they were being ushered into Hernu's office at DGSE headquarters. Hernu embraced Ferguson briefly. "Charles, you old rogue, it's far too long."

"Now then, none of your funny French ways," Ferguson told him, and introduced Mary Tanner. She was wearing a brown Armani trouser suit and a pair of exquisite boots. For a girl who was not supposed to be particularly pretty, she looked stunning.

Hernu, who knew class when he saw it, kissed her hand. "Captain Tanner, your reputation precedes you."

"In the nicest way, I hope," she replied in fluent French.

"So," Ferguson said, "now we've got all that stuff over, let's get down to brass tacks. What about Brosnan?"

"He's agreed to see us at his apartment at three today. Time for a light lunch." Hernu opened the door. "Just follow me."

IN THE stateroom at the barge, Dillon was pouring a glass of Krug and studying a large-scale map of London. Around him, pinned to the mahogany walls, were articles and reports from all the London newspapers, specifically referring to affairs at number Ten Downing Street and how well John Major was doing. And there were photos of the Prime Minister—several of them, in fact. The British press was wonderful.

The things that intrigued Dillon were the daily meetings of the British War Cabinet at Number Ten. All those fools all together in the same spot—what a target. But Number Ten? That didn't seem possible. "Fortress Thatcher" it had been dubbed by some after that redoubtable lady's security improvements.

There were footsteps on the deck overhead. He opened a drawer in the table, casually revealing a Smith & Wesson .38 revolver, closed it again as Makeev came in.

"I've heard from Tania Novikova again," the Russian said. "It seems Brigadier Ferguson and his aide, a Captain Mary Tanner, have flown over. They were due out of Gatwick at noon." He glanced at his watch. "I'd say they'll be with Hernu right now."

"To what end?"

"The real purpose of the trip is to see Brosnan. Try and persuade him to help actively in the search for you."

"Really?" Dillon smiled coldly. "Martin's becoming a serious inconvenience. I might have to do something about that."

Makeev nodded at the clippings on the walls. "Your own private gallery?"

"I'm just getting to know the man. Do you want a drink?"

"No, thanks. I've things to do. I'll be in touch."

Makeev went up the companionway. Dillon poured himself a little more Champagne and lit a cigarette. He looked at the clippings again, but all he could think about was Martin Brosnan.

ANNE-MARIE was in the kitchen at Quai de Montebello and Brosnan was going over a lecture in the drawing room when the doorbell rang. She hurried out, wiping her hands on a cloth. "That will be them," she said. "I'll get it. Now don't forget your promise."

There was a sound of voices in the hall, and she returned with Ferguson, Hernu, and Mary Tanner. "I'll make some coffee," Anne-Marie said, and went into the kitchen.

"My dear Martin." Ferguson held out his hand. "It's been too long."

"Amazing," Brosnan said. "We only ever meet when you want something."

"Someone you haven't met. My aide, Captain Mary Tanner."

Brosnan looked her over quickly—the small dark girl with the scar on her cheek—and liked what he saw. "Couldn't you find a better class of work than what this old sod has to offer?" he demanded.

Odd that she should feel slightly breathless, faced with this forty-five-year-old man with the ridiculously long hair. "There's a recession on. You have to take what's going these days," she said.

"Right. Let's get down to business," Ferguson said. Hernu went to the window. Ferguson and Mary took the sofa opposite Brosnan.

"Max tells me that he spoke to you last night after the murder of the Jobert brothers and that you've refused to help us," Ferguson began.

Anne-Marie came in with coffee on a tray. Brosnan said, "That's putting it a bit strongly. What I said was that I'd do anything I could except become actively involved."

Ferguson said, "You agree with him, Miss Audin?"

"Martin slipped out of that life a long time ago, Brigadier," she said carefully. "I would not care to see him step back in for whatever reason."

Max Hernu came across and picked up a cup of coffee. "But the professor is in a special position as regards this business. You must see that, mademoiselle. He knew Dillon intimately, worked with him for years. He could be of great help to us."

"I don't want to see him with a gun in his hand," she said. "Once his foot is on that road again, it can only have one end." She was distressed now and angry. She turned and went through into the kitchen. Mary Tanner went after her and closed the door.

Anne-Marie was leaning against the sink, arms folded as if holding herself in, agony on her face. "They don't see, do they? They don't understand what I mean."

"I do," Mary said simply. "I understand." And as Anne-Marie started to sob quietly, she went and put her arms around her.

BROSNAN went and opened the French windows, and stood on the balcony taking in lungfuls of cold air. Ferguson joined him. "I'm sorry for the distress we've caused her."

"No, you're not. You only see the end in view. You always did."

"He's a bad one, Martin."

Brosnan nodded. "I know." He leaned against the balustrade. "She seems quite a lady, that aide of yours. That scar on her left cheek. Shrapnel. What's her story?"

"She was doing a tour of duty as a lieutenant with the military police in Londonderry. Some IRA chap was delivering a car bomb when the engine failed. He left the car at the curb and did a runner. Unfortunately, it was outside an old folks home. Mary was driving past in a Land-Rover when a civilian alerted her. She got in the car, released the brake and managed to freewheel down a hill onto some wasteland. It exploded as she made a run for it. When she came out of hospital, she received a severe reprimand for breaking standing orders, and the George Cross for gallantry. I took her on after that."

At that moment Mary Tanner joined them. "Anne-Marie's gone to lie down in the bedroom," she said.

"All right," Brosnan said. "Let's go back in."

They went and sat down again, and Ferguson turned to Mary. "Your turn, my dear."

"I've been through the files, checked out everything the computer can tell us." She opened her handbag and took out a photo. "The only likeness of Dillon we can find. It's from a group photo taken at drama school twenty years ago. We had it blown up."

There was a lack of definition, the texture was grainy, and the face was totally anonymous. Brosnan gave it back. "Useless."

"Did you know that he took a pilot's license, and a commercial one at that?" Mary said.

"No, I never knew that," Brosnan said.

"According to informants, he did it in Texas some years ago."

"There is a point in all this which no one has touched on," Hernu put in. "Who is he working for?"

"Well, it certainly isn't the IRA," Mary said. "We have computer links with both the police and British army intelligence in Northern Ireland. Nothing about the attempt on Mrs. Thatcher."

"Oh, I believe that," Brosnan said. "If he'd needed any help—weapons, whatever—he'd have used the underworld. He wouldn't have gone near any IRA contact unless it was someone who'd been in very deep cover for years, someone he could really trust."

"There are the Iraqis, of course," Ferguson said. "Saddam would dearly love to blow everyone up at the moment."

"True, but don't forget Hezbollah, PLO, Wrath of Allah and a few others. He's worked for them all," Brosnan reminded him.

"You think he'll try again?" Mary asked.

"My dear, I've been in this business a lifetime," Ferguson said, "and my instincts tell me there's more to come."

"Well, I can't help you there," Brosnan said.

He stood up, and they all moved into the hall. Brosnan opened the door. "I suppose you'll be going back to London?"

"Oh, I don't know. I thought we just might stay over and sample the delights of Paris. I haven't stayed at the Ritz since the refurbishment."

Mary Tanner said, "That will give the expenses a bashing." She held out her hand. "Good-bye, Professor Brosnan. It was nice to be able to put a face to the name."

"And you," he said. "Colonel." He nodded to Hernu, and closed the door.

## Five

IT WAS colder than ever that evening, a front from Siberia sweeping across Europe. Brosnan put some more logs on the fire. Anne-Marie, lying full length on the sofa, stirred and sat up. "So we stay in to eat?"

"I think so," he said. "A vile night."

"Good. I'll see what I can do in the kitchen."

He put on the television news program. More air strikes against Baghdad, but still no sign of a land war. He switched the set off, and Anne-Marie emerged from the kitchen and picked up her coat from the chair where she had left it.

"Your fridge, as usual, is almost empty. To concoct a meal, I'll have to go round the corner to the delicatessen."

"I'll come with you."

"Nonsense," she said. "Why should we both suffer? I'll see you soon." She blew him a kiss and went out.

Brosnan opened the French windows and stood on the terrace shivering until she emerged from the front door. "Good-bye, my love," he called dramatically. "Parting is such sweet sorrow."

"Idiot!" she called back. "Go back in before you catch pneumonia." She moved away, careful on the frozen pavement, and disappeared round the corner.

At that moment the phone rang. Brosnan turned and hurried in, leaving the French windows open.

DILLON was on foot. He had had an early meal at a small café, and his route back to the barge took him past Brosnan's apartment block. He paused on the other side of the road, cold in spite of the reefer coat and knitted cap pulled down over his ears. He looked up at the lighted windows of the apartment.

When Anne-Marie came out, he stepped back into the shadows. The street was silent—no traffic movement at all—and when Brosnan leaned over the balustrade and called down to her, Dillon heard every word he said. It gave him the totally false impression that she was leaving for the evening. As she disappeared, he crossed the road quickly, glanced each way to see that no one was about, then started to climb the scaffolding.

IT WAS Mary Tanner on the phone for Brosnan. She said to him, "Brigadier Ferguson wondered whether we could see you again in the morning before going back."

"All right," Brosnan told her reluctantly. "If you must. But it won't do you any good."

"I understand. I really do. Has Anne-Marie recovered?"

"A tough lady, that one," he said. "She's covered more wars than we've had hot dinners. That's why I've always found her attitude about such things where I'm concerned strange."

"You men can be incredibly stupid on occasions. She loves you, Professor. It's as simple as that. I'll see you in the morning."

Brosnan put the phone down. There was a draft of cold air; the fire flared up. He turned and found Sean Dillon standing in the open French windows, the Walther in his left hand.

"Jeez, Martin, the years have been good to you," he said.

Brosnan, a yard from the table drawer, made a cautious move. Inside the drawer was a Browning High Power 9-millimeter pistol—one of the deadliest handguns in the world.

"Naughty." Dillon gestured with the Walther. "Sit on the arm of the sofa, and put your hands behind your head."

Brosnan did as he was told. "You're enjoying yourself, Sean."

"I am so. How's that old sod Liam Devlin these days?"

"Alive and well. Still in Kilrea, outside Dublin. But then you know that. So what do you want with me after all these years?"

"Oh, I know all about you," Dillon said. "How they're pumping you for information about me—Hernu, old Ferguson and this side-kick of his, Captain Tanner. Nothing I don't know. I've got the right friends, you see, Martin. The kind who can access anything."

"And were they happy when you failed with Mrs. Thatcher?"

"Just a tryout, that—just a perhaps. I've promised them an alternative target. You know how this game works."

"I certainly do, and one thing I do know is that the IRA doesn't pay for hits. Never has."

"Who said I was working for the IRA?" Dillon grinned. "Plenty of others with enough reason to hit the Brits these days."

Brosnan saw it then, or thought he did. "Baghdad?"

"Sorry. You can go to your maker puzzling over that one."

"Just indulge me, Sean. I mean, the war stinks. Saddam needs something badly. President Bush stays back in Washington, and that leaves the Brits. You fail on the best-known woman in the world, so what's next? The Prime Minister?"

"Where you're going, it doesn't matter, son."

"But I'm right, aren't I?"

"You always were the clever one!" Dillon exploded angrily.

"This bungled attempt to get Mrs. Thatcher reminds me of a job dear old Frank Barry pulled when he tried to hit the British foreign secretary, Lord Carrington. I'm surprised you used the same plan, but then you always did think Barry was special, didn't you?"

"He was the best."

"And at the end of things, very dead," Brosnan said.

"Yes, well, whoever got him must have given it to him in the back," Dillon said.

"Not true," Brosnan said. "We were face to face, as I recall."

"You killed Frank Barry?" Dillon whispered.

"Well, somebody had to," Brosnan said. "It's what usually happens to mad dogs. I was working for Ferguson, by the way."

"Damn you." Dillon raised the Walther, took careful aim. The door opened, and Anne-Marie walked in with the shopping bags.

Dillon swung towards her. Brosnan called, "Look out!" and went down, and Dillon fired twice at the sofa.

Anne-Marie screamed—not in terror, but in fury—dropped her bags and rushed at him. Dillon tried to fend her off, staggered back through the French windows. Inside, Brosnan crawled towards the table and reached for the drawer. Anne-Marie scratched at Dillon's face. He cursed, pushing her away from him. She fell against the balustrade and went over backwards.

Brosnan had the drawer open now, knocked the lamp off the table, plunging the room into darkness, and reached for the Browning. Dillon fired three times very fast and ducked for the door. Brosnan fired twice, too late. He got to his feet, ran into the hall, got the door open and went downstairs. Of Dillon there was no sign, but the night porter was kneeling beside Anne-Marie.

The porter looked up. "There was a man, Professor, with a gun. He ran across the road."

"Never mind." Brosnan sat down and cradled Anne-Marie in his arms. "An ambulance, and hurry."

The snow was falling quite fast now. He held her close and waited.

FERGUSON, Mary, and Max Hernu were having a thoroughly enjoyable time in the magnificent dining room at the Ritz. They were starting on their second bottle of Champagne when Mary saw

Inspector Savary at the entrance speaking to the headwaiter. "I think you're being paged, Colonel," she told Hernu.

He glanced round. "What now?" He got up and made his way to Savary. They talked for a few moments. When Hernu came back, his face was grave. "I'm afraid I've got some rather ugly news."

"Dillon?" Ferguson asked.

"He paid a call on Brosnan a short while ago."

"What happened?" Ferguson demanded. "Is Brosnan all right?"

"Oh, yes. There was some gunplay. Dillon got away." He sighed heavily. "But Mademoiselle Audin is at the Hospital St. Louis. From what Savary tells me, it doesn't look good."

BROSNAN was pacing up and down in the third-floor waiting room when they arrived. His eyes were wild. Such a rage there, Mary thought. Briefly, coldly he told them what had happened.

As he finished, a tall graying man in surgeon's robes came in. He was Professor Henri Dubois, a colleague of Brosnan's at the Sorbonne. Brosnan turned to him quickly. "How is she, Henri?"

"Not good, my friend," Dubois told him. "The injuries to the spine are bad enough, but even more worrying is the skull fracture. They're preparing her for surgery now. I'll operate straightaway."

He went out. Brosnan's face was bone white, his eyes dark.

THERE was a small café for visitors on the ground floor. Not many customers at that time of night. Savary had gone off to handle the police side of the business; the others sat at a table in the corner.

Ferguson said to Brosnan, "I know you've got other things on your mind, but is there anything you can tell us about Dillon?"

"Yes, plenty. He's not working for the IRA. When I suggested Saddam Hussein, he got angry. My guess is, you wouldn't have to look much further. An interesting point—he knew about all of you."

"All of us?" Hernu said. "You're sure?"

"Oh, yes. He boasted about that." Brosnan turned to Ferguson. "Even knew about you and Captain Tanner being in town to pump me for information—that's how he put it. He said he had the right friends, the kind of people who can access anything."

"Did he?" Ferguson glanced at Mary. "Rather worrying, that."

"And you've got another problem. He spoke of the Thatcher affair as being just a tryout, that he had an alternative target. I think you'll find he intends to have a crack at the Prime Minister."

Mary said, "Are you certain?"

"Oh, yes." He nodded. "I baited him about that."

Ferguson looked at Hernu and sighed. "So now we know. I'd better go along to the embassy and alert all our people in London."

"I'll do the same," Hernu said. "Discreetly, of course."

They got up, and Brosnan said to them, "You're wasting your time. You won't get him, not in any usual way. You don't even know what you're looking for."

"Perhaps, Martin," Ferguson said. "But we'll just have to do our best, won't we?"

Mary Tanner followed them to the door. "Look, if you don't need me, Brigadier, I'd like to stay."

"Of course, my dear. I'll see you later."

She went to the counter and got two cups of tea.

DILLON WAS IN THE KITCHEN ON the barge heating the kettle when the phone rang. It was Makeev. "She's in the Hospital St. Louis," he said. "We've had to be discreet in our inquiries, but from what we can ascertain, she's on the critical list."

"Damn," Dillon said. "If only she'd kept her hands to herself."

"This could cause a devil of a fuss. I'd better come and see you."

"I'll be here."

Dillon poured hot water into a basin, then went into the bathroom and took off his shirt. He got a briefcase from the cupboard under the sink. Inside was a range of passports, with photos of himself suitably disguised, and a first-class makeup kit.

Over the years he had frequently traveled to England through Jersey, in the Channel Islands. Jersey was British soil. Once there, a British citizen didn't need a passport for the flight to the mainland. So, a French tourist holidaying in Jersey. He selected a passport in the name of Henri Jacaud, a car salesman from Rennes. To go with it, he found a Jersey driving license in the name of Peter Hilton, with an address in the island's main town of St. Helier. Jersey driving licenses carry a photo, and the photos on this one and on the French passport were identical.

He dissolved some black hair dye into the warm water and brushed it into his fair hair. Amazing what a difference changing the color made. He blow-dried his hair and brilliantined it back in place, then selected from his case a pair of horn-rimmed spectacles. He put them on and closed his eyes, thinking about the role. When he opened them again, Henri Jacaud stared out of the mirror.

At that precise moment Makeev came down the companionway. "Good God!" he said. "I thought it was someone else."

"But it is," Dillon said. "Henri Jacaud, car salesman from Rennes, on his way to Jersey for a winter break." He held up the driving license. "Who is also Jersey resident Peter Hilton from St. Helier."

"What happened tonight, Sean?" Makeev put in.

"I decided the time had come to take care of Brosnan. He knows me too well, knows how I think, and that could be dangerous."

"I can see that. So you decided to eliminate him?"

"It was an impulse, Josef. I was passing his place, saw the woman leaving. The way it sounded, I thought she was gone for the night, so I took a chance and went up the scaffolding."

"What happened?"

"Oh, I had the drop on him."

"But didn't kill him?"

Dillon laughed, went to the kitchen and returned with a bottle of Krug and two glasses. As he uncorked it he said, "Come on, Josef. Face to face after all those years. There were things to be said."

"You didn't tell him who you were working for?"

"Of course not," Dillon lied, and poured the Champagne.

He toasted Makeev, who said, "I mean, if he knew you had an alternative target, that you intended to go for Major . . ." He shrugged. "That would mean Ferguson would know. Aroun, I'm sure, would want to abort the whole business."

"Well, he doesn't know." Dillon drank more Champagne. "So Aroun can rest easy. After all, I want that second million. I checked with Zurich, by the way. The first million has been deposited."

"Of course. So when do you intend to leave?"

"Tomorrow or the next day. Meanwhile, something you can organize for me. This Tania Novikova in London—I'll need her help."

"No problem. She has a flat off the Bayswater Road."

"First, my father had a second cousin, a Belfast man living in London, called Danny Fahy. IRA, but not active. A deep-cover man. Brilliant with his hands. Worked in light engineering. I used him in 1981, when I was asked back to do a few jobs for the organization in London. In those days he lived at number Ten Tithe Street in Kilburn. I want Novikova to trace him."

"Anything else?"

"Yes. I'll need somewhere to stay. She can organize that for me, too. I'll contact her at her flat."

"There is one problem," Makeev said. "As regards explosives or weapons—I'm afraid she won't be able to help you there. A hand-gun perhaps, but no more. As I mentioned, her boss, Colonel Yuri Gatov, is a Gorbachev man, and very well disposed to our British friends."

"That's all right. I have my own contacts for that kind of thing," Dillon said. "But I will need more working capital. If I am checked going through customs on the Jersey-to-London flight, I can't afford to be caught with large sums of money in my briefcase."

"I'm sure Aroun can fix that for you."

"That's all right, then. I'd like to see him again before I go. Tomorrow morning, I think. Arrange that, will you?"

"All right." Makeev walked up the companionway and turned. "There is one thing. Say you managed to pull this thing off. It would lead to the most ferocious manhunt. How would you intend to get out of England?"

Dillon smiled. "That's exactly what I'm going to give some thought to now. I'll see you in the morning."

He lit a cigarette and sat at the table looking at the news clippings.

IT WAS one o'clock in the morning, and Mary Tanner was sitting alone in the waiting room when Professor Henri Dubois, the doctor, came in. Shoulders bowed, he sank wearily into a chair.

"Where is Martin?" he asked her.

"It seems Anne-Marie's only close relative is her grandfather. Martin is trying to contact him. Do you know him?"

"Who doesn't, mademoiselle? One of the richest and most powerful industrialists in France. Very old, though. Had a stroke last year, I believe. I don't think Martin will get very far there."

Brosnan came in then, looking incredibly weary, but when he saw Dubois, he said eagerly, "How is she?"

"I won't pretend, my friend. She's not good. Not good at all. I've done everything that I possibly can. Now we wait."

"Can I see her?"

"Leave it for a while. I'll let you know. How did you get on with Pierre Audin?"

"I didn't. Had to deal with his secretary. The old man's confined to a wheelchair now. Doesn't know the time of day."

Dubois sighed. "I'll be in my office. I'll see you later."

When he'd gone, Mary said, "You could do with some sleep."

Brosnan managed a dark smile. "The way I feel now, I don't think I could sleep. It's all my fault." There was despair on his face. "If it hadn't been for me, none of this would have happened."

She put a hand on his shoulder. "Come on. Lie down on the couch and close your eyes. I'll wake you the moment there's word."

Reluctantly he lay back and surprisingly did fall into a dark, dreamless sleep. Mary Tanner sat there listening to his quiet breathing.

IT WAS JUST AFTER THREE WHEN Dubois came in. As if sensing his presence, Brosnan came awake with a start and sat up. "What is it?"

"She's regained her senses. You can see her now. But Martin, it's not good. I think you should prepare for the worst."

"No," Brosnan said, choking. "It's not possible."

He ran along the corridor, opened the door to her room and went in. A young nurse sitting beside her got up and left. Anne-Marie was very pale, her head swathed in bandages.

Brosnan sat down. He reached for her hand, and Anne-Marie opened her eyes. "Martin, is that you?"

"Who else?" He kissed her hand.

"I must talk to you," she said. "Let him go, Martin. Give me your promise. It's not worth it." She grabbed at his hand with surprising strength. "Promise me."

"My word on it," he said.

She lay back then. "Your hair—too long. My lovely wild Irish boy. Always loved you, Martin. No one else."

Her eyes closed gently. The monitoring machine beside the bed changed its tone, and Henri Dubois was in the room in a second. "Outside, Martin—wait." He pushed Brosnan out and closed the door.

Mary was standing in the corridor. "Martin?" she said.

Brosnan stared at her vacantly, and then the door opened and Dubois appeared. "I'm so sorry, my friend. I'm afraid she's gone."

IT WAS just after ten a.m. when Mary Tanner admitted Ferguson and Hernu to Brosnan's apartment. "How is he?" Ferguson asked.

"He's kept himself busy. Anne-Marie's grandfather is not well, so Martin's making the funeral arrangements with Audin's secretary."

She led the way to the drawing room. Brosnan was standing at the window staring out. He turned to meet them, hands in pockets, his face pale and drawn. "Well?" he demanded.

"Nothing to report," Hernu told him. "We've notified all ports and airports—discreetly, of course."

Brosnan seemed curiously indifferent. "You won't get him. London's the place to look now, and for London you'll need me."

"You mean you'll help us? You'll come in on this?" Ferguson said.

"Yes."

"But you can't," Mary said. "You promised Anne-Marie."

"I lied," he said calmly. "Just to make her going easier. There's nothing out there. Only darkness."

His face was rock hard, the eyes bleak. It was the face of a stranger. "If it's the last thing I do," he said, "I'll see him dead."

## Six

IT WAS just before eleven a.m. when Makeev drew up before Aroun's apartment in Avenue Victor-Hugo. Dillon was there to meet him. Makeev said, "The Audin woman—she died last night."

"You haven't told Aroun?"

"No, of course not."

"Good." Dillon smiled. "Now let's go in."

Rashid opened the door to them. A maid took their coats. Michael Aroun was waiting in the magnificent drawing room. "Valenton, Mr. Dillon—a considerable disappointment."

"I promised you an alternative target, and I intend to go for it."

"The British Prime Minister?" Rashid asked.

"That's right." Dillon nodded. "I'm leaving for London later today. I thought we'd have a chat before I go."

"Of course," Aroun said. "Now, how can we help you?"

"First, I'm going to need operating money again. Thirty thousand dollars. I want you to arrange that from someone in London."

"No problem," Aroun said.

"Second, there's the question of how I get the hell out of England after the successful conclusion of the venture. That's where you come in, Mr. Aroun."

He said, "Please explain."

"One of my minor talents is flying. I share that with you, I understand. According to an article I read, you bought an estate called Château St.-Denis just south of Cherbourg, on the Normandy coast."

"That's correct."

"It has its own landing strip, and it isn't unknown for you to fly down from Paris, when you feel like it, piloting your own plane."

"Quite true, my friend," Aroun said.

"Good. This is how it will go, then. I'll let you know when the job is done. You'll fly down to this St.-Denis place. I'll fly out from

England and join you. You can arrange my onwards transportation."

"But how? Where will you find a plane?" Rashid demanded.

"Plenty of flying clubs, old son, and planes to hire. I'll simply fly off the map, disappear. Once I land at St.-Denis, you can torch the bloody thing." He looked from Rashid to Aroun. "Are we agreed?"

"Absolutely," said Aroun, "and if there's anything else—"

"Makeev will let you know. I'll be going now." Dillon turned towards the door, and he and Makeev left.

Outside, they stood beside Makeev's car. The Russian passed him an envelope. "Tania's home address and telephone number. I'll speak to her about you today."

"Fine," Dillon said. "That's it, then. I'll speak to you after I get off the hydrofoil in Jersey, just to make sure everything is all right."

"Good luck, Sean."

He smiled. "Oh, you always need that as well." He walked away.

SEAN Dillon caught the express to Rennes and changed trains for St.-Malo at three o'clock. There wasn't much tourist traffic at that time of year, and the atrocious weather all over Europe had killed whatever there was. There couldn't have been more than twenty passengers on the hydrofoil to Jersey. He disembarked in St. Helier just before six o'clock and caught a cab to the airport.

He knew he was in trouble before he arrived because the closer he got, the thicker the fog was. At the airport, he confirmed that both evening flights to London had been canceled. Then he caught another taxi and told the driver to take him to a convenient hotel.

It was thirty minutes later when he phoned Makeev in Paris. "Did you contact Novikova?" he asked.

"Oh, yes," Makeev said. "Everything is in order. Where are you?"

"I'm at a place called Hotel L'Horizon in Jersey. There was fog at the airport. I'm hoping to get out in the morning."

"I'm sure you will. Stay in touch."

"I'll do that." Dillon put down the phone; then he went downstairs to the bar. He ordered a bottle of Krug and relaxed.

IT WAS at roughly the same time that the doorbell sounded at Brosnan's apartment, on Quai de Montebello. When Brosnan opened the door, Mary Tanner stood there.

"Hello," he said. "This is unexpected."

"I thought you'd be alone. I didn't think that was a good idea. Ferguson spoke to you before he left for London?"

"Yes. He said you were staying over for the funeral. Suggested we follow him tomorrow afternoon."

"Yes, well, that doesn't take care of tonight. I expect you haven't eaten a thing all day, so I suggest we go out for a meal, and don't start saying no. There must be somewhere close by that you like."

"There is indeed, Captain. I'll get a coat and be right with you."

It was a typical little side-street bistro, simple and unpretentious, booths to give privacy and cooking smells from the kitchen that were out of this world. Brosnan ordered Champagne.

"Always Champagne with you?" she said.

"I was shot in the stomach years ago. It gave me problems. The doctors said no spirits, no red wine. Champagne was okay. Did you notice the name of this place?"

"La Belle Aurore."

"Same as the café in *Casablanca*. Humphrey Bogart? Ingrid Bergman?" He raised his glass. "Here's looking at you, kid."

They sat there in companionable silence for a while, and then she said, "Can we talk business?"

"Why not. What do you have in mind?"

"What happens next? I mean, how do you hope to find Dillon?"

"One weakness," Brosnan said. "He won't go near any IRA contacts for fear of betrayal. That leaves the underworld. Anything he needs—weaponry, explosives—he'll go to the obvious place."

"Where is that? The East End of London?"

"Yes. A lot of the big men—the governors, as they call them—have gone legitimate to a degree. But all the old-fashioned crimes—banks, holdups, security vans—are committed by roughly the same group. All family men. It's in that fraternity Dillon will look for help. And as it happens, I've got what you might call the entrée."

"And how on earth do you have that?" she said.

He poured her another glass of Champagne. "Back in Vietnam, in 1968, I was a paratrooper—Airborne Rangers. I formed part of a Special Forces detachment to operate in Cambodia. It was recruited from all branches of the services. We even had a few marines, and that's how I met Harry Flood."

"Harry Flood?" she said, and frowned. "That name's familiar."

"Could be. I'll explain. In '69, when I was getting out, Harry still had a year of his enlistment to do. He was a sergeant then, and they posted him to London. Embassy guard duty. One night at the old Lyceum Ballroom, he met a girl called Jean Dark. Just a nice, pretty twenty-year-old in a cotton frock, only there was one difference. The Dark family were gangsters. Her old man had his own little empire down by the river. He died later that year."

"What happened?" Mary was totally fascinated.

"Harry and Jean got married. He stayed on and got sucked in."

"You mean he became a gangster?"

"Yes, but much more than that. Much more. He became one of the biggest governors in the East End of London."

"My goodness, now I remember. He has all those casinos."

"Right. He has the casinos, business interests in electronics, and property development on the Thames. He owns half of Wapping High Street. Nearly all the river frontage. He's extremely legitimate."

"And still a gangster?"

"Let's say he's still the governor to a lot of East Enders. The Yank—that's what they call him. You'll like him."

She looked surprised. "And when are we going to meet?"

"As soon as I can arrange it. If anyone can help me catch Sean Dillon, Harry can." The waiter appeared and placed bowls of onion soup before them. "Good," he said. "Now let's eat. I'm starving."

HARRY Flood came awake with a start and sat upright. In his dream he had been back there in Vietnam, a prisoner of the Vietcong. He was standing in a narrow pit, and the rain was pouring down relentlessly through the bamboo grid above his head. The water rose rapidly until it was up to his chest and he no longer had a footing. He struggled and kicked to keep afloat, fighting for breath. Suddenly a hand grabbed his, a strong hand, and it pulled him up through the water, and he started to breathe again.

He'd had that dream on and off for years. It usually ended with his drowning. The hand pulling him out was something new.

He reached for his watch. It was almost ten. He always had an evening nap before visiting one of the clubs, but this time he'd overslept. He hurried into the bathroom and had a quick shower.

He was handsome enough in a rather hard way—muscular, with good shoulders. In fact, not bad for forty-six, he told himself as he shaved. He dressed in a black silk shirt, buttoned at the neck, without a tie, and a loose-fitting Armani suit in dark raw silk. He checked his appearance in the mirror.

"Showtime, baby," he said, and went out into the sitting room.

His apartment was enormous, part of a warehouse development on Cable Wharf. The brick walls of this room were painted white, the wooden floor lacquered. Comfortable sofas, a bar, bottles of every conceivable kind ranged behind. Only for guests. He never drank alcohol. There was a large desk in front of a wall lined with books.

He opened French windows and went out onto the balcony. It overlooked the Thames. Tower Bridge was to his right, the Tower of London just beyond it, floodlit. He watched a ship pass, took a lungful of that cold air and went inside.

The door opened, and Mordecai Fletcher came in. Six feet tall, with iron-gray hair and a clipped mustache, he wore a well-cut double-breasted blazer and a Guards tie. The edge was taken off his conventional appearance by a flattened nose, which had been broken more than once. A useful heavyweight boxer, he had been Flood's strong right arm for the best part of fifteen years.

He went behind the bar, poured a Perrier, added ice and lemon, and brought it to Flood, saying, "Your accountant called. Some papers to sign on that market development. And Maurice was on the phone from the Embassy Club. He says Jack Harvey was in for a bite to eat with that niece of his, Myra. Harvey asked for you. Said he'd come back and have a go at the tables." Mordecai hesitated. "You know what that guy's after."

"We aren't selling, and we certainly aren't going into partnership. Jack Harvey's the worst hood in the East End."

"I thought that was you, Harry."

"I never did drugs, didn't run girls, you know that. Okay. I was a right villain for a few years—we both were." He walked to the desk and picked up the photo in a silver frame that always stood there. "When Jean was dying for all those lousy months, you know the promise she made me give her? To get out. That's why I made us legitimate, and wasn't I right? You know what the firm's net worth is? Nearly fifty million. Fifty million." He grinned. "So let Jack

Harvey and others like him keep dirtying their hands if they want."

He opened a closet and took out a dark overcoat. "Now let's get moving. Who's driving tonight, Mordecai?"

"Charlie Salter." He hesitated. "Shall I carry a shooter, Harry?"

"For God's sake, Mordecai, we're legit now, I keep telling you."

"But Jack Harvey isn't—that's the trouble."

"Leave Jack Harvey to me."

They went down in the old freight elevator to the warehouse, where Charlie Salter—a small, wiry man in a gray chauffeur's uniform—waited by a black Mercedes. He got the rear door open. "Where to, Harry?"

"The Embassy Club, Charlie. And drive carefully."

Salter got behind the wheel, and Mordecai got in beside him and reached for the electronic door control. The warehouse doors opened, and the Mercedes turned onto the wharf.

The club was only half a mile away, just off Wapping High Street. It had been open only six months, another of Flood's developments of old warehouse property. They parked, and walked up the side street to the entrance. Inside, it was warm and luxurious, with oak paneling and oil paintings. As they checked their coats a small man in evening dress hurried to meet them.

"Ah, Mr. Flood. Will you be dining?" His accent was French.

"We'll just have a look round first, Maurice. Any sign of Harvey?"

"Not yet."

They went down the steps into the main dining room. The place was almost full, waiters working the table booths busily. A trio played on a dais in one corner, and there was a small dance floor.

Maurice threaded his way through the tables and opened a door of quilted leather, which led to the casino part of the premises. It was crowded, too, people jostling one another at the roulette tables.

"We losing much?" Flood asked Maurice.

"Swings and roundabouts, Mr. Flood. It all balances out."

"Come on, then," Flood said. "Let's go and eat."

He had his own booth in a corner to one side of the band. He ordered smoked salmon and scrambled eggs; then he took a cigarette from an old silver case. Mordecai gave him a light and leaned against the wall. As Flood sat there brooding, surveying the scene, Charlie Salter hurried over. "Jack Harvey and Myra—just in," he said.

Harvey was fifty years of age, of medium height and overweight—a fact that the navy-blue Savile Row suit failed to hide. He was balding and had a fleshy, decadent face.

His niece, Myra, was thirty and immensely attractive. Her jet-black hair was caught up in a bun and held in place by a diamond comb. Her lips were blood red. She wore a sequined jacket and black miniskirt and high-heeled black shoes, for she was only a little over five feet tall. She was her uncle's right hand, had a university degree in business, and was just as ruthless and unscrupulous as he was.

"Harry, my old son," Harvey said, and sat down. "Don't mind if we join you, do you?"

Flood didn't get up, just sat there waiting. Myra leaned down and kissed him on the cheek. "Like my new perfume, Harry? Costs a fortune, but Jack says it's like an aphrodisiac, the smell's so good."

She sat on his other side, and Harvey took out a cigar. He looked up at Mordecai, who flicked his lighter without a change of expression. Myra said, "Any chance of a drink?"

Flood said, "Champagne cocktail—isn't that what you like?"

"It'll do to be going on with."

"Scotch and water for me," Harvey said. "A big one."

Maurice, who had been hovering, spoke to a waiter, then whispered in Flood's ear, "Your scrambled eggs, Mr. Flood."

"I'll have them now," Flood told him.

A moment later the waiter put the plate in front of Flood, who got to work straightaway.

Harvey said, "I've never seen you eat a decent meal yet, Harry. What's wrong with you?"

"Food doesn't mean much to me, Jack. When I was a prisoner of the Vietcong, I learned you could get by on very little." After a while Flood pushed his plate away and wiped his mouth with a napkin. "Now, what have you really come for?"

"You know what I want, Harry. I want in. The casinos—four of them now—and how many clubs, Myra?"

"Six," she said.

"And all this development on the river," Harry went on. "You've got to share the cake."

"There's only one trouble with that, Jack," Flood told him. "I'm a legitimate businessman, have been for a long time, whereas

385

you . . ." He shook his head. "Once a crook, always a crook."

"You Yank s.o.b.," Harvey said, "you can't talk to me like that."

"I just did, Jack."

Myra said, "Be reasonable, Harry. All we're asking for is a piece of the action."

"You come in with me, and you're into computers, building development, clubs and gambling," Flood said. "Which means I'm in with you into pimps, whores, drugs and protection. I shower three times a day, sweetness, and it still wouldn't make me feel clean."

"You Yank—" She raised her hand, and he grabbed her wrist.

Harvey stood up. "Let it go, Myra, let it go. Come on. I'll be seeing you, Harry."

"I hope not," Flood told him as they went out.

"THE swine," Jack Harvey said as he and Myra walked along the pavement towards the car park. "We'll have to show him we mean business, won't we?"

A dark van was parked at the end of the street. As they approached, the side lights were turned on. The man who leaned out was young, hard and dangerous-looking in a black leather bomber jacket and flat cap. "Mr. Harvey," he said.

"Good boy, Billy. Right on time." Harvey turned to his niece. "I don't think you've met Billy Watson, Myra."

"No, I don't think I have," she said, looking him over.

"How many have you got in the back?" Harvey demanded.

"Four, Mr. Harvey. I heard this Mordecai Fletcher was a bit of an animal." He picked up a baseball bat. "This should cool him."

"No shooters, like I told you. Flesh on flesh, that's all it needs, and maybe a couple of broken legs. Get on with it. He'll have to come out here sooner or later."

Harvey and Myra turned and continued towards the car park.

IT WAS an hour later that Harry Flood got ready to leave. As he got his coat on, he said to Mordecai, "Where's Charlie?"

"Oh, I gave him the nod a couple of minutes ago. He went ahead to get the car warmed up."

They went outside and started along the street. When it happened, it was very quick—the rear doors of the van swinging open, the men inside rushing out carrying baseball bats. The first to reach them swung hard. Mordecai ducked, blocked the blow and pitched the man over his hip, down the steps of the basement area behind.

The other four paused and circled, bats ready. "That won't do you any good," Billy Watson said. "It's leg-breaking time."

There was a shot behind them, loud in the frosty air, then another. Charlie Salter moved out of the darkness, reloading a sawed-off shotgun. "Now drop 'em," he said.

They did as they were told and stood there waiting. Mordecai moved close and looked them over. Then he grabbed the nearest one by the hair. "Who are you working for, sonny?"

The youth cracked instantly. "Jack Harvey. It was just a wages job. It was Billy who pulled us in."

Billy said, "You fool, I'll get you for that!"

Mordecai glanced at Flood, who nodded. The big man said to Billy, "You stay. The rest of you, beat it."

They turned and ran for it. Billy Watson stood looking at them, then suddenly picked up one of the baseball bats. "All right, Harry Flood—big man. No bloody good on your own, are you, mate?"

Billy swung, Flood swayed to one side, found the right wrist, twisted. Billy cried out and dropped the baseball bat, and in the same moment, the American half turned, striking him hard across the face with his elbow, sending him down on one knee.

Mordecai picked up the baseball bat. "No," Flood said. "He's got the point. Let's get going."

As they went along the street towards the car park Mordecai said, "What about Harvey? You going to stitch him up?"

"I'll think about it," Flood said.

## Seven

DILLON's flight from Jersey got into Heathrow just after eleven the following morning. Customs didn't seem to be stopping anyone just then, not that they'd have found anything on him. His suitcase contained a change of clothes and toilet articles, no more. He also had two thousand dollars in his wallet. Nothing wrong with that. He'd destroyed the French passport in Jersey. No turning back now.

He took the escalator to the upper concourse and joined the queue at one of the bank counters, changing five hundred dollars for sterling. He did the same at three other banks, whistling softly. Then he phoned Tania Novikova's number and got her answering machine. He didn't bother to leave a message, but went out and hailed a cab, and told the driver to take him to Covent Garden.

In his tinted glasses, striped tie and navy-blue Burberry trench coat he looked thoroughly respectable.

The driver said, "Terrible weather, guv. You live in London?"

"No. Just in town on business. I've been abroad for some time," Dillon said glibly. "New York. Haven't been in London for years."

"A lot of changes. Not like it used to be."

"So I believe. I was reading the other day that you can't take a walk up Downing Street anymore."

"That's right, guv. Mrs. Thatcher had a new security system installed—gates at the end of the street."

"Really?" Dillon said. "I'd like to see that."

"We'll go that way if you like. I can take you down to Whitehall, then cut back to Covent Garden."

"Suits me." Dillon sat back and watched as they drove into London. From Trafalgar Square they moved down Whitehall, past Horse Guards Avenue, with the two household cavalrymen on mounted duty wearing greatcoats against the cold, sabers drawn.

"Here we are, guv—Downing Street," the cabby said. He slowed a little. "Can't stop, or the coppers ask you what you're doing."

Dillon looked across at the end of the street. "So those are the famous gates?"

"Thatcher's folly, some call it. But if you ask me, she was right. The bloody IRA have pulled off enough stunts in London during the past few years. If I drop you in Long Acre, will that do, guv?"

"Fine," Dillon told him, and thought about those gates.

The taxi pulled up to the curb. Dillon got out, paid the driver and walked briskly away.

The whole Covent Garden area was as busy as usual. Dillon went with the throng and finally found what he wanted—a small theatrical shop—in an alley near Neal's Yard. A white-haired man appeared from the rear. "And what can I do for you?" he asked.

"Some makeup, I think. What have you got in boxes?"

"Some very good kits here," the old man said. He took one down and opened it on the counter. "In the business, are you?"

"Amateur, that's all. Church players." Dillon checked the contents of the box. "Excellent. I'll also take black hair dye and solvent."

"You *are* going to town." The man got the required items, put them inside the makeup box and closed it. "Thirty quid."

Dillon paid and went out whistling.

IT WAS just after six when Tania Novikova heard the doorbell. She went downstairs and opened the door. Dillon stood there, suitcase in one hand, briefcase in the other. "Josef sends his regards."

She was amazed. Since speaking with Makeev, she had expected some kind of dark hero. Instead, she had a small man in a trench coat, with tinted glasses and a college tie.

"You are Sean Dillon?" she said.

"As ever was."

"You'd better come in."

Women had never been of great importance to Dillon. They were there to satisfy a need on occasions, but he had never felt the slightest emotional involvement with one. Following her up the stairs, he was aware that Tania Novikova had a good figure. Yet when she turned to him in the full light of her sitting room, he realized that she was really rather plain.

"Would you like a drink?" she asked.

"Tea would be fine."

She opened a drawer, produced a Walther, two spare clips and a Carswell silencer. "Your preferred weapon, according to Josef. Also, this might be useful." She handed him a small bundle. "They say it can stop a .45 bullet at point-blank range. Nylon and titanium."

Dillon unfolded it. Designed like a small waistcoat and fastened with Velcro tabs, it was nowhere near as bulky as a flak jacket. "Excellent," he said, and put it in his briefcase, together with the Walther and the silencer.

He stood in the kitchen door while she made the tea. "You're very convenient for the Soviet embassy here?"

"Oh, yes. Walking distance." She brought the tea out on a tray. "I've fixed you up with a room in a hotel just round the corner, in the Bayswater Road. Commercial travelers overnight there."

"Fine." He sipped his tea. "To business. What about Fahy?"

"No luck so far. He moved from Kilburn a few years ago. I've drawn a blank, but I'll find him. I've got someone on his case."

"Does KGB's London station still have a forgery department?"

"Of course."

"Good." He took out his Jersey driving license. "I want a private pilot's license in this name. You'll need a photo." From inside the plastic cover of the license he pulled out an identical print.

"Peter Hilton, Jersey. Can I ask why this is necessary?"

"Because when the right time comes—time to get the hell out of it—I want to fly, and they won't hire a plane to you unless you have a license issued by the Civil Aviation Authority."

She took the photo. "Is there anything else?"

"Yes. I'd like full details of the present security system at number Ten Downing Street."

She caught her breath. "Is that your target?"

"Not as such. The man inside, but that's a different thing. The Prime Minister's daily schedule—how easy is it to access that?"

"It depends. There are always fixed points in his day. Question time in the House of Commons, for example. And the War Cabinet meets every morning at ten in the Cabinet Room."

"Interesting, that. Now, this informant of yours—you got him well and truly hooked?"

"I think you could say that."

"Keep it that way." He got up. "I'd better book in at this hotel."

"Have you eaten?" she asked.

"No."

"I have a suggestion. Just along from the hotel is a little Italian restaurant—Luigi's. You get settled in, and I'll check on what we have on the Downing Street defenses and see you in an hour."

"All right." She got a coat and scarf, and they left together.

The hotel room was what he'd expected: twin beds, cheap coverings, a shower room, a television with a slot for coins. Still, it wouldn't be for long, and he opened his suitcase and unpacked.

HE WAS sitting in a small booth in the corner at Luigi's drinking Champagne when Tania came in. Old Luigi greeted her personally as a favored customer, and she sat down.

"Champagne?" Dillon asked.

"Why not." She looked up at Luigi. "We'll order later."

"One thing we haven't mentioned is my operating money," Dillon said. "Thirty thousand dollars. Aroun was to arrange that."

"It's taken care of. Aroun's accountant will be in touch tomorrow."

"Okay. So what have you got for me?" he asked.

"Nothing on Fahy yet, but I've had a look at the file on Number Ten. In effect, Downing Street is now a fortress. The steel railings are ten feet high. The gates, by the way, are neo-Victorian."

Luigi was hovering anxiously, and they broke off and ordered minestrone, veal chops and a green salad. After he'd gone, Dillon asked, "And the building itself?"

"The windows have specially strengthened glass, and the net curtains are a miracle of modern science. They're blast proof."

"What about getting in as ancillary staff?"

"That used to be a real loophole—the outside catering and cleaning staff—but now they're very tough about security clearance for these people. There are always slipups, of course." Tania hesitated. "Have you anything particular in mind?"

"No, but I'll come up with something. I always do."

The waiter brought their soup. Dillon said, "Now, that smells good enough to eat. Let's do just that."

In Paris the following morning the temperature went up three or four degrees, and it started to thaw. Mary Tanner and Hernu, in the colonel's black Citroën, picked up Brosnan just before noon. He was waiting in the entrance of the Quai de Montebello apartment block. He wore his trench coat and a tweed cap, and carried a suitcase.

The day before, the three of them had attended the service at the village church at Vercors as Anne-Marie went to her final rest. The church was cold, very cold. In fact, Brosnan had never felt so cold. He sat there shaking slightly, hardly aware of what was being said. It was only when the pallbearers were carrying the coffin down the aisle that he realized that Mary was holding his hand.

Now the driver put the suitcase in the trunk, and Brosnan got in the rear with the other two. "Any news?" he asked.

"Not a thing," the colonel told him.

"So he's probably there already. What about Ferguson?"

Mary glanced at her watch. "He's due to see the Prime Minister now, to alert him as to the seriousness of this business."

"About all he can do," Brosnan said.

"And how would you handle it, my friend?" Hernu asked.

"As I told Mary, he always uses underworld contacts to supply his needs, and it will be the same this time. That's why I must see my old friend Harry Flood."

"Ah, yes. The redoubtable Mr. Flood. But what if he can't help?"

"There's another way. I have a friend in Ireland just outside Dublin, at Kilrea—Liam Devlin. There's nothing he doesn't know about IRA history in the last few years, and who did what." He leaned back. "But I'll get the fool. One way or another, I'll get him."

The driver took them to the end of the terminal at Charles de Gaulle Airport where the private planes parked. The Lear was waiting on the tarmac. Hernu said, "Captain, if I may presume." He kissed Mary lightly on both cheeks. "And you, my friend." He held out his hand. "Always remember that when you set out on a journey with revenge at the end of it, it is necessary to first dig two graves."

"Philosophy now?" Brosnan said. "Good-bye, Colonel."

Moments later the two were strapping themselves into their seats as the second pilot pulled up the stairs and locked the door.

"Hernu is right, you know," Mary said.

"I know he is, but there's nothing I can do about that," Brosnan answered. The plane then began to roll forward.

TANIA, with good news for Dillon, did not expect to find him in the hotel for lunch, so she went to her flat. As she was looking for her key in her handbag, Gordon Brown crossed the road.

"I was hoping I might catch you," he said.

"Jeez, Gordon, you must be crazy."

"And what happens when something important comes up and you need to know? Can't wait for you to get in touch. It might be too late, so I'd better come in, hadn't I?"

"You can't. I'm due back at the embassy in thirty minutes. I'll have a drink with you, that's all."

She turned and walked down to the pub on the corner before he could argue. They sat in an empty corner, aware of the noise from the main bar. "So what have you got for me?" she asked.

"Ferguson had a meeting with the Prime Minister just before twelve. When he came back to the office, he dictated a report for the file to Alice Johnson. She's one of the confidential typists."

"Did you get a copy?"

"No, but I read it. Captain Tanner stayed in Paris with Brosnan for the funeral of a Frenchwoman. They're flying in today. Brosnan has promised full cooperation. Oh, all the other branches of the intelligence services have been notified about Dillon. No newspaper coverage, on the P.M.'s instructions. The impression I got was he's told Ferguson to get on with it."

"Good," she said. "Stay on the case, Gordon. Now I have to go."

She walked out, leaving Brown thoroughly depressed.

WHEN Tania knocked on the door of Dillon's room just after two, he opened it at once. She brushed past him and went inside.

"You look pleased with yourself," he said.

"I should. First, I've had a word with my mole at Group Four. Ferguson's been to see the Prime Minister. They believe you're here, and intelligence has been notified. Brosnan and the Tanner woman are coming in from Paris. He's offered full cooperation."

"It's nice to be wanted."

"Second"—she opened her handbag and handed him a passport-style booklet—"one pilot's license as issued by the Civil Aviation Authority to one Peter Hilton."

"That's bloody marvelous," Dillon said, and took it from her.

"Yes. The man who does this kind of thing pulled out all the stops. And that's not the end. We've found one Daniel Fahy, at a farm called Cadge End, in Sussex." She unfolded a road map. "You take this road through Dorking towards Horsham, then head into the wilds."

"How do you know all this?" he asked.

"The operative I put on the job managed to trace him late yesterday. He looked the place over, then dropped into the pub in the local village and made a few inquiries. I got his report this morning."

"And?"

"He says the farm is very out of the way, near a river called the Arun. The village is called Doxley. The farm is a mile south of it. Fahy runs a few sheep and dabbles in agricultural machinery."

Dillon nodded. "That makes sense."

"One thing that might come as a surprise. He has a girl staying with him—his grand-niece, it seems. Angel, they called her."

Dillon got up and reached for his trench coat, putting it on. "I must get down there right away. Do you have a car?"

"Yes, a Mini. It's garaged at the end of my street. I'll show you."

He opened the briefcase, took out the Walther, rammed a clip in and put it in his left-hand pocket. The silencer he put in the right. "Just in case," he said, and they went out.

The car was in fact a Mini-Cooper, which meant performance. It was jet black. "Excellent," he said, and got behind the wheel.

She said, "What's so important about Fahy?"

"He's an engineer who can turn his hand to anything, a bomb maker of genius, and he's been in deep cover for years. It also helps that he was my father's second cousin. I knew him when I was a kid. I'll be in touch," Dillon added, and drove away.

FERGUSON had stopped off at his office at the Ministry of Defense after Downing Street to dictate his report and clear his desk. As always, he preferred to work at the flat, so he returned to Cavendish Square, had Kim prepare him a late lunch of scrambled eggs and bacon, and was browsing through his *Times* when the doorbell rang. A moment later Kim showed in Mary Tanner and Brosnan.

"My dear Martin." Ferguson got up, and they shook hands. "So tell me, where will you start?" the brigadier asked.

"With my old friend Harry Flood," Brosnan said. "When Dillon was here in '81, he probably used underworld contacts to supply his needs. Harry may be able to dig something out. If not, I'll borrow that Learjet again and fly to Dublin to see Liam Devlin."

"Ah, yes," Ferguson said. "Who better?"

"In '81 Dillon must have been under someone's orders. If Devlin could find out who, that could be a real lead."

"Sounds logical to me. So where are you staying?"

"At Lowndes Square, with me," Mary said.

Ferguson's eyebrows went up. "Really?"

"Come on, Brigadier. Don't be an old fuddy-duddy. I've got four bedrooms, remember, each with its own bathroom, and Professor Brosnan can have one with a lock on the inside of his door."

Brosnan laughed. "Let's get out of here. See you later, Brigadier."

They borrowed Ferguson's car and driver. On the way Brosnan used the car phone to call Flood at Cable Wharf, in Wapping.

It was Mordecai Fletcher who answered. Brosnan said, "Harry Flood, please."

"Who wants him?"

"Martin Brosnan."

"The professor? This is Mordecai. We haven't heard from you for what—four years? Damn, but he's going to be pleased."

A moment later a voice said, "Martin, I don't believe it. You've come back to haunt me, have you?"

## Eight

For Dillon in the Mini-Cooper, the run from London went easily enough. Despite a light covering of snow on the fields, the roads were clear. He was in Dorking within half an hour and continued straight through towards Horsham, finally pulling into a petrol station. "Place called Doxley—you know it?" he asked the attendant.

"Up the road on your right a signpost says Grimethorpe. That's the airfield. Farther on you'll see a sign to Doxley."

"So it's not far from here?"

"Three miles maybe, mister," the attendant said.

Dillon drove away, came to the Grimethorpe sign, followed the narrow road and found the sign for Doxley. He turned onto an even narrower road, high banks blocking the view until he came to the brow of a small hill and looked across a desolate landscape. There was a scattering of hedged fields and a river that had to be the Arun. Beside it, perhaps a mile away, he saw twelve or fifteen houses and a small church, obviously Doxley. He started down the hill. In the wooded valley below, he came to a five-barred gate standing open and a decaying wooden sign saying CADGE END FARM.

The track led through a wood and brought him almost at once to a run-down farm complex—a house with two large barns linked to it so that the whole enclosed a courtyard. Dillon got out of the Mini, knocked on the front door and tried to open it. It was locked. He turned and went into the first barn. There was a Morris van in there and agricultural implements all over the place.

Dillon took out a cigarette. As he lit it in cupped hands a voice behind said, "Who are you? What do you want?"

He turned and found a girl in the doorway. She wore baggy trousers tucked into a pair of rubber boots, a heavy roll-neck sweater under an old anorak, and a knitted tam-o'-shanter. She was holding a double-barreled shotgun threateningly. As he took a step towards her she thumbed back the hammer.

"You stay there." The Irish accent was very pronounced.

"You'll be the one they call Angel Fahy?" he said.

"Angela, if it's any of your business."

"Would you really shoot with that thing?"

"If I had to."

"A pity that, and me only wanting to meet my father's cousin once removed, Danny Fahy."

She frowned. "And who might you be, mister?"

"Dillon's the name. Sean Dillon."

The gun went slack in her hands. "Are you really Sean Dillon?"

"As ever was. Appearances can be deceiving."

"Oh, Uncle Danny talks about you all the time, and here you are."

"Where is he?"

"He did a repair on a car for the landlord of the pub, took it down there an hour ago. He'll stay awhile drinking, I shouldn't wonder."

"Let's go and get him, then."

She left the shotgun on a bench and got into the Mini beside him. As they drove away he said, "What's your story, then?"

"I was raised on a farm in Galway," she said. "My da was Danny's nephew, Michael. He died six years ago, when I was fourteen. After a year my mother married again."

"Let me guess," Dillon said. "You didn't like your stepfather, and he didn't like you."

"Something like that. So I left home and came here. Uncle Danny was great. Wrote to my mother, and she agreed I could stay."

There was no self-pity at all, and Dillon warmed to her.

"I've been working it out," she said. "If you're Danny's second cousin and I'm his great-niece, then you and I are blood related." She looked ecstatic as she leaned back. "Me, Angel Fahy, related to the greatest gunman the Provisional IRA ever had."

"Well now, there would be some who would argue about that,"

396

he said as they reached the village and pulled up outside the pub.

It was a small, desolate place called the Green Man, and even Dillon had to duck to enter the door. The ceiling was very low and beamed, the floor constructed of heavy flagstones. The man behind the bar glanced up, and Angel said, "Is he here, Mr. Dalton?"

"By the fire, having a beer," the man said.

Danny Fahy sat in front of a wide stone hearth reading the paper, a glass in his hand. He was sixty-five, with an untidy grizzled beard, and wore a cloth cap and an old Harris Tweed suit.

Angel said, "I've brought someone to see you, Uncle Danny."

He looked up at her and then at Dillon, puzzlement on his face. "And what can I do for you, sir?"

Dillon removed his glasses. "God bless all here!" he said in his Belfast accent. "And particularly you, you old fool."

Fahy turned very pale—the shock was so intense. "Is that you, Sean?" He actually had tears in his eyes as he rose and flung his arms around Dillon. "I just can't tell you how good it is to see you."

THE sitting room at the farm was untidy and cluttered, the furniture very old. Dillon sat on a sofa while Fahy built up the fire. Angel was in the kitchen cooking a meal.

"And how's life been treating you, Sean?" Fahy stuffed a pipe and lit it. "Ten years since you raised cain in London town, boy."

"I couldn't have done it without you, Danny."

"Great days. And what happened after?"

"Europe, the Middle East. I kept on the move. Did a lot for the PLO. Even learned to fly."

"Is that a fact?"

Angel came in and put plates of bacon and eggs on the table. "Sorry there's nothing fancier, but we weren't expecting company."

"It looks good to me," Dillon told her, and tucked in.

"So now you're here, Sean, and working on something, I can tell," Fahy said. "Come on. Let's in on it."

Dillon said, "What if I told you I was working for the Arabs, Danny—for Saddam Hussein himself?"

"Jeez, and why not? And what is it he wants you to do?"

"He wants something now—a coup. Something big. I was thinking of John Major."

397

"The Prime Minister?" Angel said in awe. "You wouldn't dare."

"Sure, and why wouldn't he?" Danny Fahy told her. "Go on, Sean. What's your plan?"

"I haven't got one, Danny, that's the trouble. But there would be a payday for this like you wouldn't believe."

"So you've come to Uncle Danny looking for help."

Dillon asked, "Do you still work for the movement?"

"Stay in deep cover—that was the order from Belfast so many years ago I've forgotten. Since then, not a word, and me bored out of my socks, so I moved down here. It suits me. I've built up a fair business repairing agricultural machinery, and we're happy, Angel and me."

"Do you remember Martin Brosnan, by the way?"

"I do. You were bad friends with that one."

"He'll probably turn up in London looking for me. He'll be working for Brit intelligence."

"The fool." Fahy frowned as he refilled his pipe. "Didn't I hear some fanciful talk of how Brosnan got into Ten Downing Street as a waiter years ago and didn't do anything about it?"

"I heard that story, too. No one could get in these days, as a waiter or anything else. The place is a fortress. No way in there, Danny."

"Oh, there's always a way, Sean. I was reading in a magazine the other day how a lot of French Resistance people in the Second World War were held at some Gestapo headquarters. Their cells were on the ground floor, the Gestapo on the second floor. The RAF had a fella in a Mosquito fly in at fifty feet and drop a bomb that bounced off the street and went in through the second-floor window, killing all the Gestapo. The fellas downstairs got away. You can make a bomb go anywhere if you know what you're doing."

"What in hell are you trying to say to me?" Dillon demanded.

Angel said, "Go on, show him, Uncle Danny."

Danny Fahy got up. "Come on, then," he said, and went to the door. He led the way outside and across to the second barn. It held some farm machinery and a fairly new Land-Rover. It also held an old BSA 500-cc motorcycle in fine condition.

"This is a beauty," Dillon said in genuine admiration.

"Bought it secondhand last year and renovated it. Can't bear to let it go." In the shadows was another vehicle. Fahy switched on a light to reveal a white Ford Transit van.

"So," Dillon said, "what's so special?"

There was an excited look on Fahy's face, a kind of pride, as he opened the van's sliding door. Inside, there were three large cast-iron pipes bolted to the floor and pointing up to the roof at an angle.

"Mortars, Sean, just like the lads have been using in Ulster."

"Explain this thing to me."

"I've welded a steel platform to the floor—that's to stand the recoil—and I've also welded the tubing together. Standard cast-iron stuff, available anywhere. The electric timer is simple. Once switched on, it would give you a minute to get out of the van and run for it. The roof is cut out. That's stretched polyethylene covering the hole. Gives the mortars a clean exit. I've even linked an extra little device to the timer that will self-destruct the van after it's fired the mortars."

"And where would they be?"

"Over here." Fahy walked to a workbench, where several standard oxygen cylinders were stacked, the bottom plates removed.

"And what would you need for those? Semtex?" Dillon asked, naming the Czech explosive so popular with terrorists.

"I'd say about twelve pounds in each would do nicely, but that's not easily come by over here."

Dillon walked around the van. "I think you've done a good job."

"As good as anything they've done in Ulster," Fahy said.

"Maybe, but whenever they've been used, they've never been too strong on accuracy. A bit hit or miss."

"Not the way I'd do it. I can plot the target on a map, have a look at the area beforehand, line the van up, and that's it. Mind you, some sort of fins welded onto the cylinders would help steady them in flight. A nice big curve, up and then down, and the whole world blows up. I mean, what good are gates if you go over them?"

"You're talking Downing Street now?" Dillon said.

"And why not?" Fahy said.

"They meet at ten o'clock every morning in the Cabinet Room. What they call the War Cabinet. You'd not only get the Prime Minister, you'd get virtually the whole government."

Fahy crossed himself. "It would be the hit of a lifetime." He slammed a clenched fist into his palm. "But it's all hot air without the Semtex, and like I said, that stuff's impossible to get over here."

"Don't be too sure, Danny," Dillon said.

FAHY HAD A LARGE-SCALE MAP OF London, which he spread across the table and examined with a magnifying glass. "Here would be the place—Horse Guards Avenue, running up from the Victoria Embankment at the side of the Ministry of Defense. If we left the Ford on the corner with Whitehall, then as long as I had a predetermined sighting," he said, "I reckon the mortars would go over those roofs and land smack on Ten Downing Street!"

"Would it work, Mr. Dillon?" Angel demanded.

"Oh, yes," he said, and started to laugh. "It's beautiful, Danny, beautiful." He grabbed the man's arm. "There's big, big money, Danny. I'll set you up for your old age." As Fahy rolled up the map Dillon added, "I'll stay overnight. We'll go up to London tomorrow and have a look. Now tell me about this airfield at Grimethorpe."

"A real broken-down place. What would you want with it?"

"I told you, I learned to fly in the Middle East. A good way of getting out of places fast. Now, what's the situation at Grimethorpe?"

"A fella called Bill Grant owns it. His firm is called Grant's Air Taxis. He has two planes there. I heard his business was in trouble."

"I'd like to meet him," Dillon said. "Could you show me, Angel?"

"Of course."

"Good. But first I'd like to make a phone call."

He rang Tania Novikova at her flat. She answered at once. "It's me," he said. "I'll need the money."

"Oh, yes. No problem."

"Good. I'll be at the hotel at noon tomorrow. See you then."

BROSNAN and Mary Tanner went up in the freight elevator with Charlie Salter and found Mordecai waiting for them. He pumped Brosnan's hand up and down. "It's great to see you, Professor."

In the sitting room, Harry Flood was at the desk going over some accounts. He jumped to his feet. "Martin." He rushed round the desk and embraced Brosnan, laughing in delight.

Brosnan said, "This is Captain Mary Tanner. I'm working for Brigadier Charles Ferguson of British intelligence, and she's his aide."

"Then I'll behave," Flood said, and shook her hand. "Now come over here and tell me what all this is about."

They sat down, and Brosnan covered everything in finest detail. Mordecai leaned against the wall, listening. When Brosnan finished, Flood said, "So what you want to know is, who would he go to for help?" He looked up at Mordecai. "What do you think?"

"I don't know, Harry. Legit arms dealers won't supply the IRA. I mean, most of your real East End villains love Thatcher and wear Union Jack underpants. They don't go for Irish geezers letting off bombs at Harrods. We could make inquiries, of course."

"Then do that," Flood said. "Put the word out now, but discreetly."

Mordecai went out, and Flood said, "We'll go to the Embassy— one of my more respectable clubs—and have something to eat."

AT AROUND the same time, Sean Dillon and Angel Fahy were driving along the road from Cadge End to Grimethorpe. The lights of the car picked out frost on the hedgerows.

They turned at the sign that said GRIMETHORPE, and a few moments later they came to the airfield. There were three hangars, an old control tower, a couple of Quonset huts. The door to one of the huts opened, and a man stood there. He looked to be in his mid-forties. Small and wiry, he wore jeans and an old flying jacket.

"Who is it?"

Dillon pulled up, and they got out of the car. "It's me, Mr. Grant. Angel Fahy. I've brought someone to see you, a friend of my uncle's."

"Hilton," Dillon said. "Peter Hilton."

Grant put his hand out, looking wary. "You'd better come in."

The interior of the Quonset hut was warm, heated by a coke-burning stove. Grant obviously used it as a living room. There was a table with the remains of a meal on it, an old easy chair by the stove, and a long sloping desk with a few charts on it.

"What can I do for you?" Grant said.

"I want a charter in the next few days," Dillon said. "Just wanted to check if you might be able to do something."

"Well, that depends."

"On what? You do have a plane, I take it?"

"I've got two. The only problem is how long the bank lets me hang on to them. Do you want to have a look?"

"Why not." They went out and crossed the apron to the end hangar. There were two planes there, side by side, both twin engines—a Cessna Conquest and a Navajo Chieftain.

"If things are as tricky as you say, what about fuel?" Dillon asked.

"I always keep my planes juiced up, Mr. Hilton. You never know when a job might come up. Where would you like me to take you?"

"Actually, I was thinking of going for a spin myself." Dillon took out his pilot's license, and Grant examined it.

He handed it back. "You could handle either of these two," Grant said, "but I'd rather come myself, just to make sure."

"No problem," Dillon said smoothly. "It's the West Country I was thinking of. Cornwall. An airfield at Lands End. I've got friends near there. I'd probably want to stay overnight."

"That's fine by me. I know it well. Grass runway."

They walked back to the hut. Grant said, "That kind of charter's expensive. Around two thousand five hundred pounds."

"No problem." Dillon took ten fifty-pound notes from his wallet and put them on the table. "There's five hundred down. It's a definite booking. I'll phone you to let you know when I want to go."

Grant's face brightened as he picked up the bank notes. "That's fine. Can I get you a coffee or something before you go?"

"Why not," Dillon said.

Grant went into the kitchen at the far end of the hut. They heard him filling a kettle. Dillon signaled Angel, putting a finger to his lips, and crossed to the charts on the desk. He went through them quickly, found the one for the English Channel area and the French coast. Angel watched as he traced his finger along the Normandy coast south to Cherbourg. There it was, St.-Denis, with the landing strip clearly marked. He pushed the charts back together.

Grant had been watching through the half-open door. As the kettle boiled, he quickly made coffee in three mugs and took them in.

"Is this snow giving you much trouble?" Dillon said.

"It could make it difficult for that grass runway at Lands End."

"We'll just have to keep our fingers crossed." Dillon drank some coffee and put down his mug. "We'd better be getting back."

Grant saw them off, then went to examine the charts. He was sure it was the third down—the English Channel area and French coast. He frowned and said softly, "What's your game, mister? I wonder."

As THEY drove back through the dark country lanes Angel said, "Not Lands End at all, Mr. Dillon. It's that St.-Denis place, in Normandy—that's where you want to fly to."

"Our secret," he said, and put his left hand on hers, still steering. "Tell me, how would you like a trip up to London tomorrow morning with me—you and Danny?"

"I'd like it fine, Mr. Dillon."

"Good. That's all right, then."

As they carried on through the night, her eyes were shining.

## Nine

IT WAS a cold, crisp morning, but the roads were clear as Dillon drove up to London, Angel and Danny Fahy following in the Morris van. Angel was driving and stayed right on his tail all the way to the Bayswater Road. Once there, Dillon parked the Mini-Cooper at the curb, got out and opened the doors of Tania's garage.

As Angel drew up behind him he said, "Put the Morris inside." When she and Danny came out, Dillon said to her, "You'll remember the street and the garage—if you lose me, that is?"

"Don't be silly, Mr. Dillon. Of course I will," Angel said.

"Good. It's important. Now get in the Mini. We're going for a little run round. Have a look at the situation."

HARRY Flood was sitting at the desk in his Cable Wharf apartment when Charlie brought in coffee on a tray. The phone rang, and the small man picked it up. He handed it to Flood. "The professor."

Flood took it. "Martin, how goes it?" he said.

"Is there any news?" Brosnan asked.

"Not yet, old buddy. We're doing all we can, but it'll take time."

"Which we don't really have," Brosnan said. "All right, Harry. I know you're doing your best. I'll stay in touch."

He was standing at Mary Tanner's desk in the living room of her Lowndes Square flat. He put the phone down. "Anything?" she asked, crossing the room to join him.

"I'm afraid not. As Harry has just said, it takes time. But I know Dillon, Mary. He's moving fast on this. I'm certain of it."

"So what would you like to do?"

"Will Ferguson be at Cavendish Square this morning?"

"Yes."

"Then let's go to see him."

403

ANGEL SAT IN THE REAR OF THE Mini, her uncle beside Dillon, as they drove down towards the river and turned into Horse Guards Avenue. Dillon paused slightly on the corner before turning into Whitehall and moving towards Downing Street.

"Plenty of coppers around," Dillon said.

"That's to make sure people don't park." A car had drawn up to the curb on their left, and as they pulled out to pass, they saw that the driver was consulting a map.

"Tourist, I expect," Angel said.

"And look what's happening," Dillon told her.

She turned and saw two policemen converging on the car. A quiet word, and it started up and moved away.

"Downing Street," Dillon announced a moment later.

"Would you look at those gates," Danny said in wonder. "I like the Gothic touch. Sure, and they've done a good job there."

Dillon moved with the traffic round Parliament Square and went back up Whitehall towards Trafalgar Square. "We're going back to Bayswater," he said. "Then let's go and get a nice cup of tea at my truly awful hotel."

FERGUSON said, "You're getting too restless, Martin."

"It's the waiting," Brosnan told him. "Flood's doing his best, I know that, but I don't think time is on our side."

Ferguson sipped his cup of tea. "So what would you like to do?"

Brosnan hesitated, glanced at Mary and said, "I'd like to go and see Liam Devlin, in Kilrea. He might have some ideas."

Ferguson turned to Mary. She said, "It makes sense, sir. After all, a trip to Dublin's no big deal. An hour and a quarter from Heathrow."

"All right," Ferguson said. "You've made your point, both of you. But make it Gatwick and take the Learjet, just in case you need to get back here in a hurry."

"Thank you, sir," Mary said.

As they reached the door Ferguson added, "I'll give the old rogue a call, just to let him know you're on your way."

IN THE small café at the hotel, Dillon, Angel and Fahy sat at a corner table drinking tea. Fahy had the large-scale map partially open on his knee. "It's extraordinary. Every detail's here."

"Could it be done, Danny?"

"Oh, yes. No trouble. You remember that corner—Horse Guards Avenue and Whitehall? That would be the place, slightly on an angle. I can see it in my mind's eye. From this map I can plot the distance from that corner to Number Ten exactly."

"You're sure you'd clear the buildings in between?"

"Oh, yes, Sean. Ballistics is a matter of science."

"But you can't stop there," Angel said. "We saw what happened to that man in the car. The police were on him in seconds."

Dillon turned to Fahy. "Danny?"

"Well, everything's pretimed, Angel. Press the right switch to activate the circuit, get out of the van, and the mortars start firing within a minute. No policeman could act fast enough to stop it."

"But what would happen to you?" she demanded.

It was Dillon who answered. "Listen to this. We drive up from Cadge End one morning, early—you, Danny, in the Ford Transit, and Angel and me in the Morris van. We'll have that BSA motorcycle in the back of that. Angel will park the Morris in the garage, like today. We'll have a duckboard in the back so I can run the BSA out."

"And you'll follow me, is that it?"

"I'll be right up your tail. When we reach the corner of Horse Guards Avenue and Whitehall, you set your switch, get out and jump straight on my pillion seat, and we'll be away. Straight back to Bayswater, to Angel waiting in the Morris." He stood up. "Now I've got things to do. You two go back to Cadge End and wait. I'll be in touch soon." Dillon smiled as they went out.

TANIA was knocking at his door precisely at noon. Dillon opened it and said, "You've got it?"

She had a briefcase in her hand, opened it on the table to reveal the thirty thousand dollars he'd asked for.

"Good," he said. "I'll just need ten thousand to be going on with. The rest can stay in your briefcase in the hotel safe."

"You've worked something out, I can tell." She looked excited.

He told her—in detail—the entire plan. "What do you think?"

"Incredible. The coup of a lifetime. But what about the explosives? You'd need Semtex."

"That's all right. When I was operating in London in '81, I used to deal with a man who had access to Semtex, a crook named Jack Harvey." Dillon laughed. "Amongst other things, he had a funeral business in Whitechapel. I looked it up in the yellow pages, and it's still there. By the way, your Mini—I can still use it?"

"Of course."

"Good." He picked up his coat. "Then I'll go and see him."

"YOU'VE read the file on Devlin, I suppose?" Brosnan asked Mary Tanner as they drove through the center of Dublin and out into the Irish countryside in a chauffeured limousine from the embassy.

"Yes," she said. "But is it all true—the story about his involvement with the German attempt to get Churchill in the war?"

"Oh, yes."

"The same man who helped you break out of that French prison in 1979?"

"That's Devlin. Let's put it this way. You're about to meet a most extraordinary man—scholar, poet, and gunman for the IRA."

"The last part is no recommendation to me," she said.

"I know," he told her. "But never make the mistake of lumping Devlin in with the kind of rubbish the IRA employs these days."

Kilrea Cottage was on the outskirts of the village. It was a period piece, single-story, with Gothic-looking gables and leaded windows. Brosnan tugged a bellpull, and the door opened.

*"Céad mile fáilte,"* Liam Devlin said in Irish. "A hundred thousand welcomes," and he flung his arms around Brosnan.

Mary Tanner was totally astonished. She'd expected an old man and found herself faced with this ageless creature in a black silk Italian shirt, a black pullover, and gray slacks in the latest fashionable cut. The blue eyes were extraordinary, as was the perpetual ironic smile with which he seemed to laugh at himself and the world.

Inside, the house was very Victorian. When they were seated in the living room, Devlin said to Mary, "So you work for Ferguson?"

"That's right."

"That business in Derry the other year, when you moved that car with the bomb. That was quite something."

She felt herself flushing. "No big deal, Mr. Devlin. It just seemed like the right thing to do at the time."

"Oh, we can all see that on occasions it's the doing that

counts." He turned to Brosnan. "Anne-Marie—a bad business, son."

"I want him, Liam," Brosnan said.

Devlin shook his head. "Push the personal thing aside, Martin, or you'll make mistakes, and you can't afford to do that with Dillon."

"Yes, I know," Brosnan said. "I know."

"So I hear he intends to take a crack at this John Major fella."

"And how do you think he'll do that, Mr. Devlin?" Mary asked.

"Oh, he'll work as he always has—using underworld contacts."

"Do you think he's working for the IRA?" Brosnan asked.

"I doubt whether the IRA has any connection with this."

"But they did last time he worked in London, ten years ago."

"So?" Devlin said.

"If we knew who recruited him that time, it could help now."

"You mean, give you some sort of lead as to who he worked with in London. Well, there's still your friend Flood."

"I know, but that takes time, and we don't have much to spare."

Devlin nodded. "Right, son. You leave it with me, and I'll see what I can do. Now I suggest you go to your Learjet and hare back to London, and I'll be in touch the minute I have something."

DILLON parked round the corner from Jack Harvey's funeral business in Whitechapel and walked to the door, the briefcase in one hand. A discreet bell push summoned the day porter.

"Mr. Hilton," Dillon said cheerfully. "Mr. Harvey's expecting me."

At the reception desk the porter picked up a phone. "Miss Myra, a visitor. A Mr. Hilton. Says he has an appointment." He put down the phone and returned to Dillon. "Down the hall, past the Chapels of Rest and up the stairs, sir," he said.

Dillon looked around at the coffins on display, the flowers, then moved down the hall and climbed the stairs to Harvey's outer office. There were no office furnishings, just a couple of potted plants and several easy chairs. The door to the inner office opened, and Myra entered. She wore skintight black trews, black boots and a three-quarter-length scarlet caftan. She looked very striking.

"Mr. Hilton, I'm Myra Harvey. You said you had an appointment with my uncle."

"Did I?"

She looked him over in a casual way. Just then Billy Watson came in, looking suitably menacing in a black suit, his arms folded.

"Now, what's your game?" she said.

"That's for Mr. Harvey."

"Throw him out, Billy," she said, and turned to the door.

Billy put one rough hand on Dillon's shoulder. Dillon's foot went straight down the right leg, stamping on the instep. Then he pivoted and struck sideways with a clenched fist, connecting with Billy's temple. Billy cried out in pain and fell back into one of the chairs.

"He's not very good, is he?" Dillon said. He opened his briefcase and took out a stack of ten one-hundred-dollar bills in a rubber band and threw it to Myra. "Now tell Jack an old friend would like to see him with more of the same."

Her eyes narrowed; then she went into Harvey's office. Billy tried to get up, and Dillon said, "I wouldn't advise it." Billy subsided.

The door opened, and Myra appeared. "All right. He'll see you."

The room was surprisingly businesslike, with walls paneled in oak, a green carpet of Georgian silk, and a gas fire that almost looked real. Harvey sat behind a massive oak desk smoking a cigar. He had the money in front of him and looked Dillon over calmly. "You told Myra you were a friend, son, but I've never seen you before."

"A long time ago, Jack. Ten years, to be precise. I looked different then. I was over from Belfast on a job. We did business together, you and me. You did well out of it, as I recall."

Harvey said, "Coogan. Michael Coogan."

Dillon took off his glasses. "As ever was, Jack."

Harvey nodded slowly. "Myra, an old friend. Mr. Coogan from Belfast. And what is it this time?" he asked Dillon.

"I need a little Semtex, Jack. I could manage with forty pounds, but that's the bottom line. Fifty would be better."

"You don't want much, do you? That stuff's like gold."

"It's everywhere, Jack. You know it and I know it, so don't waste my time. Twenty thousand dollars." He sat down, opened the briefcase on his knee and tossed the rest of the ten thousand, packet by packet, across the desk. "Ten now, and ten on delivery."

The Walther with the silencer screwed onto the end of the barrel lay ready in the briefcase. He waited, and then Harvey smiled. "All right. Twenty-four hours. Where can we reach you?"

Dillon stood up. "I'll contact you, Jack."

Harvey said affably, "Anything else we can do for you?"

"Actually, there is," Dillon said. "Sign of goodwill, you might say. I could do with a spare handgun."

"Be my guest, my old son," Harvey said, and opened a desk drawer. There was a Smith & Wesson .38 revolver and an Italian Beretta, which was the one Dillon selected. He checked the clip and slipped the gun into his pocket. "This will do nicely."

"Lady's gun," Harvey said. "But that's your business. We'll be seeing you, then, tomorrow."

Myra opened the door. Dillon said, "A pleasure, Miss Harvey," and he brushed past Billy and walked out.

As she closed the door Myra said, "I wouldn't trust him an inch."

"A hard little fool," Harvey said. "Yes, hell on wheels."

"What do you think he's up to?"

"I couldn't care less."

IT WAS just after six, and Ferguson was about to leave his office at the Ministry of Defense when his phone rang.

It was Devlin. "I've news for you. Dillon's control in '81 in Belfast was a man called Tommy McGuire. Remember him?"

"I do indeed. Wasn't he shot a few years ago in an IRA feud?"

"That was the story, but he's still around, using another identity."

"And what would that be?"

"I've still to find that out. People to see in Belfast. I'm driving up there tonight. I take it, by the way, that involving myself in this way makes me an official agent of Group Four. I mean, I wouldn't like to end up in prison, not at my age."

"You'll be covered fully. Now, what do you want us to do?"

"I was thinking. If Brosnan and Captain Tanner want to be in on the action, they could fly to Belfast in the morning and wait for me at the Europa Hotel bar. I'll be in touch probably around noon."

"I'll see to it," Ferguson said.

"One more thing. Don't you think you and I are getting just a little geriatric for this sort of game?"

"You speak for yourself," Ferguson said, and put the phone down.

He then rang for a secretary. He also called Mary Tanner at her flat. As he was talking to her, Alice Johnson came in with her notepad. Ferguson waved to her and carried on speaking to Mary.

"So, early start in the morning. Gatwick again, I think. You'll be there in an hour. Are you dining out tonight?"

"Harry Flood suggested the River Room at the Savoy—he likes the dance band. Would you like to join us, sir?"

"Actually, I would," Ferguson said.

"We'll see you, then. Eight o'clock."

Ferguson put down the phone and turned to Alice Johnson. "A brief note, 'Eyes of the Prime Minister Only.'" He dictated a report that included his conversation with Devlin. "One copy for the P.M., usual copy for me and the file. Hurry, please, and bring them along for my signature. I want to get away."

She went to the office quickly. Gordon Brown was standing at the copier as she sat down and started to type. She was finished in two minutes. "Another 'Eyes of the Prime Minister Only,'" she said. "But he'll have to hang on. I need to go to the toilet."

"I'll do the copying for you."

She thanked him and went out along the corridor, then realized she'd left her handbag on the desk. She hurried back. The office door was partially open, and she could see Gordon standing at the copier reading a copy of the report. To her astonishment he folded it, slipped it into his inside jacket pocket and hurriedly did another.

Alice was totally thrown, had no idea what to do. She hesitated, trying to pull herself together. After a while she went back in.

The report and a copy were on her desk. "All done," Gordon said.

She managed a light smile. "I'll get them signed."

"Right. I'm just going down to the canteen. See you later."

Alice went into Ferguson's office. She was trembling. He looked up from his desk and frowned. "My dear Mrs. Johnson, what is it?"

He sat there grim-faced as she told him, then reached for the telephone. "Special Branch, Detective Inspector Lane for Brigadier Ferguson, Group Four. Top priority, no delay. My office. Now."

He put the phone down. "Now, this is what you do. Go back to the office and behave as if nothing has happened."

"But he isn't there, Brigadier. He went to the canteen."

WHEN Tania heard Gordon Brown's voice, she was immediately angry. "I've told you about this, Gordon."

"Yes, but it's urgent."

411

"Where are you?"

"In the canteen at the ministry. I've got a report. It's important."

"Read it to me."

He did so, and when he finished, she said, "Good boy, Gordon. I'll see you at your place later. I promise."

He put the phone down and turned, folding the copy of the report. The door to the phone booth was jerked open, and Ferguson plucked the report from his fingers.

## Ten

DILLON was in his room at the hotel when Tania called him. "I've got rather hot news," she said. She told him about the report, then said, "Does any of this make any sense?"

"Yes," he said. "McGuire was big with the Provos in those days."

"And he's dead, is he? Or is he still around?"

"Devlin's right about that. His death was reported—supposedly because of infighting in the movement—but it was just a ruse to help him drop out of sight."

"If they found him, could it give you problems?"

"Maybe, but not if I found him first. I know his half brother, a fella called Macey. He would know where he is."

"But that would mean a trip to Belfast yourself. Is it wise?"

"Is anything in this life? It's no big deal. I'll be in touch." He put the phone down, called British Airways and booked a seat on the morning flight. He lit a cigarette, trying to remember what Tommy McGuire had known about him in '81. Nothing about Danny Fahy, but Jack Harvey . . . It had been McGuire who'd put him on to Harvey as an arms supplier in the first place.

He put on his trench coat and went out. He hailed a cab on the corner and told the driver to take him to Covent Garden.

GORDON Brown sat on the other side of Ferguson's desk in the half-light. He had never been so frightened in his life. "I didn't mean any harm, Brigadier. I swear it."

"Then why did you take a copy of the report?"

"It was just a whim. Stupid, I know, but I was so intrigued with it."

Detective Inspector Lane of Special Branch was in his late thirties and, in his crumpled tweed suit and glasses, looked like a schoolmaster. He leaned on the desk and said, "I'm going to ask you again, Mr. Brown. Have you ever taken copies like this before?"

Gordon managed to look suitably shocked. "Absolutely not. I swear it. Good heavens, Inspector."

The internal phone rang, and Ferguson picked it up. It was Lane's sergeant, Mackie. "I'm outside, Brigadier, just back from the flat in Camden. I think you and the inspector should come out."

"Thank you." Ferguson put the phone down. "Right. I think we'll give you time to think things over, Gordon. Inspector?"

He nodded to Lane, who got up and followed him out. Mackie was in the anteroom, still in trilby and raincoat, a file in one hand.

"You found something, Sergeant?" Lane asked.

"A rather interesting collection, sir."

The file contained copies of reports neatly stacked in order, the latest ones on top. Lane said, "Jeez, he's been at it for a while."

"So it would seem," Ferguson said. "My present operation is most delicate. A man working for me in Paris was attacked. A woman died. We wondered how the villain knew about them. Now we know. Details of these reports must have been passed on to a third party."

Lane nodded. "Then we'll have to work on him some more."

"No. We don't have the time. Let's try another way. Just let him go. He's a simple man. I think he'd do the simple thing."

"Right, sir." Lane and Mackie hurried out, and Ferguson went back in the office and sat down. "A sad business, Gordon."

"What's going to happen to me, Brigadier?"

"I'll have to think about it." Ferguson picked up the copy of the report. "Such an incredibly stupid thing to do." He sighed. "Go home, Gordon, go home. I'll see you in the morning."

Gordon Brown left. He couldn't believe his luck. The narrowest escape of his life. It could have meant prison. But that was it: no more reports. Tania would have to accept that. He went out to his car and was turning into Whitehall a few moments later, Mackie and Lane hard on his tail in an unmarked Ford Capri.

DILLON knew that late-night shopping was the thing in the Covent Garden area. He needed a wig and some clothes, and he hurried along until he came to the theatrical shop near Neal's Yard.

413

There was a nice selection of wigs—short, long, permed, blond, red. Dillon selected one that was shoulder length and gray. "Now, what about costume? I don't mean anything fancy. Secondhand?" he asked the man behind the counter.

"In here." Dillon followed him into the back. There were racks upon racks of clothes, and a jumbled heap in the corner.

He worked quickly, sorting through, and selected a long brown skirt, a shabby raincoat that was too big and a pair of jeans. Then he searched through a pile of shoes, choosing a pair of old runners.

"These will do," he said. "Oh, and this," and he picked an old head scarf from a stand. "How much?"

The man packed the clothes in plastic bags. "Ten quid," he said.

Dillon paid him and picked up the bags. The man opened the door for him. "Have a good show, luv. Give 'em hell."

"Oh, I will," Dillon said, and he hurried out to hail a cab.

LANE and Mackie were parked at the end of the street off the Bayswater Road. The inspector was already on the car phone to Ferguson. He gave him the address and said, "The card on the door says Miss Tania Novikova, sir."

"Oh, dear," Ferguson said. "She's supposedly a secretary at the Soviet embassy, Inspector. In fact, she's a captain in the KGB."

"That means she's one of Colonel Yuri Gatov's people."

"I'm not so sure. Gatov is a Gorbachev man, very pro-West."

"Are you going to notify him, sir?"

"Not yet. Let's see what she's got to say first. It's information we're after. Wait for me. I'll be with you in twenty minutes."

Meanwhile, Tania peered cautiously through a chink in the curtains. She saw Mackie standing by his car at the end of the street, and it was enough. She could smell policemen anywhere.

"Tell me again, Gordon, exactly what happened."

Brown did as he was told. She listened patiently, nodding when he'd finished. "We were lucky, Gordon, very lucky. Go and make us coffee. I've got a couple of phone calls to make." She squeezed his hand. "Afterwards we'll have a very special time together."

"Really?" His face brightened, and he went out to the kitchen.

She picked up the phone and called Makeev. "Josef, it's Tania," she said when he answered. "I just wanted to say good-bye. I'm blown.

414

My mole was exposed. They'll be kicking in the door any minute."

"Oh, Lord!" he said. "And Dillon?"

"He's safe. All systems go. And what that man has planned will set the world on fire."

"But you, Tania?"

"Don't worry, I won't let them take me. Good-bye, Josef."

She put the phone down, then called Dillon at the hotel.

"It's Tania," she said to him, and repeated the story.

He was quite calm. "I see. What are you going to do?"

"Oh, I won't be around to tell them anything. But they'll know that Gordon gave me the contents of tonight's report. He was in the phone booth in the ministry canteen when Ferguson arrested him."

"I see."

"Dillon, promise me one thing," she said.

"What's that?"

"Blow them away, all of them."

The doorbell rang. She said, "I've got to go. Luck, Dillon."

As she put down the phone Gordon Brown came in with the coffee. "Was that the door?"

"Yes. Be an angel, Gordon, and see who it is."

He opened the door and started downstairs. Tania took a deep breath. Dying wasn't difficult. The cause she believed in had always been the most important thing in her life. From the desk she took out a Makarov pistol and shot herself through the right temple.

Gordon Brown, halfway down the stairs, turned and bounded back up, bursting into the room. At the sight of her lying there, the pistol still in her hand, he fell on his knees. "Tania, my darling!" he cried.

And then he heard something heavy crash against the door below, and he knew what he must do. He prized the Makarov from her hand and raised it. He took a deep breath to steady himself and pulled the trigger in the same moment that the front door burst open and Lane and Mackie started upstairs, Ferguson behind them.

IT WAS almost eleven in the River Room at the Savoy, and the band was still playing. Harry Flood, Brosnan and Mary were thinking of breaking up the party when Ferguson appeared.

He ordered a large Scotch and gave them a quick résumé of the night's events. "One point I must make," he said as he finished.

"When I arrested Brown, he was on the phone and he had the report in his hand. It's likely he was speaking to the Novikova woman."

"I see what you're getting at," Mary said. "And you think she, in her turn, may have transmitted the information to Dillon?"

"Possibly," Ferguson said.

"So what are you suggesting?" Brosnan asked. "That Dillon would go to Belfast, too?"

"Perhaps," Ferguson said. "If it was important enough."

"We'll just have to take our chances, then." Brosnan turned to Mary. "Early start tomorrow. We'd better get moving."

They all rose and walked through the lounge to the entrance. Brosnan and Ferguson went ahead and stood talking. Mary said to Flood, "You think a lot of him, don't you?"

"Martin?" He nodded. "The Vietcong had me in a pit for weeks. When the rains came, it filled up with water and I'd have to stand all night so I didn't drown. Then one day a hand reached down and pulled me out, and it was Martin—in a headband, hair to his shoulders, and his face painted like an Apache Indian. He's special people."

Mary looked across at Brosnan. "Yes," she said, "I suppose that just about sums him up."

DILLON had ordered a taxi to pick him up at six o'clock at the hotel. When it arrived, he was waiting on the steps, his suitcase in one hand, a briefcase in the other. The run to Heathrow was fast at that time of the morning. He picked up his ticket at the desk, then put his suitcase through and got his seat assignment. He was wearing his suit, striped tie, trench coat and glasses to fit the Peter Hilton persona, and carrying the Jersey driving license as proof of identity. In the suitcase were the items he had obtained at Covent Garden. He wasn't carrying a gun—not with the kind of security that operated on the Belfast planes.

He got a selection of newspapers, went up to the gallery restaurant and ordered a full English breakfast. Then he read the papers.

ALTHOUGH Dillon wasn't aware of it, Brosnan and Mary had already landed and were on their way to the Europa Hotel when his flight touched down at Aldergrove Airport, outside Belfast. Customs officers stopped some people, but Dillon wasn't one of them, and within five minutes of collecting his case, he was outside and in a taxi.

"I'd like a hotel in the Falls Road," Dillon said, slipping straight into his Belfast accent. "Somewhere near Craig Street."

"You won't get much round there," the driver told him.

"Scenes of my youth," Dillon said. "Been in London awhile."

"Suit yourself. There's the Deepdene, but it's not much."

An army patrol passed them as they turned into the main road. "Nothing changes," Dillon said.

At the Deepdene, a shabby Victorian building in a mean side street off the Falls Road, Dillon got out and paid the driver. He went in and tapped the bell on the desk, and a stout motherly woman emerged. He took a room for just one night. She pushed a register and a key at him. "Number nine, on the second floor."

The room was as shabby as he'd expected—a single brass bedstead, a wardrobe. He left his cases and went out again, locking the door. At the bottom of the back stairs there was another door, which opened into an untidy yard. The lane beyond backed onto incredibly derelict houses, but it didn't depress him in the slightest. This was an area he knew like the back of his hand, a place where he'd led the British army one hell of a dance in his day. He moved along the alley, a smile on his face, and turned into the Falls Road.

## Eleven

B ROSNAN was standing at the window of the sixth-floor room of the Europa Hotel in Great Victoria Street, next to the railway station. "For a while this place was a prime target for IRA bombers," he said to Mary, "the kind who'd blow up anything."

"Not you, of course." There was a sarcastic edge to her words, which he ignored.

"Certainly not. Devlin and I appreciated the bar too much."

She laughed in astonishment. "What nonsense. Are you seriously asking me to believe that with the British army chasing you all over Belfast, you and Devlin sat in the Europa's bar?"

"Also the restaurant, on occasion. Come on. I'll show you."

As they were descending in the lift she said, "You're not armed, are you?"

"No."

"Good. I'd rather keep it that way."

"How about you?"

"Yes," she said. "But that's different. I'm a serving officer of crown forces in an Action Service zone."

"What are you carrying?"

She opened her handbag and gave him a brief glimpse of a small automatic. "Rather rare. An old Colt .25 that I picked up in Africa."

"Hardly an elephant gun."

"No, but it does the job." She smiled bleakly. "As long as you can shoot, that is." The lift doors parted, and they went across to the lounge.

DILLON walked briskly along the Falls Road. Nothing had changed, nothing at all. He twice saw Royal Ulster Constabulary—RUC—patrols backed up by soldiers, but no one paid any attention. He finally found what he wanted in Craig Street, about a mile from the hotel. It was a small double-fronted shop, with the three brass balls of a pawnbroker and the sign PATRICK MACEY.

Dillon opened the door and walked into musty silence. In the dimly lit shop there was a mesh screen running along the counter, and the man who sat on a stool behind it was working on a watch, a jeweler's magnifying glass in one eye. He glanced up, a wasted-looking individual in his sixties, his face gray and pallid.

"And what can I do for you?"

Dillon said, "Nothing ever changes, Patrick. This place still smells exactly the same."

Macey took the glass from his eye and frowned. "Do I know you?"

"And why wouldn't you, Patrick? Remember the night we set fire to that Orangeman Stewart's warehouse and shot him and his two nephews as they ran out. Let me see, there were the three of us—you, me, and your half brother, Tommy McGuire."

"Jeez, Sean Dillon, is that you?" Macey said.

"As ever was, Patrick." Dillon went to the door and locked it.

"What are you doing?" Macey demanded in alarm.

"I just want a nice private talk, Patrick, my old son. How is Tommy these days, by the way?"

"Ah, Sean, I'd have thought you'd know. Poor Tommy's been dead these five years. Shot by one of his own."

"Is that a fact?" Dillon nodded. "Do you see any of the other old hands these days? Liam Devlin, for instance?"

And he had him there, for Macey was unable to keep the look of alarm from his face. "Liam? I haven't seen him since the '70s."

"Really?" Dillon lifted the flap at the end of the counter and walked round. "It's a terrible liar you are." He slapped him across the face. "Now get in there," and Dillon pushed him through the curtain that led to the office at the rear.

Macey was terrified. "I'm not involved with the IRA anymore. I don't know a thing."

"I haven't asked you anything yet, but I'm going to tell you a few things. Tommy McGuire isn't dead. He's living somewhere in this fair city under another name, and you're going to tell me where. Second, Liam Devlin has been to see you. Now, I'm right on both counts, aren't I?" Dillon slapped him again. "Aren't I?"

The other man was shaking. "Please, Sean, please. I'm ill. It's my heart. I could have an attack."

"You will if you don't speak up. I promise you."

Macey broke then. "All right. Devlin was here a little earlier this morning inquiring about Tommy."

"Good. Now we're getting somewhere." Dillon lit a cigarette and nodded at the large safe in the corner. "Is that where the guns are?"

"What guns, Sean?"

"Come on. Don't muck me about. You've been dealing in handguns for years. Get it open."

Macey took a key from his desk drawer and opened the safe. There were several weapons in there. An old Webley, a couple of Smith & Wesson revolvers. The one that caught Dillon's eye was an American army Colt .45 automatic. He hefted it in his hand.

"Wonderful, Patrick." He put the gun on the desk and sat down opposite Macey. "So what happened?"

Macey's face was very strange in color now. "I don't feel well."

"You'll feel better when you've told me. Get on with it."

"Tommy lives on his own about half a mile from here, in Canal Street. He's done up the old warehouse at the end. Calls himself Kelly, George Kelly."

"I know that area well, every stick and stone."

"Devlin asked for Tommy's phone number. He called him there

419

and said it was essential to see him. That it was to do with Sean Dillon. Tommy agreed to see him at two o'clock."

"Fine," Dillon said. "See how easy it was? Now I can call on him myself, only I won't bother to phone. I think I'll surprise him."

"You'll never get in to see him," Macey said. "You can only get in at the front—all the other doors are welded. He's been paranoid for years, terrified someone's going to knock him off. It's all TV security cameras and that kind of stuff."

"There's always a way," Dillon said.

"There always was for you." Macey tore at his shirt collar, choking. "Pills," he moaned, and got the drawer in front of him open. The bottle he took out fell from his hands.

He leaned back in his chair. Dillon went round and picked up the bottle. "Trouble is, Patrick, the moment I go out of the door, you'll be on the phone to Tommy, and that wouldn't do, would it?"

He walked across to the fireplace and dropped the pill bottle onto the gleaming coals. There was a crash behind him, and he turned to find Macey had tumbled to the floor. Dillon stood over him. Macey's face was very suffused, and his legs were jerking. Suddenly he gave a great gasp, his head turned to one side, and he went completely still.

Dillon put the Colt in his pocket and went through the shop and opened the door, then locked it behind him. A moment later he was on the Falls Road, walking back to the hotel as fast as he could.

It was almost one, and Brosnan and Mary Tanner were at the bar of the Europa thinking about lunch when a hotel porter approached. "Mr. Brosnan, your taxi is here, sir."

"Taxi?" Mary said. "But we didn't order one."

"Yes, we did," Brosnan said.

He helped her on with her coat, and they went down the steps at the front entrance to the black cab waiting at the curb and got in. The driver of the cab wore a tweed cap and an old reefer coat.

"I presume you know where we're going," Mary said to him.

"Oh, I certainly do, my love." Liam Devlin smiled at her over his shoulder, moved into gear and drove away.

It was just after one thirty when he turned the taxi into Canal Street. "That's the place at the end," he said. "We'll park in the yard at the side." They got out and approached the entrance. "Be on your best behavior. We're on television," he said, and reached for the bell beside the massive iron-bound door.

A voice sounded through the box by the door. "That you, Devlin?"

"And who else, you fool? I've got Martin Brosnan with me and a friend of his, and we're freezing in this cold, so get the door open."

"You're early. You said two o'clock."

They could hear steps, and then the door opened to reveal a tall, cadaverous man in his mid-sixties. He wore a heavy pullover and baggy jeans, and carried a Sterling submachine gun.

Devlin brushed past him, leading the way in. "What do you intend to do with that thing? Start another war?"

"Only if I have to." McGuire closed the door and barred it. He looked them over suspiciously. "Martin?" He held out a hand. "It's been a long time. As for you, you old sod," he said to Devlin, "whatever's keeping you out of your grave, you should bottle it. We'd make a fortune." He looked at Mary. "And who might you be?"

"I'm Captain Tanner, British army," she said crisply.

"Devlin, what is this?" McGuire demanded.

"It's all right," Devlin told him. "She hasn't come to arrest you. Just answer a few questions, and you can go back to being George Kelly."

McGuire put a hand up defensively. "All right. This way."

The interior of the warehouse was totally bare except for a van parked to one side. A steel staircase led to a landing high above, where there had once been offices. McGuire went ahead and turned into the first office. There was a desk and a bank of television equipment—one screen showing the street, another the entrance.

Devlin said, "You live here?"

"Upstairs. I've turned the storage loft into a flat. Now let's get on with it. What is it you want? You mentioned Sean Dillon."

"He's on the loose again," Devlin said. "He tried to knock off Martin here in Paris. Killed his girlfriend instead."

"Jeez!" McGuire said. "What do you want to know?"

"Nineteen eighty-one, the London bombing campaign," Brosnan said. "You were Dillon's control."

McGuire glanced at Mary. "That's right."

"As regards weapons and explosives, Mr. McGuire," Mary said, "I understand he always favors underworld contacts. Have you any idea who he used in 1981?"

McGuire looked hunted. "How would I know? It could have been anybody."

Devlin said, "You're lying." His hand came out of the pocket of his reefer coat holding an old Luger pistol, and he touched McGuire between the eyes. "Quick now, tell us or I'll . . ."

McGuire pushed the gun away. "You win, Devlin. He dealt with a man in London called Jack Harvey—a big operator, a real gangster."

There was a thunderous knocking on the door below, and they all looked at the television screen to see a broken old bagwoman on the front step. Her wild and unkempt gray hair was tied in a head scarf, and she wore an old raincoat over an ankle-length skirt. From beneath the skirt, the bottoms of jeans and a pair of old runners showed. Her voice croaked through the speaker. "The lovely man you are, Mr. Kelly. Could you spare a poor soul a quid?"

McGuire said into the microphone, "Go away, you old bag."

"Oh, Mr. Kelly, I'll die here on your step in this terrible cold."

McGuire got up. "I'll go and get rid of her. Only be a minute." He hurried down the stairs and extracted a five-pound note from an old wallet as he opened the door. "Take this and clear off."

Dillon's hand came up out of the plastic shopping bag he was carrying, holding the Colt. "A fiver, Tommy boy. You're getting generous in your old age. Inside."

He pushed him inside and closed the door. McGuire was terrified. "Dillon," he whispered, "it's you?" He started to turn and raised his voice. "Devlin!" he called.

Dillon shot him twice in the back, driving McGuire onto his face. He got the door open behind him just as Devlin appeared on the landing, Luger in hand, already firing. Dillon fired three times, shattering the office window, then was outside, slamming the door.

As he started up the street two Land-Rovers, four soldiers in each, turned out of the main road, attracted by the sound of the firing. The worst kind of luck, but Dillon didn't hesitate. He pretended to fall, and dropped the Colt down a drain in the gutter. As he got up, someone called, "Stay where you are."

They were paratroopers in camouflage uniforms, flak jackets and red berets, each man with his rifle ready, and Dillon gave them the performance of his life. He staggered forward, moaning and crying, clutching at the young lieutenant in charge.

"Sir, there's terrible things going on back there in that warehouse. There's me sheltering from the cold, and these fellas come on and start shooting each other."

The officer pushed him away. "Check the bag, Sergeant."

The sergeant rifled through. "Some hooch and newspapers, sir."

"Right. Go and wait over there." The officer pushed Dillon along the pavement behind the patrol and got a loud-hailer from his Land-Rover. "You inside," he called, "throw your weapons out through the door; then follow them with your hands up."

While the patrol was intent on the entrance, Dillon eased back into the yard and found a manhole cover. He got it up and went down a steel ladder, pulling the cover closed. He had often evaded the British this way in the old days, and he knew the system perfectly. He crawled along a small dark tunnel, aware of rushing water, and came to a larger tunnel—the main sewer. He pulled off the skirt, wig and head scarf, and threw them into the water. Then he hurried along to another steel ladder, which brought him up near the Falls Road.

In the warehouse, the young officer stood beside McGuire's body and examined Mary Tanner's I.D. card. "It's perfectly genuine," she said. "You can check."

"And these two?"

"They're with me. Look, Lieutenant, you'll get a full explanation from my boss, Brigadier Charles Ferguson, Ministry of Defense."

"All right, Captain," he said defensively. "I'm only doing my job. Every death has to be investigated fully, or there's the devil to pay."

The sergeant came in. "The colonel's on the wire, boss."

"Fine," the young lieutenant said, and went out.

Brosnan said to Devlin, "Do you think it was Dillon?"

"A hell of a coincidence if it wasn't. A bagwoman?" Devlin shook his head. "Who'd have thought it?"

"Are you trying to say he came over from London specially?" Mary demanded. "That means he's got to go back."

Devlin nodded. "Perhaps. But nothing's absolute in this life, girl."

"Well, it's time we got the s.o.b." She looked down at McGuire. "Not too nice, is it?"

"The violence, the killing. Drink with the devil, and this is what it comes down to," Devlin told her.

THE OFFICER IN CHARGE OF ARMY intelligence for the Belfast city area was a Colonel McLeod, and he was not the least bit pleased with the situation. "It really isn't good enough, Captain Tanner," he said. "We can't have you people coming in here like cowboys and acting on your own initiative." He looked at Devlin and Brosnan. "And with people of dubious background into the bargain."

"Yes, well, that's as may be," Mary said. "But your sergeant outside was kind enough to check on flights to London for me. There's one at four thirty and another at six thirty. Don't you think it would be a good idea to check out the passengers thoroughly?"

"We're not entirely stupid, Captain. I've got that in hand. But there's no martial law here. All I can do is notify the police and airport security, and as you've been at pains to explain, where this man Dillon is concerned, we don't have much to tell them."

BUT Dillon had no intention of returning on the London flight. It was just after three when, dressed in white shirt and tie, dark suit and trench coat, he arrived at the airport by taxi and searched the departure board. He'd just missed the Manchester flight, but there was a flight to Glasgow due out at three forty-five.

He crossed to the booking desk. "I was hoping to catch the Glasgow flight," he told the booking clerk, a young woman.

"Yes, sir. There's plenty of space." She made out the ticket.

There was no trouble with security, and Dillon boarded the plane and sat at the rear. Very satisfactory. Only one thing had gone wrong: Devlin, Brosnan and the woman had got to McGuire first. A pity, that, because it raised the question of what McGuire had told them. Harvey, for example. He'd have to move fast there, just in case.

THE flight landed in Glasgow at four thirty. There was a shuttle-service plane to London at five fifteen. Dillon got a ticket at the desk, hurried through to the departure lounge, where the first thing he did was phone Danny Fahy at Cadge End.

"I'm in Glasgow, waiting for a plane," he said when Danny picked up. "I'll be arriving at Heathrow terminal one at six thirty. Can you come and meet me? You'll just have time."

"No problem, Sean. I'll bring Angel for the company."

"That's fine, and Danny, be prepared to work through the night.

Tomorrow could be the big one." He put the phone down before Fahy could say anything about that.

Next Dillon phoned Jack Harvey's office at the undertaker's in Whitechapel. It was Myra who answered.

"This is Peter Hilton here. I'd like a word with your uncle."

"He's gone up to Manchester. Won't be back until tomorrow."

"That's no good to me," Dillon said. "He promised me my stuff in twenty-four hours."

"Oh, it's here," Myra said. "But I'd expect cash on delivery."

"You've got it." He looked at his watch and allowed for the time it would take to drive from Heathrow to Bayswater to get the money. "I'll be there about seven forty-five."

"I'll be waiting."

MYRA got a key from her uncle's desk drawer and then went out to the head of the stairs. "Billy, are you down there?"

He came up a moment later. "Here I am."

"Come on. I need you." She led him along the corridor to the end door and opened it. The room was lined with shelves of box files. She put her hand on the middle shelf of the rear wall, and it swung open, revealing a treasure-house of weapons of every description. There were also boxes of Semtex on a table. She indicated one of the boxes of Semtex. "Take that to the office."

When she rejoined him, he'd put the box on the desk. "A right bloody weight. What is it?"

"It's money, Billy. That's all that concerns you. Now listen good. That small guy who roughed you up yesterday—he's turning up here at seven forty-five to pay me a lot of money for what's in that box."

"So?"

"I want you waiting outside from seven thirty on, with your BMW motorcycle handy. When he leaves, you follow him, Billy— to bloody Cardiff if necessary." She patted his face. "And if you lose him, sunshine, don't bother coming back."

IT WAS snowing lightly at Heathrow as Dillon came through at terminal 1. Angel was waiting for him, and waved excitedly. "Glasgow," she said. "What were you doing there?"

"Finding out what Scotsmen wear under their kilts."

She laughed and hung on to his arm. "Terrible, you are."

They went out through the snow and joined Fahy in the Morris van. "Good to see you, Sean. Where to?"

"My hotel in Bayswater," Dillon said. "I want to book out."

"You're moving in with us?" Angel said as they drove.

"Yes." Dillon nodded. "But I've a present to pick up for Danny first, at an undertaker's in Whitechapel. About fifty pounds of Semtex."

The van swerved and skidded slightly, Fahy fighting to control it. "Well, I'll be damned!" he said.

At the undertaker's, Myra was waiting for Dillon behind the desk in the office when he walked in. She tapped the carton with one hand. "There it is. Where's the money?"

Dillon put the briefcase on top of the carton and opened it. He took out ten thousand dollars, packet by packet, and dropped it in front of her. That left ten thousand in the briefcase, the Walther with the Carswell silencer, and the Beretta. He closed the case and smiled.

"Nice to do business with you."

He picked up the carton, and she opened the door for him. "What are you going to do with that? Blow up the Houses of Parliament?"

"That was Guy Fawkes," he said, and went downstairs.

The pavement was frosty as he walked along the street and turned the corner to the Morris van. Billy, waiting anxiously in the shadows, could see as Angel got the back door open and Dillon put the carton inside. Then the two got in beside Fahy, who drove through a couple of side streets and turned onto the main road. As the van joined the traffic stream Billy went after it on the BMW.

## Twelve

For technical reasons the Learjet had not been able to fly out of Belfast until five thirty. It was a quarter to seven when Brosnan and Mary landed at Gatwick, and a ministry limousine was waiting. Mary checked on the car phone and found Ferguson at the Cavendish Square flat. He was warming himself by the fire when a short while later Kim showed them in.

"Beastly weather, and a lot more snow on the way, I fear." He sipped some of his tea. "Well, at least you're in one piece, my dear. It must have been an enlivening experience."

"That's one way of describing it."

"You're absolutely certain it was Dillon?"

"Well," Brosnan said, "if it wasn't, it was a real coincidence that someone chose that moment to shoot Tommy McGuire. And then there's the bagwoman act. Typical Dillon."

"He wasn't on the London plane, sir, coming back," Mary said.

"You mean you *think* he wasn't," Ferguson corrected. "For all I know, the damned man might have passed himself off as the pilot." Ferguson turned to Brosnan. "I checked the flight schedules a little while ago. There were planes out of Belfast to Manchester, Glasgow. . . . No big deal to fly back to London from there."

"And there's always the sea trip," Brosnan reminded him. "The ferry to Scotland and a fast train from there to London."

"The interesting thing is the reason behind his trip," Ferguson said. "Dillon didn't know of your intention to seek out McGuire until last night, when Brown revealed the contents of that report to Novikova. And yet he went rushing off to Belfast at the earliest opportunity. Now, why would that be?"

"To shut McGuire's mouth, sir," Mary said. "And if we hadn't been early, Dillon would have got to him first. Dillon *knew* McGuire had something on him, and it was obviously the information that this man Jack Harvey was his arms supplier in '81."

"Yes, well, when you spoke to me from the airport, I ran a check. Detective Inspector Lane tells me that Harvey is a known gangster, and on a big scale. The police have been after him for years with little success. Unfortunately, he is now also a very established businessman, with property, clubs and so forth."

"What are you trying to say, sir?" Mary asked.

"That we can't just pull Harvey in for questioning because a dead man accused him of something that happened ten years ago."

Brosnan peered out the window. "There is another way," he said.

"I presume you're referring to your friend Flood." Ferguson smiled tightly. "Nothing at all to stop you from seeking his advice, but I'm sure you'll stay within the bounds of legality."

"Oh, we will, Brigadier. I promise you." Brosnan picked up his coat. "Come on, Mary. Let's go and see Harry."

FOLLOWING THE MORRIS VAN wasn't too much of a problem for Billy on his BMW. It was snowing lightly, and there was plenty of traffic all the way out of London and through Dorking. There wasn't quite as much on the Horsham Road, but still enough to give him cover.

At the Grimethorpe sign he switched off the headlamp of the motorcycle and followed the lights of the Morris at a distance, anonymous in the darkness. When the van turned at the Doxley sign, Billy followed cautiously, pausing on the brow of the hill, watching the lights move in through the farm gate.

He switched off his engine and coasted down the hill, pulling in by the gate and the wooden sign saying CADGE END FARM. He walked through the trees until he could see into the lighted interior of the barn. Dillon, Fahy and Angel were standing beside the Morris. Dillon turned, came out and crossed the yard.

Billy beat a hasty retreat and got back on the BMW. Five minutes later he was on the main road, returning to London to report to Myra.

IN THE house, Dillon called Makeev at the Paris apartment. "It's me," he said. "And it's all systems go, Josef. How does the entire British War Cabinet sound to you?"

"Dear Lord, you can't be serious."

"Oh, but I am. The War Cabinet meets at ten o'clock in the morning at Downing Street. That's when we'll hit."

"But how?" said Makeev.

"You can read about it in the papers. The important thing now is for you to tell Aroun to fly down to his St.-Denis place in the morning. I hope to be flying in sometime in the afternoon. Till our next merry meeting, then. And remind Aroun of that second million."

Dillon put the phone down, lit a cigarette, then picked up the phone again and called the Grimethorpe airfield.

"Bill Grant here." Grant sounded slightly drunk.

"It's Peter Hilton. That trip I wanted to make to Lands End— Tomorrow, I think. Could you be ready from noon onwards?"

"As long as the snow holds off. Much more, and we could be in trouble."

Grant put the phone down slowly, reached for the bottle of Scotch whisky at his hand and poured a generous measure. Then he opened the table drawer. There was an old Webley service revolver in there and a box of .38 cartridges. He loaded the weapon, then put it back in the drawer.

"Right, Mr. Hilton. We'll just have to see what you're about, won't we?" And he swallowed the whisky down.

"Do I know Jack Harvey?" Harry Flood, sitting at his desk, laughed and looked up at Mordecai Fletcher. "Do I know him, Mordecai?"

The big man smiled at Brosnan and Mary, who were standing there. "Yes, I think you could say we know Mr. Harvey rather well."

"Sit down and tell me what happened in Belfast," Flood said.

Which they did, Mary giving him a rapid account of the entire affair. When she finished, she said, "Do you think it's possible that Harvey was Dillon's weapons supplier in '81?"

"Nothing would surprise me about Jack Harvey and the empire he runs. But arms for the IRA? Mordecai, what do you think?"

"He'd dig up his granny's corpse and sell it if he thought there was a profit in it," the big man said.

"Very apt." Flood turned to Mary. "There's your answer."

"Fine," Brosnan said. "And if Dillon used Harvey in '81, the chances are he's using him again."

Flood said, "The police would never get anywhere with Harvey on the basis of your story, you must know that. He'd walk."

"I should imagine the professor was thinking of a more subtle approach, like beating it out of him," Mordecai said.

"I have an idea," Harry Flood said after a moment. "Harvey's been putting a lot of pressure on me lately to form a partnership. What if I tell him I'd like to have a meeting to discuss things?"

"Fine," Brosnan said. "But soon. We can't hang around on this."

MYRA was sitting at her uncle's desk going through club accounts when Flood called her. "Harry, what a nice surprise."

He said, "I was hoping for a word with Jack."

"Not possible, Harry. He's in Manchester at some sporting club function. But he's catching the breakfast shuttle tomorrow. He should be here about nine thirty. Look, what is this, Harry?"

"I've been thinking, Myra. About a partnership, I mean. Jack might have a point. There's a lot we could do if we got together."

"Well, I'm sure he'll be pleased to hear that," Myra said.

"I'll see you, then. Nine thirty sharp, in the morning, with my accountant," Flood told her, and rang off.

Myra sat there looking at the phone for a while, then rang the Midland Hotel in Manchester and asked for her uncle. When he picked up the phone at the hotel's front desk, Harvey, with Champagne and more than one brandy inside him, was in excellent humor.

"Myra, my love, what's up?" he said. "A sudden rush of bodies?"

"Even more interesting. Harry Flood's been on the phone." She told him what had happened. "What do you think?"

Harvey sobered up. "I think it's a load of rubbish. Why should he suddenly change his mind just like that? No, I don't like it."

"Shall I phone him back and cancel?"

"No, not at all. I'll meet him. What I'm saying is, be ready to give him the proper reception, just in case. Know what I mean?"

"I think so, Jack," she said. "I think so."

WHEN Makeev knocked on the door at Avenue Victor-Hugo, it was opened by Rashid. "You've news for us?" the young Iraqi asked.

Makeev nodded. "Where's Michael?"

"He's waiting for you." Rashid took him through to the drawing room, where Aroun was standing beside the fire.

"What is it?" he demanded. "Has something happened?"

"I've had Dillon on the phone from England. He wants you to fly down to St.-Denis in the morning. He expects to fly in himself sometime in the afternoon."

Aroun was pale with excitement. "What—what does he intend?"

He poured the Russian a Cognac, and when Rashid had passed it over, Makeev said, "He told me he intends some sort of attack on the British War Cabinet at Downing Street."

There was total silence, only astonishment on Aroun's face. It was Rashid who spoke. "The War Cabinet? All of them? That's impossible. How could he even attempt such a thing?"

"I've no idea," Makeev said. "But he seems certain."

Michael Aroun said, "If he can do this thing now, in the middle of the war, before the land offensive starts, the effect on the whole Arab world would be incredible." He turned to Rashid. "We'll leave at nine from Charles de Gaulle Airport in the Citation jet. You can phone old Alphonse at the château now. I want him out of there at breakfast time. He can take a few days off. I don't want him around."

Rashid went out to the study, and Makeev said, "Alphonse?"

"The caretaker. He's on his own unless I tell him to bring the servants in from the local village. They're all on retainers."

Makeev said, "I'd like to come with you, if that's all right."

"Of course, Josef." Aroun raised his glass. "To Dillon, and may all go as he intends."

IT WAS one in the morning, and Fahy was working on one of the oxygen cylinders on the workbench when Dillon entered the barn.

"How's it going?" Dillon asked.

"Fine," Fahy said. "This one's nearly finished, and one to go." He paused and ran a hand over his eyes as if tired. "Look, Sean, does it have to be tomorrow?"

"Is there a problem?"

"I wanted to weld some fins onto the cylinders to give them more stability in flight. I haven't time to do that now." He threw his spanner down on the bench. "It's all too rushed, Sean."

"Blame Martin Brosnan and his friends, not me," Dillon told him. "They nearly had me in Belfast. No, Danny, it's now or never."

Fahy picked up the cylinder reluctantly and carried it to the Ford Transit van. He got inside and fitted it into one of the tubes with great care while Dillon watched. Angel came in with a jug of coffee and two mugs, which she filled for her uncle and Dillon.

Dillon said, "I've been thinking. The garage where I wanted you to wait with the van, Angel—that's where the Russian woman, my contact, kept her car. The police may be keeping an eye on it."

"So what do you suggest?" she asked.

"Remember where I was staying—the hotel on the Bayswater Road? There's a supermarket next door, with a big parking area at the rear. We'll use that. I'll show you when we get there."

"Anything you say." Angel stayed watching as Fahy finished fitting his improvised mortar bomb and moved back to the bench. She said, "I was thinking, Mr. Dillon. This place in France, this St.-Denis—you'll be flying straight off there afterwards?"

"That's right."

She said carefully, "Where does that leave us?"

Fahy paused to wipe his hands. "She's got a point, Sean."

"You'll be fine, the both of you," Dillon said. "This is a clean one, Danny, the cleanest I ever pulled. Not a link with you or this place."

"If you say so," Fahy said.

"But I do, Danny, and if it's the money you're worried about, don't. The man I'm working for can arrange payment anywhere."

"Sure, and the money was never the big thing, Sean." He shrugged. "If something goes wrong, it's Angel I'm thinking about."

"No need. There won't be any risk." Dillon put his arm around the girl. "You're excited, aren't you?"

"Me stomach's turning over something dreadful, Mr. Dillon."

"Go to bed. We'll be leaving at eight. Now go on."

She went out reluctantly. Dillon lit a cigarette and turned back to Fahy. "Is there anything I can do?"

"Not a thing. Another half hour should do it. Go and put your head down yourself, Sean. I've found some old biker's leathers for you, by the way. They're over there, by the BSA motorcycle."

There was a jacket and leather trousers and boots. They'd all seen considerable service, and Dillon smiled. "Takes me back to my youth. I'll go and try them on." He turned and went out.

The leathers weren't bad at all. In his room in the house, Dillon stood in front of the wardrobe mirror as he zipped up the jacket over the bulletproof waistcoat Tania had given him at their first meeting. He pulled it snugly into place, fastened the Velcro tabs, then put his jacket on again.

He sat on the edge of the bed, took the Walther out of the briefcase and screwed the Carswell silencer in place. Next he checked the Beretta and slipped it inside his leather jacket. Then he switched off the light and lay on the bed. He never felt emotional, not about anything, and it was exactly the same now, on the eve of the greatest coup of his life. "You're making history with this one, Sean," he said softly. "History."

He closed his eyes, and after a while he slept.

It snowed again during the night, and just after seven, Fahy walked along the track to check the road. It was clear. He walked back and found Dillon standing at the farmhouse door eating a bacon sandwich, a mug of tea in his hand.

"I don't know how you can eat," Fahy told him. "I couldn't."

"Are you scared, Danny?"

"To death."

"That's good. Gives you that edge that can make all the difference."

They crossed to the barn and stood beside the Ford Transit. "Well, she's as ready as she'll ever be," Fahy said.

"You've done wonders, Danny, wonders."

Angel appeared behind them then. She was ready to go, dressed in her old trousers and boots, anorak, sweater and tam-o'-shanter. "Are we moving?" she asked them.

"Soon," Dillon said. "We'll get the BSA into the Morris now."

They opened the rear doors of the Morris, put the duckboard on an incline and ran the bike up inside. Dillon lifted it up, and Fahy shoved the duckboard in. Then he passed a crash helmet through as well. "That's for you, Dillon. I'll have one for myself in the Ford."

Dillon closed the van doors and turned. "Everybody happy?"

"Are we ready to take off, then?" Angel asked.

Dillon checked his watch. "Not yet. I said we'd leave at eight. We don't want to be too early. Plenty of time for another cup of tea."

THE early morning traffic on the road to London was slow because of the weather. Angel and Dillon led the way in the Morris, Fahy close behind in the Ford Transit. Epsom, then Kingston, and on towards the Thames, crossing at Putney Bridge. It was already nine fifteen as they moved along the Bayswater Road towards the hotel.

"Over there," Dillon said. "There's the supermarket." Angel turned into the car park, which was already quite full. "There, at the far end," Dillon said. "Just the spot."

She parked the Morris, and Fahy stopped nearby. Dillon jumped out, pulling on his crash helmet, went round and opened the doors. He positioned the duckboard and eased the BSA out, Angel helping. She shoved the duckboard back inside the van and closed the doors. He switched on the bike, and it roared into life. He glanced at his watch. It was nine thirty. He went over to Fahy in the Ford.

"Remember, timing is crucial. And we can't go round in circles at Whitehall. Somebody might get suspicious. If we're too early, delay on the Victoria Embankment. Pretend you've broken down, and I'll stop as if to assist. But remember, from the Embankment up Horse Guards Avenue to the corner with Whitehall only takes a minute."

433

"Jeez, Sean." Fahy looked terrified.

"Easy, Danny, easy," Dillon said. "It'll be fine. Now get moving."

Dillon swung a leg over the BSA motorcycle and turned to Angel. "See you soon," and he rode away behind the Ford.

## Thirteen

Harry Flood and Mordecai were waiting in the Mercedes, Charlie Salter at the wheel, when a taxi drew up outside the undertaker's in Whitechapel, and Brosnan and Mary got out. Flood opened the car door for them to get in.

He glanced at his watch. "Just coming up to nine thirty. We might as well go straight in." Flood took a Walther from his pocket and checked it. "You want something, Martin?" he asked.

Brosnan nodded. "It's a thought."

Mordecai opened the glove compartment, took out a Browning and passed it over to him.

Mary said, "For heaven's sake, anybody would think you were trying to start the Third World War."

"Or prevent it from starting," Brosnan said. "Think of that."

"Let's move," Flood said. Brosnan followed him out of the car, and Mordecai emerged from the other side. As Mary tried to follow, Flood said, "Not this time. I told Myra I'd be bringing my accountant, which explains Martin, and Mordecai goes everywhere with me. That's all they're expecting."

"Now look here," she said. "I'm the official case officer on this."

"Bully for you. Take care of her, Charlie," Flood told Salter, and he turned to the entrance, where Mordecai was already ringing the bell.

Myra was waiting for them in the outer office. She was wearing a black trouser suit and boots, and carried a sheaf of documents.

"You look very businesslike, Myra," Flood told her.

"So I should, Harry." She nodded to Mordecai. "Hello, muscles." Then she looked Brosnan over. "And this is . . . ?"

"My new accountant, Mr. Smith."

"Really?" She nodded. "Jack's waiting." She opened the door and led the way into the office.

The room was warm and comfortable. Harvey sat behind the desk smoking his usual cigar. Billy Watson was over to the left, sitting on the arm of the sofa, his raincoat casually draped across his knee.

"Jack," Harry Flood said, "nice to see you."

"Is that so?" Harvey looked Brosnan over. "Who's this?"

"Harry's new accountant, Mr. Smith," Myra told him. She moved round the desk and stood beside her uncle.

Harvey shook his head. "I've never seen an accountant that looked like Mr. Smith, have you, Myra?" He turned back to Flood. "My time's valuable, Harry. What do you want?"

"Dillon," Harry Flood said. "Sean Dillon."

"Dillon?" Harvey looked mystified. "And who the hell is Dillon?"

"Small man," Brosnan said. "Irish. Although he can pass as anything he wants. You sold him guns and explosives in 1981."

"Very naughty of you that, Jack," Harry Flood said. "He blew up large parts of London, and now we think he's at it again."

"And where else would he go for his equipment except his old chum Jack Harvey?" Brosnan said. "That's logical, isn't it?"

Harvey, his face suffused, said, "Billy!"

Flood put up a hand. "I'd just like to say that if that's a sawed-off shotgun he's got under his coat, I hope it's cocked."

Billy fired instantly through the raincoat, catching Mordecai in the left thigh as the big man drew his pistol. Flood's Walther came out of his pocket in one smooth motion, and he hit Billy in the chest, sending him back over the sofa, the other barrel discharging, some of the shot catching Flood in the left arm.

Jack Harvey had the desk drawer open. His hand came up clutching a Smith & Wesson, and Brosnan shot him very deliberately through the shoulder. There was chaos for a moment, the room full of smoke and the stench of cordite.

Myra leaned over her uncle, who sank back in his chair, moaning. Flood turned to Mordecai. "You okay?"

"I will be when Dr. Aziz has finished with me, Harry."

Flood, still holding the Walther, clutched his left arm, blood seeping between his fingers. He glanced at Brosnan. "Okay. Let's finish this." He took two paces and raised the Walther directly at Harvey. "I'll give it to you right between the eyes if you don't tell us what we want to know. What about Sean Dillon?"

"No!" Myra screamed. "Leave him alone. The man you want calls himself Peter Hilton. He bought fifty pounds of Semtex. Picked it up

435

last night and paid cash. I had Billy follow him home on his BMW."

"And where would that be?"

"Here." She picked a sheet of paper up from the desk. "I'd written it all down for Jack."

Flood looked it over and passed it to Brosnan. "Cadge End Farm, Martin. Sounds promising. Let's get out of here."

Mordecai limped out ahead of the others, dripping blood. As they got into the Mercedes, Charlie Salter said, "Harry, we're getting blood all over the carpets."

"Just drive, Charlie. You know where to go."

Mary looked grim. "What happened in there?"

Brosnan held up the sheet of paper. She read it and said, "My Lord, I'd better phone the brigadier."

"No, you don't," Flood said. "First we call at the quiet little nursing home in Wapping run by my good friend Dr. Aziz so he can take care of Mordecai and see to my arm. After that, Cadge End."

As Fahy turned out of the traffic on the Victoria Embankment into Horse Guards Avenue, he was sweating in spite of the cold. He could see Dillon in his rearview mirror—a sinister figure in his black leathers on the BSA. Then it was the moment of truth, and everything seemed to happen at once.

Fahy pulled in at the junction of Horse Guards Avenue and Whitehall on the angle he'd worked out. Some distance away a policeman turned and saw the van. Fahy turned off the engine, switched on the timers and pulled on his crash helmet. As he got out, the policeman called to him and hurried over. Dillon swerved in on the BSA, Fahy swung a leg over the pillion seat, and they were away, sliding past the astonished policeman and moving off fast. As Dillon joined the traffic the first explosion sounded. There was another, perhaps two, and then it all seemed to become one with the greater explosion of the Ford Transit self-destructing.

Dillon kept on going, not too fast, through the Admiralty Arch and along the Mall. Soon he was turning along the Bayswater Road and within minutes rode into the car park of the supermarket. As soon as she saw them, Angel was out of the van. She got the doors open and the duckboard in place. Dillon and Fahy shoved the bike and duckboard inside and slammed the doors. "Get in and drive," Dillon said to her, and a minute later they were turning into the Bayswater Road.

Dillon lit a cigarette and sat back, whistling softly.

IN THE small operating room at the nursing home just off Wapping High Street, Mordecai Fletcher lay on the table while Dr. Aziz, a gray-haired Indian wearing spectacles, examined his thigh.

"Harry, my friend, I thought you'd given this up," he said. "But here we are again, like a bad Saturday night in Bombay."

Flood was sitting in a chair, jacket off, shirtsleeve cut away, while a nurse swabbed his arm. Brosnan and Mary stood watching.

Flood said to Aziz, "How is Mordecai?"

"He'll have to stay in for two or three days. An artery is severed. Now let's look at you."

He held Flood's arm and probed gently with a pair of small pincers. The nurse held an enamel bowl. Aziz dropped one piece of shot in it, then two, then another. Flood winced with pain. "That could be it, Harry, but we'll need an X ray."

"Just bandage it up for now," Flood said. "I'll be back later."

"If that's what you want." Aziz bandaged the wound skillfully, then jabbed a shot of morphine into Flood's arm. "It will help with the pain," the Indian told him.

As the nurse fastened a sling behind Flood's neck, the door burst open and Charlie Salter came in. "All hell's broken loose," he said. "Just heard it on the radio. Mortar attack on Ten Downing Street."

Mary turned to Brosnan. "Come on, Martin. At least we know where the fool's gone."

THE War Cabinet had been larger than usual that morning, fifteen including the Prime Minister. It had just begun its meeting in the Cabinet Room, at the back of number Ten Downing Street, when the first mortar, curving in a great arc of some two hundred yards from the Ford Transit van, landed. There was a huge explosion, so loud that it was clearly audible in the office of Brigadier

Charles Ferguson at the Ministry of Defense, overlooking Horse Guards Avenue. Ferguson, like most people in the ministry, rushed to the nearest window.

At Downing Street, in the Cabinet Room, the strengthened windows cracked, but most of the blast was absorbed by the special blast-proof net curtains. The first bomb left a crater in the garden, uprooting a cherry tree. The other two landed farther off target in Mountbatten Green, and only one of those exploded.

There was surprisingly little panic in the Cabinet Room. Everyone crouched, some seeking the protection of the table. Then the Prime Minister stood up and actually managed a smile. With incredible calm he said, "Gentlemen, I think we had better start again somewhere else," and he led the way out of the room.

MARY and Brosnan were in the back seat of the Mercedes, Harry Flood in the passenger seat beside Charlie Salter, who was making the best time he could through heavy traffic.

Mary said, "Look, I need to speak to the brigadier. It's essential."

Flood turned and looked at Brosnan, who nodded. "Okay," Flood said. "Do it. We're bound to get to this Cadge End place first anyway."

She used the car phone, ringing the Ministry of Defense, but Ferguson wasn't there. She left the number and put the phone down.

THE BBC news flash came over the radio in the Morris van. There had been a bomb attack on number Ten Downing Street at approximately ten a.m. The building had sustained some damage, but the Prime Minister and members of the War Cabinet meeting together at that time were all safe.

The van swerved as Angel sobbed, "Oh, Lord, no!"

Dillon put a hand on the wheel. "Steady, girl," he said calmly. "Just stick to your driving."

Fahy looked as if he were going to be sick. "If I'd had time to put those fins on the cylinders, it would have made all the difference. You were in too much of a hurry, Sean. You let Brosnan rattle you, and that was fatal."

"Maybe it was," Dillon said, "but all that matters is, we missed." He took out a cigarette, lit it and suddenly started to laugh helplessly.

FERGUSON WAS STANDING WITH Detective Inspector Lane and Sergeant Mackie at Mountbatten Green. It was snowing lightly, and a police forensic team was making a careful inspection of Fahy's third mortar bomb—the one that hadn't exploded.

"A bad business, sir," Lane said. "To use an old-fashioned phrase, 'Right at the heart of the empire.' I mean, how can they get away with this kind of thing?"

"Because we're a democracy, Inspector. Because people have to get on with their lives. And that means we can't turn London into some East European–style armed fortress."

A young constable came across with a mobile phone. "Excuse me, Brigadier, it's urgent. Your office has been trying to contact you. Captain Tanner's been on the line."

Ferguson took the phone, spoke briefly to his office, then called the number Mary had left. She answered at once. "Brigadier?"

"What's going on?" he demanded.

"The mortar attack on Number Ten. It has to be Dillon. We found out he picked up fifty pounds of Semtex in London last night, supplied by Jack Harvey."

"Where are you now?"

"Just leaving Dorking, sir. Martin and me and Harry Flood. We've got an address for Dillon." She gave it to the brigadier, then said, "We should be at this Cadge End place in half an hour."

"Fine. Nothing rash, Mary, but don't let the fool get away. We'll get backup to you as soon as possible. I'll be in my car."

Ferguson put the phone down and told Lane what had happened. "What do you think Harvey will be up to, Inspector?"

"Receiving treatment from some bent doctor in a nice little private nursing home somewhere, sir."

"Right. Have that checked out, and if it's as you say, just have them watched. This Cadge End place is where we go, and fast."

THE track through the trees at Cadge End Farm was covered with more snow now than when they had left. Angel bumped along it to the courtyard and turned into the barn.

Fahy said, "Now what?"

"A nice cup of tea, I think." Dillon got out, went round and opened the van doors. Danny helped him get the BSA out and up on its stand. "Performed brilliantly. Good job there, Danny."

Angel had gone ahead, and as they followed her Fahy said, "What I need isn't bloody tea, Sean. It's whiskey." When he got to the living room, he wept.

Dillon went up to his bedroom. He found an old holdall and packed quickly. He opened his briefcase, which held the ten thousand dollars remaining from his expense money, and the Walther with the silencer. He cocked the gun, leaving it ready for action, and put it back in the case. He unzipped his jacket, took out the Beretta and slipped it into the waistband of his leather trousers at the rear.

When he went downstairs carrying the holdall and briefcase, Fahy was standing, looking at the television set. "They just had the Prime Minister on, inspecting the damage," he said. "Looked as if he didn't have a worry in the world."

"Yes, his luck is good," Dillon said.

Angel came in and handed him a cup of tea. "What happens now, Mr. Dillon?"

"You know very well, Angel. I fly off into the wild blue yonder."

Angel said, "Can't we go with you, Mr. Dillon?"

He put down his cup and put his hands on her shoulders. "There's no need, Angel. I'm the one running, not you or Danny. I'm the one they're after. They don't even know you exist."

He went across to the phone, picked it up and rang the Grimethorpe airfield. Grant answered straightaway. "Yes, who is it?"

"Peter Hilton, old boy. Okay for my flight? Not too much snow?"

"It's clear down in the West Country," Grant said. "Might be tricky taking off here, though. When were you thinking of going?"

"I'll be round in half an hour. That all right?" Dillon asked.

"I'll expect you."

As Dillon put the phone down Angel cried, "No, Uncle Danny."

Dillon turned and found Fahy standing in the doorway with a shotgun in both hands. "But it's not all right with me, Sean," and he thumbed back the hammers.

"Danny boy," Dillon said, spreading his hands, "don't do this."

"We're going with you, Sean, and that's an end to it." Fahy was trembling now, the shotgun shaking in his hand. "I'm frightened. If I'm caught, I'll spend the rest of my life in jail. I'm too old, Sean."

"I see," Dillon said.

Fahy raised the shotgun. "So that's it, Sean. If we don't go, you don't go."

Dillon's hand at his back found the butt of the Beretta. His arm swung, and he shot Fahy twice in the heart, sending him staggering out into the hall. He hit the wall on the other side and slid down.

Angel screamed. She stared at Dillon. "You've killed him."

"He didn't give me any choice."

She turned, grabbed at the front door and dashed across the yard into one of the barns. Dillon went after her and stood there listening. There was a rustling of straw somewhere in the loft.

"Angel, listen to me. I'll take you with me."

"No, you won't. You'll kill me like my uncle Danny. You're a bloody murderer." Her voice was muffled.

He extended his left arm, pointing the Beretta up to the loft. "And what did you expect? What did you think it was all about?"

There was silence. He turned, hurried across to the house, stepped over Fahy's body. He picked up his briefcase and holdall, then went back to the barn and put them in the Morris.

He tried once more. "Come with me, Angel. I'd never harm you. I swear it." There was no reply. "To hell with you, then," he said. He got behind the wheel and drove away along the track.

IT WAS some time later, when everything was very quiet, that Angel came down the ladder and crossed to the house. She sat beside her uncle's body—her back against the wall, a vacant look on her face—and didn't move, not even when she heard the sound of a car driving into the courtyard outside.

## Fourteen

THE runway at Grimethorpe was covered with snow. The hangar doors were closed, and there was no sign of either of the planes. Dillon drove up to Grant's hut and, with his holdall and briefcase, walked to the door. When he went in, Bill Grant was standing by the stove drinking coffee.

"Ah, there you are, old man. Place looked deserted," Dillon said. "I was beginning to worry." He put down his holdall but still carried the briefcase.

"No need." Grant crossed to his desk and sat down. Dillon saw that there was a chart on the desk—the English Channel area, the Normandy coast, the Cherbourg approaches—the chart he had checked out with Angel that first night.

"Look, I'd really like to get going," he said. "If it's the rest of the fee you're worried about, I can pay cash." Dillon held up the briefcase. "I'm sure you've no objection to American dollars."

"No, but I do have an objection to being taken for a fool." Grant indicated the chart. "Lands End, my eye. I saw you looking at this the other night with the girl. English Channel and French coast. What I'd like to know is, what are you trying to get me into?"

"You're really being very silly, old chap," Dillon said.

Grant pulled open a desk drawer and took out his old Webley revolver. "We'll see, shall we? Now just put the briefcase on the desk, and stand back while I see what we've got."

"Certainly, old chap. No need for violence." Dillon stepped close and put the briefcase on the desk. At the same moment he pulled the Beretta from his waistband and shot Grant at point-blank range. Grant went backwards over the chair.

Dillon put the Beretta back in place, picked up the chart, his holdall and briefcase, and went out trudging through the snow to the hangar. He opened the great sliding door so that the two aircraft stood revealed. He threw the holdall and the briefcase into the Cessna Conquest and climbed in, pulling the door behind him.

He settled into the pilot's seat and sat there studying the chart. Approximately a hundred and forty miles to the airstrip at St.-Denis. Unless he encountered head winds, he should do it in forty-five minutes. He switched on, firing first the port engine, then the starboard. He took the Conquest out of the hangar and paused to make a cockpit check. As Grant had boasted, the fuel tanks were full. Dillon strapped himself in and taxied to the end of the runway.

He turned into the wind and started forward. He was immediately aware of the drag from the snow, and he boosted power, easing back the column. Within minutes the Conquest lifted and started to climb. He banked to turn towards the coast and saw a black limousine down below moving out of the trees towards the hangar.

"Well, I don't know who you are," he said softly, "but if it's me you're after, you're too late."

ANGEL SAT AT THE KITCHEN TABLE holding the mug of coffee Mary had given her. Brosnan and Harry Flood, his arm in the sling, stood listening, and Charlie Salter leaned on the door.

"It was Dillon and your uncle at Downing Street, is that what you're saying?" Mary asked.

Angel nodded. "I drove the Morris van with Mr. Dillon's motorbike in it. Uncle Danny was afraid, afraid of what might happen."

"And Dillon?" Mary asked.

"He was flying from the airfield up the road—Grimethorpe."

She sat clutching the mug, staring into space. Brosnan said gently, "Where did he want to go, Angel? Do you know?"

"It was in France. It was down along the coast from Cherbourg. There was a landing strip marked. A place called St.-Denis."

"Right. Let's get going and check out this Grimethorpe place," Flood said. "You stay here with the kid, Charlie," he told Salter, "until the cavalry arrives. We'll take the Mercedes."

IN THE great hall at St.-Denis, Aroun and Makeev stood drinking Champagne, waiting for the television news. Rashid waited with them.

"A day for rejoicing in Baghdad," Aroun said. "The people will know now how strong their President is."

The announcer came on and spoke briefly. Then the pictures followed: Whitehall in the snow, the rear of Ten Downing Street, net curtains hanging from smashed windows, Mountbatten Green, and the Prime Minister inspecting the damage.

The three men stood in shocked silence. It was Aroun who spoke first. "He has failed," he whispered. "All for nothing. A few broken windows, a hole in the garden."

"The attempt was made," Makeev protested. "The most sensational attack ever mounted on the British government."

"Who cares?" Aroun tossed his Champagne glass into the fireplace. "He failed with the Thatcher woman, and he has failed now. In spite of all your big talk, Josef, nothing but failure."

Rashid said, "A good thing we didn't pay him his million pounds, as he thinks."

"True," Aroun said, "but the money is the least of it. It's my personal position with the President which is at stake."

"So what are we going to do?" Makeev demanded.

"Do?" Aroun looked at Rashid. "We're going to give our friend Dillon a very warm reception on a cold day, isn't that so, Ali?"

"At your orders, Mr. Aroun," Rashid said.

THE Mercedes reached Grimethorpe as the Conquest banked and flew away. "Do you think that's him?" Mary said, looking out.

"Could be," Brosnan said. "We'll soon find out."

They drove past the open hangar with the Navajo Chieftain inside and stopped at the Quonset huts. It was Brosnan, first through the door of Grant's hut, who found the body. "Over here," he said.

Mary and Flood joined him. "So it *was* Dillon in that plane," she commented.

"Which means he's slipped the lot of us," Flood said grimly.

"Don't be too sure." Mary looked fierce and determined. "There was another plane in that hangar," she told him, then turned and ran out.

"What goes on?" Flood demanded as he followed Brosnan out.

"Amongst other things, the lady happens to be an army air corps pilot," Brosnan said.

When they reached the hangar, Mary was in the cockpit of the Navajo. She got up and came out. "Full tanks."

"You want to follow him?" Brosnan demanded.

"Why not? With any luck we'll be right up his tail." She opened her handbag and took out her cellular phone. She moved outside, pulled up the aerial on the phone and dialed Ferguson's car.

THE limousine, leading a convoy of six unmarked Special Branch cars, was just entering Dorking when Ferguson received her call. He listened to what Mary had to say and made his decision. "I totally agree. You must follow him. What do you require from me?"

"Speak to Colonel Hernu at Action Service, Section Five. Ask him to discover who owns the airstrip at St.-Denis so we know what we're getting into. Ask him to deal with the authorities at the airport at Cherbourg. They can act as a link for us when I get close to the French coast."

"I'll see to that at once, and you take down this radio frequency." He gave her the details quickly. "That will link you directly to me at the Ministry of Defense. If I'm not back in London, they'll patch you through."

"Right, sir."

"And Mary, my love," he said, "do take care."

"I'll do my best." She closed her cellular phone and went back into the hangar. "Let's get going."

MAX Hernu was sitting at his desk at DGSE headquarters going over some papers with Inspector Savary when Ferguson was put through to him. "Charles, exciting times in London," Hernu said.

"Don't laugh, old friend, because the whole mess could well land in your lap. Number one, there's a private airstrip at a place called St.-Denis, down the coast from Cherbourg. Who owns it?"

Hernu asked Savary to check the computer, and Savary rushed out. Hernu continued. "Tell me what all this is about, Charles."

Which Ferguson did. When he finished, he said, "We've got to get this s.o.b. this time, Max, finish him off for good."

"I agree, my friend." Savary hurried in with a piece of paper and passed it to Hernu, who read it and whistled. "The airstrip in question is part of the Château St.-Denis estate, which is owned by Michael Aroun."

"The Iraqi billionaire?" Charles Ferguson laughed harshly. "All is explained. Will you arrange clearance for Mary Tanner with Cherbourg and also see that she has that information?"

"Of course, my friend. I'll also arrange a plane at once and get down there myself with a Section Five team."

"Good hunting to all of us," Ferguson said, and rang off.

AROUN and Makeev were sitting by the fire in the great hall when they heard the sound of a plane. Rashid hurried over to open the French windows. They joined him on the snow-covered terrace, Aroun holding a pair of binoculars. Three hundred yards away, on the airstrip, the Conquest landed and taxied towards the hangar.

Aroun focused the binoculars on the plane, saw the door open and Dillon appear. "So he's here," he said.

"I'll go down and pick him up in the Land-Rover," Rashid said.

"No, you won't," Aroun said. "Let him walk through the snow—a suitable welcome. And when he gets here, we'll be waiting for him."

Fifty miles out to sea, Mary identified herself to the tower at Cherbourg. She got a reply instantly.

"We've been expecting you."

"Am I clear to land at St.-Denis airstrip?" she asked.

"Things are closing in rapidly. Visibility was a thousand feet twenty minutes ago. It's six hundred feet now. Advise you try here."

Brosnan, in the copilot's seat, heard all this on the other headphones and turned to her in alarm. "We can't do that, not now."

She said to the tower, "It's most urgent that I see for myself."

"We have a message for you from Colonel Hernu. The St.-Denis airstrip is part of Château St.-Denis and owned by Mr. Michael Aroun."

"Thank you," she said calmly. "Out." She turned to Brosnan. "You heard that? Michael Aroun."

"One of the wealthiest men in the world," he said. "And Iraqi."

"It all fits," she said.

Carrying the holdall and his briefcase, Dillon trudged through the snow towards the terrace at the front of the house. The three men watched him come. Aroun said, "You know what to do, Josef."

"Of course." Makeev took a Makarov automatic from his pocket, made sure it was ready for action and put it back.

"Go and admit him, Ali," Aroun told Rashid.

Rashid went out. Aroun picked up a newspaper and sat down at the table, placing the paper in front of him. He took a Smith & Wesson from his pocket and slipped it under the paper.

Rashid opened the door as Dillon came up the snow-covered steps. "Mr. Aroun is waiting inside. Let me take your luggage."

Dillon put the holdall down but held on to the briefcase. "I'll keep this." He smiled. "What's left of the cash."

He followed Rashid across the enormous stretch of black and white tiles and into the great hall. "Come in, Mr. Dillon," the Iraqi said.

"God bless all here," Dillon said, and walked across to the table.

"You didn't do too well," Aroun said. "I was promised great things. You were going to set the world on fire."

Dillon shrugged. "Another time perhaps."

"Another time." Aroun's face was suddenly contorted with rage. "Another time? You have not only failed me, you have failed Saddam Hussein, President of my country. I pledged my word to him—my word—and because of your failure, my honor is in shreds."

"What do you want me to do? Say I'm sorry?"

Rashid, sitting on the edge of the table, said to Aroun, "In the circumstances a wise decision not to pay this man."

Dillon said, "What's he talking about?"

"The million in advance you instructed me to deposit in Zurich."

"The manager confirmed it had been placed in my account."

"On my instructions, you fool. I have millions on deposit at that bank. I had only to threaten to transfer it elsewhere."

"You shouldn't have done that," Dillon said calmly, putting his briefcase down. "I always keep my word, Mr. Aroun. I expect others to keep theirs. A matter of honor."

"Honor? You talk to me of honor." Aroun laughed out loud. "What do you think of that, Josef?"

Makeev, who had been standing behind the door, stepped out, the Makarov in his hand. Dillon half turned.

"Easy. Hands on head, Mr. Dillon," Rashid told him. Dillon complied. Rashid unzipped the biker's jacket, checked for a weapon and found nothing. His hands went round Dillon's waist and discovered the Beretta. "Very tricky," he said, and put it on the table.

"Can I have a cigarette?" Dillon put a hand in his pocket, and Aroun threw the newspaper aside and picked up the Smith & Wesson. Dillon produced a cigarette pack. "All right?" He put one in his mouth, and Rashid gave him a light. The Irishman stood there and said, "What happens now? Does Josef blow me away?"

"No. I reserve that pleasure for myself," Aroun said.

"Mr. Aroun, let's be reasonable." Dillon picked up his briefcase and started to open it. "I'll give you back what's left of the operating money, and we'll call it quits. How's that?"

"You think money can make this right?" Aroun asked.

"Not really," Dillon said, and took the Walther with the Carswell silencer from the briefcase and shot him between the eyes. Aroun went over, his chair toppling, and Dillon, turning, dropped to one knee and hit Makeev twice as the Russian got off one wild shot.

Dillon was up and turning, the Walther extended, and Rashid

448

held up his hands. "No need for that, Mr. Dillon. I could be useful."

"You're damn right you could be," Dillon said.

There was a sudden roaring of an aircraft passing overhead. Dillon grabbed Rashid by the shoulder and pushed him to the French windows. They could see the Navajo landing in the mist. "Now, who might that be?" Dillon asked. "Friends of yours?"

"We weren't expecting anyone. I swear it," Rashid said.

Dillon shoved him back inside and put the Walther to Rashid's neck. "Aroun had a nice private safe hidden away in the apartment in Paris. Don't tell me he didn't have the same here."

Rashid didn't hesitate. "It's in the study. I'll show you."

"Yes, you will," Dillon said, and pushed him towards the door.

## Fifteen

THE study, paneled in oak, had an antique desk and chair, an empty fireplace, and shelves lined with books on one wall.

"Hurry it up," Dillon said, and sat on the end of the desk.

Rashid went to the fireplace and put his hand to the paneling on one side. There was obviously a hidden spring. A panel opened outwards, revealing a small safe. Rashid twirled the dial backwards and forwards, then tried the handle. The safe refused to open.

Dillon said, "You'll have to do better."

"Just give me time." Rashid was sweating. "I must have got the combination wrong." He tried again, pausing only to wipe sweat from his eyes, and then there was a click that even Dillon heard.

"Good," Dillon told him. "Let's get on with it." He pointed the Walther at Rashid's back.

Rashid opened the safe, reached inside and turned, a Browning in his hand. Dillon shot him in the shoulder, spinning him around, and shot him again in the back. The young Iraqi bounced off the wall, fell to the floor and rolled onto his face.

Dillon stood over him. "You people never learn," he said softly.

He looked inside the safe. There were neat stacks of hundred-dollar bills, French francs, English fifty-pound notes. He went back to the great hall for his briefcase, then filled it with as much money as it could hold. It was at that moment he heard the front door open.

BROSNAN, MARY AND FLOOD HAD just landed on the strip, and Mary killed the engine. They left the plane quickly. Brosnan led the way up the snow-covered steps—the Browning that Mordecai had given him in his right hand—and tried the front door. It opened to his touch.

"Careful," Flood said.

Brosnan peered in cautiously, taking in the vast expanse of black and white tiles, the curving stairway. "It's quiet. I'm going in."

As he started forward Flood said to Mary, "Stay here for the moment," and went after him.

The doors to the great hall stood fully open, and Brosnan saw Makeev's body at once. He moved inside, the Browning ready. "He's been here all right. I wonder who this is?"

"Another on the far side of the table," Flood told him.

They walked round, and Brosnan dropped to one knee and turned the body over. "Well, well," Harry Flood said, "even I know who that is. It's Michael Aroun."

Meanwhile, Mary was moving into the entrance hall, closing the door behind her. There was a slight eerie creaking on her left, and she turned and saw the open door to the study. She took the Colt .25 from her handbag and went forward.

As she approached the door the desk came into view, and she saw Rashid's body on the floor beside it. She took a quick step inside in a kind of reflex action, and Dillon moved from behind the door, tore the Colt from her hand and slipped it into a pocket.

"Well now," he said, "isn't this an unexpected pleasure?"

"BUT why would he kill Aroun?" Flood asked Brosnan.

"Because he cheated me. Because he wouldn't pay his debts."

They turned and found Mary at the door, Dillon behind her, the Walther in his left hand, the briefcase in the other. Brosnan raised the Browning. Dillon said, "On the floor and kick it over, Martin, or she dies."

Brosnan put the Browning down carefully, then kicked it across the floor.

"That's better," Dillon said. He pushed Mary towards them and sent the Browning sliding into the outer hall with the toe of his boot. "As a matter of interest, just how in the hell did you find me?"

"A lady called Myra Harvey had you followed last night," Brosnan

450

said. "That led us to Cadge End Farm. You're getting careless, Sean."

"So it would seem. If it's any consolation, the only reason we didn't blow the entire War Cabinet to hell was because you and your friends got too close. Danny wanted to fit stabilizing fins onto those oxygen cylinders that we used as mortar bombs. It would have made all the difference to their accuracy, but there wasn't time, thanks to you."

"Delighted to hear it," Brosnan said. "So what happens now?"

"To me?" Dillon held up the briefcase. "I've got a rather large sum in cash that was in Aroun's safe, and a choice of airplanes. The world's my oyster. Anywhere but Iraq."

"And what about us?" Mary demanded. "You've killed everyone else, what's three more?"

"But I don't have any choice," Dillon said patiently.

"No, but I do!"

Harry Flood's hand slipped inside the sling, pulled out the Walther he had been concealing and shot Dillon twice in the heart. Dillon staggered back, dropping his briefcase, and fell to the floor, turning over in a kind of convulsion. Suddenly he was still and lay there face down, the Walther still clutched in his left hand.

FERGUSON was in his car and halfway back to London when Mary called him from Aroun's study. "We got him, sir," she said simply, then told him everything. "So what now, Brigadier?"

"Get back on your plane and leave at once. French territory, remember. I'll speak to Hernu now. He'll take care of it. Contact me in mid-flight, and I'll give you landing arrangements."

The moment she was off the line, he phoned DGSE's headquarters. It was Savary who answered. "Ferguson here. Have you got an arrival time for Colonel Hernu at St.-Denis?"

"The weather isn't too good down there, Brigadier. They're landing at Cherbourg and will proceed onwards by road."

"Well, what he's going to find rivals the last act of *Macbeth*," Ferguson said. "So let me explain, and you can forward the information."

VISIBILITY was no more than a hundred yards through the mist as Mary Tanner taxied the Navajo to the end of the runway, Brosnan sitting beside her. Flood leaned over from his seat to peer into the cockpit. "Are you sure we can make it?" he asked.

451

"It's landing in this stuff that's the problem, not taking off," she said, and took the Navajo forward into the gray wall and started to climb. Gradually she left the mist behind and turned out to sea. After a while she put on the automatic pilot and sat back.

"You all right?" Brosnan asked.

"Fine. Slightly drained, that's all. He was so—so elemental. I can't believe he's gone."

"Oh, he's gone," Flood said cheerfully. "And may he roast in hell."

DILLON was aware of voices, the front door closing. When he surfaced, it was like coming back from death to life. The pain in his chest was excruciating, but that was hardly surprising after having been hit at such close range. Leaving the Walther on the floor, he sat up and examined the two ragged holes in his jacket, then took it off. The bullets Flood had fired at him were embedded in the titanium-and-nylon vest Tania had given him. He unfastened the Velcro tabs, pulled the vest away and threw it down. Then he picked up the Walther and stood.

He went to the drinks cabinet and poured a brandy, looking round the room at the bodies, his briefcase still on the floor where he had dropped it. When he heard the Navajo's engine starting up, he saw it all. Everything was being left to the French, which was logical, and that probably meant Hernu and the boys from Action Service were on their way.

Time to go, but where? The best answer, as usual, was Paris. He'd always been able to fade into the woodwork there. He had the barge, and the apartment over the warehouse at Rue de Helier. Everything he would ever need.

Dillon finished the brandy, picked up his briefcase and hesitated, looking down at the vest with the two rounds embedded in it. He smiled and said softly, "You can chew on that, Martin." He pulled the French windows wide and stood on the terrace breathing deeply of the cold air. Then he went down the steps to the lawn and walked quickly across to the trees, whistling softly.

MARY tuned her radio to the frequency Ferguson had given her. She was picked up by the radio room at the Ministry of Defense immediately, and then she was patched through to him.

"Well out over the Channel, sir. Heading for home."

"Gatwick is expecting you," he said. "Hernu has just phoned me from his car on the way to St.-Denis. Exactly as I thought. The French don't want this kind of mess on their patch. Aroun, Rashid and Makeev died in a car crash; Dillon goes straight into a pauper's grave. No name, just a number. Similar sort of thing at our end over that chap Grant."

"But what about Jack Harvey, sir?"

"That's slightly different. He and young Billy Watson are still with us, in bed, at a private nursing home in Hampstead. Special Branch are keeping an eye on them."

"We're not going to do anything?"

"No need. Harvey doesn't want to do twenty years in prison for working with the IRA. He and his motley crew will keep their mouths shut. So, by the way, will the KGB."

"And Angel?"

"I thought she might come and stay with you for a while. I'm sure you can handle her, my dear. The woman's touch and all that." There was a pause, and then he said, "Don't you see, Mary? It never happened, not any of it."

"That's it, then, sir?"

"That's it, Mary. See you soon."

She sighed, switched off the autopilot, took control of the plane herself and flew onwards towards the English coast.

FERGUSON, writing quickly, completed his report and closed the file. He got up and walked to the window. It was snowing again as he looked out towards the junction of Horse Guards Avenue and White-hall, where it had all happened. He was more tired than he had been in a long time, but there was still one thing to do. He turned back to his desk, was reaching for the scrambler phone when it rang.

Hernu said, "Charles, I'm at St.-Denis, and we've got trouble."

"Tell me," Ferguson said, his stomach already hollow.

"Three bodies, but no sign of Dillon. Just a fancy bulletproof vest on the floor, with two Walther rounds embedded in it."

"You mean, he's still out there?" Ferguson said.

"I'm afraid so, Charles. I'll put the word out to all the usual agencies, of course, but I can't say I'm particularly hopeful."

453

"Why would you be? We haven't succeeded in putting a hand on Dillon in twenty years, so why should it be any different now?" He took a deep breath. "All right, Max. I'll be in touch."

He went back to the window and stood looking out at the falling snow. Then he turned reluctantly to his desk, pausing for only a moment before phoning Downing Street and asking to speak to the Prime Minister.

IT WAS towards evening, snow falling heavily, as Pierre Savigny, a farmer from the village of St. Just, outside Bayeux, drove carefully along the main road towards Caen in his old Citroën truck. He almost didn't see the man in biker's leathers who stepped into the road, an arm raised.

The Citroën skidded to a halt, and Dillon opened the passenger door and smiled. "Sorry about that," he said in his impeccable French, "but I've been walking for quite a while."

"And where would you be going on a filthy evening like this?" Savigny asked as Dillon climbed into the passenger seat.

"Caen. I'm hoping to catch the night train to Paris. My motorbike broke down. I had to leave it in a garage in Bayeux."

"Then you're in luck, my friend," Savigny said. "I'm on my way to Caen now. Potatoes for tomorrow's market." He moved into gear and drove away.

"Excellent." Dillon put a cigarette in his mouth, flicked his lighter and sat there, the briefcase on his knees.

"You're a tourist, then, monsieur?" Savigny asked as he increased speed.

Sean Dillon smiled softly. "Not really," he said. "Just passing through," and he leaned back in the seat and closed his eyes.

"The thing that struck me most about the mortar attack on Ten Downing Street was that the terrorists got away with it—yet again," says Jack Higgins of the real-life incident on which he based *Eye of the Storm*, his fifty-first novel. "It's a terrible fact that when the IRA plan their operations so carefully, they're almost always impossible to catch. That's the point I wanted to make in the book."

*Jack Higgins*

The author, whose real name is Harry Patterson, has a firsthand insight into both sides of the Irish conflict. He was born in Belfast into a part-Protestant, part-Catholic family, and lived in Ireland for twelve years. He took his pen name from a great-uncle who, he recalls, was heavily mixed up in politics. "It was not unknown to see guns lying around," he says. Perhaps because of this childhood influence—and his years spent studying sociology and criminology—Higgins has always been fascinated by those who become caught up in violence. "Because it's like a theater—a theater of the streets—people get into the Irish cause. The trouble is, in the script, people don't get killed; in reality, innocent people are destroyed."

Although he is now sixty-three and, by his own estimation, "a bit longer in the tooth," Higgins' creative output shows no signs of slowing. *Eye of the Storm* joins *The Eagle Has Flown, Cold Harbour,* and *Night of the Fox* in a lineup of his most recent books—all best sellers and Condensed Books selections. The author's energy level remains high, too. For that he partly credits his wife, Denise, who has a pilot's license and drives racing cars. She has also managed to get her husband hooked on scuba diving. "It's a whole new world," he says. The couple lives on the Channel island of Jersey.

PHOTO: PETER TRENCHARD ABIPP / © LYNN PHOTOGRAPHERS

# Jeanne Williams
# *The Island Harp*

*The harp is small and very old. It had belonged to Mairi MacLeod's grandfather, a crofter on a windswept Scottish isle. As Mairi plays it now she sings of the beauty of her island, of the courage of her people, and of the cruel fortunes they face as they are driven from their land. But no song she has ever sung prepares this young woman for the joys—and the longings—love can bring when Captain Iain MacDonald comes into her life.*

# 1

THE lochs on the black moor of Lewis flashed blue sky, sun, and scudding fluffs of cloud. On this bright August afternoon Mairi MacLeod and Catriona Nicolson came from the shieling—the beehive-shaped stone hut where the cousins had made cheese and butter while the township's cattle and sheep grazed in the summer pastures. Now it was nearing autumn, time to reap oats and barley, time to bring the animals home.

Formidable as it was on somber days, which deepened the brooding expanses of peat bogs, the moor was far from wasteland. As well as providing grazing land in grassy hillocks and hollows, early in summer it swarmed with families cutting peats that now dried beside cuts patterning the moor with squares and circles. Deep purple bell heather and hummocks of ling were courted by humming bees and drifting magpie moths and butterflies—dark green, white, peacock, and tortoiseshell. Downy white fluffs of cotton grass were not only pretty but made soft pillows and mattresses, and fairly good wicks for the fish-oil lamps.

The peat almost everywhere was at least as deep as a tall man's height. Beneath it was clay—skinned earth—where with seaweed, sand, and hard work, arable soil could be formed. When food was scarce, Mairi's grandmother would say, "There's the fine peats, whatever else we're lacking, and God be thanked for that."

Then Grandfather, in his voice that roared like the sea, might retort, "We cannot be eating peats, woman!"

"Fearchar," Gran would soothe. That was what she called Grandfather—dear man—and so did the children. "The fire shines warm and lovely. If you'd give us a song . . ."

And then the white-maned Michael MacLeod, tough and weathered as his blackthorn staff, gentled by his wife Rosanna's voice, would smile and play on the clarsach, the small harp brought long ago from Ireland, where the black or red willows grew large enough to make the best soundboards.

The clarsach had belonged to an ancestor bard who'd played at the court of Conn of the Hundred Battles. But in spite of its legendary past, the children regarded the harp almost as another grandparent, and indeed it had a name, Cridhe, which meant "heart." Draped in the tightly woven MacLeod plaid—green and black, with narrow lines of red and blue—the harp was protected from smoke and dampness.

Fearchar taught all the children to play, but only Mairi found that music could express feelings she could not put into words. She would never be able to play like Fearchar, though. When his hands wooed Cridhe, mellow tones filled the house with magic—songs of love and battle, songs of the sea and birds.

The neighbors, hearing, would come in, the other two households of the dwindled township of Aosda gathering around the hearthstone in the middle of the single long room. Red-haired Andrew Nicolson, Fearchar's cousin and Catriona's father, would tell stories, in spite of the perpetual frown of his scrawny dark wife, Morag. She had reason now to worry, poor woman, for her youngest sons, Lucas and Paul, had gone to the army of Victoria, the English queen, as had Mairi's brother Calum. The eldest Nicolson lad, blue-eyed, fair-haired Barry, was still at home with his gentle, golden Sheila. He would contest with Adam MacNeill to see whose jokes won the most laughter. Adam and his wife, Kirsty, with their three-year-old twins, weren't related to the other households. Mairi, with her younger brother, Tam, and little sister, Eileen, had lived with their grandparents since their father drowned and their mother died in childbed a few months later.

At these gatherings, or ceilidhs, Mairi and Gran served round a brew flavored more from the peat in the water than from a few precious leaves of tea, but it was steaming and warmed the insides.

Though Mairi's belly often cramped with hunger when she crept into the box bed she shared with Eileen, she seldom went to sleep without music, some laughter, and Gran's blessing of the banked fire on the stone.

This hearthstone had been the center of their family's home from before the harp left Ireland, maybe even before the Pictish folk or those who raised the Stones at Callanish, where Gran took Mairi for Midsummer sunrise, in spite of what the minister said. They were all Christians, but the old faith lived within the new one, just as Brighde, the Celtic goddess of fire and poetry, had merged with Saint Brigid, revered as the nurse of Jesus and hence very powerful.

Getting the peats that year hadn't been easy. Fearchar's back pained him too much for the digging, and Calum was off with his regiment. Calum hadn't been recruited with a guinea and a kiss from the laird's lady in the fashion of some landlords raising levies for the queen's wars. Since the breaking of the clans after Bonnie Prince Charlie's defeat at Culloden, in 1746, even chiefs who hadn't lost their lands seldom lived on them, but preferred the excitement of Edinburgh or Glasgow. That kind of high living took money.

Some lairds sold their estates outright to men who had no ties to their tenants. All over The Highlands and islands landlords saw that sheep were more profitable than farmers and refused to go on renting to families that had lived in the same place for hundreds of years. Some tenants were driven out even though their rents were paid; others were evicted the next time rents were due. The island of Lewis was owned by Mrs. Stewart MacKenzie. Her husband had been governor of Ceylon, and they had spent little time on Lewis. Mr. MacKenzie had died last year, in 1843, and it was rumored that his widow wished to sell the island. Meanwhile, her factor on Lewis, Hugh Sinclair, carried out her agent's instructions.

Calum had gone to the army for the promise of Mrs. MacKenzie's factor that his family could stay on their croft so long as the rent was paid—and paid it was, with tweed Mairi and Gran wove, with butter and cheese, and fish smoked by the peats. It was time to pay it again, this autumn of 1844, but Hugh Sinclair had given his promise, so surely the township of Aosda was safe.

Some of that fine butter and cheese that paid the rent was in the creel Mairi carried effortlessly, though it was piled high with bedding and other gear needed when the cousins lived in the stone hut and tended the sheep and cows. It was a sort of holiday at the shieling. After tending to their dairy chores, the girls could wander the heath in search of crowberries, nap among nodding blue harebells, and laugh and talk with the freedom of the young far out of earshot of their elders. Time at the shieling was delightsome, a change from the usual round of work. It must have been even more so in the days Gran remembered, when instead of three households, the township numbered a dozen, and whole families went together to the summer pastures. Now the empty homes of those gone to America or Canada or Australia were used as byres, or barns. But when Calum got home from the army, and Catriona's brothers returned, oh, then Aosda would surely flourish again.

Catriona, as she often did, was staring toward the sea. His Viking, Fearchar teasingly called her, driven to hanker after distant places and new things; Mairi was his Gael, loving her home island. "I wish I could have gone with Calum," Catriona said, almost scowling.

The long thick braid of her hair was the gold-brown of ripe barley, and her slanting eyes were tawny. Though she was only a few months older than Mairi, who had turned seventeen in May, Catriona was curved and beautiful. But Mairi knew that people called her pretty only because her red-brown hair was waving and lustrous, her skin smooth and fresh, and her smile ready. From the brass-framed mirror Fearchar had given Gran, Mairi ruefully learned that her nose was too long, her mouth too large, and her jaw too strong. Her eyes, at least, were acceptable—a deep gray, thick-lashed and wide set. As for her figure, a childish boniness was starting to round.

Mairi sighed. No wonder Calum had begged Catriona to wait for him till he had served his time. Since they were third cousins, there was no bar to their marriage, but Catriona was so impatient that Mairi sometimes wondered if this cradle friend of hers would manage to wait for her betrothed.

Mairi broke off her thought, shielding her eyes as she stared at a dark haze in the distance. "That's smoke!"

The girls exchanged frightened glances. Maybe a roof had caught. They put off their creels and made all the speed they could, leaving the cattle and sheep to come at their own pace. They splashed through the bogs in their desperate hurry.

Breath sobbing as she flew up a slope, Mairi froze at the black-edged flames devouring the peat-smoked thatch of the houses. A keening reached her, wails and screams.

Mairi saw a man thrust a brand to the last dwelling, her grandparents', while other men forced back Morag Nicolson, Andrew's wife, and Sheila, her daughter-in-law, whose baby should come any day. Kirsty MacNeill's twins clung to her skirts, and tiny Gran struggled to keep Fearchar away from their house. The men and Mairi's young brother, Tam, were away at the summer's fishing.

Mairi gasped as Fearchar wrenched free of Gran and ran into the house. What could be left in there precious enough to risk his life? Cridhe, the harp! That must be it. Mairi sped down the slope, frantically, uselessly calling his name.

How could they be driven out when the rent was paid and they had assurance from Hugh Sinclair that they were secure because Calum had gone for a soldier, and Lucas and Paul also? How could it be?

Fearchar staggered out, clothes and white hair blazing, rested Cridhe on the ground, and fell beside the harp. Gran and the others beat out the flames with their skirts.

At last Mairi was on her knees beside her grandfather. He didn't look like Fearchar at all—snowy hair frizzled to the seared skull, mouth crookedly agape. The burners gathered to stare down at him. "Must be it was his heart stopped," said a burly young one defensively. "He's not burned bad enough for mischief."

Mairi sprang to her feet. Choked with rage and grief, she hurled herself on the man, clawing at his throat. He gasped, cursing.

A blow stunned her. There was blackness.

Then strong arms raised her. "What are you about, Mr. Sinclair?" a voice demanded in Gaelic. It came deeply from the chest against which she lay. "Has war been declared on women and children and old men?"

Wincing at the throb in her head, Mairi opened her eyes and recognized black-bearded Hugh Sinclair standing above her. His hard black eyes slid away from the man holding her.

"It's their own blame, Captain MacDonald, sir. I gave them writs

463

of eviction last month. I warned them again. They wouldn't go peaceably, so I had to fetch the constables."

"The rents are paid!" Mairi cried, sitting up. For the first time she saw the face of her rescuer. Lean it was, and long, with sundarkened skin taut over cheekbones and cleft chin. Lines at the corners of his eyes, straight nose, firm, down-curved mouth, and black hair that fell in an unruly wing across his forehead. Captain, Sinclair had called him, but he wore no uniform, only gray trousers and coat, with a shirt of white linen.

A short distance away a blond youth held a gun and a brace of red grouse. She understood then. The stranger was from one of several hunting lodges the MacKenzies leased for deerstalking and salmon fishing. What would he care about the troubles of tenant folk? Wasn't it gentlemen like him who'd cleared off tenants in their thousands to make room for sheep?

"Our rents are paid," she said again. "When Mr. Sinclair came to enlist our young men for the regiment, he promised that their folk could bide on their crofts. Without that promise, never would my brother and cousins have gone." Her voice cracked. "Now Mr. Sinclair comes with constables and torches and clubs while even the few men left to us are off at the fishing!"

Letting go of the stranger, she got to her feet, advancing on the factor. "God's curse on you, Hugh Sinclair." The voice did not seem to be hers. The words came of themselves.

"Curse all you've breath for, girl," he said gruffly. "I only took back Mrs. MacKenzie's land which is hers."

"We have lived here always!" Mairi cried.

"Always is finished."

Mairi's wrath ebbed into overpowering grief for Fearchar and despair at the smoking, flaming roofs. The burners had tossed belongings outside, chests, stools, clothing, webs slashed from looms.

"You burned the box beds," she said, aghast at such waste on a treeless island. "And the roof timbers!"

Sinclair shrugged. "You could have had them if yon old man hadn't been stubborn. In spite of that and your cursing, I'm a merciful man. I'll buy the cows and sheep at the going price."

Mairi glanced at the weeping women crouched beside Fearchar. Gran, huddled with his head in her lap, knew only that her dear man was dead. Morag was praying, and Sheila pressed Fearchar's limp hands to her streaming face. He was the chief of this small clan.

"We will keep our beasts," Mairi said.

"Where will you graze them?" Sinclair demanded. "You have no land, nor can have."

"Then what are we to do? Throw ourselves into the sea? Swim to America or Australia?"

Captain MacDonald spoke suddenly. "Mr. Sinclair, having dispossessed these people, you will now see that their goods are conveyed to the lodge. They will shelter there till their men return and they can decide what to do."

Sinclair's jaw dropped. "But sir, Captain, the MacKenzie agent would not allow that, and a bad example you're setting—"

"I pay enough for my lease to have such guests as I choose." The captain's tone allowed no argument. He turned to the abashed constables. "Rig a litter and carry the old man to the lodge."

"No," said Gran. "He would rather be buried in sight of the sea. This night we'll watch with him, and tomorrow we'll take him to the graveyard. A coffin he'll have if it takes every stick left me."

"There will be a coffin," Captain MacDonald assured her. "But, good woman, it helps nothing to stay the night by these ruins."

"I thank you, sir, but this has been his home since I nagged him into giving up the sea. And 'tis the harp my Fearchar will have this night, if you will play it, Mairi."

"I will play." Mairi looked at Cridhe for the first time since the horror. The plaid that had protected it trailed on the grass, but the strings, though smoked, seemed intact. She moaned at seeing a crack in the soundboard. Perhaps she could daub it with wax.

"Lass, can't you persuade your grandmother to hold the wake at the lodge?" the captain said. "It's a grim night and grim place for you two to be alone."

"We aren't alone, but with my grandfather," Mairi said, though she couldn't keep a tremor from her voice. "Only, Captain MacDonald, if tomorrow you will send a coffin—"

"I will, and men to bear it."

"We will do that ourselves."

"Three miles to the kirk and two more to the graveyard?" he asked. "I will help, and you cannot refuse, for I'm in your brother's

465

regiment, and you must let me take his place." He nodded at the fair young man who held his gun. "Jamie, too, serves in the Seventy-eighth Highlanders."

After a hesitation, she nodded. "We will thank you, then, for taking my brother's and cousins' places."

Hugging Eileen, she bade her help herd the cattle and sheep. The women, the constables, the captain, and his gillie gathered up the jumbled heaps, stuffing smaller things into creels and baskets.

"I'll send for the rest," said the captain. And soon only two women, a dead man, and a harp remained in the smoking debris of what had been a homeplace since time out of mind.

MAIRI and her grandmother washed Fearchar in water from the spring before they dressed him in his best linen shirt and the kilt and MacLeod shoulder plaid. He'd inherited these from his grandfather, who'd worn them in the terrible Battle of Culloden.

That had been almost a hundred years before. The Highlanders were defeated with Bonnie Prince Charlie, slaughtered on the field, jailed, executed, or sold to American plantations. The Saxon heel ground the clans into the dust. Bagpipes and arms were outlawed, and for thirty-six years it was a crime to wear kilt or plaid. Fearchar, though, vowed a kilt was the best garment ever designed for wading brooks and tramping through wet heather.

"Save the plaid for Calum," Gran said. "The kilt is ample for a shroud. And we'll make your bed of blooming heather, dear man."

Mairi cut armfuls of bell and cross-leaved heather, raising a sweet-smelling bier on which they laid Fearchar, wrapped in his tartan, with his face uncovered. It was dusk when Mairi cleaned Cridhe's strings and soundboard. After she washed her hands, she sat on a rock beside Fearchar, tuning the harp.

Gran took a place in the heather, holding her husband in her arms. A scent of clover and a hundred other blooms came from the machair—earth rich with shell sand—before the dunes where oats, barley, and potatoes were thriving. What, now, would the folk of Aosda have for their food that winter? And where would they be?

If Mairi lived, she would be on the island. To keep from weeping, she began to sing from a bard of Uist who lamented his people's ruin seventy years before:

> *"Look around you and see the gentry*
> *With no pity for the poor creatures,*
> *With no kindness to their kin . . ."*

She played on, recounting Fearchar's life and their life together, telling her love and loss. Sometimes she choked and could only speak through Cridhe. Sometimes her voice rang wild with anger and sorrow, but she played till the cushions of her fingers were raw, and ended with her grandfather's favorite drinking song.

Gran was so still that Mairi thought her asleep. They had not eaten, and though it seemed unfitting to be aware of such things, her belly cramped. Morag had left them some bannocks and a kettle for boiling water. Draping Cridhe with the scorched plaid, Mairi made her way to the ruined house.

She saw with a rush of thankfulness that peats still smoldered on the hearth, their glow like a promise. Even on barren rocks above the sea, the hearthstone would make a center for a new home. And there, Fearchar, she promised, Cridhe will sing your songs. Folk of your blood will live on this island after the lairds are gone. With your songs we'll outlast them, win back our land.

Heartened by the resolve, though she had no idea of how to carry it out, she built up the fire and set the kettle on. The peat would give the water a flavor, and its heat should comfort Gran.

As Mairi located the bannocks in a basket, her fingers closed on an unfamiliar object. A metallic flask, and beside it two packets. The captain had left them. She uncorked the flask and took a nip to confirm that the pungent fragrance was that of whisky.

That, now, would ease Gran's bones, she thought with relief. Gran knew and appreciated *uisge-beatha*—the water of life—which came from malted barley. One of the packets contained raisins, which Mairi knew because Calum had once brought her some from Stornoway. Boiled, they would make the hard bannock tastier for Gran. The other packet contained a kind of dried fish.

The water reached a boil. Mairi filled the cups that Morag had left in the basket, and added good dashes of whisky. Shivering in a wind grown stronger and colder, she carried Gran's cup to the bier. Rosanna MacLeod hadn't moved. "Gran, love"—Mairi spoke in her softest voice—"here's a drop to warm you."

Kneeling, Mairi set the cup to Gran's lips. She took a deep sip and savored it. "Ah, the velvet of the *uisge-beatha*," she crooned. "Finest I've made, smooth as a kitten's paw with the claws tucked in. Michael will get a brave price when he goes to Glasgow town."

Why, she talked as if it were forty years ago! Mairi's scalp prickled. Then she remembered that Calum had once been stunned in a fall, and it had been a fortnight before he remembered who he was. Small wonder if Gran's mind rebelled at Fearchar's death and slipped back to when they were young and life promised brightly.

"I'd fancy another dram, Mairi, love," Gran said briskly. She stared down at Fearchar and slowly shook her head. "And is it my poor father's wake we're having?"

Mairi's heart stopped. Still, if believing she mourned her father was easier for Gran than accepting Fearchar's death, the delusion was merciful. "I'll bring it, dear," she said, "and a bite to eat."

While Mairi devoured a bannock, Gran ate hers with the plumped raisins and shared the fish before sipping the whisky. Sighing deeply, she asked suddenly, "Why are we out here? Why are we not in the house, and Father laid out decent on the table?"

"There's been a fire. The thatch burned."

"So a new roof's to be made along of Father's burying," Gran said, shaking her head. "But we must smoor the hearth fire anyway, for 'tis bad luck for it not to last till morning."

Mairi helped Gran up, praying that the ruins wouldn't jar her into the present. When Gran gazed around at the embers that winked from the fallen roof, she only muttered, "Well, thatch do burn sometimes, and it's a pity, but my Michael will soon have us snug again."

Kneeling, Mairi tried to concentrate on Gran's nightly blessing of the fire. Gran raked the embers into the middle of the ancient stone, with a small raised heap in the center. "In the name of the God of Life," she said as she set the first peat touching the raised center. "In the name of the God of Peace," she blessed the second. Placing the third, which finished dividing the embers into three parts, she said, "In the name of the God of Grace." Then, covering the coals with ash, Rosanna MacLeod stretched out her hand and blessed the hearth of her ruined home.

Her voice failed at the ending. Like a small child, she permitted

Mairi to wash her face, brush and plait her white hair, and wrap her in a blanket beside her husband, with heather for a pillow.

Exhaustion suddenly completely overtook Mairi. Wrapping in her shawl, she curled against Gran to warm them both. Strange, but she felt as if the captain were near, watching over them.

Gentry or not, he was a strengthening man. He had known just what to leave for Gran. Even the small amount of whisky Mairi had sipped now curled warmly in her, and she soon slept sound.

## 2

"DRINK this," the captain said as Mairi blinked and sat up, at first not knowing the thin dark face and then feeling as if it had haunted her consciousness like a dream. Something warm and vibrant passed between them, pulsing in lovely golden waves.

Mairi took the cup, and strength revived in her as she drank the steaming, fragrant tea. The captain turned and went to where Jamie, his yellow-haired gillie, was busy over a fire.

Gran stirred. Straightening her garments as best she could, Mairi went to the fire. "May I have a cup for my grandmother?"

The captain's eyes swept her keenly. "How is she?"

Mairi explained, and he nodded. "I've seen it when someone's badly wounded—a soldier denying he's lost an arm or leg."

"Gran's lost more than an arm or leg. She's lost her heart."

The angles of his face sharpened. After a moment he said, "They were blessed if their hearts cleaved together as well as their bodies. But you're too young a maid to understand."

Even with her world destroyed around her, it stung that he thought her a child. Hadn't he felt what she did—that radiating flame? "I know what's between men and women," she said, lifting her chin to face him, for he was tall, though sparely built. " 'Tis naught for shame be there loving and all decent."

He chuckled. "You *are* young, lass. As an aging man of thirty-one, let me warn you: loving and decent don't always march together."

She turned her back on him and carried a cup to Gran, who was trying to sit up. Cradling her, Mairi coaxed her to drink, but Gran insisted on putting her hair up under her ruffled white cap before she would come to the fire. " 'Tis wrong to speak ill of the dead," she whispered, "but I do hope these kind gentlemen aren't knowing what a rascal Father aye was. I'll see him proper buried right enough, but that's from duty. Now where bides the coffin?"

"It'll be here soon." The captain spread a blanket on a stone outcropping near the fire and led Gran to it, kind as if she'd been his own kin. She studied him, obviously wondering why gentry was concerned with the troubles of poor folk.

A creaking rumble sounded from the north. "That'll be the carts," said the captain. "They bring the coffin and can take your furnishings to the lodge till it's decided where you will go."

"Where but the rocks?" said Mairi. She gazed at Fearchar, and furious grief made her hate the captain for a moment—not as himself, for he had been kind—but as a regimental officer who made decisions that got lads like her brother and cousins killed, or leased lodges where starving crofters were forbidden to hunt.

The MacDonald must have sensed her mood, for he said quietly, "We'll talk of that later."

Fearchar's mourners and the coffin arrived in two carts drawn by small, sturdy horses. The drivers lifted out the coffin and then, at a word from the captain, drove beside the remaining goods and furniture and began to load them.

Mairi hurried over to warn Morag and the others about Gran's confusion. Eileen caught hold of her. "Oh, Mairi, the people were grand to us at the lodge. Will we be staying there forever?"

It was clear that she hoped to. Mairi almost rued the captain's charity, for where they must go would seem the more bleak and dreary after the comforts of the lodge estate. "We can't bide there, sweeting. Folk there can only be servants."

Eileen's mouth quivered. "Can't we be servants, then?"

"We'll not, Eileen Doireann MacLeod! Don't you remember how Fearchar said, 'Better seaweed and mussels at one's own hearth than fatted meat in the servants' hall' ?"

"Oh, Mairi, have done!" Catriona tossed her head. "The cook at the lodge needs a helper. I'm taking the place."

It was unseemly to wrangle by Fearchar's corpse, but Mairi couldn't restrain herself from saying, "You'll please yourself, Catriona, but you won't be pleasing my brother when he comes from soldiering to find you in the lodge's kitchen."

"I've told him I've no mind to starve on a croft. Get a little sense, Mairi MacLeod! We come from folk who left their homeland when it got too crowded. What if all Adam's and Eve's descendants had tried to stay huddled up close to the Garden of Eden?"

It was such a comical thought that Mairi had to laugh. The anger faded in her, and she gave her cousin's hand an affectionate squeeze as they moved toward the bier. The captain and Jamie placed Fearchar gently in the coffin, which was made not of driftwood, but of solid lumber. Women and children dropped in heather and wildflowers as they knelt to kiss the chill, gray face.

The captain and Jamie secured the lid and took places at the middle handle on either side. Carrying a coffin was men's work, and the women came to it uncertainly, Catriona and Mairi at the head, Morag and Kirsty at the foot. Had the captain and his gillie not put their strength to it, the women could never have borne the coffin across the moor to the tiny village, where men from the few families left took their places and spoke awkward condolences.

The minister, Reverend Campbell, scowled from the door of the kirk, lips tight as his purse string. As if he grudged them entrance, he stood in the door till the bearers had to pause. "When a man throws away his life for a heathenish harp," he said, "I cannot think God will show him mercy."

"I would suggest, sir, that you leave that to God." Captain MacDonald looked at the minister in a way that caused his cheeks to flush. Shoulders sagging, he went down the aisle.

The captain moved aside to let Mairi precede him. She stood beside Gran, one arm around an exhausted Sheila, the other nestling Eileen against her, through the Scriptures and a sermon full of Calvin's dark gloom: all human beings deserved eternal hell; only through God's mercy would a chosen few escape. There was no solace in the words.

Fearchar's real funeral was last night, with the sea wind and Cridhe, Mairi consoled herself. Right then, as if Fearchar's buoyant, life-loving spirit entered her, she resolved that though she mourned now, all her days she would be as happy as she could, do any kindness, and above all, sing and play on Cridhe to put heart into people cast out by their lairds and uncomforted by the kirk.

The graveyard's sandy earth was protected in some measure

from the ocean by stone cliffs that jutted into the waves. Most of the grave markers were Celtic crosses, many ancient and crumbling, the lettering scrubbed off long since by storms and blowing sand. Of names that could be read, half at least were MacLeods. Half a century ago Fearchar's surviving close kin lived on Lewis, but famine and poverty had driven them away. They had indentured themselves and sailed for America, Canada, and Australia, scattered like seabirds in a furious storm. If Mairi did not succeed in holding to the island, her whole line would be swept away from the land won by their clan a thousand years before.

As Fearchar was lowered into the grave, Mairi and the others covered him with flowers. The handful of turf that Gran tossed in resounded on the coffin. When the soil was mounded, Mairi and the rest smoothed it with their hands. Mairi wished she had Cridhe, to sing her grandfather a last song, but the gulls would do that.

"It's proper done," muttered Gran. "Let's be going, lass."

Mairi gave Gran her arm. As they reached the level she blinked in surprise. The two carts waited, cushioned with pallets.

"You'll ride to the lodge," said the captain.

He lifted Gran onto a pallet and gently assisted Sheila, while the drivers and Jamie helped the others. Mairi was starting to scramble up when she was lifted by strong hands into the cart.

No one had picked her up since she was a bairn. It was discomfiting to be handled like one, though there was something dangerously pleasant about it—realization of the captain's strength, coupled with an instinctive desire to trust it. He had a clean, good smell, and his fingers were long and tanned. She loved the feel of them. His eyes, on a level with hers now, crinkled at the edges.

Such eyes they were, deep gray with a light to them like sun on the ocean. Drawn into them, Mairi was caught in the vortex of the fathomless black pupils. He stepped back a pace, as if he, too, found their closeness unsettling.

With a flare of triumph Mairi said, "Thank you, sir, for helping me up. It was kind of you to have the carts brought."

Dark eyebrows raised quizzically. "You don't allow much helping, Mistress Mairi. Take a word of advice. If you don't let people help you now and then, you'll wear out early." He smiled. "You have a flower face, child. Don't make it wither sooner than it must."

"I could wither the more waiting," she retorted, and instantly bit her tongue. He *had* helped where it was none of his concern. It wasn't fair to vent her wrathful despair on him. Swallowing hard, she forced herself to meet his gaze, raising her will like a shield against that frightening yet unspeakably sweet sensation of being encompassed by his eyes, drained of strength. "I—I do thank you with all my heart. Without you, we would be in much worse case."

Indeed, without his succor they'd be huddling on the moors, not that they could bide long at the lodge. They must find land, get something of a start to hearten the men, who'd find such a cruel welcome when they came from the fishing. But where? With Gran demented and Sheila near childbirth, how would they manage?

"I have some proposals to set before you," the captain said. "Of course, you'll wait till your men return to make a final decision."

Before Mairi could respond, he set boot to stirrup and vaulted into the saddle of his big bay horse. The carts rumbled off. Eileen fell asleep at once, flaxen head in Mairi's lap. With great tenderness Mairi cradled her little sister, and thought yearningly of Tam, only a few years older, trying to do a man's full work at the fishing. Tam idolized Fearchar and would be wild at the loss of him.

Thinking of her brother and that grave down by the sea, Mairi bowed her head and wept for a long time.

TURRETS and round towers reared in profusion from the gray stone walls of a rambling building so immense that Mairi wondered if the English queen's castle could possibly be larger. What amazed her most was the glass—panes and panes of it, glinting from a multitude of windows. The only glass windows she had ever seen were in the kirk, narrow and small at that. The roof was of thin, flat slabs of dark gray rock—not a friendly bit of thatch anywhere.

The carts had stopped in a court behind the back of the lodge. A man was working in a bed of flowers. Think of that! A man paid to putter with flowers that couldn't serve for food!

A block of buildings formed one side of the courtyard. Boys ran out to take the captain's and Jamie's mounts and lead them inside a stable. Facing this block were eight white houses made with mortar. Each had several glass windows and a chimney.

Captain MacDonald came over in his loose, long stride. "You

473

may use the cottage where you stayed last night," he told the other women. "If you need anything, come to the lodge kitchen."

He hoisted down the twins and also helped Sheila. "You had better rest," he advised in a surprisingly gentle tone.

Sheila murmured her thanks and moved slowly off with Kirsty and Morag, the twins racing ahead to a cottage on the end.

While the captain lifted Gran and Eileen down, Mairi made haste to jump to the turf. The MacDonald gave her a half grin. "You three should be comfortable in the butler's quarters," he said.

"But the—whatever he is—the butler—"

"I don't have one. I much prefer living without the complication of a household, with all its layers of authority."

He proffered his arm to Gran, but she held back. "I do not ken this place at all. And how will my dear man be finding me when he comes from the fishing?"

"Your roof burned," said the captain matter-of-factly. "I'll send a message to Stornoway so when the fleet returns, your men will come here straightaway."

Intimidated by the vast heap of stone, Mairi at first hung back. "Sir, we would liefer stay with the others."

"That cottage is crowded enough with three women and two children," he said. His smile flashed, and she marveled at how it changed the grim lines of his face, made him seem almost a lad. "Besides, your harp is waiting by the fire in the parlor. That seems a fine clarsach. I hope you'll let me hear it."

In answer, she held up her swollen, abraded fingertips. His mouth tightened. It was a moment before he spoke. "I think you are one, Miss Mairi, to tell your harp what you'll tell no mortal."

"You would not like the songs I feel like playing now."

They had reached the lodge, and he opened the door. Now they stood in a great hall, with a massive fireplace and antlers forking from the walls in numbers that made Mairi gasp.

"There must be more antlers here than stags on the island!"

"Oh, there are plenty left, though who knows what will happen with young Prince Albert so keen on deerstalking and the able-bodied aristocracy imitating him."

"You're not one of those, sir?"

He laughed outright. "Bless you," he said. "I was feeding my family with deer off the mountain while Albert was still with his tutors. My father died fighting in one of those wars that still go on, and he left my mother with a hungry brood. I was the eldest. It's a pleasure to me now to see a stag and not have to shoot it."

Bewildered, she glanced around at the elegant furniture, soft jewel-toned rugs, and ornately framed paintings of hunting scenes. Reading her thought, he laughed again.

"No, Mistress Mairi, my captain's pay doesn't stretch to luxuries like this. My uncle's money does. He insisted on taking the lease for me when I wouldn't spend my leave in his Edinburgh house. A sore disappointment I am to Uncle Roderick, but I'm his nearest kin."

The captain pulled on a woven rope attached to a bell. Almost instantly, a thin woman in black dress and white apron and cap appeared. "Mrs. Munro," he said, "kindly take Mistress Mairi, Mrs. MacLeod, and the child to their quarters."

"As you say, Captain."

"I have business in Stornoway tomorrow," said Iain MacDonald to Mairi. "I'll leave a message for your men. Rest, and when I return, we'll talk about what you should do."

Mrs. Munro led the way down a passage that wound past countless doors till she stopped at the last one and opened it. "You'll soon be brought a meal," she said. "If you need aught, tell the lass."

The door closed. "Look at the brave fire, and a steaming kettle and teapot ready!" said Gran rapturously. "Yon great hall with all those antlers was a grue place. This is homier. And that's honest peats in the fireplace, even if that chimney wastes the good smoke."

"There's no thatch to smoke, Granny," said Eileen. She moved around the room, examining the dishes in an open cupboard, the pictures on the wall, several lamps with patterned globes that did not smell of fish oil, a settle plumped with cushions, a shelf displaying china animals.

There was a tap, and the door opened to a bright-cheeked young woman with a frilled cap. She set a big tray on a table between two armchairs. "Captain told Cook you're to sup well," she said with a lilt. She smiled at Eileen. "Cook's baking you a raspberry tart, poppet, and that crystal bowl holds *crannach*."

"What's that?" wondered Eileen.

"Toasted oatmeal and nuts mixed with honey, slathers of

whipped cream, and just a blessing of good whisky." With a bob of her head, the young woman withdrew.

At the tray in a flash, Eileen pleaded, "Granny, Granny, let's see what's under the lids!"

A mouth-watering broth thick with leeks, peas, and barley; potatoes roasted in drippings; crisp oatcakes; eggs poached in a spicy red sauce; and beside the bowl of *crannach* there were plump glazed buns studded with ginger.

Watching Eileen's eyes widen at the sumptuous repast, Mairi felt a pang at knowing that never again in her life would her little sister enjoy such food. Deciding that pride and independence could survive a few plentiful meals, Mairi began to ladle up the broth.

THE end of the day was so different from its start, beside Fearchar's bier. They had bathed in a copper tub, with scented soap. Then the three of them had put on their good dresses, Gran's the black she'd been wed in, and Mairi's—also black—her mother's bridal gown. Eileen had the heather-dyed brownish purple dress that had been Mairi's till she outgrew it.

Mairi granted Eileen's wish to go visit the twins, and turned to examine Cridhe's soundboard. As she knelt by the harp for which Fearchar had died, Mairi was seized by a tide of grief and shame.

She wasn't out of her wits, like Gran, or a child, like Eileen. How could she have gorged, reveled in being clean? She had laughed! Light-minded she was, feckless as Catriona. Fearchar, dear man. She buried her face in her arms and wept till her eyes had no more tears. Fearchar, I won't forget you. Your Rosanna will bless the fire again on our hearthstone. Cridhe will sing your songs. You won't have died for nothing, dear man.

A rap at the door brought her stumbling to her feet. It was Iain MacDonald, fresh shaved and garbed, his dark face made even browner by the white frills of his shirt.

As if he didn't note her blotched face, he stepped over to Cridhe and gazed at the old harp with unfeigned admiration. Reaching into his pocket, he brought out a small box of veined and polished stone. He smiled and said, "Out with your hands, Mistress Mairi."

She hesitated, not wanting him to see her work-roughened skin. Gently he took the clenched fists at her sides and laid them open in his palm. She trembled, as if he had bared her body. "Here," he said. "I have balm for your fingers."

Feeling as if she had just drunk deep of Gran's heather ale, Mairi scarcely felt the stinging. She yearned to bow her head to his hands, feel them warm and strong and vital beneath her lips.

This man, this stranger, had entered her heart. There would never be, her whole life long, a way to cast him out. But he was of the gentry. There could be nothing honorable between them. So there must be nothing at all.

In spite of having barely slept the night before, Mairi turned and tossed more than she rested. Perhaps the bed was too soft, the feather-stuffed pillow too plump. More likely it was the bliss that swept through her when she remembered Iain's fingers applying the ointment, his touch as healing as the balm, yet as wounding as if he had grasped her heart and held it naked in his hand.

Rare daft that was! Oh, a gentleman might lie in the heather with a girl who took his fancy. If Iain wished that, she doubted that she'd be strong enough to refuse him. But there could be nothing lasting, like the love between Gran and Fearchar.

As if Fearchar spoke to her, Mairi remembered then something he'd said. "When Cridhe sings, it's not just soundboard and strings that make the music, lass. It's that bard who brought her from Ireland centuries ago, and all those of our blood who've played her since. Something of them lives in the harp. Don't forget, ever, that you hold here not only Cridhe but the spirits of our folk."

Mairi slipped out of bed and hurried to the parlor, where she sank down by Cridhe, resting her face against the tartan, embracing the swaddled harp. The wool against her cheek felt like Fearchar's plaid, and the odor of course was his—peat smoke and heather. Mairi could almost hear him rumble, "There, lass, don't weep for me. Take care of our folk. The land will surely be ours again if even a few remain. Give them a song, and I will hear you and be glad."

I will, she promised. I will, dear man.

Catriona brought their breakfast, special bannocks dipped in egg and baked crisply golden, porridge with fresh butter, and thick slices of ham. In a ruffled white apron she sat down to have a cup of tea with them, eyes shining as she described the room she had to herself, "with a real glass window. And a little rug! Even the maids have snug lodging and plenty to eat."

"They may sleep soft and eat fat," Mairi said. "But they have no bit of land nor their own hearthstone."

"No more do you."

"I will."

Catriona shrugged graceful shoulders. "Use your wits, love. The men won't be back in time to build new houses before winter, even if they've heart for it. I talked with Morag and Kirsty this morning. They're of a mind to go to America if a way can be found."

Mairi's heart sank. Aosda had already been depleted to the fewest men who could take out a boat and work the croplands. If the others gave up, how could one household manage? She said nothing, and Catriona picked up the tray and went out.

After another cup of tea Mairi went with Gran and Eileen to see Morag, Kirsty, Sheila, and the twins. Inside the cottage, the women sat knitting by the hearth.

"Well?" demanded Morag. "What does Captain MacDonald intend for us? Has he told you?"

"He said when the men are back, he'll make some suggestions."

"He means to help us?" Kirsty asked, hazel eyes brightening. "Maybe even loan us passage across the ocean?"

"I think he will offer, but—"

Kirsty looked out the window. "If there's a way to leave, we'll go."

"So will we," said Morag. "Our exile is God's punishment."

"For what?" Mairi flashed. "For working hard, paying our rent, asking only to stay on the land our folk claimed long ago?"

"Just like your grandfather," the dark, rawboned Morag chided. "You're full of pride and those heathen songs that entice others to bootless vainglory. 'Tis a great pity yon plaided harp didn't burn with the thatch. Without its beglamouring we might have all by now been settled in good homes in America." She gave a nod of bitter satisfaction. "Andrew wouldn't listen before, but he will now."

Hot words were on Mairi's lips, but she forced them back. No use to wrangle. Turning to Gran, she said, "I'm going to walk down to the cliffs for a breath of sea air. Don't worry if I'm gone till suppertime." While Iain was gone, she hoped to find a place where a shelter could be made before winter. That would arm her against his proposals, which would surely be for emigration.

As she left the walled estate, wind, unbroken now by anything, overbore her as if a hundred invisible hands pressed against her. It was all she could do to keep her feet. Lewis winds were famous, even on this comparatively sheltered eastern coast. She wrapped her shawl tightly, bearing toward the distant glint of the waves.

A mixed day it was, clouds roiling gray, and just enough sun to transfigure the moor, rent by deep fiords cutting sharply into the land. Wind drove white spume before it. Waves lashed the serried cliffs with thundering crashes, then collapsed and eddied back, leaving pure white sand studded with glistening stones and shells. The shrill call of birds, wheeling and diving, filled the air. Beautiful it was, God's glory and the sea's, but an awesome world of wind and rocks and sea, where only powerful wings could capture a living.

Mairi looked behind and before her. Was it this way all along the coast? Surely, somewhere, there had to be a tiny haven—a foothold, however precarious. The fiords, stretching far as the eye can see, compelled her to go around, but finally, after tramping for miles, she caught in a breath and stared, giving a choked little laugh of delighted relief.

A building, or part of one! Like a tower tumbled away on one side. Why, that must be the broch! She had heard of it, though she had never been near it. Built long ago, Gran said, maybe by the Pictish folk, though no one knew for sure. The tower was situated on a small inlet, and though cliffs reared from the sea, they didn't seem as formidable as those she had skirted.

As she approached, she was seized by a kind of fear. So big it was, so fallen away and ancient. Still, the wind blew much less fiercely here, a stream danced nearby, and best of all, there was grass growing tall between the bogs and the cliffs. Not much, but it showed there was at least a scrap of soil.

Bending, she walked through the entrance that cut through the thickness of the double wall with space between. The passage was dim and smelled of moss and mold. Peering into a low entrance in the side, she saw that galleries ascended between the walls, linked by stone stairs. Mairi clambered to the top and looked slowly all around, from purple moor to cliffs to the magical sea.

479

She saw that the broch enclosed an area about forty feet across. There were tumbled stones aplenty to divide it into sections, and heather turf would make a good roof. The problem on this treeless island was to find wood for supports and rafters. Wicked it had been of Hugh Sinclair to burn the treasured roof timbers!

But these walls were here—wonderful strong walls. Gratefully Mairi pressed her face against the ancient stones.

Fearchar, we have a place! She could almost hear him laughing as she hurried down the stairs. Feet light with joy, she ran till she was breathless, then ran some more to tell her good news.

Twilight thickened on the moor ahead of her, concentrated into a shape. At first she was afraid, but then the vague shadow became horse and rider, and Iain's voice reached her, half laughing, half exasperated. "Mistress Mairi, what are you doing out here so late? They said you'd gone to walk by the sea, and I feared you'd slipped from the cliffs."

He reined his big bay horse to a stop, and she looked up with such triumph that she felt as if her face must shine with it. "I've found a place where we can stay!"

"You've what?"

She explained, ending happily, "It only needs a roof, and we'll be snug for winter!"

Even in the dimness she could see he didn't approve. "I hope the others have better sense than you, girl."

"It's the only place I found along the coast—"

"There are other coasts more hospitable than this one."

"This one is ours."

He stifled something profane. "Put your foot on mine and get up behind me. I want my dinner, even if you do not."

"No one asked you to miss it."

He fairly swung her in place behind him. "You'll have to hold on to me," he said, and laughter was back in his voice.

Strange it was and wonderful to be pressed against him, face buried against his back, hearing and feeling the deep, steady beat of his heart. Her own heart pounded till she was sure he felt it.

"Thank you, sir, for coming after me."

"I came solely because I couldn't relish my dinner while imagining you smashed somewhere on the rocks."

"I grew up near the sea. I'm careful on the cliffs."

"Then it must be the only place you are."

She didn't want to argue, not while it was so sweet to be closer to him than she would ever be again. Closing her eyes to savor the delight, she asked, "Did you leave word in Stornoway?"

"I did, at the curers. Your men should come along tomorrow."

"Fearchar's death will be cruel hearing for them all," she said. "Especially for Tam, my brother. He's scarce twelve. But with Calum and my cousins gone, he was needed to make up the crew."

"So you have no man at home?"

"Calum should be back in a year."

"You could starve long before that."

"That's not your worry, sir."

His rough laughter vibrated through her. "A poor tyke you must think me if you believe I can leave you in this condition."

"Sir, there be folk in our condition all through the islands."

"True. But when three or four families try to exist where only one can scrape a living, it's clear some must go. Thousands have left over the years because they saw the hopelessness of staying."

"I say good luck to them, and God's blessing. They can go. All of them. But I will not. I'll bide on the island. I will be here, Iain MacDonald, when the lairds are gone, and you, too."

To her surprise, he howled with laughter. Then he raised her hands and stroked the fingers to the tips. "What? No claws? I'd have sworn I had a cat behind me. No more of this, Mistress Mairi. There's the lights from the lodge. We'll soon be at our dinners."

Regret surged over her. Why hadn't she kept quiet and stored up every moment of this ride? Pressing her cheek close to him, she closed her eyes again and didn't stir till he reined in the horse.

# 3

THE men of Aosda trudged in next evening, carrying their nets. Tam's eyes were swollen in his thin, narrow face, and he didn't tug free of Mairi when she threw her arms around him.

"I—I wasn't there when Fearchar needed me," he muttered. "Och, Mairi! I didn't get to say good-bye—" His voice broke off.

"You can tell him good-bye," she comforted. "He'll hear you,

Tam. I know he will. He was proud of you taking a man's part with the fishing."

"We caught a brave lot of herring," rumbled Andrew Nicolson. His brawny shoulders bowed, as if too much had been heaped on them, and his very largeness made him seem all the more lost and vulnerable. His cousin, Fearchar, had been so much older that Andrew had respected him as head of the family, relied on his judgment. "Ever since we heard, my head's been fair spinnin'. Fearchar dead, the houses burned—it's too much to take in."

Adam MacNeill, Kirsty's husband, high-strung and impatient, gave a harsh laugh. "Don't strain yourself, lad. It'll still be true when you get used to it. That bloody Hugh Sinclair! Servin' writs on our women and an old man whilst we were away!"

Barry Nicolson crimsoned. Big and deliberate like his father, Andrew, he was slow to wrath, but fiery when aroused. He knotted his fist. "Aye, and Hugh Sinclair's thatch can burn, too!"

"I'll help!" cried Tam, green eyes blazing.

Mairi caught his shoulder and covered Barry's fist with her hand. "The factor only did as he was bid," she reminded them. "Sheila and the rest of us need you here, not on the end of a rope."

"Och, lass," Barry groaned. "What can we do, then?"

"I've come to talk about that," said a voice from the open door of the cottage Sheila, Morag, and Kirsty were using. Tall as the Nicolson men, the captain wasn't dwarfed by their bulk, but simply made them look ungainly. An impression heightened by the contrast of his well-cut gray coat, trousers, and handsome boots to their thick jerseys, homespun pants, and homemade footwear.

As they stared at him, abashed and suspicious, the captain gave his name and shook hands all around. "I won't intrude long," said Iain. "You have much to talk about. But I have a proposal you should hear. The eviction was heartless but quite legal. You cannot return to your crofts. Leaving your homeland is a sad thing, but it offers chances undreamed of here. I'll pay your way wherever you choose to go. There's a ship in Stornoway right now that sails for America next week, but if you prefer Canada—"

"Do you mean it, sir? All of us?" Adam burst out.

"All who wish to go."

Excited murmuring. Morag gripped Andrew's arm; Kirsty and

Adam embraced each other, with the twins in between them squealing delight at their parents' joy.

No doubt what they would do. Mairi couldn't blame them, but her heart contracted with pain as Catriona clapped her hands. "I don't have to think about it, Captain. I'm for America, thank you!"

"There can only be one answer, to be sure!" Morag almost shook her bemused husband. "Thank the captain, man."

As Iain's gaze swung to her, Mairi read pity in it. That turned her pain into cold resolve. Even if they all left, she would stay, she and Gran. Fearchar had entrusted her with the harp. It belonged on the island with folk who somehow managed to hold on.

"Captain MacDonald is generous," she said, cheeks burning, though she controlled her voice. "I won't beg you to stay. But before you all accept his offer, I want to tell you what I've found."

"Let me know when you've considered," Iain said, and went out.

Eyes blurred with tears, Mairi looked from face to face of these people who had been her world, who had shared the hearth and songs her whole life long. She told them about the broch.

Adam said regretfully, "Mairi, lass, were it only us, Kirsty and I might stay, but we don't want these young ones to live as we have, at the laird's whim, with never a sure footing. We will go."

Mairi bowed her head. Tam came to her and gave her a hug. "I'll stay, Mairi, and take care of you and Gran and Eileen. The lairds don't own the sea yet, or the herring in it."

Andrew brooded. At last, he said apologetically, "You'll not take it ill, Mairi, if we think the night on it?"

"Father," Catriona entreated, "you'll never say I can't go!"

He gave her thick braid a teasing fillip. "Whisht, lassie! You can travel with Adam and Kirsty. Decide for yourself."

Throwing her arms around him and even including her dour mother, Catriona gave them each a kiss. "Och! Then I'm good as away! And when Calum comes—"

"Don't make sure he will," Mairi warned. "Calum never meant to live anywhere but in Aosda."

"Well, now he can't, and if he wants me, he'll have to follow." Catriona's eyes flashed. "If he stays, I'll find a man over there."

"Lassies, don't wrangle," commanded Andrew. "Is that broth I smell? We're nigh famished after our tramp."

"There's broth." Sheila smiled. "There's sausage and currant scones, and I was just making bannocks."

"I'll bring Gran from her nap," said Mairi. For a moment she gave Catriona a hard stare before, in a breath, each said, "I'm sorry, love." They went into each other's arms and set off to the lodge together.

"Ask Mrs. Fraser, the cook, if we can't all eat in the cottage tonight," Mairi said.

"Bring the harp," urged her cousin. "Oh, Mairi, I will miss it! I'll miss you."

But you'll go. Mairi forced away the spurt of bitterness. "I'll miss you. But there'll be songs there. Learn them, Caty."

"It won't be the same."

Catriona turned to the kitchen, while Mairi went down the hall. Rounding a corner, she almost bumped into Iain. Each stepped back. His eyes searched her face. "Have they decided?"

"Adam and Kirsty want to leave." A lump swelled in Mairi's throat. "So does Catriona. Tam will stay. The others want to think."

He hesitated. "Forgive me, Mistress Mairi, but I hope you won't try to persuade them to stay against their better judgment."

"I know 'tis their lives they're choosing. I'll say naught."

He smiled a little. "Fair enough. But I could wish *they'd* persuade *you*. Why persist in this folly?"

"Can't you see?" she cried. "Folk of mine have lived on this island from the dawn of time. I will not abandon it to lairds who buy with money what belongs to the people."

"Good Lord, girl, what a soldier you'd have made!"

She shook her head. "I'd only have fought defending my home. I could never go into other lands and kill folk I'd no quarrel with." His face tightened, and she flushed. "I meant no slap at you, but that seems to be what soldiers do."

He shrugged. "Your views are disconcerting, lass, but let's cry truce. Are you taking your grandmother to see the men?"

"Aye. We'll sup together and have some songs."

"I haven't heard you play. Would you allow me to trade tunes on my Northumbrian bagpipe for some of yours?"

"Why," she said, "we'll have a ceilidh! Do come, and bring Jamie, too."

He stepped out of her way with a small bow. Odd of gentry to bow to the likes of her, but the bemused expression on his face said that he didn't mock her.

As if by common consent not to mar this reunion, no one talked of the captain's offer. Gran, with that peculiarly divided awareness of hers, welcomed the returned fishermen, while accepting that her Michael must have extended his trip. Iain and Jamie appeared with a jug of whisky and a flagon of wine. Iain filled a beautiful crystal goblet and carried it to Mairi, where she was tuning Cridhe.

"I think you'll like this." He handed her the wine, which sparkled like liquid sunshine, and poured some for himself.

She took a sip. It was delicious, with an edge of velvet fire that curved through her, so that she wondered if it came from wine or his deep gray eyes. Almost desperately she said, "Will you play first, sir?"

Under his arm he tucked the bag, covered with the MacDonald tartan—green, black, and purple, crossed with thin lines of white and red. Then he worked the bellows under his right arm, which filled the bag through a wind pipe that lay across his chest, moving the drone slides to make them harmonize with the flutelike part, which the piper fingered. When he was satisfied with the sound, Iain played the old clan melody, "The MacLeod Salute."

Applause filled the cottage. "You're a brave piper, sir," cried Andrew, lifting his cup. "I ne'er heard it played better."

"I love the pipes," said Iain, handing them to Tam, who had come close, to gaze longingly at the silver-and-ivory-embellished instrument. "But you know what they say—to make a real piper takes seven years' training." Tam looked stricken at that, but Iain added, "If you'll come over tomorrow, lad, I'll give you a lesson."

Next Iain played a march, then "The Red-Speckled Bull," singing the words in a deep, resonant voice. Now Cridhe was eager to sing. Mairi played the islands' best-loved milking song and sang of summer at the shielings. She played Fearchar's love lilt for Gran, his tune of prideful joy on the birth of Mairi's father.

Rising briskly, Gran said, "Andrew, lad, if you'll make some mouth music, I'll dance a fling for my part at this ceilidh. Captain MacDonald, will you stand up with me?"

He swept a low bow. "Honored, Mrs. MacLeod."

Andrew had a rare gift with the mouth music, developed to accompany dancers when there was no pipe, fiddle, or harp. Everyone clapped the rhythm as the two danced—Gran with skirts gathered, the captain with toes pointed in a way that showed him no stranger to flings. They stopped with a flourish amid great applause. Then the informal party continued.

It was late when Mairi noticed that Gran had dozed off with her head on Sheila's shoulder. Iain saw it, too, and got to his feet. "I've never been to a better ceilidh," he said. Perhaps, being gentry, he hadn't been to any. He motioned back Barry, lightly lifted Gran, and carried her out. Mairi followed with a sleepy Eileen and Tam.

The captain put Gran down on the big, postered bed, told Tam and Eileen good night, and turned in the door. "You have a rare gift with the harp, Mistress Mairi."

His admiration made her glow. "You're grand yourself, sir."

"You know what they say about pipers." In the lamplight his eyes were very dark, but a smile softened the firm line of his mouth. "The time comes when they demand their pay."

Something leaped between them, like those dancing fires that sometimes darted over the moor at night. "Indeed, sir, we all are in your debt and must remain so, for what could we give you?"

He took a step forward. She stood transfixed, trembling within. There was a yearning for his touch. His hand raised, brushed her cheek, but then he caught in his breath, swung violently away.

"I'm paid with your song. Sleep well, Mistress Mairi."

The door closed after him, but Mairi knew, shuddering as if released from the grasp of towering, crashing waves, that if he had taken her hand and led her down the hall, she would have gone with him, even though it was wrong and could only bring her heartbreak.

That night, when Mairi roused between fitful dreams, she wondered if Iain, in some chamber above, was restless, too; if he thought of her. Not likely. He must know many fascinating ladies who belonged in his world. Give him credit, at least. How many gentlemen would have interfered at the burning? How many would give shelter and comfort to evicted folk? How many could come to a crofter ceilidh and fit right in? No, Iain wasn't like most of his class, but there could be nothing honest between them.

Well, yes, there was. The feeling she had was honest, true as blood and breath. No matter what the minister said, she couldn't believe anything so natural and inevitable was a sin. Flame coursed through her, sweet and wild, reckless.

Long before dawning, Mairi knew she couldn't stay around the lodge that day while the fateful decision was being made. She must not plead or argue. Those who stayed must truly want to, for harder times lay ahead. She would go fetch the hearthstone. More than walls or roof or furnishings, that made a home.

As soon as she could see without lighting a lamp, she woke Eileen to whisper that she was going over the moor. Selecting their broadest creel, for the stone, though flat, was two feet across, Mairi dropped in several bannocks. It was so early that no one was about. Mists still brooded on the purple-brown moor as she followed tracks made by the carts sent to Aosda.

At first it was a hushed world—no hum of bees or hover of butterflies—but as she passed a brook, rays of diffused light beamed through rose-and-gold clouds. The moor suddenly glowed, every loch and pool luminous, bees pillaging heather, which gave out a sweet odor that permeated the senses like slow nectar.

Surely nowhere else in all the world was the air like wine or the land so magical, transmuted by every shift of light, responding to sun like a woman to a lover. Now how would you know about that? Mairi derided herself with a chuckle.

She started as a laughing voice hailed her. "Mistress Mairi! Tell me where you're going with that creel so I can decide whether we need horses or a wagon."

Blushing as if Iain had read her thoughts, she decided it would do him good to be mystified. "I'm fetching our home."

"What?" Dark eyebrows rose to the fall of black hair that curved over his forehead. "Lass, not even you would try to carry those tumbled stones across the island."

"The walls aren't our home."

"What is your home, then?"

"It'll fit in my creel."

He shook his head, smiling. "This sounds like a riddle." The harsh planes of his face softened to boyishness. "If you won't tell me, I'll have to march along and see."

"You won't be at the lodge if Tam comes about the bagpipes."

"I told Jamie to show the lad the first things, and I'll give him a lesson tonight if he doesn't see pipes as a thing of the devil."

"He was mightily taken with them." And you.

"I've heard there aren't many pipers on Lewis."

"That may be so. I've only heard them a few times. Cridhe is the only harp I know of. Of course, if the ministers get their way, we'll have no music at all."

"Music has a way of outlasting laws." Iain laughed softly. "Don't look so sad, Mistress Mairi. Cridhe may sing alone now, but in your lifetime I'll wager you see the harp come back to the islands."

"I pray that may be so, Captain. There are songs that don't sound right except from the harp."

"And some need the bagpipe."

They laughed together. That was a kind of music, the lilt of her laughter sparkling against the deep vibrance of his. He lifted the creel from her, so that the basket hung against his back.

"Och, sir!" She was horrified. He was not made for bearing such a workaday burden. "Give it back, do! I'm used to it."

He shook his head. "A girl like you should walk light and free, dance a few turns just from being young and alive."

"I walk light with the creel and can knit at the same time."

"Sing, too, I daresay!"

"Of course. There's always singing. There's songs for the quern and loom, and even for fulling the cloth."

"Would you sing me some of the work songs, Mistress Mairi?"

As she sang, Iain listened till he caught the melody, and then whistled, weaving his notes around her voice.

Then as she caught her first glimpse of Aosda a rush of grief flooded through her—the roofless houses, the trampled gardens, and most of all, Fearchar's loss. Her eyes filled with bitter tears.

"What have you come for, lass?" Iain's voice was strange. "What can be left?"

She answered by going through the entrance, with its charred remnant of a door. Better not look at the blackened bits of box beds. She knelt by the stone in the center of the main room.

Now that it was time to move the stone the deed seemed close to sacrilegious. It seemed an undertaking that required a ceremony. Closing her eyes, she stretched out her hand and thanked the

Sacred Three—Mary, Christ, and Saint Brigid—for blessing the hearth these many years. "Come with the stone," she prayed. "To save, to shield, surround our hearth, each and every night. Amen."

Feeling that the guardians gave consent, Mairi opened her eyes and caught a breath of dismay. Why hadn't she remembered to bring a tool for prying the stone from the hard-packed floor?

"So it's the stone," Iain said. He produced a stout clasp knife. "Let's see what this will do." He began to dig around the rock.

It was to Mairi both a brief and endless time till Iain tested the stone and it moved. A few minutes more and he lifted it.

She put the half-burned peats from the hearth into the creel with it. Before she could bend to slip it onto her back, Iain took it and went ahead. As she stepped outside what had been her dwelling, a current of warmth flowed with her. She knew she was taking with her all that had made a home.

THAT night they gathered again at the cottage with Iain and Jamie. After glancing uneasily around, Andrew cleared his throat.

"Mairi, lass, we've chased it up and down, whether to stay or go. Barry and I went to the broch today. If we find roof timbers, we could last the winter there, but then what? Do you believe that we'll have proper crofts again? Where we can make a living, not just starve along?"

"Andrew! Only God could promise that!"

"I'm not askin' for a promise. I just want to make sure you've thought past this one winter. You've much of Fearchar in you, lass. I always trusted him. All you need say is what you believe."

She searched her heart. "We can build soil on the rocks," she said. "For the cows, we can cut grass wherever we find it. We have a lot of spun wool and can weave it to trade for what we need. Next summer we can build houses. I believe, sure as I live, that if we can hold on, we'll have our land again."

Andrew moved his head in affirmation. "Then we will bide."

"Fools!" burst out Morag. "Why, *why,* hang on by our fingernails when the same work would get us farms in America—real farms, with plenty of land—that we'd own free of landlords?"

"You may go, and you will, woman," thundered Andrew. "But if you stay, let's hear no more of your sour carping!"

"I'll have my say first." Hands on gaunt hips, Morag glared from her husband to her son Barry. "I knew last night that the harp 'tranced you. You, too, Sheila, that should know better for the sake of the bairn you carry! It's not for any sensible reason that you trust your fate to this green lassie! 'Tis all for a song. . . ."

"Mother," began Barry.

Slumping to her chair, she buried her face in her hands. Andrew gathered her to his broad chest. "It'll work out. You'll see."

"I'll carry things when your back hurts, Mother," Sheila promised, and Barry said, "I'll make a fine wicker chair, and you'll sit in our new house like a queen." Catriona patted her mother's hand.

Morag wiped her eyes. "I must have greatly sinned to be condemned to the rocks, but I will bear it, since it's God's will."

"Captain, dear," said Gran. "Be that a jug of *uisge-beatha* you set in the corner when you came in?"

"Let's try it and see." Rising, he got the jug and filled cups and glasses before lifting his own. "Here's to those who stay and those who go! May they flourish both!"

He downed his drink, while Mairi sipped at hers. As she looked at her kinfolk who had chosen to stay, she had to confront the truth. It was she who had swayed them, she who would have to lead, hearten, and plan. Along with relieved joy that they were staying came a heavy responsibility.

Could she take Fearchar's place in grimmer times than he had ever known? If only he were here! Then, as if he spoke to her, she knew he was. He was in the harp; he was in the songs.

Reassured, she looked up, met Iain's watchful eyes. Smiling, head high, she raised her glass to him—and to the future, even though it would have to be lived through without him.

THE next days flew in readying Catriona and the MacNeills for their journey. Gran finished a warm shawl for Catriona. Mairi had no treasure to give her but her red flannel underskirt and tucked into it a small bag of dried heather blooms. "So you won't forget the moor," she said, blinking back tears as they embraced and clung in the realization they probably would never meet again.

On their last night they shared a festive meal in the cottage and held a farewell ceilidh. Mairi brought the harp, Gran a jug of heather ale, and Iain came with bagpipes, whisky, and sparkling wine.

It was very late when Mairi played "Loch Lomond," about how the spirit of one dying in a foreign land returns to the homeland by the low road—an underground path—and traveling faster than the living, reaches the beloved loch before the surviving friend. Did the low road stretch over the ocean? There were tears in most eyes.

Farewells were said in the dim light of morning. Barry was driving the wagon, piled high with belongings. Adam handed the twins to Kirsty and climbed up himself, giving Catriona a hand.

Mairi stood back with the others to watch till the wagon was out of sight. With them vanished the safe, familiar life. One arm around Eileen and Tam, and the other around Gran, she went into the cottage with all that were left of her folk. Iain had stayed away, feeling this was a private time.

"My only daughter!" Morag wailed against Andrew's shoulder.

Awkwardly he patted her back. "For sure, lass, Sheila's our daughter. When Lucas and Paul come back, they'll marry, too. We'll have a host of daughters! You have all your children living. Few women do. And I hand over any coin I earn and put up with your clatterin'."

"What we need to do," said Mairi, "is get ready for winter."

"Have you found our roof timbers, *Ceann-cinnidh*?" Morag mocked Mairi by calling her Head of the Clan.

"The captain's giving us timbers meant for a stable roof," said Andrew. "And fixed it with Sinclair for us to harvest our crops."

"What's gentry making such a fuss over crofters for?" demanded Morag, with a suspicious glance at Mairi.

"He's a good man before he's gentry," retorted Andrew.

Cheeks hot, Mairi ignored Morag's stare. "I think we'd best tell the captain we're ready to go to the broch."

"Good." Iain spoke from the open door. "The wagon's loaded with timbers. All the men at the lodge want to lend a hand."

Tears prickled Mairi's eyes. "That's mightily kind of them. But Captain, will you have to join your regiment while we're gone?"

"I must do that soon." His tone was so regretful she felt a stab of pain to know these blessed days were ending. "But Jamie and I are working, too. It's been a long time since I helped thatch." As she gazed at him in wonder he smiled. "Will you come with us, Mistress

Mairi? There's food and bedding in the wagon. We'll stay till we're finished so as not to lose hours of going back and forth."

"I make better bannocks than any of these lassies," Gran boasted. "So I'll come along. Eileen, you can make yourself useful."

Mairi hurried to the lodge for things she, Gran, and Eileen would need. Iain overtook her. "Let me put the harp in the wagon," he urged. "I'll cover it with oilskins. If it rains, it can stay dry."

"Can we take the hearthstone now?"

He gave her a whimsical look. "Won't we need it for cooking and, even more, to sit around?"

"You'll bring your bagpipes?"

"Certainly." He took the harp, Jamie the stone, and they went out, while Mairi hastened to throw necessaries in the creel.

This very day they'd start their new roof! With Iain helping. If he helped set the hearthstone and secured the roof, the place would be filled with him even when he was gone. She would be able to picture him there till he came back.

*Would* he come back? Soldiers died, not only from enemy fire but from diseases of camp and barracks. And even if he came back, what could there be between them?

If I can see him, I'll be grateful, she vowed. If we can talk and be together sometimes, I won't ask for more. I will say I was lucky. Iain took the creel from her, wedging it in the wagon, and as his hands brushed hers she knew she lied. It wouldn't be enough.

THE Aosda men set off across the moor with the lodge workers, but there was a gentle bay mare for Mairi, with Eileen riding pillion and Gran mounted behind Iain. By now it was bright morning. Skylarks had been caroling for hours; golden plovers and lapwings caroused above the moor. The party rode near enough to the sea to watch gulls and terns soaring. That water, gleaming emerald and molten silver, diademed with crystalline froth, would carry away Adam, Kirsty, the playful twins—and Catriona.

Unable to believe she'd never again see Catriona, her companion from the cradle, Mairi felt a great lump in her throat. God bless them all, she prayed. Keep them safe, bring them to a good place.

"Look, love," she said to Eileen. "See that shape that comes to a point—there, against the bay? That's the broch."

Peering around Mairi's shoulder at the crumbling tower, Eileen squeezed her mightily. "Oh, Mairi, it's like a castle!"

The wagon rumbled up behind them, and the men bringing the cattle and sheep followed close. Before Mairi could dismount, Iain sprang down from Chieftain, set Gran on the turf, and swung down Eileen. Almost as easily but much more slowly he lifted Mairi from the saddle. At his touch a tremulous thrill ran through her.

He stared at the broch, then turned toward her. "Mairi!" It was the first time he'd used her name by itself. "This is madness. Come back to the lodge. I'll work out something for you to shelter there."

Mairi gazed along the bay, around the surrounding moors, and back to the walls, drawing courage from each tuft of grass. "We must make our own land," she said, meeting Iain's troubled eyes. "Please, Captain, first of all, let's place the hearthstone."

## 4

THOUGH the lodge men and those of Aosda had never worked together, the work went smoothly. The space was divided into three parts—one for each household—all opening onto a big main hearth room, with a passage between living quarters connecting to the byre. Tam and Jamie raised walls for barn and byre. Iain and the men from the lodge set up the timbers. Andrew and Ewan Fraser, the cook's husband, expertly cut divots from heathery turf for thatching, and Eileen and Mairi cut creel after creel of heather. As she piled her loads by the wall, Mairi always stole a glance at Iain, full of pride that he knew how to peg the timbers.

It was nearly dark when the company gathered to enjoy crispy golden-brown potato scones, fish stew thickened with barley, and *crannach,* the whipped-cream-and-toasted-oatmeal treat.

"A fine start," said Iain. "At this rate, we should finish in three or four days." His eyes touched Mairi's.

And then you'll go? Mairi thought with a pang. As if answering her unspoken question, he said, "I sail Monday from Stornoway."

"No fear, Captain." Ewan grinned. "We'll finish Saturday for sure. And now, sir, could we hear harp and bagpipe together?"

Iain rose to get his pipes. Mairi took the plaid from Cridhe. As the peats on the hearthstone winked and smoldered, she and Iain joined in melody after melody, notes slipping in and out. It was a musical conversation, a language between them.

Something to remember with thankful joy every time she touched the strings. Always now, she'd hear Iain's pipes, luring her into wild flourishes, as if they improvised a dance, a dance she'd never want to do with any other man. She'd rather have had these days with him than a lifetime with someone else.

FRIDAY afternoon the dwelling was finished. Flagstones paved the floor. Box beds formed part of the wall between each household, and over heather mattresses were linen sheets, blankets, and coverlets, woven on looms now reassembled in the hearth room.

"You made this?" Iain asked Mairi, admiring the rose-purple coverlet that dressed the nook Mairi would share with Eileen.

"Of course I did. We learn our weaving early, sir."

"Could you make me a coverlet like this? It would cheer my tent and keep me warm when campaigning starts against the northern hill tribes in India and Afghanistan."

Mairi didn't want to think about that, but she could gift this man she loved. What a comfort it would be to know he slept warm in wool she had carded, spun, dyed, waulked, and woven. She pulled it off the bed and folded it. "Take it with you," she said.

"You'll need it," he protested.

"I've others in the chest." Mairi smiled, pressing the coverlet into his arms. "Take it, Captain! You've done so much for us. It would be my pleasure to think of it keeping you warm."

A swift smile brought dancing lights to his gray eyes. "When I draw it over me at night, it'll bring me to your fire, your music."

"I'll remember your pipes," she said. The sweet liquid fire that his closeness always sent through her throbbed now in her veins with special poignancy. "Will you come back to the island, sir?"

"I've already leased the lodge for next spring, though I can't be sure my duties will permit me to come."

Oh, if he were coming back, that would speed the winter! She wouldn't allow herself to think beyond that.

"Supper's ready," called Gran, and they went into the hearth room. There was crab stew and pease porridge, Gran's tasty bannocks and crowdie. Everyone helped themselves.

"Real glass!" Gran laughed as she sat down and looked out a window at the blue twilight. "Isn't it a marvel?"

The glass, Iain's gift, was a wonderful improvement on the oiled skins of the Aosda crofts, and these panes could be used, like the good lumber and timbers, when permanent houses were made. Glancing around, Mairi delighted in how comfortable and home-like their shelter was. And in the barn, the potato corner was ready, the winnowing floor clayed. Thank goodness they'd have barley and oats from Aosda to thresh there.

There was music late that night, with stories and riddles and rhyming contests. Mairi stored up Iain's every word, every smile, the proud set of his head, the grace of his movements. Most of all, as they played together, she tried to absorb the pipe's melodies so she would hear them when she played those tunes alone.

IAIN and the lodge workers were off at dawning. Mairi's heart was too full for saying much. After shaking hands with the men, including Tam, bowing to Morag and Sheila, and kissing Gran and Eileen, Iain came to Mairi. Taking both her hands, he held them between his long tanned ones, so warm, so vital that she felt as if they held her life. "Thank you for the covering, Mairi. Thank you for your music and your hearth."

"They"—her voice failed—"they'll always be here for you."

Bending his head to her hands, he kissed them. His eyes traced her face, lingering; then he gazed full into her eyes. "Oh, sweet Mairi!" he breathed. Releasing her abruptly, he swung into Chieftain's saddle. At the crest of a slope he turned to wave, and was gone.

As WHEN Catriona and the MacNeills departed, Mairi found her best solace in work. There was much of it, the most pressing to return to Aosda for harvest, for it was now early September.

Soon the oats and barley, transported in the wagon Iain had lent them, filled half the barn. Because they were almost out of grain, the men threshed some, spreading loosened sheaves on the clayed floor and beating them with a flail. By Saint Michael's Day the grain was ready for the quern, or grinding stone.

With the harvest safely in, the men and Tam fished from rocks along the shore. Some of the fish were stuck on wooden hooks for

495

drying in the hearth room, and others were salted down in barrels. Mairi and Eileen were out every possible moment gathering seaweed and sand to create soil for lazybeds, small plots among the rocks that stretched toward the sea from the broch. As a change from this, they wandered the moor with sickles, seeking out tussocks of grass to cut and dry for hay.

The peat cuttings were miles away, and it was worlds easier to bring them home by wagon instead of in creels on the back. As she helped stack peats outside the entrance, Mairi thought of Iain with worshipful gratitude. And now his wagon and team had one more expedition to make, to fetch the potatoes. When these were piled in the bin near the salt barrels, it was All Souls' Day, the eve of the ancient festival marking the change from summer to winter.

This was a time for divination, and Mairi was tempted to set up two straws in the ashes. But now that Iain was beyond her reach, she felt it wrong to seek an answer. Perhaps she didn't want to be warned that her love was hopeless, though she knew that all too well. In the end, as Gran blessed the hearth that night, Mairi prayed that Iain slept safe in her coverlet, and that he would return.

Tam went with Andrew and Barry to return the wagon. About sundown, as Mairi and Morag finished with the milking, Mairi heard a faint, distant sound. "Can that be a pipe?" she wondered.

Morag shielded her eyes. "It sounds more like a pig with its tail caught in a crack. Look, isn't that our lads long-legging over the moor? But what's on their backs?"

"Let's go see!" Eileen bounded off, like a blue hare. The women put the milk cogs on the bench and hurried out.

Tam piped zestfully, striking many a sour note, so that Morag muttered, "Lord save us, where did the child get that?" before her tone brightened. "Och, can that be a spinning wheel astraddle Andrew's shoulders? And another on Barry?"

Spinning wheels they were, and in wicker cages the men carried four red hens. In Andrew's creel was a carved stone cross for Fearchar, engraved with the dates of his birth and death. Barry's creel held a jug of whisky for Gran, and tins of tea and sweeties.

"It's all from the captain!" Tam cried. "He had the pipes sent from the mainland, from Inverness!"

"Ewan Fraser just brought the spinning wheels from Stornoway, where the captain had them made," Andrew said. "I said we could not take them, but Ewan had his orders."

"There's a note," Barry said, handing it to Mairi.

Iain's bold, slashing scrawl fitted him:

> Mistress Mairi,
>
> To ease my guilt at bearing away the covering that took you so much time and work, I'm sending something to speed your labor. The most peace I've had in my life was at your hearth. Bless you.

His writing, words he had penned to her! Blinded by happy tears, Mairi carefully refolded the paper. In all the world there was no one like him. But as Tam gave a great screech of the pipes, she winced and thought it would be only fair if Iain were here to share the racket of Tam's apprenticeship.

WHEN they reached home, Gran was brewing a pungent tea for Sheila, while Morag walked with her. She had been in labor since midday, and her fair skin was dewed with sweat. Her pains grew stronger and closer together, and she soon wanted to lie down.

Before it was over, Barry was in such a state that Andrew had to take him outside for a calming walk. Mairi took turns at giving the panting young woman hands to grip. After long hours of deepening travail, there was a protesting howl. Gran said to Sheila, "You've a fine little lass, girl. With gold hair like yours."

Gran tied the cord with two bands of linen, then washed the baby. Wrapped in a soft towel, the child was placed in Sheila's arms. "Now, dear," said Gran, eyes moist, "you can show Barry what you've done this day!"

BECOMING as much a center of the household as the hearth, the cradle during the day stood in the hearth room, where the baby, Seana Catriona, was lulled by the hum of the spinning wheels. At night she was soothed by the harp and Tam's efforts on the pipes.

When it wasn't raining or too windy, Mairi spent part of most days carrying up seaweed for the lazybeds. Tam and Eileen wandered the shore, gathering seaweed and digging silverweed roots, nutritious foods used to make the potatoes last longer.

One morning, when the baby was a few weeks old, Mairi was fetching water from the burn when the wind brought her the snatch of a cry. The men had gone fishing, and Eileen and Tam had been out since early morning, nothing unusual for them.

A small figure was pelting up from the sea. That was Eileen's yellow shawl. For her to be alone, running like that, something must have happened to Tam. Had he fallen from the rocks? Gripped with dread, Mairi caught up her skirts and ran to her sister.

"Oh, Mairi, they've stolen Tam!" Eileen gasped.

Not believing her ears, Mairi froze. "Who?" She caught Eileen's shoulders. "Who stole Tam?"

"A big ship!" Eileen wept. "We were gathering from the rocks when we saw the ship. They put a little boat over the side, and four men rowed to shore. They—they asked Tam how he'd like to go see the world. When he said he wouldn't, they took him anyway."

Holding her young sister, Mairi forced her numbed brain to function. Andrew and Barry wouldn't be home till late. If anything was done, she would have to do it. "Do you know the ship's name?"

"*The Cormorant.*"

"Did they say anything about where they were going?"

"The biggest one was laughing about how when they got to Stornoway, the captain would give them extra money for whisky, since he'd turn a neat penny selling Tam for a cabin boy."

Selling Tam! Mairi felt the hair on her nape bristle. The ship would be in Stornoway long before she could get there, but it might be several days in port taking on cargo or replenishing supplies.

Whirling with Eileen, she ran for the broch. "Put some food in a basket for me, darling. I'll get Tam back someway!"

SHE ran till her side ached, walked till she had her breath. All the time her mind worked furiously. It seemed to Mairi that her best hope lay in pleading with the captain and offering the only valuables they had. Sheila had sent silver coins given Seana by the Frasers at her christening; Morag produced a hoarded shilling. Gran gave up the silver brooch Fearchar had given her when they were courting. And into the creel had gone weaving ready for sewing, yards of warm crotal-dyed rust brown and a most beautiful length of misty blue.

498

Please let it be enough, Mairi prayed. She also prayed one of the men at the lodge could go with her. But when she arrived, the men were all out, and Mrs. Fraser took it on herself to lend her a horse.

It was just twilight when Mairi rode down the cobbled streets of Stornoway, the only town in all the Western Isles. She made straight for the harbor, where a dozen ships dwarfed smaller craft. Mairi found a safe place to tether the mare in an empty shed and hid the creel under some old nets in a corner. If entreaties would free Tam, she wasn't going to offer their treasures.

Drawing a long breath, thinking of Iain for courage, she walked along the quay, peering to make out the names on the ships. Lanterns glowed yellow from most of the vessels, and on the next-to-last ship she made out in bold black letters THE CORMORANT.

Heart pounding, she scanned bow to stern, though she realized Tam would be locked in the hold most likely. Poor lad, how frightened he must be! I'll have you off there, laddie, or die trying.

But how? No sounds came from the ship. The crew must be ashore. Was the captain? Cupping her hands, she shouted, "*Cormorant!* I need the captain! I have to see the captain."

A guffaw sounded over the water. "Ye'll find the auld devil, Cap'n Tarbert, in that first tavern open to the quay."

Mairi turned and sped toward the ramshackle huddle of taverns and sailors' boardinghouses. Gulping in a deep breath, she opened the door to the first tavern. Smoky light flickered at the draft, smearing faces with patches of yellow and darkness. A fiddler perched on a high stool in one corner. A fat, balding man moved among the tables, filling the roisterers' cups from a jug.

"Look what's here, lads!" The man nearest her, red-bearded, with a patch over one eye, caught at her skirt. "Fresh from the country, I'm bound! Sit here on my knee, lovey."

Mairi wrested away from him, dodged other hands. "Please, sir," she gasped to the fat man. "Is Captain Tarbert here?"

A heavy-bodied man with graying hair and tangled beard squinted up at her from his table. "I'm Cap'n Tarbert. Now who would you be, my pretty?"

"I have to talk to you, sir."

He weighted an arm around her hips. "What's your price, lass?"

Shivering with loathing and fear, she struggled to keep her voice

499

even. "That's my brother you have on your ship. I want him back. You stole him! You ought to be in jail!"

He burst out laughing. "Can you put me there?" he taunted.

The biggest man she'd ever seen rose up from his seat. Young and fair-haired, he shone with the brightness of a Viking prince.

"I can snap your neck and throw you to the fishes, Tarbert," he drawled in a voice of soft thunder. "And that I'll do with a right good will unless this minute you send for the lass's brother."

The fiddling ceased. "To me, lads!" shouted Tarbert, jumping up. Eight or nine men pushed their way to him, some drawing knives, others snatching up bottles or stools. "Now how loud do you crow, my rooster?" Tarbert grinned.

"I've no quarrel with your men, only with you." The stranger looked from one sailor to another. "There you are, Geordie," he

called to a tall dark man with hard eyes and a pockmarked face. "Been sportin' with more killer whales?"

"Not since the one snappin' at my heels when you dragged me out of the sea, Magnus." The man thrust his dirk back in the sheath under his shirt and came to stand by the big stranger.

"Harris! Brown! MacTavish!" bellowed Tarbert. "Haul this stinking lout to the ship and put him in irons!"

The three started forward, but in no great hurry. Geordie slipped out his knife again and they halted. "Mac," he said to a wiry older man, "weren't you dragged off the shore near Stromness? When you finally got back, hadn't your poor mother died of grieving?"

"Aye," muttered MacTavish. And he stepped back.

"I'll have the lot of you hung for mutiny!" yelled Tarbert.

"You flogged my mate to death," rasped a brawny seaman.

"Rats won't eat the grub you lay in," charged another.

The men of *The Cormorant* looked at one another. They had nothing to lose. They sauntered out of the tavern.

The captain stumbled after them, cursing. Magnus felled him with a chop to the side of the head and said to the sweating tavern keeper, "If he goes out anytime soon, he may fetch up anchored to the bottom of the harbor." His smile broke like sun from behind a cloud. "Come along, lass. We'll get your brother."

WHILE Magnus and Mairi watched from the shore, Geordie and several of the others rowed to the ship. There was no sound of a struggle with the watch, only muffled voices. Shuddering with anxiety and the bite of the wind, Mairi didn't resist when her rescuer drew her into the shelter of his broad arm.

"Won't the men get in trouble for helping us?" she asked him.

"They can hide on my boat till Tarbert fills out his crew and sails. Then I'll take them to a mainland port where they can find a ship." Above the lapping of the waves came a rhythmic plashing. "Here they come, lass. And soon as we have your brother, we'll go to a decent inn and settle you two for a sound night's sleep."

"I can't thank you enough for all you've done, but once Tam's ashore, you needn't trouble more for us."

"You can thank me by your company," he said. "I'll pay the reckoning at the inn." When she started to protest, he chuckled. "Save your breath, lass. I still don't know your name."

When she told him, he repeated it softly. "I'm Magnus Ericsson of Rousay, in the Orkneys, putting in on my way to Barra Head." Amused laughter rumbled in his chest. "There's no big hurry, though, I'm thinking." His breath stirred the ringlets that escaped her shawl, and she felt the strong, steady pound of his heart.

The grate of wood on sand put everything but Tam out of Mairi's head. She ran toward the boat, calling his name. In a moment, laughing and sobbing, they were in each other's arms.

MAIRI'S creel rested against the wall as they sat in the quiet inn, at a table near the fire. Tam devoured buttered oatcakes and hot chowder, and seemed amazingly unmarked by his experience.

"It's sorry I am to be such a trouble," Tam said. The straight look he gave Magnus held a man's responsibility for his womenfolk. "I'm in your debt, sir. I hope the winds blow me a way to pay you."

"I was paid by your sister's eyes," said Magnus.

Going to the creel, Mairi piled the woolens on a bench. "You must at least have your choice of these," she said. "It was all for the captain, to get our Tam back. Please have one, sir."

" 'Tis grand work, lass." He touched the fabrics admiringly. "If you must give me something, though, what I'd give a tooth for is a jersey like your brother's—that would fit me, to be sure." He showed the fraying cuffs and darned snags on his heavy sweater.

"Sheila's begun a blue-gray one for her husband. I'm sure she'd let me finish it for you. If you'll tell me where to send it—"

"My men won't mind some time in Stornoway. I want to make sure you're safe home. If there's room for me in your barn, maybe I could stay till the jersey's ready."

Mairi flushed. "We're not living in a proper house, sir. Three families we be, sharing an old broch."

At the seaman's stunned look, Tam cried, "But it's snug and fine inside! We've a barn and byre. I like it better than a real house!"

"It's serving us well." Remembering Iain, who had much to do with the broch, Mairi felt a stab of guilt for responding to Magnus' cheerful vitality. "If you don't mind a pallet by the fire—"

"Don't fear I'll lout about underfoot," he assured her. "I grew up in a croft. But you must be wearied to the bone. Tam, there's an extra bunk in my room. Lass, you're next to us, so no one will bother you." His grin broadened. "If you're nervous of a strange place, though, I'd be glad to hold your hand till you get to sleep."

Improper as the suggestion was, it was made in such a droll way that she couldn't be angry. She said, "That won't be needful, sir, thank you very much."

"Call me by my name, at least."

"Thank you—Magnus."

The innkeeper's wife lit them to their rooms. Mairi slipped into bed, thinking. If Magnus had no one to knit his jerseys, there must be others like him. While she was in Stornoway she should find a shop that would buy the woolens in her creel—perhaps sell knitted and woven goods made by the women at the broch. Now that they had spinning wheels, they could produce more than they needed.

Such an income would let them feed the animals and themselves—even on the small amount of arable land they had.

Exciting as the prospect was, Mairi was too sleepy to ponder on it long and drifted happily into slumber.

As THEY breakfasted next morning, Mairi explained what she wanted to do. "I think I know the right merchant," Magnus said. "Seafaring men buy from the widow Annie Gordon. She sells good quality at fair prices in her shop. You'll like Annie."

Mairi did. The full-figured young woman with warm brown eyes admired the weaving, the skillful dyeing, and Tam's jersey. "I can sell all the jerseys you can make," she said. "Caps, too, and stockings." She then named what seemed an astounding figure for the woven goods. "Bring more when it's wove, lass."

"That's wonderful!" Mairi gave Tam's hand a squeeze. "Pick out some sweeties, lad, enough for everyone. And Mrs. Gordon, I'll have a pound of your best tea, some raisins, treacle, and some good tobacco." Barry and Andrew rarely got any for their pipes. She was being extravagant, but the cloth might have gone to Tarbert.

The creel was much lighter now than when it had held the woolens, but Magnus took it from Mairi and swung it to his own back. That reminded her that Iain had done the same. Getting spoiled you are, Mairi thought, enjoying the extra lift in her step. For wasn't Tam safe, hadn't she found a grand market for their work, and wasn't it fun to pace along with a handsome young man and bask in his manifest admiration? She loved Iain, couldn't imagine loving any other man, but this one made her deliciously aware of herself as a woman. Since he probably had sweethearts in every port, she didn't have to worry about hurting him.

"You've been to France?" Tam was asking him. "And even to Spain? Oh, it must be main glorious to own your own ship."

"The *Selchie*'s not glorious," said Magnus. "More contrary than any woman, and costly. Long ago, 'tis said, one of my family's women called a selchie—a seal—from the waves to love her, and ever since, our men have followed the sea."

Such tales were common in the islands. "So when you sit down," teased Mairi, "is there a damp spot when you rise?"

"Not unless I've been in rain or water." He looked at her straight.

504

"Nor do I lose my man's body. I can love a woman not just one magicked day in the year, but all the days and nights."

Feeling on boggy ground, where a misstep could plunge her knee-deep, Mairi sparred. "Little good that'd do your wife with you always at sea."

"Oh, but lass! Think of the homecomings!"

WHEN they trudged in at twilight, Tam was embraced, as one snatched from the grave, by those waiting at the broch. When Mairi told what Magnus had done, he got a hero's welcome, and she herself was praised and fussed over. During supper she gave the news of what good prices Annie Gordon had paid for the weaving. Even Morag looked impressed.

"She wants jerseys? The kind we make for our men?"

"That very kind," assured Magnus, and again exhibited the sorry state of his.

"Why, you must have the one I'm making," Sheila said.

"Bless you!" Mairi hugged her. "I'll help you knit."

"I'll help, too," put in Gran. She studied Magnus. "The image of Michael you are, lad, though a mite bigger. You won't have seen him in your voyaging?"

"I haven't, Mrs. MacLeod." Magnus knew of Gran's delusion, and his tone was gentle. "He sounds a man I'd like to know."

For a while they sat around the fire, unspeakably grateful that none of their number was missing. Eileen rocked Seana's cradle, but it was Tam to whom her eyes clung. That night they all said silent thanks while Gran blessed the hearth.

As HE had promised, Magnus wasn't underfoot. He fished with the men till violent rain and wind kept them in, and he joined in braiding heather rope and mending nets. At night Sheila or Gran knitted on his jersey so Mairi could play the harp.

On the fifth day the jersey was almost finished. Magnus would leave next morning. Mairi felt sad, for he had become dear to her. Indeed, they would all miss him, but she felt a certain relief.

She didn't love him. She couldn't—not when she loved Iain. But if it hadn't been for Iain, she'd have fancied herself in love with Magnus, for his gaze could make her blood leap, and she loved to laugh with him. He breathed in life, fully and naturally, found it good, and didn't trouble himself with reflecting on it.

That evening Mairi was down by the burn scrubbing out milk vessels when Magnus approached. It was the first time he'd sought her out alone. She scrubbed harder, keeping her head low.

"Are you trying to wear a hole through the wood, lass?"

She straightened, shaking back her hair. "I—I'm finished." Why must she sound so breathless? "Maybe you'd help fill the vessels?"

"I'll help you in a minute."

He wasn't laughing. His mouth had as grim a tuck to it as on the night he confronted Tarbert. Tingling, voluptuous fear shot through her. The wind was rising; the sun was gone. They were alone, and she trembled.

"Let's get out of the wind." He took her hand and brought her to a small hollow grown with heather and bog myrtle, drew her down beside him. "There. Now we're cozy."

"I can't stay. I—I've got to help get supper."

"The others are managing finely," he said with dry amusement.

She tried to rise. He kept her where she was. "Magnus! Let go!"

"As soon as I've told you a story." In the hastening dusk his blue eyes were luminous. "It seems there was burning thatch, a good man dead, confusion and weeping. This gentleman happens along, an officer of the queen. He shelters the families like a fairy-tale prince, sends those who would go to America, raises a roof before he joins his regiment. Now how do you think the story ends?"

" 'Tis none of your concern," Mairi flashed, humiliated. He knew, then! Knew how she felt about Iain.

"It is my concern." Magnus' tone was equable, but his jaw thrust forward. "Don't you see I'm crazy for you? The MacDonald aided you and your folk. I credit him that, and might keep myself to myself but for a thing that's bound to ruin your fairy tale. He's gentry." His tone was soft, compassionate. "Your prince can't carry you off where you'll live happily ever after. Up that road there's only grief for you."

She flinched. "How dare you make me hear such things?"

"I dare because I love you, girl."

His honesty forced honesty from her. "I wish I loved you, Magnus. I do, as a friend. But Iain—" Her voice broke.

"I can be real for you, Mairi. Your Iain can only be a dream."

"He wouldn't—"

Magnus' mouth closed on hers. Catching her close, he held her so her hands were trapped against his heart. Overwhelmed, she resisted no more. It was as if he drank or fed from her, drawing her essence into him, filling her with his.

It was Magnus, not she, who drew back. "There's fire between us, lass. I want to marry you."

"I can't."

"Will you wither, grow old, and never even bloom?" Warm fingers on her throat, he laughed in male triumph at the violent leap of her pulse. Rising, he drew her to her feet. "I'll be back. Think on what I've said."

THAT night Gran did the final stitch on Magnus' jersey. He knelt by her while she snugged it down, blue-gray with broad red bands at throat, cuffs, and bottom. It became him well.

"May it warm you in any blast," Gran said, kissing him. "May it keep you safe till you come again."

"Thank you, Rosanna MacLeod. But to finish the wish, I'd like a kiss from the others who helped with the knitting." He bent for Sheila's shy kiss, returned it on her forehead, but Mairi he kissed full on the lips and said to her startled kinfolk, "I've asked Mairi to be my wife. Though the lass refuses now, I'm hoping she'll see what a bargain she's missing." He gave Mairi a devilish grin that set her blushing. Sobering, he looked around at those gathered by the hearth. "Mostly I want you to know that if there's aught I can do for you, leave word with Annie Gordon in Stornoway. Soon or late I'll anchor there."

"Can't you anchor closer and come see us?" Eileen demanded, hugging his arm.

"Maybe I could come and stay an hour or two." He patted the child's fair hair. "You know, if your cruel-hearted sister won't have me, I may wait for you to grow up."

Her face blazed, and she threw her thin arms around his neck. "Och, Magnus, will you?"

"If your sister won't wed me." He laughed, but his eyes were grave when they met Mairi's above her little sister's head.

507

# 5

HE LEFT next morning, striding off across the moor in his new sweater, heedless of a fine mist. With the going of that bright head, winter came upon them. All that day the wind blew colder. Before nightfall it seemed wise to bring the cows into their byre, where they'd remain confined until spring. In the foulest weather the sheep would shelter in the barn.

Winter was the time for making nets. This year, Barry, Andrew, and Tam did that, made rope, and crafted shoes. The women spent every possible moment spinning and at the looms.

Dyeing the wool before it was spun was the most exacting task, one at which Gran excelled. On a fair day, so the odorous task could be done outside, she put layers of lichen or roots, wool, and just the right pinches of staghorn moss in the big dye pot before filling it with water and setting it on the fire to boil. Gran might let someone else stir it, but it was she who dipped the fleece from time to time and decided when the sopping mass was the right shade.

It took all the women to waulk, or full, the ammonia-soaked web, and they sang together as they rubbed and thumped the cloth over a plank table, never singing the same song twice, for that was believed to harm the cloth. Singing lightened the tedious chore. When the finished cloth was given its final stretching and tightly rolled, Gran blessed it, and it was ready for sale or use.

At Christmas the cows were given some of the first and last sheaves of harvest to keep them healthy. The family had extra-thick bannocks and drank one another's health with Gran's heather ale.

"Let's drink to those who're far away but deep in our hearts." Andrew refilled the cups, called out the names, and for each, everyone took a few sips. "Catriona. Calum. Lucas. Paul. Kirsty. Adam. Magnus Ericsson. And the captain, Iain MacDonald! *Slainte!* May they all have love, health, luck, and may the mouse never leave their meal chest with a tear in its eye!"

That night, as she always did, Mairi held Iain's note to her heart and said a prayer for his safety. He had been gone now almost four months. Would he come in the spring? In summer? She didn't think she could bear it if he didn't come before fall.

A STORM WITH DRIZZLING SLEET howled over the moor in those first days of January 1845. The men, Tam, and Mairi went searching for the sheep, scarcely able to keep their feet against the gale. Crouching and stumbling, they searched out animals huddled in clefts and hollows, and took them, soaked and miserable, to the barn.

Numb to the bone and blinking against the stinging ice rain, Mairi was urging one of the last of their flock up from a bank when she heard a thin wail. "Who's there?" she shouted.

The cry came again, sounding like Seana when she was too sleepy to give lusty howls. How could a baby be out here? Calling, she worked her way along the bank. To her great relief, she could make Barry out, hurrying through the storm from the other direction.

He stopped short where the bank had eroded to a shallow cave, dropped to his knees beside a motionless heap wrapped in sodden plaids. Mairi knelt, too. As they drew back the coverings the wail sounded from between the young man and woman who lay clasped in each other's arms, so pallid and still that Mairi thought them dead. A baby of perhaps five or six months was between them.

Barry felt the pulse at the side of the woman's throat. It took him longer to find the beat of the man's blood, but in a moment he gave a relieved sigh. "Alive. But we've got to get them warm. Take the babe, and I'll fetch the lass, then come back for the lad."

"BRING in three of the cows and make them lie down," Gran ordered as they wrapped the young woman in a soft blanket. "Heat from a cow'll warm her quicker and better than anything."

"The babe's better nourished than you'd think," said Morag, cuddling the tiny dark-haired boy as she warmed some milk. " 'Twas God's mercy that you heard him, Mairi."

"Where's God's mercy that they're starving?" Mairi demanded. "Odds are they've been driven from their croft, as we were."

Andrew and Barry soon had the young man in a blanket, nestled between the cows. Tall, with his bones showing, he had russet-brown hair. Mairi half knelt beside the couple. Thank goodness the young faces were gradually losing their pinched bloodlessness. The woman's eyelashes fluttered. She moaned, and her arm moved as if to clasp something. Staring wildly, she tried to raise herself.

"Here's your wee laddie." Morag brought him over.

Folding the child to her, the woman looked at them dazedly before dread constricted her features. "Donald! Where—"

"Your husband's right beside you, love," said Gran.

Turning her head, the young woman saw her husband. Her thin face lit up. "Donald, my darling. Are you waking?"

His eyes opened, glowing as he saw her. "Katie!" Trying to sit up, he moved his head as if to clear it, and looked from one strange face to the next. "Where has the storm blown us?"

"You must have some tea, and eat," said Gran. "Then we'll talk."

An hour later the cows were back in their stalls, and Katie and Donald Gunn, warmed with broth and tea with whisky, slept snug in Gran's bed with little Alasdair between them. By supper they could sit by the hearth and eat, seeming as nourished by the fire and friendliness as they were by the flavorsome stew.

A factor had driven them from their house on the island of Harris in the heart of winter. "There were eight families in our township," Donald explained. "My sister-in-law's from North Uist, so she and my brother went to her family. Two of my cousins went to Glasgow to find work in factories. The rest scraped and borrowed to go to Canada." He shook his head as his eyes found Katie's. "I reckoned on finding work. I can build boats and carpenter. We traded our cow for a pony to carry our things, but when I got no work, we had to trade our belongings for food and lodging. Then we had to sell the pony and carry what was left on our backs."

"And then there was nothing to carry," Katie finished, when Donald could not. "We lived on seaweed and shellfish as we made for Stornoway. We thought Donald could find work there. But the storm came." Shivering, she glanced from small Alasdair to her husband. "Never can we thank you enough."

"But we won't burden you." Donald held his head proudly. "It's hard to feed one's own folk. From the little you've said, you've had your own troubles. What I would ask is, would you let Katie and Alai bide here whilst I find a place in Stornoway to fetch them to?"

"The favor would be to us if you'd stay," Andrew rumbled. "We need another man, and the women have plenty your lass can help with. Why, man, if you can build boats, maybe we could make our own and not be tied to that cheating curer!"

After a startled glance, Donald beamed. "If you can get the

wood, we can build a fine boat." He stared in amazement at his wife. "Now, lass, will you be weeping when we've found a home?"

"That's why," she said, laughing through her tears.


THAT very night three more near frozen people, from an evicted west coast hamlet, found shelter at the broch—Murdo MacKinnon, his son, Gavin, and Murdo's mother-in-law, Meggie Ross, who had unaccountably survived privations that had killed her daughter.

Again it was a story of a small community rent asunder, scattered to Australia, America, The Lowlands, while this family, trying to remain near their ancestral home, lived in a byre till they were driven from that a few days before the storm. It caught them unprotected on the moor, but they struggled on.

"Hadn't have been for that glow cast up into the night, we'd have given up," Murdo said. He was a tough, knotty little brown man with steel-gray hair and eyes.

In his mid-thirties, Gavin had butter-yellow hair and a round face. "The light called us for so long, we began to fear it a trick, but when we sniffed peat smoke, we knew 'twas a real hearth."

"Glad we are to share it," said Andrew, though three more mouths would dangerously stretch their provisions.

The Gunns and MacKinnons understood this. By the time the storm blew itself out several days later, they were out gathering laver, dulse, carrageen, and shellfish. "We don't want to use up your grain and taties," Murdo said.

"We can all eat more seaweed and shellfish," Mairi said.

"And we'll fish more," Barry added.

"We can help with that," said Gavin. "Also, you say there's a hunting lodge within a half-day's walk. I'm a stonemason. Maybe I could work in return for food and a place in the stable."

"We can use a good mason when we build houses in the spring," said Andrew. "And Donald here can build us a boat for a crew of six. Counting Tam, we'll have enough men for the first time since my lads and Calum went for soldiers."

Barry nodded. "Without the curer's charge, we'll win enough of our living from the sea to make up for what we can't grow."

"And," said Mairi, "soon as we waulk the webs on the looms, we'll see if Annie Gordon will pay what she did for the others!"

SHE DID, AND WAS EAGER FOR more, saying Gran's dyes were the best she'd ever seen, and the weaving and knitting were of the highest quality. Their own wool was almost used up, so a new supply was brought with the grain the men carried back from Stornoway. Their great triumph was in bringing sailcloth and cordage for the boat. It was February 1, three weeks since the terrible storm. The newcomers had regained their strength, though everyone went to bed with what Gran called a mite hungry corner.

Pride for the skill he could use for his family and friends gave a jaunty lift to Donald's curly head. "For twenty-five pounds we can make a good stout boat that would cost forty if we had it built."

Barry glanced from his wife and mother to Gran, Mairi, Katie, and Meggie Ross—who, it had turned out, was a notable weaver. "If we make another loom," he proposed, "can you weave as much plaiding and tweed as we carried up this time—maybe knit two more jerseys? If you can, we're assured money for the timber."

The women stared at each other. It seemed too good to be true—that their work could be the means of winning a boat.

Mairi had a sudden thought. There was small use in the six men, counting Tam, spending the winter making more heather rope than they'd soon need, while the women strained to cook, care for babies and beasts, and spin and weave far into the night. Facing the men, she said with a smile, "We might just be able to do it, lads, if you'll take on some of our work."

"*Your* work?" Barry frowned in puzzlement.

She laughed into her cousin's bewildered eyes. "Aye, laddie. Fetch water from the burn, grind the grain, do the cooking—"

"Whisht!" Andrew grinned after his first shock. "Do you think we can't do it, lass? Why, we cook while we're at the fishing."

Barry gaped at his father, and Morag's jaw dropped, but after a moment the younger man shrugged. "I never thought to do woman's work—but then it's a lot we're asking, and all the way home I was wishing there was some way to help."

"But it never entered your curly head that you could do our chores," said Mairi a trifle acidly.

He flushed and squirmed. "Och, Mairi, give over! And promise you'll never tell on us."

"We won't," said Mairi, chuckling. She thought of something

512

else, and though she was reluctant to broach it, that seemed the only fair thing to do. Looking at the Gunns and MacKinnons, she said, "If you want to go, we could loan you the passage to America."

Katie shook her head. "Who'd cross the ocean if we can live in our own dear land and speak our mother tongue?"

Murdo grinned hardily. "We want to stay and crew the boat, build a house, and make a township. You're our *clanna* now."

"*Clanna*," mused Gran, tilting her head. "That would be a good name for our township."

"And for our boat," Andrew said, and laughed. "Then there'll be no fash about which wife to name it after."

Gran clapped her hands. "That calls for a round of heather ale! Let's drink to our boat—*An Clanna*—and to the looms!"

That night, holding Iain's note to her heart, Mairi summoned up his face. His eyes seemed to dance as she told him, That's what comes of your carrying my creel, love. What will you think of it all when you come home? And when, when are you coming?

THE hearth room was busy, with all of them caught up in having the cloth and jerseys ready in time. Strange it was to see men grinding at the quern, patting out bannocks, scrubbing milk vessels, and churning, and though no Lewis man, alone, would have done woman's work, together the broch men made it a game.

From dawn to bedtime, webs grew on the three looms, while yarn twined on spinning-wheel bobbins and from distaff and spindle. Gran presided over the dyeing, and knitting needles flashed.

Not only were the MacKinnons and Gunns hard workers but Katie had a sweet, rich voice, Donald had a store of sailors' jokes, and Murdo could play gay tunes on his Jew's harp. Cridhe spent some evenings plaided in the corner, but usually Mairi was urged for "just a song or two, lass." Every night was a ceilidh. This did much to make up for the monotony of their suppers.

By early April the potatoes were planted in the hills. The cows were led from the byre, lowing with joy at being under the sky and able to wander. Soft green brightened the moor. It was a trial to stay at loom and spinning wheel during this glad stirring of the earth, but right after Easter, cloth was rolled tightly, jerseys were folded, and the men set out for Stornoway.

In four days they were back, with ash and larch from the mainland, iron fittings for the boat, and wool, with a new order from Annie, who had long since sold their winter's production.

"*An Clanna* will be beautiful!" Donald sighed. "With a steep stem and stern like the old Viking galleys, and two fine sails like wings. First thing we do is steam the ash to shape it for the frame."

For the next week, from first light to last, the men hammered away down by the inlet where the boat would be launched. Twenty feet long, the craft was partially decked. There were three planks to seat the oarsmen, and strong tholepins of ash to hold the oars.

"No more trudging to Stornoway with creels to our backs!" exulted Barry after the boat was tested for leaks and found to be watertight. "We'll take the high road of the waves to the fishing."

A boat was usually the pride of the men, but since the women had earned the money for *An Clanna,* she belonged to them, too. Sheila carefully painted on the name, and Gran blessed the boat. Andrew prayed for good winds, good catches, and a safe return. Then the men climbed in, while the women, skirts kilted above the knee, waded and shoved till the men could push out with their oars.

As *An Clanna* lilted toward the open sea, she moved like a great swan, suddenly alive. Beautiful! And watching the sails that swept their men away on depths that both blessed and murdered, each woman silently invoked the powers.

# 6

ON MAY Day morning Mairi awoke to the song of skylarks, who caroled from faintest light to darkness, intoxicated with lengthening days that told them it was time to make nests.

"We must wash our faces in the dew for beauty and health," said Gran, winking. "I've no hope for the first, but can try for the last."

Even Meggie trooped out to wet her hands on heath-spotted orchids and violet-pink blooms of butterwort. Eileen washed so enthusiastically that crystal droplets glinted on her hair, and Mairi teased, "For whom are you washing? Is it Magnus?"

Eileen flushed. With surprise, Mairi noticed that she had grown taller, and bony angles were beginning to round. "It's not a joke, Mairi. Turned eleven, I have. Some wed at fourteen."

"An ill thing," said Mairi. "A child shouldn't be put in the way of bearing children. Make no hurry, love."

"You won't be taking Magnus?"

"I won't. But henny, he's old enough to be your father."

"Magnus was twenty-six on the twelfth day of Yule," cried Eileen fiercely. "That's only fifteen years older." Her dark blue eyes glistened. "If you won't have him, didn't he say he'd wait for me?"

"Sweeting! That was a joke, to be sure."

"It won't be! You just wait!" Eileen ran for the cliffs. She stood there, a small thin shadow facing boundless sea and sky as if willing them to bring Magnus to her.

Mairi said a prayer—not only for Magnus, so kind and strong and laughing, but for those on *An Clanna* and for Iain, too, for it was possible that he was on the sea, homeward bound. Let him come soon. Let him come safe.

Suddenly as lonely as her little sister looked, Mairi turned to the others and said, "This might be a day as good as any for washing."

Gran gave her a knowing smile. "Aye, thumping clothes and treading blankets is a good way to ease your worries, lass."

Great washings of sheets, towels, and bed curtains were done in spring and fall. These were strong, beautiful linens, some older than Mairi, made of homegrown flax. That day the women knelt at the burn and pounded the linens with wooden beetles, or sticks. Gran said, "Hard work, lassies, but we would not be wanting the Fairy Washerwoman's help. When she washes a man's shirt, that man will die. Before a battle, she often has a great pile."

May she never wash Iain's, Mairi thought.

Eileen was treading blankets in a big wooden tub to free them of peat smoke. After Mairi and Katie spread out the bed curtains to dry, Mairi fastened up her skirts and got in the tub, laughing as she took her sister's hands. "Let's go around and around," she chanted. "Squish goes the dirt! Weesh goes the smoke!"

Eileen laughed, leaning far back and treading so fast and hard that she splashed Mairi thoroughly. They spun faster and faster, the women at the burn cheering them on, till Eileen stopped abruptly. Mairi tripped into her. They went down together. Giggling and spluttering, trying to wipe the water from her eyes, Mairi heard the creak of leather and the soft clump of hoofs.

She scrambled out of the tub and stood there dripping. "It's the captain!" Gran cried, and ran from the burn nimbly as a girl, hugging him as he came off his horse. Eileen wasn't far behind.

He opened his arms to them both, but over their heads his eyes found Mairi's. The joyful greeting broke from her then, and she ran forward. A good thing his arms were full of Eileen and Gran, or she couldn't have kept from embracing him. So often she had dreamed of this, pictured his return! But he was to find her on the beach or on the moor, not with other folk about—especially not just when she'd fallen in a tub!

It didn't matter. He'd come back to her. Her love was here. But his face, his dear face—what had happened to it? What had made the puckered seam from cheekbone to chin that gave a slight twist to the left side of his mouth? With a pang she saw, too, when he moved forward, that his stride, once confident and graceful, was now a limp.

Her dismay must have shown, for he stopped dead. "Do I frighten you, Mairi MacLeod?"

She closed the space between them. He was starving thin. His weathered brown skin had an ashen cast. "You—you've been hurt." It sounded weak beside her joy at his return, her sorrow for his wounds. "Is my brother all right? My cousins?"

"When last I saw them. They'd survived the worst fighting, and an epidemic that killed more of our men than the tribes did." For the first time he noticed Katie. "Has your clan increased?"

"The *clanna* has." Quickly Mairi explained the coming of the Gunns and MacKinnons.

"And we've got our own boat!" Eileen burst out. "We womenfolk made the cloth to build it, while the men baked bannocks. And—"

"Whisht!" chided Gran. "Go jump up and down in that tub, lass, instead of on the captain's toes! You, Mairi, fetch milk for him and sit down and tell him all that's passed."

Mairi hurried for a beaker of milk. When she returned, Iain had tossed Chieftain's saddle over a rock. He thanked her for the milk, his fingers warming hers a moment before he took the cup. "Chieftain limps, too," he said. "Caught arrows in the thigh and haunch in the same fight where I took one. No more wars for him, though. I'll leave him in the meadow when I rejoin the regiment."

Mairi felt as if an unseen fist had knocked the wind out of her. "When—when will you be going, sir?"

He frowned. "I'm not your commanding officer, Mairi. Call me by name. I have leave till August." He turned the scarred side of his face to her, watching her closely. "Does my scar distress you?"

"Only because you were hurt—"

He made an impatient gesture. "Don't I revolt you?"

Scarred from the crown of your head to the soles of your feet, you wouldn't revolt me, she thought, longing to hold and comfort him. "A handsome man you are, Captain," she said, trying to laugh. "A mark on the face just shows you've lived through danger."

He laughed wryly, but most of the wariness left his eyes.

"Will Calum and my cousins be home this year?" she asked.

"Calum will, but you mustn't count on his staying. When he heard of the eviction, he was for going to America. And when he learned his sweetheart was there, it settled his course."

"The devil fly off with Catriona!" Mairi cried. "We need Calum here! But when he sees our boat, maybe he'll stay."

"Don't count on that, lass. Lucas and Paul, though, mean to stay. To save more money, they'll soldier for another two years."

She was fond of her cousins, but it was Calum she'd grown up adoring. Bad enough to lose Catriona, but Calum, too!

"Now, Mistress Mairi," Iain said briskly, "tell me how you've managed these wonders—a boat, taking in six people when you'd scarce provender for yourselves. And I see lazybeds are hugging every place where there's an inch of soil on these bony rocks."

"We have done well, haven't we?" She flushed at his praise.

"But thirteen people and two babies in the broch! I thought you crowded before, but reckoned it would do for a winter."

"We'll be glad to move into houses, right enough," she admitted. "But we had grand times in the hearth room, everyone busy, with the fire warming us and always a story or song. Oh, Iain, it was kind of you to send the pipes to Tam! Set him in the clouds. He'll be after you to teach him more if you have time."

"I'll have time." After a pause he said slowly, "This leg, Mairi— They wanted to cut it off, but I said I'd die sooner. Do you know what I remember more than the fear and pain? I remember the coverlet you gave me." He smiled. "There was still a hint of peat

517

smoke in the wool. I was out of my head with fever and opium. Jamie says most of the time I thought I was at your fire, and when it seemed you were playing your harp, that would quiet me into sleep."

She shook her head. "If only I could have been there."

"I felt your hand on my forehead. You gave me to drink and made me eat. If you had not, I would have died."

"But Iain, I wasn't there."

"You played the songs I asked for. When I shivered with chills, you held me in your arms."

"Iain," she almost begged. A wild pulsing drummed in her ears. She felt suffocated, though she was breathing fast and hard.

His voice dropped. "I know it was a dream, but it was a dream that saved me. I wanted you to know." There was sadness in his eyes. "And know this, Mairi. I would rather die than harm you. Come now, and let me meet the new ones of your *clanna*."

KATIE was so awed by Iain that she couldn't answer his questions. But he won her heart by hoisting Alai to his shoulder and declaring him the handsomest baby boy he'd clapped eyes on. Seana, golden-haired and elfin, went to the other shoulder. Mairi couldn't stifle the wish that the children were theirs, made from their love.

Iain had brought many delicacies. Cheeses, figs, dates, nuts, ham, smoked salmon, and Mrs. Fraser's excellent shortbread made a brave show on the snowy cloth spread on the waulking table.

"It's like a wedding!" Katie's violet eyes were wide. "Och! If only Donald and the others could share it!"

"We'll feast them when they return," Iain promised. He was shocked to hear about Tam's abduction and gave Mairi a swift glance when Eileen praised Magnus as "just like a Viking chief— tall and strong and handsome!" Mairi's cheeks burned.

At last Iain reluctantly got to his feet. "I must go. Will you be doing anything tomorrow that I could help with? I'm weak from lying about and need to try my muscles."

"Won't you be hunting?" Gran squinted shrewdly. "Banging away at grouse and deer and any misfortunate hare?"

"I've seen too much death these last months to pleasure in killing. I want honest work, Rosanna, that puts food in people's bellies and clothes on their backs." He looked at Mairi. "I want to cut peats for the hearth and feel I've earned the right to sit by it."

"Your whim is our must,"said Gran dryly. "We'll keep you busy."

IAIN helped shear the sheep, tying the forefeet before cutting off the fleece with a sharp knife. He stared at the pile of fleece, daubed with tar and butter to keep off pests. "How will you get this clean?"

" 'Twill need a good washing," Mairi said. "But the wool in your coverlet once looked just like this."

His look was between respect and puzzlement. "You take it for granted, don't you, that everything takes work?"

"Och, no!" She laughed. "Only look at those larks and peewits rollicking, and their songs pure joy! See the sea pinks solid beyond the marram grass that bows to the white shore and blue-green sea. Not all the money in the world could make that. Yet it's free!"

He watched her so strangely that she faltered. "Perhaps you've seen such grand things that this is naught—"

"Don't say that." He caught her hands in a grip that hurt. "You see the bright first day of God's creation, and you're a part of it. No laird's gold can buy that."

She knew she was lucky—still on the island, and instead of a dazed remnant, they were a *clanna* knit together in common hopes and endeavor. But though she gloried in the marvels of the sea and moor, she longed for him as if he were a severed part of her.

Without him she could never be whole. While he'd been gone, she believed she could be content if he simply returned—that seeing and being with him would be enough. But now she couldn't be close to him without yearning to be closer; couldn't see his scarred face without yearning to caress it. She couldn't see his mouth without burning to feel it on hers.

Turning the subject to Iain's mention of lairds, Mairi said, "The Frasers at the lodge say Mrs. MacKenzie's sold the island to a Sir James Matheson. Do you know him?"

"I do. A canny Scot who's made his fortune in the Hong Kong opium trade. Unlike most Highland lairds, he can live well without squeezing tenants. He'll build roads, encourage industries—"

"And the folk?"

"He says he won't force any hardworking crofters to leave,

though he'll pay fare to Canada for all who want to go. I told him about your people, Mairi. He was impressed with your determination. I think he'd consider letting your cattle and sheep range on the moor and allotting enough arable land for sustenance."

"That would be no more than just." Mairi tossed back her head. "For he's bought with his new money earth that's mulched with flesh and bone of my ancestors."

Iain's eyes flashed amusement, which they had rarely done since his return. "I don't believe I'll tell him that."

THREE evenings later Eileen spied *An Clanna* trying to make shore in a rough sea. Everyone ran to the inlet. The boat dashed between the frothing waves, oarsmen bent double, and when the prow touched sand, Donald leaped out with the painter cable and hauled. Tam, Murdo, Barry, and Gavin leaped into the waves and helped the women shove *An Clanna* out of the tugging reach of the breakers. Sheila and Katie embraced their young husbands, and Gran hugged Tam, then stared out to sea. "When Michael comes—"

The fishing had gone well. When the sail and nets had been spread to dry, the men sat blissfully around the hearth in dry garments, savoring the fuss made of them.

"Och!" sighed Andrew, ruddy face beaming. "Wasn't it grand to stroll in and tell the curer we had our own boat and all he need tally against us was salt and barrels? We were the envy of the fishing, let me tell you!" He clapped Donald on the back. "Why, lad, if we need another trade, we could go to boatbuilding."

Barry grunted. "We have more trades than we can juggle, Father. Haven't we left the fishing to dig peats and start our houses? And before the houses are up, it'll be back to fishing."

"Whisht, lad." Murdo chuckled. "Wouldn't it be dull—the same task day after day? It's a life I'd trade for no other."

THROUGH mutual restraint, good humor, and thankfulness that they had a roof over them at all, the broch dwellers had lived in surprising harmony, but everyone looked forward to more privacy. The timber and windows in the broch, along with driftwood and a few glass panes from Stornoway, should suffice for building three houses. Till next summer, when separate homes for them could be built, Barry and Sheila would share with his parents, and Murdo and Gavin would have a small room in Donald and Katie's place. But elbow room had its costs. Three dwellings meant that many hearths, each requiring cutting about fifteen thousand peats.

Andrew located a good peat bank a mile from the broch. The men cleared the surface with spades and formed teams, one to cut with the peat-iron while the other carried the oblong chunks to the women, who spread them to dry. The cutting was hard, and the men took turns at it. After much laughing advice, Jamie and Iain could make their cuts, though the results were not perfect.

At night, Mairi no longer held Iain's note to her breast. Why dream over a bit of paper with the living man close by? But seeing him without being able to do more drove her so frantic that she was almost glad when, after the peat cutting, he was called to Inverness for the wedding of one of his lieutenants.

Still, the relief quickly vanished in missing him, so Mairi forced herself to concentrate on the house that was starting—Andrew and Morag's. Built of drystone into a slope that protected it from gales, the hearth room had a built-in box bed dividing it from the small bedroom. Byre and barn followed the gentle downward slant, and the whole was enclosed with walls six feet thick. In eight days the house was finished and the men soon went back to the fishing. In a month or so they'd return to build the others.

It was mid-June, and Iain had been gone two weeks. Why was he lingering at Inverness? Had he met some highborn lady? Fallen ill? Dreadful possibilities plagued Mairi. As the days passed, she thought of going to the lodge to learn what kept him, but she had no good excuse to spend a day on such a selfish errand.

One day Ewan Fraser, from the lodge, stopped by. He was making a survey of game on this side of the island for the new laird. "He's building a castle at Stornoway," Ewan said. "Money to burn, Sir James has. At least he's willing to spend it improving Lewis."

Here was a chance to mention Iain. "Will Sir James keep on leasing the lodge to the captain?" Mairi asked.

"So far as I know, lass, the captain will keep his lease." Ewan gave Mairi a searching glance. It must be the talk of the lodge folk, how Iain had worked at the peats. "But why is beyond me. Two weeks he's back from that wedding and hasn't gone out of the house. He's like some lost soul. Stronger in his body than when he first came, but there's something amiss with the captain in himself."

Two weeks returned, and Iain hadn't come near her! What had happened at the wedding? Who could know? Except that he hadn't come. He hadn't wished to see her. But she felt there was more than that behind his shunning her. Something had hurt him on that trip to the mainland, something that made him hide away. She was glad when Fraser went his way and she could weep.

Her heart ached, but what could she do? It was almost Midsummer, the time when she, Gran, and Eileen would go to the Stones to greet the rising sun, as their people had done since those stones were raised. Perhaps the ancient powers would guide her.

The midnight sky glowed with enchanted twilight—a luminous, living blue—as the three made their way across the moor. Gran gripped Mairi's arm, while Eileen whimpered, "I don't see why we have to do this. Not when Sheila and Katie and Morag don't."

"Their folk aren't of the Stones," muttered Gran. "But women of ours have always been there for Midsummer."

"Morag says it's heathen."

Gran made a rude noise. "When you're older, you can choose—with your conscience, not your laziness. Trot along or we'll be late."

Mairi had never questioned going to the Stones and intended to do so all her life, but it was an act without knowledge, piety without a creed. All that remained of what must have been a potent ritual was a tradition that when the cuckoo welcomed the sun, the Shining One walked down the aisle and blessed the high-summer fullness. Mairi had heard the cuckoo most Midsummer morns, but she had never seen a vision, shining or dark, though sometimes heavy mist shrouded the Stones, so that they looked like cowled giants in long robes, rapt in meditation.

Gran was so tired that though they were within a mile of the Stones, they stopped and rested in the cover of a ruined byre. Gran winced with the effort of rising. "Och, my dry old bones! On the way back, lassies, I must lie down awhile and sleep."

Approaching dawn crimsoned the east. The sky blanched gray, but vapors thinned, parted, and coalesced on the promontory of the Stones like diaphanous cloud beings. Only now and then did one of the pillars rear among constantly wreathing veils. Suddenly cold, wrapping her plaid more closely around her, Mairi followed Gran.

The Stones formed a Celtic cross—a long aisle leading to a circle from which radiated three single rows. There, with the shrouding mist obscuring anything more than an arm's length away, the three of them—old woman, maiden, and girl—awaited the dawn.

It came with a burst of rose-gold rays. Like a glimpse of a fairy world, Mairi saw the purple hills of Harris and Uig, the waters of Loch Roag, drenched with light jubilant as a shout of angels, before glowing vapors hid them, and the cuckoo called. Had she seen a Shining One pace through the clouds, she could not have been more entranced. It was one of those rare moments when matter lost its density, dissolved into particles of dancing light.

"We can go now." Gran's voice jarred Mairi. She wasn't ready.

"Why don't you and Eileen have your rest at the byre?" she suggested. "I'll come in a bit."

Gran sighed. "These long tramps draw the bones out. Give me your arm, Eileen child, and don't streak along like a plover!"

The mist hid them before the whisper of their steps faded. Mairi entered the circle, advancing between the Stones, and approached the central megalith—a great squared pillar twice her height.

How did the island look when the Stones were mysteriously set in place? No peat then. According to ancient songs, there were trees—vast forests of them. So different it was now, yet blood of Mairi's blood had built this place of worship. In spite of their brief lives, her people were like the rock underlying peat and thin soil. Perhaps that was all the message the Stones need hold for anyone.

She started forward, and as she did, Iain loomed out of the mist. "Is it you, Mairi?"

Her heart stopped. "Yes." Was he real or an apparition? His gaze probed her as no phantasm's could. What should she do?

"You haven't been to us," she said into the weighted silence. "I—I was afraid some ill had befallen you."

"Is it ill to know the truth? That I am disgusting, even to a woman eager to wed my uncle's money?" His words were slurred.

She smelled whisky on his breath. "You've been drinking, Iain."

"I wouldn't have married the lady in spite of my uncle's urging. He's hot for another heir in case I'm killed. But it was educational to watch her try to overcome her disgust."

Mairi did then what she'd wanted to do ever since he returned. She took his face in her two hands and reached to press her mouth against the scar, as if the kiss could heal. His arms closed around her, crushing her to him. Their lips sought each other's.

"I love you, Iain."

"And I love you." He tore himself away from her. "Run away, child, before I do what your *clanna* would rightly kill me for."

"Iain, I am no child." She drew him to her. "Oh, Iain, love me, make me your woman!"

Trembling, they sank to the earth. His kiss was flame and worship. His hands sent honey sweetness through her, a melting flood that swept her into a boundless sea, then left her light and floating.

"Mairi," he sighed at last against her hair. "I'd rather lose my battered soul than hurt you, but see what I've done."

She smiled at him, caressed his seamed cheek, smoothed his black hair with her hands. "See what I've done," she challenged tenderly. "My man, my laddie, you had no chance at all."

He stared at her in wonder, then traced the contours of her face and throat and said with a rueful, husky laugh, "If I didn't know better, Mairi MacLeod, I'd swear you seduced me."

"If I did, I'm not sorry."

He kissed her, and it seemed she had always known the rough sweetness of his mouth, the embrace that filled her with fresh hunger yet gave her an inexpressibly safe and protected feeling. Perfect peace. That's what it was with him after the loving.

With a shuddering sigh he imprisoned her wrists and sat up, drawing her with him, though he kept the length of his arms between them. "Sweet, sweet Mairi, this must not happen again."

She'd always known he couldn't marry her. But never to be with each other again? "If you love me—"

"That's why. You must see it would disgrace you, keep you from wedding a good man like that Magnus I've heard about."

"I won't wed anyone."

"Don't say that, Mairi. You were made to love a man—love him and bear his children." He got to his feet, bringing her with him. "I love you. Because I do, I won't come back to your island."

"Never?" It seemed a death sentence.

He made a defeated gesture. "I wish I could. Working with your people, sharing your hearth, hearing your music, all these are happiness of a kind I've never had. I thought I was strong enough to delight in your company and not seek more. I won't see you again, my darling, for your own sake. It's because I love you past all measure that I must take myself out of your life."

How could he condemn her with such beautiful, loving words? "I think I will die if I never see you!"

He gave a twisted smile. "No, Mairi. Beneath your sweetness, you're as enduring as the stones of your island. You'll live to be an old woman, head of your *clanna* and soul of your people."

"I can live without you. But I will never love."

"Love?" he mocked tenderly. "Oh, Mairi, mine! You must love. You can't help yourself. Not only me and my ruined face; not only your family. You have loved strangers—fed and sheltered and comforted them. You will stop breathing before you fail to love."

It was men she was speaking of, but he would think what he wished to. Fighting tears, she said, "You'll surely come to the broch and take your leave?"

"Yes, but this is our good-bye, Mairi." He paused. "It's most unlikely that you'll be got with child this one time, but should that chance, write my solicitor. I'll instruct him to inform me at once, and meanwhile aid you however he can." His mouth was grim. "If you conceive my child, I'll marry you."

She gasped. "You won't! I could never live among your kind,

make you scorned and outcast. What would your uncle say?"

"Mairi! If I thought you could be happy in my world, I'd marry you, and the devil with my uncle! But that would never be a life for you—away from your family and island, with me gone most of the time with my regiment." His jaw set. "But if you have a child, I won't have it doomed to bastardy on this kirk-ridden island."

He'd marry her out of duty—and what kind of life could be there for them? And the child? Too upset to speak, she huddled against her knees, wishing him gone so she could weep. Finally she said, "If there's anything you should know, I'll write. I must go now."

He raised her hands to his lips. "Don't," she cried. "If one last kiss is all I'll have from you, kiss me on my mouth."

He swept her against him, kissed her till the bones went soft in her body. "Be well, be happy. Farewell, my only love."

"You cannot go so far away that my love won't follow, Iain."

Moving away from him was like tearing away from part of her body, severing her heart. As she plunged through the Stones the rosy gold left the mist. It was gray now, and cold.

# 7

MAIRI couldn't show her grieving, and was rescued by the round of work. She learned, too, that the best help for loss was to build something that would last. Raising the walls of her house gave her pride that was the opposite of the helpless shame she'd felt when she saw that she could never fit into Iain's world. When the men went back to the fishing, the women collected stones and paved the floors, then clayed the barn floors.

When the men took in their last catch and settled with the curer, Andrew would lead a delegation to ask that Clanna be leased pasture and arable soil. From all Iain had said, the island's new owner would be impressed that they'd progressed to a community owning its own boat and producing fine woolens. Few townships could claim as much. Of course, if it hadn't been for Iain—

Always her thoughts came back to him. Would it always be that way? Would it always, always hurt? Forcibly she turned her musings to Calum. He should be home soon—her big brother. Though he'd sadly miss Aosda and Fearchar, he'd *have* to see that life on the island held fresh promise. Mairi prayed that he would stay and convince Catriona to come back.

Though Andrew and Gran, as eldest man and woman, often spoke as leaders, it was Mairi to whom everyone turned. She was, without wishing it, the real center of Clanna, much as Fearchar had been. This was disturbing. She felt too young and inexperienced for such responsibility. And then there was something else.

As July slipped into August, as some of the yellow iris began to go to fruit, she could no longer hope her monthly flow was only a few days late. She knew that she was nurturing the start of Iain's bairn. It thrilled her with wonder at the same time that she shrank from the others' knowing.

A fine example she was for them! And when other folk knew, why, what shame upon her family! The thought made her flinch from Calum's return. As for Magnus, she only hoped he'd forgotten her.

Facing now what Iain had tried to provide for, she thought in desperation of writing his solicitor, of going to the mainland and leaving the child in fosterage. The temptation was scarcely more than a flash. She could feel in her arms a baby sweet, with Iain's eyes and hair. She couldn't give up his bairn.

What, then, should she do? She'd have to tell the *clanna* after the men returned from fishing. If they could accept and love her child, it wouldn't harm the bairn so greatly to be without a father. Growing up with Seana and Alai for playmates, the child would have a family and a share in what the *clanna* owned. But what if Morag preached, if Andrew and Barry looked at her with reproach? If that happened, and it might, she must leave.

That fall Gran wanted to make heather ale, and the rose-purple blooms were at their best. The women were gathering blossoms one afternoon when a horseman appeared, on a fine black.

He rode up to them, a dark, keen-eyed man, vigorous-looking, though he was past youth. Unsmiling, though civil, he wished them a good day. "I am looking for Mistress Mairi MacLeod."

"You've found me," said Mairi. "Won't you get down, sir, and have a cool drink or bite to eat?"

"I might at that," he said, eyeing the broch. "So you really live in the ruin?"

"It was grand good shelter through the winter, sir, but now, as you see, we're building houses."

"I see. You have leases?"

Lord save them, was he the new factor? Stomach knotting, Mairi said, "This is wasteland, sir, almost on the rocks of the sea."

He scanned the lush beds of potatoes, the oats and barley ripening, the sheep foraging along the bay. With a grim chuckle he said, "It's clear there's been some work here."

"May I ask, sir, who you might be?"

He grinned at her then. "I would be James Matheson. Do I still get my bannock and sip of milk?"

Mairi's heart skipped. "You're welcome indeed," she said, and led him into the broch.

Though his dark eyes probed every corner, Sir James Matheson, now owner of all Lewis, was very pretty-mannered to Gran, praised his bannock, and drank his milk as if it were French claret.

"It's clear that Captain MacDonald exaggerated neither your efforts nor your results," he said. "I applaud enterprise and wish to encourage it. I'll instruct my factor to devise leases that will give you cropland and the right to pasture on the neighboring moor."

"The men will be pleased, sir," said Gran. "Och, I can hardly wait to tell my dear man."

"I'm sure it will be to our mutual advantage." Rising, he smiled quite charmingly. "Thank you for your hospitality. I hope I'll be welcome to stop if I ride this way again."

"Indeed you will, sir." Gran beamed. "Be sure of that."

The laird turned to Mairi. "Could I have a word with you?"

Might he have some news of Iain? "Of course, sir." Heart thudding, she went out with him to where his horse was tethered.

He studied her a moment. "You're with child, aren't you, lass?"

How could he guess? A blush scalded her. She glanced involuntarily at her waist, confirming what she knew—that she was slender as ever, thinner even, for she lacked appetite.

"It's not yet apparent." Sympathy warmed his voice. "But there's that soft glow to your skin, and your hands hover in front of you as if protecting something precious. Does the father know?"

Mairi's throat was dry. "He must not. I—I love him, sir, and he loves me. But I'll never see him again."

"Is he dead?"

"I pray not."

"Then you mustn't speak of never. Is he in the army? I'll write his commanding officer—insist you're sent a bit from his pay."

"You've struck it, sir. My lad's in the army. But I'll manage fine. It's best he never knows."

He frowned. "Do your people know?"

"I—I'm going to tell them when the men come home."

"They'll stand by you?"

"If they can't do it freely, welcome my bairn, I'll take myself off and find work to keep me and the babe."

His straight eyebrows lifted. "Captain MacDonald praised your skill with the harp."

She laughed ruefully. "Bless us, you mean I might make a living at the harp? It's long and long since anyone's done that."

"It would please me well to have a harpist at Lews Castle," he said. "I'd give you your own house, on the grounds or in town."

Mairi said courteously, "You're very kind, sir. But I want my bairn to grow up among our people. Then, you see, he'll have a family and not feel the lack of his father so much."

"I see." Sir James' tone was dry but amused. "I see you love the rascal father more than he deserves. But good luck to you, Mistress Mairi." His smile flashed as he mounted. He raised a hand in salute, and the black set off at a smart canter.

THE men returned in mid-September, jubilant that they now had leases on their homesites and, for each household, six acres of arable land near the broch. Almost as exciting was a letter from Catriona, which included greetings from Kirsty and Adam. For fifty cents they had bought land scrip for six hundred and forty acres in the Republic of Texas. "The sun shines so hotly, I'm glad when it rains," Catriona wrote. She gave special messages to each of them, asked hungrily for news, and concluded: "Every night you are remembered in our prayers. Still, we are glad to be in a country so big and beautiful, with almost everything free for the taking and hard work. Calum had better come swiftly. Men outnumber women a dozen to one. I've had five proposals of marriage. Tell him to come, Mairi, so we can start our own family! Your Viking, Catriona."

In order to take it all in, Mairi read the letter aloud three times. A laird's estate—six hundred and forty acres!

"It's sure to harm the eyes, all that Texas sunlight," said Gran.

"I couldn't live out of sight of the sea," admitted Andrew. "But Adam was more farmer than fisherman."

Mairi couldn't bring herself that night to confess about her baby. Let them enjoy Catriona's news and the pride of securing land.

The fishing had gone well, too. After settling with the curer and buying supplies, each family had silver to tuck away. If only Mairi didn't have to give her folk such news! More than what they'd think of her, she hated what they'd think of Iain.

THE heads of grain were full and heavy. It would be a fine yield, though not enough for their needs. Fortunately, there should be plenty of potatoes, and next year they'd have enough land to grow all their oats and barley. There'd be kale from new beds, and four young pullets would be laying eggs before spring.

On Saint Michael's Day the harvest was in. As everyone gathered about the hearth to eat special bannocks of new grain, Mairi resolved to tell her secret. With each breath she drew, she intended to speak, but her courage would fail or someone else would talk.

She closed her eyes, drew in a long breath. It would never get any easier. "I've something to tell you." She didn't recognize her own voice, it was so cracked and thin. The familiar faces turned to her suddenly seemed those of strangers. "I am with child."

"Lassie!" cried Gran, starting up.

Shock in all those eyes. Disbelief. "I've been offered work by the laird, so you needn't feel you're casting me out," Mairi said, painfully looking at each person in turn. "If—if you cannot love the babe—be its family—I will go away."

Tam's face was white, but he came to stand by her. "I'll take care of you, Mairi."

Eileen threw her arms around her. "If you go, Mairi, take me!"

"There'll be no going," rumbled Andrew. "You're the living heart of us, Mairi lass."

"You saved us," said Katie. "How could we not love your bairn?"

Sheila slipped an arm around Mairi, while Barry, crimsoning, struggled with words. "Does the captain know?" he finally blurted.

531

"I don't want him to. I'm afraid that if he knew, he'd want to take the child away, have it fostered on the mainland."

"Mainland, indeed!" Morag's eyes flashed. "We'll do far better here for the bairn, though the christening will be hard!"

By then Mairi was weeping, embraced by her brother and sister and Sheila. Rising from Fearchar's chair, Andrew enfolded them all in his great arms. "Don't fash yourself, lass. You'll have your bairn and rear it with our help and love. That's all that need be said."

THE new houses were roofed with timbers from the broch, which now stood open to the sky, peat-blackened walls calling up memories of its shelter. Barry pried up the hearthstone and carried it to the center of the MacLeods' dwelling. Cridhe stood draped in her plaid, so the place was immediately home. Within a week each house had enough peats to last till summer. Delving up the potatoes was the last autumn chore. The others had urged Mairi not to dig, but though she was almost five months pregnant, she was still light on her feet, and the rounding of her belly didn't show, because of her full skirts. She was carrying a load to the barn when she spied a man in a dark kilt and red jacket striding from the north.

"Calum!"

Dropping the creel, she sped to meet him, but Eileen and Tam reached him first. Hugging, laughing, weeping, brothers and sisters embraced in a tangle of arms and kisses.

"Can it be little Eileen?" Calum marveled. "Tam lad, you're nigh tall as me. And Mairi, you—you're a woman!"

He soon must know how true that was. But for this moment, how wonderful to touch him and gaze into his warm hazel eyes. He'd gone away a lad and come back a man, Mairi thought.

Andrew, Barry, Sheila, and Gran took turns at greetings. Calum met the Gunns and MacKinnons, gave reassuring news of Lucas and Paul, and devoured bannocks and crowdie as he told them something of the army. Only when he went with Mairi to fetch water from the burn did they have a chance for a private word.

"So there's a letter from Catriona? She's happy over the sea?"

"She sounded so. She says you'd better come before she flits with some Texas Ranger or other lonesome bachelor." Mairi dropped the teasing and faced him. "Will you go, Calum?"

His jaw clenched. "I've a debt to settle first."

Mairi's heart froze. "Calum! Fearchar wouldn't want you to hang or be transported!"

"It's not Fearchar I'm suiting, lass. It's myself."

She caught his hand. "Lad, don't leave us to mourn you, too!"

"Hugh Sinclair lied to me out of his black beard, and to Paul and Lucas." Calum's voice held cold rage. "Said if we went for soldiers, our folk could bide safe in our crofts. And didn't he wait till the men were at the fishing to come with torches? I won't forgive him that."

Still, as days passed, Calum seemed in no hurry to find Sinclair. He went fishing with the men and helped break the new croplands. Then, the second week of November, he stuffed his few belongings into a pack. He said he was going to Stornoway and find a ship there or on the mainland to carry him over the ocean.

"But you haven't given any warning!" Mairi protested, crying. "Oh, Calum, at least stay the night and make a proper farewell!"

Awkwardly he patted her cheek. "Come, lass! We've had a good visit. I know you can manage without me. I must be on my way."

"But Calum— You won't be looking for trouble?"

"Would I do that?" His tone was bland, but a smoldering in his eyes filled her with dread.

Mairi made a quick decision. "We need some indigo and other things," she said. "I'll walk with you and have your company. Annie Gordon's said I may spend the night when I'm in town."

He gave her a look of mingled vexation and amusement. "Hurry up with you, then. It's a long trudge, even for a soldier."

In half an hour they had started out. Mairi told Calum in more detail about her desperate walk this way almost a year before and how Magnus had rescued Tam. "And now Eileen's set her heart on Magnus waiting for her," Mairi finished.

"And from all I hear, he's set his heart on you."

"He's a sailor." Mairi shrugged. "No doubt he's courted a dozen women since he was with us."

"When the captain was wounded," Calum said in a sudden turn of conversation and with a searching glance at her, "it was said in his fever he called on a Mairi. He asked her to play her harp."

"Perhaps he thought on Mairi of the Isles, Màiri Nighean Alasdair Ruaidh."

"That Mairi is dead near two centuries," said Calum dryly. "I doubt Captain MacDonald was having dreams of her. It's said he had a rosy purple coverlet that he held to."

"We gave him that." Mairi turned on her brother. "If it solaced him, I'm grateful. And yes, I love him, and yes, I will for always."

"He's gentry, lass."

"I know. Don't fret, Calum. He'll come no more to the island."

It was dark when they stopped at Annie Gordon's. She welcomed them in and said at once that Calum could sleep in the shop. Putting another peat on the fire, she said nothing would do but for her to heat up the mutton broth she'd had for supper.

When Mairi awoke in the dark November morning, Calum had gone out. "He'll be at the harbor about his passage," Annie said.

Mairi frowned. "If he happens into Hugh Sinclair—"

"Well, you can pick out what you need from the shop. Maybe Calum will be back by then. You need indigo?"

Mairi made her purchases, including Gran's favorite toffees, and was deciding on sour-plum candies to treat the rest when a stout little woman burst into the shop. "Annie, Annie, what a moil! Hugh Sinclair's roof burned around his ears, and him trounced within an inch of his life! A lad did it who's been caught and dragged to jail. Hanging for him—or at best, hard labor in Australia."

Mairi cried out. Swaying, she leaned against the doorframe.

"She's the lad's sister," said Annie.

"Och! I'm sorry, to be sure! Had I known . . ."

As the woman withdrew with a pitying look, Annie put her arm around Mairi. " 'Tis an ill thing, love. But likely the judge will be merciful, since your grandfather died from the burning."

"Why did he do it?" Mairi wailed. "More grief it is to us if he hangs." She sobbed on Annie's shoulder till the worst shock passed. "I've met the laird. I'll beg him to do something."

"The laird's in England," Annie said with tears in her eyes.

Mairi groaned, thought desperately. "Do you know the jailer, Annie? Is he a drinking man?"

"Mother's milk to him the whisky is." Hope flared in Annie's face. "Let's go to the harbor. If there's a captain I'm friends with, maybe I can fix it for him to be off with Calum before the hue and cry is raised."

THE OVERCAST SKY THREATENED rain. Gray clouds merged with gray sea, but the wind, though chill, wasn't blowing hard. Scanning the ships riding at anchor, Annie let out a glad cry. "Mairi! The *Selchie*'s in! And who's this rowing to shore but the lad himself!"

It was Magnus bending to his oar, Magnus who leaped to the sand and ran toward Mairi, fair hair an aureole around his tanned face, while his companions hauled the boat ashore. Catching Mairi up in his arms, he kissed her cheeks and then her mouth.

"Am I dreaming? Are you the first one I see?" Looking more closely, he asked quickly, "Why, lass, have you been crying?"

She told him, Annie filling in when Mairi's voice broke. His eyes, blue with that haze of gray, darkened like night.

"We'll have Calum out of jail," he said, "and away on the *Selchie*, but that'll have to wait for dark. Let's go to your place now, Annie, while we plan what's to be done." He swept the women along with him, so big and strong and buoyant that Mairi took heart.

While Annie attended to a customer, Magnus poured Mairi some tea in Annie's private quarters and made her sit in the chair by the fire. He pulled up a stool. "Well, lass, it's a rare tangle. But never fear. I've broke my crewmen out of better jails than this." He brought her hand to his cheek. "We'll slip out of the harbor as soon as we can see in the morning. I was coming to see you. Now that'll have to wait, so I must use this little time we have."

She tried to withdraw her hand. "Magnus . . ."

He set his hands on the back of the chair on either side of her, but she was trapped more by his gaze than his arms. Her heart tripped heavily. "Well, lass. Will you wed me?"

"You know why I can't."

Still not touching her with his hands, he kissed her long and deliberately, his mouth warm and hard. He drew back, frowning.

"I've had warmer kisses from a stone." He gripped her wrists. "Is that it, Mairi? Did that man you love seduce you?"

"Seduce me he did not! But—" She took a breath and plunged. "I will have his bairn."

Magnus let go of her. He turned, yellow head bent as if he had sustained a deadly hurt. At last he said, "Will he help you?"

"He doesn't know. I don't want him to. He'll come no more to the island." She sat with her head bowed, sorry to lose his respect.

535

After what seemed a very long time, he lifted her from the chair to his lap. "You need a husband, Mairi, and a father to your bairn." He cradled her as if she were herself a child. "Wed me. The tyke will never know it wasn't got in our marriage bed."

She buried her face against his massive shoulder and sobbed until she was exhausted. He smoothed her hair, whispered tender, loving words. When she quieted, he smiled into her eyes. "After I've landed Calum safe, we'll marry, with a great feast. Proud I am to have you, and the world shall know it."

Resting in his arms gave her a wonderful feeling of being cherished and protected. He would love her child. Iain intended never to see her again; he wouldn't even know about the baby.

Every reason to wed Magnus against the single truth of her heart—it was Iain whom she loved. She moved her head in sad negation. "Magnus, in the whole world, you're my dearest friend. But I still am his." Wresting free, she stood erect. "I thank you with all my heart. But I—I cannot do it."

Magnus got to his feet. "Then there's naught more to say." He swung toward the door. "I'll warn my men. Meanwhile, you and Annie think upon the best way to get your brother out."

DARKNESS and fog pressed so thickly that Mairi could scarcely breathe as she moved with Annie through the narrow streets. Annie had a jug of good whisky under her shawl, and Mairi carried a *cruit*—a sort of lute—that Annie had borrowed from a neighbor.

"Mind now," cautioned Annie. "We've come to visit Calum and give him a cheering dram. It's up to you to sing so sweet that Angus Roy, the jailer, will sit and tip the jug with us till he's snoring. Magnus will wait for us at the net loft on the harbor."

Sure enough, Angus, a wizened, sharp-faced man with red hair, opened to them gladly, and pulled a bench into the passageway leading to a few musty cells. As Calum's face came to a small barred window, Mairi gasped at the bloody weal across his cheek. But he chuckled, and said, "If you think I look tousled, you should have a peek at Hugh Sinclair." He added regretfully, "He'll not die of his whipping, but maybe he'll be less eager at thatch burning."

"Under the new laird there'll be no evictions," Mairi pointed out. "Calum, laddie, would you had left Sinclair to God!"

"Too slow," Calum said unrepentantly.

Angus Roy nodded. "Those sorry about what you did to Sinclair will only rue that he wasn't killed entirely. If that be a jug beneath your plaid, Mrs. Gordon, I could relish a drop."

"To be sure, Angus." Producing several small cups, Annie poured out the drams. *"Slainte!"* she toasted. "Lass, give us a tune."

"I'll try, though it was only this afternoon I met this *cruit*." Mairi teased her brother by singing "Beloved Calum Is My Sweetheart," then sang the ballad of the selchie of Sule Skerry.

"Ye play fine, lass." Angus wagged his head and held out his cup, which Annie filled to the brim.

Mairi sang a dozen more, marveling that Angus could drink as much as he did and still be sitting up. Maybe he wasn't going to get drunk. Maybe he could lounge there all night. Maybe—

Her nerves had reached the breaking point when the jailer rose with a sigh and unlocked the door of Calum's cell. "I could listen to ye all night, lass, and drink your good whisky, Mrs. Gordon," he said with a roguish wink. "But ye must be off with the lad."

As the women stared at him, his shoulders shook with mirth. " 'Twas a canny notion, to wile me with music and get me drunk, but bless you, 'tis a long time yet you'd be waiting. Take that rope there and tie me up, do, so that 'twill be seen in the morning."

"You're kind, Master Angus," Mairi said.

"I've no love for Sinclair." He cocked a ruddy eyebrow at Calum. "Wasn't I a soldier meself and came home to find me mother turfed out of her house?"

As they tied him hand and foot, Angus said hopefully, "One last drop, Mrs. Gordon. To help me sleep on these plaguey stones?" He got it, and a kiss, before they slipped out into the fog and murk.

Magnus loomed as they approached the net loft. The men shook hands in the darkness, and they all made their way down to a small boat. Mairi hugged her brother tight, relief at his freedom mixed with sorrow at losing him. Then Magnus brought Mairi so close that even through their heavy clothes she felt the hardness of his bones and muscle. "I'd wed you after the bairn comes," he whispered. "I'll wed you, Mairi, any day you'll have me."

Releasing her, he joined Calum. The men softly called farewells out of the darkness; then there was only the plashing of the oars.

537

Mairi drowsed fitfully that night. At the first hint of dawn, she got quietly out of bed, dressed, and stole through the shop and into the street. Down at the harbor, anchored ships bulked against an iron sky. As she watched, the shadowy form of the *Selchie* began to move. Mairi waved though no one could see, called farewells though no one could hear. Tears blinded her as the ship merged with dark ocean and sky. She walked back to the shop.

"Hot porridge will set you right. We can breathe easy, now you've seen the ship sail." Annie was up now, briskly stirring oats into water. "Did you have good potatoes this year?"

"Grand ones, fine and firm." Mairi thought Annie was making conversation to divert her, till the older woman frowned and said, "The word is the crop is lost in Ireland, rotted in the earth."

"Poor folk. Maybe the blight will die with the winter."

"Let's pray so. But the weather's freaky this autumn. In September a strange powdery dust fell on the Orkneys. It's stayed warm much too long. I do not like it, Mairi."

A chill fingered Mairi's spine. "We've more land for grain, but it's potatoes that must fill us. All we can do is plant them and hope."

# 8

BEFORE they left for the winter fishing that started in January 1846, the men prepared the potato beds, and on good days fished from the boat for cod, ling, whitefish, skate, and turbot.

"If we had a way of getting our catch to market . . ." said Barry.

The township had an agreement to supply the lodge folk with cured fish, but there was no other local sizable demand. "When Lucas and Paul come home," mused Andrew, "maybe then we'll have two boats. That might make it worth some captain's trouble to call in here." He glanced at Mairi. "Think you Magnus would?"

"If he won't, some captain might."

While the men were away at the fishing grounds, the women started planting potatoes. After much inner debate, Mairi, heavy now in her seventh month, had told the others about the blight. She hated to worry them, but it was a threat she couldn't bear alone. The soil of the lazybeds was so fertile, though, and the seed potatoes so healthy, that she thought surely the plague wouldn't reach here. Then in the spring fearful news came that potato pits opened on the mainland held nothing but stinking slime. Mairi watched the planted beds intently.

The wheatears were just back from the south, warbling from hillocks, when Mairi awoke on the twentieth of March with cramping pains. Iain! I wish you were with me now, she thought. Wherever he was, she hoped he was thinking of her, that he still loved her, now as she fought to bring his child into the world.

She met the pangs as a swimmer the waves, trying not to be swept under, not so much frightened as amazed. In spite of her body's swelling, she had not quite believed she would bear a child. Now for the first time she realized her life would change profoundly.

She caught in her breath at a pain that clutched deep, relentlessly. When the spasm eased, she got out of bed, remembering that walking helped. Gran was instantly with her. "The babe?"

Mairi nodded.

"Best not eat anything, lassie. We'll brew you tea. When the next pain eases, start singing a waulking song that takes five minutes. By the time you scarce finish before the next cramp starts, we'll have in the other women."

The fist knotted again inside Mairi. As the contraction passed, she sang softly—three songs before the pain coiled again. Mairi walked and sang and drank the hot drafts Gran gave her.

Eileen crept in, eyes wide, and was soon sent for Katie and Sheila. They walked with their arms around Mairi, encouraging her, while that great, gripping hand tugged at her flesh, clenched tighter and tighter, till she could no longer force back her cries.

Getting her to bed, they gave her their hands to squeeze. This couldn't be natural! She was being riven apart. Screams tore from her throat. Oh, she was breaking! "Push, lass!" Gran's voice from far away. "Come, Mairi, push!"

She tried to gasp that she couldn't. Pain hurled her into fiery blackness, pain that had no ending. After an eternity she heard Gran's voice from a long way off—from another world. "Her bones are too narrow. I fear she must die, and the babe in her—"

Not Iain's child! Summoning strength from some power beyond her, Mairi bore down with all her will. "Iain!" she called.

On his name, she thought she had died, then heard a thin wail and Gran exulting. "Och! 'Tis a fine lad with the hair of his da."

Mairi lay panting, unable to believe it was over. "He's—he's all right?" she demanded when she could speak.

"See for yourself." Old eyes glowing, Gran washed the babe and placed him in Mairi's arms. "A bonnie, bold lad for sure."

Indeed, his black ringlets, damp from being washed, were beginning to fluff. He bore a clear resemblance to Iain, especially in black brows that furrowed imperiously as he howled protest against this strange new universe. Mairi nudged him to her breast.

Now her wee lad was in her arms, Mairi could scarce remember how it had been without him. She never tired of marveling at the perfection of his skin, of his thickly lashed, smoke-colored eyes.

If only Iain could see him! Her son so filled her heart that she wondered how she could still miss Iain so much and love him even more. David—Mairi would have him christened Michael David after Fearchar—was a constant reminder of him, of course, but now she needed Iain to father their child, not only as her man.

As she grew stronger, Mairi could no longer put off the hateful necessity of approaching the Reverend Marcus Guinne, minister of the kirk where Seana had been christened, and asking him to christen David. He would certainly belabor her for conceiving out of wedlock. Still, if she wanted her baby baptized a Christian soul, she would have to accept whatever reviling came with it. Sheila and Morag went on the journey with her. Morag, the only person from Clanna who attended kirk, might have credit with the minister.

She did, enough for him to pity her ties to a parcel of godless heathen. Standing on the threshold of the parsonage, the Reverend Guinne ranted at Mairi till he ran out of breath. When she said nothing of regret, his florid face went even redder.

"Do you not understand, woman? You have played the harlot. Do not think, Mistress MacLeod, that there's not been shrewd guessing over who gave you your bastard."

For him to say such a thing of the innocent child at her bosom! "You will not call my child that!"

He glared at her, then composed himself. "Well, the child must not go unbaptized. He may have his christening on Sunday."

Mairi turned to go. Guinne's voice stopped her. "Before the

540

naming," he said, "you will stand bareheaded before the kirk while decent folk come in. You will not answer whatever they say to you, for you be mightily in need of mortification."

Mairi recoiled. Even Morag looked aghast.

"See you are here early." He shut the door in their faces.

"Now I pray I never need have another babe christened by yon cruel man!" Sheila cried.

"He was over hard," admitted Morag.

"David will have his name as a Christian," Mairi said as they set off across the moor. "That's all that matters."

WHEN the rest of Clanna heard her penance, Donald Gunn said, "I can't bear seeing Mairi shamed, when she saved our lives!"

"Nor we," said Murdo and Gavin at once.

"It will only be for an hour or so," Mairi said, though the thought of it, of the prying eyes and sneers, the dirtying of her love, made her stomach churn. "I will stand there a short while, and my laddie will have his name for all his life."

Gran came and put an arm around her. "I'll go stand with you."

Katie clapped her hands together. "That's it—we all will!" As the others stared at her she said, "Those mean enough to jeer at a lone lassie may not find it so easy to gibe at strong men."

" 'Tis a grand notion, Katie." Andrew chuckled in relief.

"It may anger Reverend Guinne till he won't baptize David," Mairi protested.

"All we're doing is letting the world know that Clanna stands by its own." Rising, Andrew gathered Mairi and David into his arms. "Don't be sore-hearted, love. All we can do, we will."

"And afterward we'll have a christening feast," Gran said. "Bid all the lodge folk and send word to Annie Gordon, too."

On Sunday, in her mother's black wedding dress, Mairi stood in the kirkyard with David in her arms, but she was not alone. Her friends and kinfolk were scattered around, placing themselves as if by accident between Mairi and those passing into the kirk.

These shot curious or scornful glances at her, though none of them paused till one woman gave a sneering laugh and said to her husband, "That's Captain MacDonald's hussy and his by-blow."

Barry stepped in front of the woman. "That's Mairi MacLeod of

Clanna," he said, and gave the woman such a grim look that she gripped her husband by the arm and hurried into the kirk.

Ewan and Mrs. Fraser appeared with two men from the lodge. Ewan stopped to talk with Andrew. Mrs. Fraser spoke to Gran, and was introduced to the newer members of Clanna, but neither she nor her husband—nor the lodge men—moved on.

As the hour of the service neared, Reverend Guinne came out of the parsonage and saw the crowd around Mairi. "Go your ways in!"

Ewan Fraser smiled blandly. "Come along, then, Mairi lass, and sit you by my wife on the women's side."

"No!" cried Guinne. "She shall not go in."

"Whisht, parson!" Andrew boomed. "My cousin has done your bidding—stood outside while your righteous folk shanked in."

"She was not alone!" cried the minister. "Your whole ilk stood with her—even these folk from the lodge."

"Aye," cut in Barry, blue eyes aflame. "You'd have no doubt liked it better had folk thrown rocks and spit at her!"

The minister glared from one person to another. "Will you go into the kirk and leave this sinful woman here?"

No one moved. Guinne stared at Mairi. "I will tell you how it is, Mairi MacLeod. You have puffed up the hearts of these people. You have made idle music that filled their minds with heathen pride. I will christen your child only when you bring me that harp I have heard of, that harp for which your grandsire went into earthly flames and earlier than need be into those of hell."

"What would you want with the harp?" Mairi asked, frightened.

"You will burn it here, before the kirk, as should be done with all pipes, fiddles, and such that encourage folk to light-mindedness."

Though she knew musical instruments had been burned throughout the islands at the ministers' urging, Mairi could scarcely believe her ears. She would put herself in the fire before she would yield up Cridhe. But for her son not to have his name? Did an unbaptized soul, even a baby, burn in everlasting flames?

Mairi held David closer at that horrible thought. Her knees turned to water. All she saw was Guinne exulting, sure of victory.

Suddenly she felt the presence of those spirits of the hearth that Gran invoked each night. They were real; they were love and protection, older than the kirk. A vision of the Stones, where David was begotten, rose before her. She would carry David to the Stones and show him there. She would give him his name there, and tonight at the often-blessed hearth.

Guinne shouted, "You'll bring the harp?"

"I will not."

"Don't think another minister will grant what I refuse till you rid yourself of that devil's plaything!"

Mairi looked at him. What kind of blessing could come from his twisted heart? She thought better of God than that He would punish a baby, or that He willed all music should cease.

"Don't fret yourself, Reverend Guinne. Brigid will give my bairn his name, Christ's foster-mother."

He took a furious breath. "You prate papist idolatry! Aye, and you shall not enter my kirk till that harp is burned before it."

"Then I will never enter."

"Woman," he cried, "with every word you damn yourself! I leave you with your folly."

He flung away. Trembling now that it was over, Mairi turned to her friends. "Go to service or back home. I will come soon, but first there is a place where I must take small David."

Gran's face widened in quick understanding. "A good notion, lass. I'll come with you."

"I will go to kirk," said Morag, pale and distressed. "Och, Mairi, child, I'll pray for you!" She made for the kirk, where she went in with the Frasers.

"Shall I walk with you?" Andrew asked.

"Go make ready for the feast," Gran counseled. "We'll strike across the moor here, but it will be late ere we come home."

The others started homeward. Mairi didn't have her strength back fully. Little and dear as her burden was, her arms and back were already weary. In a short time David began to whimper. Mairi sat on a rock near a thicket of whortleberries in profuse pink bloom and nursed him. Rested, they journeyed on.

At last the Stones reared against the dark sea. This brisk April day there was no mist. The waiting pillars, with their irregular shapes, seemed more than ever a gathering of archaic beings, cloaked and hooded. Gran beside her, Mairi walked down the aisle and stood in the center at a place that emanated power. It might have been on

this exact spot that she and Iain had created the child in her arms. She uncovered him as if showing him to revered kinfolk.

"This child was got here on Midsummer morn," she told the mystery long worshipped in this place and surely still existing. "I give him the name of David Michael. Accept him. Bless him."

Gran took David then. Crooning soft words Mairi couldn't distinguish, she walked three times sunwise around the great stone. A golden eagle soared upward, tips of its great wings splayed, and as it burst through streaked clouds, light rayed on the ancient circle, giving an incandescent luminance to David's flesh, so that to his awed mother he seemed a being of sun and air.

Gran put him back in Mairi's arms. "He will be a great man of our people. Hurry now, or we'll come late to his naming feast."

THE DIM YELLOW GLIMMERING from Clanna's windows guided them the last stretch over the moor. They were welcomed to a company already merry with Gran's heather ale, whisky brought by the lodge people, and French claret from Annie Gordon. Mairi exclaimed at the presents filling David's cradle.

"We brought the silver cup," said Ewan Fraser.

"The spoon's from me," called Annie, "and the bit jersey."

Mairi praised these gifts, and also the small wicker chair from Barry, an array of animals carved from driftwood by Murdo and Gavin, and warm knit garments from Clanna's women.

The guests had contributed to the gala meal. There was cock-a-leekie soup, finnan haddie, savory bannocks filled with cod livers, potato scones, crowdie, raisin-and-spice scones, treacle tart, carrageen pudding with raisins, and a basket of sweeties from Annie.

When David was tucked in his cradle, Mairi tuned Cridhe and played a song Fearchar had composed to his harp. Cridhe responded joyfully, as if knowing Mairi had refused to yield it to the burning. When Mairi tired and Tam played his pipes, Murdo danced a fling on a space no bigger than two peats, pointing toes and arching feet with great dexterity while the rest cheered him.

Nothing would do then but to clear away the table and dance foursomes to pipe and harp. *"On your feet, my pretty little love, on your feet, my darling . . ."* Save Morag, everyone danced.

It was almost dawn when the visitors spread out to sleep through houses and barns, and Mairi and Gran were at last alone by the fire. Gran banked the ashes and arranged the peats in the name of the God of Life, the God of Peace, and the God of Grace, while Mairi brought David, still sleeping. "Thou Sacred Three," prayed Gran. "Save, shield, protect this babe. Bless him as David Michael MacLeod in this life, and after death, receive his soul."

Dipping her finger in the ash, Gran touched it to his forehead.

THOUGH she had scarce laid head to pillow, Mairi was up early to milk the cows now grazing on moorland leased from Sir James. Starting past the other houses sheltered by the slope, she was glad the men had begun building homes for the MacKinnons and Barry and Sheila, now happily expecting a new baby.

The sound of shod hoofs reached her. Turning, she saw a rider approaching on a chestnut. There was something about him—something familiar. Her heart stopped. No, it wasn't Iain. There was just a likeness in build, in the proud carriage of head and shoulders. She'd never seen this man before.

As he neared, Mairi was filled with misgiving. This man could almost be a model of Iain in thirty years. The craggy face was weathered brown, which gave the light gray eyes an icy hue. Black hair was streaked with white, and the mouth was a grim line.

"I would speak," he said, "to a certain Mairi MacLeod."

"You have your wish, sir."

"I've heard you have a son. I wish to see him."

Mairi stiffened. Gentry this stranger was for sure, but he'd no right to make such a demand. "The baby's sleeping, sir."

Dark brows joined over a hawk nose. "Would it make a difference if you knew I am Roderick MacDonald, uncle to the Captain MacDonald with whom, I believe, you are well acquainted?"

Mairi would have given anything to sink into the ground and, failing that, to run far out of sight.

He gave a harsh laugh. "Where's the vaunted island hospitality? Will you not invite me into your house?"

Hospitality was a rule so deeply engrained it was second nature, but she didn't want this man to see David. "You are welcome, sir, for the captain's sake," she said at last. She led the way to the house, but paused at the threshold. "I'll fetch you some milk."

"Never mind. I've claret in my flask." Roderick MacDonald glanced impatiently beyond her. "Are you ashamed of this child?"

"Indeed not! Come, then, and see." Mairi stepped in and went swiftly to the cradle. David slept with his face nestled against one chubby arm, dark hair clustering on neck and forehead.

"No doubting the father." Was it a trick of light or had the chill eyes softened? "Iain had that very look when I went out to India. By the time I returned, he was grown, but I remember him in my sister's arms." Shrugging off the memory, MacDonald stared at Mairi across the sleeping child. "Since this babe is his, I'm prepared to take him—pay for his fostering in some worthy home."

When Mairi stood speechless, MacDonald said, "You must see that would be an advantage to you both."

"I cannot think it an advantage to either of us."

"Come now! How can you hope to find a husband with a bastard at your knee?" His eyes slitted. "You plan to use him on Iain?"

Mairi clenched her hands. "I could have told the captain about my bairn before he left last autumn. I didn't. I never will."

The disbelieving gaze probed her. "Why? You don't seem so prosperous as to spurn a settlement."

Mairi lifted her chin. "We've enough. We'll manage."

"You are not what I expected," said MacDonald slowly. "I believe that you love my nephew, and it's clear you love your son. Wouldn't you like for him to be brought up a gentleman and educated to the level of his abilities?" His hand swept disdainfully past the view from the window. "Don't you want something better for him than this . . . . endless grubbing to barely scratch a living?"

"It can be a good life. We have our boat and cropland."

"And when the oats and barley are beat to the ground by storms? Or if the potatoes rot, as they have in Ireland?" He made an impatient gesture. "You don't seem stupid. It's likely Iain's son will be intelligent. He could become a factor, perhaps even a lawyer."

"A factor? To bully the poor? I'd rather him dead," Mairi said.

"You speak foolishly."

" 'Tis only truth. Will you kindly be on your way, sir? I must get back to work."

"You needn't work if you give me the child. Iain wanted you provided for, young woman. That's how I learned of you."

"He—he didn't tell you?"

"No. He told his solicitor—who is also mine—to send you the better part of the allowance I've made him."

So Iain had taken care for her! Even in this tense moment, that filled Mairi with joy. Still, she set herself between her son and Iain's uncle. "Once for all, you cannot have my bairn."

For a long time their eyes battled. She didn't look away, terrified as she was. He was rich, powerful, blood kin to her son. Was there some way he could forcibly take David?

"Think on it," he said at last. "I'll be at the lodge the rest of the week. After that, Sir James' agent knows how to reach me."

He turned to go. Mairi hated to ask anything of him, but the words burst from her lips. "Please, sir! Is Iain well?"

"The last I heard. Garrison duty in India, with a little skirmishing now and then with hill bandits." He looked at her curiously. "You don't hear from him, then?"

"It's better not."

"I'm glad you've the sense to see that, at least. Good day, then, Mairi MacLeod. I shall hope you decide to put the boy above your selfishness." Ducking his arrogant head, he went out.

As soon as the barley was sown, the men went off to the fishing. Though Roderick MacDonald had troubled her no more and had surely left the island, Mairi couldn't rid herself of uneasiness. It was like walking in the dark while expecting an ambush, the same sort of helpless anxiety she felt while daily scanning the potatoes in the lazybeds. The plants were so luxuriant that Mairi thought the tubers beneath must be sound, too, but how could one be sure?

In spite of heavy storms that set the women praying for their men, the potatoes thrived through the two June hoeings. Home again, the men laid up the walls of the new houses. Their tidings from Stornoway filled Mairi with loss. A mainland investor had offered Annie such a good price for her business that she'd sold it and gone off to marry an old sweetheart in Inverness. The new owner had put a tight-fisted Aberdeen man in charge of the shop.

" 'No credit,' he says, in a nasty, squint-eyed way," Andrew growled disgustedly.

"Will he buy our things for what Annie paid?" Mairi asked.

Andrew scowled. "Why should he change it?"

"Best to make sure," Mairi said.

August came, with butterflies shimmering green and blue over the heather. Mairi stepped out one morning and, as had become her habit, glanced first toward the lazybeds.

The potato plants drooped, looked withered. How could that be? Only yesterday she'd been sure the blight would miss them. Panic rising in her, she smothered a cry and ran to examine the crop.

Oh, Lord, no! The plants were blackening, shriveling, as if scorched by invisible fire. Walking the length of each of the five lazybeds, she saw not a single healthy green leaf—not one. Groaning, she fell to her knees and dug frantically into the soil, again and again exposing small potatoes that oozed stinking fluid.

Better than two thirds of their food for the year! After all their work and careful tending! Even as she sat there, fearful and despairing, she knew she must hold herself together, somehow encourage the others through this terrible curse.

"What is it, Mairi?" cried Sheila from her door. At once, Katie appeared in hers, and Morag and Gran and Eileen hurried out.

Mairi didn't have to phrase the deadly words. The others ran to the plants and stood dazed. "Och!" wailed Morag, dropping to her knees. Katie ran wildly along, peering down the blasted rows.

"Will we starve, then, Mairi?" Eileen implored.

Managing a smile, Mairi drew Eileen close in a reassuring hug. "We won't starve, darling. Don't we have barley and oats, and now kale growing finely? There's fish in the sea, eggs from the hens, and milk from our cows. Indeed, we're lucky we have so much."

"Aye." Morag nodded. "For that we must praise God."

Mairi turned to Gran. "I was only eight when the first blight ruined the potatoes, but didn't we find a few good ones? Enough for seed the next year?"

"We did," said Gran and Morag.

Without another word they all set to work.

Digging deep in every hill of putrefying sludge, the women rescued enough sound potatoes to plant a fair crop next spring. No one said what chilled them—that if any of the other crops failed, it would be a hungry winter, perhaps of near starvation.

Mairi tried for cheer. "We're lucky to have spinning wheels. We can do enough woolen goods to trade for what we lack."

They would have to find another buyer, though, one who'd advance them wool. When the men returned again from fishing, Andrew scowled to remember his encounter with Angus Mac-Bride, the Lowlander who'd bought Annie's shop.

"Says to me that he'd only pay half what Annie did. Says he can get cheaper goods from the Glasgow factories, dyed with bright colors—not the soft ones Rosanna makes out of God's own heather! Our wool is old-fashioned, says our little man."

"Merciful God!" Morag wailed.

"There, lass, 'tis not all bad news." Andrew beamed at the rest of them. "We got enough for our fish to buy all the grain we could carry home. Thanks to our boat, we can win more of our living from the sea when the land fails us."

Mairi wasn't ready to accept Angus MacBride's opinion, however. "Andrew, you didn't ask any of the other shopkeepers?"

"Nay. Belike I should have, but I was flummoxed by MacBride."

"Perhaps I should go myself to hunt a market for the goods. I can talk with the shop folk—find out if there's something different we could be making. Or there might be a captain who'd carry our goods to the mainland for a share of the profit."

"It's Magnus you mean," said Eileen with a sniff. "Oh, no doubting if you smiled at him, he'd take our wool to America!"

"It would be grand if we had enough fish to make it worth his while to stop here." Barry sighed. "If the 'taties hadn't failed, we'd be talking of another boat. Now . . . best be glad we can eat!"

Mairi started to nod agreement, then stopped. This was exactly the time to build another boat, if only there were a way to borrow. Another boat would benefit not only Clanna but employ men of other, destitute families. And if the township was to do more than live on the barest level during hard times, Clanna needed the means to earn more than subsistence. If she couldn't give little David a better life than that, wouldn't she be selfish to keep him by her rather than allowing his great-uncle to take over his rearing?

When harvest was over, with Tam for company, Mairi set out for town. At the lodge, Mrs. Fraser gave them news that the queen's government was too involved in financing far-off wars to spare money to relieve the starving Highlanders, but a few lairds were digging into their own pockets to feed their tenants or hire those in the worst need. Sir James was buying grain and employing men to improve the Stornoway harbor. They also worked at his castle.

As Mairi and Tam walked on to town, she saw sheep grazing where people had once lived, passed a huge tract set aside for a deer park. Even under the comparative benevolence of Sir James, there'd never again be enough cropland and moor grazing for crofters to survive on that alone. They must fish, and they must be able to make and sell something.

Besides MacBride's, three shops handled woolens. They sang the same tune as the Lowlander. The Glasgow mills turned out bright cloth far cheaper than handloomed goods. The spinning wheels that were the pride of Clanna couldn't compete with the speed of machines. It was the same for knitting. After buying wool, the Clanna women would get almost nothing for their labor.

Work was still going on at the harbor and castle. Tam glanced at men who were draining a bog in a distant field. "Maybe some of us men can get work from Sir James," he said.

Sir James! Mairi stopped in mid-stride. He would know the fashions in the great cities—know if there was a market elsewhere for Clanna woolens. It was surely to his advantage to have his tenants self-sufficient. If he had money for harbors and a grand castle, he might finance another boat for the township.

"Mairi!" cried Tam. "Where are you going?"

"To see the laird." Her step faltered for a moment. Then she thought of David, of Gran, and the others, and she flashed Tam a smile. "We're going to make him a proposition, lad."

MAIRI KNEW THEY SHOULDN'T approach the castle's grand front entrance, but she feared that if they went around to the back, servants would never let them see the laird. As it was, they were being roundly berated by a paunchy uniformed servant who opened the door, when Sir James himself came down the hall.

"Bring these young folk some refreshment, Talbot," he bade the man. "We'll be in my study." Smiling at Mairi, the owner of Lewis lifted an eyebrow at their creels. "No harp? When I saw you coming, lass, I thought perhaps you'd decided to become my musician. Come rest yourselves while you tell me why you're here."

"I have a matter of business to put before you, sir," Mairi said when they were seated. Gripping her hands behind her to conceal their trembling, she presented her arguments, while Tam stared at her as if she'd suddenly changed into someone he didn't know.

"I'm not begging, Sir James. That's the finest weaving and knitting in our creels. Surely it's to your advantage to help us find a market—surely it's cheaper to lend money for another boat than feed the six men who'd crew it, along with their families."

A girl in a ruffled white apron and cap brought in a tray heavy with raisin scones, ginger cakes, and a steaming porcelain teapot. "Will you pour, Mistress Mairi?" asked the laird.

The teapot was heavy, and Mairi's fingers visibly shook. She knew Sir James noticed. He waited till she'd fixed Tam's cup and hers before inviting them to sit down. "My wife is a friend of Lady Dunmore, who has, since her husband bought the island of Harris, found markets for the weavers there," he said. "I think it likely Lady Matheson would take an interest in promoting your township's products. But before you show her your goods, tell me more about this fishing enterprise."

At least he was hearing her out. "Sir James, you're giving employment to many to keep them from starving. If you'd lend Clanna enough for barrels and salt as well as another boat, we should be able to get a captain to stop for our fish."

"How will these six new families live?"

"We can build more lazybeds. If they have beasts, perhaps you, sir, would grant them moor grazing. If your wife will help us sell our woolens, the women could join us in weaving and knitting."

"You mean that you would share with them after you've borrowed the means from me. Heaven knows this island needs no more landless folk. That's the trouble now—too many people. I shall continue to pay the way of those who're sensible enough to prefer owning large farms in Canada or America." The shadow of a smile lit his somber eyes. "But you aren't sensible, are you?"

"I will never leave the island—nor will my grandfather's harp."

"And you would liefer play that harp in a peat-smoked black house than in my castle."

"The songs belong to my folk, Sir James, and I belong with them."

"You ask for much, Mairi MacLeod. It seems hard that the laird of Lewis should have to beg for a song."

"Indeed, sir, I will gladly play for you and your lady—but afterwards I must ever go home to Clanna."

"You'll entertain my guests when I send for you?"

"I cannot promise they'll be entertained, but I will come, Sir James, so long as I'm not in the middle of work I cannot leave."

"My music must wait on harvest, planting, or who knows what?"

"Songs are woven into our lives, sir, like part of the warp and weft. And our lives are woven into the web of this island."

His mouth bent down. "As mine is not, though I've bought it?"

"Lewis has changed lairds many times, Sir James, but my folk raised the Stones at Callanish. Time out of mind, our bodies have turned into Lewis earth. We are rock and soil of this island."

Her heart thudded sickeningly in her ears. Had she been too bold? She went limp with relief when at last he smiled. "I'll instruct my factor to advance to your township the sum needed for another boat and salt and barrels. You'll need lumber to build a quay and curing shed. Interest on these funds will be three percent, and the township has three years to pay. Also, the six new crewmen may each have four acres of arable land. And you need wool for weaving and knitting."

Mairi's head whirled at the enormity of the undertaking and the strange words. Interest! Percents! Sir James must have seen her apprehension. "No gain without risk, lass. Do you want to lay the matter before your men?"

That would take time. Feeling as if she took a heavy load on her shoulders, she said, "They're willing to leave business to me."

"You'll sign an agreement?"

She nodded, terrified. "But what if the fishing's poor? Or a boat wrecks? What if we can't pay?"

"You have collateral I'd accept to secure the loan."

"You'd take our beasts and furnishings? Or the boats?"

"No. Your harp is very old. I've a taste for antiquities. Should you default on the loan, I'd count the harp full payment."

Risk Cridhe! The pride of ancient forebears, the harp Fearchar had died to rescue? Looking into Sir James' dark eyes, Mairi spoke through a tight throat. "Were you the devil, sir, and we struck a bargain, I'd liefer stake my soul than my harp."

He smiled. "Oh, you could keep your harp—if you came to play it in my castle."

She groped for words. "It is being with my people that gives Cridhe her soul. If she leaves us, she'll be only wood and strings."

"Nevertheless, will you agree that the harp secure your loan?"

Cridhe, Fearchar, forgive me. For myself I never would. This is for our people, that they may live on the island. "If we cannot pay you, the harp is yours," Mairi said.

Sir James nodded and pulled a bell rope. "The agreement will be prepared while you show Lady Matheson your woolens."

LADY Matheson, a small, dark-haired woman with a plain, kindly face, admired the weaving and exclaimed over the soft colors. "I'm sure my friends in Edinburgh and London would buy all the cloth you can make, as long as it is of this quality," she said.

For all her wealth and rank, there was a commonsense air about Sir James' wife. The price she said that his factor would pay was the best Mairi had ever received for comparable work. Additional cloth would almost certainly be sold to society friends.

A thin, bespectacled young man brought in a paper, which he presented to Sir James with a bow. Sir James moved to a polished table, where a silver pen lay by a silver inkstand. "Read the contract before you sign, lass," he said. "A good rule always."

Some of the words were unfamiliar, but the meaning was clear. Mairi's heart stopped when she saw the words pledging Cridhe should the township fail to repay the loan. And though she took great care, her name sprawled across half the page.

# 9

AFTER buying wool and other necessaries, Mairi and Tam started home. The silver now in Mairi's creel made a lovely, soft chinking, and as she walked, she let herself dream. A harbor below the broch—half a dozen good boats, with her son the skipper of one of them. Fields of ripening barley and oats, ample kaleyards, big patches of carrots and peas in case the potatoes failed.

Still, there was a dark undercurrent beneath the sparkling flow of her exhilaration. If the loan couldn't be repaid, how would she live without Cridhe? What was that word the laird had used? Collateral. The true collateral for the loan was her heart and soul.

As they approached Clanna, Mairi saw two extra men working on Barry and Sheila's house. Were they from the lodge? She gave a glad cry as they dropped their thatching and ran to meet her. "Lucas! Paul!" Embracing them, she sobbed and laughed at once. "Look at you!" She gazed at her broad-shouldered cousins, Barry's younger brothers. "You're not lads anymore! Full grown you are!"

"I should hope so." Lucas had rust-brown hair and hazel eyes. At twenty-three he was a year older than fair, blue-eyed Paul. "Men we had better be, for we've brought home wives."

Andrew hurried up behind his sons. Mairi beamed at him and the others gathering around. "You've come at a good time, lads. The laird will lend us money for a boat you can help crew—and salt and barrels, Andrew! Even for a quay and curing shed!"

By then everyone had assembled. Proudly Lucas and Paul brought their wives forward. Sisters they were—Paul's small Rose looking no more than sixteen, while Lucas' Barbara was about nineteen, Mairi's age. Orphaned earlier, after their family was evicted from their croft, they'd been working in a Glasgow factory.

"Lucas feared I wouldn't leave Glasgow for a croft." Barbara laughed merrily. "I had to ask him if he wouldn't like to marry."

"I knew Aosda was lost," said Lucas defensively. "And though Captain MacDonald told us you were making a brave new start, how could we guess there'd be a proper township, with a boat?"

"Is Captain MacDonald well?" Mairi tried to keep her voice steady, but it treacherously faltered.

"It's Major MacDonald now," said Paul. "He sent his greetings."

Greetings! It was almost worse than no message at all. Did he no longer care? Stabbed deep, Mairi flinched, but forced herself to tell the good news about Lady Matheson's interest in Clanna woolens.

"We can weave and knit," Barbara said happily. Rose nodded.

"We saved our pay," Paul said. "It can go toward the boat."

"Aye," said Lucas. "And we know where to find the rest of our crew. Truth is, we could man a fleet with lads who went for soldiers to keep their folk safe in their crofts. Plenty of them went home to burned thatch—found their families gone over the waters or slaving in Glasgow. Neil MacAskill got wounded dragging me off the battlefield. His township's been cleared on South Uist. When he heard it, I told him he must come to us after he's found his family."

Andrew dropped a great hand on each returned son's shoulder. "Praised be the good God, there's room for him and three more men. Now we'd better hurry with Barry and Sheila's house! We have a boat to build before the winter fishing!"

AN CLANNA made several runs to Stornoway to fetch seasoned wood for the boat. On the last trip, Magnus' ship, the *Selchie,* followed the small craft like a whale with a calf, and off-loaded barrels, salt, and windowpanes for Barry and Sheila's house.

The last barrel was stored out of the weather in the broch passageway. As Mairi came from milking, Magnus loomed between her and the house. Taking the foaming bucket, he gave her a long look from those mist-blue eyes. "So, Mairi. Here you are, mother of Clanna, and the township growing in spite of famine. What surety did you give Sir James for all of this?"

When she told him, his mouth twisted as he heard the details. "I like it not, your being so beholden. Let me raise the money to pay him, lass."

It was tempting. Magnus would never evict them. "We can't let you go in debt on our account," Mairi said, screwing up courage to speak straight and honest. "Magnus, if you haven't forgot me—"

"Forgot?" He stared out at the *Selchie,* rising and falling in the waves. "Would I be here, Mairi, were you not grown into my heart?"

"I'm sorry—"

"I won't beg you." He slanted her a glance that made her keenly aware of him. How good it would be to rest in his arms, surrounded by his loving strength. A kind father he'd be to David. But, oh, Iain! And even if she could be a wife to Magnus, he deserved better.

She tried to say something of this, but he hushed her with a motion. "It would seem I must bide for Eileen. She is blood of your blood, Mairi. I will love you in her so well that she'll have no cause ever to envy another woman." At Mairi's frown, he said, "Rest easy, lass. No word of this she'll hear from me till she's sixteen."

"Magnus—"

He tilted his head jauntily. "Well, let us strike a bargain, head of the clan, since it'll be to my advantage to have well-to-do kindred."

"What bargain?"

"I want to see crofters stay on their land. Already I have agreements with several crews that own their boats. For a percentage of what I sell their catch for, I'll carry fish to the mainland. It's safe to reckon I can get you twice what the curers pay. How does a one-third share for me sound to you?"

It sounded wonderful after years in debt to the curer. "Come sup with us, Magnus," Mairi said. "I think you have more partners!"

BARRY and Sheila—and Paul and Rose with them—had scarcely warmed the hearth of their new house when Sheila's baby daughter was born, on a late November day. She came into the world with as little trouble and pain to her mother as possible. Her two-year-old sister, Seana, and young Alai were entranced with her, though they didn't abandon eight-month-old David.

Grand playmates the children would be—four of them, with only two years between oldest and youngest. Growing up with Clanna children, David would never feel a need of brothers and sisters. Or a father; all the men treated him like their own. It was Mairi who ached when she saw Iain's face in her son's, who would have given years off her life for them to know each other.

Murdo, who'd been elected skipper of the new boat, painted *Brighde*, or Brigid, on the graceful prow of the finished craft, and that same day the hearthstone was tamped in place in a new house built to shelter some of the expected newcomers. This house was soon filled, and room shared out in the other homes, for Lucas' friend Neil MacAskill arrived with others evicted from his village, all their belongings in the creels on their backs.

557

Neil and his brother, Gerald, were small, wiry men in their thirties. Neil's wife and little son had died of exposure after they were forced from their croft. Gerald's wife was yellow-haired Marta. Malcolm Fergusson and his wife, Flora, had a sixteen-year-old daughter, Margaret. Flora's brother, Allan Bailey, was a broad-shouldered lad of about Mairi's age.

The newcomers were welcomed and fed. All were used to crowded quarters, and so grateful for shelter that not even Morag complained. After what Barry laughingly dubbed the Clanna fleet was off fishing, the womenfolk slowly, steadily added to the many-hued store of knit and woven goods piled at the foot of Gran's big box bed. Spinning wheels hummed, shuttles flew, and needles flashed while they waited for the boats to pull up at the fine new quay and unload their catch.

When the laden boats came back into harbor, the women hurried down to take charge of the silver-gray mounds of cod and ling. They gutted, washed, and cleaned the fish, then packed it between layers of salt. Every barrel they packed was money for Clanna.

Several days later, as Mairi went out to cut kale, a horseman approached, wraithlike in the overcast, misty day, sitting tall on a big black horse. Her heart plunged. It was Roderick MacDonald. The gray eyes, so like Iain's, but without that inner light, gazed somberly from the long, weathered face. "Iain's son is well?"

"Very well, sir." Penetrated by cold of another sort than that of the bitter day, Mairi wrapped her shawl tighter to hide her shivering. "The captain—I mean, the major?"

"Missing in action. Presumed dead," he said bleakly. "I'm sorry to distress you, young woman."

An involuntary cry ripped from Mairi's throat. "Where—where did it happen?"

"Afghanistan. A skirmish with hill tribesmen. His body wasn't found. There were no survivors, but his horse was dead and there was blood on the saddle." The strained voice trailed off.

Struggling against a swirling blackness, Mairi whispered, "Will you come in, sir, and have some tea to warm you?"

"Last time you didn't want me under your roof."

Let her not cry in front of him. "You're cold now."

Mairi set off for the house. The kale beds, of which she was so proud, suddenly looked to her like graves. Iain couldn't be dead! She would have felt it, known it in her bones. Only perhaps it was different when someone died so far away; that soul might not find the low road home, the underground path traveled by spirits. She desperately needed to weep and lament.

MacDonald followed her inside. "Where's the child?" he asked.

She didn't want the man to see David, yet under the circumstances how could she refuse? "I'll fetch him, sir."

Annoyed at being caught up from the sheepskin where Eileen was marching a toy calf after a cow, David stiffened his sturdy little legs and stared at the strange man. MacDonald sat down cautiously in Gran's wicker chair. "He's the picture of Iain at that age."

Settling David on her hip, Mairi poured boiling water into the teapot and put out a mug. Sir Roderick drank the brew so quickly she marveled he didn't scald his throat.

"Your township has grown," Sir Roderick said. "But you seem to be eating in spite of the potato blight."

Why wouldn't he be gone? "We have another boat," she said simply. "And Lady Matheson is to find markets for our woolens."

He nodded. "Yes. And you owe for that boat and quay lumber, and salt and barrels." From his coat he brought a piece of paper with her signature at the bottom—the agreement with Sir James.

"I will burn this in the fire," said MacDonald, "if you will let me bring up Iain's son. I will adopt him, make him my heir. And you may stay with him, as his nurse, till he's of an age for school."

Gentry! They thought they could buy anything—and the pity was, in famine times they almost could. Mairi subdued her wrath before she spoke. "I'll say it again. I will not sell my son."

"That's not how to think of it, girl. You love the child. Do you love him enough to open the great world to him?"

Was she wronging David? Should she let him go? For a moment she wavered. Then Iain's face rose before her. She remembered how he had spoken of his uncle's world—how he had enjoyed helping with the thatch, how he found peace at their hearthstone.

"David will grow up with all Clanna to love and teach him. It was ill done of Sir James to let you have our agreement."

MacDonald slowly got to his feet. "He reckoned, as any sane person must, that you'd be glad to see your son inherit his father's

559

place. I offer not only an education and better opportunities. Your son would possess my lands and wealth."

Mairi said nothing.

With a closed, haughty face he dropped the paper on the smoldering peats. "That's all *your* son will ever have from me. Not that your loving family won't be deep in debt again long before the boy understands what you threw away when he was too young to choose."

Cold wind rushed in as he went out, fanning the crumpled paper into a small blaze. Stunned, Mairi watched it fade into ash.

They didn't owe for the boat, the shed, and the quay? Was a wisp of smoke all that remained of a debt they'd have done well to pay with three years' fishing and weaving?

There was relief in it for Mairi, but no joy. It was as if fate, in an unholy bargain in which she'd had no voice, had given Clanna this grace in return for Iain's life. She cuddled David to her breast. Only when he was falling asleep, replete and satisfied, did she put him in his cradle and draw off Cridhe's plaid. Her anguish poured through her fingers to the strings in the "Salute to the Chief" and the "Lament for a Chief." She played Iain's favorites, remembering him with his pipes at their hearth. Oh, God, where was he now, where was his body? And he had never even known he had a son.

WHEN the men knew they owned *Brighde* outright, they came to Mairi with a daring proposal. *If* the winter fishing, after Magnus' share, made a profit above what was needed to live, would the women, *if* Lady Matheson paid well for their woolens, consent to pool funds to build a larger boat for the summer fishing? Then the herring could be followed to the North Sea in July and fished till September, while *An Clanna* and *Brighde* could fish coastal waters, crewed by a few Clanna men and others from Stornaway.

"Let's ask all the women," Mairi said.

In a meeting like the one where Clanna folk vowed to treat David as their own, the women agreed to add their earnings to fishing profits for the makings of the North Sea boat.

And that was what they named it—*The North Sea*—lean and graceful as the Viking ships of their ancestors. It was a proud day for Clanna when *The North Sea* sailed after the herring on a bright morning in mid-May. In order to have her ready, Donald and the best builders had worked on the boat instead of going after the early herring, but their places on the small craft were filled by men from Stornoway, glad of having a share in the catch.

Spring brought the birds and brighter weather, a greening of the moor, and everyone sang at their work—prayed, too, when they planted the hoarded seed potatoes. Magnus had got a good price for the barreled winter catch, and Lady Matheson said she could dispose of double the output of wool goods. Mairi felt a little guilty that all went well for Clanna while famine stalked the islands.

Through the summer the women packed the fish the small boats brought in, and hoed the crops. When they went to milk in the mornings, they paused to scan the potato plants, breathing easily only after they saw the leaves were green and healthy.

One morning in August the plants looked shriveled. By noon blackened vines sprawled over the lazybeds. Frantic digging rescued a handful of small potatoes, not enough for seed. And that was the last of months of planting, tending, and hoping.

"We're lucky," Mairi said to hearten the others. "We've good carrots and peas. And the kale does finely and the barley and oats."

"There's fish," said Gran. "Milk and crowdie."

But what of the others? Mairi thought. What of those who'll have nothing if their crop rots, who somehow managed to hold out till now, but can never endure another famished winter?

Next morning Mairi kissed David, who at seventeen months was almost weaned, and with a creel of woolens, set off for Stornoway.

"I MUST borrow against my harp all that you will lend me," she blurted to Sir James.

He frowned, looking weary. "The potatoes are failing again, my factor says. But your township surely will have coin to buy grain."

"We will. But sir, many will not."

His dark eyes flickered. "Lassie," he said, "you cannot provide for others. Even I cannot, with thousands of pounds laid out. There are too many people. I'll pay the way of any who'll go to Canada, but to let them starve is doing them no favor."

If you gave them land from your deer parks, Mairi wanted to cry. If the beasts of Lowland farmers did not feed on the moor— But angering Sir James would ruin any chance of his help. "Those who'll go over the ocean, God speed them," Mairi said. "Many, like my brother, crave a fresh beginning. But what of those who feel they are part of the rock and earth and sea?"

"You've a bard's tongue, Mairi MacLeod, but I can't let it magic me into what would be cruel mercy in the long run. Those who can't win a living on this island must go where they can."

"If they had a chance—as Clanna did—"

"Clanna had you. Without you there would be no Clanna. If there were one of you in each township, it would be a different matter—though thank heaven there isn't or you'd take over the island." He shrugged. "Look you, Mairi MacLeod. Apart from employing men to improve the harbor, I've put in a brickworks, a paraffin works, and tried to start fisheries. Thousands would be starving except for my charity. Now the potatoes have failed again. Surely you see people must support themselves or emigrate."

"You want to start fisheries, sir. Our Donald Gunn is a fine boatbuilder. He could help the men of townships to build boats. Gran could teach the women about dyestuffs and show them the patterns Lady Matheson says sell handily. We can get them to planting peas and kale instead of depending on potatoes. And where there's no music, there must be pipes or a fiddle or harp. I'll teach the songs if no one remembers. Folk have to have the songs."

"Oh, Mairi, Mairi! A boat, kale, weaving, and music! That's your remedy for the islands? And likely you've asked your people, and they're willing to spend time this hard year helping others."

She held her breath as he turned to the window and gazed out over the harbor. Then he faced about. "I'll give you a chance, lass. For townships willing to build a boat, I'll supply the lumber. My factor will get seeds for planting. Strange as it will look on my accounts, I'll buy such musical instruments as you deem necessary. The expense will be charged to each township and repaid within five years—with interest."

"Do you want the pledge of Cridhe?"

"Yes. Are you willing to forfeit the harp if a township defaults on its loan—or if you exceed your own authority?"

It was one thing to borrow money against Cridhe that she herself was responsible for. How could she risk her harp on the efforts of people she didn't even know? Yet Sir James had taken her challenge and offered to do far more than she could have dreamed.

"I will sign your pledge," she said.

To PROTECT Cridhe from salt air and water, Donald fashioned a strong case lined with MacLeod tartan. Late that August and into the autumn *An Clanna* sailed the coast, crewed by Donald, Murdo, and Tam, while Gran and Mairi held to Cridhe in the boat.

In townships where people groaned over rotting potatoes and wandered the shore in search of shellfish and seaweed, Mairi and Gran promised wool for the looms and, where the secrets had been lost, showed how to make soft natural dyes for the plaids and tweeds. Mairi also showed them how to set out tiny kale plants and grow carrots and peas from seeds. None of these townships had boats, and all were joyous at the prospect of a craft.

Tam played his pipes at the ceilidhs, and Cridhe sang of Viking forebears and mighty heroes. Mairi sang Fearchar's songs and ones she had made herself—her lament for him, her conviction that the folk of the island would remain here so long as they kept their spirits strong with pride of their ancient roots.

In a few villages an old man brought out a squeaky fiddle or a grizzled soldier produced well-worn pipes and joined in the music. In townships where there was no instrument, Mairi watched those who listened most intently, then asked if they'd learn the pipes or fiddle and if the township was willing to add the charge for it to the amount owed Sir James. Later Tam, with his pipes, and Lucas, with his fiddle, would return to teach them.

While Donald and Murdo helped build a boat, two of the villagers crewed *An Clanna* on its way. By Christmas a score of villages had new boats, new hope, and their own music.

A miracle it seemed, yet only many times multiplied what had worked for Clanna. *The North Sea* was home after turning over the bountiful packed catch to Magnus to sell in an English port. The rents were paid, and after additional grain was bought, there was still a mellow clink of silver in each family's possession.

THE NEXT YEAR, IN 1848, THE potatoes failed for the third summer. The townships *An Clanna* had visited survived, and the relief plans of Sir James saved Lewis from starvation, but Clanna's fishing crews often landed on Harris and Uist to distribute their catch among the famished.

When *An Clanna* put in at Stornoway, Lucas and Paul helped Mairi carry the latest store of woolens to an office at the rear of the castle. As Sir James' bespectacled accountant counted out pennies, shillings, and pounds, he said, "The townships you heartened last year, Mistress MacLeod, paid their rents this year with woolens. Several even paid a bit on their loans. They're determined you won't lose your harp because of them."

Mairi stared. "I never told them about the pledge."

"Sir James thought they should know." The accountant shrugged. "Owing a rich landlord is one thing, but causing you to forfeit that harp with which you sang to them, that is something else indeed."

She was on her way out when Sir James overtook her.

"Well, Mistress Mairi, as prosperous as Clanna is, I keep expecting to see a gold brooch on your shawl or shoes made by someone other than your township cobbler."

Mairi flushed. "Andrew's shoes serve well." Twenty-one years old and the mother of a son, she'd no reason to gaud herself up like a young lass at a fair. "Everyone in Clanna has all needful—and to have more in these days seems near a crime."

"I was just down in the town," he said. "Your kinsmen are buying a great lot of meal and grain. What do you purpose? None of my tenants are going hungry, nor will they."

"Most lairds are not like you, sir. Along the coasts of Harris and Uist, folk are so weakened they go ill and die."

"You mean to take them food? They're not of your island."

"They're my people. Even were they not, they are starving. We wish to eat our bannocks without them sticking in our throats."

His dark eyes probed hers. At last he said, "So long as you pay your rents and support yourselves, I suppose what your township does with its little hoard is no concern of mine. But heed this, Mairi. Do not interfere with evictions or the legal rights of my fellow landlords. If you do, you will lose your harp."

Interfere with evictions? How could she do that? There were

always constables, or sometimes even soldiers forced to herd their own kind away from their houses. "I hear you, sir" was all she said.

"Mairi, I'm having guests the end of the month. It would pleasure me if you would play your harp for them."

How could she refuse him? But it went against the grain to entertain gentry while their tenants starved. "My tunes will not be merry, with famine in the land and folk driven from their homes."

He sighed heavily. "Make me no laments, Mairi! I do all I can."

"For that I thank you, sir. I will come when you send for me."

# 10

ON THE coast of Harris, where blue-green sea lapped on white shell sand from which marram grass flowed back, rippling like a mermaid's hair, *An Clanna* found a few families of crofters sheltering among the rocks, living on seabirds, shellfish, and seaweed. The 78th Highlanders had been called on to help the civil authorities evict the people. At the name of Iain's old regiment, Mairi's heart felt a crushing pain. Had he lived, would he have carried out that order? If he did, she would have wished him dead.

"I am almost ninety," quavered one old man as Murdo, Lucas, and Paul unloaded the grain. "Seventy rents have I paid faithfully to the laird. Never did I think to flit, except into my grave. And now where will that be?"

But nothing anywhere had prepared Mairi and the Clanna men for what they found on South Uist. Unlike the rocky coasts of Lewis and most of Harris, South Uist's sandy western beaches seemed gentle and hospitable, with meadows to support the livestock of many crofts. Instead, they heard shrieks and wailing even before they saw smoke curling yellow and thick from a cluster of houses. Men and women fled constables who wielded truncheons, knocking their quarry to the ground, dragging them to wagons.

"Is it dogs they've set on those poor folk?" cried Lucas.

It was. Beasts led their masters to fugitives hiding in some ditch or thicket. Paul swore, starting to turn *An Clanna* toward shore. Murdo caught his arm. "We can do naught, lad," he said in a choked voice. " 'Twas so they cleared my township. They must purpose to cart these poor folk to a transport ship."

Blackness engulfed Mairi. The burning thatch was that of Aosda, the wailing that of her kinfolk. Fearchar, ablaze, stumbled from his house with Cridhe in his arms. This time he didn't fall. He burned, but he did not die, and in that brilliant flame he sang to his harp.

She roused to Lucas' shaking her. "Mairi! Shall we put in to rescue that couple? Look—they're running as if they mean to plunge into the sea. 'Twill break your pledge to Sir James, but—"

Waves swept over the feet of the fair-haired man and woman. She held an infant to her breast. Constables stumbled through the marram grass; hounds bayed. "Put in for them," said Mairi.

In a frantic scramble Mairi took the infant, then helped the woman and man into *An Clanna*, while Lucas and Paul fought off the constables and hounds with their oars. As Murdo pushed into deeper water an officer of the constables shook his fist. "We mark you well—the name of your craft! Your laird will hear of this!"

"Let him hear!" yelled Lucas. "Damnation to your hard hearts!"

"Aye!" shouted Murdo. "Damn ye all!"

The woman was shaking, doubtless from terror and the chill of her wet garments. Mairi wrapped her own plaid around mother and child, while Lucas gave his jersey to the man.

"Will your families fear for you?" Mairi asked.

"Families?" The woman glanced dazedly around her. "My close kin have mostly died of sickness worsened by hunger. One brother I have left, and cousins. All left for Canada last month."

Her husband, a thin but strong-muscled man of perhaps Lucas' age, drew a long breath. "I am Marcus MacFarlane. My wife is Una. Our laddie is Angus. We are in your debt. Belike you can set us down somewhere along the shore."

Mairi gave their own names and said, "Why don't you live at our township for a while? There's fishing for you, Marcus, and spinning or weaving for Una."

Marcus frowned. "But your laird?"

"There's room for you," Mairi assured him. "So long as we pay our rents, I doubt Sir James worries overmuch how many we are."

"But if the constables report you . . ."

Lucas glanced at Mairi. "Lass, your Cridhe!"

Cridhe was forfeit. Mairi's heart was wrung for that, but she didn't think Fearchar would blame her. Her vision of

Fearchar, the words of his song, filled her like a battle cry.

"Sir James wants me to harp for his fine guests," she said. "I will make such a song that those lairds will never forget. Such a song that if Cridhe never sings again, this song will sound and resound through the isles so long as there is one of us left."

WHEN *An Clanna* sailed into the harbor, Mairi noticed a tall stranger among those who hurried down to the jetty. A black-haired man, taller than the other men . . . and wasn't that David on his shoulder? Her heart leaped. She put her hand over it as if to quiet it, hold it in her body. It couldn't be! Yet there was that slight limp, and now she could make out the face so often in her dreams.

The sky spun into the sea. Everything whirled around her. In the same breath she heard the MacFarlanes welcomed and Murdo call, "Major MacDonald, is it you indeed, sir?"

"What's left of me, Murdo." Strong hands lifted her almost bodily from the boat, or she would have fallen. "Mairi!" His eyes glowed from within like sunrays radiating through dark clouds.

"Iain! You—you're alive! Your uncle told me—"

"Truth as far as he knew it. It was months before I could get back to the regiment and send word."

"He might have let me know. *You* might have!"

"He never told me he'd seen you—never told me we have a son. And I still thought it best you had no contact with me." He caught a long breath and smiled up at David, who crooned, "Da! My da!"

The Clanna folk, knowing they had much to say, were walking toward the houses. Moving back to hold her at arm's length, Iain said grimly, "Why, Mairi? Why didn't you send me word of our laddie? I told you to let my agent know if you needed anything."

"Would I do that?" she cried, suddenly overwhelmed by the pain, humiliation, and grief of the past years—standing in the kirkyard while people called David a bastard, fending off Sir Roderick, mourning Iain as dead. Fighting now the strength of his hands, she whispered, "Why are you here?"

The sternness vanished. He looked into her eyes. Her body, so long sealed from love, quickened, as if frozen blood began to warm. "I've come to beg you to have me, Mairi."

Disbelieving her ears, she shook her head. "You said it yourself.

*The Island Harp*

We are of different worlds. Never could I leave my island."

"You don't have to, love. I'll live here, with you and our son. Sir James promises me a lease on land between Clanna and the lodge."

Too much to take in. "But . . . the army . . ."

"I resigned my commission. When the Highlanders were ordered to evict crofters on Harris, it was too much to stomach." He brought her close to him again. This time he kissed her long and sweetly. "Nor am I fettered by being my uncle's heir. He has married and already dotes on a healthy son. Since I plan to raise horses, he's given me the choice of his stables, but that's all I'll have from him. You see, Mairi mine, I am a broken-down, retired officer—no great catch for a woman of your resources. Sir James says you'd be close to rich had you built for yourself on what you've earned instead of trying to succor the whole Western Hebrides."

"Oh, Iain, Iain! I have dreamed of you but never, ever, did I dare dream this—"

Setting David down, he kissed her thoroughly. Wakened and roused, she answered his hunger with her own. She was no girl now, but a woman reunited with her man, her only man.

They walked toward the village in the last rays of sunlight. Then everything Iain's return had pushed from her mind rushed back with sickening force. Iain was still gentry, a friend of Sir James'. When he knew what she intended to do . . .

She would lose him. Him and Cridhe both. That was too cruel! Surely God meant them to be together, or it wouldn't have worked out this way. Look at David, proud of his father, adoring. She'd continue to help the scattered crofters. Surely that was more useful than insulting Sir James' guests. But again she saw the MacFarlanes' village burning. Again she saw Fearchar ablaze, with Cridhe in his arms, again she heard his song.

"Iain." Each word wrenched Mairi's heart and lungs. "We have to talk. As soon as David's tucked in bed."

Iain's male side-glance and pressure on her hand told her why he thought she wanted privacy. That brought a crueler pang. Well, they could sup together. David would have this one evening with his father home.

After they had supper, Gran fetched her heather ale by the fire. "Rosanna, we need some music," Iain said. "It's a long time,

568

Mairi, since I've heard your harp, excepting in my dreams."

"Get Tam's pipes, lad," entreated Gran. "Eileen, run tell the others that we're having a ceilidh! Lucas, go get your fiddle!"

Watching Iain while his grace notes wove in and out of her music, Mairi had never loved him more than in this time when she knew she must sing for her people, though that would surely drive him away. It was still early when Gran yawned ostentatiously, and said it was time they were all abed. The company took their leave.

Mairi and Iain were left alone in the soft glimmer of the banked peats. Iain rose. Mairi raised her hand. If he held her, if he wooed her, she would be undone.

"Iain, I have broken my pledge to Sir James. Cridhe is forfeit, but before I yield her up, she will sing such a song to Sir James' guests that they'll never forget it. You must hear that song."

Puzzled, he sat down. As she sang, she saw not Iain, but Fearchar. When she finished, Iain's face was set like stone.

"So this is your thanks to James Matheson?" he demanded.

"The song is not against him. It's for Colonel Gordon, who sets hounds on tenants, for the Dunmores, in Harris, and their ilk."

"If you insult Matheson's guests in his very castle, you won't be a good argument for aiding one's tenants, Mairi. And that last part of your song could be taken as a threat."

"It's a prophecy, Iain! You were there when Sinclair burned Aosda, when my grandfather died! What are manners and courtesy when such things are happening every day through the islands?"

He got to his feet. "If it would do any good, Mairi, I could understand. But you'll only anger and frighten the lairds. Let me make your excuses to Matheson. It may even be I can persuade him to let you keep your harp. Let me do that for you, Mairi."

But Fearchar blazed between them.

"This song was sent to me, Iain. It was given for Cridhe's last singing in the hands of a MacLeod. Some lairds may not know how their folk are evicted. And perhaps if they hear it in a song they know will be sung for generations, they may pause to think if this is how they want to be famed."

Iain stared at her. "You will do this?"

"I must."

"Mairi, are you punishing me? Because David, as Rosanna

told me, was baptized at the Stones instead of by the parson?"

"If you can think that—"

"I do think it." His voice rasped, but he kept it low. "I think, Mairi, that you can't forgive me for being gentry. That would always be coming between us. One thing is sure, you would always place your people ahead of me—ahead of our son, even. Perhaps you don't know it, but Matheson says you're renowned as a bard. They call you Mairi of the Isles. Here at Clanna, there's no doubt you're head of the clan. I could deal with that, I hope. But I cannot live with a wife more avenging fury than woman, who thinks any mad idea she has comes straight from her ancestors."

"That is for you to say." She wouldn't weep. Not till he was gone.

He shook his head. "Tell David his da will come see him soon."

Did he, like she, feel hollow and twisted inside? Why shouldn't they, at least this once, love again? But he moved swiftly past her, and she stepped well out of his way. Loving him would melt her, and she must be a sword.

SIR James came himself the next morning to tell Mairi that his guests were assembling in four days. The laird smiled like a man at last winning a wager. "So, Mairi, if you keep your word, for one night at least, you'll be my harper."

"I'll keep my word on more than that, sir. If you haven't had complaints from the constabulary or Colonel Gordon, you doubtless will. On South Uist the officers were coursing people with hounds, dragging them off like felons. Our boat put in to rescue a family. So I have forfeited my harp."

Matheson grimaced. "The harp without the harper is not such a trophy, lass. It would take a stony heart to leave anyone in that plight. When you're married to Iain, he won't let you go searching for woe."

Pleading and promises, she was sure, would ransom Cridhe. Before she could weaken, Mairi said, "The major and I may not wed."

"What nonsense is this?" Matheson's dark eyes narrowed. "For you, he's giving up position and place! And I know you have loved him only. What's gone amiss?"

"There's a song I must sing for your guests, if I sing at all, and Iain does not like it."

"I must suppose, then, that I won't like it, either."

"You will not, sir."

He colored. "Mairi, let's strike a bargain. Entertain my guests in seemly fashion and you may keep your harp."

"Sir, if I play in your castle, I must sing the song my grandfather brought me in the flames of a South Uist village."

Heat flickered in his black eyes like flame in peats. "You will play for me, Mairi MacLeod. What you sing is of your choosing. But if you persist in folly, your harp is indeed forfeit—and since without you it is only scarred willow wood and brass strings, it may go to the fire." He strode to his horse and didn't look back.

GRAN draped the dark green and black MacLeod plaid over Mairi's black dress and pinned it with Fearchar's gilt brooch. Kissing David a last time before Gran took his hand, Mairi climbed into *An Clanna*. Her cousins and Murdo were taking her to Stornoway.

Holding to Cridhe, Mairi felt as if she were taking an unknowing friend into battle. But surely Sir James wouldn't give the harp to the fire no matter how angry he was—or would he? If I can get Cridhe to sing sweet enough, she thought, Sir James may spare Cridhe whatever he does to me.

A HIGH-NOSED English footman escorted her to a large and elegant drawing room. Mairi tried to move like the head of a clan, dignified and gracious, though she was dazzled by the glittering of the ladies' jewels and the rustle of their flounced skirts. Lady Matheson greeted her kindly, but Sir James' aloof courtesy was vastly different from his usual pleasant manner.

Mairi settled herself on a bench, tuned the harp, and strummed, summoning Cridhe's memories, the spirits of all the harpers who had ever brought music from her strings. She sang war songs to rouse valor, peace songs played after victory. There was the haunting song of the seals, and there was a medley of waulking tunes, David's lullaby, songs for the harvest and planting, and Fearchar's own poems.

Mairi sang to Cridhe more than to the gathering, pouring out her heart, for this was the last time, unless Sir James relented, that her beloved harp would ever sing. Cridhe seemed to know it. Her notes had never been more sweet and resonant, and her strings responded, it seemed, almost before Mairi plucked them.

571

And now it was time.

Closing her eyes, Mairi invoked the spirits of the hearth, the Old Ones of the Stones, Brigid, Fearchar, the God of Life. Drawing in a long breath, she began Cridhe's last song:

> *"Oh, Mary Mother, of the Black Sorrows!*
> *I have seen townships swept, thatch pulled away,*
> *Roof and walls crashed over scattered hearth fires.*
> *I have seen strong men bound like cattle.*
> *I have seen their children wail.*
>
> *"Once this island belonged to the* clanna.
> *But now our chiefs have sold us to strangers.*
> *Lowlanders' sheep devour the land of our love.*
> *Our fields lie untilled under bracken and heather.*
> *I see our folk departing on the white-sailed ships.*
>
> *"Had we been sheep or deer, lairds would give us value.*
> *Men are worth nothing. The glens are empty.*
> *Yet some will endure between the rocks and the sea.*
> *If you would be rid of us, you must break the Stones,*
> *You must sink the islands below the ocean.*
>
> *"One day in this isle will come justice.*
> *Men will take deer from parks made of their fathers' fields.*
> *Their sheep and cattle will graze the moorland.*
> *Folk will bide safe in their homes.*
> *There will be no one with power to cast them out."*

There was silence. Drained, trembling, Mairi bowed her head. In a moment she must rise, give Cridhe into Sir James' hands. But it had been a brave song, a true song, and after Cridhe burned, the words would be sung through the islands.

She must be dreaming! That was pipe music! The pipes were playing the MacLeod "Salute to the Chief." She had heard only one piper who could so weave in the grace notes.

Looking up, Mairi stared at Iain. He wore the MacDonald tartan, and beside him was David. Iain finished the salute and bowed to her before he spoke to the gaping company. In the amazement that followed, he came to Mairi and raised her to her feet.

"I told them they could boast to their grandchildren of having heard Mairi of the Isles. And I told them you will be my wife."

Mairi's head swam. He'd come to protect her. In spite of his hurt and anger, he had placed himself between her and these gentry. Sir James approached. "That was rare piping, Major MacDonald."

The laird turned to Mairi. "I must felicitate with you on your marriage, but there is still the matter of your forfeit. Give me the harp, Mairi MacLeod."

Numbly she put the harp into Matheson's grasp. The fire was blazing. Even tough black willow wood would burn swiftly when it was more than a thousand years old.

Sir James didn't stride toward the fireplace. Instead, he placed the harp in Iain's hands. "This is a wedding gift, my friend. I hope I may be invited to the feast. The two of you should beget a line of notable harpers and pipers."

Iain and Mairi journeyed home on two horses, while David and Cridhe traveled on *An Clanna*. As she rode, holding to the saddle, Mairi cast side-glances at Iain. "I am obliged to you. I think if you had not been there, Iain, Cridhe would be ashes."

He gave her a grim smile. "I doubt it. Sir James confided to me that it would be a blasphemous soul indeed who would destroy a harp with such a lineage."

"You are still angry with me."

He let out an exasperated breath. "What man wouldn't be, to see his beloved so risk herself." He took her horse's reins and drew close alongside, circling her with his free arm, finding her mouth. "I meant only to protect you today. But when you played Cridhe's lament, I knew, Mairi, that you and your songs cannot—should not—be ruled by any man. If you will live with me in love, I will count myself the luckiest of men."

*The North Sea* crew was back from the fishing in time for the wedding, and when Magnus stopped for their catch, he stayed on for the ceremony. The way Magnus smiled at Eileen, it was clear he saw through new eyes that she was fifteen and very beautiful.

Sir James had fetched his own chaplain. There was no room for assembly in the houses, so it was under the sky, with birds calling and the distant crash of the waves, that Iain and Mairi stood before the company and their little son, pledging themselves forever. When Iain put his mother's ring on Mairi's finger and bent to kiss her, there was a stifled sound from Gran.

She was the first to embrace and bless them. Then she drew Mairi aside. "Did you see him, love? Fearchar, my Michael?"

"Oh, Gran—"

Rosanna MacLeod lifted her hand. "Hush, lassie, don't fear. He came to see you wedded; he was at my side, and joyful. But I remembered then that he died when our house burned." Tears glistened in the bright blue eyes, but Gran was smiling. "Fearchar let me think he was at the fishing till I could bear the truth—and this day I can do that, Mairi. Now go to your feast and know you have your grandfather's blessing."

As if nothing had happened save a happy wedding, Gran served around her heather ale, while Iain supplied delicacies that made this the grandest feast in memory. After the banquet Tam played his pipes while Iain led Mairi in the old Lewis bridal dance.

They danced with other partners then, and Mairi, when stopping to rest, sounded her joy on Cridhe. She could feel her grandfather's presence and knew he rejoiced with her.

By this time it was growing dark, and people dispersed to their houses. Eileen strolled off with Magnus, while Tam swung David to his shoulders, grinned a good night, and went to Andrew and Morag's house. Gran knelt to bless the hearth, as she had done so many times. "The Sacred Three to save, to shield . . ."

When she finished, she kissed both Iain and Mairi, drank to them with a final draft of whisky, and left them together. Only Cridhe, wrapped in her plaid, saw them go into each other's arms and find their marriage bed.

The lofty peaks of Arizona's Chiricahua Mountains, where Jeanne Williams and her husband make their home, seem far removed from the moors of Scotland's Outer Hebrides. But it was on a visit to Scotland in 1987 that the author became fascinated by the land and by the people of those islands.

*Jeanne Williams*

She discovered in particular that the islands' nineteenth-century ancestors had much in common with the settlers of the American frontier, whom she has brought to vivid life in her previous novels. (*Home Mountain, No Roof But Heaven,* and *Lady of No Man's Land* have all been Condensed Books selections.) Like the pioneers of the Old West, "the islanders had to battle against great odds," the author says. "First, of course, there was the condition of the land itself. And then there was the potato blight. Most of us know of the Irish potato famine, but few realize that the blight had just as cruel an effect in The Highlands and islands of Scotland." When their farms were taken from them by their landlords and their houses burned, many Scots emigrated. But others, like her character Mairi MacLeod, chose to stay behind. This time around, Jeanne Williams explains, "I longed to tell the story of those who stayed, who lived on seaweed and shellfish between the rocks and the sea, and who finally triumphed."

Though her visit to Scotland was five years ago, the author retains some vivid memories. On the island of South Uist, Jeanne Williams was a guest in a farmhouse where "a grand ceilidh" was held. A peat fire burned on the hearth, and neighbors, friends, and even the field hands entered the festivities to sing and dance till dawn. At another ceilidh two women joined with the celebrants. One woman sang, while the other accompanied her—to Jeanne Williams' immense delight—on a Celtic harp.

The original editions of the books in this volume are published and copyrighted as follows:

*The Pelican Brief*
Published by Doubleday, a division of Bantam Doubleday Dell Publishing Group, Inc.
distributed by Doubleday Canada Ltd. at $27.50
© 1992 by John Grisham

*Treasures*
Published by Delacorte Press
distributed by Bantam Books Canada Inc. at $26.00
© 1992 by Bar-Nan Creations, Inc.

*Eye of the Storm*
Published by G. P. Putnam's Sons
distributed by Bejo Sales Inc. at $28.50
© 1992 by Septembertide Publishing B.V.

*The Island Harp*
Published by St. Martin's Press
distributed by McClelland & Stewart Inc. at $26.99
© 1991 by Jeanne Williams

ILLUSTRATORS
Walter Rane: *The Pelican Brief*
Rick Johnson: *Treasures*
Michael Herring: *Eye of the Storm*
Ted Lewin: *The Island Harp*

182 220 9301